Mindplaye

For Allie, putting on the madcap that Jerry borrowed was a very big mistake. The psychosis itself was quite conventional, but it didn't go away when she took the madcap off, so the Brain Police took over leaving her with a choice – go to jail as a mind criminal or become a mindplayer herself.

Fools

The winner of the 1995 Arthur C. Clarke Award. When Marva, a Method actress, awakens in a hologram pool, carrying in her head the memory of a murder, she must think fast to find out whose life she is living and to elude the Escort Service assassins who are pursuing her.

Tea from an Empty Cup

'How can you drink tea from an empty cup?'

That ancient Zen riddle holds the key to a baffling mystery; a young man found with his throat slashed while locked alone in a virtual reality parlour. The secret of this enigmatic death lies in an apocalyptic cyberspace shadow-world where nothing is certain, and even one's own identity can change in an instant.

Also by Pat Cadigan

Novels

Mindplayers (1987)
Synners (1991)
Fools (1992)
Tea from an Empty Cup (1998)
Dervish is Digital (2000)

Collections(1989)

Patterns (1989)
Home by the Sea (1992)*
Dirty Work (1993)

* Not available from SF Gateway

Pat Cadigan

SF GATEWAY OMNIBUS

MINDPLAYERS

FOOLS

TEA FROM AN EMPTY CUP

GOLLANCZ

LONDON

First published in Great Britain in 2013 by
Gollancz
An imprint of the Orion Publishing Group
Orion House, 5 Upper St Martin's Lane,
London WC2H 9EA

An Hachette UK Company

A CIP catalogue record for this book is
available from the British Library

ISBN 978 0 575 12021 1

1 3 5 7 9 10 8 6 4 2

Typeset by Jouve (UK), Milton Keynes

Printed and bound by CPI Group (UK) Ltd, Croydon, CR0 4YY

The Orion Publishing Group's policy is to use papers
that are natural, renewable and recyclable products and
made from wood grown in sustainable forests. The logging
and manufacturing processes are expected to conform to
the environmental regulations of the country of origin.

www.orionbooks.co.uk
www.gollancz.co.uk

CONTENTS

ENTER THE SF GATEWAY . . .

Towards the end of 2011, in conjunction with the celebration of fifty years of coherent, continuous science fiction and fantasy publishing, Gollancz launched the SF Gateway.

Over a decade after launching the landmark SF Masterworks series, we realised that the realities of commercial publishing are such that even the Masterworks could only ever scratch the surface of an author's career. Vast troves of classic SF and fantasy were almost certainly destined never again to see print. Until very recently, this meant that anyone interested in reading any of those books would have been confined to scouring second-hand bookshops. The advent of digital publishing changed that paradigm for ever.

Embracing the future even as we honour the past, Gollancz launched the SF Gateway with a view to utilising the technology that now exists to make available, for the first time, the entire backlists of an incredibly wide range of classic and modern SF and fantasy authors. Our plan, at its simplest, was – and still is! – to use this technology to build on the success of the SF and Fantasy Masterworks series and to go even further.

The SF Gateway was designed to be the new home of classic science fiction and fantasy – the most comprehensive electronic library of classic SFF titles ever assembled. The programme has been extremely well received and we've been very happy with the results. So happy, in fact, that we've decided to complete the circle and return a selection of our titles to print, in these omnibus editions.

We hope you enjoy this selection. And we hope that you'll want to explore more of the classic SF and fantasy we have available. These are wonderful books you're holding in your hand, but you'll find much, much more ... through the SF Gateway.

www.sfgateway.com

INTRODUCTION
from The Encyclopedia of Science Fiction

Pat Cadigan is the working name of US writer Patricia Oren Kearney Cadigan (born 1953), in the UK from the early 1990s; she began to publish sf with 'Death from Exposure' in *Shayol* #2 for February 1978; this Semiprozine, which she edited throughout its existence (1977–85), was remarkable both for the quality of stories it published and for its production values. She later assembled much of her best shorter work in *Patterns: Stories* (1989), where its cumulative effect is very considerable; later stories appear in *Home by the Sea* (1992) and *Dirty Work: Stories* (1993). From the beginning, Cadigan has been a writer who makes use of her venues – usually Near-Future, usually urban, and usually Californian though often intensified by a sense of windswept, prairie desolation – as highly charged gauntlets which her protagonists do not so much run as cling to, never arriving safely, but surviving somehow. It is an effect also to be found in the stories assembled in *Letters from Home* (1991) with Karen Joy Fowler and Pat Murphy, each contributing her own tales.

It may be that Cadigan's first novel, *Mindplayers* (1987), failed to sustain the intensity of her shorter work, though its virtues were evident from the first (see below). Her next novel, *Synners* (1991), on the other hand, takes full advantage of its considerable length to translate the street-wise, Cyberpunk involvedness of her best short fiction into a comprehensive vision – racingly told, linguistically acute, simultaneously pell-mell and precise in its detailing – of a world dominated by the intricacies of the human/Computer interface; it won her first Arthur C. Clarke Award in 1992. The plot, which is extremely complicated, is an early exploration of the interface disease trope, where computer viruses which pass for AIs are beginning to cause numerous human deaths and to fragment human Identity; authors like Eugene Byrne have subsequently explored the imaginative possibilities of this concept, though Cadigan's work may increasingly seem to have been prescient, in some part through the anxiety of entrapment it conveys, the sense that what is happening to us is not just our imagination ...

Her immersion of her female protagonists in traditionally masculine venues – though she does not explicitly write Feminist sf – has furthermore had a salutary effect on both readers and any writer who wishes to continue to explore the prison-side of Cyberpunk. Like William Gibson's similarly enclosing cyberpunk novels – and unlike the can-do brutalism of

Bruce Sterling's generically similar works – *Synners* offers no sense that the Conceptual Breakthroughs that proliferate throughout her texts will in any significant sense transform the overwhelming urbanized world, though there is some hint that the system may begin to fail through its own internal imbalances. At the heart of *Synners* is the burning presence of a future which offers little release. Cadigan's third novel, *Fools* (1992) – which won her second Arthur C. Clarke Award in 1995 – exercises a virtuoso concision on similar material (see below).

Cadigan's next significant work is the loose Doré Konstantin series, comprising *Tea from an Empty Cup* (1998) (see below) and *Dervish is Digital* (2000), in which the dark colours of the typical Cyberpunk future are conveyed through even more unrelievedly noir tones, as Near Future detective Konstantin, gradually becoming streetwise within the Virtual Reality domains that now proliferate, engages in complex Identity games with perps and victims, sometimes Japanese. Though the series is fast and not infrequently witty, there is a sense that Cadigan has exhausted, at least for the time being, the potentials of the 1980s-tinged marriage of Cyberspace and Virtual Reality. She has explored worlds whose like we now inhabit; and like many of her readers, but sooner and more clearly, has found them wanting.

Mindplayers (1987), the first novel presented here, can be faulted for its refusal to sustain unbrokenly a book-length tale; but the compensations are considerable, for the text is free to display very considerable vigour and a good will that seems valiant, given her default darkness of vision. *Mindplayers* takes off from a concept of the human mind as being an almost literal Theatre of Memory, into which a healer may literally enter, given the proper Dream-Hacking tools. It is an intriguing notion, and uttered before its time; more than a decade into the twenty-first century, we are beginning to suspect that the truth may be something very similar: that the mind's internal narratives may be physically located and traced back and forth through the substance of the brain. *Mindplayers* was here first.

Fools (1992) expands on some of the suggestions made in the first book, though this time plotted with all the intricacy (but not the taxing length) of *Synners*. We are again in a Near-Future environment; memories are marketable and can be insertable at will into one's mind/brain. Once inside the head, these memories prove themselves to have autonomy; each of them is a narrative (or segment of a self) in its own right; and individual brains become arenas where various partial selves engage in gladiatorial combat with each other. It is a dizzying ride. Hold on.

The third tale here selected, *Tea from an Empty Cup* (1998), is even faster and more intense than its predecessors; but this time round Cadigan has chosen for her protagonist a detective whose profession it is to weave through the traps and allurements of Cyberspace, and to solve its mysteries in the

course of his job. Without Doré Konstantin to guide us, we might be as lost as we sometimes feel out here in the 'real' world. But we are not lost. We are shown the sights, we learn the streets. Cadigan remains one of our best guides. It is very good to follow her.

For a more detailed version of the above, see Pat Cadigan's author entry in *The Encyclopedia of Science Fiction*: http://sf-encyclopedia.com/entry/cadigan_pat

Some terms above are capitalised when they would not normally be so rendered; this indicates that the terms represent discrete entries in *The Encyclopedia of Science Fiction*.

MINDPLAYERS

This is for my husband,
Arnie Fenner
for love and loyalty
above and beyond

and

In loving memory of
Tom Reamy
Won't forget, Tom

I wish to express my thanks to the following people, for their considerable help and encouragement:

Gardner Dozois, Terry Matz, Lisa Tallarico, Ellen Datlow, Merrilee Heifetz, Victoria Schochet, Susan Casper, Tom Abel-lera, Jim Loehr, Ken Keller, Kathye McAndrew, Parke Godwin, Barry Malzberg, Jeannie Hund-Stuart, Robert Haas, James Gunn, Renée Duvall, Carolyn Hoppe, Cheryl Hawkinson, Mr and Mrs Robert A. Heinlein, Mr and Mrs George W. Fenner, and not least of all to my mother, Mrs Helen S. Kearney, whose contributions would fill a book on their own.

And of course, many thanks to Shawna McCarthy, caring editor, great friend.

PART ONE

Altered States of Consciousness

THE MADCAP

I did it on a dare. The type of thing where you know it's a mistake but you do it anyway because it seems to be Mistake Time.

Of course, any time I did something with Jerry Wirerammer was Mistake Time. That seemed to be Jerry Wirerammer's purpose in life. He was a cheery-looking type, very fair, all good teeth and clean hair and new clothes. He was also very crazy. His angle was skewed with respect to the rest of reality; one of those localized anomalies in human skin who always wants to make things interesting.

He came to me with the madcap, I didn't go looking for him, which proves that when it's Mistake Time, it won't do you any good to hide out in your efficiency, wondering how overdrawn you can get with the kitchen before the meal dial locks up.

Even so, I suppose I should have known better than to let him in, but I figured, what the hell – he'd gone to all the trouble of fooling the entrance security program, I might as well see what he was up to now.

The madcap was surprising. Jerry's trade ran mainly to bootlegged pharmaceuticals – hypnotics, limbos, meditative facilitators, hallucinogens. Hardware was usually beyond him unless he stole it, and he didn't like to steal. Stealing was too physical, he'd told me once.

'But this is just borrowed,' he said, handing the madcap to me. I held it up and examined it as he made himself at home on my futon. It seemed to be a professional make, not jerry-rigged (or Jerry-rigged) – cushioned helmet, wraparound eye-shield, built-in reservoirs for premeasured doses of anesthetic, sedative, and madness. 'Go ahead, Allie. I brought it over for you. Put it on. Dare yourself.'

Psychosis is an acquired taste and I wasn't sure I'd acquired it. But I was game. After all, game was the name of the game. I slipped it on. The inner cushion molded itself to my head with a snugness so comfortable I forgot I was standing up and almost toppled over.

'Whoops. Careful,' Jerry giggled, lowering me to a sitting position on the futon. 'You'll be okay in a minute.'

Less than a minute. Behind the eye-shield, I was already getting a local anesthetic. Then the connections snaked under my eyelids and around my eyeballs to the optic nerve. Big splashy color explosions when they made contact. Where had *Jerry* gotten something this good? I was aware that my

eyes were partly out of their sockets but the shield held them so securely I couldn't really feel them. Then the psychosis kicked in.

Very slick – the transition from sanity to insanity was smooth. All the neurons involved were hit at once, so there was no bad-splice sensation. The right things were inhibited just as other things were stimulated, producing a change in brain chemistry that felt as natural as changing your mind. Not a bit of dizziness or pain. I got crazy.

The actual psychosis itself was quite conventional, paranoid delusions that built up quickly, one drawing on another for substance. Jerry had been wearing a white shirt, so that meant if I heard anyone, including myself, cough within the next few minutes (I did), I could be sure that there was a machine on the roof beaming thoughts at me. Exactly whose thoughts wasn't clear, but I had to receive them: I was the One Chosen, and only moments after I realized that, I heard a voice in my ear confirm it.

You are the One Chosen, said a pleasant male voice. *Don't let on to Jerry, though. You know what a mistake that would be.*

I sure did. I let the thoughts flow into me and watched a few mildly interesting hallucinations for a while and then the alarm signaled the end. The madcap separated the chemistry it had added from my own, cleaned it out, sedated me and disconnected, replacing my eyes in one smooth stroke.

Jerry struggled the cap off my head for me. 'Good, huh?'

'Not bad at all. How'd you get it?'

He shrugged cheerfully. 'Told you. Borrowed it.'

'Yah, but who do *you* know that would loan it to you?'

He shrugged again. 'I didn't ask.'

'Probably the same people who put the machine on the roof.'

'What?' said Jerry, still cheerful.

'The machine on the roof. The one that –'

I told you not to say anything, said that male voice, now coming from a point slightly above me and to the right. I looked up in its direction. Jerry caught it and his cheerfulness faded a bit.

'Uh-oh,' he said.

'What do you mean, "uh-oh"?'

'Nothing.'

'No, you meant something by it and I want to know what.'

'Nothing, Allie, I swear. It's just an expression.'

'Right.'

'It is. Honest. It's just something I say once in a while. Uh-oh. See?'

I tried to look knowing. 'Okay, Jerry. Have it your way. But I'm in on it.'

'You are?'

'You bet. And there's nothing anyone can do about it.'

Well, I was wrong on that count. Jerry just waited until the sedative kicked

in a little more and then left me off at a dry-cleaner emergency room where, after I was sane again, the Brain Police took me into custody.

Of course, they traced the psychosis to Jerry and his borrowed madcap and got him, too. Jerry was hardly a licensed psychosis peddler, and the madcap turned out to be an experimental model he'd lifted out of someone's back room.

I didn't find out for a long time what they did with Jerry. But what they did with me was pretty interesting.

THE REALITY AFFIXER

You lose consciousness when you're dry-cleaned; afterward, you dream or you drift. When the fog cleared, I was lying naked on a slab in a boxy gray room while the Brain Police photographed everything inside and out. I could see the mug-holo taking shape in the tank on the ceiling. Unbelievable. My first offense and they were taking a mug-holo as though I were a hardcore mind criminal, and for what was basically a victimless crime at that. Was this someone's election year? I wondered. Or maybe I was still at the dry-cleaner's waiting for treatment and this was a psychotic dream.

'Haas, Alexandra Victoria,' said a female voice. Not a paranoid delusion but real, belonging to the Brain Police officer looking through the thick observation window at me.

'Yes?' I said, trying to sound casual and matter-of-fact all at once.

'You can dress now,' she said.

I sat up. A set of prison jumpjohns was lying over the foot of the slab. I put them on a leg at a time, trying to get my thoughts together.

I didn't know much about the Brain Police – not many people do unless they get into trouble with them, and those people don't talk much about it later – but at that moment, I'd rather have been facing the IRS. At least the IRS couldn't audit your thoughts. The woman on the other side of the window didn't look like gestapo; she was plain to the point of dowdy with her straight sandy hair and bare face. The uniform was more the kind of thing you'd put on if you were going to paint something yourself. She was gazing expressionlessly in my direction without looking directly at me. When I finished dressing, a door opposite the slab whispered open and I stepped through into another boxy room.

'Have a seat,' the officer said, pointing at a table and two chairs in the center of the room. She remained at the window and the desk beneath it. I could see a smaller duplicate of my mug-holo revolving in one of the two monitors set between the array of system controls.

I sat. 'Now what happens?'

Another door across the room opened and a round man in a beige sacsuit came in. The officer turned away and made herself busy at the desk. The man looked harmless enough; he wasn't any taller than I but a good deal heavier. He barely nodded to me as he went over to her. They whispered to each other for a few minutes. I stared at my hands on the tabletop, trying to catch a few words, but I couldn't hear a thing.

Abruptly, the woman crossed the room and left. I watched her go and then looked questioningly at the man, but he was busy studying the monitors. I waited a while and then cleared my throat.

'Could you at least tell me if there's anything good on tonight?'

He peered at me over his left shoulder. He said his name was Paolo Segretti and he'd been assigned to my case. 'I see you still have your own eyes,' he said, after a pause. His eyes were carnelian biogems. 'Unusual for someone in your position.'

'What position is that?'

'Mind criminal.'

'Oh, for – I put on a madcap for maybe two minutes. *Two minutes.* I didn't go out and urge children under twelve to do likewise and I didn't threaten anyone with bodily harm. The madcap was stolen but *I* didn't steal it. This is my first offense!'

'This is the first time you've been caught,' the man corrected me. 'But that's better.'

'What's better?'

'That wailing note in your voice. Now you sound more like what you are, which is a woman only a few years over the age of consent – an age I personally think is too low, but I'm sure that doesn't interest you – who took a wrong turn.' He smiled. 'You're very lucky. I mean it.'

'I know,' I said; somewhat defensively. 'I had no idea a madcap could leave you altered after it cleaned out the psychomimetics. I thought when it was over, it was over.'

'The particular madcap Wirerammer "borrowed" was incomplete; it didn't have a restore setting, which you need even with the clean-out sequence. Once you put it on, you're crazy until you go for the cure. Is that his real name – Wirerammer?'

'I don't know. I never asked.' I took a deep breath and sat up a little straighter. 'You can probably find out easier than I could. Take a look at his specs.'

Segretti glanced down at the monitors again. 'Can't. He's not my case. I can't just go barging into anyone's head as the whim takes me. I was just curious. "Wirerammer."' He pronounced it carefully. 'Nah. Couldn't be, it's too good.'

I got up and went over to look at the monitors. There was some kind of program full of numerical gibberish running on one; on the other, my nude

form was still revolving slowly next to a list of distinguishing characteristics – two moles on left shoulder, nose broken once, and so forth. I frowned at the display of my rather padded form, with my hair showing a little more auburn than it actually was, rippling down to my shoulders as though I were underwater.

'What's the matter, One Haas? Don't like what you see?'

'On the contrary. I didn't think I looked that good.'

Segretti restrained himself from chuckling. 'Have you ever heard the expression "Nobody loves a smartass"?'

'Yes, and I don't think it's necessarily true.'

'Well, it's truer than some smartasses might care to admit. When I said a little while ago that you were lucky, I didn't mean only that you were lucky Wirerammer had enough decency to leave you off at a dry-cleaner's when he realized you were in trouble. I meant you were lucky they caught you.'

'"They"? Shouldn't that be "we"? As in 'you'?'

He shook his round head. 'I'm not Brain Police. I'm your attorney. And your reality affixer.' He glanced at the watch on his shirt cuff. 'Ah, it's time.'

'For what?' I was still trying to absorb the fact that I had an attorney who was a reality affixer, or vice versa.

'For a little trip. We're going over to my office to get your reality affixed.'

I stepped back. 'Wait a minute. What if I don't *want* my reality affixed?'

'Sorry. It's mandatory after an emergency dry-cleaning for an illegal psychosis.'

Great. I wasn't sure who to curse, Jerry Wirerammer, Segretti, or myself. 'No, *you* don't go barging into everyone's mind as the whim takes you, not *you*. You're a real respecter of privacy, *you* are.'

'You're my case,' he said brightly. 'I won't take you out restrained and I'll even treat you to dinner.'

Yippee, I thought sourly.

Restraints were hardly necessary. With my mug-holo in the active file, I couldn't have used any credit and I couldn't even have gotten into my own apartment building without alerting the authorities. I was no Jerry Wireram-mer, I didn't know how to hackety-hack the security program. I was beginning to see how ill-prepared I was for a life of crime, even petty crime like being crazy without a license. But then, Jerry Wirerammer *had* been prepared and they'd gotten him, too.

Segretti took me out a side entrance, signing me out in his custody by pressing my left hand to a screen and superimposing his own print. The big Brain Police officer on the door didn't look like the type who knew much about anyone's brain; he was built more like an assassin. He also had that same lack of expression that I'd seen on the woman officer.

'Glad to be out of there,' I said as we stepped out into the deepening late afternoon sunlight. 'Are they always so emotional?'

Segretti looked at me as though he couldn't decide whether he should be amused or not. 'They get that way, dealing with mind crimes. Stuff like mind-suck, mindrape. Even the petty stuff like unlicensed psychosis. Defensive suppression of emotions, what with all the mental stuff they sort through.' He took my elbow and guided me up the sidewalk to the corner.

The city was just starting to get its second wind for the onset of evening. Overhead, airborne traffic was accumulating as it headed for Commerce Canyon; a looped holo on the belly of a crosstown express urged anyone looking for a new lease on life to visit any of Power People's 57 local outlets 'and browse our selection of over 1000 franchised personas! Rates are rea-sonable but reservations are *required!*' I shuddered slightly as the goose walked over my grave; franchised people gave me the creeps worse than the Brain Police. Segretti noticed, but he didn't comment.

'Ground traffic's lightened up a lot,' he said. 'We'll walk. It's only eight blocks and walking's good for the brain. Ever notice how after you take even just a short walk, you get a new idea? Or do all your new ideas come out of madcaps?'

I tried to duplicate the Brain Police officers' no-expression look. Segretti laughed, his chubby body jiggling in his sacsuit. 'Remarkable,' he said. 'You could be taken for one of them. I mean it.' I must have looked alarmed then because he laughed a little harder.

We started walking in the general direction of Commerce Canyon; through the gaps in the air traffic, I could just see the haze-covered lines of the buildings that rose up in man-made walls on either side of the central urban air and ground artery. In eight blocks, we wouldn't get anywhere near it, which was fine with me: the filtration systems in Commerce Canyon left a lot to be desired. I didn't care much for breathing air I could see.

'Did anyone ever tell you your brain organization is unique?' Segretti asked, still keeping a firm hold on my elbow as we walked. A woman in a red plastic workerall gave my prisoner jumpjohns a disdainful look but she gave Segretti an equally disdainful look.

'Everyone's brain organization is unique,' I said, glancing over my shoulder at the woman as she passed us. 'Even people who think alike think differently.'

'Well, I was looking at your activity readings and it seems you store a lot of information in places where most people tend to store only those things they've experienced in real time. You lead an awfully mental life. I'm sur-prised no one's ever approached you about it.'

'"Approached" me? What do you mean, "approached" me?'

'Talked to you about it after mindplay.'

'I don't mindplay.' A pair of onionheads linked together by a three-foot

chain gave us a wide berth, ignoring us as hard as they could. Onionhead marriage is about as weird as you can get without drugs. 'Wait a minute. I thought you were supposed to be able to tell whether somebody mindplayed or not.'

'Yah.'

'Well? Wasn't it in my readings?'

Segretti gave me the look I was beginning to think of as his Standard Cheerful. 'Nope. You've got the brain chemistry of someone who has mindplayed regularly, entered into altered states of consciousness.'

'That's from the madcap.'

'No, it isn't. The madcap left an entirely different sort of trace. And a madcap, by the way, is technically a form of mindplay, though not the kind we both know I'm talking about.'

We passed a dreamland where a freestanding holo of some sort of silvery bird-person was beckoning with a feathery arm. A melodious recorded voice assured us that if we could imagine it, we could dream it, and with their enhanced dreaming technique, we'd never know the difference between it and a real experience. Big deal; I never knew when I was dreaming even without enhancement. Anyway, the claim wasn't true. The human mind won't accept a script in the rem state. I'd tried it.

'Mindplay is a hell of a lot safer than madcaps or drugs, you know,' Segretti said, oblivious to the dreamland come-on.

'And a hell of a lot less private.'

'You'd be surprised. How private is it to end up at some dry-cleaner emergency room babbling every thought that runs through your head at the top of your lungs?'

'That's never happened to me before. Maybe because of my unique brain organization.'

'If it happens enough, you could lose that unique brain organization. And a lot of other stuff. Having unique brain organization doesn't automatically make you smart.'

I shrugged. 'Being smart doesn't make you smart.'

'But it does make you a smartass.'

There was a neurosis peddler on the next corner, spitting glittery little stars into the air from a pouch in his cheek as he solicited passersby. 'Are you paranoid enough? Are you sure? Paranoia's the wave of the future. Get alert, get paranoid!' He spotted Segretti and made a fast getaway down the cross street without looking back.

Segretti smiled benignly at me. 'I used to know him. Such a shame. His license was revoked a while back and what he's selling are basically his own fears and insecurities. So sad when talent goes bad.'

'Why was his license revoked?'

'Because he was selling his own fears and insecurities. Bad ethics. You use the client's own raw material, you don't impose your mental state on someone else.'

'How can you avoid it?'

'There are ways. Training.'

For some reason, I thought of the Brain Police and their blank faces.

In the middle of the third block, one of Power People's franchise outlets was having a grand opening, with a freestanding holo of a party in progress on the sidewalk in front of the store. There were hardly over 1000 personas displayed; probably just some of their bestsellers mixed in with the slower-moving types. A deliriously-in-love Nordic couple with matching gold hair and sculpted noses were discussing something with a grandfatherly man holding a bowl of pretzels. Next to him, a licensed likeness of this month's hottest holo star was laughing with the licensed likeness of last month's hottest holo star, while a tall, slender woman with large sad emerald eyes wandered among some of the other images. Very slick arrangement – it was cued to have them all turn and greet anyone stepping into the display field. Silently, though; there was no sound track. It wasn't that slick.

The grandfatherly type held out the bowl of pretzels. It passed through my shoulder and I looked the other way just in time to see I was marching through a bouncy brown-haired woman with her arms wide open in welcome. Of course, I didn't feel anything, but it still made me uncomfortable.

'It was an inevitable outgrowth of the chain method of merchandising goods,' Segretti said, smiling at me. 'It lets people be the way they'd like to be with each other, and when they'd like to be different, they can change without a lot of emotional problems.'

'Yeah, everybody wants to be somebody but nobody wants to be just *anybody*.'

'Would you deny them a little pleasure just because they're so dissatisfied with themselves they'd rather exist with an imposed persona? It's really just another form of acting.'

'Actors don't rent personas so they can act.' Segretti walked us a little faster as the afternoon began to fade. 'No, but a lot of them are licensing themselves. Acting being what it is. What it's always been. It's no different than selling their faces to endorse jumpjohns, say, or flyers or drugs.'

'If you say so. But that doesn't mean *I* have to think it's wonderful.' I remembered when they'd finally legalized franchises. My parents had gone out and put their applications in the same day. The last time I'd seen them, I still hadn't known who they were. 'Listen, I don't feel like a big sell on how wonderful it is to be alive in this age of mental marvels. Just affix my reality and let me pay my fine and I promise never to get loony without a license again.'

'I don't believe you,' Segretti said flatly but no less cheerfully.

Well, he was on target there, but I didn't say anything. The streets were becoming a little more crowded as the lights came on; apparently there were plenty of parties somewhere tonight. We went in silence the rest of the way to his office.

Segretti's office was schizy; half of it was crowded with screens of various sizes and cassette library cases piled floor to nearly ceiling. You could hardly see out of some of the windows for the stacks of books and program boxes on the sills. He had two desks, back to back, and there was less than a square foot of clear space on both of them with all the slates and styluses and even more books he had scattered all over them.

The other side of the room was completely separate, as though a tangible, if unseen, barrier ran right through the center. That side was reserved for his system. It was fair-sized, maybe seven feet by ten, with two cushioned slabs and two holes the size of small ovens, where we'd be sticking our heads. The outside of the system didn't show much, except for six monitor screens and the lighted control panel between the headholes.

'Hungry?' Segretti asked brightly.

I just looked at him.

'I've got a nice lasagna dinner on the dial. Algae instead of spinach but it tastes great, I mean it. Come on.' He led me around a corner on the cluttered side of the room and into a small, tidy alcove where an old-fashioned break-fast nook stood under a delivery box and a dial.

When the delivery box chimed and the door slid up and I smelled the lasagna, hunger hit me all at once. Segretti served us healthy portions from the dish without making much of a dent in what was left. 'Plenty of cheese,' he said, putting a fork in my hand. 'You're a bit depleted in the neurotrans-mitter department, so eat up. We're going in.'

'On this?'

'Oh, it's all fortified.'

'You could have just shot me.'

'The brain likes to take its nourishment conventionally, through the stom-ach. Shooting you full of concentrate is a strain in the long run, something you should be more concerned about. You don't go cranking up the thought machine indiscriminately or someday you'll wake up with Swiss cheese behind your eyes, I mean it. I eat.'

'Obviously.'

He didn't take offense. 'If I wanted to look different, I would. Anyone can.'

The lasagna tasted wonderful, lacking the mediciney undertaste fortified food usually had. Segretti let me diminish a fair amount of it in peace, beam-ing at me as though he'd cooked it himself. I could feel myself starting to relax

after a bit, at least physically. No tranquilizers, just the right combination of carbohydrates in the right dosage. But I didn't want to relax.

'I've never had my reality affixed,' I said, after he'd served me another helping. 'I don't see why I have to.'

'It's the law.' He frowned at the dish, then shrugged and helped himself to more.

'But why? I mean, I know what reality I'm in now.'

'Then, you'll still be in the same reality afterwards. Nothing to worry about.'

My appetite died suddenly. I sat back against the booth and pushed my plate away.

'Uh-uh,' Segretti said, gesturing with his fork and the long dangle of mozzarella cheese hanging from one of the tines. 'Keep eating.'

'I thought you referred to mindrape as a crime.'

Now I got a reaction out of him. He put down his fork and stared at me, the carnelian eyes scanning my face. 'I'm not going to mindrape you.'

'You're not? Tell my mind that. It doesn't seem to believe you. My mind has a mind of its own. As it were.'

'*You* committed the crime. I can't believe you didn't know you'd have to go through some kind of probe.'

'What I didn't know was that I'd get caught,' I mumbled, staring at the half-finished lasagna on my plate.

'The Brain Police put together an approximate picture of your history without having to access your mind. Everything you do leaves its mark on your brain chemistry, you know. Though I must say this is the first time I know of that anyone's brain chemistry deceived their analysis. I'll have to enter a note in your record that you've never mindplayed. Real mindplay is harder to pinpoint specifically than things like madcaps or drugs. Because it's so global, you know.

'Anyway, this was the fifth madcap you've taken, the third in about the last twelve months. A fair amount of hypnotics and meditation drugs. You've also limboed quite a bit with catalysts and you've tried enhanced dreaming two or three times – it was hard to tell because it apparently affected your normal dreaming for some time afterwards. You'd do better to visit a dream-feeder but instead you put on illegal madcaps that could do serious damage. Makes sense.' He pointed at my plate. 'Eat. I mean it.'

I pulled the plate over and twiddled my fork in the sauce.

'Once you have commerce in things mental,' he went on, 'you give up your right to be free of an apropos legal system. Mindplay's been around a lot longer than you have. Blame it on society. Perhaps you'd prefer to go to an enclave and live happily ever after, sans madcaps, sans Brain Police, sans any kind of mindplay at all.'

'It sounds more attractive all the time.'

'You wouldn't like it. I can tell.' He leaned his elbows on the table and looked at me with his round face all puckered up earnestly. 'It's not going to be anything like rape.'

'But you'll be in there!'

'No, I won't. We'll both be in the system, where we'll meet in mind-to-mind contact. But I won't be *in* your mind. There's only room enough for you in there. Part of you would have to be excised for both of us to fit. I'm not going to do that.'

'How would I know if you did?'

'A record of your brain activity is being kept at three separate locations. When we're through here, you'll be tested at each location and the results compared. Any sign of tampering and *I'm* under arrest and you get restored. With a large cash settlement. But you have to know.'

'Know what?'

'Mindplay. Not the piddly little stuff you've been fooling around with. Not even the stuff that most people fool around with, buying neuroses and thrills and having their dreams fed. The real mindplay – that isn't even the word for it. "Mindplay." It's always sounded trivial. But it isn't. What I'm going to do is show you a few things. After that you'll be arraigned, and what happens after your arraignment depends. You'll be given some options. Because of your unique brain organization.'

I didn't like the sound of any of it but I forced myself to start eating again. If we were going to run around inside my head, or whatever, and I really was low on neurotransmitter, I'd be no match for him.

The thing was, I was scared. Not just of him or the Brain Police, but of all mindplay. I didn't mind, as it were, an altered state of consciousness, but the idea of going naked mind to naked mind with someone …

And people did it every day, as though they were just meeting each other on the street instead of mind to mind. How did they keep themselves from leaking into each other, or from disintegrating completely into one big blob of mixed-up consciousness?

It worried me. Everything worried me. Segretti said the Brain Police hadn't accessed my mind – what a way to put it – while I'd been down, but how would I know the difference? Like a perfect crime – the locked room, no way in or out, but, somehow, someone gets in anyway, looks at every single thing in the room and gets out again, and (let's just optimistically assume) doesn't disturb so much as a speck. No on knows, no one will ever know. So, did it happen? Was the room really entered? The only person it would make a difference to would be the person who'd gotten in. Would that mean it happened only in his or her reality, and as far as anyone else was concerned – even the owner of the room – nothing happened? Or would it be like quantum, where

something might change just by virtue of the fact that it's been observed? And how would you tell it's been changed? *Could* you tell?

It worried me. It worried me all the way up to the time Segretti was satisfied I'd eaten enough and put me on one of the slabs.

'The system will administer a local anesthetic and displace your eyes,' he said, very businesslike, as his fingers danced over the control panel. 'You shouldn't feel any discomfort, though it would be a lot easier on you if you didn't still have your own eyes.'

Leaning on one elbow, I twisted around and looked at the headhole. In the soft light of his office, I couldn't see anything inside.

'Lie down, now. There's nothing to worry about.' He patted my hand.

'Do I look worried?' I said, forcing myself to lie down.

'No. The first thing the system will do is play a little game with you, just by way of getting acquainted and helping you relax. I've set it for a simple color exercise. You can just watch or participate as you choose. Once the system senses you're relaxed enough, we'll make contact.'

'What if I never get relaxed enough?'

Segretti did something to the slab and I felt it rearranging itself slightly under me, molding to the contours of my body.

'Comfortable, isn't it. Listen, I want you to understand – I won't be joining you inside your mind. I mean it. Our minds will meet within the system.'

'So you said.'

'I just want to make sure you're clear on that.'

'Okay. But I'm not willing. I just want to make sure *you're* clear on *that.*'

Segretti touched something else on the side of the slab and it glided back to the system and inserted my head in the hole.

INSIDE

The inside of the headhole was dark and pleasant smelling, like a field after a light spring rain. The smell grew stronger with every breath I took and I was just starting to feel almost calm when I felt something soft close around my neck and panic kicked in like an electroconvulsant.

Dark! And small! And close! And something had me by the neck and that smell, that smell, smothering me in pleasantness and I had to get out, get *out* –

Then the system was injecting the local anesthetic and before I could even register that my eyes were partway out of their sockets, the connections had

reached my optic nerves and it was no longer dark and small and close. The fresh-field smell seemed to be coming from me now, spreading through my awareness like haze. I was floating along with it, alert but calm, no longer burdened with a physical body.

It felt pretty good. Not ecstasy but all right, the kind of well-being you'd choose over ecstasy when you were having a bad day – and this, I thought, definitely qualified as a bad day. I had a sense of being somewhere, in some sort of location, and I thought of looking around, even though I didn't really have anything to look with.

As soon as the idea occurred to me, the colors came up. It wasn't like light coming up, though you'd have thought it would be. For some reason, it made me think of music rather than light, like music I'd been hearing for a while but had only just become aware of.

Blue came first, deep, dark, fading in from the edge of my perception. As I watched, it changed, becoming lighter. It evolved into a soft green and I automatically thought of the fresh-field aroma. I smelled the memory and knew that it was the memory, not the aroma itself. Very trippy.

A small spot of yellow blossomed at the center of my perception and sent out tendrils. Well, it was *like* that, but that wasn't precisely what I saw. I couldn't really resolve what type of movement it was, unless I changed my perspective so that I was perceiving it directly, and then I *almost* got it. *Almost*. Exactly what was going on eluded me, as though I were trying to grab hold of mercury. I stopped trying to force the colors into a coherent pattern and they sort of settled around me, the yellow changing to gold and then to orange.

No pictures, I thought, watching the colors move and change. No pictures and no sense of environment or dimension. It was a few steps away from watching patterns on the backs of your eyelids, which was a perfectly respectable way of achieving entry to certain mental states. I used that a lot myself. I'd tried all the techniques for reaching altered states of consciousness – unaided, that is, without drugs or involving another person like a mindplayer. The colors thing felt like the best solo stuff but even better, because I didn't have to concentrate so hard to keep my mind from wandering off on tangents.

The colors became a little more complex in their shadings, acquiring nuances – turquoise with a hint of stronger yellow, gold with an emphatic red underlay, red falling into purple that flickered back and forth on the border of midnight blue.

He was there, in the blue, his presence coming up the way a diver might slowly approach the surface of a dark lake.

See? No shock, no intrusion. How are you doing?

The sensation of his presence made me think of bubbles touching. There was the surface tension of his personality, his *Segretti-ness*, all the things that revolved around his actively being who he was, meeting my *Allie-ness*, the container that was me and the me the container contained, and which materials

went into the container and which into the thing contained – it was the most powerful sense of identity I'd ever had in my life.

There was a feeling of barriers going. Somewhere panic jumped in me again, but the sensation leveled off and I perceived that there hadn't been a total breakdown in my border condition or in his either. We were still separate, but we were in contact.

Suddenly, and yet somehow not abruptly, I had an orientation; the colors were rising, or I was falling, or both. Like veils drawn upward as I descended, the colors were lifting and something else was coming into focus around me.

Here we are, Segretti said.

Here was the edge of a broad field bounded by a low, flimsy wire fence; a roughly made sign on a post in front of me read WATCH THIS SPACE.

I didn't realize I was so suggestible, I said, feeling rather amused.

Suggestible? How so? asked Segretti. He had come into being (if that's the way to put it) sitting on the grass near the sign but a respectful distance from the fence.

That fresh-field smell in the system. It must have triggered this image.

Segretti smiled up at me. I looked around. Perfectly ordinary blue sky (maybe with a hint of the depth of that midnight blue behind the light day color); the field went as far as I could see in front of me. Behind me was more countryside but it was different, unbounded, grass grown up freely, the land rolling, the horizon obscured by haze.

This is what your mind looks like from this angle, Segretti said, still smiling.

What angle is this?

Your point of departure.

I shook my head, or rather, I did the mental equivalent of shaking my head and discovered I'd visualized/materialized a complete body for myself. I studied my hands for a moment; they were my hands as I'd always known them, no surprises there. I reached up to feel for my face.

Big surprise. No face. No head, even. Nothing but air.

You're all right, Segretti said, looking both amused and concerned.

I'd be better if I could find my face and everything that goes with it, I said, my fingers groping in the empty air where I judged my mouth should be.

From your perspective, you'll have a head only when you really need to feel one. To shake, for instance. From my perspective, you look quite normal. Remarkably normal, in fact, very much the way you look out there. You have a very strong physical image of yourself. How you look is, uh, how you look. Most people's inner image is a little more idealized, at the very least, and there are plenty who don't look much like their outer selves at all.

I was still feeling for my head, trying to concentrate hard enough to bring one into existence. *Suppose I want to put on a hat? Or maybe a madcap?*

Segretti's amusement took on an edge. *If you really need to do that, you'll*

find something there when the time comes. But if you spend all your time trying to feel for your own head when you're already inside the contents, you're not going to find out much about yourself or anything else.

He had a point. I looked back at the open country again, straining to see through the haze in the distance. *Well, I find it strange that my mind looks the way it does from this angle or any other, even taking my suggestibility into account,* I said. *I'm not queer for the country. That I know of.*

Segretti got up, brushing a little dirt and grass from his pants. I felt as though I should have had some kind of sensation from that – he was brushing at my visualization on himself. But I didn't feel any differently than if we'd been out in the real country in real reality and he'd brushed some dirt off himself.

Well, I'm not going to tell you about your mind, he said, *or perform a thoroughgoing analysis of your imaging. But I would guess it grows out of some kind of personal metaphor you're so accustomed to that you're not even aware of it anymore. And metaphors do tend to propagate, if you don't keep an eye on them. Since they have no discrimination, they'll go on into the unimaginably absurd.*

Good thing I couldn't see any trees; I'd have been afraid to think what they meant.

But you have to remember, Segretti went on, *that this is only what we're seeing from* this *angle. Your point of departure.*

So how do we get somewhere else and see something a little more interesting? I looked at the sign. *I don't really want to hang around here watching this space.*

Segretti shrugged. *This is* your *mind, as I keep telling you. And as I also kept telling you, I'm not going to force you to do anything.*

It may be my mind but you're making yourself at home in it.

Not quite true.

True in the sense I mean and we both know it.

For the first time, he showed real irritation; it manifested as a small swarm of noisy little insects buzzing around both of us. *All right, yes, in that sense. But if you think I'm going to go leading you around in your own mind, think again. And I do mean think. It will be quite a change for you.* The insects' buzzing grew louder. *Up till now, you've been perfectly happy to pour all sorts of junk into your head to jerk your own consciousness around, supposedly in the name of thought. Madcaps aren't thinking; limbo isn't thinking; you don't engage anything, you just lie there and have it done to you. Altered state of consciousness. You might as well alter your ear for all the good it's done your consciousness.*

I batted at the insects; now I had a head just so they could annoy it. *Okay, okay,* I said, *I'm a menial suckling, have it your way. But you're the one who dragged me in here and now you're expecting me to behave like a seasoned tripster. I just wanted to know what to do, I didn't ask you to do it for me.*

The insects faded away, along with my head.

You're right, I'm wrong, said Segretti. *Come to that, you really are taking this awfully well.*

Yah, I said, looking around again. *It's not the way I thought it would be in here with someone else. I mean, you're here but you're not invading. You're still – outside. And I like it here. I'm –* I groped for a word and found one I hadn't quite expected. *Home.*

I was, too. It was more than just getting used to it. I really wasn't enthralled with the country, and if I'd come to an identical spot out there in real reality, I'd have thought it was pretty enough but I wouldn't have fallen in love with it at first sight or anything. But in here – in my mind, I kept reminding myself – I could feel the rightness, the *appropriateness* of it. The faded grass at my feet, bending over my shoes – shoes? I wore *shoes* when I ran through my own mind? Guess so, they persisted – I might have spent my whole life standing around in that grass (in those shoes), I felt so at home. And of course, I *had* spent my whole life standing around in it (after I'd grown it … watered it? cut it? Stop. Segretti was right, metaphors propagated too damned crazily). Just as I'd spent my whole life walking around under *this* sky, the sky I'd always assumed to be over me when I didn't take note of the one out there. Yah, and that was my haze in the distance. The longer I was there, the more at home I felt. It was, as it were, *me.*

My attention wandered back to Segretti, who was staring up at the sky with a pleased expression. I looked up to see what was making him so happy, but suddenly the sun (or whatever) was too bright.

What are you looking at? I asked.

Symbols.

Where?

They happen to be overhead at the moment, probably because you're elated. Kind of a getting-acquainted euphoria. A high, as it were, and the mind's symbolism is often simplistically literal when it can get away with it. The symbols tell me that you're glad you're in here and you feel very comfortable among all your mental trappings.

I tried to look up at these too-revealing symbols again but the light was still blinding.

Don't bother, you can't see them. Not at your level, anyway. That's a very sophisticated mental trick you couldn't perform without training, I mean it, and even then lots of people never manage to get a deliberate look at their own symbols.

That's nonsense, I said. *All of* this *is made up of symbols.*

All of this is your visualization. It carries a certain symbolism, yes, but it's not the same as what I was looking at. It would be like your trying to see one of your own spontaneous facial expressions by staring into a mirror.

20

You can if you're caught off-guard, I said.

Yes, you can, Segretti said smoothly. *And when was the last time you were deliberately caught off-guard?*

I couldn't help squirming. The grass rustled with me.

That noise you hear is the sound of a mind beginning to work for a living.

It's grass rustling.

So, are you game to take the tour? he asked.

Definitely the right thing to say to me. Sure I was game. Much later, of course, I realized that Segretti wasn't always so obvious about reading symbols.

All I had to do was move around a little. But in the beginning, I was moving around a lot, just to watch the way things changed. I couldn't tell how it was going to happen – quickly, gradually, with a shimmer and a sigh or a blink and a flash – but there was high entertainment value in it, at least for someone who'd never done it before. I didn't ask Segretti any questions; somewhere between the open country and the cathedral, he'd tied a gag over his mouth.

The cathedral – now, *there* was a surprise. I'd never imagined that *I* would have a church in *my* head, but there it was, taking up a healthy portion of space in whatever area of my mind I was in. I looked around for anything that might have been a mental landmark but the only thing I found was another sign near the cathedral's front steps, so inconspicuous I might have missed it, bearing the legend: You ARE HERE. And below, in smaller letters: WHERE DID YOU THINK YOU WERE?

Segretti stayed right with me, handy but unobtrusive and still voluntarily gagged. I walked from side to side in front of the cathedral, trying to get some idea of what kind of church I'd been keeping all these years. I didn't know exactly how many years but it had obviously been around for a long time. In spots, the architecture (architecture in the mind – I wavered between acceptance and disbelief) seemed traditionally Gothic from one angle, but then from another it looked different, all clean lines and windowless, and from still another, it had a rough-hewn appearance, like a log cabin or something. I kept finding odd spots here and there that I couldn't see clearly, a hole or a patch where a hole had been or a place where the stone had changed to wood or glass or something softer, like leather. (Leather? Me?)

I was hesitant to go inside. After all, I hadn't expected to find anything like that in my own mind; I wasn't sure I was prepared for what I'd been keeping in it. But after a while, I'd seen just about all I could of the front, and for some reason, I seemed to have some kind of block about going around to the back. Eventually, I went up the steps to face the front door.

It was a big wooden door with a lot of carving on it. I couldn't quite make out what the carving was – it kept shifting and changing. When I put my

hand on it, it rippled under my fingers, sometimes changing texture so that it felt like velvet or fur or, disturbingly, flesh.

There was a doorknob instead of a chip slot. I was reaching for it when the door swung open and I was inside without having taken a step.

The room was nothing like the interior of a cathedral. It was bright with serene golden lamplight and filled with more things inch for inch than Segretti's office, all of them things that I especially liked, things I'd owned or wished I had, souvenirs of things I'd done or seen. A pile of rock crystals I'd seen in a geology exhibit when I'd been a kid were sitting in an old felt hat I'd found in a clothes bin in a secondhand shop. There was an old jacket of my father's that I'd coveted lying next to a static holo of myself on the street in front of a dream-enhancement parlor with someone I didn't usually let myself think about (unrequited love makes you feel like such a jerk). I tried to see it all and couldn't. But directly in front of me, high on a wall covered with red brocade, was a large portrait of my great-grandmother.

A goofy kind of happiness spread through me at the sight of her. It wasn't a holo but an oil painting, like the ones she'd owned. She was sitting on some kind of antique chair with a high back, dressed in a white silk kimono embroidered with delicate butterflies. I remembered her showing me a picture of it in one of her old big books (the book itself, I noticed, was on a glass-topped table, open to that page).

My great-grandmother had been incredibly old, having, by some feat of endurance, outlived even my grandmother. I'd never known her when she hadn't been bedridden, often with tubes running in and out of her. Some institute had maintained her for years, just for research because she'd been so stubbornly *not dead*. But she'd been more than that to me – she'd been so stubbornly *alive*, signing for me when my parents had gone franchise (my mother had opted for a party-animal model while my father chose the soldier of fortune, complete with memories of the Malaysian war he'd never been in).

Having outlived her time, my great-grandmother hadn't approved of mindplay or anything else that couldn't be slept off. *If you have to get messed up*, she would tell me, *get drunk. You can sober up from that, and for free. And it'll probably make you sick, which will keep you from doing it too often. If you're smart, anyway.* The institute hadn't approved of her attitude, but she'd told them that if they took away her vodka she'd withdraw from their maintenance and they could go hunt up someone else over the age of 110 to study. Nor had she given them permission even to delve her memories, in spite of the fact that her eyes had been replaced decades before and it would have been a fairly easy procedure.

Eventually, she'd begun to fail. The organism was simply wearing out, as the institute had put it. Near the end, she suddenly chose dream therapy, and

went out hooked into a dream enhancer. The dent her death had left wore smooth after a while, but it was still there.

Obviously. Here she was, enshrined in my personal cathedral. I was beginning to catch on.

The portrait showed her a little better than I remembered her ever looking when I'd known her, but otherwise it seemed to be fairly true to her appearance. There was the same wiry, colorless hair, the square forehead and gray eyes, aquiline nose, the long jaw, her lips set in some private, probably reactionary thought; I might have been looking at my own face a hundred years on.

And maybe I was. I couldn't figure out how much really was accurate memory and how much I was filling in myself ... *with* myself.

The woman in the portrait turned her head and looked down at me. *Now you're really catching on*, she said.

I stepped back in shock; around me, the cathedral shuddered in sympathy.

Gran? I said. *Are you – I mean –* I floundered, unable to find the right question.

How would I know anything? she said. *This is* your *place. I just stay here. Never expected to see you here like this. You're not drunk, are you?*

No, Gran, I'm not.

You're a lot more messed up than that, aren't you?

Yah. I sure am. I paused. *Can you come down out of there?*

I doubt it. The portrait frowned. *I told you, I don't know anything.*

There was a strange high whistle from somewhere.

What's that? I asked.

Something I do know. Telephone. Voice only. I hung onto that thing until your mother finally wired it into the regular phone for me because I liked the sound better than that beep-beep-beep. You put it in here with me. You never call, though.

The phone whistled again. I found the long flat receiver on the desk next to a large crystal bowl filled with silk lotuses and picked it up.

So, how are you doing? said Segretti.

There's a picture of my great-grandmother in here. I'm talking to it. To her, I amended, glancing up at the portrait.

Are you learning anything?

Well, she says she doesn't know anything.

She doesn't know anything you don't know is what she means.

That figures.

Don't take too much longer in there, all right? We have other things to think about.

Okay. Just let me take a look around and I'll be out in a minute. Or something. I put the receiver down and looked up at my great-grandmother's portrait again.

I have to be going soon, I told her, *but I'd like to see what's here, if that's all right with you.*

She shrugged. *It's your place.*

I could have spent something equivalent to the rest of my life rooting around in there. In a short space of time, I came across a copy of *The Love Song of J. Alfred Prufrock* (which my great-grandmother had first read to me), several musical recordings, a picture of a friendship that hadn't been active in years, and, to my great surprise, a very small holo, smaller than the palm of my hand, of Jerry Wirerammer.

He grinned up at me. *Heya, Allie*, he said.

Quickly I put the holo down on the desk where I'd found it.

I never met him, said my great-grandmother, *but I don't think he's any good for you.*

Yes and no, Gran, I said. *I have to leave. I don't know when I'll be back.*

I'll be here, she said. That had been something she used to say back when she was rooted to her bed with the tubes. *I'll be here*. I felt mildly melancholy as I left.

Outside, Segretti still had his gag on.

You can make phone calls through that thing? I said.

He shrugged.

You're not helping me.

He pulled the gag down from his mouth. *Sorry. I can only help so much. Come on.* We walked around the side of the cathedral and into an apartment.

It was my apartment – not the overpriced efficiency I was leasing, but the apartment I'd idealized for myself out of wish fulfillment and the best parts of other places I'd lived or visited. There were windows all over the place, looking out on the ocean to the east and on a city skyline from high up on the west. The differing views were almost the only things I could see coherently; the rest was jumbled up, sometimes the overstuffed leather sofa (okay, that was where the leather had come from) taking up my vision, sometimes the gleaming fully-equipped lavabo crowding everything else out.

Just decide on something and get comfortable, Segretti told me.

I concentrated, clearing away a big area and laying a futon down in the middle of it. After holding that for a while to make sure it wouldn't melt away on me, I added the right amount of humidity and a hint of joss-stick fragrance.

Okay, I said, stretching out on the futon. *No, wait.* I glanced at either side of the futon; it tripled in width. *Now it's okay.*

Segretti sat down near my head (I could feel it again, for the sake of comfort, I guess). *Relax.*

I'm relaxed.

Really *relax. Stop thinking about being relaxed. Stop talking to me, or you won't be able to hear it.*

I almost asked, but for once I managed to do what I was told. I had to lie there for a long time, but at last it started coming through to me. It was like singing, or white noise, but not really like either one of them; like the murmur of the voices of people you like who are close enough to hear but too far away really to listen to; like the sound of the voice that comes sometimes in dreams, telling you the secret of life and shutting off just as you snap to awareness of what it's saying; like something you almost see but miss; like something you almost remember; like being almost asleep and almost awake; like thinking you're awake and finding out you're asleep; like thinking you're asleep and finding out you're awake; like holding a familiar object just before you identify it; like a face you know but without a name; like teetering before you fall; like a shadow you can describe only by what it is not; like a figure that is in reality the ground; like the ground that comes forward as a figure; like …

After a while, I sensed Segretti shifting position and I was alert, just like that. *Here*, he said, and handed me a folded sheet of paper.

What is it?

Letter from your great-grandmother. Read it. Then we have to go.

I unfolded the paper, feeling rather strange. It was really a letter from another part of myself, sort of.

You find this peculiar, getting a letter from your great-grandmother while visiting inside your own head. It's peculiar having you here. Mostly you live out there, in what you call 'real reality,' in spite of the fact that this reality is just as real.

I've been here a long, long time, not just since your great-grandmother's death. For years, I kept pace with that woman in 'real reality.' When you indulged your thoughts and memories of her, it was me you were activating. Visiting me the way you just did activated me even more; I'm becoming somewhat of an entity in my own right. Because of the way you relate to me, as we used to say in my day, and because of this terribly mental life you lead.

If you think this is something, wait till you see the rest of your head. If you live that long.

I looked at Segretti. *How did you do this?*

You did it. I just helped you attain the proper mental state.

Passing the letter from one hand to the other, I could feel the paper quite vividly. It was that strange, non-tear stuff people mostly use for formal invitations. *You really didn't have anything to do with this?* I asked Segretti.

No.

How do I know that?

You'd know the difference right away. He yawned. *Listen, I'm worn out after that trick, I mean it. You can come back later if you want but I'm about to go to sleep.*

That made me nervous all over again. *What would happen if you went to sleep in here with me?*

We'd wake up unable to tell ourselves apart. The sarcasm was mild.

I'm just asking.

If it were unintentional, the system would automatically break our contact as soon as it felt the loss of consciousness.

Oh, I said. *But – unintentional? Why would it be intentional?*

Sometimes the dream state can be very useful. Or just plain unconsciousness, for that matter. 'Never mind. Let's go back outside.

How?

You could click your heels together three times and say, 'There's no place like home.'

Say again?

I felt his laughter. *Never mind. Find a blank wall and stare at it.*

I found one but it wasn't blank for long. The colors came back, possibly in the reverse order in which they'd appeared; I couldn't remember well enough. A calm spread over me again and I had a sense of the colors receding, something like a tide ebbing. Very pleasant sensation. I kept watching them forever, it seemed like, and then they faded, blurred, and resolved themselves into Paolo Segretti's face.

OUTSIDE

He let me go home. He had to: I made bail. Of course, I wasn't about to jump. I couldn't afford to lose any money or start over as a fugitive from a stupid offense like being psychotic without a license. I had to go right back the next afternoon, anyway. It seemed the disposition of my case might go differently than the usual thirty days and thirty dollars or whatever the penalty was. Usually a fine for the first offense, but not always. The law was not that crazy about people being psychotic without a license. I could hope for leniency – which was better than Jerry Wirerammer could hope for. This couldn't have been *his* first offense. I wondered what they'd done with him.

I mooned around my efficiency – no spectacular views from any of the three windows. There was a futon but not as wide as I'd have liked, and I was still on the verge of being overdrawn with the kitchen. I was homesick for the apartment in my head, just as though it were a true, separate place I'd visited. Maybe in some way it was.

In the midst of all the mooning and sulking and wondering, I found that

Segretti had been right – I really could feel the difference of having been in mind-to-mind contact with someone. He'd left a sort of aftertaste in my thoughts, a sense of intense familiarity, as if I'd seen him every day for years or something. It was a purely mental phenomenon, what some people call the 'pressure of presence.' He felt even more real to me than my great-grandmother. Maybe I had a picture of him in the cathedral now.

No, I thought, it wouldn't be there, not in the cathedral. There had to be another place where I'd keep people like Segretti. I didn't feel like trying to figure out where at the moment, though he clung to the top of my mind like a tune I couldn't stop humming. Just to distract myself, I went into the kitchen and calculated how much I could get out of the dial.

It was a little more than I'd originally thought, which elated me all out of proportion. In the throes of delight, I ordered up the budget protein-algae casserole and ate it out of the wrapper on the counter. There was even enough credit left for a drink and a quarter, or for a moderate-to-weak shot of something moderate-to-inferior. My great-grandmother wouldn't have approved. If you had to get drunk, she'd said, make sure it's something worth getting sick on.

Maybe I had a soporific in my also-depleted goody bag, in which case I could try to sleep everything off. I checked the head of my futon; the bag was still there, and I laid everything out on the smooth black cushion.

One soporific, from Jerry Wirerammer, of course; one limbo spansule, two meditative facilitators, also from Jerry Wirerammer; a sleeping capsule in drop-dead strength, courtesy of the Wirerammer larder; one of the new minor hypnotics, Jerry Wirerammer stock; and a breath mint. Probably also from Jerry Wirerammer.

I popped the breath mint and stretched out next to my pharmacy, trying to decide which, if any, would get me through the next twelve hours, or at least give me a running start on them.

Somehow you always ended up doing that sort of thing alone. Where had my life gone, I wondered – into a lot of funny pills and spansules? What happened, and when? I hadn't always lived like this.

Well, there had been the separation from my parents, when I'd moved to live closer to my great-grandmother. I'd spent some time with her but the institute people hadn't cared for me hanging around slipping vodka to her, and since she'd been bedridden, we couldn't exactly go out doing the town or even a small portion of it. Friends – yah, there'd been friends, but they'd all drifted away when they'd started mindplaying. I could see why. What would I have to say to someone like myself now? I was just talking to my great-grandmother the other day – she lives in the cathedral upstairs. Sure. Saying it out loud would make it seem lame. Even just thinking it out that way made it seem lame.

So much for friendship, or anything deeper. There was a little of that, mostly superficial contacts, outside of the Unrequited. I could have lined all of them up next to the drugs and they'd have come out one for one except for the Unrequited because I'd eaten the breath mint.

I rolled over onto my back and stared at the meditation mandala on the ceiling. The colors reminded me of the colors from the relaxation exercise Segretti had hooked me into. The program had probably drawn on them, I realized, and for some reason, the idea was rather comforting.

So the course of action seemed to suggest itself. I looked at the meditation facilitators. Jerry Wirerammer Vat No. 44. They were actually mild hallucinogens – I used them regularly. Meditation was such a loose term; you can do almost anything mentally and call it meditation. Maybe, I thought, I should have told Segretti and the Brain Police I meditated by ingesting bouts of paranoid schizophrenia, and seen if I could have gotten around the freedom-of-meditation statute, which didn't cover psychosis.

What the hell. I slapped both patches onto the side of my neck directly over the blood vessel and stared up at the mandala, thinking about the cathedral and my great-grandmother.

After a while, the mandala began to shimmer, the colors loosening their boundaries. I looked past them, trying to recreate the whole scene of the outside of the church in my mind's eye. The extra neurotransmitter in the hallucinogens kicked in, giving me a boost that enabled me to picture it in more detail than I'd have been able to manage unaided, but I never achieved the detail I'd had with Segretti.

Segretti – his aftertaste was stronger than ever under the influence of the facilitators. I couldn't picture the cathedral without him standing outside with his gag on, frozen in place but very present. I let him stay there and concentrated on getting a firm visual hold on the front steps.

I went up those steps four times, and every time I got to the door it dissolved into the mandala. On the fifth try, I almost lost it. The colors threatened and then suddenly I found myself inside the cathedral.

There was hardly any light at all this time. All I could see was my great-grandmother's portrait and not very well at that. There was no possibility of getting it to speak to me. Nonetheless, I concentrated on it for a long time, trying to move a little closer to it.

What light there was faded away. I didn't even get the mandala back; I just fell asleep.

CONSCIOUS CHOICES

Segretti laughed. 'Well, what did you expect?'

'I tried not to expect anything,' I said, not entirely truthfully. 'I thought maybe once I'd been in, I could go back whenever I wanted.'

'Someday you might be able to do that, but you don't have the brain paths right now.' I stared down at the thick protein drink he'd given me. We were back in the boxy gray room at Brain Police headquarters where I'd first met him, sitting across from each other at the spare little table. Two expressionless Brain Police officers had escorted me through the maze of corridors, placed me here, and left without bothering to speak a word. Maybe they'd thought I was some sleazoid mindrapist. Or maybe they hadn't thought anything at all. It was hard to tell. They seemed more cut off from everything than I'd ever been.

When Segretti had come in, bearing the protein drink like some kind of priceless gift, I'd had to force myself not to jump out of the chair and run over to him. The sight of his round face and pudgy little body reactivated his mental aftertaste, turning it into a small storm of associations I hadn't been aware of. Somehow I knew he was probably feeling tired because it was morning and he didn't hit his stride until afternoon, and that he was already hungry for lunch, which he wanted to eat in his office. He'd also just finished discussing me with someone, probably one of those deadpan Brain Police officers. I had no idea how I knew something like that; it was just that *familiarity*. I wondered if I felt as familiar to him as he did to me and, if so, what he did about it.

'News on your case,' he said to me. 'Care to hear it?'

'I think I can guess. Plead guilty to a lesser charge of going crazy without a license or plead not guilty and be tried for one count of failing to report a stolen madcap, one count of receiving a stolen psychosis, and one count of second-degree insanity without a license.'

He was impressed in spite of himself; I could tell by the way his mouth curled at one corner. 'Or you can shut up and listen to the third option.'

Chastened, I gulped my protein. The fishy flavor was unpleasant but it was breakfast.

'Your third choice,' he said, when he was sure I would stay shut up, 'is to do something.'

'Community service,' I guessed, not without a hint of weariness in my voice.

'In a way. You can become a mindplayer.'

I blinked at him. 'Me? What kind?'

'Any kind you want. Thrillseeker, belljarrer, dreamfeeder, pathosfinder, neurosis peddler.' He grinned. 'Reality affixer.'

'Justice goes poetic, huh?'

'Your brainwave and activity patterns along with the results of yesterday's reality-affixing have been previewed by the presiding judge and a consulting panel. In light of the potential demonstrated by your brain organization and native mental abilities, the judge and panel both feel that justice would be served if you entered mindplay training with the goal of becoming a professional of some kind. Your criminal record would be erased a year after your certification.' His grin flattened. 'Or you can just go to jail.'

The bottom dropped out of my stomach. 'Really?'

'Well, not right away. You'd be fined and go to jail for your second offense, which you will inevitably commit. It's your decision. What's going to happen?'

I set the fish-shake aside and leaned forward, resting my elbows on the table. 'You probably know me better than anyone. What's going to happen?'

Segretti looked troubled. 'I don't know. I mean it. If you want, I could draw you a decision tree. But just making a guesstimate on the different outcomes, I'd say most of the other courses have you ending up subsisting from offense to offense, possibly incarcerated as a career mind criminal, though that sounds extreme to me. More likely you'd get burned out from one thing or another. Or one thing *and* another.'

'I didn't ask you that.'

'I know.' He smiled again. 'But no matter how well you know someone, you can't predict the future.'

I pushed the fish-shake further away. 'You know – and you *know I know you know* – that I'm going to go for the mindplay thing, if for no other reason than to lose the criminal record. Once you're a convicted mind criminal, you're locked out of anything but menial work, even if it was a victimless crime, because nobody trusts you not to tamper with reality in some way, your own or someone else's. I don't want to spend the rest of my life swabbing out some neurotic's vomitorium.' I sat back in the chair. 'You also know that I'm hooked. Once you've taken the trip, you're never the same afterwards.

'But I want you to know that I still feel like I'm forced on this. The choice is really no choice at all. And how do you know, once I get to some mindplay institute, they won't find something in my head that will weed me out as a crank?' I paused. 'Or do you keep your finder's fee anyway?'

Segretti just looked at me without anger or recrimination, but he looked at me for so long that I thought I'd squirm completely out of my skin.

'Someday,' he said slowly and quietly, 'I hope you'll know the rewards of finding something of value and quality in the most unlikely situation. And

how that doesn't require the extra incentive of material gain. "Surprised by joy," as it were.'

I sat there studying the table top. There wasn't much to study, but I memorized every featureless inch in front of me.

'The best place,' he went on, 'is J. Walter Tech, up north. They've been the best for the last sixty years, almost from the beginning. Started out in another line of work entirely, became one of the pioneering mindplay institutions on the basis of thorough studies of human nature.'

'Where you went,' I said.

'Where I went.'

I jerked my head at the desk under the observation window. 'You can punch me up an application anytime.'

'Not necessary,' Segretti said cheerfully 'They've already accepted you. I mean it.'

Oh.

So it was all over but the court appearance, which had been reduced to a formality. The judge gave me a speech about how failure to find my niche in life (unquote) was a mitigating circumstance, and that my mental abilities warranted all-out effort at rehabilitation, with the added warning that if I dropped out, they'd snap me back into court with all charges reinstated. Next case.

Which happened to be Jerry Wirerammer. They wouldn't let me stay and hear the outcome but the recommendation had been for an Exploratory – the Mental Strip Search. Or, as Segretti put it, death by embarrassment.

It wouldn't actually kill him. You could survive someone knowing every single thing about you – every single thing you'd ever done, said, seen, or thought, not just exposed but examined and analyzed. You could survive that. Therapy helped.

Jerry Wirerammer in treatment. I couldn't picture it. I didn't much like it, either. I thought about what Segretti had said: once you have commerce in things mental, you give up your right to be free of an apropos legal system. How apropos was the Mental Strip Search, really?

And I was going head first, as it were, into the whole thing, legal system included. (Head first made me think of the headhole in Segretti's office; the thought of that small dark place was enough to give me reminiscent horrors.) As if I were condoning this ultimate invasion of Jerry Wirerammer's privacy, or of anyone's, career mind criminal notwithstanding.

There were some things about mindplay that just weren't very nice, Segretti told me the day he saw me off on the underground tube. He treated me to another of his lasagna dinners in his office. I sat with my back to his system so I wouldn't have to look at the headhole but it seemed as though I could feel it gaping at me the whole time.

'Appeal is automatic. And at least they aren't going to incarcerate him,' he said, digging into his portion heartily. 'They're not going to offer him the same chance they did you. Most likely they'd simply let him loose afterwards to put himself together however he can.'

'That's a hell of a thing to wish on anyone.'

'He's not an innocent. I've seen his record. Wirerammer, indeed. The boy's a burglar. You're lucky you never went mind-to-mind with him. Jerry had the rather tacky practice of cloning memories and fencing them. Half your life would have been all over town, I mean it. How *that* for invasion of privacy?'

'My life isn't interesting enough to fence.'

'That's what you think. Suppose you found out some burnout case was having your great-grandmother? Or reliving one of your love affairs?'

The idea and the headhole behind me combined to kill my appetite. Again. 'Okay. I hate it. But I hate the Mental Strip Search, too. Getting a taste of your own medicine isn't medicine.'

'What would you suggest they do, dry-clean his criminal tendencies out of him? That would be much worse, wouldn't you say? I would, I mean it. And dry-cleaning wouldn't work, anyway. They'd have to go to a full wash, maybe even with surgery, a procedure that was outlawed generations ago before mindplay was hardly more than an experiment. To prevent the government from correcting people into obedient robots. Mindplay was never meant to be mind control.'

I leaned my elbows on the table and cupped my chin in my hands. 'It's just as bad. Choosing between having every detail of your mind exposed or being *corrected* isn't much of a choice. The Mental Strip Search is just one step removed from brainwashing. If authorities are allowed just to look at any-thing they want, the next logical thing to do is to allow them to mess around with the arrangement.'

Segretti nodded at me. 'You're not the only one who thinks so. There's a move on now to ban the Mental Strip Search as cruel and unusual.'

'Is that the way you feel about it?' I asked.

'I'm a lawyer. I deal with the law as it is, not how I feel about it.'

'Yah, but you're a person, too. You have to have some feelings about it. *I know.*'

'Yes, I know you do.' Segretti's smile was gentle.

I sat up straight and stared at him. 'And that's not all you have feelings about, either.'

'Pardon?' The smile vanished and he took on that Brain Police kind of expressionlessness.

'After that first night you brought me here, I had this – aftertaste in my brain –'

'In your mind.'

'Yah, that, too. This aftertaste. Of you. Like, I don't know. Like you were the only person who'd ever gotten to know me so well. And you affix realities for – god, I don't know how many people you've gone mind-to-mind with. And they all leave that mark on you, don't they? That aftertaste. How do you handle it? How does *any* mindplayer handle it?'

Segretti glanced down at his plate for a moment. 'How do you handle what *is?*'

I squinted at him. 'What's *that* supposed to mean?'

'The aftertaste, as you put it, comes with the territory. You learn that *any* contact, face-to-face or mind-to-mind, leaves its mark on you. In mindplay, it's a bit more profound –'

'*That's* an understatement.'

'– it's a bit more profound, but no less impermanent, really. The mind is a dynamic system. More information comes in, rearranges everything. Impressions fade. Unless, of course, you reinforce them with continued contact. Just like anything else.'

I thought it over. 'I don't think I can deal with that.'

'It's just a matter of training, I –'

'– mean it,' we said together.

Segretti burst into hearty laughter. 'It really is, though,' he said. 'And there's nothing wrong with any of it. What are you so afraid of?'

I opened my mouth and then hesitated. 'It would take too long to tell you.'

'I know. Finish up, now. You've only got half an hour till the northbound tube departs and you should board at least ten minutes before.'

'Paolo –'

'What?'

'Are you really trained just to forget me?'

'Oh, not forget.' He laughed a little. '*Recover from* would be the more appropriate term, I think.' He shook his head. 'As long as it's alive, the mind is a most resilient thing. You'll see. Mindplay makes it work a lot harder than it's ever had to, but what's wrong with pushing the limit – of anything?'

'But if you get pushed over the limit instead … ' I shrugged. 'Forget it. I guess I'll recover from you, too.'

'It's better to recover from something than to have been numb to it. I mean it.'

'I know you do,' I said.

When he left me at the tube station, it was like watching my mother walk away. Not the mother who'd bought herself a franchise personality, not her. I wondered if other people were hit so hard by their first mindplay experience, or if it was just because I was so much older and had that much more resilience to learn.

The Mental Strip Search was declared unconstitutional before they got

a chance to do it to Jerry, even though it made me wonder what they'd find to do to him instead. By then, I'd been at J. Walter Tech for over a month, and they were doing plenty to me.

J. WALTER TECH

'Pyotr Frankis wants to see you.'

I sat up on Jascha's bed, wincing at the give of the mattress. 'I'm going to ache like hell in an hour. Why can't we use *my* bed?'

'Because I paid a fortune for this one and all the equipment's built into it,' Jascha said, his mustache twitching. It was gilded today, as were his eyebrows. 'I've already fixed up special connections so you won't have to stick your head into the cavity.' He straightened the wide neck of his sweater for the millionth time. A few more yanks and it would be an off-the-shoulder number, which wouldn't have been so bad. Jascha was an attractive man. It wasn't exactly protocol to think of your dreamfeeder in terms of his desirability, but I did it anyway. I couldn't really help it. The familiarity reinforced by repeated mindplay didn't discourage me, either.

Jascha remained professional about it, neither emphasizing nor glossing over the pertinent elements that turned up from time to time *in* my dreams. His matter-of-factness made me marvel; he fed elements into my dreams nearly every day and watched the outcome as I made my way through the various events and images and symbols. Having your dreams fed was a lot better than enhanced dreaming. Jascha's judgment was unerring as to what elements should be added to a dream to make it stronger or stranger or more complex, whatever the therapy seemed to call for, which also made me marvel. But it didn't make me want to be a dreamfeeder.

I swung my legs over the side of the bed and rubbed the small of my back. An hour, hell; I was starting to ache now. Jascha shook his head at me.

'I suppose I could put in a bedboard for you.'

'I'd appreciate it.'

'I'm sure you would. I'm just not so sure it'll help.'

'Neither am I. But I told you the first time you plugged me in, I've never dreamed lucidly and I never will. I'm incapable of it. No matter how bizarre it gets, I just can't tell when I'm dreaming, even if you signal me with the most obvious symbols. If you can't tell when you're dreaming, it's impossible to take control and start steering things around.'

'A lot of impossible cases have lain on that bed –'

'No kidding.'

'– and they were all dreaming lucidly by the last time they disconnected and got up.' His gold-flake eyes narrowed. 'If I put in a bedboard, will you stop saying it's impossible?'

'I'll stop *saying* it. But you'll still have to turn in the readings to Pyotr Frankis.' I paused. 'When does he want to see me?'

'As soon as you're feeling alert. I'd give it at least two hours if I were you. You were dreaming pretty hard, especially toward the end.'

'You put that stuff in.' I yawned and rubbed my eyes.

Jascha pulled my hands away from my face. 'Not all of it. And I told you not to do that.'

'Old habits die hard.' I got down off the bed and left him puttering around with his system, getting it ready for his next appointment.

By the time I got back to my apartment, five levels below Jascha's office in the peculiar maze of the J. Walter Tech building, my postdream lassitude was wearing off and I was feeling a little nervous. Carbohydrate time. The dial in the kitchenette produced a fair lasagna, but nothing approaching Paolo Segretti's. I dialed it up anyway and ate it picnic-style on the floor in front of the dataline, while the news babbled at me.

In the seven weeks I'd been at J. Walter Tech, I'd mainly spent my time plugged into Jascha's dreamfeeding system, absorbing technical information about brains and systems and mindplay in general, or hooked in with Pyotr Frankis. There had been a few dips in the pool for training in dealing with consensual reality, and a fair amount of socializing in real time with the other mindplayer candidates. That was J. Walter's official term for us: candidates.

The candidates were a pretty mixed bag, without many overt similarities. J. Walter's program was just as diversified: there was no set time when everyone's training began or ended. You started when you came in and you left when you were finished. The average length of stay was around a year, but that was just a statistic; the only time frame that meant anything at J. Walter was your own.

They didn't expect you to replace your eyes, either, which was something else I liked about the place, although I'd thought that would be a requirement when I'd arrived. My arrival had been rather low-key. Jascha had met me at the front door when I stepped out of the groundcab that had brought me from the tube station in the center of town. J. Walter sat on the fringe of the mid-urban area, housed in an old stone building that looked as if it had been some kind of temple once, before it had been built up and added onto; flanking the wide front steps were a couple of stone lions, almost featureless. The curious minimalism of their faces gave me pause until Jascha explained they'd been reconstructed from the days of acid rain, but the finer details had been lost.

Jascha had explained a lot to me in the beginning. He'd showed me to my living quarters, an efficiency slightly smaller than the one I'd left behind.

Along with the usual features, including meal dial and lavabo, it had its own scaled-down system and the dataline that was presently telling me what was going on in the rest of the world.

It was easy to lose touch with that sort of thing at J. Walter. Hell, it was easy to lose touch with night and day, you spent so much time plugged in to one thing or another. It surprised me how quickly I got used to that, being plugged into a system, with or without someone else. The awfully mental life I'd been leading, I supposed. As though I'd been training for something like this for years.

But then, it helped that it was Pyotr Frankis I'd first plugged in with and not Jascha, probably because Pyotr Frankis wasn't real.

I finished the lasagna, tossed the pan in the disposal, and settled down in front of the dataline again. They were running old footage of the Malaysian war split-tank with present-day scenes of the Restoration, ten years after. It might have been anywhere. The Malaysians didn't look too happy. I wondered what they would have made of my father.

Sometimes I thought about calling my parents, but mostly, like now, I thought of not calling them. As far as I knew, they were still franchised. Being franchised doesn't leave a lot of room in your head for anything else, or so it seemed. The easy life, if you could qualify. Surprisingly – or maybe not so surprisingly – plenty of people couldn't. I'd never cared to find out, even just for curiosity's sake, but something told me I was completely ruined for it now.

Closer to home, the dataline told me, mindsuck was on the upswing again. There was an interview with one of those impassive Brain Police officers. The sight of him emotionlessly reeling off some of the latest cases so unnerved me I switched off and put a music spike in the deck, Coor and Lam's *Transcontinental Elopement*. It was nearly ten years old but I never got tired of listening to it, maybe because I'd never listened to the whole thing. But it was 408 hours long and somehow I'd never found time for one of those listening parties where everyone gets together and camps out for the whole two and a half weeks it takes the piece to run. Too busy putting on madcaps or hanging in limbo, I guessed. That was where my life had gone, too.

And here I was hanging around again, except now I was preparing myself for a visit with Pyotr Frankis. What a name – Pyotr Frankis. I wondered who had made it up for him. Pyotr Frankis, Jascha – Slavs all over the place, it would seem. Just like my great-grandmother. I felt for her in my mind about the same way you'd feel for a stray piece of food in your mouth with your tongue, but as usual, I had no sense of her beyond a particularly intense memory. Paolo Segretti felt about as vivid to me, though his aftertaste had faded quite a bit over the weeks.

I looked at the clock over the dataline. There was another hour before I had to present myself to J. Walter's system. No one had said I had to stay in

my apartment, so I went down to one of the outside courtyards, using the exterior gallery promenade. The claustrophobia I'd felt when Paolo Segretti had stuck my head into his system seemed to have extended itself to elevators and laterals and other small enclosed spaces. Even the tube ride up to J. Walter had given me some bad moments.

The garden courtyard was beginning to fill up with people taking a break between mindplay appointments. Waving to a few familiar faces, I found the Extremely Identical Twins, Dolby and Dolan, having a late lunch at a small round table under an elm. They were both the same fraction over six feet tall, with the same amount of minor plumpness around their middles. Their straight reddish-blond hair grew at the same rate and fell into the same patterns (and cowlicks). Their taste in clothing ran to the same kinds of loose, frothy shirts over leggings, though they stopped short of dressing exactly alike, and their eyes, too, were different. Dolby had malachite biogems while Dolan had opted for reproductions of his (or their) original hazel pupils. They claimed not to know which had been born before the other; apparently, no one had ever told them.

'Allie,' they said almost simultaneously as I joined them. They adjusted their chairs so they seemed to be exactly the same distance from me on either side and offered me the same portion of their identical tomato sandwiches.

'Thanks, but I just ate,' I told them. 'I'm murdering time before I have to go see Pyotr Frankis.'

'Murdering time,' said Dolby. 'Sounds too serious. How is it, being mentored by a composite?'

'Does it feel different than hooking in with a real person?' Dolan asked. 'Clare mentors us. Never both at once, though.'

'It's different,' I said. 'Though I'm not sure I could explain how. Part of it is the way it draws so much on me for a lot of things. Hooking in with a real person, that doesn't happen in quite the same way.'

'It sounds like you're inventing your mentor as he mentors you,' said Dolan. 'Weird,' Dolby added. They paused, looking at each other intently.

'But probably no weirder than anything else,' Dolby said, and offered me part of his sandwich again. I took some, figuring I could use the extra fuel, and then had to take some of Dolan's to even them out. No weirder than anything else. And Jascha couldn't understand why I was unable to dream lucidly. How could I? *Everything* was absurd, whether it was dream real or really real, so how was I supposed to be able to tell when I was dreaming?

'We've finally come to a decision,' Dolan said, holding off on finishing the last bite of his sandwich so his brother could catch up. 'I'm going to be a belljarrer and Dolby's going to be a thrillseeker.'

I looked from one to the other, suppressing the urge to laugh. The Twins had been at J. Walter for two months longer than I had and they'd been com-

ing to a decision every week. 'I thought Dolby was going to be the belljarrer and you were going to be the thrillseeker.'

'We talked it over,' Dolby said. 'Dolan is really more suited to belljarring. I'm slightly better at finding a thrill in someone's mind than he is.'

'Actually,' said Dolan, 'I'm slightly better at inducing sensory deprivation is what it is. Positively no trauma, none whatsoever. I'd ease you into the belljar so carefully, you'd never miss your senses.'

'I'd find you a thrill you'd never forget,' Dolby said, not to be outdone. He popped the last bite of his sandwich into his mouth at the same moment as Dolan. 'But it would be a safe one, too, not something that should stay buried in your mind. There was this woman I heard about whose big thrill – true case – was walking a dog.'

'That doesn't sound terribly thrilling to me,' I said.

'*She* got a big charge out of it, though. Of course, it had to be a certain kind of dog and the walk had to be in a certain place and go on for a specific amount of time – I can't remember all the details. But it's pretty exciting work. I mean, it *can* be, looking for bona-fide thrills in people's minds. You know, most people are looking for thrills and they don't really know what they are. And most of it's a lot more than walking a dog.'

'I hope so,' Dolan said. 'For your sake.'

They gave each other another one of those looks. 'Are you sure you don't want to be a thrillseeker?' Dolby said after a moment.

'We decided,' Dolan said. 'I'm better at belljarring than you are.'

'You could both be thrillseekers,' I said.

They stared at me.

'Well, surely you've thought of that, haven't you?'

'Yah, we have,' Dolby said uncomfortably.

'But there's a problem. The Kibitzing Factor.'

'We do things differently, see –'

'And we'd be jumping in on each other's work even worse than we jump in on each other's sentences,' Dolan finished in a rush.

'Oh,' I said, mollified. 'Well, I suppose it'll work even better with one thrill-seeker and one belljarrer. After people are overstimulated from Dolby, they can go to you and take a rest under the belljar.'

The Twins nodded together. 'That's the idea,' said Dolan. 'It'll work out just fine.'

Unless he decided to become a pathosfinder and Dolby chose to go into neurosis peddling instead. I couldn't picture either of them as pathosfinders – they didn't seem to have the temperament to work with artists, helping them find what was basically the soul in their work. Pathosfinders delved other kinds of professionals as well, usually as part of some kind of therapy, but I couldn't picture that either.

Twin neurosis peddlers was a more likely scenario, I thought. I could just see them giving people some kind of obsessive-compulsive ritual or a minor recreational fetish. I was considering neurosis peddling myself. If I knew anything, I knew neurosis.

And then again, I thought, anything could happen and all three of us might end up as reality affixers. *Oh, sure,* said a small voice in my mind. *But in three different realities.*

The Twins began another discussion of who should be the belljarrer and who should be the thrillseeker. I listened to them until the appointment chime on my collar went off.

PYOTR FRANKIS

The attendant on the system worked as fast as he could to minimize the lapse between the time I stuck my head into the system and the time the connections touched my optic nerves, but I still hit the relaxation exercise with a bang. There was no way to modify the institute's system the way Jascha had changed his for me, rigging up a blindfold-type sling to secure my eyes while I was plugged in. The institute's system was worse than Paolo Segretti's had been; it molded right around your face and fed you air instead of letting you breathe undisturbed. No matter how much I relaxed myself before climbing onto the slab, every nerve in my body turned into an alarm bell as soon as I put my head in the hole.

The system was patient, once I was inside. It just kept washing colors over me, working with my synesthesia to get me down off the ceiling of my skull and into a receptive mode.

Pyotr Frankis always appeared after the colors began to fade rather than feeding himself in as one of them, the way Segretti had. Probably because he wasn't real, I figured. Except, when I was hooked in with him, he felt as real as anyone did.

He looked real, too. His composer(s) had made him a fairly diminutive person, always dressed in dark, loose clothing that seemed to be hiding a bony frame. His straight black shoulder-length hair was starting to get a little white in it, just like anyone real. The silver eyes, however, were just a little too much, at least in my opinion. They would catch light at odd moments and glow at me. I'd thought I might laugh about that effect but somehow I never did, even afterward.

Today, there was a pause between the end of the relaxation exercise and his

appearance. I waited, drifting bodiless in some kind of undefined open space, and then I saw them.

Snakes.

Well, that was new. They congealed out of the air – or whatever – moving slowly, floating along with me. I didn't know anything about snakes but something told me they weren't the kind even an expert could have identified. They were all colors, some bright, some pale, some dark, some almost invisible. It wasn't unpleasant, having them there with me, and I was no longer given to snap judgments about symbolism so I wasn't upset by them. They swam through the nothing for a while and then, almost casually, they all grabbed their tails in their mouths and began to spin.

I tried to back off but it was like trying to recede from my own shadow. They stayed with me, spinning faster and faster, becoming rings of colored light, giving off sparks. I felt something vibrating inside me, answering somehow. Sympathetic excitation.

Then they were gone and Pyotr Frankis and I were sitting across a desk from each other.

What was that? I asked, breathless, as it were.

Alerted Snakes Of Consequence.

Pardon?

Pyotr Frankis smiled at me. *It's a joke. Altered States Of Consciousness. Alerted Snakes Of Consequence. Life is funny, Allie. You should remember to laugh. But that's not to say you shouldn't watch out for the Alerted Snakes Of Consequence all the same.*

The environment switched without so much as a blink to a large empty room. Pyotr Frankis and I were sitting on the floor in the center of it, reddish-gold afternoon sunlight pouring over us from the oversized mural windows to my right. Outside I could see a hazy city skyline that looked vaguely Byzantine. The environment tended to switch without warning when I was hooked in with Pyotr Frankis. I wasn't sure whether it was a peculiarity of his program or something of my own, perhaps a sort of mental nervous twitch.

Pyotr Frankis was looking at me dreamily, stroking his own hands one against the other as though he were a magician preparing for his next trick. *Now*, he said, *tell me you can't dream lucidly.*

I can't. I'd try, except I don't know when I'm dreaming so I don't know when to try.

Try now, he said.

Now? But I'm not asleep now.

No, but you're dreaming.

Well, yes and no, I wanted to say but I had a sense of not wanting to argue with him. Instead, I got up and went across the room to one of the windows. The skyline seemed to shimmer like a mirage, the haze more like red dust

resting thickly in the air. Minarets and spires gleamed in the sun, swollen to three times its normal size as it floated downward. Far off, I could see the points of a familiar cathedral.

Without thinking about it, I put my hand through the glass. It felt as though I were reaching through something warm and soft. The sharp points of the buildings touched my fingertips. I was a giant; the skyline outside was miniature.

I touched the cathedral, running my hand over the roof, the spires, the buttresses. My fingertip was larger than the front door. I could find no evidence of the patched places I'd seen when I'd visited it before. Some things were visible only from very close up.

My hand closed around the tallest spire. In one stroke, I could have pulled the cathedral up like a root. If I did, would everything come with it, or would I just pull the housing off the foundation, leaving everything inside exposed?

My attention pulled back, turning inward so that the mental flow of time halted. Not this; you don't go exposing your private places just for the sake of having done something. I let go of the cathedral.

Abruptly, I was sitting on the floor again, facing Pyotr Frankis. There were still indentations from where I'd been holding the spires.

No one is prepared for such an extreme action, Pyotr Frankis said. *Not you, certainly not me. Mental activity does not need to be so drastic. If I were real, I would be unable to cope with being a witness to such an act of self- exposure. And even so, it might have done something to my configuration.*

But suppose I took you there and showed it to you?

That would be different, he said. *A revealing rather than an exposing, which is quite something else. It would be in context, and so appropriate for you to do that.* He laughed a little. *Or would you really like to try ripping off your undergarments before you remove your outer clothes?*

Oh. I heard something slither dryly across the floor behind me but I didn't turn around. *Alerted snakes of consequence?* I asked.

I told you to watch out for them, said Pyotr Frankis, mildly amused. *Say it with the capitals. Alerted Snakes Of Consequence.*

Alerted s-s-s-S-snakes of conse-con – I shrugged. *Sorry. I guess I just can't accept them. I mean, they're a joke. Aren't they?*

He was smiling at me.

All right, then, what are they? Really.

Is really *the word you want to use, Allie?*

I did my best to convey *glare* as a total sensory experience, which amused him.

Think of them as … oh, perhaps something you hadn't thought of. How much of the consequence of anything can you foresee? And everything has consequences, Allie, especially in the mind. You have to be – he beamed like a small sun – *alert.*

Okay. I'm alert. What now?

We were sitting on a bench in a courtyard not unlike the one where I'd left the Twins, except this one was an island in the middle of an endless sea of low shrubbery. Pyotr Frankis was on my right, gazing up at the pale blue sky. *I see forever,* he said. No, what he'd actually said was, *I can see this is going to take forever,* but somehow it had gotten compressed. He reached over almost casually with his right hand and pressed the palm to my forehead, which materialized as soon as he made contact. I jumped. There was pressure and a flash memory of the last several days. Tendrils from his fingers unwound, going deeper, touching even earlier events.

Switch. The memory probe was over and now we were ambling along the green bank of a river, Pyotr Frankis still on my right, closer to the water.

I have some things for you to do, he said. *Perhaps they will help. First, you will fast two days out of seven. Two days in a row, forty-eight hours. Only water those days, lots of it. Start today, as soon as we finish. Spend at least an hour every other day in the pool, longer if you can manage. Take walks. Dream vigorously.*

Except for the fasting and the frequency in the pool, I do all of that already, I said.

Now do it in a mode of following my instructions.

All right, I said, *but tell me something – all I've done since I've gotten here is have my dreams fed, paddle around in the pool, and meet with you. When do I take the other forms of mindplay?*

The time will come. This is just the beginning for you, Allie, and everything begins in dreams. He smiled up at me. Being closer to the water, he was shorter than I was. His silver eyes gleamed as he leaned forward and kissed me. Nothing much, just a brush of lips (I'd gotten so used to being without a head that it was somewhat jarring when it sprang into existence for any reason). Then he turned and went toward the river.

He didn't do anything so ostentatious as walk on water. He just walked into the river and disappeared beneath the surface.

Colors fell over me like a soft rain of veils.

GOING FAST

Two days out of seven. It was hell. I took to marching through the city by myself (walks he wants me to take, I'd think, well, I'm taking them, this is a walk, maybe I'll walk off the edge of the world, lucid walking, we could call it), glaring straight ahead without really seeing anything. Then I'd feel bad because

I knew that wasn't in the spirit of what Pyotr Frankis wanted me to do, so after I could eat, I'd go out again and look at real reality as though I were a tourist.

There were still regular appointments to keep with Jascha, fasting or not. My dreams had to be fed even if I went hungry. The fasting dreams were not all about food, but they always contained some element involving consumption, much more so than the dreams I had when I wasn't fasting. Jascha would feed in some element – an image of a piece of sculpture, a stranger entering the room, music playing – and whatever it was, I would find some way to consume it.

But never lucidly. I still behaved as though I were in real reality, even as I was absorbing a futon or a holo-tank. If it continued to frustrate Jascha, he didn't say anything about it.

The pool was a different experience. The hookups were buried in the J. Walter sub-basement, a collection of pods watched over by several attendants who installed people and removed them again like batteries in a power pack. I had to spend half an hour breathing myself into a near trance just to get near one of those pods. The attendants didn't seem to care. They were a curiously bland group, all of a kind; I often wondered how they'd come to do what they were doing, and what they'd been doing previously. But after a bout of swimming around in consensual reality, it was a relief to surface to one of those nondescript beige uniforms who would help me out of the pod without comment and send me off.

The pool fascinated me, as it did just about all the candidates and even the resident mindplayers, who dipped into it almost as often as we did. You couldn't always tell who was who in the pool – people wouldn't necessarily manifest in a form you would recognize from the outside world. Sometimes you couldn't even tell which were the real people and which were pool phantoms, a phenomenon nobody understood completely. The prevailing theory was that they were leftover waking dreams or visualizations that had taken root in the reality, like feedback loops or something. Aside from the general bizarreness of the phantoms' existence, it meant that you couldn't always be sure of exactly how many people were really in the pool at any one time.

After my first few dips in the pool, I stopped trying to figure that out while I was still in, although I had a feeling Jascha wouldn't have approved. Not lucid enough. Well, there were times to be lucid and times just to go with it, I reasoned. Maybe someday I'd strike a balance.

Entering consensual reality was different from meeting someone mind-to-mind in a system. Things were already in progress; you had to visualize a place for yourself in the middle of whatever was going on. Breaching the boundary conditions of the environment (or whatever) was sometimes easy, sometimes not. Occasionally, I found myself watching for several mental minutes before I could get the gist of what was going on and find a place for myself in it.

After that, it was almost easy. Sort of. You had to concentrate to hold up your end of the reality. If your energy flagged, you'd find yourself locked out of the action, watching as though from behind a transparent screen. Eventually, you learned how to keep pedaling, as it were, without devoting the greater part of your attention to it.

In spite of the strong mental image Paolo Segretti had said I had of myself, I was surprised to find I didn't always join the pool in an easily identifiable form. Pre-existing conditions might dictate something entirely different than how I usually saw myself and my unconscious (or something) complied. It was quite natural. The day I faded in to find a playground scenario in progress, I joined as another child. Another time, the pool was flying a jet stream so I came in as a flyer, complete with flashy paint job and chrome accents.

Scenarios seldom persisted for very long, however, and there wasn't always a great deal of continuity. The pool system provided a back-up environment in case things dissolved, so we wouldn't all be drifting around in our private conceptions of limbo – a pool of the swimming kind, with deep end, diving board, and even a smell of chlorine. But you still had to work to keep your part in it going.

Generally, I took a walk after a session in the pool even if I was exhausted, probably as a reaction against knowing I'd been shut up in a pod barely larger than a body bag. I'd walk halfway across the city sometimes, past the business district, through the residential area, all the way to the lake harbor, and then grab a flyer back.

I began to get into a kind of rhythm that wasn't exactly a routine but more a matter of knowing what I had to do and what I could leave open. It figured, I thought; Pyotr Frankis had to exist the same way, since he wasn't real.

Well, *I* felt real enough. The only times I didn't feel quite real were on fast days, when I wasn't sure I could generate enough presence to hold my place in real reality, let alone in something as trippy as the pool. Nonetheless, I managed, not always lucidly, and I might have gone cycling my way through my life almost indefinitely, except that McFloy showed up. And that changed everything.

THE EYE TRICK

I was eight hours into another bout of fasting and the pool had gone pastoral, rolling hills bounded by lightly wooded areas, mountains in the distance under an overcast sky. The pastoral scenario was a variation on a recurring environment, fairly undemanding in terms of how much it took to make

a place for yourself in it. The air seemed charged with collective conscious energy. Must be a full pool today, I thought, settling down in a small stand of trees on the fringe of the forest. Whenever the pool was full, the situation simplified to accommodate all the presences at work in it. I coasted for a while, watching two men directly in front of me set up a sketchy campsite with a barely realized lean-to and some vague equipment. One of the men was very old, the other just out of adolescence. The Twins, I guessed and wondered how they appeared to each other. How I was seeing them wasn't necessarily how they were seeing themselves.

A little ways off from them, someone in a clown suit was juggling an inde-terminate number of brightly colored balls. No, not balls – eyes. That had to be Felicity, I decided. Felicity was about to leave J. Walter at any moment for a career as a thrillseeker. She had all those thrillseeker characteristics, extro-version, tendency to act out, energetic style, the dramatic gestures Pyotr Frankis had accused me of, as well as real talent for finding bona-fide thrills locked in the unconscious. But there was one last step for her and it hadn't come yet. She had explained some of it to me not in the pool but one night when insomnia had hit us separately and we'd found ourselves in one of the Common Lounges, the only people awake in the whole world. In real reality, she was an expansive kind of person, always looking as though she were tak-ing up more space than she actually was. Perhaps it was the hair, which seemed to have been colored by a primitive artist and designed by an admirer of Van de Graaff. In the pool, she often manifested as an odd element that somehow always found a niche. A clown juggling eyes in the country wasn't the most unusual thing she'd ever done with herself.

There were a few other people sitting on the grass, some alone, some in small groups of two or three or four, some wildlife running around, stray flowers appearing and disappearing as someone thought about them and then forgot them again. Someone I couldn't identify waved at me, an andro-gyne wearing an expensive-looking velvet suit. I waved back. Overhead, the trees whispered in the wind and I heard a faint mumble of thunder from far away.

The androgyne melted into existence next to me, leaving the little group she'd been sitting with. It's hard to say what happened next. When you're in mind-to-mind contact with just one other person, the exchange is fairly clear-cut. But there was something about the pool that tended to make cer-tain things blur. Kind of. Maybe it was the fact that everyone was acting on everyone else all at the same time, just by being present. Or maybe it was because the contact wasn't as direct in the pool. Individual events could take on a virtual aspect and you'd have to figure out what happened later, after you were out in real reality.

Some kind of contact was made, some exchange took place. Eventually,

I looked up and saw a man sitting in one of the trees directly above me. The androgyne was gone.

This is my first time in, the man in the tree said. The words were quite clear, not muddied the way a lot of first-timers' were. I was impressed.

What are you doing up there? I asked, standing up to get a better look at him. If his words were clear, his face wasn't. I seemed to be looking at him underwater.

Getting the lay of the land. Pause. *As it were.*

As it were. And then I was in the tree with him, perched on a branch at right angles to his. I didn't know whether that was my idea or his, or maybe someone else's entirely, like the androgyne. Another branch obscured my view of him, so I broke it off. For a few mental moments, his image rippled in front of me, as though he couldn't decide on something. Then it cleared and I nearly fell out of the tree.

Jerry Wirerammer.

Jerry Wirerammer and none other. The same insubordinate sandy hair, the same cat's-eye biogem eyes, the same mildly goofy expression of *Who, me?* and *Come on, dare yourself* all at once. The tree began to sway.

Did I do something wrong? he asked.

Not Jerry Wirerammer. Definitely not. *Did I do something wrong?* was not a Jerry Wirerammer question.

We were sitting on the ground, some distance behind the campers, whose lean-to had vanished. Somewhere in there I'd told him he looked like someone I'd known once and he'd acknowledged it but he still looked exactly like Jerry Wirerammer.

If Jerry Wirerammer did not exist, it would be necessary to invent him, he said. *The spirit of Jerry Wirerammer moved upon the waters and found it good.*

What? I said.

I was just thinking, he said. *Jerry Wirerammer sounds more like a force of nature than a person.*

You were talking like he was God.

Isn't God a force of nature?

The scenario was evolving as we spoke, or whatever we were doing. Now it was a large indoor room with grass carpeting and odd potted plants in the corners. The person who had been the androgyne was now more female than male; she was traveling around the room a few inches off the floor. I couldn't find the Twins. Maybe they'd become plants for a while.

It's disconcerting. You looking like that, I told him.

I don't know how else to look, he said, almost sadly. *I think I've always looked this way.*

I've never seen you before.

Well, I did tell you it's my first time in the pool.

There was music, something I couldn't quite identify, and we were all outside again on a terrace, attending a formal evening dance under an impossible sky of multicolored stars.

Does it always change this quickly? he asked.

Not always.

I may have danced, alone or not, but I kept returning to him. We sat at a tiny metal table in the same respective positions we'd occupied in the tree. For a while, the eyes Felicity had been juggling sat in a pile on the table between us and he examined them all carefully, occasionally handing one to me. We talked, but I wasn't always sure what we were saying.

Not Jerry Wirerammer, he said at one point, *but McFloy. Just McFloy, nothing else.*

There's always something amusing, if that's the word, about one-name people. You wonder what they do when they run into two-name people whose first or last name duplicates their one. Three-name people like me rarely run into two other people with names that duplicate two of their own – the equally amusing possibility of Alexandra, Victoria, and Alexandra Victoria all swimming around in the same pool.

He picked up a little of it from me; someone else caught more of it and passed it on to little effect. The music faded away and there was the sensation of a lot of time passing without any time passing at all. Eventually, the environment moved back inside, but the terrace was still visible through a pair of tall French doors.

McFloy looked around the brightly lit room from where we sat together on an indeterminate antique divan. *I liked it better outside,* he said.

And then we were outside again, just him and me, looking back at everyone still inside from the other side of the French doors.

That's pretty good, I told him. *Not many people can manage that on their first time in the pool.*

I'm a prodigy, he said distractedly, reaching into his jacket pocket and pulling out an eye. Not one of those Felicity had been juggling. It had a gold-flake pupil. *You recognize this?*

It looks like Jascha's.

He balanced it on his palm. *He doesn't know I have it. Should I give it back to him?*

That gave me a chill. *Yes. Right away.*

He rubbed the eye between his hands and then paused, smiling at me. A man materialized on my left. He had two eyes, but the right eye was blank. It changed to a gold-flake biogem; McFloy's hands were empty. The man turned to me; he didn't look at all like Jascha and he melted away when I tried to speak to him.

Not terribly ethical, I said, *borrowing a piece of someone without his*

47

permission. The eyes Felicity was juggling were of her own imagining, they didn't really belong to anyone.

That wasn't Jascha. It was a phantom. Some people leave them behind, I've noticed. They can persist for mental days before they finally fade away. McFloy smiled Jerry Wirerammer's loopy smile at me. *Here's something else you should know about.* He reached into his pocket again and held out a gold-flake eye – the same one.

Very prodigious, I said, feeling uncomfortable. Jerry Wirerammer had been in the habit of cloning mental bits from other people, too.

Jascha was still here when I joined the pool. And he still doesn't know. He never will. Unless someone tells him. He closed his hand around the eye. When he opened it again it was gone. *See?* he said, smiling at me. His right eye was now gold-flake, mismatched to the other one. *Everyone's got a blind spot. Never mind, I haven't diminished him. I've just cloned something of his and now we both have it. Allie.* A new eye appeared in his hand, not a biogem. The pupil was brown with green flecks.

I put my hand up to my eyes, but there was nothing to feel because I had no head. My blind spot. I moved to the center of the terrace, wishing the eye back into the head I didn't have. It vanished from his hand.

Don't worry, Allie, I haven't diminished you, either, he said, still grinning at me in the loopy way. *What I'm really interested in is your mind.*

Time to go, I thought, and went.

The damnedest things affect you in the damnedest ways. I kept seeing those eyes resting in the palm of his hand, first the gold-flake biogem and then my own. Quite a mental trick, and he'd accomplished it effortlessly, or so it seemed. I wondered if anyone at J. Walter knew there was a prodigy loose who was capable of appropriating other people's points of view. Or maybe I was the only one bothered by it. People traded points of view all the time in real reality – figuratively, of course. So maybe it was just the way it translated so literally into the eye trick in the pool that bothered me. Maybe it was just my initial resistance to mindplay resurfacing.

I looked for McFloy in real reality but almost no one seemed to know him, with the exception of Jascha.

'I'm dreamfeeding him, the same way I am you,' Jascha told me somewhat shortly when I questioned him. I couldn't stop looking into those gold-flake eyes. Did he have any idea someone had stolen part of his vision? But if it wasn't actually missing from him, had it been stolen at all?

'I was just curious,' I said, hoping I sounded harmless enough. 'I'd never met anyone named McFloy and he looks exactly like Jerry Wirerammer.'

'No, he doesn't. Not out here, anyway. He leads an awfully mental life, too.'

I kept looking at Jascha as I stalled with talk about McFloy so I wouldn't

have to get up on that too-soft mattress, and gradually I became aware that I was reading his Emotional Index by sight.

Training in reading an Emotional Index by sight or while you're in the system was rather vague. Somehow, you were just supposed to start doing it. It was easier in the system, since things tended to become palpable. Sight-reading in real reality was a lot less certain. So much depended on body language of a particularly subtle sort – movements performed in a certain order, the tilt of the head, certain facial expressions of course, but you couldn't always depend on that, either. It had to be a gestalt kind of thing, where you were perceiving everything at once, situation and mood as well as appearance. When you could make it work, however, it was extremely revealing. Not quite mindreading, Jascha liked to say, but more like being able to read the graffiti on the walls of someone's skull.

The graffiti on the walls of Jascha's skull said he was troubled, by McFloy and by my questions about him. He didn't like McFloy, or he didn't like something about him, which was almost the same thing, and he had to work extremely hard to hold it in.

It was a little embarrassing, as though I'd peeped into his room and caught him talking to himself or something. After a long moment, I realized he was staring back at me just as hard; he knew I'd been reading him.

'Hey,' I said, hopping up onto the techno-bed to cover my embarrassment. 'Lucid living. You know?' The bed didn't give the way it usually did. I pressed the mattress with both hands. 'You put in a bed board!'

'I told you I would,' Jascha said, almost sullenly. 'Think you can dream lucidly now?'

'No.'

I was right about that, too.

Maybe it was because of Jascha's reaction as well as my own curiosity about McFloy but I started spending more time in the pool. Neither Pyotr Frankis nor Jascha commented on it; the attendants installed me and took me out with their usual neutrality. And McFloy was always there, as though he lived there. If Jascha hadn't told me he was dreamfeeding him, I might have come to believe McFloy was actually one of the stronger pool phantoms, invented by all of us because he didn't exist. It wasn't that he didn't seem real, but then even the pool phantoms seemed real while you were in.

McFloy and I became shadows to each other, always within easy mental reach. The pressure of his presence was unmistakable; I always knew him, no matter how he appeared, and his image would always resolve itself into the form of Jerry Wirerammer. Like a mental landmark for both of us.

Occasionally he did the trick with my eye again, producing it from a fold in his clothes or some other hiding place, once from his mouth, which was

rather alarming. I couldn't reciprocate with one of his cat's-eyes; the mental acrobatics of just appropriating his point of view without his help were beyond me. Reading his Emotional Index wasn't easy, either. It seemed to be something he was already familiar with and was able to guard against, showing me only the more predictable feelings without the undertones. Once in a while I caught him out, but not often. Not often enough, as far as I was concerned.

The walks in real reality took on an intermission quality, as though I were using them to rest up for dreamfeeding with Jascha or the occasional conference with Pyotr Frankis or the pool. Maybe mostly the pool.

Maybe? Well, I fooled myself about that for a while. Mindplay never meant you couldn't fool yourself as much as you wanted. I took to the pool as though I were trying to emulate Pyotr Frankis in his form of existence, meeting McFloy in the sky, in realms built out of group fantasies, in places that were so common I wasn't always sure I was really in the pool, except that I would look over and see him in his Jerry Wirerammer suit.

Eventually, I realized he'd had my eye for longer than when he'd first shown it to me on that terrace. I wasn't sure why I hadn't caught on sooner. Maybe because I couldn't live lucidly enough. I wondered if he had a complete collection of eyes. But mostly I wondered how I could find him, out there in real reality.

You don't need to find me out there, he said. *It's enough that you found me in here. What I'm really interested in is your mind.*

We were sitting in another variation of the pastoral scenario where I'd first met him; his words startled me several inches off the grass. I hadn't mentioned I'd been looking for him out there in real reality.

Come down, he said, amused. *I didn't mean to alarm you. The sensation of searching has been pouring out of you for some time.*

That obvious? I reached down and dug my fingers into the aqua grass, trying to pull myself down again; my buoyancy fought me.

For anyone who wants to see it. The cat's-eyes shimmered. *Everything is obvious for those who want to see it.* His left eye was blank now; he was holding one of the cat's-eyes out to me. *What would you like to see, Allie?*

I was fasting that day, and very hungry. I took the eye from him.

What I'm really interested in is your mind.

That's the sort of thing you should think over, especially when a mindplayer says it to you. Even a mindplayer candidate. The first thing I saw were a series of parquet deformations. He watched them with me as the patterns evolved, drawing on the shapes in the pool reality.

Do you keep this running all the time? I asked. There was no answer. The deformations cleared and we were floating in the system pool. Some kind of

mist or fog was rising up from the water, thickening in the humid air. I was disappointed; I'd thought he would show me more than a few of his personal visuals.

We're the last two left, he said. *There's no one else in the pool but us.*

I might not have known it if he hadn't told me, and with anyone else it might not have mattered. I could detect no difference in the feel of the hook-up; it wasn't as though we were hooked in only to each other, and yet now we were. The only thing between us was the pool itself.

This was bound to happen, he said, treading water lazily. *With all the time you spend in the pool now. Sooner or later you were bound to end up alone, or just with one other.*

With you, I said.

With me. His admission stirred the water gently. The fabric of my thoughts rippled in sympathy. His left eye was open now, brown with green flecks in the pupil. I was no longer holding the cat's-eye in my hand, but I knew where it was.

Let me look at you, he said.

In the act of letting him, we bypassed the pool medium and it vanished. Now we were hooked directly in with each other, by virtue of the eye trick, an exchange of vision.

Paolo Segretti's carnelian eyes had changed to cat's-eye in the memory, shimmering as I accused him of being about to mindrape me. Pyotr Frankis's cat's-eye pupils caught the light more intensely than silver and shone like small, distant suns. Jascha asked me about a bed board, the cat's-eyes alternating from light to dark with each small movement. As though they'd been there with me all along and I was only seeing them now. Even my great-grandmother's portrait looked down at me with them, casting their light over everything in the cathedral.

Did anyone ever tell you you lead an awfully mental life? someone asked.

He moved through all of it, touching the memories carefully, handling the pieces of my life as though he were looking through a small box of treasures. I could feel his curiosity, his amusement and compassion and, strangely, envy and a kind of longing as he went back and forth among them.

Where did my life go?

You are the One Chosen. (That one seemed to amuse him greatly.)

On the contrary. I didn't think I looked that *good.*

Hey. Lucid living. You know?

Alerted Snakes Of Consequence. Life is funny, Allie. You should remember to laugh.

McFloy's longing seemed to swell in volume like music or water; it flowed in between the memories and I felt myself resonating in sympathy. My resonance drew him in further. Something in him gave, or perhaps it was

something in me. The cat's-eye he'd given me seemed to blaze up brightly, illuminating both of us. Surrounded by the elements of my life, he could not do anything but consent to my own request.

Let me look at you, I said. *Let me look* –

Panic flashed briefly, but it was too late for him to be afraid.

Getting the lay of the land. As it were.

I think I've always looked this way.

The powers of visualization greatly exceed the stage of development in this subject; he can already produce a fully-realized mental scenario with a minimum of detail-smudging. This is virtually unheard-of in regenerated subjects at so early a stage. The recommendation is for training, beginning with the subject's discharge from the facility –

I think I've always looked this way.

What I'm really interested in is your mind.

I could have held all of it in my two cupped hands. He was only two years old. Beyond two years was the solid blackness of nonexistence.

Mindsuck.

Everything stopped. McFloy was gone. I found myself alone in the pool, staring at a single cat's-eye biogem floating in the water. I grabbed it up just before it would have sunk.

I tried to get Jascha to talk to me about McFloy but he refused. Under any other circumstances, I would have considered it none of my business, except I still had a sense of McFloy when I thought about things, about Paolo Segretti and Pyotr Frankis, about my great-grandmother, even about the holo display I'd walked through a lifetime ago when Segretti had taken me to his office and introduced me to mindplay.

It was the eye, of course, McFloy's cat's-eye, that I'd saved from the pool.

I locked myself in the efficiency, put out a Do Not Disturb flag and shut off the dataline. I needed time and space to think but I wasn't ready to go under a belljar to do it.

Even if I hadn't had his eye, it wouldn't have been hard to put the bare bones together. Two years before, McFloy had been someone else and someone had sucked him. It happened, mostly to artists of some kind, holographers, composers, dancers, actors, writers, generally just as they were about to achieve their first recognition. Full-blown celebrities were more inaccessible and their minds more traceable to the chop shops where mindsuckers parted them out and sold off the memories and talents to people who craved the overlay of someone else's experience on their own.

It had happened to McFloy. No, not to McFloy but to someone else entirely, who had then been taken mindless but with his brain intact to a hospital quarantine where a new mind had grown into the vacant neurons and axons – and

behold the man, McFloy, born full-grown from his own empty forehead. In his own words, a prodigy.

I could get a glimpse of it through his cat's-eye, if I concentrated, brief scenes from his hospitalization, a fleeting memory of a doctor's face. But mostly what I could see through his eye was myself, perched on the branch of a tree, sitting on a terrace under the stars, suspended in the pool, about to accept his eye and give him one of my own. I looked amazingly like myself; I couldn't tell whether that was because he actually saw me that way or because that was how I saw myself even through his sight. But the reason didn't matter as much as finding him and reversing the eye trick. He'd been right when he'd told me he hadn't diminished me.

He'd added to me, and I wasn't sure if I could live with that. It was hard enough living just with myself.

I couldn't find him, in the pool or in real reality.

Mindplay candidates came and went. Felicity made the last step, whatever it was, and went off to seek thrills in the minds of the hard-core jaded. New faces, a rainbow of new eyes, rushed in to fill the place she'd left. The Twins and I remained. The Twins and I and, somewhere, McFloy. J. Walter was a big place; I hadn't met half the people I knew from the pool in real reality. It wasn't hard to find strangers and I found them in droves, sitting in the Common Lounges, loitering in courtyards, passing through the halls, but none of them felt familiar, I could find no sense of McFloy in the plain faces, the polished ones, the dyed ones, nothing of McFloy's essence looking out from any of the biogems that looked at me, cat's-eye or not.

The days slipped through my hands less lucidly than ever.

Jascha fed me a flower. It turned into an eye. Cat's-eye. The dream trailed away into a non-event and Jascha woke me with a curtness that had become routine with him, at least as far as I was concerned.

'Still no lucidity,' he said, making himself busy with the connections by cleaning them carefully with a sonic needle. In the wall over the bed, the monitors were dark and silent. He'd recorded the dream to analyze later, I knew; there wouldn't be much to analyze this time.

'Maybe if you weren't mad at me,' I said, 'I'd make some progress.'

He looked up from the connections with genuine surprise on his face. The gilding had worn off his mustache and eyebrows. He appeared younger without it. 'Mad at you? I'm not mad at you.'

'You're mad at someone. Or something.'

'It's not anger,' he said, going back to his busywork. The needle vibrated around the nearly invisible tips of the connections. He pulled a drawer out from the wall and carefully stuck the connections into a bowl of solution.

It must have been somewhere in the dreams, I thought, forcing myself not to smile. It must have been in the dreams, the memory of McFloy looking at me through Jascha's perspective with those cat's-eyes. Maybe Jascha felt invaded or used or something. But it hadn't been *him*, not really. His Emotional Index indicated some kind of anger but perhaps he wasn't thinking of it that way.

'I'm putting in a recommendation for a pathosfinder,' Jascha said abruptly.

'For what?'

'For you.'

I sat down on the bed again. 'For *me*? Why?'

'You're stalled. Or stalling. We're just rerunning the same pattern over and over and you're not any closer to dreaming lucidly than you were when you first came here. A pathosfinder might be able to shake something loose.'

I laughed a little. 'If you want to shake something loose, a thrillseeker would be more appropriate. Maybe what I need is a nice, homegrown thrill.'

'You've been thrilled enough. That's the whole point, Allie. You're letting things happen to you but you're not making anything happen. You're in the passive mode.'

'Not always,' I said, feeling stung. 'I hold my own in the pool.'

'You've got a lot of help in the pool. Consensual reality nudges you around some, but you still float a lot.'

I hadn't been floating that last time with McFloy but I didn't say anything.

'Don't look so unhappy,' Jascha said, sitting down next to me. 'I'm trying to help you, not hurt you.'

I stared at my hands, which were gripping each other in my lap. 'I don't think it's a pathosfinder that I need, Jascha.'

He was amused. 'Well, what, then?'

'Someone else entirely.' I got up and left.

'I'm *still* putting in the recommendation,' Jascha called after me. I didn't have to look at him to know he was angry, or something, again.

I found the Twins glued to a dataline in one of the Common Lounges, watched a news item about a pair of women called the Lady Bugs.

'Who are they?' I asked Dolan.

'Listen,' Dolby said while Dolan kept staring at the two identical women on the screen.

' … another day in court for the former Dolores Messer and the former Iris Feder,' said the newscaster's voice. 'The panel of judges is still deadlocked over the women's request, the first of its kind. What happens in the end will set a precedent, the repercussions of which are incalculable. Counsel for the women has been silent, unlike the LadyBugs themselves … '

54

The woman on the right leaned forward, grinning away, and spoke into an unseen pick-up. 'We are simply fighting for our right to be different by being the same. We don't feel there's an issue here at all.'

'No, we don't,' said the other one. Her grin was looking a little forced. 'If we want to be identical, it's our perfect right. The problem is that no one else is identical, not as identical as we want to be.'

'It's not as if we're asking the government to pay for it, or –'

I reached for the remote and lowered the sound a little. 'Why are they called LadyBugs?' I asked.

'They're as alike as LadyBugs,' Dolan said, giving in and looking at me.

'Even more alike than we are. Amazing.'

'What's the problem?' I said.

'They want their brainwaves synchronized,' Dolby told me. 'Jiggered around within the area of the patterns traced by both their brains so they'll match perfectly, apex to trough. Completely congruent.'

'Nobody wants to make the adjustment, though,' said Dolan. 'Permanent alteration of brain tissue as well as the mind. Mind control. Nobody wants any part of it, so the LadyBugs are suing.'

'Suing who?'

'The Mindplay Bureau. To make them get someone to do it.'

I looked up at the screen. One of the grinning LadyBugs waved at someone. 'They're crazy.'

'Oh, yah? You think so?' Dolan sat up a little straighter on the couch and squinted at me.

'You don't know,' said Dolby. 'You're not a twin.'

'Neither are they, really. I heard their names, they're not even related.'

'Kinship without blood ties. Haven't you ever felt it?'

'And besides,' Dolan added, 'maybe if they were related, they wouldn't feel the need to be so much alike. Think how compatible they are. And they're not even getting married.'

'They're not even *lovers*,' said Dolby. 'They told the news. They're just very best friends who have found that the person they each want to be is a combination of the two of them.'

I was lagging several beats behind them. ' "Compatible." Why do you think they're compatible?'

'Are you kidding? Aren't you compatible with yourself?'

I gave a short laugh. 'Depends on who you ask.'

'Well, *you* can't imagine. The Joy of Congruence is completely beyond you.'

'I hope you won't be offended if I take that as a compliment.'

As soon as I said it, the word lit up in my head. Except it was spelled *complement*.

'Are you okay, Allie?' asked Dolan, taking my hand. 'What's wrong?'

'Maybe you better sit down,' Dolby said and half pushed me onto the couch next to his brother. 'You looked like someone told you you were going to die.'

Complement. When two elements combine and make each other whole. Kinship without blood ties. Sometimes a thing isn't fully in existence until it is named, and then there's no turning away from it.

I *had* to find him now.

I stayed nearly to the limit of my neurotransmitter in the pool and he never showed up. Exhausted, I went comatose for five hours afterward with an IV patch releasing a tyrosine compound into my neck and came out of it still feeling mildly dead.

For some timeless interval, I floated in half-consciousness, dreams flickering in my brain. Eventually McFloy appeared, looking more like Jerry Wirerammer than ever, and I was overjoyed to see him again.

We were back on that terrace, where he'd first done the eye trick. I could hear the people and the music inside as clearly as I'd heard them when we'd been in the pool. The goofy Jerry Wirerammer smile suddenly turned kind. *Not a single thing that's passed between us has been real and yet you've been hunting me like the hound of heaven.*

It is real and you know it. If it weren't, I wouldn't have something that belongs to you. And you wouldn't have something of mine.

But it happened in a dream. How can a dream be real? The smile faded a little. *You'll just have to keep it. If it's so real to you. I'm hardly real, myself.*

I'll find you. Then you can tell me that in person. Unless you're too unreal.

Ghost lightning danced bluely in his hair. *It's the most real part of me that you have, Allie. Nothing of me could ever be so real.*

The eye was there in my hands. I lifted it up to look at it. *Why are you hiding from me?*

The answer, if that's what it was, was so garbled I couldn't make sense of it. There were hints of fear, a strong feeling of wistfulness, a sense of being inadequate, of being full-grown and only two years old. And something else, something I didn't call love for fear the word would shatter him and scatter the pieces beyond my ability to call them back.

It went on for a long time and then, suddenly, I caught a coherent thread. *– said I was a prodigy and sent me here. They told me it was the best thing. Half my life wasn't real. In the quarantine where this person came into being, this McFloy came into being in a dream where they gave me language and humanity but no history. But here, I learned to do what you call the eye trick, to see with others' vision. It's the only time I'm real. When I see through someone else. When I see through you.*

The eye in my hands was glowing like a coal.

I shouldn't be. I should never have come into being.

I wanted to look at him but the eye wouldn't let me. *It's no different for any-one else, really,* I said. *Who ever asked to be born?*

Pyotr Frankis is more real than I am. You're the sum of everything you've done. What do I have but a little of someone else's vision?

There was nothing but the eye now; and me.

But I gave something to you. No one else, just you. For me, it's too much and not enough, all at once. I don't know how to be real on my own. You take it. Make me real. Somewhere, then, I'll live for real, even if it's just in a dream. Your dream.

Why, McFloy?

A little amusement, followed by a memory of a memory. *You are the One Chosen.* The memory faded. *I love your life, Allie. I love you.*

In the pupil of the eye, I could make out the form of a snake in a perfect circle, mouth gripping its tail.

Where are you? I asked. Did I really expect an answer? This was *my* dream. Wasn't it?

The phone's chiming startled me awake, shattering the dream. I rolled over on the futon, putting my back to the screen. Taking a phone call was about the last thing I wanted to do.

On the fifth chime, the recorder kicked on.

'I really expected you to be there,' Jascha said, sounding miffed. I rolled over again and looked at the screen. Jascha was looking straight ahead, like someone having a mug-holo shot, an expression I still knew pretty well. His own screen was showing him a Not-In reading. 'I called to tell you I've made an appointment with a pathosfinder for you. Her name's Benedict, she's quite good. You're to see her this evening, after supper. I'm putting a page out for you so you can't pretend not to know about it.' He paused, looking troubled, seemed about to say something else, and then disconnected.

I wanted to laugh out loud. I didn't need a pathosfinder to help me learn how to dream lucidly any more. The clock over the dataline told me it was an hour until supper. Maybe that would be enough time.

Where are you? The beach was miles long, stretching far ahead of me. The tide was coming in under the afternoon sun and it seemed as though I could feel every grain of sand under my bare feet. The seashore scene was relatively rare in the pool, at least when I was there. It felt especially strange today, built up from minds new to me. I wondered how many people were in the pool today.

After a while, I became aware that someone or something seemed to be pacing me, but when I looked around I couldn't see anything, only a little movement in my peripheral vision. I let it be and kept moving, holding McFloy's eye.

If I hadn't been hungry, I told myself, it never would have happened. Damn

Pyotr Frankis and his bright ideas about fasting for enlightenment. If fasting really had anything to do with enlightenment then millions of people throughout the ages had died of the secret of life. And the secret of life was, in its entirety, that starvation hurt like a bastard.

Several people wading at the edge of the waterline beckoned to me. I paused, scanning them carefully, even though I knew it was unlikely that McFloy would be among them. Overhead, seagulls called out to each other with almost human voices.

There was another movement in my peripheral vision. I turned and saw that a large umbrella had materialized on the sand to my left. I trudged up to it and sat down in the shelter of its shade. I was tired, I realized. Tired enough to sleep.

I lay back on the sand, resting McFloy's eye on my chest. There was a moment of dizziness and disorientation; it seemed as though I could feel every little bit of movement in the universe, the rise and fall of the waves, the earth turning and turning as it swept around the sun, the whole solar system traveling on the fringe of the galaxy as it revolved in endless night.

A thousand faces snapped into focus on the inner bowl of the umbrella, a good many of them my own. The rest were McFloy's.

Everyone has a blind spot, said McFloy's faces.

I was asleep and dreaming in the pool. Nobody did that very often in the pool but it happened once in a while. From everyone else's perspective, I would seem to have vanished. That included McFloy. I was more like a pool phantom now.

My dream self sat up. The beach scene appeared in a kind of negative to me, an orange sky burning over violet sand. I raised my hands but there was nothing to see. Dreaming, I was invisible even to myself. I looked back at where I'd been lying and there I was, asleep with McFloy's eye resting on my chest. Beneath my closed lids, I could see my eyes moving back and forth as I dreamed lucidly. I turned away and paused, staring at the handle of the umbrella. It was a snake. A Snake. Just a joke, but that didn't mean I shouldn't watch out for them.

The beach seemed to brighten, the light very hard, almost blinding. I concentrated into the orange glare on the water and eventually I saw him, standing near the water's edge a little to the left of my focal point, still decked out in all his Jerry Wirerammer glory.

Carefully, not wanting to wake myself up, I moved my perspective a little closer to him. The tide rushed up around his feet and slid away again, taking a little of him with it, as though he were made of sand.

No, I thought. Don't. Please don't.

You don't know, said the McFloy faces in the umbrella. *For you, staying real is effortless. You'll always be real. You've had a lifetime to get used to it.*

The sea was becoming rougher now. The waves came in higher, hitting him in the back, and McFloy was smaller when they washed away.

I knew as soon as I came here I wouldn't be able to stay, said the McFloy faces. At the waterline, McFloy himself said nothing, but I thought I saw a chancre in him, as though he sensed I was nearby.

There are other places to go, I said silently. A gull was calling, except it sounded like an alarm bell for some reason. The sea looked as if it were boiling; far out, larger waves were building, rushing toward the shore.

I don't mean J. Walter, McFloy's faces said. *I mean here. This reality.*

If we could have met, I thought, you could have seen how real you were to me.

I'll always be real to you, Allie. More waves crashed over him, melting his shoulders, eroding his body. Remember that I never really took anything away from you. Remember what I gave you. Let it be your third eye if you want. If there could be such a thing.

That damned gull kept screeching. I struggled to wake myself up. From the corners of my eyes, I could see people gathering on the beach. The air quivered with their agitation.

A hard, high wave rose up and I thought I could see a thousand phantoms in its glassy wall. McFloy turned and looked directly at my sleeping self. He smiled; *Allie,* he said silently. Then the wave pounded down in an explosion of fiery orange froth.

The people on the shore scattered, several of them popping out of existence as they ran. The gull screamed and screamed and screamed.

The attendant was tapping my face lightly with her fingertips. 'You in there? Say something.'

'I'm – what. What's going on?' I could still hear the seagull, except it was unmistakably an alarm bell now.

'Who are you?' demanded the attendant. 'Do you know who you are?'

'Sure. I'm –' I looked down. My hands were still cuddled up to my chest, cupped as though I were holding something, but of course there was nothing there. 'I'm Allie.'

'Good. You can go.' The attendant gave me a little shove toward the door and went to the pod next to the one I'd occupied, yanking open the cover. All around me, the attendants were pulling people out of the pods as soon as the indicators on the covers showed their eyes had been reinserted by the pool system. I found my way over to a chair near the door and sat down, trying to clear my head. Being yanked up through two altered states was a lot like taking a hard one to the skull. My eyes felt as dry as cotton balls.

I don't know how long Jascha was standing over me before it finally registered on me that he was there.

'I was afraid I'd find you here. You're supposed to be with the pathosfinder,' he said.

I pushed myself up from the chair. The room was empty now except for the attendants gathered around one last closed pod in the center. The indicators on the cover were dark, inactive, except for the ones measuring blood pressure and respiration. Low-average readings; the person inside was still alive.

I went over to them. 'Aren't you going to open it?' I asked the one who had pulled me out.

Behind me, Jascha said, 'Allie, I don't think –'

'It's okay,' I said. 'I knew him.'

The attendants looked at each other. All of a kind. I don't think I'd have recognized any one of them if we'd met again in the next two hours.

The readings on the cover of the pod began to fail. Another indicator light went on to show that emergency life support was standing by. If I didn't see him before that happened, I'd never get another chance.

I pushed past several of the attendants and knelt to unlock the cover. Someone made a move to stop me and then thought better of it for some reason. Later, I thought Jascha had probably told them to let me go ahead.

I didn't take a long time. Just long enough to know that he didn't look the least bit like Jerry Wirerammer.

'Flat-line,' said one of the attendants. 'All readings.'

It took me several moments to realize he wasn't talking about me.

Jascha helped me up. 'Call Stanwyn, the belljarrer. Right away.'

'I don't want to go under the belljar,' I said, but no one seemed to hear me.

HOW TO FIND YOUR PATHOS

The Lady Bugs had been grinning out of the screen for several minutes before I registered on them. I tuned out the audio. It had been two days since I'd come out of the belljar and I just wasn't in the mood to hear about their struggle.

The door chimed. I gave it some thought before I got up and answered it. It was Jascha. I let him in anyway.

'You've missed two appointments. Should I phone the Brain Police and tell them you've reconsidered?'

I wandered back to the sofa and curled up on it. 'I've overdone the mind-play lately. I have to sit things out for a while.' I reached for the remote, intending to shut off the screen.

'No, leave it on. I'm dying to see what happens with those two. I think

they're loony, myself, but its going to be a landmark case.' Pause. 'You did as much as you could.'

'I know,' I said, a little impatiently. 'So did you.' Jascha settled himself on the couch a respectful distance from me. 'You were in shock. You had to go under the belljar. Shut down the organism, let it rest. You can't still be mad at me for that.'

I didn't say anything. All I could think of was how much it reminded me of McFloy's time in the darkness while he was regenerating. In the five hours I had spent under the belljar cut off from all sensory input, his eye had shown it to me. Not a lot, because he couldn't remember it consciously; just little flashes that resonated with my own absence of light and sound and feeling. Resonating. McFloy and I had done a lot of that in a small space of time and I hadn't always realized it.

'Look,' Jascha said after a bit. 'It happens sometimes with mindsuck cases. Not often, but it will happen. It's too much for some people to be forced to full maturity in the space of a year.'

'Two years.'

'All right, two years, if you count the year he spent in quarantine along with the year as an outpatient. They were impressed enough with the strength of his mental life to send him here, thinking we'd make some kind of mindplayer out of him.'

I shrugged. 'He might have made it.'

'He didn't have a chance. I knew it as soon as he taught himself to do the eye trick. A person who has to mooch bits out of other people because he can't find enough in himself can't make it.'

'The eye trick. Yah. I know all about the eye trick. That one got by me. Just because I was hungry. I had to consume something, and there he was with something I could consume. His eye.'

Jascha moved a little closer to me. 'There's all kinds of hunger. When you love somebody –'

I groaned loudly. '*Please.* Spare me. When you say stuff like that out loud, it always sounds trivial.'

'You were the only one he gave an eye to. Everyone else he just took from. I don't think that's so trivial.'

'No, it isn't.' I paused. 'Sometimes giving can be like taking, Jascha. Especially when someone gives you part of himself.' All he'd been interested in was my mind. Whenever I closed my eyes, I could call up the image of that third eye as clearly as life, the cat's-eye pupil shimmering. Except now I always saw it with the Snake making a circle inside it.

He said he hadn't diminished me, I remembered. And he hadn't. Except by his death.

'Pyotr Frankis wants to see you again,' Jascha said after a bit. 'That was what I came here to tell you.'

'You could have phoned.'

'I also came to escort you personally to his hook-up.'

I sighed. 'Can't it wait? I told you, I've overdone the mindplay, I need time just to breathe in and out in real reality. Feel real air on my face, hear real sounds, see real things. I feel like I've been in dreamland for a hundred years. Maybe *I'm* getting less real now than I used to be.'

'He's going to pathosfind you.'

'Pyotr Frankis? He's not a pathosfinder.'

'He's whatever his configuration says he is.'

I supposed that was true enough, but – Pyotr Frankis?

'What about your pathosfinder friend?' I said. 'The one I didn't keep the appointment with.'

'Pyotr Frankis and I agreed that it wouldn't work to bring a third party in on things at this point. Before McFloy's drowning, it might have –'

'Drowning?' I stared at him. 'Is that what you re calling it?'

'What else would you call it?'

I thought about it. 'Dissolution. Disintegration.'

'It's the same thing, really. They had to, uh, they had to drain the pool.'

'What?'

'They had to shut it down and run the program bit by bit.' Jascha looked at me. 'Searching for his remains.'

'Did they find any?'

'Some. The rest is so embedded in the program now it doesn't make any difference whether there's anything of him there or not.'

I stared at the LadyBugs on the dataline screen without really seeing them. 'Then, it's like … McFloy *is* the pool.'

'No,' Jascha said firmly. 'He disintegrated.'

'If you shatter a hologram,' I said, 'you can pick up any one of the pieces and regenerate the whole picture. And the mind is a hologram.'

'Not without life, it isn't. The pool is not alive. And neither is McFloy, anymore.' Jascha glanced at the clock. 'Pyotr Frankis is waiting for you.'

I got up. Jascha leaned over to shut the dataline off.

'No, just leave it on. If a dataline is running and there's no one there to watch it, has anything really happened?'

Jascha frowned at me. 'What kind of silliness is that? Do I have to send you back to mindplay kindergarten?'

'There is no mindplay kindergarten.'

'Congratulations,' Jascha said dryly.

We were walking on the bank of that river again, Pyotr Frankis and I. The scene felt a little sketchier than usual. I wasn't exactly putting my heart into it.

Always the dramatic gesture from you, Pyotr Frankis said. *Even the dramatic non-gesture.*

I'm tired of mindplay. It's nothing but trouble.

You might as well say you're tired of thinking. Or that you're tired of life.

Uh-huh.

But you are not. He stopped and gave me a little shake. *Pull yourself together now. That's all you have to do.*

That's all? What kind of a pathosfinding is this, where you just tell me to pull myself together?

His amusement rustled the trees around us, made the river gurgle. *I could give you a lot of double-talk, but yes, that's really all. Come now; give yourself to your concentration. You can visualize better than this.*

A tree that had been a vague blur on the other side of the river came into focus. I recognized it as the tree McFloy and I had been sitting in when we met, and I looked away, half-afraid I'd see him on that same branch, getting the lay of the land again.

Ah, Pyotr Frankis said, studying the tree. Abruptly, we were standing under it. I made a move away from it but he kept me there firmly and yet somehow without real force.

You see now how things can be and not be simultaneously in the mind, he said. *I hold you here without holding you. Now, this is how you pull yourself together.*

What happened next wasn't clear. For some timeless interval, I seemed lost in a jumble of half-formed images – Paolo Segretti, the Brain Police, Jascha, my unlucid dreams, Jerry Wirerammer, my old efficiency. The pieces of my life. You don't keep the pieces of your life in any particular order, they're all over the place.

When the storm cleared, I was standing in front of the cathedral.

It had been a long time since I'd seen it close up. It looked the same on the outside, except it seemed heavier, more solid, as though the whole structure had been reinforced.

Things hadn't changed much inside, either. Some of it had been rearranged but my great-grandmother's portrait was still in the same place and the pose hadn't altered.

I found the eye right away, of course; it was on the table near the crystal vase and the phone and the small holo of Jerry Wirerammer. I held it up to the light. In the cat's-eye pupil, the Snake was clearly visible, still gripping its tail with its mouth. As I watched, it revolved very slowly. Marking the passage of some private time, I thought; maybe sometimes the Snake revolved more quickly. Perhaps there were times when it actually spun.

Ouroboros, said my great-grandmother's portrait. *Alerted Snake without end.*

It was just a joke, I said, putting McFloy's eye back on the table. *Altered states. Alerted Snakes.*

All right, then, altered state without end.

I gave a short laugh. *I suppose you're right. And everyone's got to go somewhere, don't they. Only – when I go, where will that leave you?*

We'll be wherever you are, of course, my great-grandmother said matter-of-factly. *Altered state without end.*

She means it, said a familiar voice. I turned; Paolo Segretti was sitting on an antique divan, plump enough to be real.

Where have you been? I asked.

Here. Where I've always been. You just never got around to me before.

I went over and sat down next to him, surprised at how comfortable the stiff-looking divan actually was. *I didn't think I'd gotten around to you now*, I said.

You triggered me, Segretti said amiably. *I don't just run around in here on my own.*

You told me once that there was only room for me in my mind. That part of me would have to be excised for someone else to fit.

That's true.

Then, how can part of someone else be here in my mind?

If it's here, then it must he part of you. Just as I am. Are you going to use it? he asked.

Use what?

That part of you. The eye was in his hands. Then it vanished and reappeared in his own head, replacing his left carnelian biogem. *I see*, he said thoughtfully. His features blurred, taking on some of McFloy's characteristics.

Something in me leaped to do something about that. Abruptly the eye was gone and Segretti was completely Segretti again.

Suppressing the eye isn't going to solve anything, he said and his voice sounded a little like Pyotr Frankis's.

You bet it's not. I need a dry-cleaning, not a pathosfinding.

It won't work. Look. Segretti held up a mirror. McFloy's eye looked out at me from my left socket. *You can't dry-clean out part of yourself.*

It's not me. It's him, it's McFloy.

Oh, it's you, all right, whether you want to claim it or not. For better or worse. If you'll pardon the expression.

I lowered the mirror and glared at him.

You want to dry-clean something out just because it hurts? It was Pyotr Frankis sitting next to me now. *Sorry. Can't accommodate you.*

You refuse to understand. But that's all right. I reached up and took hold of my left eye, pushing my fingers into the socket.

Stop! Look at what you're doing! Pyotr Frankis held the mirror up again.

My left eye was my own once more, brown with green flecks. I looked over at the table. McFloy's eye was back where it had been. *Do you see? If you try to cast it out, you'll end up crippling yourself.*

I sat back on the divan, feeling suddenly drained. On the table, the eye gleamed at me in the soft light of the cathedral. *All right*, I said after some immeasurable mental time. *Then, I'll live with it. But in my own way.*

Pyotr Frankis laughed. *Of course in your own way – who else's way could it be?*

His, I said. I got up from the divan. *Can we go now?*

Pyotr Frankis nodded. *I'll wait outside for you.* He was gone and Segretti was in his place. *And I'll be waiting in here for you*, Segretti said. *Altered state without end.*

And in McFloy's eye, Alerted Snake without end. I headed for the door, pausing at the table. Jerry Wirerammer's holo looked up at me and grinned hugely. That Jerry. What a kidder. Next to the holo, McFloy's eye trembled. I pointed at it.

STAY, I said firmly.

So where else would it go? said my great-grandmother's portrait.

I looked up at her. *You know what I mean*, I said, and got out of there in a hurry.

Pyotr Frankis and I met in the room with the large windows and the alien skyline outside. *It's like being a ghost without being dead*, I said. *Which I guess would make the system a haunted house.* I paused. *Or me. Can a haunt be haunted?*

I cannot answer that, Pyotr Frankis said, *on the grounds that the theorem of incompleteness makes it impossible.*

What?

That there is nothing on this level of existence that can fully explain this level of existence.

What? I said again.

If a haunt is haunted, it's on a different level of reality.

Not this one.

But which level is this? I asked.

Whatever level you're on, of course.

I remembered the sign in front of the cathedral: YOU ARE HERE. (WHERE DID YOU THINK YOU WERE?)

I think I've had a satori, I said. *Is there a light bulb on over my head?*

In here, you don't have a head. You must also be careful not to mistake a satori for a sartori, which is the realization that you haven't got a thing to wear. The silver eyes twinkled, sort of.

More jokes.

65

Life is funny, Allie. Try to remember that, or tragedy will overtake you and wash you away. In a different fashion, perhaps, but just as thoroughly.

I looked out the window. The cathedral spires were visible just as they had been the other time. I no longer had the urge to go over to the window and toy with the idea of pulling the cathedral up like a flower. Or a weed. Even at that distance, it seemed as though I could feel McFloy's eye where it rested on the table.

Tell me, I said, *what the difference is between reality affixing and pathosfinding.*

Pyotr Frankis was amused. *In reality affixing, you come to me and say, Am I here? And I help you see what you need to see so you can answer that question. In pathosfinding, you come to me and say, I'm here, but am I any good at it?*

There was a rustle of snakes – Snakes – somewhere out of my field of perception. I laughed.

That's reducing it to rather simple terms, he said. *But my configuration tends to do that.*

I'll accept it. But then I have to tell you, I don't think it was successful.

Pyotr Frankis' silver eyes gleamed. *Why not?*

I showed him the scene of myself in the cathedral, ordering McFloy's eye to stay there.

Where else would it go? he said.

You know what I did. Locking it up. I don't think you meant for me to do that.

You do what you need to do, Allie. A Snake materialized between us, coiling lazily. *As for pathosfinding, why do you think the results have to be immediate?*

The Snake looked at me expressionlessly. Of course; what kind of expression could a Snake have?

The mind is a dynamic thing. It will go on and on, changing, reshaping itself, Pyotr Frankis said. *Someday you may go to your cathedral and find it's become a shoe-box. And everything that was in it ...* He paused, looking at me solemnly.

And everything that was in it will be pretty jammed together, I finished for him.

His laughter filled the room. *All right, have it your way, Allie.*

I will, I said. *My way and no one else's. But that's what I've been telling you.* I let it go at that.

In spite of my having locked the eye in the cathedral – or maybe because of that – he began to appear in my dreams. Not the ones I had by appointment with Jascha but in the ones I had in my off-hours, the dreams I was allowed to keep for myself. It was as though he knew the difference. He would emerge from strange countrysides, appear in mirrors, walk through open doors. He

was just a dream phantom, little more than a memory. Always, one of his eyes was blank.

I should have been afraid, but somehow I never was, not in the dreams. He was just there, taking it all in. If he got in my way, I simply moved him aside and went on with the dream. He might have been watching a play or a holo program. Near the end of the dream he sometimes offered a comment, but not always. Eventually, I started taking his presence for granted even while I worked around him, never allowing him to change anything or participate. My way and no one else's.

The change in my dreaming processes extended to the ones I had with Jascha. 'You're dreaming lucidly all the time now,' he told me after one of our longer appointments. 'You're not letting the dreams run away with you. I told you you'd be able to do it someday.'

I was lying on the techno-bed, staring out the window. Below was an empty stone courtyard. No one sat on the sterile benches in the late afternoon sunlight. In the middle of summer, the place looked cold. 'If I have to dream my life away, I might as well be in the pilot's seat. Or at least the navigators,' I said without actually realizing I was speaking aloud.

'You're catching on,' said Jascha approvingly. He tucked away the connections and shut down the system. 'You want to go somewhere?'

I looked at him in surprise. He was gilded again, his skin newly polished. The gold flakes in his eyes struck sparks. 'Don't you have another appointment to feed someone else's dream?'

'I'm taking the rest of the afternoon off. You don't think people mindplay without a break, do you?'

Why not? *I* did.

There was an empty flyer waiting at the stop a block down from the stone courtyard. Jascha hired it and shooed me in. 'Where are we going?' I asked, plopping down on the worn overstuffed cushions in the back.

'Somewhere. Everybody's got to go somewhere.' He leaned forward and spoke to the control deck. 'Overfly the city.'

The flyer lifted immediately, rising at a steep angle. We strapped ourselves in.

'I'm not normally letting anyone make a decision for me these days,' I said.

'Understood.' Jascha turned on the dataline screen in the ceiling. I groaned at the sight of the LadyBugs and he shushed me. 'No, listen. It's the ruling, they said it would come today.'

' ... precedent-setting ruling that the LadyBugs have, indeed, made a psychotic request and thus are petitioning for a license for psychosis, which is their right under the law. The approval has already come in from the local registrar, and tomorrow the LadyBugs will report to a psychosis clinic for their brain-wave synchronization. The National Institute of Mental Activities

is drawing up specifications that will describe this new form of psychosis and name it formally.'

'I always said they were crazy.' I reached over and turned down the sound.

Jascha nodded, smiling at me. I leaned back against the cushions and watched the toy skyline glide by below us.

'Why so deadpan?' he asked me after a bit.

'I was just thinking. If I'd been able to afford the LadyBugs' lawyers, none of us would be here right now.'

'Yes, but where *would* you be?'

'Of course, if I'd been able to afford the LadyBugs' lawyers, I probably wouldn't have been *there*, either.'

'Where?'

'Hanging around an efficiency with an overdrawn kitchen, waiting for someone like Jerry Wirerammer to show up –' I stopped. It was the first time I'd thought of the real Jerry Wirerammer in some time. 'I wonder what ever happened to him.'

Jascha's expression was unreadable, 'If you wait a few minutes, you'll probably find out.'

'What's that supposed to mean?'

'Just wait.' Jascha was looking up at the screen again. The story on the LadyBugs wound down and faded to a commercial. Jascha turned the sound up. It was for the Power People franchise but I stifled the urge to groan again.

The overdone camerawork showed hordes of dreary, dull people marching along; suddenly, a golden arrow materialized and touched the shoulder of a middle-aged man. He stopped and looked heavenward with an expression of childlike wonder.

'Have you ever wished you were more than just another warm body in a world of warm bodies?'

The scene switched to a party, where our hero was standing in a corner with a drink in his hand, nodding his head thoughtfully. Someone passed him a platter of artificial-looking hors d'oeuvres and he sent it on without looking at it. The sound of a roomful of people giggling madly came from off-camera.

'Have you ever wished you had more personality? The kind that could, enchant, amuse, *involve?*'

Switch to our man alone in a room. He hesitated, then went to the phone and punched the buttons with enthusiasm. Switch to a view of the phone monitor. A ridiculously beautiful woman appeared: 'Power People – we have the person you want in your life!'

'You can be enfranchised!' crowed the narration. 'It's simple, it's fun, and it's not as expensive as you'd think! Due to the breakneck pace of scientific and technological research, personality rental is the most reasonable it has

ever been – and with our seasonal specials, you can pay even less!' Quick succession of shots of our man going to Power People for consultation, then sticking his head into a system, after which he was wheeled into reconstructive surgery ('On the premises!' the narrator said assuringly). I thought of the LadyBugs, but it wasn't quite the same thing. Getting franchised involved an overlay on the core person, the mental equivalent of a mask, if a bit more complicated. The physical surgery wasn't absolutely necessary but most people seemed to prefer going the whole route. Rampant brandname-ism. They wanted everyone to know which designer personality they had.

'Over a million outlets worldwide, waiting to serve *you!*' Pause; final shot of our man, now unrecognizable as a ridiculously handsome type, being entertaining at a party with a woman under each arm.

'And just *look* at this weeks *specials!*'

We looked. Portrait of a striking older woman staring off into space. 'Anya Mukherji, a real person who modeled her life on Indira Gandhi's!' Change to a slightly younger woman with sequins glued to her bald turquoise head. 'Yvette La Due – the life of any gathering, anywhere, any time!' The portrait winked. Change again, another face. 'Jerry Wirerammer – if there isn't one in every crowd, there ought to be!'

I didn't gasp or yell or even move. He must have sold himself for salvage to pay the fines, I thought, and somehow Power People had found something in him that real people wanted. I thought of McFloy finessing his image out of me without my even knowing it. But then, McFloy had only been two years old, his own life hadn't been enough.

So when had that ailment ever been confined to recovering mindsuck victims?

'Now you know,' said Jascha, and he shut off the screen as a story on the breakup of the Coor and Lam composing team was fading in. 'Do you want to talk about it?'

If Jerry Wirerammer did not exist it would be necessary to invent him. 'No.' It didn't make that much difference. Jerry himself was probably wandering around somewhere tickled to the point of spasm that people were paying good money – or bad money – to feel like they were him. And they all lived happily ever after. As each other.

'Look, I know you must be feeling a lot of things about it right now –'

'I'll just keep my feelings to myself for the time being, if that's all right with you.' And everyone had to go somewhere, McFloy, Jerry Wirerammer, even me. Except that by licensing himself for franchise, Jerry had gotten to go and stay at the same time. Just like – I clamped down on the thought and shut it off.

'Deadpan Allie,' Jascha said.

'What? That sounds like a bad neighborhood.'

Jascha laughed a little. 'Just a thought.'

DEADPAN ALLIE

I wasn't sure who I surprised more, Jascha or myself, when I took the pathos-finding option. Pyotr Frankis wasn't surprised at all, but then, surprise probably wasn't in his configuration. The Twins would have been surprised if they'd had time; they were packing to leave the day I told them. Oddly enough, they were unleashing themselves as twin neurosis peddlers on an unsuspecting world.

'It's the only way,' Dolby said as he rearranged the contents of one of Dolan's suitcases. 'Otherwise, we'd never be sure if we were in the right roles.'

'What about the Kibitzing Factor?' I asked, sitting on Dolby's bed and handing some of Dolby's things to Dolan, who was, of course, repacking one of Dolby's suitcases.

'Kibitzing is neurotic,' Dolan said cheerfully, holding a tube of depilatory in one hand and a bottle of cologne in the other. 'We'll be able to roll with it, work it right in with no problem. This looks like my stuff.'

'Of course it does. All my stuff looks like your stuff.'

'Not all of it,' Dolan said a little darkly.

'Well, *that* stuff looks like your stuff.'

'Then, where's *my* stuff?'

'With your other stuff.' Dolby held up two identical items.

Dolan frowned. 'That looks like *your* stuff.'

'Yes, I know,' Dolby said patiently. 'I just explained that to you.'

'No, wait now. There's a dent in the middle of this tube, see? I saw a dent like that in your tube.'

Dolby looked at the tube he was holding and pressed it with his thumb. 'There. Now they're both dented and it doesn't make any difference.'

'But I want my tube –'

It was too much. At any moment I expected to find Alerted Snakes crawling out of the walls. I jumped up and grabbed Dolan in a clumsy hug. 'I'll say good-bye now. I've got a full schedule this afternoon.' That was a lie but they were driving me crazy. Just as well I hadn't gone into neurosis peddling after all; I just didn't have the temperament for neurotics, or anyone who wanted to be that way.

Dolby rushed over for an identically clumsy hug and I felt sadder than I'd wanted to allow myself. J. Walter was full of new candidates I barely knew now and the last stretch of my training would be rather lonely. Once again, I'd set myself up to go it alone. I'd probably end up packing to leave by myself and wondering where this part of my life went.

'We'll let you know where we are,' Dolby said.

'And maybe you'll drop by for a little fetish or something,' Dolan added. 'Have I got a fetish for you.'

'I've got one, too,' Dolby said, glancing at him.

'Great, I'll get a two-fer if I'm ever in the neighborhood.' I headed for the door before a small war could break out.

'Allie,' one of them called after me (I couldn't tell who without looking).

'What,' I said, pausing with the door open.

'Pathosfinding?' Dolan said. 'That'll be good for you.'

'It'll be good for somebody,' I said.

Dolby grinned. 'So will you.'

Jascha was waiting in the hall for me at my efficiency.

'You haven't come to cross-examine me about my decision to be a pathosfinder, have you?' I said, pressing three fingers to the print-lock panel.

He shook his gilded head. 'Pyotr Frankis gave his approval so I have nothing to say about it.'

I opened the door and stopped. My futon had been exchanged for a much wider one.

'Your doing?' I asked, looking over at him.

He shrugged. 'I always felt bad that you were never able to get comfortable on my bed.' He wandered over to the couch and sat down. His Emotional Index could have been a flashing LCD display but apparently he didn't mind. I closed the door and kept my distance.

'It wasn't so bad after you put in the bed board,' I told him.

'But it wasn't the same.'

I went over to the futon and sat down on it. 'You did your best.'

'Deadpan Allie.'

'What.'

'Nothing. Just Deadpan Allie. I used to be able to read you with my eyes closed. Or out. Now I have to be mind-to-mind with you, feeding your dreams. And sometimes even then I'm not always sure. Not right away, anyhow.'

'Pathosfinders can't go spraying their own feelings all over their clients' minds.'

Jascha nodded. 'Benedict told me you were a quick study. But I'm not a client.'

'You're my dreamfeeder.'

He smiled. 'Yah. When you put it that way, it sounds as good as it is. Being your dreamfeeder. At least I did that, even if I wasn't really the one who got you to dream lucidly. But I'd like to think that I helped in some way.' He fell silent for a moment. 'There's a lot I would say now but I don't want to make

anything sound trivial. And I'm not deadpan. But I've been about as professional as I can be with you and I've reached the limit. So I guess what it comes down to is, if you can't be comfortable on my bed, maybe I can be comfortable on yours.'

There's all kinds of hunger, he'd said. There were all kinds of fasts, too. Pyotr Frankis' had been over for weeks. It was time to end this one, too.

Very ethically, Jascha ceased to be my dreamfeeder. I wasn't taking much in the way of dreamfeeding by then, anyway. Mostly I worked with Benedict, first in a monitoring mode and later on the receiving end. Her approach was different from Pyotr Frankis', which still seemed like more of a reality affixing to me than anything else. But I was getting somewhere, and everyone had to go somewhere. Some things happened and some other things didn't, and at one point I found I'd gone to a place where I married Jascha.

Pyotr Frankis had been right: life was funny. It was also reasonably good and so was the relationship. And after the divorce, I got a job.

PART TWO

Altering States of Consciousness

THE PATHOSFINDER GETS A JOB

'Kid,' said the big little man on the couch, 'it's a good thing you're a pathos-finder and not a neurosis peddler. Neurosis peddlers are a buck a gross in this town.' He rolled over onto his back and watched the dancers on the ceiling. A year before, I might have rolled over to watch them, too, drawn by the faint, classical music flowing under our conversation, but Jascha had tipped me off to that tactic. Let prospective employers divide your attention like that and they can get you to agree to all sorts of things without your realizing it, the more unscrupulous ones using posthypnotic suggestions keyed in with symbols. Or they can use subliminals to convince you that you don't want the job, if *they* don't want *you*. It saves them the trouble of arguing with you. So I held my position, reclining on my left side with my hands composed in front of me, resisting the urge to pick at the lamé upholstery. Only someone as successful as Nelson Nelson would have lamé couches. I was dying to look at the ceiling; whatever those dancers were doing up there, he was enjoying immensely. But I kept watching him watching the holo until he acknowledged my self-control and rolled back over onto his side to face me.

'All right,' he said, smoothing out a wrinkle on his loose tunic. Loose tunics were all the rage these days; even I was wearing one. 'All right.' He touched a button on the low desk between us and the music faded. 'Bolshoi, about seventy years ago, just before they went weightless. They're all twelve feet tall now. You like ballet?'

'A lot.' I was glad I hadn't sneaked an eye at the holo. I would have been lost in the performance until he wheeled me out a side exit, couch and all.

'Me, too. You're good. Takes more than a holo-tank to frag your concentration, isn't it so? Sure. But you'd be surprised how many get caught in that little trap.' He lit a cigarette. 'Want one? Imported. Straight tobacco, I wouldn't try to drug you. I hate drugs.' He tossed me the pack and I plucked it out of the air.

'Thanks,' I said, lighting up by the glowhole in the couch frame.

'You impressed? That I can throw around imported tobacco?'

'More satisfied, actually.'

Nelson Nelson laughed. 'You'll do. All right, you can work for me. That's a privilege, kid, I don't employ many people. I've got a client waiting-list that could stretch to the moon and I like it that way. We'll start your training as soon as you move in.'

'I'm already trained,' I said, feeling like I had nothing to lose. If he let me get this far, he wasn't about to throw me out now. 'J. Walter made me the best pathosfinder in town.'

'I know that. Here's something else I know: the best institutes in the country don't train people in how to work. All my staff I train myself. I'm gonna strip you down and build you back up again. When I'm through with you, you'll be the best pathosfinder in the country If you're not, you can sue me and I'll settle with you for any amount. What's your full, legal name again?'

'Alexandra Victoria Haas.'

'Okay, Allie, just a few things before I show you around. You don't like what you hear, get up and walk. Fair?' He nodded for me. 'Fair. You're gonna have to lose those eyes.' He paused, waiting for my reaction. 'That scare you?'

'No, I –'

'Okay. I didn't know. You don't see a lot of people wearing the eyes they were born with any more. I thought maybe you were queer for organics or something. A lot of agencies let you keep them until they wear out, but I say, why wait? You're gonna be hooked up to the system more often than anyone in any other profession. Living eyes weren't made to be popped in and out that often. Pretty soon you've got a couple of rotten eggs endangering your optic nerve. The eyes I'm gonna give you reattach to the muscles easier, not to mention the optic nerve, which I already mentioned.' NN took another pack of cigarettes from the desk, waving away my offer of the pack he'd tossed me. 'Keep 'em. Happy birthday.' He lit up again and blew smoke toward a far corner of the room. 'They come in here from the best institutes in the country thinking they can get away with a little fudging. But you can't fudge in this business. The last time I had the best pathosfinder in town on that couch, he was a chubby little guy who wanted to hook up to the system through the ears. Said it was just as good. *I* said, "How you gonna hear me tell you what a lousy job you're doing with your ears plugged up like that?" He took a stroll. He's not the best pathosfinder in the country, that's for sure. Then there was the guy with a *socket* in the back of his head. *I* said, What are you, a federal employee or just a freelance zombie? *He* said he could hook directly into the vision center of his brain, bypassing the optic nerve altogether I showed him out. I don't have that kind of equipment.' NN leaned forward and squinted at me. '*You* don't have any sockets in *your* head, do you?'

'No, I –'

'Just checking There may be a better method than the optical system, but as far as I'm concerned, it hasn't been invented yet. Hooking up through the ears is complicated, time-consuming. Ever seen the inside of an ear? What a *mess!* Going in through the ear is like hacking your way through a jungle when there's a perfectly good freeway with no traffic on it you could use instead. And connecting right into the visual center of the brain is more direct, sure, but the

brain doesn't like that. It likes to get its pictures through the optic nerve, the way it *always* gets its pictures. Sockets in the head! Goddammit, why do people think they have to break into the skull like burglars when they've got two perfectly good entrances right here?' He pointed two fingers at his own eyes and I thought for a moment he might accidentally poke himself.

'NN, I'm all for the optical system,' I said quickly, before he could draw another breath. 'J. Walter's system could accommodate organics or replacements. But I came here knowing your policy.'

'Then, there's no problem.' NN's smile was blissful. 'It's so nice when there's no problem. I just hate it if I want to send somebody out on a job and it's no-go because the eyes are rotten eggs and the optic nerves infected and I have to spend even more than I lost on the job getting the mess fixed.'

'Not to mention the person in question having to sit around blind for months,' I added.

'That's right, Allie. You take care of your part, I take care of mine, and everyone gets rich. But you won't have to worry about the eyes I'm gonna give you as long as you treat them right. I got a contract with the best eye house in the hemisphere. The retinas are guaranteed – you couldn't detach them with a twenty-mule team. The company kicks in for replacements if they spoil and the tissue is replaced every five years. They're the finest eyes in the world. If you don't think so, you can sue me and I'll support you for life.'

We laughed together, both of us knowing he could probably wiggle out of that one even though he was recording.

'Your new eyes can be just like your old ones or you can have your choice of the weird stuff or any biogem you like – bloodstone, onyx, fire opal, cat's-eye –'

'I'll take cat's-eye,' I said before I even realized it.

'Ah? Good for you. I like it. It'll be striking. Like a trademark. Good for business. You'll get a following.' His foxy old face was all lit up. 'I can see it now – Deadpan Allie, sees in the dark.' He winked at me, popped his own eyeballs into his palms, and then clapped them back into the sockets without breaking the connections. 'See? They're that easy. What do you think?'

'I think it could give new meaning to the sentence, "My eyes dropped to my soup."'

NN guffawed so heartily his couch shuddered. 'Not bad, Deadpan. I can see already you're going to do well with us. You want to look at the setup?'

We took his private lateral to the west wing, where the system was housed. I hesitated before getting into the lateral; it was only seven feet square. NN noticed and said nothing. He knew how I felt about small enclosed spaces from my profile and was probably waiting to see if I'd throw up on a moving conveyance or save it for later, after I got home. Some employers keep testing you right up to the day they ask you to leave.

It took about a minute to reach the west wing. NN kept me distracted with chatter. Just about the time I got the urge to punch holes in the walls, the lateral stopped at a darkened room, dimming its own lights. Blinking into the darkness, I could just make out the supine form of what seemed to be a headless man on a table. From the neck up, he was engulfed in the system, which took up most of the room. A pair of bloodstone eyes were waiting in a clear bowl of solution.

'That's Philbert,' NN told me. 'I'm switching him from pathosfinding to dreamfeeding. He was a good pathosfinder but we both thought it was time for a change. There are hook-ups for twenty more in here, not that I keep twenty more around to use them.'

Stepping into the room, I looked around. I couldn't see much detail but I could tell it was the biggest mindplay single system I'd ever encountered. It rose from floor to ceiling, the latter invisible in the gloom so I couldn't tell if it ended twenty feet up or two hundred. I got the impression that if I yelled, it would echo. Areas of it jutted out like promontories on a cliff born in the mind of a cubist sculptor. Nothing showed, no wires, no dials, no lights, just a black facade, part of it eating a man's head. The man's body twitched a little. NN beckoned me back into the lateral.

'There's another lateral moving in behind this one. Someone else wants in,' he said, pointing to a flashing blue light next to the doorway.

'Only one entrance?' I asked as we rotated and started back to his office again.

'A couple of emergency exits but besides those, yeah, just one. Keeps it private. You know, sometimes you come out of there and you don't want anyone to see you for a while.'

My couch was gone when we returned to his office. He sat down on his and turned on the holo again. 'That's all, kid. For now. Any questions?'

'Not yet.'

'Still want to work for me?'

'Sure.'

He leaned back on one elbow and cocked his head. 'You really are deadpan, kid.'

I wasn't sure if I was amused. 'How'd you hit on that nickname?'

'It's in your profile. Go back and cash in your apartment or wherever you're living – say, you haven't become a Two, have you?'

'No, I'm single. Uh, not married.'

'Good. I don't lust after taking on half a couple at this level of development. But I don't discriminate. One of my people is a Four. Anyway, you move in here tonight. I want you living at the agency while I train you and for the first year after. Then you can live wherever you please as long as you can get here when I need you. Suit?'

I nodded. 'Just one other thing. Why is it –'

'– that I bother with educated people if I insist on training them over from scratch? Everyone wants to know that. If you weren't already trained, I wouldn't know you were trainable. I let the institutes weed out the failures and the missionaries for me. See you tomorrow.'

I left him to the Bolshoi and slipped a tube back to my apartment.

Jascha's face looked a little older in the phone screen. Maybe it was because he wasn't using gilt these days. 'I'm not surprised Nelson Nelson took you, Allie,' he said. 'And don't kid yourself, he probably knows all about you. There are all kinds of ways they can get around the privacy seal in your records. The smart ones can, anyway, and he's about the smartest one there is.'

'"Kid." That's what he calls me. "Kid." It's weird. Like meeting someone from a past time.'

'Yah, well, he's *old*. How old I'm not sure but he's probably giving your great-grandmother a run at the record.'

There was a long silence while we just looked at each other at an exorbitant per-minute charge. 'Listen, I think I'm going to be incommunicado for a while. While he strips me down and builds me back up again. Unquote. Jesus, all I could think was, "Not *again*."'

'That's the way he works. You'll be okay, though. He'll see to it.' Another long pause. 'I'm, uh, well, I'll leave callback so you'll know where to reach me.'

'Do you *want* me to call you?'

'Who else would you call – Pyotr Frankis?'

I gave a short, uneasy laugh.

'Ah, Christ, Allie, everybody's got to have someone to trust. I could have done worse than to be yours.'

And I had done worse than to be his. But all I said was, 'Thanks, Jascha.' I couldn't even bring myself to tell him about the cat's-eye biogems.

The screen blanked as Jascha disconnected. I sat there, feeling pretty disconnected myself. Another part of my life over with. Or maybe vice versa.

I began to understand a little of how McFloy had felt. I had a past but everything in it seemed to be receding from me faster than the speed of light. The way I'd been cut off from my old life (such as it was), the days of the drugs and Jerry and madcaps and then J. Walter and Pyotr Frankis and McFloy and Jascha, I might as well have been a mindsuck starting over myself.

I was still sitting in front of the screen pondering how it was I kept ending up alone contemplating my life when the phone beeped, startling the hell out of me. It beeped twice again before I jumped for the answer pad, thinking it might be Jascha calling back to say he wanted to see me the instant I was out of training. And I'd do it, I thought in the split second before the screen lit up.

And if he wanted to give it a try again, I'd do that, too, what the hell, I didn't have to drift through my own outer life without any ties –

'Heya, Allie.'

The features looked a little more world-weary than I remembered them but they hadn't changed much. I closed my eyes briefly, seeing that face in my mind's eye, or in some mind's eye. Identical, except I could discern the differences in spirit that moved behind each one.

'Jerry what are you doing calling me?' I said. 'I thought the conditions of your sentence specified no contact with –'

He giggled. Same old Jerry Wirerammer giggle. 'Hey is that any way to greet an old war buddy? After all we've been through together. Didn't you get even a little nostalgic seeing me around?'

I squinted at the screen, feeling uneasy. 'Is this the *real* Jerry Wirerammer, or a Power Person?'

He giggled again. 'Oh, it's really me, all right, Allie. They wouldn't let me clone off my memories. Not legally, anyway. Whaddaya say, can I come see you?'

'I'm not supposed to see you, Jerry. What are you doing calling me after all this time anyway?'

'Because we're old friends, like I said.' He looked hurt. 'And it wasn't any too easy to find you, either, even for an old hack like me. I had to access your great-grandmother's records.'

'I ought to report you,' I said darkly.

'Come *on*. Give an old friend a few minutes before you go off to be a big hot-wire mindplayer.'

I stared at the face on the screen. Identical to McFloy and yet it didn't look a thing like him. In some ways, at least. Of all the images in my head, why had McFloy pulled out that one? Maybe because of the weakness he'd sensed I'd always had for Jerry. Or maybe because I felt responsible for Jerry's getting caught. He hadn't had to take me to the dry-cleaner's that day a million years ago. He could have left me insane and gotten away.

'Allie?' Jerry said hopefully.

I sighed. 'Where are you?'

'No problem, I'll come up.'

'No. I'll meet you somewhere. Just tell me where you are.'

He thought for a moment. 'There's the fetishizer's on the east side where I've been doing a little work. I'll meet you there. Say you're there for me and go into the back room –'

'I'll meet you out in front, on the sidewalk,' I said.

'Why? I thought you were worried about being seen with me.'

'I'll pass you off as a Power Person or something if it comes to that, but I'm not walking into some fetishizer's back room alone. Give me the address.'

He punched it in and a tiny line of print ran across the bottom of the screen. 'Half an hour okay with you? Or is something wrong with that, too?'

'Half an hour's fine. Just be there because I'm not going to wait.'

That giggle. 'I've done a lot of things, Allie, but I've never been late to do them.'

I disconnected and found myself rushing for the door. I forced myself to slow down. Why the hell was I hurrying to consort with a known mind criminal, especially when it would violate the conditions of my own sentence – or rather, reprieve. Jerry had been the one who'd been sentenced.

Running out to see McFloy's face. But even as I thought it, I knew that wasn't it. Well, that wasn't *all* of it. Not even most of it.

It's just a way of putting a real end to the days of drugs and madcaps, I thought as I pulled my credit chip out of the stash bag at the head of the futon (old habits die hard). Just a way to tell Jerry good-bye once and for all.

And I really believed it, too.

'Actually,' Jerry said with that goofy smile, 'I'm in kind of a tar baby.'

'Why am I not surprised?' I asked the low, gray ceiling in the fetishizer's back room. We faced each other over a workbench where a small mindplay system was lying half-assembled, spilling it's guts into the grainy surface. I still didn't know much about hardware but I could see that a lot of the connections were definitely Jerry-rigged. 'Something to do with the "work" you've been doing here?' I gestured at the system. 'Illegally.'

Jerry spread his hands. 'Hey, even a convicted mind criminal retains the right to turn a screwdriver if he wants to. Nobody has to know what on. I've got to eat, don't I?'

'What's the matter, are the residuals from Power People running a little slow?'

'You know I can't collect on that. All proceeds go to the state. The No-Profit law – no criminal shall see material reward from the commission of a crime blah, blah, blah, and blah. They could make a big-budget holo about my life and I wouldn't even see a free ticket to the premiere.' He shrugged. 'Crimes not supposed to pay. I get by, the state and Power People are getting fat. Real fat, from what I hear. Maybe there ought to be a law that no one should be able to profit from someone else's mind crime.'

'What did they do to you?' I asked.

He gave a carefully casual shrug with one bony shoulder. 'Oh, nothing much really. Some enforced belljarring with amnesia, a few thousand hours' community service, some fines. They let me hook up with Power People to pay those. My contracts up with them next year but they'll probably sign me on again. The Jerry Wirerammer property'll outlive me, I think. Which is kind of the problem.'

The fetishizer poked her head through the black curtains in the doorway. 'Are you getting anywhere near finished with that system?'

Jerry held up a screwdriver. 'Still working. My consultant here tells me half the parts are obsolete.'

'You said she knew how to update them.' The fetishizer glared at me. I didn't glare back. She was a husky woman, laced into an old leather oversuit with nothing underneath. The pupils of her eyes were black spiders, and at either temple, her long black hair had been molded into two horns that looked sharp enough to pierce flesh. Giving people fetishes was a hell of a way to make a living and you wouldn't have thought there'd have been enough of such a specialized trade to keep fetishizers in business, but there was. You could get the same thing from a neurosis peddler but a fetishizer was far cheaper, if somewhat cruder in approach. Or so I'd been told.

The door buzzer went off in the other room, signaling a new customer and saving me from having to say anything to her. Jerry had hustled me in past her with some double-talk about my being a hardware expert. She'd taken an instant loathing to me and told him I'd better be worth the extra fee. Which Jerry had apparently pocketed, figuring it would be all right with me.

'What's going to happen to you when she finds out you're no further along on this pile of junk after I leave?' I asked in a low voice.

'Maybe she'll kill me,' Jerry said cheerfully. 'And maybe I should let her, which would solve all my problems. Of course, she's treading lightly herself with the law these days, so maybe she'll just beat me up a little, which won't solve anything and will probably get me caught.'

'Caught for what?'

Jerry winced. 'Bootlegging.'

I almost didn't need to ask. 'Bootlegging what?'

'Myself.'

I had to try not to laugh. 'Oh, chris*sakes –*'

'Hey, I've got to *eat,*' Jerry said plaintively. 'I wasn't seeing anything from Power People, I could hardly get any work, for a while I had to sleep in a parking space, not even a flop but a *parking space,* and once I got towed off when the meter ran out – and I didn't even have a *vehicle. You* try living that way sometime. Then when somebody offers you a deal that'll make you a little more than sub-subsistence, you'll jump for it without a second thought, too.'

I stared at the disassembled system so I wouldn't have to look at Jerry. 'That's great. Who are they, the same people you used to fence stolen memories to?'

There was a long pause. 'How'd you know about that?'

'Did you think I wouldn't have been told?'

'Well, what do you care? I never got any of yours.'

'I never gave you a chance at them. Lucky for me.'

'I wouldn't have done that to *you*, Allie. We're old war buddies.'

'*What* war?'

'The war of life.'

I wiped my hands over my face. 'I don't think I can handle philosophy from you, Jerry, so just tell me what it is you think I can do for you and let me get out of here before your girlfriend decides to beat me up a little along with you.'

Giggle. 'You got any money?'

'Not much. Not enough to buy you out of either contract.'

'It wouldn't be for that.'

'Jesus, Jerry, *why*? Bootleggers usually clone their goods off one of the enfranchised people. Why couldn't you just let them work from one of your copies –'

'Well, they were. But then they found me, and everyone knows you get better results from the original template.'

'Is that what you are to yourself now – an original template?'

Jerry shrugged. 'You think differently when something like Power People gets through with you.'

'And whose fault is that?' I slipped my credit chip out of my shirt pocket. 'Never mind. I've got a little money on this. Not much. I won't be needing anything after today, you can have it. But maybe you should just turn yourself in. Or leave town.'

'Forget it. I'm travel-restricted. They'd just catch me, and I'm not going under the belljar with amnesia again.'

I couldn't blame him for that. I was about to say something else when the fetishizer reappeared in the doorway, looking meaner than ever.

'Well?' she said.

Jerry jumped up. 'We've got to go out for a part.' He ran around the bench, grabbed my arm, and pulled me toward the back door.

'*What* part?' the fetishizer asked, staring at me with those spider eyes.

'A part you don't have,' I said and slipped out the door before she could say anything else. Jerry was right on my heels.

We hurried up the narrow alley to the street. 'What's she going to say when you go back without a part?' I said as Jerry pulled me past a trip parlor.

'I don't know. Don't worry about her now.' Jerry kept pulling me along the street, looking at the storefronts until he stopped abruptly in front of a memory-wipe place. 'You got that chip?'

'You can't use it until I sign it over to you.'

'Don't sign it over to me, sign it over to them.' He jerked his thumb at the memory-wiper's.

'What? Why?'

Jerry looked at me as though I were mildly retarded. 'I've got to get rid of the memory of bootlegging myself before Power People calls me in for template renewal tomorrow, of course. Otherwise they'll find out what I did.'

I blinked at him. 'Jerry, if you can't remember what you did, how are you going to avoid the bootleggers?'

'Oh, they'll put me on callback here and resell me the memory. I've done it before. And who says I want to avoid the bootleggers? They're the only thing between me and starvation.'

I shook my head. 'I thought you wanted me to *help* you.'

'This *is* helping me.'

'I don't think so.'

'Come on.' Jerry herded me into the memory-wiper's.

The woman behind the counter looked like a raccoon, down to the black band painted over her eyes and the little black nose and whiskers grafted onto her face. She was actually kind of cute, if animals were your weakness. Right then, I wished they were mine instead of Jerry.

'Hey-*yo*, Rammer-Jammer!' she said, showing her sharp little teeth in a grin. 'Thought you were about due for another visit.' The bright animal eyes took me in eagerly. 'Bringing me new trade, too.'

'Not me,' I said, 'I'm just the wallet here.'

She spread her hands, showing off her raccoon claws, which weren't so cute. 'So that's pretty handy, having a wallet that follows you around. The usual, Rammer?'

Jerry nodded. 'She'll pay you, Bandit. Including the callback and resell.'

'That's all right by me, it's your memory. But don't you think there's some things better left forgotten?'

Jerry disappeared through a doorway at the back of the shop without answering. The raccoon-woman beckoned to me with one claw as she turned to a console at her right. 'Cash or chip?' she asked me.

I put the chip on the counter and somehow she managed to pick it up without the claws getting in the way. She saw me staring.

'Just like fingernails,' she said, 'only more useful in case of an emergency.'

I nodded. 'I'm signing everything on the chip over to you for Jerry's account. Can you keep my name out of it?'

'No problem, milady.' She pushed a small pad of numbered squares at me. 'Enter your unlock code and I'll do the rest.' She worked on the console for a minute, checking a screen I couldn't see on the other side of the counter. 'Personally, I wouldn't use a "bearer" chip – too easy for people like your friend the Rammer-Jammer to hackity-hack the unlock code.'

'I never cared to pay the feds for a personal account ID.'

'Can't fault you for that.' She made what I supposed was a raccoon noise as she looked at the screen. 'There's a little left over even after the callback and

resell. Sure there isn't something *you'd* like to forget about? Like the Rammer-Jammer maybe?'

I shook my head. 'Too many associations. It would wipe out half my life, maybe more. I've never really understood how some people can just come into a place like this and forget whole blocks of things so easily.' The raccoon-woman clacked her claws together. 'Well, for some of us, it's just this episode and that episode, one thing after another, and not too much relates to anything else. It's one way to live. Not the worst way. Nothing haunts you.'

'Yah. I'll wait outside for, uh, Rammer-Jammer.'

'Right. Come back any time,' she called to my back.

I found an empty parking place a few feet up from the wiper's, fed the meter a token, and sat down on the curb. Jerry came out twenty minutes later looking relaxed, refreshed, and ready to goof up anything. He glanced at me, did a double-take, and came running over.

'Allie! What the hell! I never thought I'd see *you* again!'

I opened my mouth to say something and then realized he'd had to wipe the memory of calling me along with his bootlegging. 'Just passing by, Jerry. Some coincidence, huh?'

'Yah, synchronicity in all her glory. Heya, I'd invite you for a drink or a pop but, you know, I don't think we better take a chance on getting seen together.' He looked up and down the street. 'I don't care about me, but they'd go hard on you.'

'Yah.' I looked at the meter; there was another five minutes on it. 'Listen, I've got to sprint. You want a parking place for five minutes?'

'Yah, sure!' He sat down and stretched his legs out. 'You're a real friend, Allie.'

'I sure am. Seeya, Jerry.' I walked off as fast as I could without running and without looking back. One thing after another and not too much relates to anything else. And I'd thought *I* was disconnected.

THE PATHOSFINDER DOES A JOB

I canceled my lease, sold off the big stuff to General Stores, and took one suitcase back to the agency. I found my new quarters easily enough, even though there seemed to be no one to show me around. The big building was a windowless maze inside, but the laterals and passageways were color-coded.

My name was already up on the apartment door – as Deadpan Allie, not Alexandra V. Haas – and the door was set to my handprint. It opened to a three-room apartment superior to anything I'd had in the last several years. I had cooking privileges in the elaborate kitchenette or I could dial up meals.

There was an area set up for entertaining, complete with stocked bar; NN apparently believed in socializing. He probably liked having his staff talking shop and picking each other's brains. I wouldn't have called the bedroom luxurious but it wasn't a monk's cell either (if there were any monks left). The bed was big enough for five and firm enough for me and I wondered how Jascha had managed to include that in a recommendation.

There was a conch shell sitting in the middle of the bed. I tossed my suitcase into the autovalet and sat down. There was a note in the shell reading simply, *Welcome*. It wasn't a cultured shell but the real thing, unpainted and unvarnished. NN sure was ostentatious. I put it carefully on the nightstand and dialed up a mushroom-and-algae casserole for supper. I found an orientation program cued up and ready to run on my dataline so I lingered over my food, reading about the history of the Nelson Nelson Agency and NN's personal feelings about mindplay.

What he had to say didn't differ much from J. Walter's line, except for a small paragraph on the last page. NN felt that mindplay was a necessary tool for the evolving, expanding mind, and that the next evolutionary step would take place in the brain, generated voluntarily by humans themselves. That was nothing new. There were plenty of people in the if-god-had-not-meant-for-humans-to-mindplay-he-wouldn't-have-put-ergot-fungus-on-bread camp, and a lot of them had been at J. Walter.

Eventually, I found myself nodding out at the screen. I undressed, sent the empty casserole down the chute, adjusted the room temperature, set the bed for six hours, and slept hard.

The next day, and every day after for six months, were all-hours full. I had my eyes out early that first morning and spent the following three days waiting for my optic nerves to heal while I got acquainted with Rich Lindbloom. She had the apartment next to mine. NN had assigned her to be my seeing-eye person. She was a big one, almost seven feet. After I got my eyes, I saw that she was also navy-blue-skinned and orange-haired. Not a permanent dye-job, she told me. She liked to switch around. NN employed her as a thrillseeker. I thought she was a walking thrill all by herself.

Most everyone else besides Rich and Philbert, who was still switching tracks – Fandango, the neurosis peddler; Deacon and Sara, the belljarrers; and the other pathosfinder, Four L.N. (a single parent with three cubs, something you don't see much) – were in and out as business required, mostly out. NN made himself scarce as well once the training began. He slipped in a few times while I was sleeping to check my brain wave personally. I guess he liked what he saw because he never bothered to wake me.

I spent a lot of time letting the system eat my head. There was no way to modify it in a fashion that NN would allow, but at least it didn't grab your face. I had to take all the mindplaying over again, too, administered by the

appropriate employee, who approached things as though I were an actual paying client. NN wanted me to be on the receiving end of the agency's preferred techniques. Fandango came up with one of those cleanliness obsessions for me with a side tendency to become sexually aroused by the color orange. The bit with the orange was pretty interesting, if kind of kinky. I wondered where she'd learned it.

Rich dug down into my mind, found a thrill, and arranged it for me. I was kind of nervous about that but she showed good judgment about what could be brought up out of my subconscious and what should have stayed buried. It was a very satisfactory thrill, though I suspected she was getting back at Fandango for making me go into rut every time she brushed her hair.

Philbert finished switching tracks, so I let him practice his dreamfeeding on me. He was pretty good – he had to be or Nelson Nelson wouldn't have kept him around – but he was no Jascha. I managed to keep him from picking up any of that feeling from me, though. They didn't call me Deadpan Allie for nothing.

Belljarring I couldn't look forward to; it still felt too much like being buried alive. Or something. Deacon was sensitive to my dislike of being cut off and worked to give me an impression of people-just-in-the-next-room without stimulating any senses. It lasted half a day and it was just fine, when it was over.

Four L.N. and I spent some time hooked in together so I could get the feel of how he worked. Interestingly enough, he'd been at J. Walter several years before I had and there were overtones of the institute technique, especially in the relaxation exercises. But through the years in private practice, his methods had evolved into something that was actually quite different. What I noticed mostly was how skittish two pathosfinders were when they were hooked in mind-to-mind. The first couple of sessions were like The Great Stone Face Meets The Other Great Stone Face. When we were finally able to let out some with each other, I saw he had developed a persona that was strictly activated within the system, his own mental mask. It made me wonder if he hadn't had a franchise personality at some time in the past, but of course he didn't tell me.

And once in a while, when there was a free moment, I paused in front of the mirror in my apartment and looked at myself with those eyes. Of all the biogems I'd had to choose from, what had possessed me –

Bad way to put it. Try again. Why *those?* That's all. Just *why.*

Because I liked them. Honestly, truly. And what I liked best about them was that they didn't look a thing like McFloy's eyes in my head. If anything, they seemed to be more me than McFloy. I hung onto that thought.

Training concluded, NN gave me a week to breathe in and out in any fashion I chose, so I went off with Rich to a sky-island owned by the agency. It was

about the same as any of the other flying resorts circling the world, except it wasn't crammed to the weight limit with tourists and businesspeople on working vacations. Entertainment was the finest in music, dancing, even some theater, works in progress or recently finished, things that wouldn't see popular release for months. Rich told me it was all provided by the agency's clients who chose to pay partially for services by playing the island. We spent a lot of time free-fall sailing and exercising mindlessly and I decided I could get used to being a member of the Jetstream Set.

It was all so wonderful I was suspicious of what would be waiting for me when I bounced down out of the clouds again. Probably a killer assignment, Rich theorized. NN's vacations weren't usually so lavish. We were both right.

Jascha's phone asked who was calling. I punched in my code and instead of an answer blank, it tossed up a videotaped message. 'I've left J. Walter and gone back into private practice,' Jascha said. He was using gilt again and also a little face paint, just a tasteful floral spot design. The resolution on the answer tape wasn't good enough to let me see exactly what kind of flower it was. 'This is my office number, but if you need to, you can pry my home code out of the answering machine. I've put you in as one of the very few who can access it. Just tell it your name.' He paused and I almost shut the screen off, thinking the tape was over.

'I've remarried, Allie. I guess I should have told you that in person but I wanted you to know before you called. You *can* still call me. If you want to. I want you to. I just don't know how you'll feel about it. So it's up to you. I'll always take your calls. I've just got this screening process because I'm not with an agency.' He glanced at something, or maybe someone, beyond the screen. 'I don't know if you *will* call now. In case I don't hear from you for a while, I bet you're a hell of a pathosfinder ... Deadpan.' The screen faded to white with an asterisk cue. I punched in an end-it and plugged into my system access for a round of calming influences. Just a few mental hours of mental fingerpainting. I mean, what had I expected, after all?

One minute to the week my time off was over, I found myself reclining on the couch in NN's office, listening to him tell me about Marty Oren, the actor who had started to make sensations two years back just before he'd retired to an anti-mindplay enclave with his new wife.

'But now he's back on the outside, wife and all,' NN told me. 'He tried old-style theater while he was in and apparently found it extremely unsatisfying. How you gonna keep 'em down on the farm, I guess. He was vague about it on his preliminary application. Truth to tell, I think the adulation of a few hundred people was too little for him. Anyway, his old company kept letting

him know regularly they were ready for him any time he wanted to come back. So he's back. He and Sudella Keller are in Restawhile, Kansas.'

'Restawhile? *Kansas?*'

NN shrugged. 'It's kind of a year-round resort-cum-village, very quiet. Ideal for making a transition back into the mainstream.'

'Transition? How do they live in those enclaves – in mud huts?'

'Not exactly. It's a difference in sensibilities. Without a transition period, the culture shock could make him psychotic. Kind of like if you took an eighteenth-century hermit and dropped him smack into the middle of Commerce Canyon out there.' He jerked his chin at the window.

'Marty Oren isn't an eighteenth-century hermit. After all, he grew up –'

'Only recently. He's just twenty-two years old, a comparative baby.'

'Compared to who?'

'You. He went through his second puberty in that enclave. And don't look at me like that, a lot of experts call the years between eighteen and twenty-four second puberty.'

Involuntarily, I felt my face with my hand.

'Relax, Deadpan. It's just because I know you so well. Didn't know I knew you so well, did you? Well, I do. You don't have to agree with me about second puberty, you just have to do your job. Besides Oren's well-being, there's also his wife to consider.'

'What's she going to do – make the transition with him?'

'Hell, no. She's just as anti-mindplay as she ever was. She's your stumbling block.' NN smiled pleasantly. 'All these jobs have stumbling blocks, did I ever mention that? So it's going to be hard for you to work with him while she's there. The only thing you've got going for you is her respect for his personal choices, but she's bound to inhibit him in some way.

'*Also*, Oren's always had this bitter streak he's had to keep in check, which I think is why they've always worked him with pathosfinders rather than dreamfeeders, like some actors. After being out of things for two years, he needs a pathosfinder more than ever. That's why the company asked the agency to handle him instead of turning him over to their resident pathosfinder. Next month, they want to put him into rehearsal for *Two Moon Night*, the play about the guy who died alone on Mars.'

'I'm familiar with it. Isn't that kind of industrial-strength material to start him off with? I mean, a man in that part has to go through all kinds of things – raptures, hallucinations – he's got to run the emotional gamut. Experienced actors have taken year-long recuperations after doing *Two Moon Night* because they were too wrung-out to work afterwards and Oren's been out of touch for, what, two years?'

'If he's not ready for it, you'll tell them.'

I was really looking forward to something like that. NN's smile was

broader and more benign than ever. 'If he's as sheltered as you say, I don't think he'll be able to deal with it. We could just phone the company now.'

'Your compassion is showing, Deadpan.'

I sat up and folded my arms. 'Empathy's a bitch.'

'What isn't?'

'So I get him into shape for the play. Or I try to get him into shape. Then what?'

NN looked blank.

'What about his wife? He can't very well move into a city with her.'

'They haven't let me in on their plans.' NN sounded just a bit sour. 'I imagine she'll be staying in Restawhile when he's working. It's far enough out in the country that she can avoid most problems if she's careful. Anyway, they want to stay together. Don't ask *me* why. Neither one of them is about to give so much as an angstrom in their viewpoints. He's going to mindplay, she's dead against it. It's going to screw his emotions around.'

'It could be a good source to draw on.'

'I doubt it, but use your own judgment. They're both a couple of very defensive people right now.'

'I'm not sure if I'm going to be able to make any progress, then. The ideal thing might be to work with both of them, but if she won't – well, it's their time.'

'And their marriage. Don't bust it up.'

Maybe I should have told him my new hobby was not busting up marriages. 'I won't. But they can't blame me if after he –'

'They most certainly *will* blame you, they're the sort of people who tend to lay blame for their own messes. So watch where you step. He probably wouldn't sue us but she most definitely would. And I don't want that, not at all.'

'Is she well-connected?'

NN flipped on the ceiling holo and the familiar Bolshoi music filled the room. 'Sort of. She's my daughter.'

Oh.

I went underground tubeway to Wichita and rented a flier to take me and my equipment east to Restawhile. I spent the time on the tube getting acquainted with Marty Oren's old notices and re-reading *Two Moon Night*. It was a powerful piece of work, heavy on emotion and full of tenuous science, with the potential to be a tearjerker instead of an honest study of a dying man.

When I got a look at the flier in Wichita, I nearly turned around and went home. It was an airplane converted to computer autopilot and seemed to have been put together with masking tape and spit. It did fly, albeit roughly; the rolling Kansas landscape, pretty as it was, gave it a lot of trouble. By the

time I got to Restawhile, a hamlet nestled around a lake, it was late afternoon. I circled the lake several times before I realized the autopilot was locked in an electronic argument with itself as to whether the water could be landed on. I ended up landing the thing myself and took a few turns on pontoons before I found the dock I wanted. I might not have found it at all, except Sudella Keller was standing on it, watching.

She looked large in her loud, flowery-print muumuu, but when I climbed out of the cockpit and onto the dock, I could see she was nearly swimming in diaphanous material. Her wide, elegant face was made up subtly but effectively and it bore absolutely no resemblance to NN's foxy pink features. Her eyes tilted up at the outer corners without actually being Oriental. Her nose turned- up, too. Great body engineering. Apparently bodyplay was all right if mindplay wasn't. Interesting. I chided myself for being catty, but it didn't make things any less interesting.

We just stood taking each other in for a few seconds. 'You must be Sudella Keller,' I said, making an extra effort to be cordial.

'You must be Daddy's thug,' she said, also quite cordial.

Ah, I thought, court is in session, the judge is on the bench, and I'm already in contempt.

'I could have told by your face who you are,' she said. 'Deadpan Allie. What's so important about being deadpan?'

'A professional mindplayer has to remain neutral at all times. We aren't judges of human behavior. Clients have to remain unaware of our approval or displeasure, so they won't attempt to gain either.'

'Well, I see you've swallowed Daddy's menu first course to dessert.'

I almost asked her why she was so bitched at Daddy, but it wasn't my business. Instead, I asked if it would be all right to bring in my equipment.

'I'll show you your room. Then you can decide whether you want to or not. It isn't much bigger than the inside of your flier and you didn't mention how long you'd be staying.'

'I'm not sure. But I don't have much with me.'

'Good thing.'

She led me down the pier to the house. It was an old-fashioned cottage with a bare minimum of conveniences, none of which were in the broom closet they called a guest room. It had a water bed taking up most of what space there was. I stood in the doorway staring at it and trying not to think about my mattress back at the agency. 'Nice woodwork,' I said lamely.

'It'll be pretty cramped.'

'Doesn't worry me,' I lied. 'Where's Two Oren?'

'Gone fishing. Know anything about fishing?'

'Not freshwater. Just mid-Atlantic shark-fishing.' I winced inwardly. If I couldn't be more deadpan than to one-up fish stories, I was going to make a

bigger mess than the one I was supposed to straighten out. But somehow it seemed to have been the right thing to say; she almost smiled at me. Perhaps she was surprised that I didn't spend all my waking hours letting Daddy's system eat my head.

I had already decided to sleep on the roof and was wheeling the last components of my portable system over the extendable ramp from the flier to the dock when Marty Oren came home, rowing himself in a rowboat. I stopped to watch, wondering what part of the lake he'd come from that I hadn't spotted him from the air. He looked tired, disgusted, sunburned, and very attractive. His hair had grown down below his shoulders and was plaited in two gold braids. The gold was strictly his own, probably maintained from childhood by something in his diet. As he got closer, I saw that his face was more angular than it appeared on holo. Lots of cheekbones. Your basic leading man.

When he reached the dock, I leaned down to give him a hand up and was surprised to see that he had cat's-eyes. They looked better in his head than they did in mine.

'Deadpan Allie.' He smiled warmly. Inside, I felt a chord being twanged, which is what's supposed to happen when a leading thespian smiles like that in your direction. I didn't make anything of it but I was sure plenty of people had tried to in the past.

'Nelson Nelson gave you a big build-up,' he said and something changed in his face. He had shut himself off from me at his own mention of his father-in-law. It was as sudden and effective as a slap. 'We'll have some food and then get started. If you haven't eaten.' He looked back out over the water, which was turning gold as the sun began to edge toward dusk. 'Nice day.'

'Lovely.'

I wheeled my equipment ahead as we walked down the dock to the house together. Sudella was waiting like a statue at the door.

The meal was roast duck, which Marty cooked in an old microwave, a real, functioning antique, taking all of twenty minutes, including the algae. We sat around the table passing each other orange sauce (which stirred a few decidedly unusual memories) and not saying much. I felt like I was in a holo period piece, complete with anachronisms. Marty and Sudella loosened up a little but it was more resignation than relaxation. I tried reading Marty's Emotional Index by sight but I couldn't get much feeling for his state of mind. Sudella's was only too clear.

Afterward, they cleared the table, leaving me the coffee. I pretended not to watch them as they put the reusable dishes in the washer. For a few moments, their guards went way down. Obviously they loved each other a great deal while being in conflict with each other's desires – pretty normal. But the love

part seemed strangely intensified, like sunlight reflected on water, as though one of them were wearing an amplifier. It bothered me. If I could have delved Sudella – but by law I couldn't even ask her. I'd just have to work their puzzle with half the pieces.

They dawdled by the dishwasher as long as they could but finally Marty came over and sat down across from me.

'Do you want to start?'

'Only if you think you can.'

He glanced at Sudella, still over by the dishwasher. 'I want to get this over with as soon as possible.'

'This isn't something you can rush, remember. There's no way I can tell how long it's going to take until we're in.' Peripherally, I saw Sudella cross her arms and stand up a bit straighter, ready for a siege.

'I hadn't thought there'd be much to do. It always went pretty smoothly before.'

'You've been out of touch.'

'Well, I've always worked with pathosfinders, so I'm used to it. Or I was.'

Sudella suddenly turned and strode out the front door, leaving it open behind her. Marty started to get up.

'Sit where you are. Sudella is showing us a great deal of courtesy. I think we should respect her by accepting it.'

'But she left because –'

'A lot of the right things get done for the wrong reasons. If I gave you a soft purple sponge, what would you do?'

'Hold it in my hands and squeeze it.' He twisted in his chair.

'If I gave you a green hat with a brim all the way around, what would you do?'

'I'd see if it was my size.'

He went on for close to half an hour, longer than usual, but I thought he would enjoy playing *What Would You Do?* Most people did. They forgot it was less a game than a relaxation exercise geared to provide a pathosfinder with some hints about what kinds of things were wandering around in their heads. He got involved in it, and by the time I asked the last question his answers were spontaneous and his mind was (mostly) off Sudella.

I gave him one of NN's expensive cigarettes to keep him busy but idle while I wheeled out my apparatus and put it together. It was like playing with a giant set of cub's blocks, three big pieces and five smaller ones. When I finished making the connections, I had a portable version of NN's cubist cliff, looking off-balance but actually quite stable. It wouldn't eat our heads; instead, the connections were external, so as to keep the system as compact as possible.

I pulled out the drawer with the four connections and the thermos tank of solution for our eyes. 'Ready?'

'Do you know there are no longer any actors alive today who still have their own eyes?' he asked suddenly.

'Does that bother you?'

'It seems strange. Drawing on life and looking at it through artificial eyes.'

I remembered my own eyes with some fondness, but it was rather nice not to have to put up with having my astigmatism worked on every few years. Pushing the tank over, I showed him how it was compartmented so we wouldn't be groping for our optics later. He made three tries at getting his eyes out before I did it for him: his eyes were deepset and he was out of practice. After I hooked him into a relaxation exercise, I made a quick check of his connections. The tissue and insulation would be good for another year at most; then they would have to be replaced or he'd go blind. I wondered how he'd planned to do that from an enclave, or if he even knew what condition his eyes were in.

After a minute of deep breathing, I hooked myself in, making my presence felt gradually, so he wouldn't feel like I was bursting in on him. He was in the middle of a chromatic, making colors. Surprisingly, he didn't seem to have any enthusiasm for it. I made a few with him – navy blue to jade blue to scream blue to milk blue, and he yielded the whole thing to me with juvenile boredom. Maybe I'd relaxed him too much and he was getting antsy. I put the colors aside and indicated we could start.

Nothing happened.

I prodded again and then again before I got any results. We were in a bare, sterile room, no windows, no doors, nothing, just smooth white walls. The Infamous White Room; most people are stunned to find out how common an image it is. Marty was sitting in one corner with his legs stretched out in front of him, hands resting on his thighs. I seemed to be invisible.

Marty?

The figure in the corner slumped and became a marionette. I was suddenly awash in waves of *reassure me, reassure me.*

Not my job, I told him as neutrally as possible. *Let's do some work.*

The marionette persisted a little longer, as though he thought he might get me to believe he really did need reassurance, that he wasn't just a pawn by sheer stubbornness. Then everything faded, leaving us in limbo, aware of each other's presence but alone. Lots of people felt that way, though few were so textbook in expressing it.

You have to help me, I said. *I can't carry us both.* Not strictly true, but the idea was to keep him thinking for himself rather than following my lead.

No response. I checked his vitals; he was still conscious. He just didn't seem to care.

Well, that was a hell of a note – my first job and the client was more deadpan than I was. It was more than a hell of a note, though; it was all wrong,

and in the worst way. So. I could fumble around for a while and get nowhere or I could give him a direct mental jab.

Disregarding NN's warning, I showed him a visualization of Sudella watching us from across the room and then suddenly walking out. He clamped down on his reaction quickly, but not quickly enough to hide a sense of responsibility or obligation for something that Sudella may have done for him that was, to his way of thinking, somewhere between a service and an outright favor. Then the rest came out of him involuntarily and I saw that if I were willing to pick up doing this service/favor where Sudella had left off, I could gain his responsibility/obligation in her place.

They don't call me Deadpan Allie for nothing. I let it pass and took his Emotional Index, looking at all the little domino feelings that led up to the reaction. I had to take it several times just to be sure. It kept coming up *like* hunger but definitely *not* hunger – like someone who wanted food just because it was there.

Over his protest, I went for a walk through his life. He tried to keep me distracted with the recent past, his sense of triumph and accomplishment after each performance. It disturbed him that I noted only his orgasms during applause. I went back further to the time before he became an actor, for a look at his family.

He'd been a Three, an only child between two parents, a tripod, which some diehard experts were still claiming as the most stable of family configurations. I found it unusual that it was *so* nuclear. Pressure on each corner of the triangle had remained constant until sometime after he reached puberty, when his corner had begun to spike up and down before ascending rapidly out of plane. So much for the stability of the tripod.

His first mindplay experience had been a full two years after he'd come of age, at eighteen. His first acting audition had paired him with the company's pathosfinder. I went back and checked carefully to make sure I hadn't missed any suppressed thrillseeking or illegal madcaps but there was nothing.

The company's pathosfinder had been an incompetent. No, not really – just overworked. It figured. The emphasis had been on turning out performers in a hurry. Rather than working with Marty Oren's inexperienced mind, the pathosfinder had done a rush job, teaching him by example rather than helping him find his own answers. After being the focus of a tripod, Marty had simply accepted the attention and mimicked the appropriate responses.

He'd gone on to his next play with conditional notices; apparently someone had noticed there was something lacking in him. Then he'd suddenly switched companies but the next pathosfinder was no better. The troupe was on a tight schedule and they got exactly what they wanted from him. By the time he'd joined his present company, his mimicry of real emotions had been perfected. All he had to do was reflect the pathosfinder's expectations back to the source.

I sat on my anger and told him he should have gone for help. A feeling of *I didn't need help, I was doing fine on my own* came out of him.

We can put this right, I said.

Put what *right?*

He became an observer while I searched around for things he cared about. A two-dimensional image of Sudella slipped by me before I could catch it, turned sideways, and disappeared. I went after it through a long hall lined with locked doors. He made no attempt to stop me as I jerked them open; I received the distinct impression that somehow it no longer mattered.

Sudella's image, still two-dimensional, stood in a room of mirrors with a fixed smile on its face. Mirrors; he'd done enough with mirrors. It was time for someone to do something else. I ignored the toy Sudella and looked deliberately into his mirrors to be sure he could see what I was doing. If everything he cared about was two-dimensional, he could deal with me alone.

I plucked my eyes out of my head.

It was a purely figurative act but the feeling of reality in it hit him hard and he couldn't maintain the mirrors. Vision heightened rather than destroyed, I went back to the locked places I had forced open.

The hallway was shadowy, empty, abandoned, a place no one had ever come to. I went along it slowly, pausing at each of the doors to look into the rooms beyond.

They were all empty. There was nothing to see in any of them and no sign of anything ever having been there. Occasionally there was a strong smell of something spoiled but it was just a smell. Once I heard something large and wet shift its weight, but it was only a noise.

I let him close the doors after me, locking each one tightly, not against me but because there was no point to leaving them open. It was just a place in his mind. His body was an instrument rather than a live thing, his face a device, his eyes windows where no curtains had ever hung. He didn't hate. He just couldn't care.

In his own way, he was possibly one of the best actors of all time. Only there was no audience for his best performance.

And there was no such classification as emotional criminal. Which, I reminded myself, was a good thing for all of us.

Emotional cripple, then. But I wasn't a doctor. I couldn't even diagnose him, officially. I was only there to help him with what he had. If it wasn't there, I had no job to do. I started to withdraw.

Wait, he said.

I waited a long time. Then a landscape began to form around us, all from him though I could feel him trying to draw on me. I clamped down and he didn't like that much, but I wasn't about to let him tap me. On his own, all he

could manage was bare earth under a colorless, sunless sky, none of it feeling terribly real.

Help?

I didn't say anything. He strained a little and I felt the ground against my feet, like cardboard.

Better? He was looking around for me now and I jumped into his blind spot. *Allie?*

There's nothing more to do, I told him.

Nightmare purple flickered like heat lightning; fear. He was capable of a few emotions. *Are you going to turn me in?*

As what? To whom? It's not against the law to – to be the way you are.

Can't you tell me what to do? He was still looking around for me, confused. But he had a big blind spot; there was room enough in it for me, Sudella, and most of the country. *I need a pattern to follow, that's all, for me it's just as good …* Suddenly we were in a huge empty theater. He was onstage; I was looking up at him from the audience. He smiled down at me triumphantly. No blind spot here; he knew exactly where to find everything and everyone in his theater. I had to withdraw quickly or I was going to give him what he wanted after all.

I jumped up and hurried along the row of seats toward the aisle. He laughed a little and suddenly the aisle had receded to a vanishing point; the row of seats was endless. I paused, trying to form a clear picture of the aisle as it had been, without letting him see it, too.

See? he said. *This feels good, doesn't it? It feels real, doesn't it?*

Didn't you think someone would find out someday? I asked him, covering the image of the aisle. I almost had it. *Another actor, a better pathosfinder, or even Sudella?*

Sudella's two-dimensional form appeared in the row behind the one I was in. She was smiling and applauding.

Sudella loves the reflection of her love. And youth is forgiven many things, including it's callowness. I am as good a mirror out there as I am in here. The world is my oyster. I am the pearl.

There was a time to argue the case that youth won't persist forever, or even as long as it thinks it will, and a time to cut and run. I lunged for the aisle, which materialized just as I hit it. Before Marty could react, I tossed him into another innocuous relaxation exercise and broke the contact between us. The image of the theater persisted, fading slowly as I ran, and ran, and ran.

Eventually, I reached a small, safe, private place in the system, where I could take a few free mental breaths before I had to go back into real reality, or whatever that was out there where Sudella and Marty went through their shadow play of a relationship.

Even real reality is full of unreal things, said a voice. It sounded a little like

Pyotr Frankis's and a little like Jascha's, with the intonations of Paolo Segretti. I didn't look around; at the moment, I didn't have enough will to visualize anything more than mental fog. *Some will choose an empty exchange over a real one. Because they refuse to see that it is empty.*

Abruptly, I was facing a cat's-eye with a Snake around the outer rim of the pupil, holding its tail in its mouth.

The emptiness is real.

I had no reply. The eye faded away as I let myself be drawn out of the system.

When I disconnected and put my eyes back in, I saw that Sudella had come in out of the dark and was standing behind Marty. She was very pointedly not looking at the eyes. They *are* a bit grisly when they're out if you're not hardened to that sort of thing. I reached into the drawer and ran down a line of switches. Each of Marty's limbs gave a small jump, separately and then all together. Sudella made a gasping noise.

'What are you doing to him?'

Nothing, compared to what he tried to do to me. 'Making sure his motor controls haven't suffered. Routine.' I unhooked him, popped his eyes back in, and turned him around to Sudella before he could say anything. He stared up at her open face, which was filled with longing and compassion and love for him. Sudella in the empty theater, applauding for all she was worth.

'You must be exhausted,' I said. 'Why don't you lie down?'

'I think I will.' He turned back to me and I saw a trickle of blood leaking from the corner of his left eye. Sudella wiped it away with her fingertip.

'He's hurt.'

'He's all right, he just ruptured a capillary. It happens sometimes, when you're out of practice.' I nodded at Marty. He gave me that smile again, but this time all I could see were lips and perfect teeth. For an empty package, he sure had a beautiful wrapper. Then he went into the bedroom and shut the door.

'Now what?' Sudella lifted her chin belligerently.

'Now I leave.' I started dismantling my apparatus under her startled gaze; she hadn't been expecting that.

'Marty will explain everything. He's decided to return to the enclave with you. He's –' I paused. 'He's who he is.'

'I know.' She took a tiny step closer to me. 'He never needed your stupid mindplay. It's indecent to go running around in a person's mind like that. You find things out you shouldn't know.'

I stopped what I was doing and leaned on my equipment. 'Why not? Why shouldn't we know?' I asked gently.

She looked at me and for a moment it felt like we were hooked in together.

Of course. Rudimentary telepathy. Not developed enough to be useful, just enough to hurt.

'Some of us can live with our illusions.' She looked down at her arms, which were folded tightly against her chest. 'For some of us, it's good enough if you can't get the real thing.'

'If that's what you want to settle for.'

'If the alternative's nothing at all, what choice have you got?' She was close to tears now. 'Maybe we can't know ourselves as well without mindplay but it's the human condition to struggle for it. It's the human condition to try alone.'

I didn't comment on Marty Oren's condition. I didn't have to. It might have been different if she'd mindplayed – and then again, probably not. He wouldn't have given her an eye. He didn't have one to give.

Nelson Nelson didn't have much to say about my report, but then I'd left out what I knew about Sudella being telepathic. It didn't make any difference; the only one it really mattered to was going back to the enclave with Marty Oren.

He made a business of getting the receipt chips for my expenses in order, scrutinizing each one on the screen in his desk before punching them into final entry. I made a business of lying on the couch not looking curious.

'So tell me, Deadpan,' he said after a bit, 'how it was that you caught his problem when it eluded people who had been practicing for years?'

I was ready for that one. 'I had no expectations. I didn't stereotype him and I was thorough. You said I'd be the best pathosfinder in the country – I did a superior job.'

'Only it was too superior, eh?' NN waved away anything I might have said. 'Forget it. You did what was best for everyone. The theatrical world won't come to an end without him.'

'What about those pathosfinders who aggravated his problems?'

'He's got only *one* problem. I congratulate you for not dismissing it as a superficial manifestation of an overblown ego but recognizing it as the fabric of his reality. Woo, what a speech, eh, Deadpan?' He rubbed his wrinkled pink chin with one finger. 'Say, you'd make a good reality affixer.'

'No, thanks.'

'Good, because I don't need one. Yet.' He rolled onto his back and put his hands behind his head. 'I've turned their names in for recertification testing. The Mindplay Bureau may get around to calling them in sometime. Bureaucracy stinks.'

I shifted position uncomfortably. 'Look, if they aren't found and stopped, we might as well go back to lysergic acid and watching the ceilings roll by. Without holo-tanks.'

'Incompetence and mediocrity are everywhere. But what do you think you're here for?'

'Pardon?'

'It's the nature of any discipline to stagnate for a while, for the superficial to be received as something of depth and meaning. Mindplay doesn't mean that people won't go right on believing what they want to believe. Even – *especially* – in the name of *love*, of all things. But sooner or later some smartass comes along and points out the emperor is naked.'

'And nobody loves a smartass,' I said.

NN gave me a sharp look. 'How right you are, Deadpan. Now get out of here and leave me alone with the Bolshoi.'

I got. I didn't like the sound of *What do you think you're here for?* Just what did *he* think I was here for? Some pathosfinder – my first job was a success because the patient died, as it were. As it were. One session with me could end a career. What the hell *was* I here for anyway?

I didn't get an answer for a long time.

JERRY WIRERAMMER REDUX

'Heya. Remember me?'

I shook my head at the phone screen. 'The correct question, Jerry, is, do you remember *me?*'

'I never forgot you, Allie, I just didn't remember everything. But I do now. So you'e a big hot-wire mindplayer these days.'

'And real busy. So tell me you're not calling to get another memory wipe.'

He giggled.Same old Jerry Wirerammer giggle. 'No, nothing like that. I gotta remember everything I can, can't forget a thing.'

'Well, it's nice you remembered me, but I've just come off a job and I'm tired –'

'Yah, saw it in the dataline. That holographer, Bonspere. Did you know you got coverage on that one?'

'Strictly gossip-column, society-screen stuff, Mr Up-Town tells on your favorite celebrities. I didn't think you'd care to follow that kind of news, Jerry'

He gave me his goofy grin, but it looked a little strained. 'Oh, yah, all information is valuable. Whaddaya say we get together and talk over old times? And new times.

'Allie, please?' No grin, no giggle.

'I'm too tired for you right now; Jerry.'

Then how about tomorrow? Or the day after,' he added quickly, before I could say no again. 'Or any time you say. *Please?* I wouldn't ask if it weren't real important.'

Real important. The words echoed in my tired brain. The damned thing about it was, I *wanted* to see him and I couldn't kid myself about why. It was like a last connection to McFloy, even if I didn't give McFloy another thought as soon as I was with Jerry. That face. As long as it existed, it would haunt me.

But then, it would exist as long as I did, wouldn't it?

I brushed the thought away. 'You can't come here, Jerry.'

'Yah, I think the Nelson Nelson building's beyond even my considerable talent for hackity-hack. But that's okay, you can come here.' He punched the address in and disconnected before I could put him off till the next day.

I was impressed by the west-side address, impressed by the maxecurity luxury of the building, even impressed by the size of the elevator/lateral that took me up to the extra-private penthouse apartment levels stacked atop the rest of the structure, very impressed at being delivered directly into the living room. But I was most impressed at being greeted by three Jerry Wirerammers.

They stood side by side by side, grinning at me goofily and looking pleased with themselves. I turned to get back into the elevator/lateral.

'No, Allie, it's okay!' The Jerry Wirerammer on the left end darted forward and grabbed my arm. 'Here I am. This is me.'

I studied his face carefully. It seemed to be the original. I walked over to the other two for a closer look and right away I could see the differences. They were small, perhaps even unnoticeable to someone who didn't know Jerry as well as I did, but now that I saw them, I knew I'd never get them confused. The middle one didn't have the grin quite right – it was almost a sneer with cynical undertones – while the other one had tense eyebrows. Almost before I realized it, I'd taken their Emotional Indices. The one with the tense eyebrows was scared, probably of me but of something else as well; the middle one didn't believe in something, probably Jerry as well as me, and might have been ready to do something dangerous about it.

Jerry stepped up and put his arm around my shoulders. 'This is her, this is Allie. The pathosfinder who did your friend Bonspere. I told you I knew her. Allie, this is –'

'Shut up,' said the scared Jerry. 'She doesn't have to know anything other than we're you.' And then, absurdly, he giggled.

'Oh, she knows more than that,' said the other Jerry. 'Maybe not everything but she can tell us apart. Can't you, Allie?'

I shrugged, forcing myself not to dive for the elevator/lateral as the doors whispered shut behind me. 'It's harder to fool a mindplayer, I guess.'

'Ah,' said Jerry, 'she *can* tell us apart but I bet she can't tell which is the bootleg.'

The other two stiffened. I pulled away from Jerry and headed for the elevator doors. 'Great to see you, Jerry, gotta sprint.'

He caught me in half a hug, half a restraining hold. 'Heya, *heya*, Allie, there's no hurry!'

'Let me go, Jerry. I haven't seen a thing and I don't want to see any more.'

He pushed my face into his shoulder. 'Leave us alone a while, how about?' he said to the other two over my head. 'We got some things to talk over. You know how it is when you haven't seen someone for a long time.' Giggle.

There were two answering giggles. Twenty minutes max before that would have driven me killing mad. I could hear the dry brush of their feet on the thick white carpet; then, silence.

'Are they gone?' I said into Jerry's shoulder.

'Yah.'

'Then, let go of me.'

He released me and stepped back with his arms up. 'Heya, you're free.'

I glanced at the elevator doors. 'And you're not. Am I right?'

Jerry looked sheepish. 'Sometimes life is just one tar baby after another.' He tilted his head and squinted at me. 'Is there something wrong with your face?'

'My *face*?'

'Yah. Did you get the nerves cut or something? You haven't changed expression since you came in here.'

'Just a habit.'

'Then, you really *are* Deadpan Allie.'

'You knew that.'

'Yah. I just didn't know it so much. You want a drink? Birch beer or something?' He went across the room to a fancy bar near a mural-sized window that looked out over the skyline. It was just starting to get dark; Commerce Canyon was a murky spot against the coming evening. I followed after him slowly, taking in the expensive freestanding holos, the harsh lines of the nouveau furniture, and the indirect wall-well lighting growing brighter as the daylight faded.

'Hell of a place, isn't it?' he said, setting a tall glass of birch beer on the bar. 'Lots better than fetishizer back rooms.'

'Different,' I said, sliding onto a tulipesque stool in front of the bar. 'Not necessarily better. What do you need me to do for you now, Jerry?'

'Like I said, talk over old times.'

'Our old times consist mainly of your bringing me drugs and madcaps.'

'Yah, those were the days. I thought we could talk about them.'

'*Jerry*. I think I just said about all there is to say about them. You want me to describe them in detail? How my old efficiency looked, what I was wearing, what you were wearing, how many times you used the lavabo?'

He grinned a little too brightly. 'Sure. Why not?'

'*Why?*'

'Because if I don't come up with some more memories for those two guys, they're probably going to kill me.' He grabbed my hand as I started to get off the stool. 'Okay, not *kill* me. I mean, not *dead* kill Probably. But they'll be mad enough to kill. And then I don't know what they'll do but maybe afterwards they won't kill me even if I beg them to.'

'Who are they? No, don't tell me. I don't want to know. Just explain to me why they seem so enamored of being you.'

Jerry grinned goofily at a point somewhere over my head. 'I don't know if it's that they want to be me so much as it is they don't want to be them. If you see what I mean. Maybe you could understand that better if you knew just how much I wish I weren't me right now.'

'Yah, I think I can understand that pretty well.'

Jerry pushed the birch beer at me. '"Drink up, Shriners." Anyway, these two guys, they're just a wealthy married couple, bored, they've spent so much with Power People, they should probably be half-owners. So one of them rented the Jerry Wirerammer property and liked it so much he talked his husband into it, and *I* said he could buy direct from me and I'd give him a break on the price.'

'You're bootlegging yourself on your own now? What about the bootleggers you were working with?'

'Jerry Wirerammer's still moving well for them, they've got no complaints.'

I touched my face casually; ever the professional, I still hadn't changed expression. 'Don't you see the problem with that? Or are you that much dumber than I ever thought?'

Jerry shrugged theatrically. 'Heya, it's not something I'd make a habit of. I just wanted to give these guys a break. Mostly, I let Power People and, uh, the other company do the selling for me.'

'How did you meet these two?'

He looked pained. 'You know, that's the one thing I can't remember. I guess it's not important.'

'Only to them. So they aren't happy with the product?'

'Sure they are.' Jerry's grin faded a bit. 'They just wish there were more of it. They keep after me for more memories. I've given them everything, including stuff I didn't even know I had. But I'm going dry. I need help. And here you are.' He pushed the glass a little closer. ' "Drink up, Shriners." '

I shook my head.

'Come on, Allie, all you have to do is talk over old times with me. Prime the old memory pump.'

'Jerry, you were a long time ago. It's like someone else's life to me now.'

'No problem. They've got equipment here.'

I blinked.

'You know, enhancers. It'll be like reliving everything.'

'You're not getting access to my mind. That was the one thing you never talked me into and you're not going to talk me into it now.'

He looked down at the glass of birch beer. 'Yah, that was the funny thing about you. You'd do just about anything except mindplay. That was before you became a big hot-wire mindplayer, though. They have to pay for you now, right? Suppose I offered to pay?'

'Call the agency in the morning. Nelson Nelson'll put you on the waiting list. If you want to hire a pathosfinder.'

Jerry leaned his elbows on the bar and rested his chin on his hands. 'I'm not asking for anything you haven't got, Allie.'

'You don't get in. That's my final word.'

'Well, I had a feeling this was how it would go, but I was hoping.' He nodded at the glass. ' "Drink up, Shriners." '

'How come you keep saying that? What are "Shriners." '

'I don't know. It's something I picked up from my two, uh, fans. They say it all the time. "Drink up, Shriners." Sounds kind of cute.'

'Actually, it sounds like maybe you've picked up more from them than they have from you. They aren't really very much like you, Jerry.'

'They're resting their imprints right now. They were me all day. You should have seen them then.'

I was glad I hadn't. 'Listen, I think I can help you after all.'

He perked up, complete with goofy grin.

'No, not that way. Suppose I get you out of here.'

Jerry waved a hand at the expensive room, including the mural window. 'Get out of here? What for? So I can go back to sleeping in parking spaces and rewiring fetishizers?'

'Does all of this really mean that much to you? It's just *stuff*, Jerry. It's just expensive *stuff*. You're risking your – your *self* for a goddam nouveau *couch!*'

'What else is there for me? I'm a convicted mind criminal. I'm a mind *felon*. I'm out of the game you're playing in, they didn't offer me a rehab deal.'

'Not that time. But maybe they did once?'

He mirrored my expressionlessness back at me, with an edge. 'I don't remember.'

I nodded. 'Yah. I guess you also forgot that things you can't remember still happened anyway.'

'I'll tell you what I *do* remember – taking someone to a dry-cleaner's when I could have pissed off and gotten away.'

'*I* remember who gave me the madcap.'

'And *I* remember there wasn't any gun to your head to take it, either.'

We stared at each other. 'Old times,' I said after a few moments. 'Those were the days.'

Jerry burst out laughing. Not giggling but laughing. 'Yah, they sure as hell

were. I remember how you'd do just about anything to light a fire in your brain. Sometimes I used to wonder what you were after.' The laughter subsided. 'What *were* you after?'

I blew out a breath. 'You're asking me *now?* I'm not sure. Lights. Colors. Patterns. A glimpse of Something.'

'Like that mandala on your ceiling.'

A vivid picture of the old mandala sprang into my mind. 'Yah. I used to wander around in that for hours, just … ' My voice died in my throat.

'Go on,' Jerry said helpfully. 'You used to wander around in your mandala for hours, just what?'

I reached over and tipped the glass of birch beer toward Jerry. He jumped back with a small yell.

'What did you do *that* for?' he said, grabbing an expensive towel and mopping at the mess.

'Just to let you know I'm onto you.'

'Not a terribly deadpan thing to do,' he said, dumping the saturated towel in a small sink behind him and grabbing another one.

'I was deadpan all day. You should have seen me then.'

'Glad I didn't,' Jerry muttered. I felt a brief prickle of gooseflesh. 'But that's okay if you want to stop now. You've given me enough to work with.'

'I have?'

'Sure.' Giggle. 'Your offer to get me out of here still open?'

'Why?' I said suspiciously.

'Because I need to get out right now.'

'All right. I'll get you out.'

Big grin. 'Hey, Wirerammers!' he called.

A door near one of the freestanding holos slid back and the ersatz Jerrys appeared in the doorway side by side. Neither of them was grinning.

'She says we have to go to her place,' Jerry said, gesturing at me somewhat sheepishly. 'You know how it is when you haven't seen someone for a while.'

'Does she have equipment?' the scared one asked.

'"Does she have equipment." She's Deadpan Allie, she's got all the equipment in the world.'

I hopped off the stool and headed for the elevator doors. 'Come on, Jerry, gotta sprint.'

'Wait a minute,' said the angry one as Jerry hurried after me. I jabbed the call panel next to the doors and kept my back to them.

'The faster we get out of here, the faster I get back with the goods,' Jerry said. 'Don't worry, it'll be great.'

The elevator arrived and I was so relieved that I didn't notice until we'd dropped fifty floors that it wasn't the same one I'd come up in, but a much smaller one.

'Sorry,' Jerry said casually, as my breathing became audible, 'but you were in a hurry. Otherwise I'd have called the big one. When did you become a claustrophobe?'

'I don't remember,' I said with some difficulty. Mercifully, Jerry didn't giggle.

We hit bottom and I spilled out into the lobby. Jerry sauntered after me, watching me with great interest. 'Your face really does work after all,' he said as he punched an exit code into the front door.

'You can feel privileged that you got to see it,' I said, taking deep gulps of the night air.

'I never wanted to see you in trouble. That's why I took you to the dry-cleaner's in the first place.'

An airbus went by overhead, the underside lit up with a new advertising campaign for Power People. Jerry's face was not among those on display. He glared up at it for a moment.

'Come on,' he said and led me down the steps to the front gate, where he had to punch in another exit code.

'Where do you want to go now?' I said. 'You can't stay with me and I don't think a visit to a memory-wiper is a good idea.'

'Oh, I'm going back there,' he said. 'Just like I told them. Did you really think I wouldn't?'

'Jerry –'

'But first I've got to get to a memory lane.' He punched another code into a stone stanchion on the left side of the gate. 'I'm calling the car,' he explained. 'I'll drop you off at the agency on my way.'

'Why are you going to a memory lane?'

'They can take the stuff we talked about and plug it into a more elaborate scenario. Those two'll never know the difference. It'll be easy to fool them since I've never gone mind-to-mind with you.'

A private flyer swooped down and landed almost silently in front of us, the door opening automatically, like a mechanical bird wing offering shelter. I hesitated; Jerry gave me a gentle push inside.

I settled into the green velvet cushions while Jerry gave the flyer the agency's address. 'That little bit we talked about isn't going to be enough,' I said.

'Yah, it will. When they get through with it at the memory lane, it will. Never been to one, have you? Stupid question, yah. In two hours, you and I will have a history rich enough to make a holo and two sequels over.' The flyer lifted smoothly. I didn't bother strapping myself in.

'Why didn't you do that before?'

He grinned at me, but not goofily. 'I have. With other things. I've been saving you for last. I wasn't going to get to you unless they got greedy.' He shrugged. 'So they got greedy.'

'If you've been saving me for last, you should have had plenty of material.'

Now he looked confused. 'Yah, you'd think so, wouldn't you? But, I don't know. I got down to you and then I needed you to be there. Damnedest thing.' He giggled but it didn't come out quite right.

Organ fatigue. I stared out the window at the city lights passing below us. All the little intrigues and counterintrigues Jerry had been indulging in to keep himself one step ahead of everyone he was double-crossing. The mental strain was beginning to translate into something physical – too much memory-wiping, too many strolls down memory lane to get falsified memories. Probably stripping the myelin sheathing off his axons like cheap paint. He was losing himself. How long before he woke up one day with Swiss cheese behind his eyes?

I forced myself to look at him again. He was lying back on the cushions with the trademarked Jerry Wirerammer grin on his face, staring at nothing.

'Jerry.'

'What,' he said brightly.

'Has it occurred to you that you can't keep this up?'

'Who's going to stop me?' He paused. 'You going to turn me in?'

I shook my head. 'I should. It would save you. Maybe I will.'

'No, you won't. Because I asked you not to. I know what I'm doing.' He sat up a little. 'I choose to do it. If they caught me and put me under the belljar with amnesia now, I'd come out a baked potato, I know that. You've been under the belljar, haven't you? Imagine it with amnesia, nothing to draw on to help you through the sensory deprivation. It's cruel and unusual, and they keep doing it because none of *them* knows what it's like. The crazy thing is, you don't remember what it's like yourself afterwards. But your subconscious gives you a little glimpse now and then. You walk around with the creeps for the rest of your life.'

'They couldn't Strip-Search you. It was disallowed.'

'I'm supposed to feel grateful? They whipped me but thank god they didn't use the really big whip?'

'There's a bright side to everything, Jerry.'

'You're such a smartass.'

'And nobody loves a smartass.'

'Except another smartass.' He slumped down on the cushions and closed his eyes. 'I know what I'm doing. And you can't stop me unless you want to get in trouble yourself and I don't think you do. You want to stick with being a big hot-wire mindplayer, Allie. And I'll stick to what I've got. I'm living in the outer world and I'm locked out of the one you live in. You're living in yours and you've turned your back on the outer world. That's how it is.'

The flyer made a gentle landing on the agency roof. The door swung upward to let me out.

'I won't call you again, Allie.' I stepped over him out onto the roof. 'Unless I really need to,' he added as the door closed again.

FANDANGO

'But if you'd gone into neurosis peddling, what would you do to relax?' said Fandango. She'd taken to hanging around my place in her various neurotic drag. This week she was dead white all over with a coating of lanugo. Early Petulant Child, she called it; it looked more like the Invasion of the Giant Baby to me.

'Huh?'

'Neurotics should never go into neurosis peddling. It only encourages them.'

'*I'm* neurotic?'

'Sure you're neurotic. All you pathosfinders are neurotic. You have to be. You're always looking for what things *mean*. It's part of your job, of course, but it's still neurotic.'

'And what about you? You're not neurotic?'

She shrugged. 'Oh, sure. But it's different for me. I'm into it as an art form, like all neurosis peddlers. Can you honestly say you have an appreciation for neurosis as another form of art?

'No.'

'Well, there you have it. You're stuck with pathosfinding unless you quit and you can't quit. You're under contract until you make back what NN invested in training you, plus a twenty-percent profit. That fancy vacation you took with Lindbloom is included in that figure, you know.'

I hadn't known. Or rather, I hadn't read my contract carefully enough, but it didn't matter that much to me. After all, I had nowhere better to go.

Fandango popped up off the floor where she'd been knotted up like a sheepshank or something and dialed herself another birch beer. 'Anything for you?'

I held up my glass to show her I was only half done with mine.

'You're the first one I know of that the old fox hired in right out of an institute. Everyone else here had a few years in private practice. Were you some kind of prodigy at J. Walter?'

'No,' I said, laughing a little. 'Not me.'

'*Ah*.' Fandango ambled over, clinking her ice cubes. 'Then *he* was the prodigy.'

'"He"? "He" who?'

Fandango blinked. Moonstone eyes; they didn't really become her. 'Whoever it was that left such an indelible mark on your life. Or *she*, excuse me.'

Indelible mark; that was one way to put it. 'Sorry, I hadn't realized we'd

gone from a discussion of my hiring to, uh, something else entirely. You were right the first time. He. Yah, he was. A prodigy, I mean.'

'I know what you mean, I'm following this conversation. After all, I started it.' She lit on the couch next to me. 'So tell me, was *he* the reason you went into mindplaying?'

I laughed again, shaking my head. 'No, not *him.*'

Fandango's smile got broader. 'Out*rage*ous, Deadpan. *Another* one. Quite the vixen, were you?'

'Oh, no, not *me.*'

Now she looked puzzled. 'Well, then, who?'

'Who what?'

'Who was the vixen?'

I broke up completely. 'It wasn't anything like that, Fandango,' I said when I stopped laughing.

She drew back a little, frowning at me. 'What's the matter with you?'

'I don't know what you mean.'

'You need a life, Deadpan. Hey, listen to that, that's the second time I've called you Deadpan. *That's* what I mean: What kind of a life have you got just pulling down the big ones for Nelson goddam Nelson?'

'Hey, give me a little time. I'm new in town.'

'Not that new. You've been here, what, a year?' I nodded. 'A year and what have you done? I'll tell you what you've done. You've done Nelson goddam Nelson's son-in-law, you've done that punchy holographer, and you've done the Dancing Barbanos.' I grinned at her reference to the half-dozen members of the revival dance company. I'd helped their sincerity but not the fact that there wasn't much interest in reviving things like square dancing and demishawn.

'I also did that performance artist,' I said. 'The one who'd spent a month in creative trance.' And then there'd been Jerry, but I'd been refusing to think about that.

'Oh, yah. I remember your performance artist. A few more like that and nobody would need neurosis peddlers. All right, you've got quite the list of accomplishments. What have you got for yourself?'

I tried my best Deadpan face on her. 'That's a rather personal question, don't you think?'

Suddenly all the neurosis-peddler facade was gone from her face and we were just person-to-person on the couch. 'You know what a mindplayer is without a personal life?' She tossed back her drink and held up the glass with just the ice cubes in it. 'This.'

'Well, I lead a very mental life,' I told her.

'Yah. Your personal life's all in your head, right?'

'Something like that.'

'You go and visit your phantoms regularly in whatever kind of little home you have for them in your mind? Tell them everything that happens to you, maybe feast your inner eyes on that old lover preserved for all time just the way he was?'

Some deadpan. I was staring at her with my mouth hanging open.

'Allie, for chrissakes, *I'm a neurosis peddler!* I know every mental kink and twist and trick there is, *what do you think I peddle, pancakes?*'

In spite of everything, I couldn't help laughing a little. 'I never thought of that.'

Fandango bounced on the couch cushions impatiently. 'Goddammit –'

'Okay, *okay*,' I said, 'I was listening to you, really, I was. I understand what you're trying to tell me. I'm just, I –' I spread my hands. 'It's not that easy.'

'You want me to give you an exhibitionistic streak for a while? Great way to meet people.'

Oh, my god, I thought. 'Well talk about it after the next assignment.'

'What – you got another one already?'

'"Already"? It's been close to a month since the last one. NN left a message in my dataline last night. I've got to see him' – I glanced over at the clock above the screen –' in about an hour.'

'You didn't tell me that,' Fandango said accusingly.

'You didn't ask.'

'What were you going to do, throw me out when the time came?'

I shrugged. 'That's what you do to me. Except you're usually over here these days so you just flounce out when the time comes.'

'Flounce?'

'Or slither, or toddle, or whatever.'

Fandango got up to dial her third birch beer. 'You go ahead. Take your assignment, do your usual brilliant job with it. And after that, you see living people.'

'I'm going to see living people on the assignment.' I smiled into her petulant glare, just being obtuse. Also being wrong.

NEARLY DEPARTED ...

'Three things,' I said, and held up a matching set of three fingers.

Nelson Nelson looked tolerantly amused. 'Run 'em.'

'One –' I curled my index finger. 'I don't do empaths. Two –' I bent my ring finger. 'I don't get physical. Three –' I pointed the remaining finger at the old fox on the other side of the desk. 'I don't rob graves.'

The couch creaked as NN rolled over onto his back and folded one arm

behind his head. 'Is that all that's bothering you? Kitta Wren hasn't been buried.'

'I don't do dead people. If God had meant me to pathosfind dead people, she wouldn't have invented the Brain Police.'

A broad smile oozed over NN's saggy features as he reached for a cigarette. He was smoking those lavender things again. They smelled like young girls. 'What's the matter, Allie? Are you scared of a dead person's brain?'

'I'm scareder of some live ones I know. Fear isn't the issue. I just have certain beliefs, and this job you're asking me to take goes against every one of them.'

'Such as?'

Sighing, I shifted position on my own couch and scratched my forearm. That vulgar gold lamé upholstery giving me a rash. You can dispute taste but you can't stop it. 'Such as, death is the end. Of art, I mean. The end means there is no more. Dead people should be allowed to rest in peace instead of having their brains plundered and looted for any last bit of – of treasure, like Egyptian tombs.'

NN looked at me with mild admiration. 'Eloquent. Really eloquent, Deadpan,' he said after a moment. 'You're probably the most eloquent mindplayer this agency has ever employed. Someday you might talk yourself out of a job. But not today.' He winked at me. 'Actually, I respect your feelings. Those are good feelings. Especially for someone who trades on the name Deadpan Allie.'

'Being deadpan doesn't mean I don't have feelings. I just don't show them.'

'You're showing them now. And I personally don't share them. I feel there's a lot of validity in, say, going in and getting the last measures of unfinished music from a master composer who dropped dead at the harpsitron, or mining the brain of a gifted writer for the story that remained unwritten in life. Postmortem art is highly regarded and a large number of artists, including Kitta Wren, sign postmortem permissions. It's a sort of life after death. The only one we know about for sure.'

I scratched my rash some more and didn't say anything.

'Kitta Wren *wanted* a postmortem. It's not grave robbing. If she hadn't signed the permission, that would be different.'

'Kitta Wren was a five-star lunatic. I read her specs while I was waiting for you. She had a psychomimic's license and when she wasn't writing her poetry, she was going boing-boing-boing.'

'Ah, but she was brilliant,' NN said dreamily. I blinked at him, astounded. I'd had no idea he liked poetry, or anything else besides the Bolshoi. 'When it came to her work, she was totally in control. Somehow, I always thought that control would bring her down. In a thousand years, I never would have thought anyone would kill her.'

I wanted to tear my hair and rend my garment. 'NN,' I said as calmly as I could, 'I *hate* murder. I am *not* the Brain Police. If they want to find out who did her, let them send in one of their own to wander around in her mind.'

'Oh, they will,' Nelson Nelson said cheerfully. 'Right after the postmortem.' A cloud of lavender smoke dissipated over my head as NN flipped his cigarette into the suckhole in the center of the desk. 'The Brain Police can't do anything until that's taken care of. Otherwise whatever poetry is left in there could be fragmented and irretrievably lost.'

The rash had crept up past my elbow. I kept scratching. 'You know, there are mindplayers who postmortem for a living.'

'I'll pardon the expression. Wren's manager hired you. Come along, now, it'll take you somewhere you've never traveled.'

'I've never been to the heart of a white dwarf star and I don't see why I should go.'

NN exhaled with a noise that was almost a growl. 'Do you *want* to work for me?'

'I'm thinking.'

He gave me that oozy smile again. 'Deadpan, this is important. And you might learn something.' He raised up on one elbow. 'Just try it. If you can't do it once you're in, fine. But *try.*'

I sat up, scrubbing my arm through my sleeve. 'All right. But just don't make a habit of signing me up for postmortems.'

The agency's system would have removed my eyes for me but I'd come to prefer doing that little chore myself for some reason. After I lowered them into the bowl of solution, I lay down on the slab and felt it slide me headfirst into the system. Even blind, I could sense the vastness of it around me as it swallowed me down to my neck. You could have spent the rest of your life wandering around in it but all I wanted at the moment was a little basic reality affixing and reassurance. If I was going to run barefoot through a dead lunatic's mind, I needed all the reinforcement I could get. After letting the system eat my head for an hour, I almost felt ready.

I hadn't been gassing Nelson Nelson as to how I felt about postmortems just to cover a corpse phobia. To me, you ought to be able to take something with you – or at least make sure it goes the same time you do – and if it's your art, so be it. Hell, there were plenty of living artists around with a lot to offer. Stripping a dead person's mind for the last odds and ends seemed close to unspeakable.

I supposed the appeal was partly what Nelson Nelson said – life after death. But there seemed to be more than a little thanatophilia at work. Art after death made me think of sirens on rocks, and I wasn't the only one who heard them. Occasionally there'd be an item in the dataline about some

obscure holographer or composer – holographers and composers seemed to be particularly susceptible, or maybe there were just more of them – found dead with a note instructing that an immediate postmortem be performed because the person had been convinced that the unreachable masterpiece so unattainable in life could be liberated only by the Big Bang of death.

So there'd be the requested postmortem and the mindplayer who hooked into the brain, which was all wired up and floating in stay-juice like a toy boat lost at sea, would come out not with a magnificent phoenix born of the poor deader's ashes but with a few little squibs and scraps from half-completed thoughts that had turned in on themselves, swallowing their own tails for lack of substance, vortices that had gone nowhere and now never would. Some people aren't happy just with being alive. They have to be dead, too.

At least Kitta Wren hadn't been one of those. The information Nelson Nelson had dumped into my dataline was freckled with little details but was rather sketchy taken all together. I punched her picture up on my screen and sided it with her bio.

She'd been a very ordinary woman, squarish in the face with a high forehead and medium-brown untreated hair. Her only physical affectation had been her eyes. Since the advent of biogems, many people had at least a semiprecious stare. I hadn't seen very many people with my own preference for the shifting brown of cat's-eye and it takes a certain coloring to carry off diamonds, but Kitta Wren had something I'd never seen before.

Her eyes seemed to be shattered blue glass, as though someone had deliberately smashed the gems before putting them in. Her pupils were spiderwebbed with white cracks. I enlarged them for detail and then paused. Wrong again. Her eyes weren't spiderwebbed with cracks – they were spiderwebbed with spiderwebs, thickened as though coated with dew or frost. Come into my lunatic parlor. I wondered how much they had to do with her psychoses.

She'd gotten her first psychomimics license at nineteen and spent the five years after that almost continuously crazy with a few months off here and there for extended periods of writing. Later, she had begun limiting her psychotic times to summers while she worked on a cycle of poetry. The result, a long series called *Crazy Summer*, had given Wren her first major recognition. From there she'd gone to being crazy only at night, then only during the day, and once she'd spent six months orbiting the moon in high mania.

That was the other thing that was bothering me, of course: the whole psychosis thing. All those madcaps I'd taken leading me step by step to contact with this madwoman who also happened to be dead but still crazy. Did I believe in the Cosmic Practical Joke? And how much funnier was it going to get?

When Kitta Wren had died, which had been – I punched for the date – just the day before, she'd been a week into a general schizophrenia no one seemed

to know anything about. Cause of death – I blanched – disembowelment. There was a photograph of her office where she'd gotten it. She'd been strong all the way to the end, walking clear across the room before collapsing. Dead just under an hour when her manager had found her. Not too bad. Five hours was about the limit for an untreated brain. After that, it's not worth trying to hook in with. No suspects and no murder weapon; the Brain Police were holding off their investigation of her brain until after the postmortem. Standard procedure, as their technique tended to wipe a mind clean.

Under Miscellaneous, I found a small picture of Wren's manager, a gold-skinned androgyne named Phylp with fan-shaped eyebrows. The request for a pathosfinder was entered as well. It seemed Phylp wanted someone who wouldn't treat her like just another deader. Sounded to me as though Phylp was hoping Wren hadn't left behind as little as s/he suspected.

... WE ARE GATHERED HERE ...

A morgue is a morgue is a morgue. They can paint the walls with aggressively cheerful primary colors and splashy bold graphics, but it's still a holding place for the dead until they can be parted out to organ banks. Not that I would have cared normally but my viewpoint was skewed. The relentless pleasance of the room I sat in seemed only grotesque.

The other two people in the room with me didn't seem to feel that way. One had introduced himself as Matt Sabian, postmortem supervisor. The other was unmistakably Phylp. S/he overshadowed Sabian despite the latter's silver hair, garnet eyes, and polished skin. Phylp was the flashiest androgyne I'd ever seen – most of them preferred no higher an appearance profile than anyone else, but Phylp handled major talent. It was probably advantageous to have such a memorable manager. If anyone could remember the talent after seeing the manager, the talent had to be pretty major. Show biz.

'I understand this is your first dead client,' Sabian was saying. The absurdity of the statement made me want to laugh but they don't call me Deadpan Allie and lie.

'Up until now, I've worked only with living minds, yes.' I sneaked a glance at Phylp, who was more arranged in a chair than seated.

'You shouldn't have any trouble,' Sabian said. His voice had an odd hint of disappointment. 'Your own mind will have to provide a good deal of visualization, except for her memories and the like, so I hope you're not given to overly bizarre symbolism. And you have to realize that you'll be *in* the mind,

not just in contact with it, as you would be with a living mind. A dead mind can't respond to anything outside of itself. You'll find that everything in a living mind is present in a dead one. Except life, of course. We leave this world as we come into it – without thoughts, personality, memories, talent. When life fades, it leaves these things behind, just like any other material item. Which is why there'll be room for you inside of it.'

I didn't like the sound of that but I couldn't decide exactly why.

'You'll have to actively stimulate the mind to obtain anything, as it can't offer it voluntarily,' he went on, seemingly pleased to be lecturing. 'It takes life to do that. It'll be very much like hooking into a computer program of Kitta Wren's identity.'

'But it's not really that simple, is it?'

Sabian was about to answer but Phylp spoke up for the first time. 'That's why I wanted a pathosfinder for her.'

'Pardon?'

'Someone who would understand that it's not just a matter of searching out data. I want whatever it is that comes out to sound alive. Because she was alive when she created it.'

Sabian pointedly did not look at Phylp, who returned the favor. It clicked for me then. Sabian, postmortem supervisor. If Phylp hadn't insisted on hiring a pathosfinder, Sabian would have been on this job. A nice sweet plum of a job, too, doing a postmortem on someone of Kitta Wren's stature. I did a sight reading of his Emotional Index but I couldn't tell who he was angrier at, me or Phylp.

'How well did you know Kitta Wren?' I asked Phylp.

'Not at all. I managed her, but she was a stranger to me.

That was a lot of help. 'What about family?'

'Only two brothers. One is at the South Pole. The other is under the Indian Ocean in a religious trance.'

'Do you know anything about her early life?'

'Only that her parents gave the children to the state and vanished.' S/he spread her/his hands gracefully. 'That's all anyone knows. In the five years I've handled her, she never showed the slightest inclination of opening up to me or anyone else. It was a major disclosure if she told me she liked her contracts.'

'That extreme sort of self-isolation isn't exactly normal behavior for a poet, is it?'

Phylp frowned at me. 'Nothing about her behavior was *normal*. She was crazy. All the time she was crazy, and when she wasn't, she wanted to be. God knows what she got out of it.'

Her poetry, apparently. I turned my attention back to Sabian. 'What about the psychotic dead mind? Is the psychosis still operating?'

'Very much, though in a strictly mechanical way.' He thought for a moment. 'But it probably doesn't know it's dead.'

I hesitated. 'Which do you mean – the psychosis or the mind?'

'Both, I would think.'

'How does a mind not know it's dead?'

Sabian lifted his head slightly. 'How does yours know it's alive? It's the same question, really.' Not the way I saw it, but I let him go on. 'Minds contain information, but it takes the presence of life for them to know anything. What does a computer program *know*?' The polished face stretched in a tight, triumphant smile, as though he'd given me a glimpse of Big Truth.

'And where is the brain now?' I asked after a moment.

'Here.' Sabian got up and went to a panel in the nearest wall. He punched a few buttons and a section just below opened up. There it was; what had waited behind Kitta Wren's spiderwebs in life now hung in a tall, clear canister of stay-juice, trailing wires like the streamers on a Portuguese man-of-war. The wires went down through the bottom of the canister to the maintenance box, which kept a minimum number of neurons firing. Two more wires leading from the visual center were coiled on top of the canister.

'We're still within the optimum time to go in. One more day and the neurons will begin to cease firing efficiently, and after that, deterioration will be rapid. I hope you'll be able to get everything on the first try.'

Looking at the thing in the canister, I hoped so, too.

They left me alone so I could set up my portable system. There was a lot to be said for the ritual of preparation as a form of relaxation therapy; I never needed it more than I did just then. I took my time, working silently and trying not to look at Kitta Wren's mortal remains while I let my thoughts wander.

Eventually I found myself thinking of Jerry Wirerammer and the madcap. A logical association; this was the first time I'd been near a psychosis since my arrest. But it was quite a different thing to deal with psychosis than it was to be psychotic yourself. Given the choice, I would rather have been crazy, but it didn't seem to hold the same attraction for me as it once had. You grew up, Deadpan, I told myself; you grew up and found out reality is crazy enough on its own. Any reality.

Pulling out the drawer with the connections and thermal tank for my eyes, I paused. A living client I would have hooked into a relaxation exercise such as making colors, building landscapes, or running mazes, but what could I do with a dead one? Aside from the fact that it couldn't initiate any action – could it get any more relaxed? I laughed to myself. A little mental humor. Sabian had said I would have to stimulate it. I settled on some abstract moving visuals, made the connections, and then dragged over a chair.

Despite my apprehension, it didn't take any longer than usual to calm myself into a smooth, alert state of receptivity. I had positioned the thermal

tank of the maintenance box next to the canister, where I could reach it easily. When I was absolutely sure of its location, I thumbed my eyes out and let them down into the solution. It never ceased to amaze me how well I could function blind; training had given me superior short-term eidetic memory.

The connections crept under my eyelids and found their way to my optic nerves. After a few moments, body awareness faded and I was through the system, into Kitta Wren's mind.

Normally I would have made my presence felt gradually so as not to startle my client by bursting in like an invader. But this client couldn't know that trauma; besides, I was going directly into the visual center instead of using the less abrupt route through the optic nerve. After the slight disorientation of passing through the barriers of personality and identity, I found myself in the thick of random pictures and arbitrary memories. So this was being inside a mind. It wasn't so different from being inside the system, or anywhere else. Everybody's got to go somewhere. Around me, the mind seemed to tense as it felt the addition of something new and unpredictable. Then it ground on as before, leaving me as just another thought.

The abstract-visuals program was still running and I was awash in lazy spiral rainbows and harlequin rivers. I set it for gradual fade-out, and as it went, more of the brain's own pictures appeared, some of them mundane objects remembered for no reason, some of them vignettes from Kitta Wren's life. I let them swirl around while I decided on the best way to go about the postmortem. Hitch a ride on a memory? Follow a random thought? Get hold of some false starts or blind alleys and reconstruct them?

I'd immersed myself in one of her false starts (an image of a walk in the rain in the middle of the night) when the mind tried to think me. There was almost no warning. I was busy receiving multiple over- and undertones accompanied by the memory of the false start's creation and the frustration Kitta Wren had felt before finally giving up on finding anything to do about it. Taste of rain dissolving on lips and tongue and the first line: *Do I drink the rain or does the rain drink me … drink? Think?* I was searching it for possible salvage when the mind clamped down on me and the old, unfinished poem together.

It thought the poem piece by piece, starting with the memory. It remembered the night and then the season (why not the season and then the night, I wondered), and then moisture, pausing to associate it with varieties of wetness. I was overwhelmed by the smell of the ocean, followed by a brief image of a coffin covered with barnacles lying on the sea bottom. The taste of rain returned more strongly, eradicating the picture of the coffin *(my brother, that's all)* but not quite managing to suppress a fleeting thought of snow. *Drink the rain … the rain drinks me … drinking the rain I am drunk and am drunk by drunken rain …* The mind niggled and gnawed out each variation

from the original line (what was this big fascination with rain, anyway?). When it was through, I was next.

There is no way to describe being thought, or being about to be thought. If you imagine yourself in, say, a play, it's still not the same, at all. If you imagine yourself recorded on holo, yourself being the recorded image – no, who can imagine that. I still can't, and I was there. I couldn't imagine what it would be like to be thought, either, except I didn't think it would be a very good thing.

Hurriedly, I made a mask of my face and then took it off. The mind reached for me in its purely mechanical probing and I threw my face into its processes. Traveling at the speed of thought, my face was everywhere as the mind tried to find the correct association for it. I saw it materialize on the smooth, blank surface of a writing slate before I slipped through a half-remembered dream – images of cold stone carvings on a cathedral wall and a quick impression of writing about a mad cathedral, which gave me a chill. But it wasn't my cathedral. I made sure of that before I let myself settle down on Kitta Wren's back burner.

There isn't a mind in the world that doesn't have a back burner and it was usually a lot more difficult to get a client to open it up. Sometimes the incomplete puzzlements and notions stewing there were capable of growing into full-fledged ideas; other times, they changed into false starts or shrank away into un-existence. Kitta Wren's back burner was so full of images that some were teetering half-dissolved on the edge of forgotten, as though she had deliberately pushed every idea that occurred to her to the back burner and waited to see which ones wouldn't disintegrate. Not the most productive way to work. I propelled myself through them to see what I might be able to glean, which, I thought, would probably yield more results than looking at false starts and blind alleys. I was learning.

It was like looking at a holo-collage of a beginning holo student. Kitta Wren's inner voice faded in and out where she had found words to go with the pictures. In quick turn I was looking up from the bottom of a deep, narrow hole at a circle of innocent blue sky, staring across the surface of a bed at eye-level, watching two people, their faces in shadow, touch hands while their low, womanly voices murmured to each other (each was Wren herself). I was caught in a storm in the desert with rare rain beating straight down (there was that rain again), observing a street scene populated only by machines, my cheek pressed against the pavement, tasting an empty cup and pretending there was something in it. That one caught my interest; I reviewed it to see where she'd gotten it.

Something from nothing, that intelligent-sounding inner voice said. *Something from nothing.* I saw a chrysanthemum in the bottom of the cup; it metamorphosed from live to painted-on. The center of the flower was an eye. *Something from nothing. I fill me with something from nothing.*

I began to get the feeling I wasn't alone. Which was absurd – even *she* wasn't there any more. I turned my attention from the cup and waited. Possibly what I'd felt was the mind reaching for me again. Lowering my energy level as much as possible, I moved in among the jumble of unfinished ideas and waited. Rain punched dents in the sand; the sideways view of the street shimmered in the soggy desert sky like a mirage.

The mind spasmed. I had given it a new combination of thoughts by the way I had juxtaposed her old fragments. It fixed on me and the madness hit.

That was what I had felt approaching, her psychosis, and it struck like a concentrated, highly localized storm. I thought my perception of it had been colored by my exposure to her preoccupation with rain but it remained stormlike even after the mind separated me from its own concepts, and I realized the nature of what Kitta Wren had done to herself.

Had she been alive, I would have been witnessing a localized psychotic episode, a variety of seizure meant to produce not a physical convulsion but an altered state of consciousness. Except there was no consciousness.

The seizure tore into her ideas and images and they scattered in all directions, falling flat because there was no one to pick them up and use them. The rest of the mind practically came to a standstill while the storm raged on. She'd been hoping for a literal brainstorm, a creative madness that would tear through her mind, stirring her thoughts into new and better patterns, giving her the stimulation she had refused to seek in the larger world outside herself. The mind seemed to shimmer and its perception of me grew vague. I slipped away down to an area of learned reflexes and automatic behavior to wait things out. As soon as the seizure had passed, I would go back, collect her ideas, memorize them, and get out. Phylp had been wrong. I would have to treat this strictly as a data-retrieval operation, I couldn't deal with the mind as though it were living –

Reaching for a cigarette with only a dim awareness of the act I/she felt the first pain. I/she looked down at the slate on the desk and the stylus in my/her hand. It gleamed like a knife. (Memory run; it was a go; humans keep memory packrat style, who would have thought this one would be in Habits and Mannerisms?) But it couldn't cut away the blankness of the slate to reveal the words that were stuck in my/her mind.

Then I was past the memory pocket and the mind had me again. Tropism – I should have known. Minds were meant to live and be conscious. There had been no consciousness, but now there was mind. If consciousness was there, then the mind must be alive.

Alive. It pulled at me and I passed through the psychosis like a kite in a high wind. The madness clutched at me, searching for a way in, almost as if it were a separate, living intelligence as alien as I was. I tasted anger and spat it out; it came back at me as a sea of strange faces registering disappointment,

confusion, hate. Kitta Wren's view of the world, vinegar laced with poison. The mind dragged me onward and I went, trailing the madness and the memory and the madness of the memory through the fireworks display of her life.

Something from nothing. I looked to see who she was speaking to but there was no one. Just a personal affirmation. *Give me nothing; I take nothing. Offer me nothing; thank you. His eye may be on the sparrow but the Wren looks out for herself.* She had worked hard for her unhappiness and her mind showed her efforts to me as though they were trophies and prizes. A coffin under the Indian Ocean, something she'd never seen, an image invented and embellished for her own meditation of bitterness. A silhouette in a blizzard at the bottom of the world. Empty pedestals labeled *Mother* and *Father* and an arena of thick, sweaty faces demanding a show, their greedy voices orchestrated by a golden-skinned androgyne. *Give them what they want; something from nothing. Give me nothing. You take something.*

In her office, she faced the invisible, hungry multitude. The mind tried to push me back into the memory but I clamped down on my energy level again, pulling the image of the desert over me.

I watched through the hard beat of the rain as the seizure leaked into her visual center, causing the slate on the desk to swell to enormous size. She backed away from it, hallucinating patterns on the slate. The patterns become faces. *Give them what they want.*

The pain doubled her over. She straightened up slowly, both hands on her belly. There was a dark stain on the stretchy material of the secondskins, just below her navel. *Something from nothing. Give them what they want.* Her fingers gripped the cloth. Psychotics frequently displayed extraordinary physical strength. And some had a touch of telekinesis, undiscovered, unusable until a moment of crisis. Any crisis; it didn't matter if it took the form of a hallucination brought on by an anxiety attack.

Her hands fell away. The woman who could not open up finally did, and thirty years of misery poured out. She didn't even moan.

The memory went black, along with everything else. Then the mind stirred itself and probed through the desert storm, finding me easily. Kitta Wren might have been dead but her mind wanted life. Any life. Mine would do.

Listen, she said. The memory was so worn now only her words remained. *All they want is the show. Give them what they want, but never ask anything of them. Something from nothing. The Wren looks out for herself.*

I pulled back, preparing to withdraw. The mind flexed and the feel of it was plaintive now. Without warning, I was face to face with the image of Kitta Wren as she had been, spiderwebs glistening in her eyes. They still looked like shattered gems at first glance and they always would.

Unbidden, the memory came to me. Not one of her memories but one of

mine. And with it came the thought that there could be a variation on the eye trick.

I concentrated on that thought, sending it toward the image in steady waves. After some timeless mental interval, new lines appeared in the webs, running like fissures. The mind fought, trying to maintain the solidity, but this was right. The cracks crept slowly over her face. I had to strain to keep them going, but they went, dividing her forehead into a myriad of little territories, fragmenting her cheeks, sundering her mouth. The image shudder, almost held, and then just came apart, every piece sailing away from every other piece. When they were all gone, so was she, and I withdrew without difficulty.

The first thing I saw after I put my eyes back in was the brain in the canister. The stay-juice looked milky now, a sign of imminent decay. Without really thinking about it, I leaned forward and shut the maintenance box off.

Nelson Nelson held up an official-looking chip-card. 'This is a lawsuit.'

I nodded. He put the card down on his desk and picked up another one.

'And *this* is a lawsuit.'

I had my own card and I held it up. 'And *this* is a countersuit. In case anyone actually has the nerve to go to court.'

NN looked tired. 'Everything's already being settled out of court. The agency took your side, of course. No one can say I don't back my people, isn't it so?'

It was sure as hell so. But I could tell by the way that puckered old mouth was twitching that he'd probably thought about filing against me, too, for taking it upon myself to shut off the maintenance box. If the morgue laboratory had not come out and said that the composition of the stay-juice had indicated degeneration beyond the point where the mind could be reentered, I would most likely have been signing my next thirty years of salary over to Nelson Nelson.

'Why'd you do it, Deadpan? What got into you?'

'She was dead. And nothing at all got into me.' Not lately, I hoped.

'Sabian says the brain couldn't have deteriorated so quickly between the time you went in and the time you came out.'

I didn't attempt an answer right away. The brain had been a lot deader when I came out than it had been when I'd gone in. I didn't know if that was really because of what I'd done to Kitta Wren, and I didn't want to know. 'Maybe the solution was defective. Or hadn't been changed often enough.' That was the argument in my countersuit, anyway, that Sabian had allowed me to hook into an unstabilized brain which caused me to act in an irresponsible manner by shutting my client off instead of calling for him so he could decide what to do. Sabian was just bitched because it meant he couldn't enter

the mind after I was through to do his own little postmortem, to see if there was anything I'd missed that he could sell Phylp. He wasn't gassing me. Nobody filed a lawsuit over a protocol violation.

NN shrugged. 'Phylp's charge is more serious.'

'Seriouser and seriouser. It'll never hold up. S/he got all the postmortem fragments I could find. I had them all memorized, I did my job. It's not my fault s/he thinks none of them were worth the effort. And I can't be sued for wrongful death of someone who was already dead.'

'It's a little more complicated than that, Allie.'

'That's what it amounts to. Phylp's charging that before I broke contact –'

'*Prematurely* broke contact.'

'– I dissolved her Self and killed her a second time, compounding that by turning of the box.'

'That's the way it looks in the transcript of your report.'

'That's the way it was.'

I thought Nelson Nelson was going to choke. I sat up, rubbing the small of my back with both hands.

'Just between you and me, NN, yes. That's exactly what I did.'

He reached down and fiddled with something on the side of the desk facing him. Of course; he'd been recording. He was always recording. This one would have to be doctored.

'You know how a dead body will twitch when you send a current through it? A dead mind'll do the same. It takes more than current, but it's a fair comparison. They had the neurons firing so well, it didn't know it was supposed to be dead and it tried to use me to come back. '

'Could it have?'

'I don't know. It didn't work. I killed it.'

'But what do you think?'

I sighed. 'Possibly I might have ended up incorporating elements of her personality and some of her thoughts and memories. Then you'd have had to have me dry-cleaned to get rid of her.'

NN raised his invisible eyebrows. 'Now; there's an interesting situation.'

More interesting than he knew. 'Not for me. I wouldn't want any of that woman in me.'

'I mean in terms of the legal definition of existence. If such a thing had happened and the agency did have you dry-cleaned, would we, in fact, be killing her all over again?'

I glared at him. 'No. She was *already dead.*'

'But if she returned to life in you – well, never mind, Allie. Its just an intellectual exercise. At this point.' He waved the subject away. 'All this aside, tell me. Did you learn something?'

From a bitter woman who had literally torn herself apart? 'I learned she shouldn't have been buying psychoses. She was already fogged in.'

'No, now really, Allie. Wasn't there anything in there at all – some insight, or a vision beyond – ah, any filial knowledge of any kind?'

I lit a cigarette by way of stalling. Tell him about altered state without end, everybody's got to go somewhere even if they might not be real after they make the trip? Oh, sure, he'd love it. Except – what had happened to Kitta Wren? If there was an answer to that – or an Answer – it wouldn't have been in a dead mind because you couldn't ask the right questions in there.

So ask a living mind. Unbidden, the thought came to me with a mental image of an eye with a shimmering gold-brown pupil rimmed with a very Alert Snake, a completely realized eye, marvelously detailed and absolutely unshatterable. Even if I could have shattered it, I knew where the pieces would have gone.

I shoved the thought aside. Instead, I lay down on the couch again and blew smoke at the ceiling. 'Life's a bitch. Then you die.'

I could almost hear his mouth drop. There was a long, thick moment of silence and then he began to laugh. 'That's a good one, Deadpan,' he said finally, wiping his eyes. 'You know, sometimes, I can't tell when you're kidding.'

I just nodded, still deadpan, as though he had caught me out. What the hell. He probably wouldn't have believed me. And then again, maybe it would have been worse if he did.

PART THREE

Alerted Snakes of Consequence

OLD HOME WEEK

You will go down into darkness before you die.

You will go down into darkness before you die. You will go down into darkness before you die.

You will –

'Light!' I yelled, sitting up and flinging the cover away from myself. Every light in the place went on and that awful, hateful voice stopped, as it were, dead. As it were.

I sat there looking around at the apartment, making sure I was anchored in real reality. Bed, check; Picasso sheets, check; system access in the wall, check for sure; body, heartbeat, sweat, check, check, check. Definitely back in the real world and not down in darkness of any kind.

It was her, of course. Nelson Nelson would have corrected me and said, *It was she* but the hell with it. *Her*. It was *her*. The growl of that word fit Kitta Wren better than grammar.

Shoulda put yourself in for dry-cleaning, Deadpan, I thought. The lawsuits had all been settled, I was halfway through the minimum mandatory rest period before I could take on another job; there was no reason why I couldn't have. Except I'd really thought she was gone.

Well, the agency s system had a superior dry-cleaning program and there was no time like the present. I got up and shimmied into a caftan.

To my relief, no one else had felt called to mindplay in the middle of the night. I stepped off the lateral into the semidark of the enormous system room. Behind me, the lateral hummed slightly as it moved away. The darkness should have made me nervous but I guess I was too relieved to be out of the little box to be troubled by anything else. I hopped up onto the slab, started to remove my own eyes, and then paused. What the hell; for once, I'd let the system do it. Besides, I hadn't prepared a bowl of solution and I was feeling too jumpy to do anything so responsible.

The system had a light, humanish touch. My eyes came out smoothly, the connections going to my optic nerves almost at the same time. I could feel the initiation program running through my vital signs and responding with a near-hypnotic relaxation exercise, colors in motion, to focus my attention. Colors in motion was a bit more involved than color building. You had to add particular kinds of motion to each one – spinning, flapping, swinging, pulsing, flowing – all the kinds of motion you've ever seen. Sometimes you

see patterns of different things in the colors, rotating wheels, pendulums, birds' wings. It's actually a great way to focus your attention and calm down without having to work too hard at it right away.

Meanwhile, the system was reading my immediate needs. It had the dry-cleaning program all cued up and ready to go as soon as my mind drifted away from the colors. With me, that usually happened as a result of an accumulation of associations – one idle thought would lead to another and eventually I'd find myself poised for a mental leap. It wasn't really necessary to make a deliberate entry into a dry-cleaning program – it'll just kick in when you're ready to open up for it – but I've always preferred jumping to being pushed, as it were. As it were.

After a short mental moment of limbo, I found myself standing in what seemed to be either an office or a store, staring across a counter at a man who looked like the result of a liaison between my great-grandmother and Nelson Nelson. Except he had cat's-eyes.

Is something wrong? he asked.

Was something wrong. I just looked at him.

Yes, somethings wrong, I know, he went on. meant, besides that.

Your appearance is … sort of disturbing.

I just incorporate elements that seem to be appropriate. Do you think they're inappropriate?

No, I said, *I just hadn't expected them. It. Oh, hell, you know what's wrong. I don't really have to tell you anything.*

Not if you don't want to. However, experience has shown the human need to express one's self outweighs any benefit of expeditious thought-reading.

A mental laugh feels pretty much the same as a real-reality laugh. *Nelson Nelson wrote you, didn't he?*

Not the whole program; just the flourishes.

Flourishes. As it were. Well. *There was this dead woman, a poet. I did a postmortem on her mind, scavenging for lost fragments of art.*

A terminal had materialized on the counter in front of him. He was working the keyboard and nodding at me.

Her mind was attracted to my life. Her mind and her insanity – she was insane when she died. I disintegrated her mind but I think some of it splashed on me. I heard her voice in my sleep. No visuals, just the voice. She said, You will go down into darkness before you die.

He looked down at the screen for a moment and then up at me again. *And you are –?*

Allie, I said, feeling bewildered. *Alexandra. Deadpan Allie. I'm a pathosfinder.*

Got it. He did something else to the keyboard and smiled at me. *Yes, I did know that. I just wanted to make sure you did.*

I'm not that far gone. You can tell that, can't you?

Uh-hun, just wanted to make sure you could.

Another one of NN's redundant flourishes; I let it go. *Okay, when do we start?*

He shoved the terminal aside and reached for my hand. I felt the most realistic sensation of skin against skin and then I was gone.

CLEAN, NO STARCH

Afterward, the dry-cleaner put me into a sleep mode and let me dream it off, which I found superior to the programs that would just let you drift. I dreamed about Pyotr Frankis and Snakes. We were walking through a desert-type area together and I was surprised to see how diminutive I'd dreamed him. He was telling me something about multiple levels of consciousness but it was as though his words were bouncing off me; I forgot what he said as soon as I heard it. There were movements in the sand around us, a wiggling that sometimes appeared as a snake, sometimes just bare sand showing indentations from an invisible snake.

Excuse me, Pyotr Frankis, I said at one point, *I'm trying to concentrate on what you're saying but the snakes are back.*

Ah, he said, and at last I heard his voice quite distinctly. *I told you to watch out for them. Say it. With the capitals, Alexandra.*

Alerted ... s-snakes of ... c-c-c-c – Konsequence. That still wasn't it, was it?

Keep practicing, you'll get it. Pyotr Frankis' smile was sunny. *Even so, you've made so much progress. You're altering states of consciousness now.*

Yah, but – somehow, it just hasn't been what I expected.

What had you expected?

It was easier to show him than to put it into words. I stopped and looked past him to my right. Jascha was standing there, smiling thoughtfully.

Pyotr Frankis nodded. *I see. Come, we have to keep going.* He took my arm and urged me forward. *You expected to be like Jascha? But you're not a dreamfeeder.*

No, but – I jerked a thumb to my left. Marty Oren and Sudella Keller were sitting at a campfire cooking something in a beat-up old pan. They looked up and glared at me as though I were an intruder. Pyotr Frankis and I kept going. *That was a mess. And then there was –*

A coffin appeared a little further on from Marty and Sudella; there was an empty canister on top of it. *And you know what an even bigger mess that was.*

Pathosfinding can be messy work. No matter how deadpan you are. Pyotr

Frankis pulled me along a little more quickly. We trudged through the sand, the snakes flickering on either side of us, sometimes visible but mostly not.

Well? I said after a mental minute or so.

Well, what? Pyotr Frankis was going faster now, almost yanking me along behind him.

That's all you're going to say – 'Pathosfinding is messy work'?

Isn't that true?

Yes, but …

But you want to be like Jascha. Clean hands, clear conscience, rest at the end of the day. Jascha reappeared ahead of us and to the right, this time with his techno-bed. *What makes you think it was ever like that for him? Don't you know anything about dreamfeeding?* Pyotr Frankis slowed for a moment, looking over his shoulder at me. *Ah, it's Jascha you don't know about.*

Hey, I was married *to him.* But as soon as I said it, I knew how lame that was. Marriage was no substitute for knowing anyone. *Well, he was my dream-feeder for a while at J. Walter. As you know.*

I know. He gave me a hard tug, trying to get me to catch up even with him. *How do you think it is, rifling through people's dreams, introducing elements and symbols and watching what happens to their minds.*

Cleaner than pathosfinding?

Different. Another hard tug. *Different from pathosfinding but no cleaner, as you put it.* Tug, tug. *But you're as clean as you can be. Especially now. You do work clean, Allie. That's good. Remember that. You do work clean. But you are altering states of consciousness And you have to live with the consequences.*

But I'm only supposed to alter a client's consciousness, not my own!

You can't alter anything without altering yourself. So you must alter yourself lucidly. Or you'll never get out of the dry-cleaner's. He was hauling me along so quickly now I was stumbling.

Wait – slow down – I can't –

No slowing down, Allie, nothing waits, not even your own mind.

Our hands parted. Pyotr Frankis went on a few steps and then turned to look at me. *It's all here, Allie. Everything you do, everything you've done. It all lives in you. Its everything you can't dry-clean out because it* is *you.* A hard wind suddenly sprang up and Pyotr Frankis lifted into the air like a kite, spreading his arms and legs. *XXXXXXXXXXXXXXXXXXXXXXXXXXXXX XXX!* he said.

What? I yelled over the wind. It was starting to carry him away.

I said, XXXXXXXXXXXXXXXXXXXXXXXXXXXXXX! he yelled back.

What? WHAT?! I still can't understand you!

Truth and information are not the same thing! he shouted, and he shot up into the sky instantaneously, shrinking to a tiny black dot that hung briefly in the air and then winked out.

I stood staring up at the spot where he had been. That wasn't what he'd been trying to tell me, that truth and information weren't the same thing. He'd been saying something else but I just hadn't been able to get it. $XXXXXXXXXXX$ $XXXXXXXXXXXXXXXXX$. I focused my concentration; there was a sizzling sound. It had been pressed into the sand in front of me in green glass symbols: $XXXXXXXXXXXXXXXXXXXXXXXXXXXXX$. Okay, now I'd retain it and work on a translation later. Probably take me the rest of my life, I thought.

The desert began to fog over. Getting on time to wake up. I was letting myself go with it when, ever so faintly over the sound of the wind, I heard someone calling my name. At first, I couldn't tell what direction it was coming from; then I turned around and I saw him, far, far away He was waving at me, and in spite of the distance and the fog, I could see the expression on his face, even the glimmer of his cat's-eyes, and I could feel the difference, the *pressure* of his presence, nothing like the way the image of Pyotr Frankis had felt. This wasn't a dream phantom, the way it had been in my dreams at J. Walter. A dream phantom could only appear, like a ghost; it couldn't take any action beyond that.

Still with you, Allie. I'm still here.

No. It had only been the eye trick. Just his eye, and the eye was locked in the cathedral. Not him. Not *him*. Only a living mind was a hologram.

It's really me. I'm still with you.

Couldn't be. You couldn't have someone else – *really* else – living in your mind. That was a fact.

It's really me, Allie.

Truth and information are not the same thing.

The desert faded.

JASCHA

'What I'm sure Pyotr Frankis was trying to tell you – or rather, what you were trying to tell yourself – is simply that you're an accumulation of events,' said Jascha. He sat on the couch with his arms spread out along the back, more comfortable than he probably should have been. I kept wanting to ask him if his wife knew where he was; I honestly couldn't guess whether she did or not. I felt like I both knew and no longer knew him, and whether this was because he was a different person now or I was, I couldn't tell, either. Sometimes it felt one way, sometimes the other. Life as an either/or experience.

I was knotted up on the chunky table Fandango had talked me into putting in as a space-taker-upper right after I'd finished with Kitta Wren. More furniture,

she'd kept saying over and over. You need more stuff to touch and see and sit on. Later on, when you don't need it any more, you can get rid of it. But see if it doesn't make you feel better. Damned if she wasn't right about it, too.

'That sounds plausible enough,' I said to Jascha, before a silence could definitely fall between us. 'Now explain why you decided to drop in on me now, even though I didn't call you.'

'Because you *didn't* call,' he said simply. 'I gave it a little while, and when you *still* didn't call, I figured I'd better see what you'd gotten yourself into.'

'You already knew what I'd gotten myself into. This agency.'

'You're still a smartass.'

'And nobody still loves me.'

Well, that did make a silence fall between us. I plowed into it before it could get too thick. 'What about the last part of the dream? With McFloy.'

'We've been over that. Like you said and I said. Impossible. You can acquire bits and pieces like neuroses, or elements fed to you in dreams, and things that rub off on you from other people – like the stuff with Kitta Wren – but you can't hold an actual separate identity that isn't you in your mind. I promise you that's a fact.'

'Truth and information aren't the same thing. I promise *you that's* a fact.'

'So you told yourself. But you have to admit that they do coincide often enough to let us all get around in the world safely.'

I shrugged.

'And you've been dry-cleaned. The program couldn't have missed it if it were there.'

'It wasn't written to clean out a whole entity. Just pieces, characteristics.'

'And we've just said you – as an entity – are an accumulation of events. Which are pieces and characteristics.'

'But when it's a whole person, it becomes more than that. More than the sum of the parts.'

Jascha shook his head, which was very lightly gilded now, so lightly you almost might not notice. 'And a dry-cleaning program doesn't clean out the sum of the parts. It knows which parts belong to the sum and which don't. Just as you did with that stuff of Kitta Wren's.'

I felt a chill. 'If I hadn't had myself dry-cleaned quickly enough, it might have taken root. Become part of the sum.'

'Maybe. And then again, maybe not.'

I glared at him. '*That's* helpful.'

'No, now really. Why do you turn out to be one kind of person and not another? Because one event fits the configuration that you are and another doesn't.'

'Now you're talking like everyone's a composite like Pyotr Frankis.'

'Pyotr Frankis is manufactured. He's an android, really – discorporate, but

still reprogrammable. His configuration can be altered by the manufacturers in any way. Or, I should say, can be altered on the manufacturers' level. But not on *his* level, by him.'

The incompleteness theorem. I didn't feel any warmer.

'On the other hand, you, like all human beings, are a composite on a different level than Pyotr Frankis – a higher level, we all fervently believe. It's not a matter of simple reprogramming. If your configuration were such that it allowed whatever rubbed off on you from Kitta Wren to become part of your –' He thought a moment. '– your pattern, then that's what would have happened and I doubt you would have been able to dry-clean it out so easily, if at all. Of course, your configuration – *you*, I mean, I'm tired of that word – might be able either to keep the stuff from Kitta Wren or slough it off equally in character.' He shrugged. 'I'd have to do a bottom-up analysis of your core personality to tell and I'm nowhere near qualified for that kind of thing. Nobody is. No ones been able to prove any of that stuff conclusively one way or the other – it's all just very strong theory.' He laughed. 'That's the thing about mindplay. The rules change when they change and everything is true unless it isn't.'

I groaned. 'I thought God didn't play dice with the universe.'

'God doesn't play dice with the universe. He plays dice with you.'

'Everywhere you go, smartasses. It's astounding that anyone ever loves anyone.'

That shut us both up for a long moment. Then Jascha laughed again, a little nervously. 'Well, just trust me when I tell you there's nobody in there. Except you, of course,' he added quickly.

'Why *did* you come to see me, Jascha?' I asked, smiling at him.

His answering smile was studiously carefree. 'I thought that by now you'd probably need a crazy dream explained to you. And I was right. I also wanted to ask how you like your eyes, now that you no longer have your own.'

'They're fine. Great. I like them.'

'Any particular reason you chose cat's-eye?'

I felt my smile fade a bit. 'They seemed to be the right choice. I always did like them.'

'They look fine. Very becoming. They don't look – they don't look bad at all.' He seemed to be about to say something else and then changed his mind.

I wheedled two extra Restaurant-of-the-Month chits out of Nelson Nelson on the phone, making him extremely suspicious when I introduced Jascha through the screen. But he gave me the chits and we had a fine if strange dinner at a place called In The Raw. Which everything was, including us.

Okay. It wasn't a very nice thing to do. But it wasn't Jascha and his wife I was trying to put a wedge between.

*

'Didn't come home last night,' Fandango said matter-of-factly.

'Sure didn't,' I said, dialing up birch beers just for something to do. Then I changed my mind and ordered ginger beer, just for something else to do.

'It's good to have a life.'

'Sure is.'

'And you're not going to tell me about it.'

'Sure won't. But have some birch beer.'

She took the glass from me with a pouty look. 'Thanks.' She got halfway through the glass before she couldn't contain herself any more. 'So at least tell me who he is, now that you've got yourself a life.'

'Someone from a while back.' I settled on the table with my back to her 'From a previous configuration. Somebody else's life.'

WIRERAMMER AND WIRERAMMEE

The phone screen didn't light up. I tapped the side of the unit once gently and then a little harder. Still no video. I was about to tell whoever was calling that my monitor was out when words began scrolling up from the bottom.

NO VISUAL OR AUDIO TRANSMISSION AT THIS TIME. URGENT YOU COME TO THE FOLLOWING ADDRESS WITHIN THE NEXT 6 HOURS, NEXT 2 HOURS OPTIMUM. ACKNOWLEDGE FOR ADDRESS TRANSMISSION.

I watched the words float upward. WHAT FOR? I typed, knowing damned well what for.

CONFERENCE, came the answer, REFRESHMENTS PROVIDED. ADDRESS AS FOLLOWS ...

I stared at the address for a long time before I took it down. What the hell. If I went out there now, maybe I'd be back before dawn, or at least before Fandango found out I'd spent another night somewhere else. Before I left, I packed a few bearer chips. Just in case.

It was nicely decorated for a vegetarian restaurant. I was always amazed at what you could do with vegetable fibers in the way of furnishings. Not to mention clothing – there was an old-fashioned host wearing a suit probably made out of hydroponic cornhusks. He seated me at a tiny table in an alcove that would have been away from the crowd if there'd been a crowd and left me with a vegetable-fiber menu that was probably edible in a pinch, if not particularly tasty: I glanced at it and then pretended great interest in the holo

loop running in the wall next to me. It was an agricultural scene from perhaps three centuries ago, full of sweaty laborers in ragged clothing picking a crop. The crop they were picking happened to be cotton, but it was the thought that counted.

It ran one full time and had started over again when a man sat down across from me. He was wearing a turban and two halves of two different pouch suits that were almost the same shade of brown, which was nowhere near as jarring as the plaztoid mask glued to his face. Plaztoid eventually melts into the flesh, permanently altering the appearance, and never for the better. It reminded me of ritual scarification, except most people didn't wear it by choice. Burn victim, I thought, and then corrected myself: uninsured burn victim. A moment later I corrected myself again: Jerry Wirerammer.

'Don't say that name,' he said in a low voice as I opened my mouth. 'I'm not *that person* any more. Legally, I mean. But I'm still ... you-know-who in essence, unless or until they catch up with me.'

I tried to look at him without seeing the plaztoid. 'Who is it this time? Your two fans, the bootleggers, or Power People? Or someone else altogether?'

'The bootleggers. They –' He broke off. 'Is there someone behind me?'

I glanced over his head at two women making their way through the main room toward the door. 'Just a couple of people leaving.'

'Tell me when they're gone.'

I watched the women leave. From the way they looked at the host, I didn't think they'd be back. 'All clear. Go on. The bootleggers.'

'They finally bought out my contract with Power People. I stopped moving well for them and they were happy to give me up. The bootleggers didn't know my popularity had fallen off and they weren't too happy about the deal. And Power People wouldn't buy me back.'

The idea that he might have spoiled his own market with bootlegs (and with bootlegs of bootlegs) probably hadn't occurred to Jerry.

'So they went to court. Filed against me claiming I'd cost them money. The court ruled I was liable for the loss.'

'And you don't have the money.'

'They wouldn't take it if I did. After Power People sold me off, my, uh, other business associates found out I'd done a little business of my own on the side and now they want me.'

'But they've got you.'

'No, they want *me*. They're going to wipe me and part me out for salvage.' He picked up the menu. 'You hungry?'

'No.'

He tossed the menu aside without looking at it. 'Good. Let's go. I don't want to hold still for too long.'

I let him herd me out of the restaurant onto the street. Three onionheads

linked together on a short chain marched past me, two of them giving me a glare. The third one winked. Bored and hoping for trouble, apparently. I looked the other way quickly by way of declining. There was nothing that would ruin a night faster than getting stomped by a three-way onionhead marriage. Well, almost nothing.

The evening had suddenly grown chill; I bought a disposable jacket from the autovalet next to the restaurant while Jerry fished several bits of paper out of his various pouches and rifled through them hurriedly.

'Now what?' I asked him, pressing the jacket closed. It was a little too large, and the wavy line print was enough to give you a headache if you looked at it too long, but it was pretty warm for a street product.

'Five minutes,' Jerry said, looking at one slip of paper and stuffing the rest into one of the chest pouches. 'There's this mobile party we can pick up, if its running on schedule.'

'And if there are openings for both of us,' I added.

'There should be.' Jerry scratched at his plaztoid-covered cheek absently as he looked up and down the street, which was empty now except for the retreating figures of the onionheads. 'I've hooked onto this party before. They've always got room for a couple more.' He rubbed his arms against the cold.

Without thinking about it, I put an arm around his shoulders. 'Listen, I'm not exactly in the mood to join a party, especially a mobile one. Why don't I just take you home?'

He shook his head without looking at me. 'My place is sealed off. They put a private security company on it. They'd pick me up if I got within a hundred yards of the front door.'

'I meant my place.'

He turned to stare at me in surprise. The plaztoid didn't allow him much in the way of expression but I could see it in his eyes. '*Your* place? You'd do that for me?'

'The Nelson Nelson building is pretty impregnable, as you pointed out to me once.'

'Maybe not for them. You don't know. They could get in just about anywhere.' Jerry glanced down the street again. 'Even if they couldn't, I'd have to come out sometime. And they'd jump on me immediately. Better for me to stay out here in camouflage. No camouflage for me at your place. I'd kind of stick out, don't you think?'

I had a brief, half-assed idea of passing him off as Fandango's husband, but it was better not to drag her into Jerry's problems. I knew from experience that once you were in Jerry's problems, it was damned near impossible to get away from them. Besides, there was no guarantee that Fandango would go along with it. Even if she did, NN would probably find out and evict him.

The mobile party's chartered airbus arrived, descending in a contained

flurry of music, laughter, and general noise. A purple androgyne in a gold-dust stocking thrust his/her head out of one of the windows and whistled to us. 'Two more!' s/he called over his/her shoulder. The front door slid down and became a ramp leading up to the admission port. The bored navigator didn't even bother looking at us.

'You want on, get on,' she said, staring at her console. 'Otherwise don't hold us up, we're on a schedule.'

'Room for two more?' Jerry asked, tugging me up the ramp after him.

The navigators diamond eyes glinted. 'Two more, eight more, twenty-four more. What's the difference?'

Jerry stopped short at the admission meter and turned to me. 'You got any money?' Giggle.

I handed him one of my chips. He held it in front of a small screen. The navigator jerked a thumb over her shoulder. 'Step to the rear of the party, please, watch your step, no brawling, dueling, or acrobatics while the party is in motion. Next stop, the Boom-Boom Room high atop the scenic Glorioso Building in Commerce Canyon. Rest, refueling, lavabos, and first aid.' The door slid up again, bumping my ass.

The main party area of the bus was a cross between a regular airbus and someone's living room. It was full of people lounging on benches, on the floor, holding onto handstraps as they ate or drank or talked, sometimes with some-one else. The purple androgyne who had greeted us from the window threw him/herself on Jerry's shoulders like a long-lost relative, babbling something I couldn't make out. With an apologetic look over his shoulder, Jerry allowed himself to be drawn over to a built-in seat by one of the windows. I grabbed the nearest empty spot, wondering if I should cab home from Commerce Canyon or hang in for a few more stops to look after Jerry. A mobile party provided pretty good camouflage but it wasn't going to run forever. Maybe he was plan-ning to go home with someone. Like the androgyne, who was now sitting on his lap listening intently to whatever Jerry was whispering into his/her ear.

Someone passed me a platter piled untidily with food and drugs. I handed it on without taking anything.

'First mobile party?' someone said close to my ear.

I turned around and looked into a gilded male face. His gilt wasn't genuine and had been poorly applied; hairline cracks threaded the golden areas along the cheekbones and temples, and the part on the bridge of his nose looked ready to flake off at any moment. The silvery biogems ruined the desired effect anyway.

'Yah,' I said, pulling back a little against the acceleration of the bus. 'First time ever … '

(*But that's not true*, said a small voice in my mind. *You've been to mobile parties before. Lots of them.* Unbidden, a scene from the pool came to me, all

of us in flight against an impossible jeweled sky over a blue-green earth while one figure soared higher than anyone, suddenly swooping down out of the sun, catching me and taking me down to a terrace outside a ballroom, where an eye sat on a small table –)

The window seat where Jerry had been sitting with the androgyne was now occupied by three women in diaphanous ragbags. I looked around and saw what might have been the back of Jerry's head disappearing into the small crowd at the rear of the bus.

'The facilities are back there,' the badly-gilded man told me. 'If you care to use them. I usually like to wait till I'm on the ground, myself. Just an idiosyncrasy.' He pushed the platter of drugs and food at me again. I shook my head. He held it out to a passing man in a bright pink explosion of feathers, who took it and balanced it on his head as he went on.

Abruptly the music, which had stopped when the bus had let us on, started up again. It was Coor and Lams *Transcontinental Elopement*, the third Urban Chase movement, full of lumpy, discordant percussion. I winced. As soon as we touched down on the Glorioso Building, I was going to sprint for a cab, with or without Jerry. There'd been no reason to come along with him and he'd never actually asked me to, just taking it for granted that I would. Why he wanted me with him when he was so concerned about being camouflaged was beyond me anyway. I got up, intending to ask the navigator how soon we'd reach the Glorioso Building, when my new friend caught my arm.

'On the other hand, if you'd like to try the facilities while we're in motion, I could be persuaded to experiment,' he said, with a tentative smile. The bus hit a small air pocket and his near-jowls trembled.

I pulled away from him. 'Body functions are things I prefer solo, thank you. I think.'

'Body functions? Who said anything about peeing? The *facilities*. The *equipment*.' He touched my arm lightly. 'Swap memories. Its a great way to get to know each other.'

I looked toward the rear of the party. The purple androgyne had reappeared alone, giggling to the man in the pink feathers.

'Goddammit,' I muttered and threaded my way hurriedly through the bus, which suddenly seemed more crowded, as though everyone on it had decided all at once to come to life and party harder. The bus itself seemed bigger, too, all of a sudden. I swam through it, dodging eager hands and the hyperactive arms of a woman dressed like a flamingo, who was either dancing or having an inner dialog with gestures.

At the rear of the bus was a small compartment with an opening near the floor just big enough for me to crawl through. Once I did, I almost backed out again – it wasn't much bigger than three of the pods from the pool at J. Walter put together, dimly lit by one small glowball.

Jerry and some other guy were lying on a tangle of blankets, on either side of a small mindplay unit I recognized as a memory-exchanger. They were already plugged in and the system was running. It didn't take long. They were finished before I could begin to feel seriously closed in.

The other guy disconnected and sat up first, groping for his optics in the half-tank hanging off his side of the exchanger. He popped his eyes in, blinked at me, and broke into a goofy grin. It didn't fit his carefully sculptured features.

'*I* know you,' he said cheerfully. 'You're … no, don't tell me, the name's on the tip of my brain. You used to … ' He rubbed his forehead. 'There was something you used to do … something crazy … ' He struggled a moment longer and then shrugged, crinkling the gold braid on his shoulders. 'It'll come to me later maybe.' He glanced at Jerry's still form. 'Did you want to be next? He's ready.'

I moved away from the entrance hole so he could crawl out.

'This guy's a charge,' the man said. 'He's really full of it. I think I got the better end of the deal. All I gave him was my ex-wife and my ex-husband.'

I crawled over to Jerry, who still hadn't made a move to get up and disconnect.

'Come out of there,' I said in a low voice, putting my hand on his chest. 'I'm not coming in after you.'

Jerry sighed, his eyelids fluttering slightly against the connections snaking under them.

'I know you can hear me. Come *out*. This is Allie and you know I won't go in there with you.' I paused. '*Jerry*.'

That got him moving. He sat up quickly, fumbling the connections to the system as he removed them from his optic nerves. I was tempted to put his eyes in for him but I couldn't bring myself to touch them.

'What are you doing?' he said, his eyes watering profusely. 'I figured you'd just get off at the Boom-Boom Room and be happy about it. And I told you not to use that name.'

'What are *you* doing? Is this National Gangbang Jerry Wirerammer Night?'

'For chrissakes, don't use that name!' he said, looking worriedly at the entrance. 'I'm getting more camouflage, what do you think I'm doing? I'm cloning my own memories and passing them out while I clone memories from other people and lay them over my own. That way, if they catch me and put in a probe, they'll find all these memories from other people and think I'm somebody else. And if *my* memories start showing up all over town, maybe they'll think someone else got me and parted me out.' The plaztoid mask crinkled a little. 'It's brilliant. They'd never suspect.'

I tried to think under the clang-bash of the music. 'It won't work,' I said.

'Yah, it will.' Pause. 'Why wouldn't it?'

'Because underneath all the memories is your unmistakable configuration – your Jerry Wirerammer-ness.'

'*Will you stop using that name!*' He gripped my arm roughly.

'All right, your you-know-who-ness. No matter how many memories you take in, they're still someone else's. You remember them as Jer – as you-know-who.'

'Not if I layer on enough memories. I know how to do it – I've seen someone do it before. Just layer on enough of them and they'll dominate your mind. You start believing you're somebody else for real.'

I stared at him. 'Then you lose. Either way. Either the bootleggers get you or you smother yourself.'

'I'll take the chance. Besides, you were just saying I couldn't obscure my basic you-know-who-ness.'

'But you can dissolve it. I know. Because *I've* seen someone do *that* before.' More than once, I added to myself.

'I'll *take* the *chance*, Allie. Now, do *you* want to contribute a memory or two to the cause or are you going to crawl out and give someone else a turn?'

I crawled out into a forest of gaudy legs and managed to stand up with some difficulty. The purple androgyne gave me a bright goofy grin and a wave. I looked away and headed for the front of the bus.

'Mind if I sit up front here on the floor?' I asked the navigator.

'Damned right I mind,' she said without taking her eyes off the gridboard in her lap. Through the windshield, the lights of the city glittered while no one looked at them. 'It's bad enough I have to fly around with a buncha urban booboes partying themselves into flat-line. I'm not going to have any of you cozying up to me, and plenty better than you have tried. Get back where you belong. Go take a drug.'

I didn't have the energy to plead a case of mistaken identity with her. Instead, I stayed as close to the front of the party as I could so I'd be able to get out in a hurry. By the time we landed at the Glorioso Building, I'd counted a dozen people crawling in and out of Jerry's compartment. And those had only been the ones I could see clearly.

'Welcome to the Boom-Boom Room, foremost open-air rooftop nightateria in the state!' sang the woman with the gold birdcage enclosing her head.

'How do I get transportation out of here?' I asked her, waving aside the menu of delights she was trying to hand me.

'The aircab stand's on the west side,' she said, missing a beat. 'You can see the sign. Sure you don't want to stay a bit? The new holo display's up, you'll love it.'

I brushed past her, looking for the sign through giant three-d phantoms of

warriors in spiky armor and princesses in spiky armor and angels in spiky armor. Spiky armor was apparently the next phase.

'Looking for me?'

It was the man with the bad gilt-job. I shook my head.

'Oh. I'd kind of hoped … the facilities here are better, you know … '

I found the cabstand sign glowing hotly yellow through one of the spiky-armored angels, who was swinging its sword through a gaggle of touristy-looking types oohing and aahing at each pass. Another woman with a birdcage around her head offered me a tray of drinks as I headed for the stand; four people in a huddle called for me to join them. Canned music came up from somewhere and blared at the sky, cuing all the angels and warriors and princesses to dance. I was out of breath by the time I reached the stand and sank down on the empty bench. Pressing the call panel, I sat back and closed my eyes to wait.

Sometime later, a voice said tentatively, 'Allie?'

The purple androgyne was standing over me, looking concerned.

'We're all worried about you. You don't look happy.'

'Well, don't worry. I always look this way.'

The androgyne sat on the edge of the bench next to me. I could see his/her eyebrows were actually tiny purple feathers. 'But we all want you to have a good time.'

'What do you mean, "we"? Who's "we"?'

The androgyne looked surprised. 'All of us Jerry Wirerammers, of course. I remember all those crazy things you used to do, putting on madcaps and going nuts, and –'

I moved away slightly. 'Get out of here. Go back to the party. With the rest of the Jerry Wirerammers. However many there are now.'

'But you'd always try anything to light a fire in your brain, I remember –'

An aircab hummed overhead. I jumped up, diving into it as soon as it landed.

'Allie, wait! It's going to be a hell of a party, from here we're going on to the hallucination pits –' The closing door cut him/her off in midgiggle.

I gave the cab the agency's address. Only after it had lifted off was I able to sit back and un-tense a little.

Until it occurred to me that I hadn't seen Jerry before I'd left. The real Jerry, that was – if there was a real Jerry any more.

Sure there was. A person was more than just an accumulation of memories –

One thing after another and nothing relates much to anything else.

Yah. That was Jerry, all right. Distributing memories of me as I'd been back when he'd been bringing me drugs and madcaps and nothing further than that.

Some people aren't enough by themselves. They find ways to make themselves more. Some of them litter the world with themselves like confetti, said a quiet

voice in my mind. *That's where the pieces go. Flying on the mental wind. Disintegrating in a dead brain. Drowning in a pool.*

The image of Pyotr Frankis's face rose up in my mind, except it wasn't completely him. He looked a little like Jascha and a little like Paolo Segretti and a little like –

The Snake revolved slowly in the pupil of the eye. Jerry's face appeared in the center, grinning goofily; the way it was in the holo portrait I'd found in my cathedral.

I'm locked out of your world and you've turned your back on the outer world. But he'd still found a pool to drown himself in.

If Jerry Wirerammer did not exist, it would be necessary to invent him. And if he did exist, it would be necessary to liquidate him.

'Destination!' the cab said loudly and I realized it was the second time it had spoken to me. Sleepily, I waved a chip at the pay screen and got out.

VARIATION ON A MAN

Well, I should have seen it coming, especially after Jerry. But I'm convinced (still am) that the Pearl Necklace Episode caused Nelson Nelson to give me the Gladney case.

All mindplayers can pretty much count on getting Pearl Necklaced sooner or later, but messing around with the past the way I had, I'd brought it on myself. And it's a far more vivid experience for pathosfinders than it is for neurosis peddlers, say, or belljarrers, who don't spend as much time in direct mind-to-mind communication with their clients, or at least not in quite the same way.

My Pearl Necklace came during a routine reality affixing. Reality affixing was mandatory for mindplayers by federal law, and mandatory reality affixing still went against my grain as much as it had the day Paolo Segretti had told me I had to go through it with him. There was something about having to have my perceptions stamped *Acceptable Per Government Regulatory Standards* that still irritated me. On the other hand – or lobe, if you will – I'd brought that on myself, too. A mindplayer who insists on imposing her own meanings on everyone else's mentality is not someone you'd want running around loose with other people's minds.

At least it wasn't time-consuming. All I had to do was go back into the agency's system and let it probe me for ten minutes' real time, if that. NN told me I should go at it as a particularly intense session of meditation and as long as I was myself, I certainly had nothing to feel uneasy about.

As long as I was myself. Yah, I thought about that one. If McFloy was in there as a full separate entity, the system would help me find him, and if he were a delusion, it would help me neutralize him.

As long as I was myself. And so, given the circumstances, who else would I be? The system stimulated this particular question and up came the Pearl Necklace.

Infinitely long, every pearl holding a separate moment in the life of Deadpan Allie, it showed me a series of completely self-contained events, touching each other but not really connected. Suddenly, I couldn't see where the sum was greater than the parts and it hit me: *I have not always been as I am now.*

Nothing to it out in real reality – you take it for granted. But it's a terrifying realization when made purely within the confines of your own mind with no physical life-landmarks to refer to. *I have not always been as I am now* – and I couldn't remember being any different. Nor could I conceive of what I'd be like in the next moment.

The bottom dropped out and I felt as though I were felling toward disintegration.

And then I was fine again and the Pearl Necklace was gone. The foundation of everything I'd lived was under me. The system ran through the rest of the reality-affixing procedure and then disengaged. I put my eyes back in and went off to have a nap.

Naturally, the crisis was reported to Nelson Nelson. I knew it would be, but he never mentioned it. Instead, he called me into his office to give me an assignment.

'In your work with artists,' he said, while I lay on the couch and tried not to be obvious about the rash the tacky upholstery was always giving me, 'what would you say your primary objective as a pathosfinder is?'

I rested my cheek on my left hand and thought it over. 'To assist in reaching a level where inward and outward perceptions balance well enough against each other so that –'

'*Allie.*' He gave me a Look. 'This is *me* you're talking to.'

'Help them move past irrelevant and superficial mental trash to the real feeling, the real soul.'

NN raised himself up on one elbow and actually shook his finger at me. 'Never, *never*, never essay-answer me.'

'Sorry.'

His eyes narrowed. He had brand-new pink jade biogems and they made him look like a geriatric rabbit. 'Don't be sorry. In spite of your initial choice of words, you're right. Would you also say that, in many cases, the pathosfinder is responsible for helping an artist locate the creative on button, as well as helping to enhance the soul in the work?'

For someone who didn't like essay answers, he was pretty fond of essay questions. 'In many cases, sure.'

Now he looked satisfied. 'That's why I'd like to put you on the Gladney case.'

'Rand Gladney? The composer? I thought he'd been sucked.'

'He was. But he's out of full quarantine now and his new personality's grown into mature form. Of course, he's not really Gladney any more and never will be again.'

'Have they told him who he used to be?'

'Oh, yah. Every detail. He wanted to know. Most victims of involuntary mindsuck do. They're all intensely curious about their former lives and the doctors figure honesty is the best policy. Better for them to hear about it in a sheltered environment where they can learn to deal with it. Anyway, I thought this would be a good opportunity for a pathosfinder to work with an adult who has no history whatsoever and help him become an artist.'

Terrific, I thought. 'What kind?'

'Good question.'

I didn't groan. 'Well,' I said, 'is there any indication that he has ability as a composer?'

NN gave me his that's-your-problem grin. 'You'll know after you delve him.'

I ran through the bare minimum of information on Gladney that NN had dumped into my dataline while my portable system was being overhauled. With some relief, I saw that Gladney's potential wasn't as vague as NN had made it out to be. Prior to having his mind stolen, Rand Gladney had been a composer of middle-high talent with a fair number of works that had settled into the cultural mainstream. At the time of his erasure, he'd been approaching a turning point in his career where he would have either ascended to greater ability and prominence or settled slowly into repetition and, eventually, semi-oblivion. In seven years, he'd peaked twice after his breakthrough. And that was just about all NN wanted me to know about the Gladney-that-had-been, other than his media notices.

The Gladney-that-was-now had been out of full quarantine for a month, though he was still hospitalized and his movements were restricted. I pored over all the background information on rehabilitating mindwipes just as though I were interested in it only for the sake of the case. It was a precarious business, like trying to stand with your hands both on and off someone at the same time. Personality regrowth began with the restoration of language, first by system and then by humans. If the humans didn't replace the system at precisely the right moment in regrowth, you ended up with a person unable to think in any mode but a mechanical one. People like that made great logicians but they were lousy on theory. Most often they resolved the conflict between the definite and the indefinite in their lives by suicide or voluntary

mindwipe, which were pretty much the same thing. There were very few brains hardy enough to redevelop a mind after a second erasure; the myelin sheathing on the axons just wouldn't stand up to that kind of abuse.

I paused. Mechanical? Not McFloy. I searched the data to find out what happened to a mindwipe if the humans replaced the system too early in language restoration, but there was nothing about that in there. Maybe nothing was supposed to happen. Even when it did.

In any case, Gladney (who was apparently still going by that name for the sake of convenience) had passed all the critical points in redevelopment and become a person, again or for the first time, depending on your point of view. He was certainly not the same person – the man who had emerged from the blank brain was (probably?) reminiscent of his former self but no more that self than he was anyone else.

The extreme convolutedness of such a situation was easier to accept, I'd heard, if you had even more of a mystical bent than mindplayers usually did. Funny, I hadn't really thought of myself as being especially mystical – but if I wasn't mystical, what was I? Maybe someday I'd get one of those impossible bottom-up core personality analyses and we'd all find out I was just in this for the visuals.

I filed the idea away for later consideration and went over Gladney's aptitude tests. His new personality had grown in with a definite talent for music, and more – I was rather startled to find that he now had perfect pitch. The previous man had not. It made me wonder. Was perfect pitch something that had shown up due to some alteration in Gladney's brain chemistry brought about by mindsuck? Or was it just due to different brain organization? Or a brand-new configuration? And how important was it for me to know?

'Truth to tell,' said the woman with the carnelian eyes and the too-short apple-red hair, 'we ended up selecting you for your business name. Anyone operating as Deadpan Allie must have quite a lot of control over herself.' She smiled brightly Her name was Lind Jesl and she looked less like the chief doctor on the Gladney case than she did someone finishing up her own recovery. Except for the carnelian eyes and the hair, she was as plain as possible, her stout body concealed in a loose gray sacsuit. The office we were sitting in was even more austere, a cream-colored box with no decorations in the way of wall hangings or sculpture. Even the computer desk was all folded into a stark, bare block. The whole thing reminded me of the infamous White Room image from Marty Oren's mind. McFloy had come up in a place like this. I tried to keep the thought far away.

'Of course,' she went on, 'your self-control will be vital when you delve our boy. An involuntary wipe is supremely sensitive and impressionable, even at such an advanced stage of regeneration. Just the experience of you probing

his mind is going to make quite a mark on him. Your flavor, as 'twere, will leave a bit of an aftertaste.'

As 'twere. 'I'm very careful.'

'Yes, certainly you are.' Her gaze snagged briefly on my equipment piled up beside me before she gave me her five-hundred-watt smile again. 'And we wouldn't have hired you if we weren't as confident of his ability to think independently as we are of *your* ability to refrain from exerting too much influence.'

She was putting a lot of emphasis on the very thing guaranteed by the fact that I was licensed to pathosfind in the first place. 'What kind of results are you looking for?'

'Ah.' Five hundred watts went to six hundred as she folded her pudgy hands and plunked them on her stomach. 'We're hoping you'll help him learn how to combine the various elements that make up a composer into a whole that will be greater than the sum of the parts.'

I blinked.

'We know that he has a musical *bent*. A definite leaning toward music, an affinity for playing instruments which tends to accompany perfect pitch. But as yet, these things are fragmented in him. He's having difficulty achieving a state where they all work together. In fact, I'd say he has yet to achieve it, even for a few moments.'

'Isn't that just a matter of, well, practice? And experience?'

'Usually. But I know Gladney. *This* Gladney. There are signs of a definite barrier of some kind that he just can't or won't find his way around. We don't know for certain because we haven't delved him since the very early part of the regeneration. That was, oh, nine months ago, which goes back further than his memory. Delicate Plant Syndrome, you see – if you keep digging up a delicate plant to see how well the roots are taking, it dies.' She sat forward, her hands disappearing into the voluminous cloth of the sacsuit. 'We feel he's ready for mind-to-mind contact now, but with a pathosfinder rather than a doctor. We want him to feel less and less like an invalid and more and more like a person.'

'How long has he been in quarantine altogether?'

'Altogether, it's been a few weeks over a year. He was delivered to us two hours after the mindsuckers got him.

'We're hoping to release him completely in another six months at the most. Depending on how much progress he makes with you. It could even be sooner. Or later.'

'Have you let him hear any of his old work? The previous Gladney's music, I mean?'

'Yes and no. Which is to say, he's heard it but he doesn't know who composed it. We've removed all identification from all the recordings we've given him, not just Gladney's.'

'Does he react any differently to the Gladney compositions than he does to any of the others?'

'He reacts to all music rather guardedly. He puts them through a mental sorting procedure and he *can* tell whether or not different pieces of music were composed by the same person with an accuracy of close to ninety-eight percent, on the average. I suspect he might also be able to arrange a composer's works in the correct chronological order as well. He's *very* bright. But –' Jesl spread her hands. 'Something inside isn't meshing. As 'twere.'

As 'twere. Had I invented this woman? 'Has he tried to compose?'

'Oh, yes. Some short things he won't play for us. We had to bug the synthesizer we gave him. According to our musical consultants, his work shows potential. There are moments when it *almost* breaks through, but it always stops short of achieving – well, fullness. As 'twere.'

As 'twere, oh, god. I considered the possibility that the evaluation of the consultants might be faulty. Perhaps the musical direction he was taking was just different from the old Gladney's and what he wasn't achieving were their expectations. I'd just have to see for myself.

'When can I meet him?' I asked.

'Right now, if you like. We've fixed up a room for you not far from his so you'll be within easy reach of each other. I'll take you down there and then we'll visit our boy.'

The room they'd given me was an improvised efficiency with a freestanding lavabo unit and jury-rigged meal dial. The bed was a hospital bed disguised as a civilian one – not very wide but, to my great relief, as hard as a rock.

I'd brought only a few personal things with me, which I didn't bother to unpack. I debated taking my equipment with me to Gladney's room and decided against it. He might feel too pressured if I appeared wheeling my system with me. I wanted some extra time myself, just to see what this twelve-month-old adult was like on the outside before I went inside. I hoped he wasn't a prodigy.

The man lying on the bed had once had the pampered good looks found in most people of celebrity status. Over the months he'd lost a good deal of it, the way an athlete or dancer will lose strength after a period of inactivity. He was still attractive but his appearance was changing, veering off in another direction. Typical of a regrown mindwipe, I'd read. In a few months, it was possible he would be so changed that no one from his previous life would recognize him.

He got up for Jesl's brief introduction, touching hands with me gingerly, as though he were afraid he might burn himself. Something like bewildered panic crossed his face as Jesl made a quick but unhurried exit, leaving us on

our own. I wouldn't even have to think about reading his Emotional Index; he was all but thrusting it on me.

'So. You're my pathosfinder.' He gestured at a small area arranged around an entertainment center, minus a dataline, with a few chairs and a space-taker-upper table. He'd probably set it up himself but I could tell he wasn't completely at home with it.

'Anything you'd like to ask me about?' I said, sitting down. The chair gave like soft clay under me and I realized I was in another one of those damned contour things. I wondered why they'd given him a contour and then remembered it was supposed to be a boon to the lonely. I was going to have a rough time being deadpan if it started any funny stuff with me. Fortunately, it seemed disposed to let me sit in peace so I decided to tough it out rather than change seats.

'I hardly ever use that one,' Gladney said, watching as it molded itself to support my elbows. 'I can't get used to it. But it's fascinating to watch when someone else is in it.' He turned his attention to my face. 'What are those gems – your eyes?'

'Cat's-eye.'

'Everyone here at the hospital has biogems. Even some of the other wipes. Dr Jesl says I can order some whenever I want to but I don't feel I can yet. *He* had biogems.'

'Who?'

'Gladney. The original one, not me. After he was sucked, the hospital replaced them with standard browns.' He smiled. 'I remember how surprised I was when they told me almost everyone has their eyes replaced with artificial ones. It still amazes me a little. I mean, my eyes don't feel artificial. But then, I guess *I* wouldn't know the difference, would I?' His smile faded. 'It's strange to think of you going into my brain that way. Through my eyes. It's strange to think of anyone else in there except me.'

Sure was.

'And yet there have been a whole lot of people in there,' he went on, rubbing his chest absently. 'Mindplayers, for *him*. And then the mindsuckers. The hospital's system, the doctors. And now you.'

'Actually, that isn't the way it is,' I said. 'We'll be in mind-to-mind contact in the system but I won't really be *in* your mind. There's only room for you in there –' I paused, suddenly overcome by déjà vu. I didn't need a memory enhancer to know that I had repeated nearly word for word what Paolo Seg-retti had told me four years ago just before my first mindplay experience. I'd even sounded like him.

'Anyway,' I continued quickly, 'mind-to-mind contact is a way of life. Not just mindplay but many forms of higher education. And people buy and sell various things. Neuroses. Memories –' Nice rolling, Deadpan, I thought. You had to bring it up.

'Yah, I know. People buy and sell.' He lifted his chin with just a trace of defiance. 'They steal, too. I made them tell me about it, and what they wouldn't tell me, I looked up. How Gladney's mind was stolen because there was some guy who admired his work so much that he wanted to *be* Gladney. So he had Gladney embedded in his own self, not just overlaid the way those franchises do.' He paused. 'Power People. What a concept. Anyway, he went crazy. Trying to be two people at once, while Gladney didn't want to be him.' He slouched in his chair and rested his head on his right hand, digging his fingers into his wiry brown hair. 'I asked them why they didn't just take Gladney out of him and put him back but they said they couldn't do that after he'd already been implanted. Even if they'd found the suckers before that, it would have been impossible because this brain' – he tapped his head with one finger – 'had already begun developing a new mind. Which is me. Doesn't seem fair.'

'Fair to whom?'

'Gladney. He just disintegrated. Evaporated when they cleaned him out of the other man. And here I am. Variation on a theme.' His gaze drifted away from me to something over my left shoulder. I turned to look. He was staring at the synthesizer near the bed. It was a small one, taking up about twice as much space as my portable system did when assembled. The keyboard looked a little dusty.

'Use it much?' I asked.

'From time to time.'

'I'd really like to hear something you've composed.'

'Ah?' Panic. 'You would?'

'To get acquainted with your music.'

'So that after you get into my brain and find my music box, you'll know whether it's mine or not, huh?' He waved one hand. 'Never mind. You don't go into my brain, I forgot. I've done nothing but short pieces and I don't think of any of them as complete. Not when I compare them to other things I've heard.'

'I would still like to hear them.'

He hesitated. 'Would a recording be all right? I don't like to play in front of anyone. I'm not an entertainer. Not a performance entertainer.'

I could hardly believe he was going along with it. 'A recording would be fine.'

He got up and puttered around with the entertainment center for a minute, keeping his back to me. Abruptly, music blared out of the speakers and he jumped to adjust the volume.

'Set it to repeat once,' I told him.

He turned to me, ready to object, and then just shrugged and thumbed a shiny green square on the console before sitting down again. 'Just a musical doodle, really,' he said, apologizing for it before it could offend me.

In fact, it was a bit more than that, a dialogue between piano and clarinet, admirably synthesized, but even my ear could tell it was too tentative. And it wasn't complete at all. It was more like an excerpt from a longer piece that had yet to form. I was no musical authority, but on the second time through I could pick out spots where a surer composer would have punched up the counterpoint, let the two instruments answer each other more quickly. There might have been the makings of a canon in it. I toyed with the idea that he'd been misidentifying Bach as the old Gladney.

'How did you compose it?' I asked after it had played through again.

He frowned.

'Did you just sit down at the synthesizer and fool around until you found a sequence, or –'

'Oh.' He laughed nervously. 'That's a funny thing. I heard it in a dream, and when I woke up, I went to the synthesizer to play as much of it as I could before I forgot it. First I just played all the notes. Then I put them with the appropriate instruments.'

'Was that how it was in the dream – piano and clarinet?'

'I don't remember. I just remember the music. Piano and clarinet seemed right.'

I knew what the answer to my next question would be, but I asked it anyway. 'What was the dream about?'

He was rubbing his chest again. 'Gladney.'

Jascha, thou shouldst be with me at this hour. Instead of the one who was with me.

I managed to talk him into playing a few more of his incomplete compositions. When his discomfort went from acute to excruciating, I gave him a reprieve and told him I was going to get some rest. His relief was so forceful I could have ridden it out of the room and halfway down the hall.

There was a message in my phone, an invitation from Dr Jesl to have dinner with her and the other medicos working on Gladney's habilitation. I begged off and asked her if she could supply me with dupe recordings of Gladney's recent attempts at composition without his knowing it. Also some of the previous Gladney's work for comparison. She could and did and I spent most of the rest of the day and a good part of the evening in an audio-hood.

Maybe if I'd known more about music – the real hardcore stuff, mathematics of progressions and so forth – I'd have been able to pick out more similarities (or differences) between the two Gladneys' work. I called for recordings by other composers he'd listened to and played portions of those as well. Our boy, as Jesl called him, hadn't been trying to crib from Bach or anyone else. He had avoided being derivative as much as possible, admirable in a beginning talent and also evident of already well-developed self-control,

which is good only when it doesn't grow into inhibition. What he had borrowed from other composers was mostly technique – my ear was good enough to pick that up.

I listened to the piano-clarinet piece again and again. It wasn't a copy of the first Gladney's work, but compared to the first Gladney's other pieces, there was something terribly related-sounding about it – as though he was picking up where that man had left off. Or at least trying to.

He'd been unable to tell me exactly what had happened in the dream where he'd heard it, just that he'd known the dream involved the first Gladney. That was somewhat unsettling and would have been more so if he had composed all his music after dreaming about that former person, but he hadn't. I would have found that reassuring if the piano-clarinet piece hadn't been so obviously superior to all of his other attempts.

Variation on a theme, he'd called himself. It nagged at me.

I waited until he had been escorted off to some kind of day-to-day culture orientation workshop early the next afternoon and had Jesl let me into his room so I could set up for our first session. That way he wouldn't have to receive me as a guest with all the attendant awkwardness again.

The bed, I decided, was the best place to put him; he'd be more receptive lying down. Not that he wasn't terribly receptive, all things considered. I mentioned to Jesl how surprised I was that Gladney would be so cooperative with me immediately. She told me that was another characteristic of rehabbed wipes; they became accustomed to being probed in various ways.

I was assembling the system when the question I hadn't wanted to ask finally broke through and asked itself.

Could I really do this job?

Sure. I'd been mind-to-mind with a wipe before. Valuable experience.

That wasn't all it was. Another mindwipe. What if he dissolved himself, too? What if I got in there and he pulled the image of Jerry Wirerammer out of me? *What if he tasted too much like McFloy?*

Calm suddenly washed over me. I sat down on Gladney's bed and did a little measured breathing. Gladney was not McFloy. It was just that simple. Gladney wanted to *be* and he wanted it on his own. McFloy had never gotten far enough to find his own life enough for him. And Jerry didn't even come into it, not like McFloy. All right. It would be all right. I would go in and do the job deadpan as hell. It would be like righting an imbalance, to do for him what I hadn't even had a chance to try to do for McFloy.

By the time Gladney returned, I had the system assembled, the compartmented tank for our eyes ready on the stand by the bed, the optic-nerve connections primed, and a relaxation program ready to run the moment he was hooked in.

He didn't seem surprised to see me, only a little resigned and nervous. 'You're not going to want to hear any more music, are you?' he asked.

'No more recordings, no.' I patted the bed. 'Come get comfortable. We don't have to start right away.'

He smiled, stripped off his overshirt and chaps (it never fails to amaze me what will come back into style) and flopped down on the bed in his secondskins.

Rather than play one of the usual preparatory games like *What Would You Do?* or *What Do You Hear?*, I eased him into chatting about his rehabilitation – or habilitation, looking at it from his point of view. I thought I'd learn more about his state of mind from simple conversation than from games. After all, what past experience did he have for a game? It would only oblige him to be inventive and pull his concentration from the situation at hand. Chitter-chat was the right approach. He had some rather astute observations on modern life, as any outsider would, and I hoped he wouldn't lose them when he became an insider.

Eventually, he began winding down. I let him get away with some delaying tactics, going to the bathroom, taking his vitamins – delaying tactics can be important personal preparation rituals, provided they don't go on for too long. When he began talking about having something to eat, I made him lie down and start breathing exercises.

He was a good breather, reaching a state of physical receptiveness more quickly than a lot of more experienced clients I'd had. When the time came, I removed his eyes for him; just pressed my thumbs on his closed lids and out they popped into my palms as smoothly as melon seeds. Gladney didn't even twitch. The connections to his optic nerves disengaged with an audible *kar-chunk*. Hospital eyes were always a little more mechanical than they had to be. After I placed them in the left side of the holding tank, I slipped the system connections under his flaccid eyelids. A tiny pulse in the wires told me when he was hooked into the mental fingerpainting exercise I'd selected for him. Mental fingerpainting was about the right amount of effort for someone on his level. The system supplied the colors. All he had to do was stir them around.

I breathed myself into a relaxed state in a matter of moments but I waited a full minute before popping my own eyes out and joining him in the system. I wanted to give him time to get acclimated. Some people experienced a disorientation not unlike sudden weightlessness and they needed a minute alone to right themselves before they have to get used to another presence.

My materialization was even more gradual than usual to spare him any trauma. I used Pyotr Frankis's old trick of coming in as another color, oozing in greenly and then revealing myself as a second consciousness. Bright lights flashed as he recognized me, some of them nightmare purple, but it wasn't

me he was afraid of. There was a little fear from not having a body to feel but he was becoming accustomed to that. He was edgy about something else entirely – quick images of traps snapping shut, closet doors slamming. But there was a certain amount of exhilaration, too, at being in a realm where almost nothing is impossible.

The images began to flow more continuously from him, rolling over us in a tumbling series, gargantuan confetti. Most of them were portions of dreams, scenes from books he'd read; some were strange scenes he was visualizing in the heat of the moment, just to see if he could. I stabilized and moved with his attention, reminding him gently that I was still there. The image of my own face came, followed by a series of others that gradually became more bizarre. The undertones running out of him indicated this was how he imagined everyone else in the world to be – exotic, different, mysterious, alien, existing on a plane he had only the haziest conception of because he lacked a past.

I emphasized my presence before he could become so caught up with his grotesque faces as to get hysterical. He steadied, his energy level decreasing. I felt him adjust something and there was a sense of balance being established, as though two large masses floating in space were settling into orbit around each other. *Space* was a good word for it. The feeling of emptiness surrounding us was enormous and vivid enough to induce vertigo, if I'd suffered from it. Which I didn't.

This is me. So much nothingness to be filled. He was unaware that he'd said anything; it simply came out of him as everything else had. There was a brief image of the previous Gladney and he tensed at the thought. *Somewhere. In this big emptiness …*

The Gladney-that-had-been image drifted away from us and disintegrated. His thought remained incomplete. He was at a loss now, drifting nowhere, so I gave him a new image as a prod, a very simple one: the synthesizer. As soon as he saw it, he reflexively reran the music, the piano-clarinet piece. I could hear little extra things in it this time, notes and embellishments absent from the recording. He was on the verge of rolling with it, letting it come the way it had been meant to, when hard negation chopped down like a guillotine blade.

We were left in silence. If he could have withdrawn from me, he would have, but he didn't know how.

I waited, making my presence as unthreatening as possible while I took his Emotional Index. He registered in peculiar fragmented sensations of movement rather than in visuals, because everything was movement for him. I could see that now. The universe was movement, the movement of vibration. Like a tuning fork. Even he himself was a tuning fork and right now he was vibrating in the key of fear-sharp. One octave up, I could hear a whiny echo

of guilt. The intensity of it ebbed and I turned the music on again. This time he didn't shut it down, just pulled back from it as far as possible and allowed it to replay as the original recording.

We'd get nowhere at this rate. I had to get into the music – *inside* the music. I slowed down my time sense and concentrated, tightening myself until I was small enough to slip in between the notes. At that level they thundered, no longer recognizable as music; my consciousness vibrated in sympathy. Concentrating a little more, I felt the thundering rumble of the notes become more ponderous and now I could detect something else within the vibrations, faint but present nonetheless. I would have to concentrate even harder to find out what 'it was, but to concentrate that forcefully is to alter your state of consciousness in such a way that you're not actually *conscious* in the sense of *awake*. I would not be able to monitor Gladney. From his perspective it would seem as though I'd gone from being real to being imaginary.

It came slowly. The notes swelled until I could perceive only one at a time and I let the nearest one swallow me up. It was a piano note, G, perfectly formed in perfect pitch, a universe created by the oscillation of a string in the air (that was how he saw it, not as synthesized but as the real thing). Each sweep of the string through space created the universe of the note anew, the string reaching the limit of its swing before the ghost of itself opposite had disappeared. And within the note –

He looked up with a smile of mild interest. The face was unmistakable in spite of all the changes he'd been through in the last year and a half.

Come closer, he said.

Gladney?

The same. The smile broadened. *Well, not quite the same.* Those pampered good looks in full flower; the well-tended skin, the sculptured jawline, the hair brushed straight back and falling nearly to his shoulders. His face was the most solid thing about him; the rest had been sketched in vaguely. I could get no undertones from him, no feelings, no images.

He locked me in here, he said. *So I won't get out and take –*

The note passed away and we were in another. Gladney was standing on a high hill in the middle of the day.

– what used to be mine. He looked around. In the distance the horizon ran wetly, melting upward into the sky. *I live in the music now. He can't come in unless I get out.*

It wasn't possible. If anything had been left of the old Gladney's mind after the suckers had finished cleaning out his brain, it would have shown up while he was still in quarantine. This had to be a delusion of the present Gladney some kind of kinky survivor guilt. And besides, you couldn't hold a separate identity that wasn't you in your mind. Someone had promised me that was a

fact, and truth and information weren't the same thing, but I couldn't think about that now, I had to be deadpan.

The outdoor scene disappeared as the note went on; now we were in a vague representation of the old Gladney's recording studio. He looked up from the piano he was sitting at.

Can you prove who you are? I asked him.

You see me as I was. Isn't that enough?

No. The Gladney-that-is has perfect pitch – that could easily translate to his being able to reproduce his old appearance. If you are really the Gladney-that-was, you can tell me something about yourself that the Gladney-that-is has no knowledge of.

The delusion spread his hands. *He's studied up on me thoroughly. They gave him access to newstapes, vid-magazines, performance spikes.*

There's still plenty he doesn't know, I said. *The private things. Certain memories, feelings. Tell me something only your family could confirm as true.*

His face took on a defiant look but there was no more feeling from him than there would have been from a holo transmission. That in itself would indicate he was a fabrication, I thought, but my merely telling Gladney that wasn't going to help him. His intellect might believe me but his emotions wouldn't.

Tell me something, I prodded again.

He rose and leaned on the top of the piano. *Don't you think a man with perfect pitch would be able to interpolate the private feelings of another man who had grown from the same brain?*

The studio was gone. He was leaning on a small table in a quick-eat while I stood just outside the entrance. I could hear the drumming of his fingers on the table.

Tell me a fact, then. Just one fact he couldn't possibly know.

He straightened up. *The mindsuckers damaged me. I remember only what he knows.*

A logical cover, I decided, but I was unsure what to do next. Arguing with a delusion would only strengthen its sense of presence. Even just acknowledging it was giving it something to feed on. Confronting it was Gladney's job, not mine. I was going to have to get him down in the music with me.

The note passed; we were in a bedroom now. Gladney lay crosswise on a futon with his arms folded behind his head. He was looking at me upside down and I could see how much better he was defined.

I'm residue, he said happily. The upside-down smile was grotesque. *I'm a myelin ghost. You can't get rid of me without physically damaging his brain.*

I hooked my feet under the futon and willed myself upward. His bizarre upside-down smile rushed away from me as I grew through the ceiling of the

phantom room, up into the emptiness to the limit of the note. The piano string swung across a sky made of the present Gladney's face. My abrupt appearance gave him a surge of alarm that nearly dislodged me.

Where were you? he said, demanding.

You know. The piano string moved between us. I stretched out my arms. *Take my hands before that string comes back.*

No.

Why not? It's your music.

No!

From the corner of my eye, I saw the string return to view, slicing through space. *Please, Gladney. Don't let that string put another barrier between you and your own work.*

Panic at the idea of being cut off from his music made him grab my hands. Half a mental moment later panic at the idea of meeting his delusion head-on made him freeze. The piano string came closer; shortly it would pass through my wrists and fragment my concentration.

I can't pull you in, Gladney. You have to jump on your own.

I'm afraid!

Why? Say it!

I'm afraid because –

Say it!

He'll get me!

Who?

Gladney!

You *are Gladney.*

No!

Then, who are you?

There was no answer. The piano string had nearly reached us.

What *are you?* I asked. *Are you a composer?*

His affirmation was all he needed to send him under the string just before it would have severed my hands. He stared after it with both horror and elation and then we were rushing down into the music together in the push of his admission.

The delusional Gladney watched us descend. The real one made a soft landing on the bed beside it, still gripping my hands. Without thinking, he tried to pull me onto the bed between himself and the other.

The bedroom vanished. We were on an underground tube, the only three in the coach. I moved around behind Gladney and he had to let go of me. As soon as he did, the delusional image vanished. Gladney was startled, but not half as much as I was. He moved forward with his hands out in front of him, groping the air.

He's not here. Is he?

I didn't answer. I was still trying to figure out what had happened. Delusions didn't go away just like that. Nor did they have enough volition to come and go like consciousness.

Is he? Gladney half-turned toward me and I saw that his eyes were closed. Either he was making use of a fairly sophisticated mental maneuver, a sort of sneaking up on his own blind side, or he was faking it to stay blinded to the situation. I couldn't tell which; his undertones showed only confusion.

Suddenly his hands seized on something invisible. The delusion rematerialized, caught in Gladney's grasp. The air around them crackled with sparks from Gladney's terror.

I can't let go!

I'd expected that; I hadn't expected to be unable to tell which one of them had said it, though.

We went from the tube to a raft in the middle of the ocean, bright sun beating down on the water. Gladney still had hold of the delusion. His eyes were open now. A shadow passed over us; high-flying piano string.

High A-sharp, Gladney said, automatically identifying the note. All right, now I knew which one was talking. *We're getting close to the end of the melody.*

And then they both said, in unison, *What do I do with him then?*

You're asking me? It's yours. What do you do when the music's over?

We were in the lower branches of a large tree, then back to the tube very briefly *(B-flat grace note,*Gladney said), in the bedroom, on a windy rooftop several thousand feet above the ground. Gladney was forcing us more quickly toward the end of the song – well, one of them was. It had to be the right one; delusions couldn't act on their own, only in reaction. The images began to blend into each other, flickering and flapping. Gladney and his delusion flashed on and off in a variety of positions, Gladney still holding on, as though they were wrestling or dancing. Or both. The music went from slow-motion subsonic to recognizable melody, both Gladneys dancing-struggling in time to it. The delusion offered no resistance now but Gladney was too preoccupied to notice. The struggle became a tumbling, end over end over end over end. I saw Gladney's hospital room, the synthesizer, Gladney himself standing before it, staring it down as though it were an enemy Dr Jesl appeared briefly, carnelian eyes blind to the two figures tumbling past her through the entertainment center where Gladney sat studying a newstape of the Gladney-that-had-been on the holo screen. The tumblers rolled on, to the vision of a dimly remembered dream, that dream of Gladney, the old Gladney, lifting his head to the sight of three people, visible only from neck to thigh, rushing forward at him. The dream Gladney – the Gladney-that-had-been – cried out, fell back, and vanished, and then the tumbling men were beyond the original end of the melody. But still they went on and the

music went on with them, piano and clarinet finally making contact, playing together and opposite each other in complement.

After some unmeasurable mental time, the tumbling began to slow with the music. And when it stopped, there was only one figure, not two. He drifted in emptiness, excited and drained all at once.

Enough. Before he could think of doing anything else, I cued another relaxation exercise and wrapped it around him. As soon as he was completely absorbed in mental fingerpainting, I broke the contact between us and withdrew.

It took a minute or so for his vitals to calm down. I changed the exercise from fingerpainting to simple abstract visuals. He was overstimulated, in need of a passive mode. After his pulse went down below eighty, I disconnected him from the system and put his eyes back in.

The moment he saw me, he broke into a sweat. 'Don't try to talk,' I told him, covering the system connections and slipping them into the drawer in the largest component.

'I *can* talk.'

'Sure. I didn't want you to feel like you had to.'

He turned his face away while I dismantled the system. His breathing was extremely loud in the room. Rhythmic. I let him be. The inexperienced were often overcome by an intense feeling of embarrassment after mindplay, particularly pathosfinding. It took some getting over.

'Listen,' he said, after a bit, still not looking at me. 'He was there. He was really there, alive in me. And I'd just come out of nowhere, a figment of my own imagination.'

'You can't have his past,' I said as gently as I could. 'And there's no such thing as a ghost, myelin or otherwise. It's always just you.'

He shook his head. 'Not any more. Before, it was like that. But you took me down into the work –'

'You went on your own.'

'Doesn't matter. You helped me go down and get him. Not get rid of him – I've *got* him.'

Well, reintegrating a delusion would feel like that. If we prized our illusions, we were even that much more jealous of our delusions because they felt so much more real. *Really* real. A few more sessions and he would adjust to being exactly what he was, no more and no less, and he would accept his music as something that had always come from the desire to compose it, not at the behest of something beyond his control. I let myself out.

Dr Jesl phoned me sometime later, rousing me from a doze. 'Our boy has a supreme mad on for you,' she said. 'Thing is, I can't tell just what it's all

about. I don't think he knows, either Struggling with new emotions, as 'twere.' She sounded more amused than worried.

As 'twere. I was too exhausted to explain about mindplay embarrassment compounded by the loss of a self-imposed handicap. 'He'll get over it,' I told her.

Which he did. Or seemed to. But it spooked me later on, when he correctly identified all of the old Gladney's music without anyone identifying it for him.

When he was stronger – when we were both stronger – I allowed myself an afternoon off. I left him at his synthesizer working on a new piece with difficulty but also with the determination of those who become real and stay real. I locked myself in the hospital room and cried for McFloy, for his not being able to overcome the survivor guilt, for being ultimately unable to fill his own empty cup, for all the stupid emotions that had gotten in his way, that wouldn't get in my way They wouldn't call me Deadpan Allie for nothing, ever.

Deadpan Allie cried herself comatose. But just that once. I still had to finish taking care of Gladney.

And I didn't cry for Jerry Wirerammer.

LAST CALL

I sat staring at the screen in mute amazement. The goofy grin, the let's-make-things-a-little-more-interesting tilt to the head, all intact, all just as I remembered them from a thousand years ago when I'd had an overdrawn kitchen and an urge to put on madcaps.

'Hello, Allie.'

'Jerry ... is it *really* you?' I said when I could speak.

He looked embarrassed. 'Well, actually, it's not. I'm a Power Person. Sort of.'

If someone could have died of the creeps, I would have right then.

'I'm, uh, a bootleg,' he went on. 'Kind of a bootleg, that is. I had one of the bootleg templates. Later I got hold of the original.'

I didn't want to hear about it. 'What do you want? Why are you calling me?'

Giggle. 'Just to say hello, I guess. And let you know everything's really all right. I still exist, in a way. Here and there. I don't know about *there*, of course, but I'm *here*. Not totally, I mean. But sort of totally. It's a funny sort of existence but it works.'

'What about ... what about the original?'

He shrugged. 'I'm not sure. My memory doesn't go that far. I know some-one was after him and I imagine they got him, whoever they were. I'm not too clear on that. And it doesn't matter any more anyway.' He paused. 'That's all, I guess. I just had this urge to call you.'

'Thanks,' I said and pushed the disconnect pad.

He was going to haunt me no matter who he was. Some people wanted to be somebody, some people didn't want to be anybody, some people wanted to be everybody, and some people wanted everybody to be them. Hell of a thing, I thought, and called Fandango over to drink birch beer with me so I wouldn't have to think any more about it for a while.

WE ARE NOT AMUSED

'Great minds,' said Jascha, 'think alike.'

'Sure. Also not-so-great minds.'

It wasn't a big bed and it wasn't even as firm as I'd have liked, but it was a bed and it wasn't at the agency and Jascha was in it with me, so all was right with the world. For the moment. Through the open double doors opposite the bed, the sun was just starting to come up over the bay, which was only lightly misty this morning.

'Want me to close them?' Jascha asked, reaching for the remote on the nightstand.

'Nah. Leave the doors open. I don't mind.' We had settled into an innocent cuddle, if any cuddle can be innocent when the people in question are naked. Jascha pulled the sheet up a little higher against the morning coolness.

'You tired? Or still all wound up?'

'Neither. Just sort of calmly alert.'

Jascha breathed a theatrical sigh of relief. 'Of course, that's assuming I'm not being premature,' he added.

'If you're tired, Jascha, go to sleep.'

'I'm just kidding, Allie. Jesus, what's happened to your sense of humor? You do remember kidding, don't you? You used to be awfully good at it.'

I turned my head away from the hard red sunlight and closed my eyes.

'Anyone's capable of developing delusions under the right conditions.'

'He correctly identified all of the old Gladney's music on his own. Not guessing. Which has to mean that was the old Gladney in there. Not a delu-sion. Which has to put the lie to your contention and everyone else's that you can't accommodate a completely separate mind in your own mind.'

'No, it doesn't,' Jascha said firmly. 'The fact that he correctly identified all of the old Gladney's music means that great minds think alike. The new mind was born in the same brain. It had to have –' he floundered for a moment, '*resonated* somehow with the creations of the old mind. Sympathetic vibration. Kinship. Perfect pitch. He used a fantasy of the old Gladney to deal with the survivor guilt and it became a delusion.'

Resonated. Oh, yah. 'That's one way to explain it.'

'That *does* explain it.' Pause. 'Sure you don't want me to close those doors?'

'I'm sure. I want to look at the bay.'

'And how can you do that with your eyes closed?'

'All right, I want the doors open so I can look at the bay if I want to.'

Silence fell for such a long time that I thought Jascha had gone to sleep. I was half-dozing myself when he said, 'The best system in the world won't reach into your fantasy life unless you offer it up. You don't do that.'

'Ridiculous. I do, too. I live a good portion of my life in fantasy. Remember? I lead a very mental life. They told me that way back when I was a mind criminal. It's far truer now than it ever was. Jascha, you weren't there in mind-to-mind contact with him. You don't know.'

'True. I only know what you've told me. Including how you helped him resolve things.'

'And what about Jerry Wirerammer?'

'I don't know. He doesn't seem to be part of this very mental life you lead.'

'Sometimes I feel as though he almost straddles it – the outer and the inner. Someone else's inner; I never went mind-to-mind with him. He said I'd turned my back on the world he had to live in.'

Jascha slipped his arm out from around me and sat up, rubbing his shoulder. He'd left off having himself gilded again; natural silver was starting to appear in his hair. Otherwise he looked about the same as he always had. 'Well, my divorce is final,' he said after a bit.

'It is?'

'As of a few minutes ago. It must be after 6:30. I think they said sunrise would be about 6:41 this morning.'

I pulled the sheet up to my chin. 'Do I say I'm sorry? For my part in it, anyway.'

'Don't be ridiculous.' He leaned his chin on his knees and stared out at the bay. The light mist was burning off rapidly. 'It was one of those interim relationships, bound to come to an end.'

'Then, why'd you get married?'

'I needed the permanence.'

'Excuse me?'

'All right, I needed the feeling of permanence so I could have had it if I'd wanted to.' He looked at me sideways, smiling.

'Oh. Well, why didn't you say so? That's something I can understand.'

Jascha cuffed me lightly and got up to use the lavabo. It was big enough for two if you didn't mind getting your elbows tangled up all the time. I stayed in bed, squinting at the sun and its reflection over the water. I'd come to Oakland alone after finishing up with Gladney, but on the second day, I'd returned to my hotel room to find Jascha sitting on the balcony and his grip in the autovalet. What the hell. If he'd gone to all the trouble of tracking me down, I could let him stay. It wasn't until later that I realized I was relieved to see him. Not just a friendly face, but him, Jascha. And maybe much later, I'd think more about what all that meant, but not now.

I slumped down on the pillow and closed my eyes again. I'd wrapped up Gladney's case in four sessions total, including the first one. Once we'd excised his myelin ghost – or integrated his delusion, depending on your point of view – everything had broken for him. Perfect pitch tends to take on a life of its own. My personal feeling was that the present Gladney was better than the previous, but that could have been a matter of taste. Anyway, his career had begun reviving – or taking off – when I'd left the hospital. It was my own career I had some doubts about.

Of course, I could probably quit now. It had been four years since Paolo Segretti had given me the choice and I'd fulfilled my end. I could walk away from the agency, from mindplay, from everything, even go live in an enclave if I wanted to. (Maybe look up Marty Oren and Sudella. Not that they'd understand why I was there.)

Only that wouldn't take care of the problem. It would only give me even less control over it – if I really had any control over it now.

I opened my eyes as Jascha stepped out of the lavabo, freshly washed and massaged, his hair and beard still slightly damp. 'Next?' he said.

'Nah. I think I'll just lie here in my own sweat and grit until Nelson Nelson calls me back for another assignment, or until hell freezes over, whichever happens second.'

Jascha threw himself down crosswise on the bed. 'Quite a self-pity showcase you're running here.'

'What would you do?' I sat up a little. 'Honestly, now.'

'I'd forget it, Allie.'

'It was just supposed to be his eye. Just the eye trick. But he's there. *Him*. Maybe it was just the eye at first. And then he re-formed around it as an integral part of my mind.'

Jascha looked puzzled. 'Then, what's the problem? We've been over this. If it's an integral part of you, then it can't be anyone else.'

'I don't *think* it can be that simple. He was – I was –' I stopped. *XXXXXX XXXXXXXXXXXXXXXXXXXXXXXX*. No, not quite. But I almost had it.

Jascha got up and slipped into a pair of light trousers and a white shirt rich

with delicate blood-red embroidery. 'Let's go out. Walk around. Be in the world. That's your problem more than anything.' He reached over and yanked me across the mattress. 'You're always talking about the world this and the world that and this reality, that reality, and real reality, but it isn't real to you.' He pointed at the bay. '*That's* the shade, as far as you're concerned. *That's* your fantasy. You can dream lucidly now but you've forgotten how to *live* lucidly.'

'Yah, I think I already mentioned that myself, leading a very mental life and all that. I can also refer you to Jerry Wirerammer, whoever he is now, if you want further testimony.' I got up and went to the lavabo. 'I do know what my problem is, Jascha,' I said, punching the controls on the door for a hard needle shower and even harder massage. 'It's what makes me such a good pathosfinder. And I know how to cure it, but I'm not sure I'd like living in an enclave.'

'It doesn't have to be that extreme,' he said.

'Maybe not for you.' I stepped into the lavabo.

Living lucidly. We took a slow open-seated caravan through the hills, gawking with the other tourists at the houses jammed into the hillsides. Ancestral homes, most of them; they were just about impossible to buy. About the only way to acquire one these days was to be born into it. Jascha and I didn't talk much, except to point out some miraculous architectural feat showing through the trees.

The caravan paused for lunch at the summit of one of the hills, overlooking more of the bay. The restaurant was picnic-style – one of those on Nelson Nelson's Restaurant-of-the-Month Club brochures, I noted. I tried to picture NN reclining on a blanket on the grass gnawing on spiced chicken wings; the image moved me to laughter, which amused the other tourists and alarmed Jascha when I wouldn't tell him what I was laughing about. I didn't want to tell him I'd lapsed back into mental living. Living lucidly was all right but not very much happened. (If you were lucky ... but then no one would have called what Jerry Wirerammer had been doing living lucidly.) I decided to wait and be disturbed about my attitude later.

On the way down the other side of the hills, the caravan passed an enclave. We'd have missed it if the tour guide hadn't pointed it out. There wasn't much to see, just a wire fence mostly hidden by trees. I stared after it anyway, wondering if there was some way I could get a closer look at it before I had to go back to the agency.

Enclaves were such odd things. You could conceivably live on the outside, never engaging in mindplay, and maybe just seem a little odd to everyone else. I knew that well enough. I also knew it was like deciding to be a hermit in the middle of a city. You'd be out of touch, out of step. Eventually, you'd want to be with people who weren't having their dreams fed regularly

or weren't having a thrillseeker delve them for new and better forms of excitement.

Only … I looked around at the other people in the caravan. Unless we were all in the pool or hooked in together through a mindplay system, I was as separate from them as the people in the enclave were from me. We were all enclaves, really. Maybe the difference in an enclave society was really just perceived, in spite of what NN had said back when I'd done my first job with his son-in-law. So why bother to shut yourself away? Might as well stay out here; who knew the difference?

And then again, maybe it was something about the culture, I thought. Something about being surrounded with people who make mind-to-mind contact would eventually bring you in to be one of them or drive you away completely –

The leaves behind the enclave fence parted and I saw the face looking out at me. Just for a moment; then the caravan rounded a bend and the face disappeared behind a tree. I twisted around, crawling half out of my seat trying to get a last look.

'What is it?' asked Jascha, mildly irritated.

I looked at him. Was it possible to lie, *really* lie, to a person who has actually touched your mind? 'Just trying to live lucidly, Jascha,' I said. 'Trying to get a better look at the scenery.'

'You've got to look while it's happening,' he said. 'Otherwise you miss seeing it the way it should be seen.'

I settled back into my seat. 'My mistake. Thanks for the tip.'

The expression on the face behind the fence had been sadly wistful. For the brief moment I'd seen it, I'd actually been unable to decide whose face it had been – Jerry Wirerammer's, or McFloy's – when it couldn't have been either. Just a trick of the light. And the mind.

Be alert, said a small voice in my head.

I ended up cutting the vacation short by a day. I left Jascha a note. It was easier than arguing with him. I also paid the bill on the room, though I knew that wouldn't make it up to him.

He left his own note on my phone back at the agency. *Did I mention that living lucidly includes loving lucidly? And if you won't marry me again, will you at least try to see that you have something of mine even though we never did the eye trick? It's just as real, though. And just as unreal, come to that.*

But we were too divorced.

LUNATIC BRIDGE

'There's divorce and there's divorce,' said Nelson Nelson. 'You ever been divorced, Deadpan?'

I lit a cigarette, using the time to decide if NN was asking me an honest question or just gassing. I had no doubt the old fox could have wormed his way into my personal data; most employers can. And he was a great one for gassing questions he already knew the answers to. He'd told me once he did it because he was interested in other people's realities. I could have given him the long course on that one.

'No,' I said after a bit. I don't know whether he knew enough to believe me or not, but he looked satisfied.

'Certain philosophers say real divorce is rare because few people ever make truly solid connections with each other.'

'Philosophers?' I tapped my cigarette over the suck-hole in the desk. 'There's a philosophy of divorce?' You hear all kinds of things in the mind-play business.

Nelson Nelson laughed. 'If the human race lasts long enough, there'll be a philosophy for blinking your eyes.'

'And we'll know the new Messiah by the way she walks on bullshit.'

'Now, now, woman. Bullshit has its uses as a lubricant. You'll come to realize that by the time you're my age.'

That depended on what you were trying to lubricate, but I didn't tell him that. I shifted around uncomfortably on my couch. NN's practice of conducting business in a reclining position was getting tiresome and that damned vulgar upholstery was making me itch worse than ever. 'So who are these philosophers of divorce?'

NN looked wise. 'The other members of my Restaurant-of-the-Month Club, actually We suppered in the jet stream last night and the subject came up with the cranberry soufflé.'

'You discussed a case?'

NN's forehead puckered. His eyebrows were nonexistent these days, which made a frown one of his more peculiar expressions. 'Allie, I didn't get to be one of the biggest mindplay agencies in the hemisphere through indiscretion. Someone else brought the subject up. I listened.'

Manipulated the conversation and then picked someone's brain was more like it. 'Did you hear anything that would help me?'

'Hard to say. I'm old enough to have seen several swings of the togetherness pendulum. For a few years, sometimes even as long as a decade, everyone's

getting Two'd and Three'd and Gang'd. Then suddenly everyone's an island again and nobody wants to be committed to anyone else. But regardless of what people want, or think they want, they clump. They can't help it. Even self-proclaimed social outcasts align themselves in some way with other outcasts. No one ever wants to be totally outside the system.'

I scratched some more and didn't say anything.

'Take an extreme case of clumping gone to bond,' he went on in his listen-to-this-you-could-learn-something voice. 'You remember the Lady Bugs from a few years back?'

I nodded, still scratching away. 'They were big news when I was at J. Walter Tech.'

NN smiled with half his mouth. 'They were big news everywhere in the mindplay business.'

'Don't tell me,' I said, sitting up. 'The LadyBugs have split up, one of them wants to be a ballet dancer, and I'm supposed to pathosfind her.'

NN gave me one of his Looks. 'You get some funny ideas, Deadpan. The LadyBugs are still happy as sandbags and loony as Klein bottles. You follow contemporary composers?'

I shrugged. 'Why?'

For answer, he thumbed a button on his couch frame. Music came up out of the walls and floated down from the ceiling and I damn near fell off the couch.

'Allie?'

'That's the Poconos Movement from *Transcontinental Elopement*. Jord Coor and Revien Lam. Their work is unmistakable.'

NN looked satisfied. We listened for a bit while I got over the creeps. The Poconos Movement was one of the more favored doses of the whole piece, all frisky piccolos and galloping guitars. You wouldn't have thought piccolos could describe the Poconos so well, but they did.

'Still with me, Deadpan?'

'Oh, sure.' I squirmed into another position, scratching my left calf with my right foot and clawing at my ribs. 'I always liked Coor and Lam.'

NN turned the volume down a little. 'Likewise. It has great spirit, isn't it so? Coor and Lam produced a fine body of work together, right up until a year ago, when they went their separate ways.'

'Yah. Which one hired me?'

'Coor.' NN raised himself up on one elbow. 'And if you don't stop that scratching, I'm going to have you flayed alive to save you the trouble. What in *hell* is wrong with you?'

'I'm allergic to this goddamn gold lamé.' I stood up, trying to scratch everywhere at once. My overblouse clung to me, snapping with static when I pulled it away from my slight if perennial potbelly that I could never seem to

exercise off. Fusion power we licked; static cling has us on the ropes. It's a funny world.

'Here.' Nelson Nelson produced a small tube and tossed it to me. 'Suddenly everyone's allergic to gold lamé. I had Lindbloom in here about a thrillseeking and she could barely hold still.'

Well, that sounded like Lindbloom, gold lamé or no gold lamé.

'Better?' NN asked as I swabbed cool blue jelly on my arms.

'Much. What is this stuff?'

'Home remedy. Take it with you.'

'Maybe I ought to leave it here. For next time.' I glanced at the couch.

'Deadpan, I'm hurt. You're sneering at the future I looked forward to in the dear, departed days of my youth.'

'Excuse me?'

'Gold lamé. Back when I was a kid, they promised us a clean, glorious future where positively everything would be covered with gold lamé. Gold lamé curtains, gold lamé furniture, gold lamé clothes. They stopped making the stuff fifty years ago and now I have to have it specially manufactured. But I figure I'm entitled.'

I pulled up one loose pantleg and smeared his home remedy on my thigh. 'Tell me about Jord Coor. And I wasn't sneering.'

'There's not much for *me* to tell you; I put all the information in your dataline and you were too sneering. Coor's trying to put himself together for a solo career and having a bad time of it. The six-month hiatus he took after the split has stretched into a year and he's feeling desperate.'

'He waited another six months before hiring a pathosfinder?'

'Some people have to take the long way home just so they know they've been somewhere.'

'Is he really ready to try it alone?'

'*He* says. That's something you'll have to determine. As always.'

'What about his ex-partner?'

'Out of sight but traceable. Part of their separation agreement was a clause promising a certain amount of cooperation in any future individual endeavors, musical or otherwise.'

'Was their split really that amicable?'

'Who knows? Divorce is a funny thing.'

Sure was. 'But they weren't married. Or were they? I don't keep up on celebrity statistics.'

NN would have raised his eyebrows if he'd had any. I couldn't wait for them to grow back. NN did some odd things and I had yet to figure what it was he was acting out. His dear, departed future, maybe. 'Well, not in the conventional sense. But they worked mind-to-mind for ten years. What do you think that means but marriage? *More* than marriage. Follow?'

I nodded.

'So if you should have to look up Revien Lam for some reason, don't hook in with both of them. Don't put them in a composing situation together.'

'But they don't want to compose together.'

'Who said so?' NN snapped. 'Did I say so?' He shook his head. 'Deadpan, the thing you gotta remember about divorced people is when they have a real crisis, they think about jumping right back into the old situation, even if that's the worst thing they could do, and it usually is. But it's a known quantity and people clump. Don't clump them, Allie. The whole music world would love to see them back together again and they don't really want to be back together. Which, paradoxically, gives them common ground and pushes them closer together. Follow that?'

'Yah.' I finished applying jelly to my other leg. 'And I didn't sneer. They don't call me Deadpan Allie and lie.'

'You sneered. Inside if not outside. I could tell.' He cut off the music and put the Bolshoi Ballet on the ceiling holo by way of dismissing me and having the last word. 'It's a mutually wished-for and consummated divorce, Deadpan. Leave it that way.'

Fandango sneaked up behind me and propped her chin on my shoulder. 'Hi. I'm your two-headed transplant.'

I kept staring at the readout screen. 'I'm not going to encourage you.'

She tickled me under the chin with one of her dreadlocks. The damnedest things come back into style. 'Why are you researching the Lady Bugs?'

'I'm looking at a case of extreme togetherness that worked. Or has yet to fail, I'm not sure which.' I pushed back from my desk and went down the three steps into the living room to flop on the couch. Fandango tagged after me, pausing at the bar to dial up a couple of birch beers.

'You think there's a difference?' she said, handing me a glass before she climbed into the pouch chair across from me. 'Between something that works and something that has yet to fail?'

'Glad you asked.' I waved at the coffee table. *Full Day*, another Coor and Lam piece, came on softly. This one was only twenty-four hours long, looped for continuous play. 'According to something I read by one of the leading experts on human relationships – who happens to be a member of NN's chapter of the Restaurant-of-the-Month Club, by the way – there are three main theories on the patterns that two-person bondings of any type follow.'

Fandango turned her bloodstone eyes on me. The bloodstones were new. With the dreadlocks, they made her look like a cross between a werewolf and a witch doctor. I didn't mention that to her. She'd have just gone and added fangs for effect. 'Let's hear it. I know you're itching to tell me.'

'Don't use that expression. One theory says that a two-way partnership

lasting until the death of one or both partners never reached its ultimate peak and thus never got the chance to deteriorate. Another theory says that all partnerships end before the actual split. In the last stage of the relationship, there are really just two sets of elements thrown together behind a facade of unity.' I put my birch beer down on the coffee table. If I was going to lose this potbelly, I couldn't be pouring birch beer into it. 'The third theory states that all partnerships are illusions. One personality dominates and absorbs the other. I guess the LadyBugs would be a rather extreme example, in a way.'

'The LadyBugs are loono and have licenses to prove it,' Fandango said, with not a little disdain.

'Then there are all the variations on those theories. The most interesting one postulates that whatever happens between two people, a third entity is created which can, in some cases, attain such definition and strength as to be a completely different person.'

Fandango finished her birch beer and hung out of the chair to set the glass on the coffee table. 'And what does all this tell you?'

Several things, none of which I wanted to think about at the moment. 'It tells me experts probably work alone and not in partnership.' I stared at the meditation mandala on the ceiling. Researching the LadyBugs, I decided, was the wrong approach. They weren't partners, not the way Coor and Lam had been. I thought of the Twins – I hadn't thought of them in such a long time. They weren't it, either. Congruence wasn't necessarily complement.

'Turn up the music, will you?' Fandango said, sinking down a little more in the chair. 'It just entered my circadian peak.'

I obliged her. Only her head was visible in the pouch chair. I'd never cared for the idea of being swallowed by a piece of furniture, no matter how comfortable it was supposed to be, but then, it wasn't my chair anyway. Fandango had dragged it over to my apartment from her place. That was the advantage of living at the agency – you could get out of your apartment and take it with you.

The LadyBugs were still grinning from the console in my work area above the living room. I abandoned the mandala and wandered back to my desk to punch for Jord Coor's entry. He was an emphatically plain man with a wide face and long, straight black hair. His eyes were the same flat black. Onyx biogems, according to his data. The overall effect was *blah*, as though his life's ambition was to pass unnoticed. Not the acter-outer type, which probably meant there was more than the usual amount of energy pent up behind that broad forehead. If he ran to form at all, he was prone to what I called the creative tantrum, as well as to bursts of creativity alternating with blocks. His being half a partnership had probably masked a lot of that.

After a while, I punched for Revien Lam's picture. The screen swallowed

Coor and delivered his ex-partner's image with an electronic burp. Time for another tune-up. Revien Lam seemed to have tried to make himself as different from Coor as possible. He'd had a bleach-out, hair and all. Against his color, or lack of it, the sapphire eyes were startling. His features were pointy where Coor's were blunted, the face almost an inverted triangle. Only the knobs of his jawbone kept him from looking too pixieish.

Just for the hell of it, I shrank Lam's picture and recalled Coor's, putting them side by side. They stared at me and I stared back.

Art makes strange mindfellows.

It was hard to imagine the two of them hooked in together, Coor through the left eye and Lam through the right, like a variation on the eye trick, I thought uncomfortably, working both in real time and the eternal Now of mind time. A rather trippy experience.

And a very long trip at that. Ten years of such continual mind-to-mind contact was a lot more intimate than two people should have been with each other, as far as I was concerned. They had to be a couple of pretty rugged individualists to have kept themselves sorted out.

'Rugged individualist,' I said aloud.

'What?' asked Fandango, coming out of her musical trance.

I looked over my shoulder at her. 'I said, "Rugged individualist."'

She waved at the coffee table and the music lowered.

'Who?'

'Just a thought. Go back to your rhapsody and forget I said anything.' I turned back to the screen and stared at the ex-collaborators some more.

If you stare at something long enough, sometimes it will begin to look wrong. Lam's picture was on the right and Coor's was on the left and the arrangement was making me uncomfortable to the point of irritation. I tried looking at them with my right eye covered and then my left. Feeding an image into one hemisphere of the brain alone can sometimes give you a different perspective on something, but I'd never been that good at isolating my visual fields without mechanical help. All I was getting out of the effort was more uncomfortable.

When I switched the pictures around, I felt a lot better, even with both eyes open. Aesthetically, the new arrangement was more pleasing, though I was damned if I could have said why. I sat back and put my heels up on the desk, gazing at the pictures through the V-frame of my legs. The system had placed Lam's picture on the right when I'd called for Coor's. Maybe if I'd made the placement myself, I'd have liked it better? I shook my head. That wasn't it and I knew it. I rested my gaze on the dividing line between the pictures for several seconds and then nearly fell out of the chair.

The resemblance between them was so marked I felt like an ass for not having seen it immediately. It wasn't exactly a physical resemblance and yet

it was. The similarity lay in their expressions, especially in the eye and mouth areas – the same things that make the long-married look alike. I had the screen enlarge those portions and remove the distinguishing coloration.

I marveled. It was almost possible to forget which features belonged to which man. Just for the hell of it, I patched Coor's eyes and mouth into Lam's face and vice versa. The old eye-and-mouth trick. My system wasn't programmed for fine-detail graphics and the result was crude, but not unreasonable.

'And what does that tell you, Dr Frankenstein?' Fandango said, hanging over my shoulder again. I patted her wiry hair.

'Take a nap and stop sneaking up on me.' I punched for pictures of Coor and Lam as they had been prior to their becoming collaborators, careful to keep Lam on the left and Coor on the right.

The youthfulness of their faces startled me. I checked the dates. The pictures were fourteen years old, which made it something close to two years before they'd met. At twenty, Coor had that I'm-an-adult-I-know-things look to him while the seventeen-year-old Lam appeared to be the sort of twink you could sell a perpetual-motion machine to.

I made more enlargements of their features and side-by-sided them one at a time. There was a definite similarity of expression around their eyes even then, as though they might have been looking at things in the same way, literally as well as figuratively.

I punched up pictures from three years later. A year into the partnership, Lam had dyed himself black with red accents. The struggle for differentiation had already begun.

Forward another three years. The haunted look of Lam's opal eyes was reflected by Coor's. I went to my auxiliary screen and called up a list of their compositions from that time. *The Freak Parade. Persimmon Dances. The Abstruse Pillow.* I listened to short excerpts from each one on the phones. It was easy to hear the conflict, but they'd conflicted so well together.

I jumped ahead to their last full year together. Coor looked weary and Lam looked crazed. By then it must have required incredible effort to keep from merging. Lam had been in the first stage of his bleach job, and it struck me that his decision to be bleached this time instead of dyed was probably a strong statement of his perception of what was happening between himself and his partner. And there was Coor, looking the same as always, making a statement by making no statement.

I leaned my elbows on the desk and looked from one face to the other. If I'd been shown all the pictures and then been asked to guess which man had hired me, I'd have probably picked Lam, not Coor.

And what about Lam? I punched for any available data. There wasn't much – some vital statistics, a facsimile of the separation agreement, and his

last known address, two years out of date. Probably safe to assume he'd given up music entirely. Considering how he'd been pulling away even from the beginning, it was in character – another and final way to differentiate himself from Coor, a pattern of behavior he was locked into for good.

'And what does all *this* tell you?' said a voice in my ear. Fandango was still lingering behind me.

'It tells me some people gain freedom by trading one form of bondage for another.'

'Yah? You don't have to tell *me* that. I'm a neurosis peddler, remember?'

'Well, you asked.' I frowned at the screen. 'I think my basic problem here is just training someone to be a unit after being half a team for ten years.'

Fandango crouched beside me and wagged her dreadlocks. 'Ah, they never should have broken up.'

'That's a matter of opinion,' I said, amused. 'An opinion that my client's been struggling against. Maybe Lam, too, for all I know.'

'Sorry. I guess I can say it because I won't be doing the dirty work. But speaking as a member of the listening audience … ' She made a face, which, considering the way she looked, was quite an accomplishment. 'Maybe I don't know what I'm talking about. All I do is make people wash their hands a lot and associate sex with the color orange. But maybe it's better to be half of something wonderful than a whole nothing at all.'

I couldn't answer right away, and when I did, my voice sounded just a little sharp. 'It hasn't been determined that Jord Coor is nothing on his own yet. If it had, I wouldn't be on this job.'

Fandango stared at me with mild surprise. ' 'Scuse me, but did I just say something?' She waved a hand carelessly. 'Oh, never mind. Pardon my nose. And mouth, too. All I meant to say was that this kind of mindplay only post-pones having to admit something like the truth, huh?' She got up and bounced back to the pouch chair, dreadlocks flying, and hopped in.

'Thanks for the moral support,' I said.

'Anytime.' She turned the music up again.

'This part of Massachusetts used to be such a mess that they put a two-hun-dred-year ban on external construction even after they cleaned it up. It'll be another eighty-four years before you see anything but naked landscape. If then.' Jord Coor's square face was impassive in the near twilight. I wasn't sure that I hadn't met someone even more deadpan than I was. He pointed to the horizon. 'Those low hills are called monadnocks, according to the locals. About half of them are occupied, hollowed out, like this one.' He tapped his foot on the soft dirt.

'Pretty,' I said.

He almost smiled. 'For over a century nobody knew that. It was all defaced

with factories, ugly little industrial towns. Poison all over the place, in everything. I've seen footage.' A small wind pushed a strand of hair over the lower half of his face and he tossed his head to shake it away. The motion put us unexpectedly eye to eye. The onyxes were like two bottomless holes.

'I thought this would be the ideal place to hide out, weather the first of the separation. Really go underground, in a place that was also coming back into its own.'

I pretended to study one of the few tall evergreens around us while I sight-read his Emotional Index peripherally His analysis sounded a bit simple to me but the set of his body said he was sticking with it, as though his partnership with Lam had been something imposed on him rather than something he'd entered into voluntarily. The no-longer-wished-for bond was now perceived as bondage or indenture. Human beings have a tendency to rewrite reality. I *don't love you anymore* would become *I never loved you to begin with*; it's no good now so that means it never was. I wondered if I'd be able to get him past that. I would have wondered plenty else but I refused to let myself dwell on any of it. They didn't call me Deadpan Allie for nothing.

A chill crept into the air as the sun slid closer to the lumpy line of monadnocks. Jord gestured at the manhole we'd climbed out of earlier and I nodded. The hole led down to an uncomfortably small elevator that took us back into the big empty chamber at the top of the stacked rooms he persisted in calling a house.

We went down to the living room, which was five times larger than it had to be, considering what he used it for, which was very little. A designer who apparently went to a lot of parties had shaped it so that it was punctuated with conversation areas and gathering spots, all around an off-center bar. It had an untouched, still-not-broken-in look. Jord just wasn't ready to make himself at home. Not a good sign.

He wasn't ready to begin work, either; he was treating me like a guest, or maybe an insurance agent, anything but a pathosfinder. Well, the first meeting was always uncomfortable, but Jord Coor's avoidance beat even Gladney's. He sat me in one of the nooks around the bar and dispensed Moxie and chitchat until I was bloated and more knowledgeable about north-central Massachusetts than I could ever have wanted to be. I let him run. He could run but he couldn't hide. Eventually he was going to blurt out something having to do with the reason I was there, and that would give both of us the momentum to go to work. Best for him to make the first move. Better to jump than be pushed.

When it came, it came without preamble. He looked up at me from his fourth glass of Moxie and said, 'I just want it back.'

'It?'

'Whatever it was I had before I met Revien. Sometimes I can almost feel it.

It's almost there. But it's like stepping forward and finding the floor is suddenly gone. Nothing there, just emptiness. And I realize all those years with Revien – I've come away half an artist.' He set his glass on a small shelf by his elbow. 'That's how it feels, anyway. I've been changed.'

'Did you expect that you wouldn't be?'

'Changed, certainly.' His face hardened even more. 'Changed but not diminished. Not shortchanged. As it were.'

As it were, indeed. I nodded for him to go on.

'Apparently what we added to the partnership we subtracted from ourselves. Or what I added to the partnership *I* subtracted from *my* self. I don't know about Revien.' He gave a short, humorless laugh. 'And you'd think I *would* know, wouldn't you. Ten years in and out of each other's heads, you'd think we had no secrets.' He stared past me. 'But we were only half hooked in. That was close enough. Early on, we went all the way, hooked in both eyes, just to try it. Only twice, though. It was too much. Felt so strange, as though we were asleep, dreaming, and discovered there was someone else dreaming the same dream.' His gaze slid over to me. 'Have you ever felt that way with a client?'

I was proud of the fact that I didn't hesitate. 'Mindplayers are specially trained not to get loose and runny around the borders, though most people don't have problems keeping self divided from non-self. It sounds like an effect, uh, peculiar to your relationship.'

'Perhaps it was.' He nodded slowly, staring at something past my right shoulder.

'Who first brought up the idea of separating?'

He took a deep, uncomfortable breath. 'I don't know if it's a matter of an idea that came up. More like a sub-theme that was always there and evolved into being the main melody. We were always pulling apart as much as pulling toward each other.' He frowned, wobbling between a hasty retreat from the subject and a headlong plunge into the problem.

What the hell, I thought; sometimes you can't jump without a little tiny nudge. 'This might be a good time for the first session,' I said casually. 'While it's at the top of your mind.'

He licked his lips, preparing an objection.

'It doesn't get any easier,' I added.

His smile was sudden and unexpectedly warm. 'No, I don't suppose it does, does it?'

He hadn't exactly cooled by the time we got up to his studio but I could tell by the jittery way he kept wiggling his fingers he was trying to build up some kind of resistance. The studio wouldn't let him.

It was a strange room, windowless and just big enough to keep a claustrophobe from stampeding. The acoustical walls and ceiling caught every little

sound and seemed to focus on it, making each noise into something significant before it was gone. In the center of the room, a marvelously restored barrelhouse piano stood back to back with a techno-crazy chunk of synthesizer bristling with wires and stepladdered with keyboards, as though inviting comparison and choice.

'A synthesizer won't always do the job,' Jord said as I touched the rich old wood of the piano. 'Sometimes there's no substitute for the real instrument.' One hand hovered over the yellowed keys, his fingers automatically falling into position for a chord. Instead of playing it, he looked up at me. 'What made you choose cat's-eye biogems?'

'I found them interesting.'

'Look toward the light.' He lifted my chin and studied my eyes. 'Revien would like eyes like those. They shimmer. The same way he does.'

I pulled away from him gently. 'Revien shimmers?'

'It's hard to explain.'

'Then, don't explain. Show me.' I went over to my system stacked by the far wall and began putting the components together. I could feel him watching, unspoken objections and excuses piling up between us, thickening the air.

'This is smaller than most of the systems I've seen,' he said suddenly, from just behind me. I had presence enough not to jump. After you've been pathosfinding a while, you get to where you can not only sense an Emotional Index without looking but also judge a client's physical position relative to yourself. I hadn't thought a client could come up behind me without my knowing.

'My agency developed this model,' I told him, keeping busy with the connections so he wouldn't know he'd startled me. 'This one's only for pathosfinding and memory enhancement, which is why there's so little to it. Your last pathosfinder probably had a standard, multipurpose system.'

'Revien and I used a composing box. It wasn't a lot bigger than this. Are you sure it'll do the job?'

I was grinning on the inside. 'Back at the agency, we've got a system the size of a small canyon. You have to let it eat your head to use it. It does a job and a half, just about anything by way of mindplay, but it wouldn't do anything more for us than this does. Which is to provide a medium for the meeting of our minds. It works, but only as well as we do. You know how it is with machines.'

He moved around to my right, frowning at the assembly. 'Revien used to call our composing box the lunatic bridge.'

'Why?' I asked, pulling some pictures out of a drawer.

'We'd send a piece of ourselves down the wire into the box and the two pieces would fuse into the lunatic that composed the music.'

I didn't raise my eyebrows. 'Interesting. Did you – do you – see it that way?'

'A lunatic on a bridge?' He wouldn't let the smile come. Attempting to out-deadpan me, maybe. 'I tried not to. Try not to.' He glanced at the sheaf of pictures I was holding.

'This is something my agency developed strictly for musicians. Some are flat photos, some are still holos, other are repros of old paintings. You take a good look at them, and tell me what you hear. Are you more comfortable lying down or sitting up?'

'Lying down. I'll get some mats out of the storeroom.'

'Just one mat. I'll sit up, if that's all right with you.'

I pushed the chair at the synthesizer over while he fetched a mat and went about molding into a contour for himself.

He almost froze on the first picture, but we'd built up too much momentum and it carried him into the exercise whether he liked it or not. But he took his time with the holo of a man and a woman in the middle of a glitzy blowout. The woman was Lindbloom, several years younger, before she'd started dyeing her skin. Even in plain flesh-tone, she was striking, which may have contributed to his stalling. People liked to stare at Lindbloom.

'A lot of laughter and chatter around these two,' he said at last. 'An old Coor and Lam piece playing in the background – *Transcontinental Elopement*. The man's caught between nostalgia and looking ahead, mainly to possibilities with the woman. But she doesn't think in terms of past or future, it's all a big Now to her. When she gets far enough from one experience, it's like it happened to someone else. She's timeless and that's her strength. He isn't, and that's his weakness.'

For someone who had been slow to begin, he was making a strong showing. I went on to the next picture, a low aerial view of some half-aboveground homes in Colorado, with Pike's Peak taking up the background.

'Wind,' he said after a bit. 'Rustling. The air is colder than usual for the season. No birds singing. There's a faraway machine noise; no one could identify it even if they could hear it. They're all dug in, hiding, and they don't make a sound.'

He barely hesitated on the third picture, a repro of the Magritte of a man with an apple obscuring his face. 'He's trying to talk but the fruit muffles him. All that comes out are these "*mmf-mmf*" sounds.'

The Magritte was the real breaker; he went quickly through the other nine pictures. By the time he finished, he was agitated and antsy, ready either to get started or to beg off for the night. I pulled the connections out of the system and untangled the wires.

'Eyes,' I said, kneeling down beside him. Obediently, he popped them into my cupped hand. I put the system connections at his empty eyelids and let them crawl in to engage the optic nerves. I had programmed a tonal exercise

for him instead of the usual color or pattern-building. Judging from the way he sagged on the mat, I'd chosen well.

I took half a minute to examine his eyes. Brand new and well taken care of. I put them in the left-hand compartment of the solution jar, consciously choosing that side, breathed myself into near-trance, and then I popped out my own eyes.

I had intended to let him feel my presence gradually to avoid contact shock, but he seemed to have been waiting for me. At the first taste of contact, he drew me in with a smoothness born of years of working mind-to-mind with someone else. I hadn't expected him to receive me so easily. Old responses live long, die hard, and frequently leave a troublesome corpse.

But that was normal next to what I found, or what I didn't find. There were no visuals – absolutely none. My mind translated the lack into the dark of eyelessness. The urge to visualize was almost overpowering but I managed to check it.

The tonal exercise was still running and that was my next surprise. Most people seem to hear bell-like sounds when you hook them into a tonal. Jord Coor's reaction was something completely new to me.

He heard seagulls. Very musical seagulls – their cries complemented and harmonized the way they never did in outside reality. It wasn't unpleasant, but in the sightless night of his perspective it was rather spooky. I prodded gently, thinking that perhaps he'd been waiting for a sign from me before he turned on the pictures.

Sea? I asked. Actually, I wasn't sure whether I'd said *sea* or *see*.

A secret sea, he answered, without disturbing the gulls. I caught under-tones of surf, a whispering rhythm and the not-quite-voice of the wind fading in and out. A perfect sound-picture, waiting for someone to add sight.

Do you never visualize? I asked. Carefully.

It's the sound that matters. Or is it just pretty pictures you want, holo? The last word came out more like *hollow*.

It's a matter of what you *want*, I told him. The cries of the seagulls died away as the exercise came to an end. We let it go. His presence grew stronger, becoming a pressure in the darkness, filling all the space around my own self. New sounds began, all the pleasurable sounds he could remember, footsteps on a hard surface, people's voices humming, the sharp musical clang of metal on metal, whispers, whistles, whales. His mental ear had remixed them into a harmoniousness not present when he'd first heard them.

Some would say all this is music in itself, he said. *But it isn't. It needs trans-lation. Interpretation.*

A tumble of conventional music drowned out the sounds. Shreds and snatches of various things, including old Coor and Lam compositions, passed

through me, as though he was trying to find the frequency at which I'd vibrate.

I felt for his Emotional Index. He was in a sort of performance mode. I let him go on throwing music while I did a gradual spread, sliding around him and into his terrain. It was exceedingly strange without visuals, but not unpleasant. Texture began to mix with sound and I had a sudden, vivid physical impression of him standing with his eyes closed, listening. What he was listening for, I couldn't quite tell – the music within that would be sparked by the sounds without, or perhaps the elusive music of the unconscious spheres. I couldn't make out whether this was a memory or the image he held of himself in the act of composing. His mind was stew, everything melting into and flavoring everything else, much more so than I'd found in many of my other clients.

Stew is a wonderful thing, free of the overcompartmentalization and learned behavior that can (and does) cripple some artists. But stew could be too thick and formless, a mass in which ideas lost definition and coherence and ultimately dissolved, leaving behind only a hint of what they might have once been, just old seasonings boiled out and gone dead. Jord Coor had not yet achieved this state, much to my relief.

I kept coming across abrupt, intense concepts and ideas sticking up like barbs – barbs and bait combined. The temptation to supply the missing visual element was nearly overwhelming. Trying to move around the barbs rather than directly into them was impossible; I'd come to depend on visualization the same way I depended on my physical sight. I sank down deeper into his terrain, careful not to probe too hard, looking for some sign of suppression.

It was like sinking blindfolded into a sensory-stimulation tank. Very sensual man, this Jord Coor. The undertones said he'd just never been terribly taken by the visual experience. He was not an habitual admirer of sunsets or scenery, his earlier bit of showing me the Massachusetts countryside notwithstanding. Most of his concentration had always been on the auditory and, after that, the tactile.

He answered my question before I asked it. *Revien. He liked pictures. Always Revien. He supplied the pictures, if that's what you're looking for.*

I was still troubled. There should have been pictorial memories stashed about here and there, pictures of Revien's pictures, but I couldn't find them. Either Jord had buried them that deeply or – highly unlikely – Revien Lam had taken them with him, in a kind of mindwipe. (And if so, had the mindwipe been forcible, or submitted to? Or, even more disturbingly, had Jord forced them on his partner? Expulsion? It was too much to think about at the moment.)

Sinking deeper now. Not much effort needed, he was drawing me down in

a movement that felt like an embrace. The sensations became more intense, taking on a sort of insistence. Sensory offering, all fragments wanting completion. I began to get that besieged feeling I always got when a client was trying too hard.

Easy, I told him.

Mild wave of surprise from him. *But it's always this way.*

You're coming and going in all directions. Do you have a focus?

His mind went immediately to Revien Lam. I felt it instead of seeing it, but the thought was unmistakable. A memory of what it had been to share his presence, intense but dreamlike, something that might have happened only in his own imagination. And now a sensation of stretching out, reaching across a distance that might have been the span of a table or the emptiness of a universe, reaching for con

fall

fall

falling plummeting down a long tunnel and nothing nothing nothing tact.

In the distortion of mind time, it was over before it had begun. I might have lost consciousness. It seemed that way. I found myself at rest far above the terrain, in the upper, superficial layers of his sense-memory. His energy level was markedly diminished.

Always, he said. *Always like that. Without him.*

I reached down into him again but his mind was drifting now. It was like pushing into layer after layer of silk streamers floating in midair, and about as substantial. I could receive no clear impression of anything except fatigue. Quitting time.

Just before I withdrew, it came to me, a wisp from a wisp, an actual visual that lasted for half a thought-beat, if that long.

Revien Lam, at last, of course. With a wire winding out from one eyelid like the trail of a dark tear.

Jord Coor was more than happy to have me leave him alone. I wheeled my equipment down to the big, emptyish guest room (taking the ramps instead of that box of an elevator) and plugged into the long-term eidetic fixer. Reviewing a session so quickly – or, rather, reliving it – wasn't always the wisest thing to do in terms of wear and tear on the psyche, but I had to study this one.

It didn't take long for hindsight to kick in and show me what had been wrong with the whole session in the first place.

He had drawn me in so quickly on first contact that I hadn't consciously noticed – there had been no personality-identity barriers to pass through, not even so much as a mild mental fence.

Why hadn't I noticed, I wondered. Had I just assumed they'd been there the way they were in every other mind?

My professional reflexes spoke up, maddeningly in the voice of Nelson Nelson.

Think about it, Allie. Those barriers would have proved an inconvenience to him and Lam. My brain helpfully provided the image of his office, picturing him in working recline behind his desk. I began to get a psychosomatic itch. Gold lamé *And maybe that's your key, Deadpan. Help him build up his barriers again – help him by helping him resist your help.*

I'd never gone mind-to-mind with the old fox so it was rather unsettling to find I'd given him a position in my mind as a persona for self-dialog. But then, there was no one else. No one else appropriate, anyway.

Which just goes to show you, he/I went on, *that the most affecting contact isn't always mind-to-mind. Is it, kid?*

I disengaged in a hurry, itching to get away from him.

I let a day go by before the next session, hoping the breathing space would allow us both to regroup. But when we hooked in again, it was more of the same, more stew, more chaos, that long reach toward something followed by the fall and the weightless, drifty mind-state of exhausted semiconsciousness, or quasiconsciousness, or something.

'The blank spot,' Jord said after we unhooked. He was lying on the mat in the studio, blinking at the ceiling. 'The place where I used to compose. Nothing there any more.'

I had no intention of accepting that, but after three more sessions, I began to think I was licked. It was astounding just how little information I was getting from him. Most people's minds teem with associations, memories, and all the rest of the mental furniture that accrues during a lifetime. Stew notwithstanding, his seemed to be all put away or suppressed – I could receive only the briefest of impressions concerning episodes in his past that didn't involve Revien Lam. Did he really expect me to believe that for ten years there had been nothing in his life but composing with his partner?

In another few sessions, he might have convinced us both. Except that would have meant Big Obsession and there was none of that unmistakable, dangerous flavor in his mind.

Still, the only visual I could get from him was that same image of Revien Lam. Sometimes it was as static as the flat pictures I had showed him. Other times it was alive, the movements barely discernible, dreamlike but still there.

It was the lone visual that gave me the idea. Nelson Nelson would have advised against it, and five days before, I wouldn't have considered it myself. But we were falling into a feedback loop. If I could not shift him away from

the idea of Revien Lam as a missing part of himself, then perhaps Lam – the Lam in his mind – could serve to trigger new reactions.

'Just one eye this time,' I said, when-we began the fifth session.

He looked up at me from the mat. That studied expressionlessness left his face like a mask melting away, leaving behind naked panic.

'Why?'

'It could be helpful to use a method you're accustomed to.'

He almost flinched from the wire I held out to him; for a moment, I thought he would refuse. Then he took the connection, removed his left eye himself, and handed it to me.

I'd known doing a variation on the eye trick with him would result in a very different type of session, but even so, I wasn't prepared for the bizarreness of it. It was something like being awake and asleep at the same time, only much more so. More like being only partially in existence. I had to adjust my concentration radically and I wasn't sure that I hadn't asked too much of my mind. I might not have managed at all if it hadn't been for Jord Coor himself.

He fell easily into our configuration, his mind coming alive – *really* coming alive. He had no problem at all with the mix of textures. Mind and outer reality spilled over into each other for him, each one feeding the other. Now he could generate visuals, picking up little bits from his right eye. I saw myself as he saw me, a sort of professional mechanism sitting in a chair, steady, composed. The visual of Revien Lam oozed over into outer reality and shimmered in and out of being around me, a cross between a hallucination and a ghost. Sometimes it faded out on its own; sometimes Coor blotted it out. But the feel of him was always there, or rather, the feel that was the lack of him.

There was never any point of stability or equilibrium; he teetered back and forth between perceiving first the outside world and then the inside of his mind as dominant. The remaining eye remmed occasionally with dreams cannibalized both from actual vision and the mind, A keyboard that seemed to be a hybrid of the piano and the synthesizer spread out before us, a hallucinatory horizon. The keys sank as ghost hands danced on them. I couldn't tell whose hands they were; the music itself was inaudible.

Something new? I asked.

You cant hear it either? The right eye fixed on me momentarily. *I think it might be something Revien and I were working on before he … went.*

Can you turn up the volume?

But the keyboard was already gone. There was a sensation of movement forward, acceleration, and then outside reality paled. An image of Jord Coor appeared with his back to me, walking away.

Jord?

He paused and turned toward me slightly.

Where are we going?

The corner of his mouth twitched so realistically I almost forgot I was seeing a mental image. Very briefly, I had a glimpse of his face in the outer world, duplicating the movement.

Jord?

He began walking again. I traveled along in his wake, undecided as to whether I wanted to catch up with him. He kept glancing over his shoulder at me, always the left shoulder, his eye hard and too bright. We were moving through a landscape that I couldn't quite make out, except that it felt bleak and barren, a wasteland or badland, an old dream.

Eventually, I felt us descending. The landscape darkened and rose up canyonlike. No stew here; everything was locked away behind rock. Nothing grew here. You could wander around in it for the rest of your life with empty hands.

The landscape leveled off after a while and I could discern a lighter area ahead. The end of the wasteland, I thought. So basic and literal. I should have expected it in this man.

And then Jord himself was gone – or at least, his mental image of himself was missing, though a good portion of his concentration remained, urging me forward wordlessly. I didn't like the feel of it, but I went. There was no firm reason to pull back and I was curious. The undertones barely registered, as though he had managed to vanish and remain at the same time.

Abruptly, I was standing at the edge of an abyss. I waited. There was light coming up from somewhere.

Jord?

Far away, I caught a slight movement. Jord Coor and I faced each other across the chasm. His head was a blur. I looked around, trying to find something to cross the gap with.

Then the light grew brighter and I saw he was walking toward me on empty air.

No, not air; a bridge that formed itself under him with each step. Lunatic bridge.

Halfway across, he stopped. There was a long, frozen moment when nothing happened and it seemed as though nothing would. I leaned forward and saw him clearly for the first time.

The right side of his body was blank.

With no more thought than anyone would have given to inhaling, he yanked me to him.

It would have taken a lot more magnetism than he had to eat me alive but it was still a bumpy experience. Rather than pull back against him, I rushed down, through, and out the other side. His realized half brushed me like tentacles, not quick enough to latch on and incorporate me. A halfhearted

disappointment followed in cold waves as I kept moving, going back up the wire to break the link.

'I *am* sorry,' he said, for the fourth or fifth time.

'It's all right,' I told him while I puttered around with the system. I still felt off-balance, with a psychosomatic brownout in my right eye. So much for the eye trick. But it hadn't really been such a close call; subconsciously, I'd probably been prepared for an attempt at absorption. Still, it's rattling to have someone try to merge with you, change you into part of them, even if you have no affinity for it. 'You didn't hurt me.'

Jord fisted his left eye in a childlike way. 'I knew you weren't Revien, I really did. I knew it the whole time but I was going to take you anyhow.' He drew his legs up and rested his elbows on his knees. 'I guess I've been incomplete for so long, I'll take anyone.' No more of that careful expressionlessness now; all masks were off for good. I'd seen that look before, on people who had just realized how alone they really were in their own heads.

And in people who had discovered their lives weren't enough.

'He's got it, you know,' he said. 'Revien. He's got the other half of me. He *is* the other half of me now.'

We do indeed adore our delusions, I thought as I tested the connection he used. Still good. I didn't tell him he was mistaken. I could have talked at him for the rest of the day and most of the night and maybe have made him admit he might possibly be wrong, that he'd only atrophied and he really was complete, just unused to working alone. And the next time we hooked in, it would be the same thing all over again. I was going to have to get him to demonstrate things to himself.

But the only way I could do that was to get a different perspective on him and the old partnership. And that was something only Revien Lam could give me.

Nelson Nelson was grumpy about it. Or perhaps he was just irritated at having to interrupt his viewing of the Bolshoi to take my call. It amazed me that anyone could watch *Swan Lake* and *Coppélia* so often without tiring. Seeing him through his ceiling holo was unsettling; it felt like I was going to drop down on him and mash him into his itchy gold lamé.

'Sure, I can find Revien Lam for you. It'll take a little while, so you might want to use that time to work with your client a little more.'

'NN, the man tried to *eat* me. He's close to pathological in his insistence that Revien Lam either has half of his ability or is half of his ability. I've got to feel it from Lam's point of view.'

'Feel *what*?'

'The partnership. As it was. All I can get from Coor is an absence of

something and he tried to fill the absence with me. Granted, it wasn't the strongest effort in the world – I'd probably be hospitalized or something if it had been – but he still tried.'

'And you really think Revien Lam can help you, even indirectly?'

'It's more information than I can get from Coor and that's *got* to be helpful.'

NN actually harrumphed. 'Seems to me any pathosfinder worth her neurons ought to be able to delve someone skillfully enough to get all the information she needs. Or is it that you believe him?'

Apparently no one had ever tried to eat NN. Well, who would have wanted to actually *be* that old fox anyway? 'Any pathosfinder worth her neurons also knows when to back off from her client and find her data elsewhere,' I said evenly. 'My man's on the defensive. The only way I can reach him effectively is to show him I've got the information he's hiding from himself. And the only way I can get it is from Revien Lam.'

We stared at each other through our respective screens. To be fair, I think I had the upper hand, literally – it's hard to stare someone down when you're lying flat on your back.

'I'll have Lam's location for you in a couple of hours. But I still think you're wrong. And what are you going to tell Coor?'

'I'll think of something. The truth is always good.' I switched off before he could object.

Actually, I had no intention of telling Coor the truth, or at least not the whole truth. A lie would have been pointless and cruel, since he'd have felt Lam's impression when we hooked in again. I could hide plenty from him, but he knew what Lam's mind felt like firsthand.

I ended up telling him I was giving us both a couple days' thinking space. There was a certain amount of truth in that. He surprised me by being disappointed and apprehensive rather than relieved. I'd thought he would have appreciated the respite.

It wasn't until I was on my way to upstate New York that I realized he'd just gotten used to having me around. Sometimes it didn't do a lonely person any good to keep him company. Another entry to the list of things I should have known.

That Revien Lam had chosen to alight in an area not terribly far from his ex-collaborator wasn't so surprising. It would figure that they'd prefer similar geographical areas, in spite of Lam's continuing struggle for differentiation. But where Jord Coor was living completely alone in an underground enclosure, Lam had opted for the Park.

I'd heard of the Park, though I'd never been there before. It was a sort of continuously running circus/ picnic/freakshow/camp for those who didn't

want the party to end. The Park population, which varied from week to week, roamed freely over a few hundred acres of weather-shielded country-side, eating, sleeping, and playing as the spirit moved them. There were no clocks, no calendars, few rules. Violence was punishable by immediate, per-manent expulsion, but other than that, the Park people did as they pleased. It was probably the best way to lose all touch with reality short of buying a psychosis.

A lot of people tried to lose themselves in the Park for just that reason. Some could and some couldn't; the rest, the hard-core Park People, would have been lost anywhere. The Park just kept them from cluttering up the rest of the world.

I wondered what Revien Lam's motivation had been for signing himself into the land of silk and funny. Whatever it was, I was willing to bet it had something to do with wanting superficial contact with lots of people. Ten years of extreme intimacy was the sort of thing that could give a person a real appreciation for the superficial.

My first glimpse of the Park was shortly before sunset from the air, in the back seat of a flyer while the pilot snored behind the stick. Tents and pavil-ions dotted the rolling green landscape while people streamed among them like currents of confetti. The Park wasn't an easy place to find someone, but NN's office had contacted a guide for me, to help me find Revien Lam. I wondered how I was supposed to find the guide.

The pilot snored through the landing, leaving me to unload my own equip-ment at the front gates of the Park. People accumulated along the flimsy fence to watch me, drifting over like colorful bits of cloth blown by an idle wind. It was an amazingly quiet audience – no chatter, no laughter, hardly a whisper. Maybe, I thought, they'd all just gotten up. Or had yet to go to bed. Or sleep, anyway. The faces, mostly dyed or polished or both, weren't solemn. A few of them looked apprehensive, some even envious (of what, I won-dered). Most of them had what I could already identify as a 'Park Look,' as distinct as the sound of a regional accent in a voice. Had Revien Lam traded in his likeness to Jord Coor for a facial uniform worn by a multitude?

I wheeled my equipment up to an ornate little kiosk at the entrance. There was no one inside, no bell to ring for service, and no indication that I should either wait for someone to take charge of me or just go in by myself.

I looked left and right at my audience lining the fence. They stared back, unmoved. I thought of cows. Finally, a man with a stiff fringe of apple-red hair detached himself from the group on my right and ambled over. He almost stopped, his gold starburst eyes looking me and my equipment over critically. Somehow, I had failed to measure up as anything sufficiently inter-esting to make him stop.

'Excuse me,' I called after him.

He turned in slow motion without actually ceasing to wander away.

'How do I go about finding someone in here?'

His expression said I was sixteen different kinds of fool. 'You look around.' He moved into a loose gaggle of men and women on their way to a tall green tent.

No one else along the fence showed any inclination to come forward and offer any hints, suggestions, or hellos. I moved my equipment further inside the entrance, trying not to feel overly conspicuous. A laughing group of people playing some kind of game with big balloons materialized and surrounded me, allowing me to be part of their playing field briefly before they gamboled away, shedding one of the balloons. It bounced gently at my feet and I picked it up.

'That was an invitation,' said a female voice behind me. I turned around.

You see it all, eventually; all the ways people play with their bodies. Dye-jobs, bleach-jobs, certain kinds of transplants, alterations that border on mutilation. You see people displaying just about anything of themselves, but this was something that could have been an image straight out of someone's troubled head, come down the wires of a mindplay system and into outer reality to be made flesh. Sort of flesh.

She let me stare at her. From a distance, I might have thought she was wearing a very close-fitting helmet that ended a few inches above her eye-brow's, with her long hair hanging out from underneath. But up close, it was too easy to see her skull was made of glass.

Well, not real glass, of course, but something transparent. It was nauseating and fascinating all at once. There are certain kinds of minds a pathosfinder should refuse to enter; I was fairly sure this was one of them.

'I was a pathosfinder once,' she said.

Surprise number two. 'You must be my guide.' It would be hard not to choke NN for this when I saw him again.

'I'd have known you were a pathosfinder anyway. Just by that look on your face. All pathosfinders get that look. Even the ones named Deadpan Allie.'

'What look is that?'

'Like you're trying to see through solid objects.' She caressed her transparent skull with her fingers. 'Watch out. This is what you're headed for.' Her young-old face showed a peculiar mix of remembrance and mild aversion. 'It's what you're really after, you know. Letting everyone dip into your head, dipping into everyone else's. What makes you think anyone'll have need or desire for you in here?'

'I thought my office explained.'

'They did.'

I could have sworn her brain changed color, flushed. 'Then, you do know where I can find Revien Lam.'

'In a way. Once we get to him, you'll have to figure out how to find him on your own.'

I nodded, thinking she must have been a pretty lousy pathosfinder.

Her lips stretched in a hard smile. 'Only because of the telepathy. Mindplaying activated it, since you didn't ask.' She patted her skull again delicately, the way other people smoothed their hair. 'I'm used to receiving thoughts. It's made me a different person. Many different people.' Her right lobe swelled slightly. 'Do you know how many different people you are? Or have you stopped counting?' She frowned. 'Well. Never mind. I'll take you to Revien Lam. He's one of the tent people. It's a long walk.'

An hour later, I knew for certain she hadn't been gassing about that. I plodded after her, struggling with my system. You want to feel really awkward, push eight components of a supposedly portable mindplay system on a dolly through a free-form gathering like the Park, where the most anyone has in the way of encumbrance is a toy or something to eat. I took to reading Emotional Indices at random, including some of the balloonatics, who reappeared twice more to make an invitation.

There were a lot of anxious people in the Park, just from what I could tell by sight. It was catching; I could feel it beginning to chew at me around the edges. Glass-Skull (I realized belatedly she'd never told me her name) seemed unaffected by it, for all of her telepathy. She marched through groups lounging on the grass or milling around aimlessly or spilling in and out of the carnival-colored tents which apparently dispensed food, toys, and other kinds of amusements, just for the asking. The daily charge for living in the Park had to be fairly high. You just never think there are that many rich people in the world.

My guide didn't slow down until we reached the shore of a small lake in the center of a lightly wooded area. On the other side, I saw a collection of the standard multicolored tents with the standard multicolored people passing in and out of them in the eternal quest for diversion. Glass-Skull gazed at them across the quiet water while I shifted from one tired foot to the other.

'Would you like me to tell you what you're thinking?' she asked without looking at me.

I shrugged.

She laughed and led me along a dirt path around the pond, pausing again at the outskirts of the tent grouping.

'Which one is he in?' I asked, since she didn't seem disposed to go any farther.

'The largest one,' she said, pointing to a red tent trimmed with gold braid and tassels. 'It's a sort of dormitory, so you won't have any privacy. Except, of course, in your own mind. A luxury some of us wouldn't be able to stand

even if we were capable of having it.' She put her hand on my arm as I was about to wheel my equipment forward. The contact was electric; I felt my mind jump in response. Being touched by a telepath is always a jolt.

'You can go on by yourself.' She let go and stepped back, and I was relieved to have her pressure fade from my brain.

The tent wasn't exactly crowded but there was an aroma of healthy bodies, or a healthy aroma of bodies, that made the air heavy and close. It reminded me less of a dormitory than it did of some kind of ward that had been abandoned by its keepers. I left my equipment just inside the entrance and took a walk around, stepping over the people strewn about. Two men and a woman invited me to join what seemed to be a complicated game of marbles – played, I noticed undelightedly, with biogem eyes – and burst into high laughter when I declined. A baby-faced woman with wiry metallic hair and silver eyes pressed an orange into my hand. I dropped it surreptitiously on my other side and maneuvered between a man who was tattooing something upside-down on his naked chest and the woman who was dictating it to him.

I knew Lam immediately. His natural skin tone was just beginning to come back from the bleaching but his flesh still looked tight and stretched, too delicate for exposure to direct sunlight. He was lying on a scatter of pillows as though he'd been tossed there, head thrown back and eyes closed. I stood over him awkwardly.

'Revien Lam?' I had to say his name twice before he raised his head slowly and looked at me.

My first thought was that he'd had a stroke. The two sides of his face seemed to have little to do with each other. Each eye perceived me independently, traveling over my face in separate patterns. Then he covered his right eye and said, 'Do you know me?' The words came out with an effort – *Do. You. Know. Me.*

'Not exactly. I know Jord Coor.'

'Ah.' He covered his left eye, surveyed me briefly with the right again, and went back to looking at me with his left. I knew, then. I moved up to crouch at his left side and put my lips close to his ear.

'When did you have it cut?'

'*Cut.*' His mouth worked silently. I'd have to be more specific.

'When did you have your corpus callosum severed?'

'Cut. *Cut.* Three months after Jord cut. After we cut. Cut ourselves apart.' The words came a little more quickly now, as though he were getting back into the practice of speaking out loud. His head turned and the sapphire eye glittered at me. 'You are –?'

'I'm a pathosfinder working for Jord Coor.'

He turned his head all the way toward me and let his right eye have a look. 'Music,' he said, and hummed a little.

'You've had your visual fields rechanneled, too, haven't you?'

He went back to looking with the left eye alone. 'Completely divided. Right up the middle. Complete sep. Aration. Two brains from one. What the hell, it's company.'

'Company?'

'Company. Not so lonely in here with the two halves. See, completely divided, *but*. One final cord. One *spinal* cord, still. I can feel each other.'

We're schizophrenic and so are we, as Jerry Wirerammer had said once, inaccurate but witty. 'Is there someplace we can go to talk?'

He waved one hand clumsily. 'I live here. Nobody cares.'

'I'd like to delve you. If you'd give permission.'

'Permission.' He nodded. 'But still can't go outside. Skin. Even after dark. Wind hurts sometimes. But really, nobody cares in here.'

If those were my choices, those were my choices. 'Would you be willing to hook in with me?'

He frowned and went to his right eye. 'Repeat?'

He must have been one of those people whose verbal and comprehension skills were spread over both hemispheres like birdshot. 'Would you be willing to hook into my system with me –' I pointed to it over by the tent entrance, 'meet me mind-to-mind?'

Back to the left eye. 'Which mind did you want to meet?'

'Either. Both, if possible.'

He gave me a funny little smile, a composite smile from two faces. 'Do our best. Haven't been delved since the split, without Jord, eye to eye. To eye.'

As it were. I went to get my system.

It must have been about the strangest place I'd ever set up, but nobody, including Revien Lam, paid much attention to me while I went about my business. He went back to daydreaming or dozing or whatever it was he did with his two hemispheres. As soon as I was ready to go, however, I found myself with a sudden dilemma. Did I hook in with him one eye at a time or both together? I considered asking him and then decided not to. Depending on which hemisphere took the question, the answer might be different. I went for the left eye first, removing it for him and plugging him into the same tonal exercise I'd used on Coor.

I put my hands up to my own eyes and paused. Now, what about me? Should I use both eyes or just one – and if only one, *which* one? I ended up removing both. Since I had no idea of what I was going to find in there, it was probably best to go at it with all my concentration.

The tones translated to this half of his brain as his own voice singing syllables – *la, la, la, da, da, da.* The visualization was weak and fuzzy but I could make out his image of himself as a creature with a big head and a

negligible body. The head was stretched and distorted at the top, too wide, forcing the eyes to look in two different directions. The left eye was bigger than the right.

The syllables suddenly became words. *It got so lonely,* he sang. *I never knew it could be that lonely. A peculiar thing. The nature of attachment and disconnection. The top of his head stretched wider. One and one equal one, sooner or later. Couldn't let that happen, we knew it. Merge into one person and we'd never sort him from me. But so lonely. Now I feel the ghost of his essence – or the essence of his ghost.*

I cast around some but I couldn't feel it in all the fuzziness.

Other side, he said.

I unplugged just long enough to switch the connection to his right eye and give that side a minute with the tonal. Then I went back down the wires.

It really was like entering a different mind. The personality barrier here was thicker than the one I'd gone through when he'd been hooked in through his left eye.

The moment I pushed through, I heard them – seagulls. The same ones Jord Coor had had, singing the tones. I lost my equilibrium and found myself sprawled belly-down on sand, the damp grains rough against me. The sunlight was nearly blinding. A very well-realized wave grazed my fingers.

Revien?

The tonal faded away and the beach went with it. I pulled myself together just as the abyss formed. Lam had me floating disembodied over it, like a dream observer.

Whose abyss is this? I asked the empty air.

Ours, came the answer from below me.

The image was beyond absurdist, impossible. A chasm could not have just one side or a bridge that connected that side with itself. My inner eyes crossed, uncrossed, crossed again; the visual steadied down, translating into a Möbius strip. A composite of Coor and Lam was standing on it.

This is where I live now, the composite said, touching Coor's dark hair on the left side and pressing Lam's cheek on the right. *Hidden away like the bastard child I am. I'm even still composing music, but he can't get at it.* Just beyond the composite, a pale image of Revien Lam shimmered in and out of existence; Lam's awareness leaking through from the other side via the spinal cord (final cord).

Why can't he get at the music? I asked.

Other side. Have to send it to the other side for it to come out.

But if Coor's composing ability is really here, you should be able to express music using this side alone.

Not outwardly. The ability to express is not what he left here. Only the ability to compose.

And your own ability to compose? Is that here, too? There was no answer. *Lam's ability*, I clarified.

Yes. You can see that, can't you?

Then you're not two opposite halves rejoined. You're the same side, superimposed. You're congruent, not complemented.

The composite wavered. *Coor is the complement to Lam. The congruence is complement.*

No, I said reasonably, *if you were hooked in through opposite eyes –*

I stopped. I'd forgotten that in a normal, undivided brain, the optic nerves fed equally into both hemispheres, not right into right and left into left, the way they did in Lam's mutilated organ. The notion that maybe Coor wasn't deluded about Lam having a portion of himself crept up on me, and I wondered belatedly what would have happened if I'd hooked into Coor through his right eye rather than his composing eye.

I was moving forward to examine the composite more closely when the visual cracked like a whip. For something like an eternity or a thought-beat, everything was jumbled and whirling. Then it all came back into ultra-sharp focus and I was standing on the edge of the abyss, where I'd been in Jord Coor's mind. No more Möbius strip – there was a real bridge across the chasm with three figures on it: the composite, Revien Lam, and Jord Coor. The *real* Jord Coor, blank on the right side, not a delusory presence. He was right there with us, in the Park, in the tent, in Revien Lam's mind.

Why hadn't it occurred to me that he would follow me, that he would suspect what I'd been up to? That he might even have been hoping I'd do it, or even pushed me into it, just to sneak up on both of us mind-to-mind?

Withdrawal and disconnection would take too long. I rushed toward them but it was already happening. They each had hold of the composite and were pulling at it, stretching it like heat-softened rubber. The whole visual shuddered and bucked, pushing me back.

This is between us! Jord said hostilely, and I wasn't sure whom he was talking to.

You have no right! Lam hurled repulsion at him and somehow managed to draw him closer. *Mine now! Mine!*

You stole it!

You forced me to take it! You gave it up willingly!

I strained toward the bridge and they almost merged in their joint effort to knock me away. I backed off quickly.

You're part of me now, whether you wanted it or not, whether I wanted it or not! Lam said.

I have a right to be whole!

The composite between them was becoming a shapeless blob.

You refused to be whole, you gave away, said Lam.

Not gave. You just couldn't give back. You sucked it all without giving in return! You wanted to be part of me, the better to love yourself!

Then, that's how it is, Jord said. *We've both been after the same thing all along – you want me and I want me.*

The composite suddenly swelled and enveloped both of them. A million images spewed from the bridge, scenes from their respective pasts, now juxtaposed, double exposures. I pulled back even further. There was just one figure on the bridge now; it kept shimmering and changing. Sometimes it was all Coor, then all Lam, then various mixtures of the two, Lam dominant, Coor dominant, both equal. Shimmer. Melt. Change.

I withdrew, put my eyes back in, and without looking at the two limp bodies still hooked into my system, went outside and vomited into the grass.

'I did warn you,' Glass-Skull said. She wiped my face with something damp. 'How many different people are you?'

I looked up at her, still trying to pull myself together enough to call NN and ask him if this meant my license had just been voided.

She smiled. 'Go ahead. Think about it. Everything you've done. The institute. The pool. A little bit of one mind here, a little of another there.'

McFloy on the beach. McFloy doing the eye trick.

'It's more than being modified,' Glass-Skull said. 'You're transformed. You're polluted, stained, dyed, altered. And you will never be the same.' She rubbed her head gently. I swear I saw her brain writhe in its transparent case.

I leaned forward and vomited again.

ALERTED SNAKES OF CONSEQUENCE

I had no memory of being taken from the Park. My mind spliced outer reality to my very mental life without segue, just like a scene-change. Freeze on our heroine; ten years later, we pick up her story.

But it wasn't ten years, not that I knew the difference at the time. I didn't know anything at all, outer, inner, or in between. Eventually, or something, I found myself looking at a familiar face.

Are you lucid yet?

Forget it, I told Jascha. *Lucid dreaming, lucid living – forget it, just forget all of it.*

I was sitting on the techno-bed in his office, watching the sun come up over the bay. He was standing near the lavabo, looking at a monitor.

Every time you think you're doing it, something else comes up on you and changes everything. It's like old Glass-Skull said. You get changed, altered. Polluted. That's a good word, polluted. Jerry Wirerammer, now there was an idea. He was one of the polluters as well as a pollutee, but he was more, of a polluter. Not like me. And he never got me. But you did. Every time you fed my dreams, Jascha, you fed me a little of yourself. I can prove it.

He tilted his gilded head to the side. Jascha was the only person I knew who could really wear gilt without looking overdressed and overpriced.

I can prove it because you're in here. I think, therefore you are. You think, therefore I am.

Something moved on the bed; a Snake rose up to attention like a cobra, but it wasn't a cobra.

Alerted Snake of Consequence. I said it right this time, didn't I, Pyotr Frankis? I looked over at him, sitting behind his desk, nodding at me with a funny little smile. *But where are the rest of them? All the Alerted Snakes Of Consequence, they should all be here now. It's time. Good thing we're not Freudians, isn't it?*

The Snake moved a little closer without having moved. Or maybe it was my perspective that had shifted. *Deadpan Allie,* the Snake said. *But not terribly, I'd say.* The Snake bore a resemblance to Paolo Segretti. *Not terribly deadpan right now.*

It's my state of existence, I'll take a break if I want to. I looked down over he right side of the bed. There was a Snake on the floor next to the futon, not coiled but in a Snakey impression of a person lying on his side resting on one elbow with one knee drawn up. They were talented, these Snakes, but then, they'd have to be.

You're taking all this so hard, said the Snake. *What's the problem? What's the real problem?*

The real problem, I began emphatically, *the real problem is …*

Some kind of immense time went by, something long enough for dinosaurs to live and die in. The Pearl Necklace went by with it, the pearls passing like compartments on a nonstop northbound tube.

We've already covered that, Jascha said reasonably. *You're the accumulation of everything you've done. No problem there.*

No, now wait a minute here, I said.

Where?

Here, dammit, here!

Oh, you mean here.

I was looking around my old efficiency at J. Walter. The LadyBugs were on the dataline, looking vibrant and identical. Except they also looked a little like Snakes, too. *We're just fighting for our right to be different by being identical,* said the one on the right. *What are you fighting for?* asked the one on the left.

I'm fighting for my right to be not interfered with.

The LadyBugs were replaced on the screen with the Twins, Dolby and Dolan, Tweedledoo and Tweedledah. Tweedledoodah. *Aren't you compatible with yourself?*

Depends on who you ask, hey, Allie? said Pyotr Frankis, standing next to me.

Well, don't ask me, I said. The Twins gave way to Jerry Wirerammer.

Heya, Allie.

I turned away from the dataline and found myself facing the desert where Pyotr Frankis and I had walked together after I'd had Kitta Wren dry-cleaned out of me. *That was the turning point,* I said. *Kitta Wren. Up until her, I wasn't having any trouble. The punchy holographer, the Dancing Barbanos, the performance artist – none of them got to me. Got into me, I mean.*

No?

The Dancing Barbanos were performing an airy dance just above the horizon like a mirage. It seemed to be a Virginia reel in demishawn.

Not the way she did.

But it's gone. Dry-cleaned out, said Jascha.

But he isn't.

Why can't you just say your love for him isn't? Why can't you just admit that and be done with it?

Because he did the eye trick. It was the eye trick, not love.

A phantom beach, ghost waves moving over the dry desert sand. *I love your life, Allie. I love you.* The beach was gone; all the Snakes were lined up in front of me like limber sticks.

Alerted Snakes Of Consequence, one of them said.

You've got to watch out for us, said another.

When you love somebody –

Don't, I said.

Why not? It isn't trivial.

You bet it's not. Because that's right where he is. I locked it up in the cathedral, and if you say it, it gets out, and if it gets out, he gets out, and I can't have that. They're not supposed to call me Deadpan Allie for nothing.

Just like that, I was standing in front of the cathedral. The carving on the front door was a portrait of Fandango. *You know what a mindplayer is without a personal life?* she said. The portrait melted and changed into Jerry Wirerammer. *How about a personal life with no mind-player?*

And then I was inside, leaning against the door. Pyotr Frankis waved to me from an open panel at the bottom of one of the stained-glass windows. The window design showed a woman lying on a futon looking at a row of pills and spansules and other things. The window next to it was a depiction of the same woman with the top half of her head covered by a madcap, as a

man with a goofy smile looked on. The bottom panel popped open and Paolo Segretti's round face beamed at me. *There's only room for you in here*, he said.

That's what you think, I told him. *The rules change when they change and everything is true unless it isn't.*

Truth and information are not the same thing, said my great-grandmother's portrait.

I looked at the table below the portrait. The eye struck sparks of light like small fireworks. If it gets out, he gets out –

But he'd gotten out once. After I'd dry-cleaned out the last of Kitta Wren, when I'd been in the desert with Pyotr Frankis. Not just part of myself, somebody else. The entity McFloy, along for the ride because his own life hadn't been enough. All he'd been interested in was my mind.

If you try to cast it out, you'll end up crippling yourself.

All right, then, so I don't cast it out. I lock it up for good. Except once in a while, it gets out by itself. *He* gets out by *himself.*

I love your life, Allie. I love you.

So who asked him to? He'd come to me with the eye, I hadn't gone looking for him.

What's so bad about that? asked the Snake, tracing the pattern of the meditation mandala on the floor in front of me. *Maybe it's better to be half of something wonderful than a whole nothing at all.*

Half or nothing shouldn't be the only choices! It wasn't fair! They had a chance to live apart, to learn to be separate again but he followed me, Coor followed me to the Park and he barged in and Lam didn't have a chance after that …

Jascha shook his head. *Then, it fits their configuration to be one instead of two. For shame, Allie. Is that why you wanted them to be apart? Were you pathosfinding them in terms of yourself? That's not very deadpan. That's not deadpan at all.*

For a moment, I reeled with uncertainty and the whole cathedral swayed with me. Then I steadied. *No. I wasn't imposing myself on them. But I wanted to learn how to separate myself from him.*

Jascha picked the eye up and looked at it. *But it's part of you. How can you separate yourself from yourself?* And then, before I could think to stop him, he raised his hand and hurled the eye at me.

I fled, through the countryside I'd first come to with Segretti, through the big room where I'd sat with Pyotr Frankis, past the river where we'd walked, past the bench where McFloy had drowned himself, into the desert again where undecipherable green glass symbols were burned into the sand. The Snakes paced me, wriggling along faster than snakes should have been able to travel.

Are you going to use it? asked one of the Snakes.

It's not supposed to be possible, for someone else to be resident in your mind, I said as I ran. *Not for real.*

Real? In which reality did you mean?

This one. That one. Whatever one we may find ourselves in. I was beginning to tire but I kept slogging through the sand, not daring to look over my shoulder. The state of my existence –

It's your state of existence, the Snake said, *but it's my reality. And that's the truth.*

Truth and information are not the same thing! I said. *And neither are reality and state of existence!*

xxxxxxxxxxxxxxxxxxxxxxxxxxxxxxx.

Green fireworks burst out over the sky. *Brava!* Pyotr Frankis from somewhere. *Olé!. Revelation is beautiful, isn't it?*

My energy gave out. I fell to my knees in the sand. The green glass symbols were gone. Pyotr Frankis smiled down benignly from where he floated in the sky. *Do you see now?* he asked. *Do you see that even though you alter yourself, you alter as yourself?*

In my own way.

Who else's way could it be?

Choose: Half of something wonderful or a whole nothing at all.

Choose: A whole self, or just an accumulation of elements that soon wouldn't be more than the sum of their parts. Madness. Fragmentation. Jerry Wirerammer.

They came in a series of flashes, a thought-beat long and an eternity, framed by the graceful Snakes: Marty and Sudella (she was applauding with her eyes closed); Kitta Wren, dissolving; Gladney-that-was and Gladney-that-had-been, fusing. And finally, the figure on the Lunatic Bridge, shimmering and changing as it displayed all the aspects of Coor and Lam together.

Realities. States of existence. They can coincide, but they can never truly meet. Reality fluctuates, but existence is. Or is *not*.

I turned around to face the eye. McFloy was standing there.

Still here, Allie. Still with you.

Which one of us, McFloy? Which one of us is which?

He smiled. *Yes.*

I wasn't sure who actually said it, but it didn't matter. The holo I'd kept of Jerry Wirerammer appeared briefly. *It's a strange existence, but it works.* And then there were just the Snakes, dancing in the air, cutting curlicues and Möbius strips with their perfect bodies.

You will go down into darkness before you die –

Light, I thought.

– but you won't go alone.

'Light!' I yelled.

LIGHT

NN visited me every day in the hospital. He always showed up at mealtimes, relentlessly cheerful, applying the nutrient patch to my arm himself and chattering away about only the most innocuous things. He didn't bring up what had happened until I reached the point where I could keep down somewhat substantial fluids, but he was very brisk and all business when he did.

I was about to have my noontime frappé when he lit on the edge of my bed and said, 'You know, in a way, it's always been true that we're made of all the lives we've ever touched. Even before mindplay.'

I set the frappé aside. 'Thanks. Let me write that down somewhere. Or are you recording?'

'Now really, Allie, what's so alarming about that?'

I glowered at him. 'I'm trying to adjust. It isn't easy on the gut level out here. Do I look like a boardinghouse to you?'

Nelson Nelson picked up the frappé and stirred it with the straw. 'I don't understand. The readings said you were so happy at the very end there.'

'What "very end" where?'

'When you called for light. Very unusual, you know, for someone hooked into reality affixing to speak aloud. Almost impossible, they say.'

'*That* was a reality affixing?'

'Don't look at me. It was your reality.' NN offered me the frappé. I pushed it away. '*Allie.* Think straight for a minute. As a personal favor to me. What's so terrible about your reality?'

'We're not discussing my reality, we're talking about my state of existence. I *said*, do I look like a boarding-house to you?'

'Well.' NN shrugged. 'You're as Allie as you ever were. Maybe not so Deadpan at the moment, but we'll make allowances for trauma, and that's all it is, you know.

'You saw something bizarre happen to a couple of weak people and you were in mind-to-mind contact with them when it happened and it triggered your own unresolved dilemma.'

'That's not supposed to happen! I've been dry-cleaned, I've been reality affixed, I've been trained –'

'*Please.* The mind is a very capricious thing! You've begun talking about it as though it were a suit of clothes. You think you can have that much control over it? *Please.* You want to dry-clean out the most Allie parts of yourself? Affix your reality so the neurons line up like little soldiers?' NN looked down at the frappé and then set it aside. '*Please.* You're making me *sick*.'

I looked down at my hands, which had fallen folded together on the sheet. 'They aren't weak.'

'Pardon?'

'Coor and Lam. They aren't weak people. The Lady Bugs are weak people but not Coor and Lam.'

'Oh.' NN was mollified. 'Well, you would know better than I. You delved them. Coor and Lam, I mean. But, uh, I would like to know how you came to that conclusion.'

'The Lady Bugs wanted to *be* changed. Coor and Lam *did* change. By their own actions. They tried to deny it for a while and then they *were* weak. But when they came together in the system –' I shrugged. 'It's not really so surprising that Coor followed me to Lam. Maybe he didn't even really have to follow me. Maybe Lam was drawing him all along, and when I finally went to him Coor had to follow. Maybe they'd have gotten together sooner or later. I just made it sooner than it might have been otherwise. They're not suing us, are they?'

NN shook his head.

'Didn't think they would. Coor and Lam might have, but not Coor-and-Lam –' I stopped. The thought burst on me all at once. Coor and Lam. *Cœur et l'Âme.* They hadn't started out that way, but the potential had been there all along. Some people resonate. Whether they know it or not. Whether they believe it or not.

I sighed. Was I going to have to adjust on every level of reality?

Maybe. NN was right. I had been pretty happy toward the end of the reality affixing – who had done it, anyway? I concentrated, feeling for a trace in my mind. The agency's system, of course; it was the only one I'd ever worked with that didn't have a facade personality. Good thing, too. I hadn't needed one more character running around in the system with me, confusing things. There was just room enough for me and McFloy, and the other pieces of our life adding up to more than the sum of our parts.

It's hard to adjust to that, said a silent voice in my head. Taking the next step.

I remembered that figure on the misnamed Lunatic Bridge, the third person that was Coor-and-Lam.

It's no wonder you didn't want to take it. But you did. You're not the Allie you were. But you *are* Allie just the same. So, all things considered, you have a right to post-mindplay depression. Or is that postpartum?

That's funny, I thought, I don't feel like a mother. Or a child. Why am I lying here in bed talking to myself like I'm somebody else?

I looked over at NN and felt myself grinning. He leaned forward and frowned at me slightly. 'What are you grinning about?'

Nothing I couldn't live with. The state of my existence. And sometimes it was real. 'Just something someone gave me once. A point of view, as it were.'

'"As it were." Deadpan goes hysterical, then cryptic. You probably wouldn't even tell me the truth as to whether you've been divorced or not.'

I would call Jascha as soon as the old fox left me in peace. It was nothing we couldn't live with.

'I've never been divorced,' I said. 'Never in my life.'

'There's a good Deadpan.' NN picked up the frappé and shoved the straw between my lips just as the door opened and Jascha walked in, looking gilded and worried and real.

Sometimes things happen that make people start resonating with each other. Thank you, McFloy.

'Now, suck,' NN said, 'take it all in.' And I did.

FOOLS

*This one is for
George and Marguerite Fenner,
my parents-in-law,
with love and thanks*

Special thanks to:

Sheila Williams, Gardner Dozois and Susan Casper, Ellen Datlow, Cheryl Cordes, Jim Cappio, Dwight Brown, Lawrence Person, Glen Cox and Jill Engel, David Garnett and Frances Jobling, Mike Resnick, Malcolm Edwards, Merrilee Heifetz, Beth Meacham, Lisa Tallarico-Robertson, Jeannie Hund, and the Delphi Wednesday Night Irregulars.

An additional round of thank-yous to Jim Brunet, Allen Varney, Laurie Mann, Carl Fink, Larry 'Wombat' Hammer, Katherine Lawrence, Lenny Bailes, Tappan King, Connie Hirsch, Rick Wilber, and Nathan/EVPA, for their suggestions and commentary about word-processors.

PART I

Fool to Remember

Everywhere I looked in Davy Jones' Locker, I saw me, or people who wanted to be me. And the club wasn't even half full yet. I knew I was going to love being Famous.

The holo fish floating through the deep blue holo water flickered, vanished, and then reappeared more vividly than before. I could relate; I'd just flickered into existence myself, it felt like. A small price to pay for being Famous, these little lapses. Happened whenever I had to fine-tune the system, nothing terribly serious. All I had to do was give myself a few minutes to get oriented, take a few deep breaths, and it would all come back to me. It always did.

I caught sight of my new manager on the other side of the club, talking to some of the employees. I gave him a cheery wave to cover the fact that I could not, at that moment, remember his name. Post-mindplay amnesia can be *so* embarrassing.

He froze in midgesture, both hands spread in front of him, and stared at me as if I had two heads or something. Migod, I thought, what was *his* drama? Had I come out too early, should I have still been in back putting on another coat of paint for La Grande Entrance later?

I gave a big, exaggerated shrug à la Constanzia, the role I had just finished playing at Sir Larry's. It would have been just like Constanzia to jump the gun this way – maybe I could blame it on leak-through. For all I knew, it *was* leak-through. My manager started to take a step toward me and one of the employees pulled at his sleeve. I was pleased to see that she had already been made over with the Look, though I doubted she had been enfranchised completely. It wouldn't have been much like me to be serving refreshments in a club, even a club like Davy Jones' Locker.

She said something to my manager and then pointed toward the back room. He looked torn, turning from her to me and back again, long white hair swinging with the movement. I made a dismissing gesture to tell him that he didn't have to worry about me right now and went for a stroll to admire the decor. I'd been to Davy Jones' plenty of times, but tonight, it was all mine, hired for the debut. My manager certainly knew what would make

me happy. I was going to have to figure out some way to keep his name from melting out of my memory all the time. It was the least I could do.

The club was starting to fill up now, but for some reason, nobody seemed to notice me wandering around. Maybe because I wasn't really dressed up – I still had on my street clothes, which were as nondescript as a person could get and still remain visible. Well, I'd just have to rely on my manager or my valets or both to drag me back to the dressing room at the proper time. After all, what was the point of being Famous if you couldn't leave the little details to the people who were supposed to take care of them?

On the other side of the main room, the funhouse mirror was already running and drawing a crowd, so I decided to go over and have a fast look. Once the party really got going, they'd be lined up half a dozen deep and climbing all over each other for a turn in front of it.

An oyster bed faded into existence in front of me on the floor. The jeweled shells opened to disgorge pearls that rolled into the golden sand. It was very pretty, but I'd seen it about a million times before. Not so much pearls as chestnuts; I'd have thought I rated something a little less overexposed. I tiptoed through it so as not to spoil the illusion. Hackneyed or not, there was no reason to be rude.

I was a good ten feet away from the mirror when I suddenly got the strangest urge to turn around and run for the nearest exit as fast as I could. More than an urge – it might have been some kind of inner alarm going off. Mi*god*, I thought, I wasn't getting one of those tiresome body-image problems where you get all mirror-phobic and start starving yourself, was I? I'd heard that sometimes happened to people after they became Famous – something about seeing yourself in so many different places that you developed some kind of aversion. I'd have thought that I would have been the last person to suffer from something like that.

Then I saw the more likely explanation for my sudden case of dread – i.e., Em-Cate, big as life and twice as gruesome. She was actually *preening* in front of the mirror, admiring her reflection, which had come up as a silvery-white shark. Typecast again, I thought, feeling nasty. Why on earth had she come here? She'd known as well as I had that the invitation had been only a formality. I couldn't imagine Em-Cate wishing me well under these circumstances or any others. There had never been any love lost between us at Sir Larry's but now that I was going to be Famous and she wasn't, she had dropped all pretense and had been openly displaying her revulsion for me.

Well, the timing on this thing could have been a lot better, too. My manager could have made the franchiser wait until I'd finished with the role at Sir Larry's before announcing I was under contract. But the contract with the franchiser wasn't going to interfere with the play – I had promised Sir Larry's. Of course, as soon as the last performance was over, I'd be lucky to get fifteen

minutes to gather up my personal belongings and clear out, probably with Em-Cate dogging my every step to make sure I didn't make off with something that belonged to the theatre. And like what – a jar of pancake, for God's sake?

Professional jealousy was a monster. I hoped to *God* that it would never happen to me. I liked to think that if they'd gone for Em-Cate instead of me, I'd have been big enough to hold my nose, grit my teeth, and say, *Congratulations*. Or maybe just *Good-bye and good luck*. Or, okay: *Good-bye*.

She'd been such a pig about things that I would have sworn she'd have flung herself off the tallest building in Commerce Canyon sans parachute before she'd attend a party in my honor. But it had been an open invitation for anyone and everyone at Sir Larry's; no other polite way to handle it, really. Almost everyone had told me they planned to come, though the director had begged off, claiming artistic differences. Just what I would have expected from a man who mainlined Fosse, but at least Bayles wasn't a hypocrite.

If Em-Cate thought I was going to let her presence sour things for me, she could write up her own scenario and stick it in her eye. I sidled up next to her and said, 'Enjoying the show, Em-Cate?'

She turned away from the mirror and blinked up at me. (She also hated me because I was taller. Tonight, she must have forgotten her stilettos, which would have brought her up to about the level of my nose.) 'Pardon?'

'I *said*, "Enjoying the show, Em-Cate?"'

She blinked some more, a habit Bayles had practically had to beat out of her, since it tended to leak through to her character. 'Why, yes. Yes, I am. Thank you.' She gave me a puzzled smile and went back to admiring the shark.

M*igod*, I thought, the bitterness of her jealousy knew no bounds – now she was pretending she didn't even know me! I felt so bad for her. Well, for a second, anyway.

On Em-Cate's right, Twill Carstairs – of *course* he made it up – paused in his admiration of his own reflection, a stingray wearing a bow tie on the stinger, to look at me curiously. Twill and I had always been on good terms, even though I knew he really didn't approve of what I was doing, and probably wouldn't have accepted an offer like it himself. Which was too bad – with the right ad campaign, lots of people would have wanted to be him.

'Looks like another satisfied customer already,' he said, glancing at Em-Cate.

Was he referring to himself or Em-Cate? 'Well, I'm still an entertainer, Twill,' I said. 'Even when I'm just helping you entertain yourself.'

His square face took on a wary expression, as if I had said something patently untrue. Maybe Em-Cate's rotten mouth had finally gotten to him and he had decided I was scum after all. Or had he and Em-Cate hit up the

pharmaceutical buffet early and scrambled their brains? I smiled at him and turned to the mirror.

Oh, *very* clever. Instead of a shark or a stingray or some other fish, I had an aquarium filled with all sorts of exotic-looking fish. Em-Cate and Twill were staring at it curiously.

'If you're thinking something about small fish in a big pond,' I said, 'keep in mind that it's *my* pond.' I gave them both a farewell salute and moved off.

'Was that ... you know,' I heard Em-Cate ask as I moved away.

'If it is, I don't like how much she's giving away with it,' Twill answered.

Well, *that* made *no* sense whatsoever. Maybe they hadn't waited to hit up the pharmaceutical buffet and picked up some cheap risers before they got here. Best to get back to the dressing room and stay out of trouble, I decided. I looked for my manager – dammit, what *was* his name? – but I couldn't see him or any of the employees he'd been talking to. Davy Jones' was getting more crowded by the moment; he was probably searching for me even more frantically than I was searching for him.

'I thought they'd sent you home.'

I turned around. Sovay's bleached face had soaked in every bit of blue light. It made him look slightly luminous. 'Are you *serious*?' I said. 'Go home and miss my *own* de*but*?'

His expression went from wary to openly amazed.

'Mi*god*,' I said wearily, 'is everyone on some kind of new drug that makes everything I say sound astonishing?'

' "Migod," indeed,' Sovay said slowly. 'I suppose what I really find astonishing is what some people will do to other people for the sake of a profit.'

Given our history together, Sovay was probably the most entitled to a say about what I was doing. But mind-to-mind contact hardly meant that he owned me, not as a fellow performer, and not personally. After all, he was married full-time, a fact he had gone to great pains to impress on me.

'I don't see where the choice I made constitutes my "doing" anything to you or anyone else at the theatre,' I said. 'So I decided to pursue the franchise rather than continue onstage – so what? I didn't try to force anyone to go and do likewise. I didn't even suggest anyone for the recruiter to talk to, though I'm sure if I told him *you* were interested in a no-obligation interview, he'd be happy to meet with you. He's a great recruiter and an even better manager.'

'Who do you think you are?' Sovay said, that fragile, bleached skin wrinkling with concern. He should have taken a semi-immobilizer to prevent overexpressing before he was repigmented. Unless he actually *wanted* his face to look like crumpled paper for some reason.

'Okay, okay, I know,' I said, 'you're getting little flashes of Constanzia, aren't you? It's not really leak-through, just a little flashover, and that's quite normal, nothing to do with the franchising programs. It's just that she's the

freshest portrayal and, frankly, she's my favorite.' I spread my hands and wiggled my fingers. 'It's a tickle to have a grand gesture for every occasion.'

Sovay put a finger to his mouth, caught himself, and stroked his chin instead. 'Do you know,' he said, 'tickling is actually a very sadistic thing to do?'

I rolled my eyes. 'Even if you tickle yourself?'

'You can't tickle yourself.'

We stared at each other for a long time. Mindplay amnesia had not affected the memory of how he had felt mind-to-mind and how I had felt to him. He had been as surprised as I had; Sovay, the man of stainless, no-rust virtue, devoted to his plump little drab of a wife, discovering love-at-first-contact.

There hadn't even been time for second thoughts – when you're mind-to-mind in a system, the speed of thought makes the speed of light look like a snail's pace. Perhaps if there had been time to consider, my nobler instincts might have won out, but I hadn't had that option and neither had he. Personally, I'd always thought we'd done the best thing for everyone. Some things you just have to get out of your system. Once it had happened, we'd gone on with the character interplay and it had been the best session I'd ever had with anyone.

Thank God his guilt-storm hadn't hit until after we'd disconnected – I couldn't have taken such an onslaught myself. I'd told him over and over that his wife needn't ever know, that it wasn't as if he'd been unfaithful to her in fact or in act. A fantasy for two is as unreal as a fantasy for one, after all. But he just couldn't seem to allow me to reassure him; it was something he had to work out to his own satisfaction by himself and I supposed he had. I didn't know for sure because we'd stayed out of each other's head after that, and he never discussed it with me.

But though he seemed to return to normal, there were times when I would catch him looking at me in an odd, almost suspicious way, as if he were sure that whatever I was thinking threatened him in some way. I figured he was just afraid that if I went mind-to-mind with anyone else, the whole dirty little story would spill out into the middle of whatever scene we were working on. I wanted to reassure him, tell him I could keep a secret and that just because I was mind-to-mind with someone didn't mean I felt compelled to show everything I had. But I had never been able to bring myself to say anything at all to him. His whole being, which I knew better than I'd ever planned to, warned me to keep my distance.

Now he was probably afraid that someday, someone would run up to him on the street, declare undying mental lust, and demand to relive the entire experience.

Poor, silly scared boy. Part of me wanted to tell him his fears were groundless. Another part of me said to let him suffer. That he didn't seem to understand me as well as I understood him was a pretty telling thing.

'You know,' I said after a bit, 'if you devoted a little cold rational thought to things – just a *little* – you'd be a lot better off. But as long as you drag around all that sad baggage, I can't help you. You can't even help yourself.'

'That's all right,' he said. 'Maybe *I* can help *you*.'

I laughed and moved off toward where I thought the dressing room might be. Sovay helping me – what a novel idea. The man was fine as long as he was pretending, but put him in a real situation, even an unreal-real situation of the strictly mental variety, and he fell on his face.

A bright yellow fish with spines all over it sailed by me and then circled around for another pass, closer this time. I was appalled to see that it had the Look, too. Mi*god*, I thought, club employees were one thing but the party decorations, too? Whose brilliant idea had *that* been, the club's or my manager's? The price of being Famous, I supposed. I made a shooing motion, hoping that whoever was on the holo controls was paying attention and would send it away or make it disappear altogether. I was going to have to have a little talk with my manager about this. Franchises were one thing, but fish seemed just a little undignified.

The fish hung there in midair, staring at me with its freakish human eyes. Then it blew a kiss at me. Heart-shaped bubbles floated upward. I had to laugh out loud in spite of myself – never let it be said that *I* couldn't take a joke – and looked around to see if anyone else was catching this little encounter.

Only Sovay, still staring after me with a forlorn, pitying expression. Mi*god*. Who did he think he was feeling sorry for, anyway?

Maybe only himself, I thought suddenly, watching the fish blow more heart-shaped bubble-kisses at me. Its face looked even more human now. I stepped back; having to focus on it at such short distance was making me dizzy. I hoped my eyes hadn't picked this moment to go glitchy on me. Scant minutes before my actual debut, I didn't need my eyes spinning like loose marbles. I had to find the dressing room and my manager *now*.

There was a slight commotion across the room and I saw the employee who had the Look, surrounded by a number of other employees. She was upset about something. My manager was bent over her; when he moved away slightly, I saw it wasn't the employee after all, but someone else who had the Look. Enfranchising on the premises tonight? Quite a vote of confidence in the product, though rather unorthodox.

Well, if they were going to pull out all the stops, they could have at least changed her clothes. She looked like she'd spent a bad week with ragpickers turned fashion terrorists, and they'd won. I'd have been upset in that outfit myself.

Faint snatches of what they were all saying to each other came to me through the underwater sound effects, which had come on without my noticing. ' … clothes … ' she was saying. ' … itch *stole my clothes!*'

I couldn't help laughing a little. If fashion terrorists really want you, they'll get you, no matter how careful you are. It was funny, even if she couldn't really be expected to see the humor in it.

' … *can't* … stampede her … won't … clean wipe … ' My manager was physically restraining her and she was practically hurting herself, trying to get away from him.

' … *me* … derstand that? … thinks … *me!*'

My manager had both arms around her and was trying to drag her into the back room. Forget the fashion terrorists, I thought, nauseated, this had to be an enfranchising gone wrong. How *awful*; especially the timing. If this hurt my image, I was going to sue the pants off everybody, including my manager, who apparently didn't have the sense to carry emergency tranks.

The sight was making me even more nauseated. I turned away and found the fish had moved up even closer. Its face was even more human and for a dizzy moment I thought I was back on the other side of the room, looking at a reflection in the funhouse mirror.

That face was *definitely* in the wrong place, I thought.

The dizziness intensified.

Okay, the last thing I remember is throwing someone off a cliff.

Now I am standing in the bottom of a swimming pool filled with holo water and fancy holo fish and a couple hundred souls who are getting a lot more out of this experience than I am, as most of them probably remember how they got here and those that can't don't care anyway.

This, they say, is the lot of the memory junkie: bad living, bad cess, tough stuff. I know I am not exactly in a position to complain to karma-rama, but who ever sets out to be a memory junkie on purpose? Ten thousand people buy and sell memories every day. Me, I'm the ducky luck-out who gets the thunderbolt in the head: junkie-junkie-junkie. The crazy side effects are just another fringe benefit. But what the hell, I always did say that anyone who wasn't pulling a fugue state here and there just wasn't trying.

The light in the swimming pool is the appropriate underwater mood-indigo murk, but my eyes are adjusted, which must mean I've been here awhile. I glance around in what I'm hoping comes off as casual, trying to get a feel for the social climate in my immediate vicinity. Apparently, I have not been throwing money, marriage proposals, or punches around carelessly, since nobody is looking except a weird, puffed-up fish with prickles all over it, floating in front of me and glowing like a radioactive yellow ghost. It's got eyelashes about an inch long on its bulgy eyes, and instead of a standard fishy mouth, there's a little Cupid's bow, red lipstick and all, blowing fishy kisses at me in tiny, heart-shaped

bubbles – yow! Isn't *that* a hell of a thing to find coming after your bait.
But what's worse is, the face is familiar.

The thing darts right at me. Instead of letting it swim through my
head, I dodge to one side and it sails up and away, twitching its tail fins.
Not that it would have hurt or anything; I just didn't like the idea.

A few feet off, I see this guy watching, and he's got kind of a fishy look
himself, like he disapproves but he's too prim to say so. He's wearing
one of those lighter-than-air sacsuits, the kind that billows out if you
even twitch, making him look like he really is underwater. His skin is all
bleached out, prepped for a tint – I can tell by the way it glows blue. The
chin-length hair is a darker blue blot around his head. I don't know him.
Maybe he's the fish's friend. So let *him* pucker up.

Then I realize there's some kind of something going on behind me,
and that's what he's really looking at. Yah, that makes more sense; I
can't be important enough for anybody to disapprove of. But then, who
knows what kind of changes have been playing while I've been fugued
out?

Whatever the big attraction is over there, it's drawing people and
holo fish from all over the pool. Angelfish are swimming through me
before I can get out of the way, and I hate it. I've heard about this kind
of thing, this is how they throw a party uptown – if you're some kind of
high power celebrity priv, they send all the party decorations your way
so you can make La Grande Entrance. I'm not sure what I'm more curi-
ous about, who the celebrity is, or why I'm in on it.

There's a break in the crowd all jockeying for position and I see her.
It's that bad old kissy fish! Or rather, it's the person the fish was mod-
eled on. She must be Famous. I wonder if she knows what they've been
putting her face on around here. Pretty good face; if I had those custom
cheek bones, I'd show them off, too. But jeez, on a *blowfish*? At least
they didn't try putting the hair on, too. I guess a hairy fish was too
sprung even for the priv'd-out joychildren who run this place. Whoever
that might be.

The people around her are all working hard to get noticed and she's
looking a little shaky about it, like she's not so sure she wants to be
there. One woman wrapped in scarves keeps moving back and forth in
front of her like she's dancing. Boy, I've heard about professional pests,
but I never saw one in action before. If it was me, I'd just relieve her of
the waking state and use her ass for a foot-rest, but Miz Famous looks
too blown out to blow up. There's a guy in a chef's outfit and a lady ang-
ler complete with a fishing rod and waders, somebody else dressed like
a court jester, two Madonnas, one Pre-Raphaelite and one postmodern,

a human torch whose holo flames have a bad case of static, the fakest-looking samurai I've ever seen in my life, and, all told, a lot more horse's asses than there are horses. Suddenly, I get this very loony flash that all these people are holos, just like the fish, and Miz Famous and I are the only real people here.

And then I think, *No, that's some other place*, but I'm god*damned* if I know what place that could be. But I *almost* know. It's on the tip of my brain. Maybe some old memory I bought to feed my beast of a habit, repeating on me like bad chili.

Miz Famous turns and sees me then, and there's no doubt from the look on her designer face that she knows me. That's a good one – *nobody* Famous would know me or anybody like me. I sure don't know her. I don't know her name, I don't even know what she's Famous for. Whatever it is can't be anything to do with me.

So what am I here for anyway?

Abruptly, the image of that cliff pops into my head again, a memory of looking over the edge into some foggy nowhere. Can't be her I threw over, unless she can fly without a plane.

A tall guy with sanitary white hair puts a hand on her shoulder, telling her something he obviously thinks is very important Now, him I do know ... but that's all I know. I don't know if I like him or hate him or owe him money or worse, so I step behind a big underwater plant. A memory junkie can't be too careful

Then this other guy in a purple satin tuxedo steps in front of her and I get a real funny feeling. Something about him makes me think I ought to go home to the Downs where I belong as soon as possible. I'm not sure where this place is, but from the look of the crowd, it's a long walk home if I can't catch a freebus.

I have *got* to tell Anwar about this. I don't think he'll believe me. He'll think I've been feeding the beast again and he'll start telling me how I'm gonna have to do something to take care of what I owe.

Of course, if I hang around here long enough, I can maybe build up a memory I can pawn. Any pawnshop'll pay more for firsthand stuff like this. Not enough to take care of the whole debt, but maybe enough to keep me out of any immediate trouble.

I look over at the Famous person again. She's turned out in full Brain Police drag – grey tunic over jumpjohns, visor cap sitting on the back of her head, even a trank-pak clipped to her belt. Jee-*zuz*, how did I miss *that*? Everybody else must be in on the joke, but I personally do not find a whole lot of humor in it.

Well, I was leaving anyway. I turn away and almost run right into the

guy in the sacsuit. By the look on his face, I can tell I was right the first time after all, he definitely does not approve of me. And then I wonder if he meant to cut me off, and maybe that Brain Police getup on the Famous person isn't a joke. But when I look back to see if she's coming for me, she isn't wearing it anymore. She's wearing some bad designer crap that's supposed to look like something you fished out of the trash. Figures; the guys who put the Emperor in his new duds are still getting rich these days.

I ain't laughing. I throw someone off a cliff and then I'm hallucinating Brain Police in water over my head? Even if it's just holo water, that sounds like a karma-gram to me.

I move away from the guy in the sacsuit, looking for the exit. It's slow going, what with all the marine and other life I don't care to get interactive with. I get to the far side of the pool and there's another big group of people jamming things up, except they're all mostly side by side, with other people trying to wedge themselves in between them. Stupid party games of the privs and Famous? I go back and forth trying to find a way around them and then some fool of a priv in mink shorts, so hyped out that his moonstone eyes are practically spinning in two directions, grabs my arm and says, 'Here, let's check what *you* look like, game-girl.'

I'm just about to smack him and tell him *I'm* no game-girl when I see what's really going on. The whole wall is one big funhouse mirror, hottest toy of choice for the filthoid rich. Whoever's running the mirror controls tonight must know these people, because the reflections look pretty pointed. One woman reflects as a shark, and the resemblance is too good. Another woman gets an octopus, and I can see the family resemblance in that one, too. One guy's a sponge, and the one holding my arm is some kind of tube-shaped worm thing. There's a few eels, another sponge, a stingray with a bow tie on the tail, a giant seahorse (with studded bridle and bit, yet – wonder what *he* does for fun), and a lobster with only one claw.

This is all supposed to be real big fun, but for some reason, seeing myself in that mirror is 'bout the last thing I want to do. But then Mink Shorts shoves me out in front of him, yelling, 'Squid! Squid! Squid!'

Now, I never thought I was the squid type, but what I see in the mirror doesn't make any more sense. I'm an aquarium, filled with assorted fishes I don't know the names of. This is supposed to be clever?

Everybody's staring. Then there are two new reflections on either side of me. Not fish, people wearing the same outfit. I turn to look at each one, thinking maybe the mirror operator is witty enough that I'm going to find I'm standing between a couple of holo fish. But no, they're

people on this side of the mirror, too, and the twin outfits are uniforms, not acute fashion-itis. At least they're not Brain Police uniforms, just hired help doing security duty.

'Madam, you'll have to go now,' says the one on my right.

Which is exactly what I figured he was going to say, except for the *Madam*. That's a bonus.

I pass the sacsuit on my way to the egress. Now he looks almost happy.

When we get outside, I see I'm on the rooftop of the Royale Building, in Commerce for-God's-sake Canyon. I also see that I have just been thrown out of the legendary Davy Jones' Locker, which I should have figured was where I was. Where else do they have holo water over everybody's head? An old-fashioned marquee card on an easel informs what part of the world that can read that it's closed tonight for a private party. Jee-*zuz*. What am I doing this far uptown? When I get fugued up, I get damn-the-torpedoes, no-prisoners fugued up.

The security guards walk me over to the transit area and ask me which do I prefer, the freebus pad, the air-taxi, or the valet-service salon for owners of private vehicles?

'What do *you* think?' I say, and they take me right to the freebus pad, sit me on the bench, and practice their servants' bows. In lieu of a tip, I look impressed. A very hotwire private club, Davy Jones' Locker, so exclusive and fancy you're supposed to tip the guards when they throw you out. I was on the lookout to buy a memory from anyone who'd been to it, but I never ran across anybody who had one to sell. Made sense; the type of clientele the Jones' got wouldn't be out selling their memories. And even if they were, I probably couldn't afford to buy.

And *then*, just as if my karma's getting all kittenish and contrary, I stick my hand down in my pocket and my fingers close around a wad of currency that is definitely more money than I am supposed to be able to ever hope to see.

Wild.

But what's even wilder is that I have a matching wad in my other pocket. Good thing, I'd probably be walking lop-sided if I didn't.

This is not exactly the place for an audit. But I've got to have at least a hint, so I pull just the very top of one wad out of my pocket and peek at the number on the outside bill. The light from the overhead floodlamp shows me the figure real clear: $100.

My head begins playing Sousa victory marches, all brass. I push at the corner of the top bill with my thumb, trying to flip it up and see if the one underneath is the same nice round number. The wad shifts and I see that I was mistaken. It's not $100. It's $1000.

I slide over to the darkest end of the bench and try to think. Lotteries don't pay off in cash, and if I've inherited a fortune from some rich relative I didn't know I had, I wouldn't have been thrown out of Davy Jones'. So who did I kill?

The memory of the cliff blooms in my mind like a dandelion on fast forward. My inner eye can see the grassy edge, and the foggy nowhere below. If I could just make the picture in my head a little bigger, maybe I'd see who I threw over it.

Then I'm off on a fast hope trip. Memory junkie, yah, maybe I've been feeding the beast after all and this is somebody else's memory. Two seconds later, the trip's over. This can't be something I got from someone else because I didn't get a rise out of it. The only memories I get junked up on are someone else's, no matter how dull they are. Someone else's vacation at the shore, someone else's wedding, someone else's frigging trip to the grocery store and I'm totaled, buzzed and rebuzzed. But the day I killed somebody – ha, and ha. Doesn't even raise a blip.

Across from where I'm sitting, the overhead rail lights up and I can hear the freebus droning in the distance like a bored hornet. Better hurry home now and see if I'm hiding bloody clothes in the shower. After all, who says this is my first kill? Maybe I *really* screwed up and got myself a murder jones from somewhere.

The freebus pulls in and the few souls peering out the windows at me look a lot more murderous than I feel. Even the stick-tender looks like a thug and that's just a holo, one of those cosmetic urban improvements they put in to make you feel like you're getting personal service from all the impersonal automateds.

Yah. Who else is gonna be on a freebus this time of night, Brain Surgeons For Jesus? They're all gonna figure anyone who climbs aboard at the Royale is a priv and they'll pick my bones clean before we hit upper midtown.

Instead of getting on, I walk over to the air-taxi pad, feeling everyone on the freebus staring daggers into my back for causing an unnecessary stop. But us killers don't sweat that small shit, ha, and ha, I think to myself, and that gives me that old sick feeling of impending doom in the pit of my chest. Anwar's always telling me that's just being short on potassium, and a banana a day keeps impending doom away. Ha, and ha. But not if that feeling of impending doom means impending doom, which it sometimes does. Anwar always covers his ears when I say that.

The freebus drones away. The backwash of cool night air feels prima, which causes me to take a better look at how I'm dressed. Normally that rooftop wind would go right through my quik-wear and chill me to the bone.

Yow ... none of *this* stuff came out of a vending machine, not even recently. I was so blown out about the wads, I never even noticed the quality of my frigging pockets. I have to stop, close my eyes for a second, and look again, just to make sure this isn't another hallucination like the Brain Police rags.

Nope. This is what *real* people put on their real bodies. Black tailored jacket that feels like velveteen over a silver Latin Revival shirt, and black don't-care pants, one size covers the earth. The shoes are standard shitkickers, but they're *new* shitkickers. Now that I'm aware, the shirt is just a little tight under the armpits, and the sleeves on the jacket fall short, but Jee-*zuz* all the same. On me, these are not clothes. They're a disguise.

So what am I disguised as?

As *not-a-killer, what else?* says that voice in my head, the one everybody's got that tells them what a fool they are. Well, yah, of course, this ought to fool whoever I meant to fool. I fooled myself with it. Didn't I?

'Excuse me?' says a polite, amplified voice. I almost drop dead of cheap surprise. 'Up here,' the voice adds.

There's a woman in a glassed-in booth on top of the taxi stand. Not a holo, but a real person. This is how they do it uptown, real people to serve their real selves.

'Hello?' I call up to her.

'No need to shout, I can hear you. May I summon a taxi for you, madam?'

I stick my hands in my pockets and grip the wads tight. Just making sure they're still in there. 'Yah. *Sure!*' Bring 'em on – hell, call two so I have a spare.

'At this time of night in this area, the only air-taxis available have drivers. Will that be satisfactory?'

It will be Expensive is what it will be, but for once, that isn't my biggest worry. 'Just what I wanted,' I say, feeling extravagant.

'There will be a five-to-eight-minute wait, according to traffic patterns,' she says, glancing down at something in front of her. I can see only the glow of the screen lighting her face from below. 'The refreshment service is through for the night, but beverages are available from the automated dispenser-wall to your left. Complimentary, of course, for your convenience.'

For *my* convenience. That's a new one, but I could get used to it. I wave at her and go over to see what the carriage trade gets for free.

No hard stuff, according to the panels in the wall – three kinds of coffee, half a dozen teas, soft drinks, fortified water, prehangover treatments, and all fancy-label. I'm getting more impressed by the second.

I decide to see if free Brazilian coffee out of a vending wall has more going for it than the poison I usually drink. When I press the panel, a screen lights up right in front of me and shows a little home movie of an antique silver pot levitating and pouring coffee into a commuter cup. A moment later a chamber below the screen opens up and I smell it even before I reach in for it. The commuter cup is identical to the one on the screen. Nice touch.

The screen says, *Enjoy the Royale's private blend often! Come again soon!*

'Beg me,' I say. And then I *taste* the coffee and I think, fuck it, cancel the taxi, I'm going to live here, right here in the taxi stand. Maybe I can work the booth, calling rides for privs and making polite announcements about only human-driven air-taxis available. Us killers can do polite as well as anybody else.

Then the taxi sets down on the landing pad and I'm impressed all over again – it's running in whisper mode, so as not to bother the privs with too much noise. The driver pops the rear door for me and I climb in, clutching my coffee with one hand and still holding on to one of my wads with the other.

Kind of a letdown here, because the interior of the cab is slightly on the shabby side. Privs are hard on their toys. The clear plaz panel between me and the driver is open – I guess there aren't too many priv stick-up artists, at least not in this part of Commerce Canyon.

'Destination, please,' says the driver politely. Yah, I can definitely get used to this. Without thinking, I give him my address.

He turns around and looks at me so hard that I get scared. Maybe I'm a publicly wanted killer, with my name, address, and description all over the dataline.

'That's a *Downs* address,' he says, like he's telling me there's shit on my shoes. I just sit there thinking it figures, humans won't go to the Downs.

He sighs and takes off his overdecorated livery cap. Underneath, his black hair's been knitted into a dizzy herringbone design now mostly flattened from the headgear. 'There are only eight rooftop pads in the Downs that serve air-taxis,' he says, talking real slow, like I might not understand one word in three, 'two in each quadrant. Four are clustered near the center, four are spread out on the perimeter. If you tell me where that address is located, I can let you off at the pad closest to it.'

'Oh,' I say. I'm supposed to know this, except I never had any reason to, till now. 'Northwest quadrant. Um, inner.'

But he's still glaring at me. I try my impression of a polite smile on him, but apparently that's not what he's been waiting for.

'I have to charge you fare-and-a-half,' he says sourly, 'because I've got to come back from there empty.'

'*Oh*,' I say again. Yah, that figures. It's not like he's just going to happen on a bunch of privs looking for a ride back to uptown after a sleaze-along. I finish the coffee and toss the cup in the suckhole. 'That's okay,' I tell him. 'Fare- and-a-half, let's do the thing right.'

Now he gives me an up-and-down, waits like he wants to ask me something else, then shrugs and turns around. As we lift, the partition between us slides shut. Maybe he thinks he's got the first ever priv stickup artist in his back seat. Nah, just a killer. In spite of myself, I feel like a rich kid on National Greed Day – the only time I ever get airborne is if I'm strapped into a showboat on my way to a court appearance. This way is definitely better.

He swings the cab around to get into the correct flight path and I have a farewell view of the Royale from the back window.

A small group of people who have just come out of Davy Jones' are hurrying across the roof to the taxi stand; one of them points up at the cab and they all look. Guess they think I took their ride. Just as they're turning toward the glassed-in booth, the taxi rises and levels off and I see only the jeweled summit of Commerce Canyon getting smaller behind me.

' ... of the line. We're here. *Hey!* Second time, end of the line!'

The driver's rapping on the partition. I didn't even know I fell asleep. Groggy, I dig around in one of my wads and find a smaller bill in the center, which I push through the fare slot. This does not make him happy.

'What is this?' he says.

'What is what?' I'm still all full of this crazy dream about an old guy falling out of a sky island.

'What are you, somebody's pet bank robber? I'm set up for fare strips and bearer chips. What is this currency?'

Was there some kind of banking coup while I was asleep? 'What's the matter with it?'

'You want to buy shoes, it's great. But I don't have an accounting system that works with it.'

I start getting scared and then all of a sudden, this weird calm comes over me out of nowhere. He's telling me about his accounting system like *my* life depends on it? 'I don't know accounting, I'm paying fare-and-a-half. *I'm* paying you. You work it out.'

He looks like I just spit on his upholstery. Then, when I think that maybe he's going to slide back the partition and punch me, he takes the currency. 'This was a lot more trouble than it was worth.'

'Your accounting system is more trouble than it's worth,' I say, and pop the rear door myself.

'Wait a minute!' But I'm already out and walking away. The down-shaft to the street is closed, I'll have to take the outside stairs, but walking ten flights down isn't so bad. Besides, the idea of being shut up in a downshaft is enough to bring on a case of the short-breath tonight. I get to the fake wrought-iron stairs when the driver takes off. Guess he decided he didn't feel like pushing it any further in the middle of the night on a Downs rooftop. Maybe he's afraid I'd kill him; us people who use currency are probably capable of anything.

I'm halfway to the street when I think to ask myself where I'm going. It's such a good question, I have to sit down on the steps and come up with an answer worthy of it. Go home, sure, crawl onto the futon, pull a blanket over my head, and hope I wake up knowing everything-and-a-half. Except I do *not* want to be alone with *that* picture in my head. Now that I'm out of the club and back in the Downs where I belong, it's start-ing to give me a case of impending short-breath. Impending doom. And me without a banana.

Oh, hell, I think, getting up and going the rest of the way down to the street. I'll just go to Anwar's. His place is only about a block from where I am right now. I'll tell him about it and he'll give me a banana, or at least a place to spend the night while I try to unkink this thing and fig-ure out who I threw over that cliff, and when, and why.

Which begs the bad old question, do I really want to know any of this?

Jeez, but I wish my mind would make up its mind. Ha, and ha.

I'm halfway to Anwar's when I'm about to pass a twenty-four-hour pawnshop.

Cause for pause. I want to get off the street as fast as possible, but I know I've done business with this place. Something of mine might still be in the inventory, and for once, I've got enough money to buy it back.

I'm thinking about going in ... and thinking about it ...

... and when I come to, I'm hanging on a parking meter at the curb, about to topple over into the gutter.

Dizzy spells now, for chrissakes. I'm getting to be a real hazard to navigation here. I've got half a mind – ha, and ha – to forget the pawn-shop and just run off to Anwar's, get indoors before I pull a really big blank and wake up in a crib or worse.

And then I think, hell, I'm here, I might as well go in. It'll save me a trip later.

Behind the counter, the pawnbroker raises an eyebrow at me and goes on combing her white hair.

'Can't stay away, eh?' she says. 'What's the good word?'

Far back in my mind, something jumps, and I hear a small voice say, *Tell her.*

Tell her? Tell her what? For a moment it feels like my head is full of cotton fuzz.

'We're having one of those nights, are we?'

We're having one of those lifetimes is what we're having. But at least I can remember her name. 'You got anything of mine, Ofrah?'

She looks at me for a long second before she runs one hand over the screen sitting to her right on the counter, moonstone eyes going side to side, then rolling up in her head while she consults deep inventory. This goes on for almost too long before she says, 'Nothing but what I had.'

'Who took it?' I ask.

Her look says I'm the craziest thing since eyes first popped. I start to reach into my pocket and something tells me very strongly that I shouldn't bother; she's not going to tell me who bought my stuff while I was off in uptown adventureland.

She notices the movement and her mouth twitches. 'Void again, are we?'

I open her mouth to tell her, no, I just won the lottery or something, but I stop again. Instead, I take my hand out of my pocket and shrug. 'Even an uptown priv gets financially embarrassed from time to time.'

'Privs have credit ratings. You don't even have a good word.'

I give her another bad word, wondering if I have finally achieved the early stages of complete mental meltdown; there's some block that won't let me tell her for once I am holding more money than memory. I want to ask her what I said the last time I came in, what I was doing, what I was like, and why I didn't put in for a call-back-and-retrieve, but somehow I know she's not going to tell me even if I beg. She'll just keep giving me that bored look.

I turn away to leave and catch sight of a pair of bald heads just outside the door. Great, this is just what I needed – a pair of onionheads with insomnia, looking for someone they can claim violated their marital space and then stomp into blood pudding. For all I know, they've been following me since I left the cab on the roof. Onionheads'll do that when they're bored enough.

They spot me and grin at each other. Yah, they're ready. They can't come in and get me because they can't claim a challenge in a public space less than ten thousand feet square; that's the law. I turn back to Ofrah.

'So,' I say, feeling humble, 'can I go out the back door?'

Ofrah gives a short laugh; she's seen the onionheads, too. 'Yah, sure enough. For you, that's free. You don't even need a good word.' She jerks

her head at the curtain behind her. 'Run like hell. Onionheads got long memories, even if you don't. Come back when you've got a good word.'

Grind my nose in it, Ofrah. I give her one last bad word by way of farewell. The curtain takes me right out to a back alley and I run like hell. Exactly like hell.

'Ah, Christ,' says Anwar. 'Do you do this just to torment me, or are you now a practicing psychotic?' In the tiny security screen, his face looks like an unmade bed, probably as much the fact that I woke him as the low-res. But he buzzes me in and he's waiting with a cup of coffee when I get up to his apartment. Sort-of coffee – after the uptown Brazilian, I can taste every chemical and additive they put in those instant cubes. But it's the thought that counts.

'You're true,' I tell him, sipping and not making a face. 'You're the truest of the true, and the truest one I ever knew.'

He scratches himself through his robe. 'Yah. But –' he yawns – 'one time, Marceline. One goddam time *only*. You either give yourself up or you don't come here anymore, because I don't need this kind of trouble.' He yawns again and plumps down next to me on the broken-down framework of cushions that passes for a couch.

My heart sinks. With the picture of that cliff in my head, this can only mean I'm a known killer now. 'Maybe I can plead amnesia,' I say. 'Or being fugued out. They give you a break for that, don't they?'

He smears his dark hair back from his forehead and peers at me through slitted eyes. 'Who! *Who gives you a break for amnesia?* You *must* be psychotic, because nobody on Bateau's payroll is that stupid.'

I pause in the act of taking another sip of poison. 'Bateau?'

Anwar throws both hands up and claps them over his face. 'Mother of God, she's forgotten she works for Bateau. Shit, I might as well wake up all the way. If I go back to sleep again tonight, I might never wake up again. How could you do this?' He gets up and marches toward the bedroom. 'Finish that,' he calls over his shoulder. 'We got a fast date in a memory lane.'

Jee-*zuz*, it just gets worse, I think unhappily, pouring the rest of the coffee down the sink in the kitchenette. I work for Bateau. I see the cliff again in my mind and I know what I do for him. That's a real balls-up throw-up. Anwar comes out of the bedroom buttoning a faded orange shirt and finds me leaning over his sink, spitting out the taste of vomit.

'Ah, *shit*,' he says. 'I want to tell you it's not that bad, but we both know that'd be a lie. Or we'll both know when you get your mind right with the lord.'

'Debts got that bad, did they,' I say, wiping my mouth on my sleeve, forgetting it's too good for that. I grab a rag off the counter and try scrubbing the spot I made. 'Debts got so bad that I work for an Escort service. Is that right?'

Anwar takes a breath. 'You'd better hope so.'

I think I ruined the frigging sleeve. 'Huh?'

'You'd better hope you're Escorting for Bateau. Still Escorting, that is.' He comes over and flicks one of my lapels. 'Because this is not what you were wearing a week ago when you disappeared.'

'I didn't disappear,' I say, but I don't know if I did or not. It feels like I'm lying but I can't tell for sure. That's wild.

'Oh? Vacation in Tahiti, perhaps? Or just a bender at the shore? You been *nowhere* for a solid week, and when somebody's nowhere for that long right after a job, Bateau assumes the worst.'

I have to swallow before I can speak. 'And what is the worst?'

Anwar looks at me hard under the kitchenette light. 'You're really asking me that,' he says. 'You're really and frigging truly asking because you don't frigging *know*. Jesus *wept*, Jesus wept a fucking *river*.'

'If I didn't know I worked for Bateau, how could I know what the worst is?' I ask; reasonable question.

'Look at you!' He grabs my jacket and shakes me. 'You're dressed like a – like a – a friggin' *taxpayer*, like some goddam day-wage priv! The clients tip, but they don't tip wardrobe, and *you* don't get enough to buy rags like this, not unless you skip and go into business for your self!' I think he's gonna hit me; instead, he does something a lot stranger. He wraps both arms around me, tight.

Something goes *beep*. At first I think he's squeezing me so hard I popped an eardrum or something, but then there's another beep, and I realize it's him. Still hanging on to me with one arm, he reaches down and fiddles with something at his waist. 'What's that,' I say into his chest, 'Bateau's first-alert system? Is he coming over to get me now?'

'No. It's a pump. Shut up.'

'A pump? What's it beeping for?'

'Overloaded capacity. I had to turn it off. Shut *up*.'

I manage to pull away from him so I can breathe. 'Look, I didn't know I disappeared. I didn't know that I was supposed to appear anywhere. If I've been out for a week, someone took me out and kept me out. And what the hell are you wearing a pump for?'

'The only way you're gonna convince Bateau is to get your bad old ass to a memory lane and come up with the goods from the job. You'd better have them. Floating a deal yourself and then crapping out on the memory and claiming hijack is an old dodge. Bateau hasn't bought that one for ages.'

'What if it's not a dodge?' I say, thinking about the wads in my pockets. Christ, if that's how I got them, I *must* have been psychotic and no wonder I can't remember a thing.

'Then you're twice fucked. He assumes the worst, remember? You got to get to a memory lane *now*, pull up everything you can remember and offer it to him on a silver platter. He'll still pop you out himself and take his own look inside, and that ain't gonna be the best day you ever had. But at least you'll have everything right up where he can get at it the easiest way.'

He's telling me I'm gonna have Bateau running barefoot through my mind; I can't believe this. I don't want to believe this, I don't even want to think about this. I rewind a few steps. 'What's the pump for?'

Now he looks as mad as some onionheads I know of. 'What's it for, she says. What does anybody wear a pump for?'

'I *know* what a goddam pump is goddam *for*. What the hell are *you* pumping out?'

He makes a noise that might have been a laugh in its former life. 'You,' he says. 'I'm pumping *you* out. And every time I come face-to-face with you, the motherfucker goes off the scale and I have to shut it down.'

I'm still trying to get my mind around that one when he drags me out of there.

Predawn in the Downs is dead time. The curbside parking spaces are full of illegal doubles and triples, mostly rooster-boys and gofers, it looks like. Later, the meterheads will clear them out, hauling them off in wagons for the grievous offense of exceeding the two-hour limit. They're not supposed to do that, they're supposed to clear them out around the clock, but the meterheads get a cut of the fines, which increase with the time, and I guess that improves the quality of their shitty meter-reading lives. The offenders get several hours of sleep and free use of the jailhouse lavabo before they go to court. So maybe everybody's just doing everybody else a favor after all.

And who am I to criticize? An Escort is not exactly in a position to watchdog the public morals. And I'm not exactly in a position to be critical about Escort services, either. I can see how I'd end up like this. I can't name an addict, *any* addict, who didn't end up doing something hinky to feed the beast. Escorting is about as hinky as you can get, and if I didn't know that before, I sure as hell know it now by the way it's so solidly *gone* out of my memory. Like I deliberately threw it out.

Which was a very stupid thing to do, seeing as how I work for Bateau, and that's about the worst news I've gotten in recent memory – ha, and

ha – unless it's the fact that I have also just surfaced from a week as a missing person. I don't know what was in my mind when I did that, but I hope to hell whatever I was holding is recoverable, buried safe and intact. Because even the kindest-hearted pimp – that's agent to you – will rip your brains out through your nose for freelancing on the sly.

And while we're on the subject of bad news, I'm wondering if I should tell Anwar we should watch out for incoming from low-flying onion-heads. Nah, I'll just ruin his night even more. As it is, he'll probably never forgive me for forgetting his pump. I'd rather think that memory got swept out along with all the stuff about Bateau, because I wouldn't want to be the kind of person that would deliberately forget that about somebody. Just because I'm a hypehead doesn't mean I got *no* heart at all. Though the fact that he's wearing a pump and I'm not isn't lost on either one of us, even if we're not saying anything about that.

The pump has to be Bateau's idea, but we're not saying anything about that, either. We don't have to. It tells me a lot about what kind of life I live now. Maybe when I get my memory back, I'll be able to figure out why I ever wanted to live this way.

But then I don't have to worry about it because we're at the memory lane, and Anwar's shoving me through the front door.

You Must Remember This is one of those places privs like to claim they've gone into on a sleaze-along. I saw some actually come into the waiting room once, about half a dozen of them moving like they were roped together in some kind of onionhead-style marriage. For all I know, they were. They looked around and then one of them said loudly, 'Dear me, I thought there was a bar at this address,' before they all shuf-fled out again. And it's not even that bad, by Downs standards.

There's nobody in the waiting room and the wall screens are all blank except for one running General News off the dataline. The guy working the front is busy watching something in his desktop. I almost know him; it's so close, I actually start to say his name, but it vanishes off the tip of my tongue.

When he sees Anwar, he leaps out of his chair with an eggsucker's grin. Business must really be in the toilet.

'You got anyone for a general all-around boost?' Anwar asks him, jerking his thumb at me.

'This is a memory lane – what do *you* think?' the guy says, still smil-ing. 'Sally's taking them walk-in.'

Like You Must Remember This has a full appointment book? Who are they putting on for? I glance down at myself. Maybe for these fancy clothes I'm wearing.

Anwar grabs my arm. 'Go on. I'm buying. Last time ever – come out with the goods, or don't come out.'

He shoves me toward the door the guy is already holding open. I step into a long narrow hall and a woman sticks her head out of the nearest doorway.

'Booster?' she says.

'How'd you guess?'

I don't recognize her. She's got glossy black hair, golden skin, onyx eyes. The effect is heiress-with-a-bad-attitude. But then someone else comes up the hall to me and forget the heiress – this woman is starving to death. She's not just scrawny, she's bones wrapped in skin. A strip on the left side of her chest says SALLY LAZER in raised black letters. One skeletal hand closes around my arm and I have this wonky flash that *she's* an Escort and all this is just an hallucination. That hand feels real enough, but all us hypeheads know that it doesn't have to *be* real to *feel* real.

She steers me firmly into her room and the way she's got my arm, it's like she thinks I might bolt on a whim, which makes me wonder if maybe I've got cause to. Then I see the sandwiches.

Actually, I smell them first. She's got this big bad old platter of sandwiches on a desk, not edible polyester but real food. You can always tell the real stuff by the smell, and if I closed my eyes, I'd think I was in a deli. She acts like they aren't there, not letting go of me till I'm sitting on the chaise across the room, next to her system.

'Can you take your own eyes out, or shall I do it for you? No extra charge for the service.'

I put my legs up on the chunky cushion before she can do that for me. The chaise shifts under me and for a moment I'm afraid I sat down on one of those live things that'll mold itself to any position, but it's only a plain old adjustable. I'm still wondering why Sally Lazer would be working in a Downs joint if she's scale enough to afford stuff like this when she comes at me with a long-handled scoop.

'Don't point that thing at me,' I tell her and pop out my left eye. She's got the holding tank ready for me and I hurry up and do the other eye before she thinks I've decided to leave the job to her after all But Jesus, what's her hurry? Does she actually have a full appointment book, or do skinny people just have to move fast before they lose so much weight they disappear altogether?

Her system connections are brand-new, I can tell by the way they latch on to my optic nerves, no pull, no jerk, just smooth. Am I the first person she's used them on? I'd ask, but the sensory cutoffs kicked in, and that's a relief, because the smell of those sandwiches was starting to get sickening.

The relaxation exercise is some kind of sequential color-building thing, simpler than what I'm used to, but I'm not too picky. The last few hours have me docile enough to be a herd animal. Any minute I'm going to be chewing my cud.

I get the space of maybe half a thought-beat to wonder if I'm going to regret this more than not. Then I'm down in it, alone in the system with fast Sally Lazer.

It's Davy Jones' Locker all over again, except all the people and fish are gone. There's just me and the mirror in the moody underwater half-light. Just me and the mirror, literally – I don't even have a reflection yet. That makes me think this was an even worse idea than I thought when I first saw old Sally Lazer.

And speaking of old Sally, where the hell is she? I wave a hand in front of the mirror to see if I can stir up an image for myself. Nothing happens in the mirror but I get a faint sensation of a distant, answering movement that might be Sally signaling her presence. Maybe her mind's as skinny as her body. That could be me carrying over impressions from outside, or she might really be starving to death.

Meeting someone mind-to-mind in a system, even the stripped-down kind dedicated to one function, you still get a fair amount of personal stuff in the drift, snatches of the other person's inner life. But I'm getting damned fucking little from bad old Sally Lazer. She's like the first draft of a facade personality for a system, operational enough for a test run but barely there otherwise.

Some kind of time passes, hard to tell what. Time in the system is a stretchy old blob, thick and slow in some places, brittle and fast in others. That's all subjective, and only low-ballers who fell off the turnip truck yesterday believe that old story about the hypehead who died of old age in three clock-hours.

Sally Lazer – right, the name wants me to believe she's built to travel at the speed of light, but she'd have to be a machine to work at the same speed every time, even down to the way her own inner time passes.

Maybe she can't get herself in synch with me and that's why she's holding back. I wait for her to figure it out so we can live at the same pace in here. Anwar's paying for this but if I'd known she was this stumble-headed, I'd have made her pay me.

Anytime you're ready, Sally.

No answer.

... Sally?

It doesn't pay to get puffed up when you're on the business end of

someone else's system, but it's a triple-A, all-wool bore to hang fire with minimal visuals and nothing to do.

About the time I'm thinking I'm going to envision the exit and get the hell out of here, a feeling comes over me, like dust settling. At first, I think it's carry-over from what I was thinking before about being a herd animal; the weirdest shit will boomerang on you. But this isn't me. It's Sally. Sally is ... chewing?

Chewing. Sally's not eating, just chewing.

Come on, get it right – herd animals don't come in extra-emaciated economy size. Then the deli smell-taste rolls in at gale force, damn the torpedoes and no prisoners. Sally's chewing away, chewing and chewing and I can tell by the feel that this is what Sally Does. We all got one Thing we *Do*, each one of us, and this is Sally's: she chews.

I can't shake the bad old feeling that she's overridden her own cutoffs and she's really chewing. You're supposed to disable outside-world movement when you're hooked into the system so you won't sleepwalk, but Sally *Does* this so through-and-through, I swear if I put my eyes back in this second, I'd find her sitting at that desk blindly chewing sandwiches with the wires trailing out from under her sunken eyelids.

My stomach declares mutiny. The taste is bad enough, too strong to be good, but she's killing me with this not swallowing. Chew-and-swallow is how it's supposed to go, but Sally only chews. *Only.*

Talk about fed up, ha, and ha. I wish that were funny. I try to concentrate on swallowing, thinking that'll teach her to hook in with me and force her bad Old Thing on me. Sally doesn't even notice. Nothing gets her when she's in peak-experience nirvana.

I stare at the mirror, concentrating. Something's got to come up in it pretty damned soon. *Okay, Sally*, let's see *what you're up to.*

The mirror fogs over and the image comes in slowly. Some kind of office ... but did anybody ever have an office like this? It's full of fat furniture, pudgy overstuffed chairs that look like they're fighting with each other for space, a desk with weird old bulgy sides – even the lights are globes with the texture of excess flesh.

Guess I found the secret Sally-land she lives in. She won't last long in this business, putting her Thing in the clientele's face, even in the Downs. Maybe she's an ex-fetishizer who can't kick the old subroutines. Fetishizers are just cut-rate neurosis peddlers with no brakes on their missionary mode. If I'd known she was one of those, she couldn't have paid me enough to come in here. And Anwar's buying.

And then I see her, crouching in the middle of all those obese chairs, too busy even to know I found her. What a *bitch*.

I start to move toward her and run a little moment of truth when

suddenly there's a new image in the mirror between us, blocking Sally from me.

Her. The Famous person, the one with her face on the fish. What the hell?

No, I'm wrong, it's not her after all, it's someone else altogether.

No, wrong again. No, not wrong, exactly, just not quite right. Now, what the fuck is that supposed to mean? How do I *do* this shit to myself?

Wait a minute, says the other woman in the mirror. *This is what you're looking for.* She holds one hand out, waving me closer to the mirror. There's something shiny in her palm.

I've killed before. That's okay. That's right. The guy was asking for it.

That's how it goes when you bet your life on a roulette wheel and lose. I remember:

An antique roulette wheel in a sky-island. A *sky-island* – if the Royale is uptown, a sky-island is like ... heaven. They were all overdressed there, period costumes from some time in the past where everybody over-dressed, and it was like they were all moving in slow motion. Who could move any other way under all those layers of brocades and silks and lace?

The guy was wearing stiff-looking black clothing, funny stand-up shirt collar, funny tie, and a coat that split into two panels – tails, he called them. Skin the shade of rich hardwood, but only here in the sky-island. Anywhere else, he was little more than a pile of dark ashes, tubes growing out of every hole he had and a few holes he never used to have.

The siege of adult-onset progeria, he told me. *Happens when the body has taken too many rejuvenation treatments – the cells suddenly react to the restoration drugs by accelerating the aging process.* Like Nature gives you only so many reversals before she slams her hand down on the fast forward button.

But in the sky-island's main gaming salon, he was in full healthy bloom in the golden light slanting through the windows running all around the place. On one side, you could look out and see the sun hang-ing above the cloud line, waiting; on the opposite side, the sky had deepened, evening just beginning to show itself. Also waiting.

And the roulette wheel went around with a rapid ticking sound, a ball skipping over the little holes, color changing from red to white to black on each bounce. The wheel was antique but the ball was strictly today – the old-fashioned kind didn't used to change color. He had these tokens – no, he called them chips – instead of money, and he put some on only one number for each spin. Sometimes the pile of chips shrank after the wheel spun, sometimes it grew. He was the only one playing

because he was the only one who had any of those chips. Everyone else including me was watching, and waiting, just as the sun waited on one side and the night on the other.

I remember:

He was real happy. More than that; there was a place called *happy* and he was in it. *My life has been filled with many sophisticated ways to be happy and unhappy, to win and lose,* he said, *but in the end, it really comes down to some relatively simple thing like this: a roulette wheel.* I didn't know much about it and he didn't tell me anything except that sooner or later the wheel must turn against you.

I knew the moment it began stealing from him. There was nothing different about that spin, but the pile of chips never grew larger afterward. It just kept shrinking little by little, until he had just one chip left. So many numbers, and just that one chip. He picked it up, holding it between two fingers at eye level between us. I was supposed to choose the number this time.

Had to be that way; that was how he needed it to be. I took the chip from him and put it on a number right in front of me. And all of a sudden, that was the most beautiful thing in the world, that chip sitting there on that losing number.

In all the complexity born of sheer duration, he said, *that's what ultimately belongs to me, to anyone: beauty, and loss.*

And the wheel spun, the ball bounced, changing colors over and over again, and came to rest in a number I hadn't noticed before: 00.

House number. Everybody *loses.*

Everybody except me. None of the chips on the table were mine.

The windows on the sun side of the island blew open then; the wind rushed through, fluttering everybody's silk and lace and scattering all the chips, before it died. The guy got up from the table and offered me his arm.

You can ... Escort me now, he said.

We walked over to the open window together, and there was absolute silence as he climbed up onto the sill. He looked out over the plain of clouds for a few moments before he turned and held out his hand to help me up. That was okay, I could go that far. The dress he'd put on me was heavy and itchy but I managed to get up there with him.

The sun was still waiting.

I've enjoyed every moment, he told me, stepping away from the frame behind him and holding on to me as he balanced on the thin sill. I got a good grip on the part of the window behind me. He took one foot off the sill, and he looked as if he were about to step out onto the clouds and stroll away.

Every moment, he said, and I knew I was going to have to be the one to let go. He wanted to, but he just couldn't make that last move. Lots of them couldn't. That was mostly what Escorts got hired for.

Only this far, I reminded him.

House number, he said. Everybody *loses.*

Everybody with chips on the table. That was okay, too, nine times out of ten, it came down to this. They got used to the company and forgot that the end had to be first person singular. I didn't mind holding him there. The link between us was telling me everything I wanted to know.

Including the exact moment to let go of his hand.

There was no pause, no in-between; he just went, fell backward, straight down into the clouds and disappeared.

Like that, I was back inside the island. The rest of them were lined up at the window now, single file and in an orderly fashion. One by one, they went, too, still gliding in slow motion.

That was what they all believed, too, that it all went when they did. Even the ones that were sure they knew better. Hell, that was what it felt like, the absolute end of

... the line?

Good-looking guy, too much makeup and overdressed, holding some kind of skinny book out to me. He's overdone the makeup and the clothes so much that it takes a while to see he's the guy from Davy Jones', the first person I saw when I came to. *You want to check the line? You want to check –*

The line? No, I know how it goes. Except I don't. But somebody does. Memory junkie, tourist in other people's lives; no memory ever gets wiped clean away, it always leaves traces, associations. Associations can reconnect.

... feed the beast ...

And there's Sally, chewing and chewing. Threw me a little bone I could gnaw on myself, but it's never my own memories that junk me up. That didn't even make a mouthful for me.

What else *you got, Sally?*

The other woman can't run interference for her. Sally's head snaps around as fast as a snake striking and I know down to the root that it was a bad old mistake to mix it up with this one. Her goddam cheeks are *crammed,* for chrissakes, and she's chewing, chewing, chewing like she's really just all mouth, all the *inside* of a mouth and nothing else is real to her, in here or out there.

She senses me thinking all this and the taste in her mouth goes bad.

Sickening enough before, but that's too much. I move closer, trying to see what she's doing. Jee-*zuz*, she's got my memory loss there and I didn't even feel her working on it. I can't feel it now. She might as well be working on someone else for all it means to me.

No, now that I'm aware, things start occurring to me, some of it making sense, some not. The images come in flashes –

– *check the line?*

– walking along some twisty dirt road out in open country, knowing that the cliff is waiting at the end of it. I'm not alone but like in one of those silly elementary dreams, I can't turn my head to see who they are, or even how many. All I know is, when we get to the edge of that cliff, one of us is going over it.

And Sally is chewing and chewing, in time to my heartbeat. Or *someone's* heartbeat.

You want to check the line?

No, not yet. We're getting closer to that cliff. One of us is going over it, as sure as God made little green brain cells. And while we're on the subject, who *is* God now, anyway? God is

Chewing. Flecks of food glisten on the lips and I think I'm going to let fly with the bad old technicolor shout right there.

You'll get some odd effects off the mirror.

She's chewing right the hell at me, trying to block it. But I'm a memory junkie; anybody's but mine; and I'll take it. This is my life, and this is my life, and this is –

Chewing. The edge of the cliff is ragged, as if a giant hand came along and broke off whatever was there before, and this is what's left, this is –

– *the line?* He's stuck in my mind like a fish hook, like he's really there, too, dangling, one more filament among all those loose ends –

– in deep water, just holo water but sounds like a karma-gram to me. I can tell it's a bleach-job by the way his skin soaks up the murky blue light and reflects it. Hair like a patch of darkness –

Like a tapestry that's become unraveled. The sound of his voice is warm and textured enough to wrap up in like a blanket. *All the threads are still there, but the picture is gone. You just have to wave them all back together the way they were. Or you could make an entirely different picture.*

Memory of a smile like a blessing.

Yah. *Oh*, yah. Someone else's memory of someone else's man. Is *this* what she got Famous for? If it isn't, it's gonna be, if this is what the carriage trade gets when they come in and say they wannabee Famous, too, so strap 'er on and let 'er rip –

Does he know she kept him? Does he know it's on a hair trigger and he's alive because she put up the mirror when they did it?

You realize, of course, this means the truth is what you make it. Try not to forget that.

Lover boy, you don't *have* to tell that to a memory junkie.

Did you want to check the line?

We're at the edge of the cliff. Long walk finished, journey over, the proverbial moment of truth is at virtual hand: *my* hand. This is what I Do. We all have one Thing we Do. Chewing is Sally's, but this is mine, this is
 Over.

Over the edge of the cliff, *that's* the line and that's the end of the line: surprise good-bye.

Sorry it has to end like this, but I couldn't let you stay and you wouldn't go. Better you than me, because I've got a life to go back to now and all you'd leave me is

Chewing. Sally's image gets up and comes toward me with this look on her face like whatever she's chewing is poison. Her gaze moves in a slow left-to-right scan, and I can feel the process going on inside her: reality check. I already know what the result will be. My reality doesn't fit hers, or hers doesn't fit with mine.

Chewing: her bad old Thing was a signal to something. Someone?

Someone *else*. Whoever should have been looking into this mirror at her isn't supposed to be me –

Abruptly, someone says in a cheery little voice, *What's the good word?* I was in the pawnshop twice last night, but it was me only the second time. The first time –

Sally tries to clamp down on that, too, but she's been too open to me, because that bad old Thing, her signal, got an answer somehow, the right answer, the answer that told her go ahead, this is the one.

Except I'm not the one. Mistaken identity. Except it *isn't*. I *am* the one, because I threw somebody over a cliff who didn't want to go, somebody who offered me the only thing that could have stopped the long fall and the surprise good-bye. And somebody else, the one that called me to the cliff in the first place to throw that someone over, she never knew what happened until it was too late. So now I'm the one.

I have half a moment to think Sally's one of those silent psychos, the ones who are never crazy outside where you can see it. The one *what?* Who does she think she's been waiting for, Neo-Jesus? Or just her One True Love?

The mirror goes blank. I don't have to check the line, now, I know what's coming up next. It's too stupid, too sickening, and there's no way to stop it.

This is going to put me off mouths for good, I think.

Just before it happens, I finally understand that I'm not standing in front of the mirror anymore, but in it.

Sally turns her head and spits.

You *know* it's going to be a bad day when you come to in some rude Downs joint with a famine fancier standing over you like one of the Four Horsemen of the Apocalypse on holiday, and there's some ratatat hypehead you can only vaguely remember tapping his foot for you out in the waiting room. Worse when you realize those connections the famine fancier is holding have just come out of your eye sockets. All I could think was *migod,* over and over like a mantra.

'I said, that's all.' She wound the wires around one bony hand. Those skeletal fingers *touched my eyes.*

Migod, I thought, *I'm going to be sick.*

She looked pretty amused, touching either side of her mouth daintily with her little finger, as if she'd just finished a hearty meal. Christ, what *could* she have eaten? I didn't want to think about *that,* nor about how I could have possibly thought letting someone like this run around in my head was a good idea.

Well, it hadn't been *me,* of course. That was just one of the hazards of being a Method actor. Without warning, you could fall into character and run off, especially if you were close to a performance date, when a character was always on a hair trigger.

Normally, though, Sir Larry's had some of the staff on wrangler duty, ready to flip us back to normal with a code word if it looked like a character was getting out of hand. Sir Larry's was terribly conscientious about that these days, ever since the time Em-Cate's game-girl character had achieved escape velocity and hid out at the shore for three weeks. They'd finally found her working out of a house of ill repute that she'd set up all on her own and which had been responsible for a minor crime wave at the very height of the vacation season. What a monster hue-and-cry there'd been about *that.* I smiled at the memory, though I shouldn't have – if any of the subsequent lawsuits had gone to court, Sir Larry's would have been wiped out. It couldn't have happened to a nicer person – just a nasty bitch like Em-Cate.

And so: what had happened to the wrangler who should have been watching *me?* And what had I been doing the night before? I was wearing my party clothes, so I must have been out somewhere. But the last thing I remembered was –

– throwing someone off a cliff –

I winced with annoyance. The damnedest associations can trigger leakthrough from a character.

'Something wrong?' asked the famine fancier.

'If you actually *meant* to scramble my brains, no,' I said, a bit snappishly.

'Oh, you'll be spotty for an hour or two, till it really takes,' she said, tucking the connections into the top of her system. 'Don't try to worry anything into coming up. After the associations resettle, things will start occurring to you all on their own, without any prompting.

'Oh, *very* comforting,' I said. 'You won't mind, then, if I sit around here till things start popping.'

She found that pretty amusing. 'There *is* a back way out of here, you know.'

'How considerate.'

She laughed. 'You're not the first person who's gotten her memory back in here and decided she didn't want to go out the same way she came in. Go all the way down the hall and turn left. If you change your mind again, though, you'll have to come around the front, because the back door won't open from the outside.'

I put the turbo on my exit, swerving around a desk with a mostly empty platter on it.

'See you around the ward,' the famine fancier called after me. One of those *witty* farewells. I shuddered at the idea that she'd been touching my mind. Famine fanciers had to be the most obscene creatures on God's green earth, and they proliferated only in lands of plenty. *Migod*, I thought as I pushed out the back door into a narrow alley, *don't let me have come in to get a diet from her.*

No, the hypehead I was dodging had brought me in here. Or rather, he had brought my character in. That much I could remember, thanks to leak-through, but not much else. Except that he wasn't the type who would just fuck off quietly, even if I showed him that the person he'd thought I was, was just a character from a play. Maybe *especially* if he knew –

I'm pumping you out. And every time I come face-to-face with you, the motherfucker goes off the scale and I have to shut it down.

That had to be a line from the play. Migod, I *hoped* it was.

You want to check?

Sovay's image floated in my mind. I didn't know why my mind had seized on him to play ringmaster for my associations. Well, actually, I did know; I was just surprised, even now, that he'd been the one to stick.

Migod, I thought suddenly, looking back at the exit I had just come out of. I hadn't done *that* with that hypehead, had I? Or, well, not me, but my character. That would have been just like Marceline, but I couldn't get enough leak-through to know for sure. The things I endured for my art.

The alley ran the length of the block and came out on a side street. I wasn't sure exactly where I was, and it was obscenely early in the morning besides. Didn't I *ever* sleep when I was in character?

I felt in my pockets. Mad money still there – what a relief. I'd be able to take a taxi back to Sir Larry's. And wasn't I going to nuke somebody when I got there. At least one wrangler would be looking for a new job by lunchtime, and a certain director was going to lose a lot of sleep worrying about a lawsuit.

The thought of lunchtime made my stomach turn over. There was nothing in it except for that minor burning sensation you get from drinking poison like cube coffee. Now that I was aware of it, the minor burning blossomed into a full-scale ache, most of it hunger. No pleasure in that, thank God, which meant I hadn't caught the famine fancy from that awful woman.

What I should do, I decided, was find some place to sit down, get something to eat, and let my spotty memory un-spot in peace. Then I could go back to Sir Larry's and read the riot act from a more informed position. In fact, the more I thought of it, the more I thought it would be better if I *didn't* go rushing back there as fast as my little legs would take me. They couldn't do the play without me – I'd made sure that was written into my contract – and my prolonged absence would definitely throw the fear of God into some people.

And all I was really suffering from was a little characterization amnesia. Some people, like Twill, who was always so wound up he had to have his reality affixed after every performance, or Sovay, who was almost too serious even for me, would have panicked if they'd found themselves in a Downs hypehead joint *sans* a chunk of memory. But I'd always said that if you were going to work the Method a hundred percent, you couldn't let a little thing like a blackout stampede you. After all, whatever you didn't remember the character probably did, and you just had to get the leak-through reenabled.

Which was not to say that it didn't *feel* funny, and I'd seldom felt funnier than I did right then. Not to mention being too hungry to think straight. I went over a block on the vague recollection of having been to a video parlor/doughnut shack there, but when I got to what I thought was the right place, there was a dreamland there instead. They weren't open for business yet, but they were testing their sidewalk holo display and there were unicorns and gryphons and djinn and exotic dancers flickering in and out of existence all over the sidewalk.

I stopped to watch. It wasn't like I hadn't seen the same kind of thing a hundred billion times before, and very few of these places ever showed much in the way of originality – I mean, *migod*, if overuse of gold-scaled dragons were a felony, a lot of people would have been doing life without parole. But it was diverting to see the place running through its catalog, promising all sorts of inspirational visions and signs and wonders and whatnot. All you could really get in there were your own boosted dreams, of course – if you wanted *real* visions and signs and etc, you went to a dreamfeeder and paid

real money for the good stuff. But few people in the Downs could afford that kind of freight – if they could, they sure wouldn't have been living in the Downs.

I became aware of the turn of my own thoughts. Watching the sidewalk show was helping to unbind my mind and reenable leak-through. That was just the way I'd been taught to do it, of course – you keep yourself distracted with something attention-getting but not too demanding and pretty soon the gears of memory would engage. And if mine didn't, I thought smugly, Sir Larry's Storefront Theatre would be out-of-pocket for the patch job, not me. They were notoriously stingy about that kind of thing, but they'd have to take responsibility this time.

'Cuba?'

I jumped. The pimp had materialized at my elbow as if he were a holo himself. For a moment I thought he *was* a holo. He was a wiry little man in scream-green ersatz-angora, the kind of fuzz that ought to have balloons stuck all over it.

'I said, "Cute, huh?" ' He jerked his head at the display. I looked; a gryphon was preening itself on its hind legs.

'Never really thought of gryphons as "cute," ' I said, 'but as they go, it's not bad.'

He stroked my arm and I drew away, resisting the urge to wipe the place where he'd touched. 'I didn't mean the gryphon, I mean the *real* animal. Wait for him, he comes back any second now. *There*. Don't miss him.'

A well-developed exotic dancer dressed (barely) like Hercules with cheap gilt on his hair and some genuine dancing ability did a turn around the projection area, threatening to remove his loincloth.

The pimp nudged me and I drew away farther. Now I was hugging the wall. 'So? Cute?'

'Cuter than the gryphon,' I said. 'Go away, I'm null-and-void.'

'Sure you are.' He felt the material of my jacket between his thumb and finger. 'That's why you dress uptown and cruise downtown. Come on, taste the good life. Don't miss that train.'

'Told you, I'm null-and-void. Really. Spent the trust fund in a thrillsville. I'm on my way home to beg Mommy and Daddy for a loan.' My character would have handled him much better, I was sure, but it seemed like I could never fall into character when it would have been most advantageous. Off-stage, anyway.

'Sure, and I bet your taxes must be killers. Deduct it, business entertainment.'

I brushed his hand off and walked away. Hercules danced across my path and I veered around him, even though it's really nothing to walk through a

holo image, or have one walk through you. But I never could stand it myself. It made me feel like a ghost.

'Tonight you'll wish you did it!' the pimp called after me. I didn't doubt it; I was always rather suggestible when I came out of character.

I spotted the video parlor/doughnut shop several doors down, next to a soundtrack shop that promised ZILLIONS of GREAT TUNES To Enhance Your Holiday or Your Day-2-Day – Or Let Us CUSTOM-COM-POZE The **PERFECT SCORE** For YOUR Life, From REAL COMPOSER ANA-LOGS!!! Today's specials, I saw with some amusement, were Bernstein, Mozart, and Elf man.

Right. They were probably holding hands under the table with an obses-sive-compulsive clinic. Doctor, I just can't get this damned tune out of my head. All right, just hold still, this won't hurt a bit, one thousand dollars please, next. I could hear a little of the Elf man as I went into the parlor; it certainly was catchy.

The doughnut aroma hit me like a fist in the face; a moment later, my mouth was watering so much that my salivary glands stung. Totally illegal, of course. Appetite gas was against the law in establishments that provided any kind of entertainment or diversion, even just video, the idea being that the entertainment was enough inducement for the customers to stay and eat. And even if it had been legal to gas the trade here, the concentration had to have been about five times the limit allowed in the available space. God, I thought, living in the Downs was like living under siege in a minefield.

I went over to the doughnut counter anyway. The gas was active in my sys-tem now and if I didn't eat here, I'd end up somewhere else, pounding down a dinner for eight or worse.

I took a tray from the dispenser and lined up behind a scruffy local in one of those technicolor quilt-suits everyone had been wearing last year. The colors were barely moving; it needed a recharge but quilt-suits were so passé, I couldn't think of a single place that would have done the job.

As if that were my worry. Well, when you were waiting for a memory boost to take, your mind would wander. A bit of the old carbo express was probably just what I needed. Or what I thought I needed. I chose half a dozen assorted artery-killers from the counter, three of them dripping custard. But I also managed to force myself to take one edible poly. Damn that gas.

I dug a couple of small bills out of my mad money without displaying the wad and stepped up to the collection box, looking for the cash slot.

'Won the lottery, did we?'

The local in the quilt-suit was eyeing the money with a half smile that had more in common with rictus from nerve damage than it did with any real expression. I made a polite noise and pushed the currency through the open-ing on top.

'You know, that don't give change,' she said, brushing at strawlike hair the exact shade of chicken gravy *(damn that gas)*.

'It don't? Doesn't?'

''Zack change for cash customers or losers-weepers. That's how they make up the overhead and pay for friggin' *gas. You* oughta know that.' Her gaze went to her own tray and then to mine. She had one doughnut.

'If I'd known that, I'd have gotten three more custard-filled,' I said. 'And I think I'll just go back and get them right now.'

'Can't do that,' she said, catching my arm. 'Go through again, they charge you again. You must really be scorched this time.' She pinched my sleeve between her fingers. 'Musta really been worth it, too.'

'Thanks for the tip.' I pulled away from her as politely as I could and walked toward the rear of the place, where a tall skinny man in a stained duster was wiping off an empty table. I hurried over and slid into one of the two chairs, flicking on the tabletop screen.

'Chit?'

I paused with a doughnut halfway to my practically drooling mouth and frowned up at him. 'What?'

He tucked the end of his washrag into a band around his arm and held out his hand. 'Chit. *Chit.* Freelance worker here. Extra service not provided by shitty bad-food-dealing owners. Come on, gimme a chit, baby needs a new pair of nose-filters.'

'*What?*' I said again.

He turned and made a beckoning motion; a boy about eight years old sidled up to him and pressed close. He had his own washrag.

'Baby of the family. Nose-filters wearing out, can't work in family trade without nose-filters. See?' The man tilted the boy's head up to show me his nostrils. 'Go crazy, eat till stomach explodes –'

I was already shoving a small but overly generous bill at him. 'Here, *please.* Thanks for the service, buy that kid a decent meal, too, while you're at it.'

The man took the bill and held it as if he'd never seen such an outlandish thing before. 'Chrissakes, she doesn't got a chit.' He gave the bill to the boy. 'Tell Mom to stash, try to convert later. And *you*,' he added, leaning over me, 'you go home. No place to be spending *cash.*'

The kid had run over to a corner booth where a woman and three other children had apparently taken up residence. I saw the boy say something to the woman, who looked over at me with a disapproving expression on her tired face. As I watched, one of the other kids slid out of the booth and hurried over to a table that had just been vacated, pulling a washrag out of his back pocket.

'So?' the man said, as if I had spoken. 'Good luck. Could have been you.' He moved away, scanning the room for anyone about to leave.

'Fortune really smiling very good on you, I guess.' The local in the quilt-suit plunked herself down at my table and folded her arms expectantly.

I transferred two doughnuts from my tray to hers. 'Okay? *Now* will you leave me alone?'

She shook her head at my largesse, laughing a little.

'Here's what they gonna carve on *your* tombstone: "All balls, no brains." What I get for callin' you in feeds me here for a *year*.' She picked up one of the doughnuts I'd given her and took a large bite. Custard flowed over her fingers and I winced. I hadn't meant to part with one of the custards.

I turned to the screen and was annoyed to find that it was jammed in browse mode. That figured; once you stopped eating, they didn't want you taking up a table because you wanted to watch some program all the way through.

'So now that you in thrill-and-chill for yourself, where you gonna run your stable from, uptown?'

I didn't look away from the news footage. 'I don't know what you're talking about.'

'Sure can't run 'em from here, unless you plannin' the violent overthrow of the crowned head.'

'Look,' I said wearily, 'I had a bad night and a badder morning. I just want to eat my doughnuts and go home. Please leave me alone.'

'Marceline, Marceline,' she sang, wagging her finger in my face. 'Don't *tell* me you got no clue.'

I frowned. How could *she* know the character's name? Well, how else, I thought suddenly, feeling uneasy. Obviously this was another friend Marceline had made while she'd been on the loose. When I finally did get some leak-through from the character, I was probably going to want to forget it all over again.

'Marceline, you know what your agent says about you?'

'*You* talked to my agent?' I said, surprised.

'So? My agent, too.'

Migod, I thought; that was a possibility I hadn't considered – not a friend of Marceline's, but another actor.

'Your agent says you been dead for a week.'

I couldn't help laughing bitterly. 'I'm not surprised. Half the time he can't remember my name. Especially when he talks to casting directors. So you're with him, too? Which theatre are you with? I don't remember you from Sir Larry's.'

'Theatre.' Her pasty face broke into a broad grin. '*Damn*. That's *good*. When it's an act, it's theatre. Sure, *I* shoulda thought of that. This Larry got any slots to fill at his place? Maybe I'll chuck our agent, too.'

'The troupe is full up right now,' I said carefully, 'but without an agent, you couldn't get an audition anyway.'

'No? All-poacher, all the time? That's the best one I've *ever* heard, and I've heard them all. Hope they put some bodyguards on you, because Bateau says now that you dead, you got to be down and be quiet.'

'Sorry, but you lost me completely,' I said.

'Yah, I know. Bateau's sorry about that, too.'

'Bateau who? I have no idea who you're talking about.'

Her face lit up even more. '*Shit!* You don't! You wiped!'

'Actually, it's just a little characterization amnesia. I didn't really get my memory wiped. In fact, I just had a boost and as soon as the right associations connect up with each other, I'll be back to normal.'

Her head wagged from side to side. 'Doping works maybe two times if you're desperate. After that, there's no fooling yourself. Thought you knew that.'

'"Doping"?'

'You know, pull the memories out and then have them put in again. So you can get a rise. Like blood-doping, pump the blood out, pump it back in again, makes you feel like Super-Duper-Man. Never had to do that after a hard week, I'd be surprised about it.'

I spread my hands. 'Oh, you've got *me* confused with the character. That's not actually who I really am.'

'No? Who, then?'

'My real name is Marva. And *I'm* not the memory junkie, *she* is.'

'Who?'

'Marceline,' I said patiently. 'Apparently, you've always met Marceline, and not me. *I'm* Marva, and the *character* is Marceline. Got it? Marceline is a character in a play.'

She clapped her hands, producing a cloud of powdered sugar. 'Ha! *Now* I got it! Some very nice people! They're *too* good, make a memory junkie go all the way! *Damn!* But, okay.' She used her sleeve on her mouth and sat up straight, squaring her shoulders. 'So, *Marva*, you like being Famous?'

I used a napkin to brush powdered sugar from my jacket. 'Oh, I'm not Famous yet, though I have resume'd a couple of franchisers and there's been some interest. No offers yet, and it's something I'd have to think long and hard about ... ' My voice trailed away. Even as I was saying it, it didn't sound right, for some reason. The gap in my memory yawned like a bottomless pit, but for the life of me, I couldn't imagine what was supposed to have been there. Except that I was pretty sure, now that I'd said the word, it had something to do with a franchiser ...

The thought blossomed in my mind like a poisoned flower. Had I done some kind of business with a franchiser while I'd been Marceline?

Some instinct was screaming yes. But what reputable franchiser would do business with someone who was obviously not herself?

'Still thinking?' said the woman, amused. 'Well, this must be a test run, eh? How you liking it? Ah, dumb question, you don't even know you like it or not. Because *you* think you're true.'

You're true … the truest one I ever knew. Another line from the play? I remembered saying it to someone …

You want to check the line?

'I want to check my brain,' I muttered.

'Check your brain at the door when you see Bateau. Easiest way to go, save him the trouble of pulling it out your nose.' She got up. 'Thanks for the doughnuts. And try to remember, if it was you, you'd have done the same as me, even for a friend.' She sailed away, swerving around tables while I blinked after her.

Theatre of the absurd, I thought, glad to be left in peace. The appetite gas wasn't working as hard on me as it had been, so I could nurse my last two doughnuts.

On the screen, an androgyne was gesticulating earnestly and silently in front of an enormous product map of Wisconsin. I pressed for volume up; nothing happened. Figured; of all the tables in the place, I'd had to pick the one with the malfunctioning screen and now there were no other tables vacant. Oh, well. Twill always said the dataline was nine times more entertaining with the volume off anyway.

The androgyne got more and more exercised until I thought s/he was going to start trashing the set. A small legend appeared at the bottom of the screen: Cheese Advocates Join Dairy Strike. It made me wish I'd thought to get some coffee to go with the doughnuts.

I started to bite into the edible polyester when my gag reflex suddenly came to life. *Damn* that famine fancier. Before I could work up a good mad, the screen gave a jump as the channel browser kicked in again and suddenly I was looking at my own face.

Migod. It wasn't any still I remembered posing for. As I stared, the pov pulled back from the head shot to a three-quarters body. The still began gyrating in melty near-animation through several different poses and costumes – all the roles I'd played at Sir Larry's. I'd seen similar things often enough to know that it was an ad for a franchise, but I couldn't tell which one.

Damn. I banged on the volume button and then the speaker, but to no result. My image was replaced by that of a large man in a chef's outfit doing a jerky dance while he flipped a pancake in a frying pan. Dammit, why weren't these things closed-captioned? I tried to pull down a menu and got a message telling me I couldn't have a menu in browse mode.

Shitty cheap public screens – I gave it a last hard slap and the image disappeared under an onslaught of static.

'*Perfect*,' I muttered, sitting back and looking around. The place was not full of people I'd have felt comfortable asking to share a table and screen with.

Hell with it, I thought. Time to go home and find out what I'd gotten myself into. Or what Marceline had gotten me into.

You want to check the line?

Yah, I sure did want to check the goddam line.

The skinny guy's youngest kid started working on the table before I was all the way out of the chair.

'Sovay's in rehearsal.'

Apparently, today was my day for bad hardware karma; Rowan's pearlized brown biogems were the clearest things on the static-filled phone screen. From what I could make out, she was as impassive as ever, as if she had no idea who I was. So like her. She was always detached, remote. I'd thought it was because she didn't really approve of Sovay's career or any of the people around him, but someone – Twill? Sovay himself? I couldn't remember that either – had told me that she was that way about everything, which made me wonder how she and Sovay had ever met, let alone married.

'Would you give me the number at Sir Larry's?' I asked her, squinting through the static. 'I don't have it on me at the moment, and I seem to have misplaced my memory as well.'

'Um,' Rowan said. I waited, thinking she might be looking it up.

'Don't put it on the screen,' I said. 'I've got a blizzard on this end.'

'Oh? I can see you fine here, but I wasn't going to. I really don't think Sovay would want to be disturbed right now. If you want to record a message, I'll see he gets it when he comes home later.'

I almost bit a hole in my lip. Weren't we high-handed these days! Maybe Sovay actually had told her what had happened between us, a very stupid thing to do unless he really *wanted* a lot of domestic problems. Or maybe it had something to do with my selling out to a franchiser – if I had. I must have; no franchiser, no matter how sleazy, would dare advertise anyone it didn't own the rights to. And we'd just see about *that*. They could plead inno-cent and we-had-no-idea-really all they wanted to, but if Marceline had sold me out, the contract would be invalid.

'If it's something urgent,' Rowan added, 'you could leave me your number and I could call Sovay for you and see if he could call you back right away.' She paused. 'How did you know he'd be at the theatre this early?'

'Look,' I said, trying to stifle my impatience, 'I know the routine at Sir Larry's, we're about to go from preproduction into full rehearsals. For the last few weeks, I've been preparing with the Method and I've been a little out of touch. All I need is the number of the direct line into the rehearsal hall and then I'll leave you alone.'

She blinked. 'The Method?'

'Come *on*, Rowan,' I said, and she jumped a little. Maybe Her Majesty wasn't used to being addressed so casually. 'I've been having what we call a less-than-perfect day. I'm running on no sleep at all, so give me some cush here. I wouldn't have bothered you at home if I absolutely hadn't had to.'

The static thickened enough to obscure her so completely that I was afraid she'd hung up on me. Then a small red light blinked in the lower left corner of my screen, indicating everything in her phone buffer had just been saved for later replay. Fine by me; maybe Sovay would find her attitude interesting. Her image faded back in again and to my surprise, she gave me the number at Sir Larry's.

'Thanks, Rowan,' I said, and she winced at the use of her name. Migod, what *was* her problem anyway? We'd only met about six dozen times and I'd called her by her first name without getting that kind of reaction. Maybe that silly Sovay had told her.

'D-do you want to leave a number where you can be reached?' she asked.

Migod, what did Madam Cool-And-Remote have to be stuttering-nervous over? Maybe something that had nothing to do with me, I thought – maybe Sovay had gotten a Call, the kind of Call we all wanted to get, from Some-body Big. *Loved you in your latest, darling, how would you like a slot with a national company?* Yah, I'd have been breaking out in hives myself about something like that.

'Same number I've been using,' I said, 'but I wasn't planning to go back there yet. If I can't get through to anyone at Sir Larry's for some reason, tell Sovay I'll keep checking the various message boards and services. Thanks again, Rowan.' I reached for the hang-up button.

'Wait.' She leaned toward the screen. 'I don't know what number you've been using. You'll have to give it to me.'

'Sovay knows,' I said.

'In case he's forgotten, then. Or lost it.'

She waited and I restrained myself again. Treating me like a stranger wasn't going to change anything that had happened between me and Sovay, so what did she think she was accomplishing? Maybe just a little self-gratification; maybe that aloofness was her way of hiding a childish streak as broad as a full moon. I shrugged and gave her the number at my apartment. 'See you around the Storefront,' I added. Through the static, I could see her staring at me openmouthed as I disconnected.

The first time I tried Sir Larry's, I was bumped to call-waiting limbo. Somebody was tying up the line talking to an agent, probably. The second time, I got the recording from the box office giving an abbreviated schedule and the proper hours to call for tickets. That bitch Rowan had given me a number I could have looked up myself, not the rehearsal studio's direct line.

I was so frustrated, I hung up and fumed for five minutes before calling back and punching in my bypass code. Probably there'd be no one in the office and I'd have to record a message.

No static this time; the words came up quite readable:

INVALID SEQUENCE ... REPEAT ENTRY: _____

I wanted to scream. Damned cheap public phone was probably garbling the numbers now instead of the visuals. I tried again anyway. I got the INVALID SEQUENCE message twice more and then Sir Larry's hung up on me.

I tried again on another phone, with the same results. I started to move to a third telephone and then hesitated. It could have been some kind of technical problem in the area node, I thought uneasily, or my bypass code might actually have been invalidated.

I decided I didn't want to know. Calling for a ride was just a big waste of time anyway, I thought, lifting the privacy hood and stepping away from the phone. I'd just spring for my own cab, go right to Sir Larry's, and get this whole mess straightened out.

The comm center was starting to fill up with odd types who seemed to be less interested in the phones and message boards than in who was using them. One free soul was using one of those illegal line-biters to collect any leftover time-credit previous callers might have left behind – just right out in the open, not even trying to conceal what she was doing. Yah, this was the Downs, all right, and I'd be damned glad to be back uptown where I belonged.

He must have spotted me as soon as I stepped out onto the sidewalk. I was scanning the street for a cab and there he was at my elbow, spitting little glittery stars into the air from the corner of his mouth. Street vendors did that all the time in the Downs, but for some reason, it really turned my stomach this morning.

' 'Ey, ya noya-nuff?' he said, sending a cascade of stars over my shoulder.

'Yah, I'm annoyed enough. Now skin off,' I said. 'Unless you want to earn a fast tip by telling me where I can get a taxi.'

'Not annoyed,' he said, chuckling out more stars. 'Paranoid. Are you *paranoid* enough?'

I looked at him, making a face at his smelly leather armor. 'For one day, yah. Now, *skin off*.'

'Heya, day's young. *Very* young. How do you know *They* won't be coming to get you by lunch? Gotta think ahead. *They* know all about *you* – why shouldn't *you* know all about *Them*

I groaned. There wasn't a single taxi in the thickening vehicle traffic. 'All I want to know about are cabs. Why can't you get one when you want one? It isn't even raining.'

He put a dirty hand around my upper arm. '*They* took all the cabs. And if

you were paranoid, you'd know where. And why.' He wiggled his tangled eyebrows at me and blew out another stream of stars. My stomach did a slow forward roll. 'Come on, it's a done deal anyway, ain't it? You know there's something going on, you just can't figure out where to. You buy some paranoia from me, you'll be so here-and-now, you'll be reading the future in the traffic patterns the way happy idiots read what happens in the daily news. Live hot, only the dead are cool. Whaddaya say?'

I jerked away from him. He took a step toward me and then jumped back. I was holding a steel comb, sharpened points aimed at his face. He raised both hands, blew a star-laden kiss at me, and hurried off.

He wasn't half as surprised as I was. I examined the comb. Everything had happened so fast, I couldn't even remember doing it. Obviously, the comb had to have come out of my hair. Except I never wore combs, my hair was –

I caught sight of my reflection in the tinted window of the comm center then, and I had the *weirdest* flash that it wasn't a window at all, but a funhouse mirror. I went over to it, ignoring the derelicts making faces at me from the other side. *Migod*, the street vendor had been right – obviously I *wasn't* paranoid enough. Even worse, I thought, touching that round face and the brown rat's-nest that was supposed to be hair, I had absolutely no sense of design.

Characterization amnesia was one thing, but I'd never in my life forgotten that I'd gone into full costume. For that matter, I'd never gone into full costume while I was still working on a character. Sir Larry's cos turners wouldn't even look at a design sketch until the week a production was scheduled to open, much less execute something.

So what did this mean ... had I jumped the gun for a reason I couldn't remember anymore? And something this extensive – migod, no wonder Rowan had been acting so strangely. I was completely unrecognizable.

A hand clutched my upper arm again. I turned away from the window and whipped the comb up. 'I told you to skin –'

Green fingers plucked the comb out of my hand, flipped it over and around like a magician's prop, and made it vanish into a matching green sleeve. 'Very dangeroso,' said the green man, still holding my arm. His hand felt strong enough to snap the bone if he'd cared to. 'I keep saying you shouldn't be allowed to have things with sharp points on them, Mar, but nobody listens to me.'

I tried pulling at his fingers and he tightened his grip so much I could feel the muscle bruising. 'Nah-nah-nah.' He grinned. His teeth were a lighter shade of the same green, a kind of rain-forest emerald. I made a mental note never to dye my own teeth if I went color-mental. 'You've got an appointment you're long overdue for. Bad to be any later.'

'You've got the wrong party,' I said. 'I'm just passing through here –'

He grabbed my other hand and took a long, hard look at my fingertips before seizing my chin and taking an equally good look at my eyes. He had telemicro; very pricey feature. I was impressed, not to mention relieved. My finger- and retina-prints would tell him he'd been fooled by a chance resemblance and that would be that.

It seemed like ages before he refocused on my face.

'Same old mess, eh, Mar? Let's go.'

'*Wait* a minute,' I said as he dragged me up the sidewalk.

He laughed and kept going, much to no one's dismay except mine. I barely got a glance from the gofers sharing a parking space and a bottle. This was the Downs, after all, people dragged each other away on a regular basis. I had to dance along with him in double-time or fall down and let the pavement sand my skin off.

'Please,' I said, 'you're hurting –'

He swung me around square-dance style and I saw the side of a van coming at me. I closed my eyes and felt someone catch me just before I would have hit.

'You *really* stunk it up, running out the back door like that, Mar.'

I opened my eyes. My friend the maniac who had taken me to the memory lane a thousand years ago this morning. His name popped into my mind out of nowhere: Anwar.

'I don't know you, either,' I said, without much hope. He kicked open the side door of the van and tossed me inside.

'This is a mistake,' I said into the carpeted floor as the green guy drove us away from the curb. Anwar was sitting on my back. 'Whoever you think I am, I'm really not. I'd know if I were, really –'

'Thou shalt not fucketh around,' laughed the tint from the driver's seat. 'But if you do, don't be stupid about it.'

'But I'm not –'

Anwar gave me a glancing swat on the back of the head. 'No more garbage, okay, Mar? I bought amnesia before breakfast, but it's closer to lunch now. Nobody runs out the back door of a memory lane because they can't remember anything. *You* wouldn't cover for me for the same thing and you know it. So do me the service of not trying to bury me up to my eyes in bullshit. Just as a thank you for the coffee, if nothing else.'

I had a vague memory of drinking a cup of coffee-flavored chemicals last night while in character. 'Not *that* coffee,' I said.

He gave me another swat. The van accelerated.

We didn't travel long before the van went over a bump and began descending. The light coming through the windows faded, leaving the interior in near darkness. I kept telling myself that this was good, the sooner we got to

wherever they were taking me, the sooner they'd find out the tint's telemicro had malfunctioned. Then they'd kick me out and my worries would be over.

By the time we stopped, I almost believed it. But as the tint got out and walked around to open the side door, I decided Plan B was better – the moment I was out, kick him in the crotch and run for it.

The door slid back and I tensed, waiting for Anwar to pull me up. Something cool touched my upper back, spreading out to my shoulders, up my neck, and around to my face. There was just enough time for a regret before the Vitamin Q in the transcutaneous patch Anwar had stuck to me took over.

Q-up and calm down, a billion strung-out hypeheads can't be wrong, as the saying went. I calmed way down, beyond the level of bothering to notice what I was doing or where I was. The buzz had it that you could counteract Q by sheer force of will if you really needed to, but that had always sounded like pharmaceutical folklore to me. Even if it was true, my will just wasn't up to the dosage.

I began to notice the world again just as we stepped off a lateral or elevator (I had no idea if we'd gone up, down, or sideways) into an immense, airy-looking space, with a sunken area in the middle of it. Sunken living rooms had been all the retro-rage last year, I thought idly, still too Q'ed to care, but they'd always looked like furnished swimming pools to me. Which reminded me of *something*, but all I could think of for some reason was a fish and a line …

'Well, another country heard from,' someone said from across the room. Part of my mind knew it should have been panicking; another part was try-ing to log the memory of the disconnected feeling exactly for possible later use. You can't take the woman out of the Method or the Method out of the woman.

On the upper level directly across the sunken area a small man in white pajamas was standing in front of a desk. He pointed at the couch lining the sunken place with a careless gesture.

As soon as I stepped on the carpeting, I knew for certain that I was still heavily drugged – no power on earth could have made me walk on it other-wise. It was one of those crawly, half-alive things that's supposed to feel so good on your feet, though I'd always thought people bought them to have sex on. And then there'd been that kinko guest director from last year, who had bought one to have sex *with* …

Pajamas did a slow walk halfway around on the upper level, passing out of my peripheral line of sight. I was staring at the carpet fibers, working away on my shoes in a vain attempt to stimulate them.

'This wasn't *my* idea,' the tint said.

'I was afraid she'd panic and try to run,' Anwar said defensively. 'So I dosed her.'

'Quite all right,' Pajamas said breezily. 'I think you did the right thing,

Anwar.' I hadn't seen him come down into the sunken area but suddenly he was bending down and looking into my face. 'I even think I like her better this way. Not so prone to trivial debate.' Pajamas looked up and to my right. 'Though I don't imagine she does much for *you* like this. Does she? Or does she?'

Deep in my mind, something stirred, as if there was some part of me that hadn't been affected by the Q. I had no feeling one way or the other about that, either. The sensation of alertness was a strangely isolated thing, like an air bubble going from deep under the ocean to the surface.

Abruptly, my vision gave a jump and something happened in my left eye. No, in the left side of my field of vision. It was like seeing through a window with a crack in it … a window, or a mirror, where everything on one side of the crack was slightly displaced, so that it didn't match up with the other side.

Interesting, I thought; was I falling into character, or just having a stroke? I was still too dosed to be any more than mildly curious.

Pajamas took hold of my chin and lifted my face, frowning.

'What?' said Anwar.

Pajamas turned my face one way and then the other. 'Something just happened in there.' He let go of my chin but I held the position, not really wanting to look up at him but not having any reason to move. 'This is the last time I ever put a memory junkie on the payroll. Much too unstable.'

'I don't think –' Anwar started and Pajamas made a cutting motion at him. 'That's good. Because thinking's not what I pay you to do, Anwar.'

The left side of my vision became unusually vivid. I could feel a sort of mental searching or groping, as if I were trying to remember something. Except I wasn't.

Aliens, I thought, bombarding my head with thought-control rays. So this was schizophrenia. And even *that* didn't feel like my own thought. Maybe this *was* schizophrenia.

'– no surprises,' Pajamas was saying. 'What I always liked best about you, Marceline. In the six months you've been in my employ, you've never *once* surprised me. Until now. And that makes me feel' – he looked pained – 'unhappy.' He picked up my hands and held them. 'Now. I have to have what's mine, dear. The good girl you used to be would understand that.'

Marceline. Well, that explained it; the character had slipped the leash, achieved escape velocity, and formed some liaisons without my knowledge or cooperation. God only knew what she'd been up to –

I had a sudden absurd flash that God had chewed me up and spit me out before the rest of what Pajamas had said registered on me. Six months? *Six? Months?!*

Impossible. I never worked on a character for that long; nobody did. Let alone in full costume for the duration –

Unless Marceline really had managed a complete break with my life. But that would have meant I'd been a missing person for half a year with no one looking for me – even more impossible. Even if the rest of the troupe had hated me as much as Em-Gate did, none of them would have let me go missing for six *days* without pursuit – the lawsuit for negligence would have left me owning all their sorry asses. These people, Pajamas, the tint, Anwar, they all had to be crazy, or their minds had been tampered with –

Well, of *course*, I realized. We'd *all* been tampered with. This had to be an improvisational exercise – long and involved, but an improv just the same. The scene at the memory lane must have been part of the scenario and I must have been playing it just fine until I'd fallen out of character, thanks to a certain ham-handed famine fancier.

And so Anwar must have given me the Q to try to induce the character to resurface. But he'd overestimated the dosage and turned me into a zombie. No real harm done; the Q was starting to wear off now. My alertness was increasing, except it still felt strangely distant … as if the Q were wearing off my body, but not me. But wasn't that impossible, too? I'd have to ask someone.

You want to check the line?

Check the reality, Sovay, I thought. Pajamas let go of my hands. They fell limply onto my thighs. Anwar and the tint got me up on my feet. I was at least a head taller than Pajamas. He folded his arms and looked up at me, still with that pitying expression.

'For all your faults, Marceline, you were really a damned good Escort. I'll miss you. Your technique was –' He kissed his fingertips to the air. *Ham,* I thought at him. I felt like laughing out loud, never a good sign. If we didn't break within the next minute or so, I'd have to disrupt things and tell them I still wasn't back in character. They'd all probably have a group tantrum over the wasted time and effort, but it wouldn't have been fair to let things go on any longer if I couldn't react properly. Out of character, I was just *terrible* at improv.

I concentrated on making my mouth move to produce the words *We have to stop,* saying them over and over in my head. Then I cleared my throat, and my voice slid out thick and low, like a slowed-down recording.

'Jee habba cop.'

Pajamas blinked at me. 'Pardon?'

Migod, I thought, exasperated. The split-vision effect intensified. Whatever was doing it was now affecting my speech center as well. I'd have to warn Anwar not to give me so much Q in the future.

I swallowed and cleared my throat again for another try. Before I could make a sound, the left side of my vision gave a funny jump and I could no longer remember how to talk. But my voice came out anyway.

'She had a cop,' I heard myself say. 'She was a cop. She was Brain Police in deep undercover.'

Pajamas looked from Anwar to the tint and back to me. 'What *are* you talking about?'

I'm *not talking*, I tried to say, but my voice went on without me. 'That last trick ... *client*. The actor. She was Brain Police in deep undercover. That was why she wanted an Escort. To kill the cop. We killed a cop.'

Pajamas took a step back as if that would somehow help him see me better. 'To refresh what seems to be your suddenly failing memory, the client is a silly stage actor who couldn't purge herself of some useless character she'd made up for some stupid flop of a play.'

Migod. This fool of a scenery-chewer was actually so caught up in the improv he was going to fit whatever I said into the scenario without questioning it. 'That's what she told you,' I continued, unable to stop myself. 'And me. But she was Brain Police in deep undercover. The cops set her up with a life and if she had too many personalities, well, who's counting anyway? She wasn't even supposed to find that one, but she did. Or rather, her lover did. I got the whole story when I threw the cop over the cliff.'

Pajamas' face was wary. 'All those silly stage actors are multiples, and they're all Method actors. They believe they're whoever they're supposed to be. That's not *our* problem, unless you start believing it, too.'

My head went from side to side. 'The cop was the real thing. And –'

– and she's still here.

I finally managed to will my voice to shut off but the unspoken thought burned slowly into my mind like a shot of absolute truth. It didn't make any sense whatsoever. The character was a memory junkie, but unless there had been some kind of major script rewrite while I'd been unconscious, Escort services and Brain Police didn't figure into any part of the plot. Unless Marceline ...

But then, that would mean this wasn't an improv.

Just how out of hand had things gotten?

'That's got to be horseshit,' the tint was saying. 'Stupid delusions. She's a crunching *memory junkie*, she's got a whole head full of horseshit. She wants to be somebody else anyway, she probably believes she's God on the even-numbered days.'

Pajamas gave him a look. 'Today *is* an even-numbered day.' He frowned at me and then went up to the upper level to fiddle with something in his desktop. 'Hm. The client's mailing address has changed from that dreary storefront theatre to some very nice people. Moving up in the world. Perhaps Souse was right and our girl here has just been indulging in a little persona pattycake.' He chuckled. 'Dear Souse. I'd give her a raise, but it would just go to her head, and she'd waste it all on bad doughnuts, anyway.'

'Should we go get the trick?' asked the tint.

Pajamas rubbed his palms together slowly, as if he were mashing a bug

between them. 'Yah,' he said, coming back down to stand in front of me again. 'I think we should talk to her. It might have been just some silly character, or it could be our girl here got all mixed up and she's having a delusion or two from the persona overlay. Or it might be the real thing. There's no way to tell without having a look at the trick. Maybe she'll tell us where our girl has been for the last week.'

'And what'll we do with *our girl* in the meantime?'

The tint gave me a hard poke.

'Hold for later disposal, of course. I want to get the both of them together. If the trick actually conned our girl into dumping a cop, there should be a lot of very interesting information locked up in here.' He tapped his index finger on my forehead. 'Box her at three-quarters capacity. That ought to keep her motor idling well enough without anything wearing out too soon. Most of them don't even realize they're in a system when you run them at seventy-five percent.'

'Then go visit some very nice people and bring the actor in. *Alive.* But fast. If it's the real thing, it'll take time to jigger her memory. I don't plan to go down for a cop-kill.' He pinched my cheek. 'If it comes to that, that's what *you're* here for.' He made a brief dismissing gesture.

I waited for everyone to break out of character. Instead, Anwar and the tint walked me out of the sunken area and back into the elevator/lateral. Elaborate, extended exit, I thought desperately. They weren't *really* going to drop me on a slab, pluck out my eyes, and plug me into a system … were they?

The door closed. Anwar gathered my hand into his as the lateral began moving to the left. I started to shake. The Q had all but worn off now and I knew it wasn't an improv.

'Aw,' said the tint. 'Lovers' farewell? And here I thought you were off the stuff, Anwar. Maybe we oughta stop at supply and get you a bigger pump, eh? Just to keep you honest.'

'Sure,' said Anwar. 'Let's do that. I don't think this one's working right and I've had all I can take of her.'

The tint chuckled. 'Gotta cancel out those nasty old brain chemicals that make you think you're in love before they make you do something everybody'll be sorry for. Maybe you oughta go all the way and get your blood changed.' He turned to the control panel.

I started to say something. Anwar gave me a hard shove. Then the tint was lying on the floor of the lateral with blood welling up from the gash in his forehead where Anwar had slammed his face into the wall.

'This'll buy you two, maybe five minutes,' he whispered to me, pulling me into a far corner of the lateral, which had begun to descend now. 'You're a big pain in the ass, Mar, but I can't let them do this to you. Supply's on an exit

level. You shove us out there and take this thing to the out-door. Then run like a rabbit. I'll tell a story.'

'Where do I go?' I said, feeling helpless.

'How should *I* know? Go back to where you've been for the last week, I don't know!' The lateral came to a stop and the doors opened. Anwar hauled the tint up and threw him out bodily before turning to me and pointing at his chin. 'As hard as you can.'

I didn't get it.

'*Punch* me, goddammit!'

I'd never punched anyone in my life. My fighting experience was limited to stage combat, showy stuff that wouldn't even smear anyone's makeup. Then the funny vision on the left flared suddenly, spreading over to the left and I felt –

sorry, this is all for shit and it isn't even my own fault except for taking the job. But there was no choice about that, either, Bateau doesn't exactly let us pick and choose the clientele. I want to tell Anwar to keep wearing a pump because feeling like you can't let something happen to somebody in this business is pretty goddam inconvenient. He's better off pumping out whatever that funny stuff is that makes him think he loves me. And I want to tell him I'm sorry that I don't need a pump myself, and whether it's because of something that being a memory junkie did to me, or whether it's that fatal flaw that makes me a memory junkie in the first place – none of that makes any difference. But maybe that I can feel sorry about it counts for something. Maybe being sorry makes me a better person than when I was just someone who couldn't feel too bad about anything.

Above all, though, I'm sorry I'm hitting him instead of anyone else. And if you always end up hurting the one you don't want to hurt, then maybe that means I lo –

He was staggering backward out of the lateral. I saw him start to fall over the tint and then the door slid shut. The flavor of whatever thoughts had just been in my head was still whirling around but I couldn't catch the sense of it. My hand slapped the exit button without any prompting from me and the lateral started moving again.

I must be of two minds about this, I thought giddily, holding a hand over my mouth. I wasn't sure whether I wanted to laugh or cry, but I knew if I started either, I wouldn't stop until Pajamas caught up with me again and finished me off. And maybe not even then.

– *two minds about this*. No, not really. Not anymore. The funny split-vision effect was all gone now, leaving me with a strange, off-balance feeling. I thought

I'd go crazy waiting for Pajamas' voice to come out of some hidden speaker and tell me there was a reception committee standing by, but the lateral kept moving in silence. Then it began to slow and I had a fast flash of panic until I saw the words STREET EXIT flashing on the control panel. I hugged the wall next to the door and held my breath.

The door slid open; nobody barreled in to grab me. I risked a peek. The small, enclosed vestibule was empty and the out-door, plain, grey, blinking FUNCTIONAL in bright green at the access panel, looked so unremarkable, I suddenly wasn't sure that the last few minutes hadn't been some kind of delusional waiting dream.

No; the hand I'd used to punch Anwar hurt too much for a delusion. I rushed for the out-door.

'You'll need your keystrip to reenter.'

I whirled around, flattening against the out-door, but there was still no one in the vestibule.

'Weather and traffic patterns are available from the wall console to the left of the exit,' the voice added politely. Standard canned exit message, I realized, and looked for the console.

The compact screen was displaying a short menu, but there was nothing on it about me. Glancing nervously at the lateral, which was still standing open as if it were waiting for me to change my mind and get back in, I tapped the access panel.

'You'll need your keystrip to reenter,' the voice reminded me, and that was all. The exit swung open silently.

Run like a rabbit.

I tried, but my hand was throbbing so much, all I could manage was a peppy dogtrot. But at least I found a cab before my endurance gave out.

The driver charged me fare-and-a-half because she wasn't licensed to pick up anywhere higher than lower midtown and so would have to go back empty. I'd expected that, but I didn't like it anyway. The pick-up boundaries were supposed to be for the benefit of the populace and the ground cabs alike, to keep the drivers from stepping on each other's toes and spread service evenly throughout the city. But people seldom took cabs within a service district, so now it was just half again as expensive to get from one part of the city to the other.

I wasn't in complaint mode; I just paid the extortion, added a barely acceptable tip, and climbed out. The sight of Sir Larry's Storefront Theatre would have been reassuring if I hadn't been so drained. I didn't even want to flay anyone alive anymore. All I wanted now was a few answers and twenty-four hours of undisturbed coma. Then I could get back to my real life.

Or not. I was about to punch in my entry code when I caught sight of the

mini-marquee on the front door. The schedule for the season was scrolling along at a leisurely, readable pace, but it was the time/date display, blinking in alternation with the box office phone number, that got my attention. I watched it through five cycles, just to make sure I hadn't picked up some kind of reading deficit. The date given as today's was a week later than it should have been.

Go back to where you've been for the last week. I remembered the phone rejecting my bypass code. 'Shit,' I muttered and tried my entry code anyway, hoping that wasn't out-of-date as well. Damned memory lane, damned famine fancier; my brains were probably scrambled so badly that I'd have to see a doctor.

By some miracle, the entry code was still correct. I went through the empty lobby and stopped in the open doorway leading to the theatre. There were half a dozen people on the large, in-the-round stage. Rehearsal in progress.

Em-Cate spotted me first and broke out of the group, moving to the edge of the stage as I came down the center aisle. Her hair was stoplight red now, or maybe arterial-bleeding red; it matched the angry flush coloring her cheeks. Em-Cate hated being interrupted even more than she hated being called Catey. The rest of them turned to look at me, but the only one who showed any sign of recognition at all was Sovay. His skin was all bleached out and under the soft yellow lights, it was the exact color of urine. Very unfortunate, I thought.

'Deliveries in the rear,' Em-Cate said snappishly, fists on her hips. 'How many times do we have to tell you people that? Who gave you the entry code, anyway?'

In spite of everything, I couldn't help chuckling. 'I'm not here for a delivery.'

Twill moved to her side and said something in a low voice. All I caught were the words *Davy Jones*'. Em-Cate gave him a disbelieving look and then turned to me again. 'Sorry, but the troupe's full up now, no vacancy. Whoever you think you are.'

'That's an interesting way to put it, Em-Cate,' I said, boosting myself up onto the stage. 'But what I'd really like, among other things, is a new bypass code for the phone so I can call in the next time I need a ride home. The cab from the Downs cost me a fortune and a half.'

She turned to the others, who all looked bewildered. I was rather bewildered myself. Except for her and Twill and Sovay, I only half recognized most of them and there was one woman I couldn't place at all. I wondered if I'd be able to get Sir Larry's to foot my restoration bill.

'It's a situation for certain,' Em-Cate said, 'and it's all yours, Sovay. You're the one who said it was just temporary and if she was removed from the context, it wouldn't happen again. But look, here she is, all pumped up and ready

to play the part. What about *that*, Sovay? What do you think we should do, throw a welcome-back party?'

Migod, I thought; had I gotten so badly messed up that I'd crapped out on a performance and been fired?

'Em-Cate,' Sovay said warningly.

She gave him a dirty look. 'It's a *situation*. How do you think we should handle it now, Eisenstein?'

'Einstein,' Twill muttered.

Em-Cate gave him a swat. '*Eisenstein*. The great director. Sovay must think he's another one.'

'Shut up,' Sovay said. He was staring at me with a pained expression. Abruptly, I realized I was biting my nails.

'Well, obviously, I've had a fairly serious glitch,' I said. 'All I'd really like to know at the moment is why I was just left to stumble around in somebody else's life instead of being rescued and treated. Is the competition around here getting that cutthroat?'

Sovay's pained look intensified. Migod, I thought, I *had* been fired. Fired and – I glanced at the woman I didn't know – replaced. The woman looked away from me and I realized I was biting my nails again. What an incredibly vile habit. Leak-through from the character, perhaps? Just my luck – when I finally started getting something from her, it wasn't anything useful, just disgusting.

'Do you remember anything about being at Davy Jones' Locker last night?' Sovay asked me. 'And getting thrown out?'

'*Thrown out?*' I gave a humorless laugh and held out some of my disastrous hair. 'Looking like this, I'm not surprised I got challenged. But didn't any of you very nice people bother to tell the bouncers I was in costume?'

There was a short but heavy silence. 'It was a private party,' Em-Cate said snottily, 'and it was for some very nice people, not for us. There are still those who won't sell their souls to be some very nice people.'

'Shut *up*,' Sovay said. 'Can't you see she doesn't get it? It doesn't mean any-thing to her.'

'Nothing ever meant anything to that woman,' Em-Cate said. 'She was always just out for what she could get and this was the only way she could ever get anyone to say anything good about her, going off to be one of some very –'

'*Turn it off!*' Sovay barked.

Some very nice people ... suddenly, it was starting to make sense.

'Please,' I said, taking a step toward him. He looked as if he wanted to back away and if he had, I'd have fallen apart right there. 'I think I'm in some kind of serious trouble with this character, but I can't remember. I woke up this morning in a memory lane in the Downs and I was missing a week. Then I

saw myself in a dataline ad –' I lowered my voice but the acoustics were too good. 'I think for a franchiser. I think I did something, made a deal or something, in character. And I think the character did something else as well, because a green guy and another guy kidnapped me and threw me in a van and took me to –'

'*Don't*,' Sovay said.

I pulled my fingers out of my mouth and wiped them on my pants. 'Sorry. They –'

'I mean don't tell me anymore. Just *don't*. I don't need that kind of trouble. The only thing I can tell you to do is go back to the memory lane you woke up in and have them finish the job.'

I stared at him. It would have been a pretty bad joke, but he wasn't kidding. 'Have you lost your mind? Or am *I* short in that department?'

'Good question, don't you think?' Em-Cate was standing right behind me now. 'Whose mind got lost? And is it finders-keepers?'

Sovay let out a noisy breath. 'We can't just leave her to –'

'Oh, yes, we *can*,' Em-Cate said. 'We are *not* responsible. This is *not* our business and I refuse to be a party to anything even remotely connected with it.' She gave me a hard look. 'Regardless of who suffers.'

'She's right,' said Twill. 'If we put ourselves in this, we all might end up in a van. If you want to take that ride, fine. Not me.'

'Or me.' Em-Cate turned her back abruptly. 'Rehearsal's scrubbed. Everyone out of the pool.'

They all jumped down from the stage, rushing for the stairs down to the dressing room as if they were running from – well, whatever I'd just run away from. Except for Sovay. Em-Cate looked back at him, shook her head, and followed the rest of them.

I waited for Sovay to do something or tell me something, but he just stood there with that pained expression on his no-color face, as if he were the one in trouble.

'Well,' I said with a weak laugh, 'I guess I can assume I'm fired, too. On top of everything else.'

'*Christ*, I feel so bad for you.' It burst out of him like he was confessing a secret sin he couldn't live with a moment longer. 'And for me. And for everything that happened. I wish I didn't know. I wish I didn't know *you*.'

'Quite an extraordinary expression of sympathy,' I said after a long moment. 'Thanks, I don't know where I'd be without your friendship and support.' I turned away from him.

'Where are you going?' he asked quickly.

'Well, let's see. Unemployment office should be my first stop, I guess. I take it my termination notice is on file? Then I guess I'll get my resume rewritten, put my name in for next season's cattle calls –' I pretended to think hard and

then snapped my fingers. 'Oh, yah, guess I'll hit a body clinic and get out of this ridiculous costume since it tends to encourage kidnapping.'

He caught my arm before I could jump down off the stage. 'Listen, M-mar ... ' Pause. 'Marva. *Marva.* I can't get over it. It really *is* you. Isn't it.'

The expression on his face was startling; it was as if he were transfixed. 'Is *that* what this is all about – Em-Cate and Twill and everyone else *just don't recognize me?*'

Now he looked as if he were on the verge of tears. The boy always could run an emotional gamut on short notice. 'I recognize you. I remember ... ' His voice died away.

'Yah, I remember, too.' I shrugged. 'But not as much as I've forgotten. Which I don't think was by choice.'

'No, it wasn't.' He took a breath. 'If I could figure out some way to help you – to help *you*, Marva – I'd do it. I miss you.'

This was a light-year and a half from the never-again-I-love-my-wife agonizing I was used to hearing. It threw me so much I almost missed the strange emphasis he'd placed on my name. *You, Marva.* What in hell was *that* supposed to mean?

'I still care,' he went on, embarrassed. 'I couldn't let it continue between us. Not because it didn't mean anything but because it did.'

I waved his words away. 'Me, Marva as opposed to me, *who? Who*, Sovay? Me, the character? Me, Marceline?'

'Marceline's –' He cut off so sharply that he didn't even breathe. But I could hear the rest of the sentence so clearly in my head that I wasn't sure that he hadn't said it after all.

Marceline's not a character.

I had the sudden wild notion that I hadn't really gotten away from Pajamas and this was my mind chugging along at seventy-five percent of capacity in a box.

Marceline's not a character.

Like a shot of absolute truth ... like *another* shot of absolute truth, straight to the brain ...

... and the cop's still here.

Marceline's not a character ...

... and the cop's still here ...

You want to check the line?

Marceline's not a cop ...

... and the cop's not a character ...

... and Marceline's still here ...

My head was full of noises and voices and a jumble of pictures that didn't make any sense – Sovay, Sir Larry's, Davy Jones' Locker, the Downs at three A.M., Anwar. They whirled around and around like leaves in a cyclone, blur-

ring, melting into each other to form a new image, unfamiliar but vivid and detailed and unmistakably mine:

The edge of a cliff, high above some enormous, vague space. I felt a flash of something like agoraphobia, except that wasn't quite it – this was more than being afraid of too much open space, this was a fear of nothingness, of nonexistence –

A hand clamped onto my upper arm on the exact spot where the green guy had grabbed me, putting bruises on my bruises. The pain cleared my vision and I saw I was teetering on the edge of the stage.

'Easy,' Sovay said, pulling me back a few steps. 'You looked like you were going to faint.'

'Not faint. I was going to do something, but it wasn't faint.' I stared at the edge of the stage, seeing the cliff superimposed on it.

'Ah, the prodigal has returned!'

I looked up; the man coming down the aisle toward the stage had a thousand-watt smile, but as he got closer, I could see it didn't really fit him. He had a long, bony face surrounded by a lot of wiry white hair so dried out, I was afraid it would catch fire from the scented cigarette he was smoking. His expensive clothes didn't really fit him, either, as if he were wearing a costume put on in a hurry. I almost placed him … something about last night and Davy Jones' Locker …

The woman walking behind him didn't flick any switches, either, but she was wearing one of those don't-recognize-me getups, a floppy hat and sunglasses big enough to cover the upper half of her face.

Somebody Big, I thought, replete with Mrs S.B., or maybe Somebody Big and *Mr* S.B. Come to Sir Larry's to give some actor the Big Break everybody was praying for. I looked at Sovay. His gaze was locked on the guy, who was now climbing up onto the stage as if he owned it.

'There's no smoking in here,' Sovay said thinly.

'Sorry.' The guy dropped his cigarette on the stage and stepped on it. 'You've no idea how glad we are to see *you* again. What a *dreadful* mistake last night.'

He was talking to me, I realized, and thought of the ad I'd seen in the video parlor. Still smiling, he reached for my arm. I stepped back, shielding the sore area, and he gave Sovay a murderous look.

'I didn't say a thing,' Sovay told him. 'Talk to her. You'll see.'

I rubbed my bruised bicep. 'Are you the one running that commercial?'

'Commercial?' the man said, trying to glare at Sovay and smile at me all at once.

'Word is out now,' Sovay said. He walked over to where the woman was waiting, one elbow leaning on the edge of the stage and her hand cupping her chin, ostentatiously bored. She reminded me of someone. 'You know, I almost wish I could hear you explain.'

She refused to look up at him. Speaking of explanations people wanted to hear, I thought; whatever had happened between them must have been pretty poisonous. Apparently Sovay's virtue wasn't as stainless-no-rust as he wanted the world to believe.

'I think I can figure it out myself,' I said, ambling over closer to Sovay. 'You people made a franchise deal with me, or rather, someone you thought was me. It was actually one of my characters. Maybe she really fooled you, or maybe you just let yourselves be fooled, but it doesn't matter now anyway, because the whole deal's invalid.'

'Ah. Is that how it is.' He glanced over at the woman.

'Erase the contract and we'll call it an honest mistake,' I said. 'No lawsuit, no charges. I'll even give back fifty percent of whatever you paid me for an advance. You can think of the other half as a rental fee.'

'That's generous of you,' he said.

'I'm a generous person. But I don't want to be a franchise.'

'Are you sure about that? Maybe you should read the contract you signed. That *she* signed, excuse me. It's a very sweet deal.'

'I'm sure it is, but it's not for me, thanks all the same. All I ever wanted to do was act in legitimate theatre.'

'Now that's dedication,' the man said. 'If you insist. Come back to the offices with us and we'll take care of it immediately.'

'Thanks, but you can just zap it to me net-mail,' I said. 'I'll trust you.'

The man hesitated and glanced at the woman again. 'You did leave some personal property with us. We'd like to return it to you.'

'You can mail that, too,' I said. 'I don't mind. Or I'll pay for a courier.'

'Against our policy. We have to put it into your hands personally.'

'Then *you* pay for the courier.'

He was struggling like mad to hang on to his patience and losing. 'Look, it won't take you any time at all.'

'Do as he says,' Sovay said suddenly. He was pointedly not looking at the woman now, though he was still standing over her. Migod, did I want to hear *that* story. 'Go with them. They'll take care of everything. They have to; there's a witness.'

I didn't like the sound of that and it must have showed – Sovay suddenly gave me a quick hug around the shoulders. 'Go ahead,' he said in a low voice. 'After, you'll remember everything.'

'Suppose you just fill me in and I take your word for it.'

'I can't,' he said heavily. 'I don't know anything.'

He stared down at the woman. 'All right? *I don't know anything.*'

She nodded without looking at him. 'Yah. I heard you.' Her voice sounded extremely familiar, but, as usual, the memory was just out of reach. It was maddening.

'Okay,' I said to the white-haired guy. 'But I want to come back here afterward.'

'We'll take you anywhere you want to go,' he said.

I moved toward the edge of the stage and damned if he didn't grab my sore arm. I tried to pull away but he insisted on helping me down from the stage. The woman was already heading back up the aisle as fast as she could go.

At the doorway, I paused to look back. Sovay was still standing there on the empty stage, staring after us. Or staring after *her*, except she was already gone. I wanted to call out to him that I'd be back, but the white-haired guy was already pulling me through the doorway to the lobby.

There was a private little-stretch humming at the curb, complete with driver. I started to hang back, trying to think of some excuse to go back into the theatre, but the guy hustled me into the back of the stretch. The woman was hugging the far end of the forward-facing seat, staring out at the traffic as if it were the most fascinating sight she'd ever seen. The guy planted me on the opposite seat, still hanging on to my arm as if he thought I might try to dive out the other door.

I leaned forward and looked at the entrance to the theatre, hoping like mad that Sovay would come running out, yelling for us to stop.

Yah. Maybe tomorrow. The guy pulled the door shut and there was a hiss as freshened, scented air blew into the interior. Suddenly, I had the strongest feeling that just as we went airborne, I was going to discover I was getting sleepy.

But nothing of the sort happened. Nothing happened at all, except that the guy finally let go of my arm. The woman didn't even take off her sunglasses.

The room would have made *prima* rehearsal space. It was twice the size of the warm-up room at Sir Larry's, with plenty of pads for floor work, freestanding exercise barres, and a lavabo with more attachments than I could identify functions for.

'Nice?' the guy said as I looked it over.

'Yah.' I pulled my head out of the lavabo and slid the door shut. 'I've never seen a five-speed pulsator before.'

'The item most requested by our people,' he said. 'We have about two dozen installed all over the building, so no one ever has to wait.'

'Very considerate.' I stepped away from him. 'And thanks for the tour, but let's get this over with. I don't want to be Famous, and I wouldn't want it even if you had three dozen lavabos on this floor alone. I don't want people walking around thinking they're me.'

'Maybe they aren't.' The woman had come up next to me without making a sound, so close that I could see twin reflections of my startled face in her big, stupid, dark glasses. Smiling, she plucked the floppy hat off her head and dropped it on mine.

I knocked the hat away, irritated.

'Maybe that's not who they think they are at all.' She pulled off the glasses. It took me about five full seconds to realize I was looking at my own face. My *original* face.

Freeze-frame.

Somewhere, that cliff is still waiting for me. Waiting for someone. If you put in a cliff at the beginning of Act I, someone has to go over it by the end of Act II. Chekhov's Law, isn't that how it goes? It applies even more in here than on any stage out there.

In here. That's a strange way to think of it, really: sometimes the strangeness jumps up and hits me full on. Only in my line of work does the mind become imbued with such essence of **place**. Well my line of work and Marva's. Marceline's, too, I guess, but I don't know *as* much about her. Yet.

But that Marva – talk about self-destructive. Ha, and ha, as Marceline would say. She hasn't been saying much of late. My conscience is bothering me about her, in spite of the fact that I had no choice, not if I wanted to live. I had no choice, and now she has no chance. I outnumber her.

But there is no time for the contemplation of moral dilemmas, even one as critical as this is. The lights are going to come up soon and we have to give the performance of our life … lives? We have to get out of this intact before we can figure out what to do about Marceline's stolen life.

Not that I'd call her an innocent bystander. After all, she came to kill me. Even after she realized who and what I was, she was going to go through with it, fling me over that cliff. Marva's cliff.

Should have seen that Marva was too good … too **real**. The hazards of being multiple sometimes overwhelm even the most rigorous Brain Police training. But I should have seen it coming, been prepared for it.

In legitimate theatre, they're prepared for it. A hazard of Method acting, it's called **achieving escape velocity**, which gives it the sound of true accomplishment, worthy of awe. Is that what really sells tickets – a freak show? Come see the human who dreamed so hard of being a butterfly that she sprouted wings and flew away?

In the old days, Method acting had nothing to do with multiple personalities. Not so overtly, anyway. In the old days, there were two kinds of actors: the ones who disappeared into their roles, and the ones whose roles disappeared into them. But maybe in the end, it was just as hard to tell which was which.

Marva found out. She shouldn't have been able to; she wouldn't have, except for Sovay. He was the one who came upon me unawares in the depths. Maybe **he** was the one who was too good, not Marva; too good at delving the layers of personality, identity: He was too good, and Marva wanted him too much.

Being in deep undercover, I couldn't do anything about it. She had to live what she would, after all, if I was ever going to get a lead on the bootleg-ging operation. And that was what I'd thought was my greatest danger, that in the process of delving her mind, bootleggers would come across that closed-off room that she had no knowledge of and no access to, and they would find out she was a Brain Police officer in deep undercover. I had never thought it would actually be her lover who would find me and give me away to her.

I don't think he meant to. From that moment to this, I really don't think that was his intention. But as soon as he knew, she knew; they were hooked in mind-to-mind, after all. They shouldn't have been, given her enormous attraction to him and his own Infatuation. People who want each other so much shouldn't get too much of each other. The knowledge gave him a trauma, but that was nothing compared to what It did to her.

She shouldn't have been able to Initiate a split but, as I say, she was too good. She had already achieved escape velocity, she was Marva and she loved it. She wanted to go on being Marva, not some nobody Brain Police officer.

So she split off her new, more aware self from the old Marva character and if she hadn't, I'd be dead now, long gone over the border that divides life from death. Courtesy of the Escort she hired to do exactly that, take me over the border.

But just because she had achieved escape velocity didn't make her the ori-ginal. That was still me, always me, and I wanted to live a lot more than she wanted me to die.

In my more generous moments, I admire her ingenuity in hiring an Escort to get rid of me. It was a true Method solution: If a character can believe she's alive, then she must believe she can die.

But here's something she didn't consider: There's life after death, if you want it badly enough.

Lights coming up. It's showtime.

The show must go on.

I was belly-down on the stage at Sir Larry's. Mostly Sir Larry's – some of the details were different, or missing altogether, little textural things tipping me off that they'd taken the liberty of relieving me of my eyes as well as my conscious state.

I should have been upset, but whatever it took to run the emotional gen-erator was missing. That wasn't an effect of whatever drug the guy had used to knock me out – I could feel the drug wearing off, but the sensation was distant, like the vibration of water running down a drain in another room. This had more to do with why I was flat on the floor of the stage ... *flattened* on the floor of the stage ...

You're getting warmer.

The words were neither thought nor voice; more like something I was remembering, vivid but definitely in the past. Information at one remove; remembering my lines, except this time I had no lines. I wasn't flattened on the stage, I *was* the stage ...

No, I was the whole damned theatre, including the stage.

Em-Cate would love this, I thought, walking over a rival's back to do a part.

Em-Cate is not your rival, memory said, if memory it was.

Who, then?

And there I was. No, not me; the woman with my face.

Some very nice people ...

Some Very Nice People.

Of course. Rather a cutesy name for a franchise, but the type of people drawn to franchising love that kind of cheap cleverness. It's part of what makes them crave a persona overlay. There must have been some complementary quality that makes an actor want to be Famous – i.e., get franchised – but I had no idea what it was. I'd never wanted to be Famous. What I wanted was –

– to stay in existence. To live.

Obviously. All right. Nothing like starting at the basics.

The rival for your existence. Think.

The woman with my face started to move around the stage in a series of warm-up exercises I recognized as my own – a little yoga, a little t'ai chi, a little ballet, and a little kitchen sink. I could see her from any and all angles now, and it was like watching a burglar enjoying stolen property.

Now I got it: she was really here. This wasn't an image or a memory, we were hooked in together mind-to-mind. She didn't know I was aware of her because I wasn't supposed to be. I was supposed to be –

– standing on the edge of the cliff.

Escort/memory junkie, just doing my job. This one was pretty unusual – Escorts didn't get many calls from actors asking to be rid of a troublesome personality. But what the hell, it was work. Didn't much matter as long as somebody died.

No. For the millionth time, no. That was Marceline, the character I'd been developing. Sorry, the name of the play and the general plot seems to escape me for the moment, but that's just a memory glitch, probably brought on by a stupid famine fancier in a cheap memory lane who insisted on work with her mouth full. But anytime now, it was going to come to me, I was going to remember everything about Marceline –

Marceline's not a character.

Marceline began to fade in on the stage, the image of how I looked now in full costume. Except if she wasn't a character, how could this be a costume?

She was materializing in response to the movements of the woman with my face, I realized. Like a conjuring trick …

Or like the creation of a character for a play, except the character was someone who really existed and the play was my life … my *new* life …

I hadn't been franchised – I'd been bodysnatched.

Is that the way it was? A lost-soul memory junkie with a yen for more than a persona overlay. *Give me a whole new life, give me somebody else's life because I'm sick of mine. Give me her life, yah, that one there. The actress. I'll take her. I'll be her.*

They'd given her my personality in an overlay and then given her my appearance as well, while they'd made me over to look like her, imprinted me with her –

Even as I thought it, I knew it wasn't quite right. Bodysnatchings weren't unheard of. There were plenty of sad cases walking around looking to hijack someone else's life and leave their own bleak existences behind, and changing their own appearances to match wasn't beyond most of them.

But surgically altering the *other* person … not to that extent. It was easier just to suck the mind out, scramble the finger and retina-prints, and dump the rest in a cipher ward.

The cliff reappeared with the three women and my attention zoomed in on the one in the middle, the woman that the Escort was there to kill.

Me?

She looked like me, but there were differences.

A new image blossomed in the middle of the scene: one of us – me? the bodysnatcher? – standing in the semidark of Davy Jones' Locker, wearing a Brain Police uniform. Me? Or some character I couldn't remember creating?

The memory hung in midair just beyond the edge of the cliff. I couldn't touch it without going over.

I turned away and found myself looking at the funhouse mirror in Davy Jones' Locker again, except it was a million times longer than the real thing, stretching as far away from me as I could see. Farther than that. I was alone, but the mirror had plenty of reflections anyway, side by side by side, reflections with no one to cast them, reflections waiting for someone to claim them. Or waiting for someone to claim?

The reflection I was supposedly casting turned to face me. *The mirror is in the eye of the reflected.*

What?

We're going to find out how good an actress you really are, she said. *In the old days, they didn't use imprints to create characters. People just did impersonations and tried to be convincing. How convincing can you be?*

How convincing can I be as what?

She gestured at the image next to her; how I looked now, the Escort's original appearance.

My point-of-view moved closer. Her features showed more clearly, that round, homely face surrounded by that terrible faded brown frizz passing for hair, that bulky body dressed in ragpicker *du jour*, and not the chic *du jour*, either. This was stuff that stronger, faster ragpickers left behind.

Can you convince them you're her? Because unless you do, you'll really be her. And no one will ever believe otherwise. Can you convince them? Can you convince her?

What, in here? The Escort's reflection was aligning herself with me now. I couldn't move away.

In here, out there everywhere … She can't stay in contact with you while this one takes control – too risky for her. She could get herself confused with you.

You have to keep this one from taking over and then convince them she has. So they'll let you go.

Oh, was *that* all. And how did I manage this minor miracle? Was there a miracle kit in here somewhere?

Abruptly, I was back in Sir Larry's again – *was* Sir Larry's again. The Escort's image was standing in the middle of the stage, a marionette sans strings. Somewhere in the theatre – in me – was the remote control for her. I let my awareness spread itself out as if I were doing one of those full-body relaxation exercises where you concentrate on each part of yourself …

Found it; With the control came a small flood of information, names, faces, locations, and a flash-shot: the sight of my own face rushing at her, pulled by some tropism from the empty space beyond the edge of the cliff one scant moment before the fall.

More images came up in bursts, scenes from the area of the Downs where I'd been doing characterization research. She knew them all as if she had seen them with my own eyes … or as if I had seen them with her own eyes …

Onionheads, rooster-boys, street-corner neurosis peddlers, sidewalk holos meant to jump-and-jive you into the dreamlands for a cheap dose of REM-pix, and the featureless one-roomer where I'd been staying on a short-term lease. Hustlers passing off cheap fixations and compulsions and calling them real neuroses, dreamlands fronting for chop shops that sold stolen memories and the last scrapings from sucked-out minds to hungry junkies (like me?). Anwar, who had suddenly had an attack of something like decency. Bateau sending (me) on another out-call, saying, come back with something good, come back with something I can use, that's what I keep you for, come back and I'll fill your head with all the things you can't get enough of and can't have for real, but most of all, come back. Come back.

Yah, I'll come back, if I have to walk through a hail of fire, if I have to kill them instead of just taking them to the edge and letting them go over them-selves. And whatever I find in the lives they leave behind is mine to take with me, at least until Bateau takes it from me, and sometimes I call him a pimp

instead of an agent, but I ain't no uptown day-wage priv. I got less than nothing
but other people's memories make it like there's something. And in here, who
knows the difference?

The vertigo of being in two places at once was almost overwhelming. I
wanted to stop and reach for the Method instead, but something held me
back until I got used to what I was doing. It felt so strange. How did those
old-time actors do it, how did they become other people and still know that
they weren't?

My eye sockets hurt, so I know I'm not in the system anymore, but
where I really am I want to find out without anyone knowing. I've got
this crazy memory of being at Bateau's and getting away, but I was deli-
rious or something ...

Shit, the damned memory lane Anwar took me to. That skull-and-
bones bitch must have shot me with a bad load. She used me for a dump,
scraped out the bottom of the barrel of whatever chop shop she was
fronting for, and while all the junk she shot into me went playtime, I
fugued out. Christ knows who or what I've been claiming I was. My
memory's all jumbled up, I remember things about a theatre and some-
one named Sovay and some other guy with white hair –

And her. The client. No, fuck Bateau's fancy talk: the trick. Much bet-
ter word for her, trick. She was a trick, all right, they're all tricks in the
end. Especially in the end, where they always try to drag you along with
them. They can't help it, drowning people will do the same. But that's
not *my* problem, my problem is getting out of the thrill-and-chill alive
and in one piece. That's the *real* trick.

Well, I'm alive, but I don't know how many pieces I got now. Worst
thing I could have done was take that job. I tried to get Bateau to let me
out of it, but he was all excited. Go on, go ahead and kill that personality
for her and while you're in, grab for all the goodies you can, let's see what
we come up with while the client's still alive and maybe of some use.

And what do you know: she didn't have much, not the one who hired
me. It was the one she wanted to kill who had all the goodies, because
she was the one in charge after all. Surprise good-bye, followed by a sur-
prise hello. I got a little more than anyone figured I'd get, and all I have
to do now is unload it without getting chilled myself. If Bateau knew she
was a cop –

Jee habba cop.

Shit, did *I* say that? Does he believe it?

And the cop's still here.

He doesn't know *that* yet, but if he gets his hands on me again, he'll
find out, and I'll get the chill with no thrill.

Unless I can make him think it was all just runaway memory after the fact. Then give him some cop stuff. She must have had plenty when she sank her hooks into me and reeled herself in off that cliff, and it must all still be there –

'Are you awake?'

I was still too drugged to startle. The trick leaned over me looking all you-poor-baby and I was supposed to buy it. 'You can sleep a little longer if you like,' she went on, too friendly. 'The operation was a success, the patient died, and all's right with the world.'

I get it. I'm supposed to think it just happened, what we did last week, I'm supposed to think we're just finishing up. The game is, I pick up and go home, walk right into Bateau a week or more out-of-date. He takes a can opener to my head and that's *my* problem. And their problems are all solved, because when I go, the cop goes with me and no one's left to tell the tale.

And a tiny little voice in my head says, *Sovay*. For a moment I get him confused with Anwar and I can't remember which of us had who, or, for that matter, how. Was he there, too? Was he there, watching from a safe distance while we balanced on the edge of the cliff?

No. I know that one for sure, he couldn't have hidden from me. But he'd been there. He'd left traces. And he could claim all he wanted that he didn't know, but when Bateau took that can opener to my head, Bateau would see where he'd been and what he knew, and even if he didn't know it anymore, Bateau would make sure he couldn't know it again. Just in case.

I got to get out of here *now*. Maybe I can tell this Sovay he's got trouble, maybe not. He should know he does, just because he knows her, but he probably doesn't. If he were really smart, he'd have gotten himself a pump like Anwar's.

I sit up, ready to go, and then freeze. I'm back in my old rags from last night. If my fancy clothes are gone, that means my wads are gone. Son of a bitch, how cheap can they get?

'If you're all done with me,' I say, 'you can call me a cab. Right after you pay me.'

Ha, and ha – who says I can't think up stuff? She wasn't expecting that one. She looks off to her right and this white-haired guy comes over, and I almost choke, because it's Coney Loe in uptown drag.

So *now* I get it. We *are* talking bootleggers and bodysnatchers and who knows what else, if Coney Loe's involved. Anybody fooling with bootlegging and body snatching has got to have a Downs connection and there's none better than an information junkie like Coney Loe. He lives to find out everything and then spills his guts. Got to say he looks

good in uptown drag. Hell, he almost looks natural, except I think the last natural thing he ever did was breathe in for the first time.

She makes Coney come across with a fistful of currency – not as much as I was holding when I came to in Davy Jones' Locker. After having that much, I'm ruined, I want it all back, but what can I do?

'There,' he says, pressing a pile of bills down on my hand and closing my fingers around it. 'Your fee, and a tip you can hype out on.'

She gives him a look. 'Maybe we'll beat that errand boy's vocabulary out of you.'

'Call her a cab,' he says, jerking his head at her. They have a glare contest for a few seconds and then she stalks out of the room.

'Temperament,' he says to me. 'You know how these actors can be. Even after they get everything they want.'

I swing my legs over the side of the bed, barely missing him as he steps back. Just as my feet hit the floor, I get the oddest damned sensation, this damned feeling that I'm not moving. More like I'm being steered. Used.

Sometimes, you eat a bad memory somewhere that gives you the being-used creeps. You find yourself taking a little daytrip to the scene of somebody else's crime all because you've got the memory of what happened and where. Like the memory knows somehow it's in the wrong head and it wants to get back to where it started.

I want to shut down, take a breather, and figure out what I could be remembering now, but whatever's making me move isn't in the mood to stop.

'Something wrong?' Coney's giving me a wary look.

'Hangover,' I growl at him. What does he know about it?

She steps back in with this big, bad old smile. 'I took the liberty of calling your agent instead of a cab. He's sending a van for you. A free ride's better than fare-and-a-half, isn't it?'

The adrenaline rush is like a punch in the gut.

'You sure you're all right?' Coney says, and for a minute there I can almost believe he wants to know.

'*Hangover*,' I growl again. 'Just show me the way outta here, I'll wait outside.' If I can hit the sidewalk before Bateau's van shows, I can sprint for it.

'This way,' she says, crooking her finger at me. I follow her through this big old empty room with a lavabo in the middle of it, to a lift that isn't much more than a cage on a pulley and a chain. Moving around still feels funny to me, like my body is an exoskeleton and it's a bad fit.

The lift is so slow it's painful. I'm slouching in the far corner and she's at the control panel like she thinks I might jump her, which reminds me

of being at Bateau's in delirium. I can remember how I got out of there now. Poor Anwar, I hit him with everything I had and it must have hurt. Not likely I'll get a chance like that again.

And *then* I remember what Bateau said before that, in his office. *Bring the actor in alive. And fast.*

Oh, boy. Bateau must have wet his pants laughing when she called him to come pick me up. Do I tell her she's taking this ride with me, or do I just let it be a surprise?

'What?' she says suddenly, and I realize I've been staring at her. 'Nobody can prove a thing,' she adds. 'She's gone, and her memories are gone. All I have to do now is purge my own memory of the knowledge that she was ever there, and I'm home free, warm, and dry.'

Now, I know, I just *know* that she's talking about that cop, the one she had in her head, or thought she had in her head. Well, fuck her. Let Bateau have at her with everything he's got. What choice did I get in any of this anyway? It's not like we voted. Let *her* get the box and I'll be home free, warm, and dry for a change. Bateau will find out how things really are, and take her apart instead of me.

'You'd better purge the memories when you're through with them,' she says then. 'You don't want to risk getting caught with them if they actually get a search warrant. And they *will* come looking when she doesn't report in. But if they can't find a trace of her, they'll just have to give up and leave us all alone, and I'll be free to live my life the way I want to. I just hope for your sake that your pimp knows how to hide the database.'

The database. That's it. That's what Bateau will want, when he knows it exists. All the Brain Police have one locked up in their minds, all the things they have to know, but that they can't get at until they really need it. The only problem is, I don't have it anymore. I used to. I can even almost remember what was in it, but I put it somewhere, and I'm god-damned if I can remember where –

From nowhere: chewing.

Oh, Jesus, *her?* Did I give it to that skinny bitch in the memory lane? Or did she just help herself to it like it was a platter of fucking deli sandwiches?

Like *that* matters. What matters is that I get it back again. It's the only thing I can offer Bateau to make him believe I'm still with the program.

'Tell me,' she says, 'is it hard for memory junkies to forget, or are you used to your memories coming and going?'

She's got that look, belligerent and knowing, one-up-on-the-world.

*

The urge to gloat was going to be the death of her. 'Yeah, sure,' I say, 'they come and go and one's as good as another if you want to get a rise.'

The elevator thumps to a stop and the outer door rattles open. We're at the far end of a large, airy, glassed-in lobby and it's a mob scene, people all over the place. She starts to get off but I hang back. This tall guy in a silvery uniform strolls by and gives me a wink.

'It's all right,' she says, and she looks like she doesn't know whether she wants to laugh at me or swing on me. 'It's just the catalog. They're all holos.'

Now I can see that. The tall guy is looking about six inches too far to my left, about the usual margin of error for guidance software. But it's still pretty great holo; no static, even though it's indoors, and real solid, you can't see through them unless you get right up close or unless there's a bright light right behind them.

'Doesn't this scare off the trade?' I say.

She's trying to pull me out of the elevator. 'Don't be ridiculous. This is what everyone comes here for.' I hold on to the door, trying to see if there's a van parked at the curb outside. But who says Bateau would send the same van, or any van? Maybe he wouldn't even send Anwar; maybe he figured out what Anwar did and Anwar's treading time in a box now.

'You got another way out of here?' I say. 'Back door, trapdoor?'

She blows out a heavy, put-upon breath. 'Look, why don't you just go back to your life? You're not me, and you'll never be me. If I'd known you were such a quick study, I wouldn't have –'

Boom – like that, I've got both hands around her throat before I even know it. Someone is yelling –

'I *know* what happened, you incredible bitch!' I yelled into that face, my stolen face. The feel of Marceline broke apart like wet tissue; so much for the masquerade. '*This* is my life and *you* stole it!' I slammed her against the wall. '*You're* the one going back to that pimp, not me! *You're* the Escort –'

She was making choking noises and pulling on my wrists. I could squeeze the life right out of her, I realized. I was bigger and heavier now, I could literally kill her in the old-fashioned, down-and-dirty way and suddenly I really wanted to do that. Let her find out what it was like to go all the way to the brink of death and be forced over it –

She's not going to go willingly.

The memory came up with such force and feeling that I thought I'd been instantly transported to some other place, *that* other place, the cliff where it had all happened –

That's what you're *here for, that's why I called you. She's just a character, just a useless character who put down too many roots and believed she was real. I can't use her anymore but she keeps trying to take over.*

I remembered; I remembered saying it. But if *I* said it ... who was I choking?

Her face was a deep red. I let go, shocked at the sight and at myself. Coughing, she staggered away from me just as the front door slid open. I stepped into the crowd of holos as the green guy came striding in, a graft bandage on his head marring the green. Anwar was right behind him. The pump on his belt was bigger.

I slipped behind a holo of a woman in a billowy outfit of scarfs; she was swaying back and forth with her arms spread, dancing in place to whatever music she'd been hearing when they'd scanned her. With only a wall behind, it was all but opaque. Still coughing and clutching her throat, the body-snatcher staggered through the image of some man in a glittery quasi-military costume cracking a soundless whip and directly into the tint.

'Where is she?' the tint demanded, digging a hand into her hair and pulling her head back. A sad-faced clown in a hobo outfit broke into silent laughter, holding his stomach and pointing. All the woman could do was cough and try to shake her head.

'*Where?*' yelled the tint and jerked his head at the holos. 'Look around!' he barked at Anwar. 'Keep your eyes open!'

The dancing woman made a sudden small leap to the left; I leaped with her, spreading my arms behind hers and matching her movements as best I could. The projection was so high-res, I could just barely see through her head as Anwar walked toward the center of the lobby, letting various characters pass through him as he scanned the display.

The woman leaped to the opposite side and I managed to go with her again. The long, filmy scarf around her neck flew back and ripped through my head. I felt nothing – having a holo go through you is less than having a shadow fall on you – but I was afraid of interference breaking up the image. But nothing happened, not so much as mild static, even when she took an unexpected step back and I found myself wearing the image like an exoskeleton. That was all right; I had her choreography pretty well figured out. All I could do was keep moving and hope it didn't make any sudden and dramatic changes. If she did anything even mildly acrobatic, I was finished.

Anwar continued his slow walk through the room. I was swaying in place when he stopped five feet away and turned to look directly at the holo. I forced myself to keep swaying instead of jumping out of my holo skin and bolting for the door. At that distance, he had to see me. At least, he had to see something moving inside the image like a double exposure that didn't quite match up.

Maddeningly, he just stood there and kept watching, and now his eyes seemed to be looking directly into mine. I kept moving with the image, waiting for him to reach forward and pull me out.

Instead, he reached down and shut his pump off in mid-beep. I dropped my arms and stood there as the holo woman jumped to the left, but at the same moment, he turned away.

'She must have run out just before we got here.'

The tint was dragging the bodysnatcher toward the front door. 'Come on, we'll see if we can catch her out on the street,' he said. She was struggling, trying to pull out of that bruising grip. I actually felt sorry for her. The tint swung her around in a casual way and gave her a solid punch in the face. She went down with her mouth bloody and I heard her head hit the floor with a nasty cracking sound.

'Jesus!' yelled Anwar. 'Couldn't you wait for me to patch her?' He flicked a glance in my general direction. I caught up with the holo and started dancing again.

The tint picked her up and slung her over his shoulder. 'No. I couldn't. Head injury won't bother Bateau.'

Anwar followed him out, glancing over his shoulder in my direction again. I danced with the holo for a full count of thirty after I saw the van pull away from the curb and then took off in the opposite direction.

It wasn't until I'd gone three blocks that I realized there hadn't been so much as a squeak out of the guy upstairs. Coney Whoever, I could remember having known the name, but it was obscured now. There wasn't any time to wonder about him anyway.

Somehow, Sovay's face in the monitor actually managed to get paler. 'No, don't come back to Sir Larry's,' he said, leaning forward. 'That's the first place your Escort service friends'll go looking after Some Very Nice People.' He paused, looking pained. 'I'm going out the door now. Meet me at home in an hour.' He gave me his address and disconnected before I could tell him I already knew it.

I raised the privacy hood and took a careful look around the tube station. Other than a few stragglers who had missed the late afternoon rush, a security guard relieving her boredom by zapping cockroaches off the wall with her prod, and a forlorn-looking hypehead who couldn't seem to relieve his boredom at all, there was nobody around.

No matter how far uptown you got, the tube stations were all alike, little branches of life in the Downs. The only difference was, the uptown stations closed at midnight and the security force cleared the stragglers out by putting them all on the last tube going downtown.

It wouldn't take me an hour to get to Sovay's by tube – he lived at the lower

edge of what was officially an uptown district, though the property values said midtown – but I didn't want to stick around here until the evening trade started coming out.

I left the phone kiosk and went out to the platform, feeling conspicuous. The guard gave me a once-over, but apparently decided I wouldn't be as diverting as cockroach electroshock. The hype was slumped on a bench, asleep with his eyes open or having an out-of-context experience, I couldn't tell which and didn't care.

I leaned against a tiled pillar and tried to smooth myself into a state of alert calm. There was nothing else I could do, until I saw Sovay. Marceline was thoroughly dormant again for the time being. Sleeping deeply; maybe what she dreamed came to me as memory, I thought idly. Maybe on some level, she wanted her old life back as much as I wanted mine. I wondered how she thought she could have pulled it off. A persona overlay from a franchise was never as deep and substantial as the franchiser wanted you to believe; eventually, it would need to be renewed. But with me completely out of the picture, Some Very Nice People wouldn't be able to do that – there wouldn't be an original to provide the feel of growth and change that was part of the state of continued existence, and you couldn't get that from a template, no matter how richly detailed an artificial reality you kept it in. So how had any of them expected to continue any of my personas?

The mirror, I realized. She must have gotten the mirror when she snatched me.

But the mirror *still* wasn't the original. And maybe Some Very Nice People didn't care about that. Maybe they were just going to use her to grind out whatever personas she came up with on her own, and so what if they weren't exactly top of the line? An outfit that would steal someone's life probably wasn't working in terms of a standard of excellence, I reflected, feeling dour. They just wanted to sign *Marva* on the work, with or without my cooperation.

A small movement caught my eye. Someone was peering around a neighboring pillar at me, a ragged skinny guy with the face of an urchin who's been stricken with progeria. I stared back at him boldly. Something told me he was more nervous about me than I was of him and there was a sour satisfaction in being able to intimidate someone else for a change.

He circled his own pillar, glancing around furtively and pushing at the uneven shock of dull, sand-colored hair falling down over his forehead. I turned away and watched the dark hole of the tunnel for the tube.

Why had this snatch worked so well, I wondered. Why had the Escort slid into my persona with such ease, why didn't she think she needed to draw on me anymore? And why wasn't she ever confused and disoriented? Even people who bought top-of-the-line persona overlays from haute operations like Power People would get some identity problems ...

I looked at the aging waif again to make sure he wasn't sneaking up on me. He had his back to me, busily writing something on the pillar with a marker. I had to press my fingers against my lips to keep from laughing. The Age of Fast Information, they called it, the crown of creation – technologically speaking – with a myriad of nets that would accommodate almost any form of communication and expression from facsimile calligraphy to detail holo that would fool your mother (or a pimp's hired help), and none of it had managed to displace the urge to kilroy. The virtual still couldn't hold a candle to scribbling on the walls.

The tube slid into the station with a hushed, windy roar and the waif looked up, startled. He zipped past me to board the last car. I strolled along the platform to the next one so I could sneak a look at what he had felt so compelled to leave as a trace of himself.

The letters were a little shaky, like a child's attempt at script: *Jerry Wirerammer lives!*

The name meant nothing to me, but I felt a sudden, strong surge of empathy.

Me, too, Jerry. Me, too.

'It's not a bootlegging or a bodysnatching,' Sovay said wearily, leaning back on an untidy pile of pillows. Pillows were what passed for furniture in the softly lit living room. At least, I was assuming it was a living room.

'Then what is it?' I said, trying to punch a cushion into a support for my back.

'Marva told me about it, until I made her stop telling me.' He insisted on referring to me in the third person and it was getting on my nerves, but I didn't say anything. After he spat out whatever grotesque lie that woman had told him, I could bite his head off if I wanted to. He gazed at his bleached-out hands. The skin looked fragile. 'I'm due at the colorist's in the morning. It'll take a few days to set the pigmentation evenly.'

'That's really fascinating. And what did *that* Marva tell you?'

He ignored my emphasis. 'She said she'd discovered she had a … an *aberrant* persona mixed in with her characterizations. She didn't give me many details about how she found it, or what she'd already tried to do about it, if anything. Just how she was going to get rid of it.'

I blew out an impatient breath. 'And what was that?'

He looked at me. 'Hiring you. That is, hiring an Escort. It just happened to be you, and you just happened to be … a quick study.'

I sat up straight, pushing both hands into the small of my back. 'And what's *that* supposed to mean?'

'You imprint fast. And I have to say, it looks thorough. You've got her mannerisms, her vocal inflections, even her posture. Everything. It's a complete

impersonation. You'd probably make one hell of an actor. I don't know what you really are, other than an Escort.'

I wiped my hands over my face. 'The reason it's such a complete impersonation is because it isn't an impersonation. She switched places with me.'

Sovay gave a short laugh. 'Nobody's ever done that. Switching's probably impossible, all the experts say so.'

'Not this kind. Not the kind where you have yourself altered to look like the persona, and then have the original altered to look like you. Which is what she did, with Some Very Nice People's help. Then she tried to send me off with a covering imprint while she took over my life, but apparently, the imprint didn't take, so they picked me up again and –' I had to stop. The look on his face said he thought I was wallowing in some cheap delusion, probably bought from a street vendor in smelly leather armor and a mouth full of glitter.

'And just how could she do all that?' Sovay said. 'Escorts make good money, but they don't get to keep it. Their pimps take most of it. For her to rig something like that would have cost her all of the take on half a dozen jobs. So how could she have paid for it?'

'Some Very Nice People did it for her on the condition that she go to work for them afterward,' I said. 'When she snatched me, she must have gotten the mirror as well. She can work off the debt for the surgeries by churning out cut-rate personas. The mass-market formulaic stuff, knockoffs of knockoffs, stereotypes. Doesn't take any real talent to do that. Besides, she's used to working off a debt. That's what she's been doing for her pimp. She was over her head in debt to him because of her addiction to memories. Selling memories is one of his other businesses, the man is a regular conglomerate.'

Sovay blinked at me. 'Marva was the only person I ever knew who called it "the mirror."'

'Yah, I *know* that. Since I'm Marva.'

'But Marva sold out to Some Very Nice People *before* she found out about this aberrant persona,' he said, shaking his head. 'We were in the middle of rehearsals when she told me she was taking Some Very Nice People's offer to become a persona hack. I should have forced her out of the production as soon as I knew she was going to do that, but I didn't.' He gave me a strangely searching look. 'I liked her, you see. I liked Marva a lot and I was hoping that she might get so caught up in the play we were doing that she wouldn't go through with it.' He paused. 'I did everything I could to get her to change her mind.'

'She got her mind changed, all right,' I said darkly.

'The only reason I'm talking to you at all,' he said, sighing again, 'is, I can't help thinking there might be more than just an imprint of Marva in there. You remind me too much of the way she was before Some Very Nice People

shook a fortune under her nose. I guess she was always wavering between art and the Big Score, and the part that wanted the Big Score won. While you got imprinted with the other part.'

I wanted to throttle him, but this time I managed to control myself. 'I *am* Marva. Not part of Marva, the only one there is. Unless you think I'm the aberrant persona she called the Escort to get rid of.'

'No, I know that was somebody else. I, uh, saw that for myself. Marva told me you managed to get rid of it for her. Which was when I told her I didn't want to know anything more, and she didn't have to bother coming back to Sir Larry's. She informed me that she hadn't planned to come back but there was just this smallish problem with the Escort. A problem of a delusional nature.'

'And what was that?' I asked.

He looked hard at me. 'The Escort seemed to believe *she* was Marva, and no matter what she or the Nice People did, the delusion just wouldn't go away. Even a solid week of custom dry-cleaning wouldn't get rid of it.'

I felt the goose walk over my grave, but I ignored it. 'So what did they do with the Escort?'

He shrugged. 'I don't really know, I hung up on her. It was all very disappointing and sordid, but I didn't know how sordid until I saw you at Davy Jones' Locker. Some Very Nice People had brought you there, with Marva. For imprinting, I believe; they were debuting her that night as their latest persona hack and they couldn't put it off. So I imagine they'd decided to use you as an example of what great work she could turn out. If they couldn't rid you of the delusion, then they'd use you as a walking advertisement. You know – 'See, folks? Even a downtown hypehead can be a star, another satisfied customer.' Except a full-blown delusion won't take an imprint. You came out of the back room wearing her clothes and passing yourself off as the real thing. But when you saw the real Marva face-to-face, you switched over and became the Escort again. The delusion's way of protecting itself from the truth. I did what I thought was the right thing and got you away from them by having you thrown out.'

'And what inspired that bit of altruism?'

'I felt sorry for you. You looked so … at sea. If you could get home as yourself, I thought, maybe the delusion would stay buried and you could go back to your life.'

I tried to think. It was all too preposterous, but those were the times we lived in. 'I don't know how to prove to you who I am. Who I *really* am. Which was why she did it this way. It's complicated, but it's the perfect crime. If I just turned up blank with my features carved off – or dead – there might have been a police investigation. Because *you knew*. You could connect her with me.'

He looked confused. I didn't blame him; I was starting to confuse myself.

'You could connect the Escort, the bodysnatcher, to Marva, the actor. Do you see? So the Escort had Marva the actor – *me* – made over to look like *her*. Then she and her Very Nice People could just send me back to the Downs to get my brains blown out by an angry pimp. That would take care of the evidence, no one would have wondered about another Downs garbagehead biting the dust.

'But now the pimp's got *her* instead of me, and the game's changed. When he runs barefoot through her head, he'll know everything and more.'

'What are you going to do about it?' Sovay asked.

I gave a short laugh. 'Nothing. Why should I? She's back where she belongs and I can reclaim my own life. Game over.'

He raised his eyebrows but said nothing.

'What would *you* do about it?' I asked.

He mumbled something about the police.

'Then *you* call them. You don't believe me anyway. It's easier for you to believe I'm some kind of greedy, venial ... *bitch* ... who'd turn her back on a career in legitimate live theatre – and you – for a pile of easy money in the franchise business.'

He was gazing at his fragile-skinned hands again. Maybe he was thinking about how long it was going to take for the pigment to set evenly.

'You and I were lovers once,' I said. 'Sort of lovers. *Closer* than lovers. Does that describe the person you knew?'

He looked up. 'It describes one of the persons I knew,' he said evenly.

'Touché.' I sighed. 'Well, I'm out of ideas.'

'Then try *this* idea: Once there was an actor, a married man, who became infatuated with another actor in the troupe. He controlled the attraction very well, until it came time for the two actors to create characters to play opposite each other in some production that is best forgotten now. The two actors found that their mutual attraction was a stumbling block to the creation of the characters and decided they should resolve their real-life emotions toward each other so that they could get on with the business of acting. As well, she was about to do something he thought was foolish and wasteful of her talent, and he thought he might be able to get her to change her mind. So they hooked in together mind-to-mind –' He paused and took a breath. 'It was not a good idea. He discovered that she wasn't the person he thought she was ... and unfortunately, she discovered that, too.

'She was doing exactly what she was supposed to do, you see. This foolish and wasteful thing was all part of a plan that had nothing to do with him or his feelings. His interference messed everything up in the worst possible way, because he went barging in with that idea of the person he thought she was. It set up a conflict in her, between the person she really was and the person she wanted to be.' He gave a short, humorless laugh. 'Are you lost yet?'

'Close,' I said. 'Yah, what the hell. You lost me.'

'I sure did.' He gave that laugh again. 'Funny how that works, how you can lose someone by finding her.' He made a face. 'Okay, straight out: Marva was a persona for someone else. I inadvertently helped her achieve escape velocity. At the same time, her … mirror … created the reflection of what I saw in her. That's what it was there for in the first place – to create characters. So she ended up with two aberrant personas to jettison instead of just one. One of them is you. Or rather, it's who you *think* you are.'

'And who's the other one?' I asked warily.

'It's her.'

Rowan was standing in the doorway holding a shopping sack. She'd put on a little weight since I'd last seen her in person and the few lines in her face were slightly deeper. I braced myself for a confrontation and then remembered she wouldn't recognize me as Marva.

'This is the one I told you about,' she said, coming over to Sovay, 'the one who called and left Marva's number.'

'It's all right,' Sovay said, 'I know her.'

'But who is she? And how does she know me?' Her gaze went from Sovay to me and back again.

I groaned. 'Don't even *try* to explain it to her.'

Rowan's face hardened. 'I *knew* it. I *knew* this would happen.' She turned to Sovay. 'So, what shall I do now – set up an appointment schedule for you, install a revolving door and a waiting room? How many do you think we'll get, anyway – a dozen? Two dozen? Maybe all of them! Won't that be something!'

Sovay got up and tried to put his arms around her but she shoved him away.

'Marva sells out to a persona mill and all the hypeheads and wannabees get a little bonus with their overlays, they all get the experience of being my husband's lover! Tell Some Very Nice People they should *advertise* it as a special – free with every Marva, your own personal *Sovay-fuck!* You could collect royalties, then it might even be worth it!' She swung the shopping sack at him. He caught it and held on, his gaze never leaving her face. For a long moment they just stood there as if they'd been frozen in the middle of a tug-of-war. Then her shoulders slumped as all the fight went out of her.

'Sorry,' she said in a flat voice.

He turned to me. 'You'd better go.'

'At the risk of getting an answer,' I said, 'where?'

'If it were me,' he said slowly, 'with Some Very Nice People on one side and an Escort service on the other, and no one but me in the middle – I'd have my memory wiped and hope I wouldn't be fool enough to want it back again.'

'Forgive and forget?' I asked sarcastically.

'Forget first,' he said. 'Then there's nothing to forgive.'

*

Night was falling after the longest day of my young life – my young stolen life – and I was standing on a sidewalk in lower uptown with no idea what to do next. *Hello in there, who's got the survival instincts?*

No answer, not even a *How good an actor are you?*

Well, hell, I decided, I'd go home. No one would expect me to show up there. I could even remember the address. East midtown was closer to the Downs than I wanted to be, but it was better than wandering around on the street until a van pulled up at the curb next to me.

The neighborhood looked familiar, and the building was the same as the one in my memory, and the access code worked on the first try, but as soon as I walked into the apartment, I was lost. That damned famine fancier in the memory lane had probably eaten all my at-home memories; the thought of her turned my stomach.

By the smell of the overprocessed air, the place hadn't been opened for over a week. It took me fifteen minutes to find the controls to adjust the ventilation. Then I explored the three rooms, trying to get a feel for my own life.

I didn't live quite as simply as Sovay – I liked furniture, though not too much of it and nothing too expensive. Of course, I thought, looking at the faded upholstery on the couch and the mismatched flea-market table and chairs in the kitchen, most stage actors didn't make salaries that would cover genuine cherry wood credenzas and solid oak bedroom suites.

At least the clothing in the closet was better than this ragpicker ratatat I had on. I grabbed a silk pullover and green trousers, tore off the rags, and took a quick turn in the lavabo. I came out feeling like myself again until I discovered the clothes wouldn't fit.

Migod, I thought, and burst into tears.

Now, that was the *damnedest* thing. After everything I'd been through, I was going to pieces over a *shirt*.

Did *anything* in this life make sense?

Well, it's always the little things that'll break you down. After a bit, I pulled myself together and found a roomy set of jump johns that were only a little bit short. Then I scrolled through the online directory looking for an overnight body carving clinic. There were plenty of them in the listings – in by nine, under by ten, up by dawn, out by eight – but I was looking for any notes I'd stored about vanity work. There were none.

Must be in my personal directory, I thought, and punched in the request for it.

The directory came up empty. I frowned at the screen. That had to be a mistake, I thought, and tried again. Still empty.

Screwy system; probably some kind of network glitch had wiped the

record. It happened from time to time. I punched for the household records to see if anything else had been lost.

According to the utility and banking files, I had moved in six months before. Was that right? Migod, I couldn't remember; I couldn't even remember my previous address. *Damn* that famine fancier – I was going to sue her so hard, it would turn her inside out.

The request for a previous address turned up another blank. That must have been some bad old glitch, I thought uneasily, and asked for my communications records. Even if everything else about me had been lost, the record of dataline use was eternal, etched into the system itself.

There was nothing older than six months.

I tried again and got more nothing, and still more nothing on the third try. Either there had been a nationwide dataline meltdown that I didn't remember, or … I was six months old?

I felt the same kind of damped-down panic from when Some Very Nice People had had me under and the bodysnatcher had tried to imprint me with the Escort's persona – I wanted to get hysterical, but something was holding me back. Maybe it was all really a mistake, I just hadn't entered my identifying codes right. Maybe these were substitute codes I'd entered during a previous bout of characterization amnesia and that starving fool in the memory lane had restored those instead of my real access codes. Maybe I was just the victim of a terrible incident of misfiling.

I had a good laugh over that one. I laughed while I scrolled through the directory looking for a reputable mindplayer who specialized in reorganizing fragmented memories. I was still laughing when the lock popped off the front door and the tint came barreling into the living room with Anwar. At that point, I could see no reason to stop.

The last thing I used to remember is throwing someone off a cliff.

Now I remember standing in the bottom of a swimming pool filled with holo water and fancy holo fish and a couple hundred souls who are getting a lot more out of the experience than I am. Hot-halle-damn-lujah, I finally got one, a memory of somebody's visit to Davy Jones' Locker, so exclusive, strictly uptown privs or visiting royalty, *if* they know somebody. My memory jones goes into overdrive; I think what I'll do with this one is, I'll remember it to death and then I'll pawn it, and when dry season hits, I'll buy it back and knock myself out again. Ofrah'll do that for me, she's holding plenty-all-else against those sudden droughts us memory junkies all hate so much.

So, let's see, what have we got here … yah, we got the holo water and the holo fish, yah, hell of a thing to find coming after your bait, uh-huh, we been through all that, and now dodge to the left, dodge to the right,

sashay round and wave at our friend in the lighter-than-air sacsuit. Doesn't look like much of a party boy.

But the dancing boy in the barely there loincloth, he looks like quite a lot of party boy. Except now that I think of it, he's at the wrong party.

Obligingly, he vanishes while he's tugging on his waist-band. Nobody noticed he was here and now nobody notices that he's gone. Well, you can't have one reality getting mixed up with another. If that were supposed to happen, we wouldn't have to be all different people, ha, and ha –

I'm trying to fast forward to the part where I find the funhouse mirror, but something is keeping everything moving at a real-time pace. I don't appreciate that, these are *my* memories, I ought to be able to enjoy them in whatever sequence or speed I want. But okay; plod-plod-plod and here's the mirror –

And here it goes again, screwing up the realities. I'm supposed to be seeing fish – tube worms, sharks, all that stuff. But instead, what I see is an audience in a theatre.

What the hell, I take a bow.

But when I turn around, I'm still in Davy Jones' Locker. I'm still in over my head, for an audience. Sounds like a karma-gram –

You know you're having a bad day when you come to in a rerun.

How good an actor are you?

Migod, that was the one thing I was never going to get over: the monotony of repeated rehearsals.

You want to check the line?

And then everything went rewind and then to fast forward and I understood that it wasn't real, not a bit. Pajamas – Bateau – had me in the box. How long had I been here, I wondered, and how long was I going to last?

She's playing for time is what she's doing. They all try that near the end, the tricks. Excuse me, clients. *So,* they'll say, hanging back, fidgeting with some old favorite memory they don't want to let go of, *so how did you happen to become an Escort? Do tell, it must be fascinating.*

Fascinating like a tracheotomy. One day I woke up with so many bad debts that I got a visit from a collector who told me I had two choices – column A was where I got taken to a chop shop and parted out any old way they could manage, and column B was where I got to kill off people who wanted to die anyway and raid their minds for valuables. So which column would *you* have picked? Do tell, it must be fascinating.

Actually, what I tell them is a lot of stuff about believing in freedom

of choice and how when you want what you want, you ought to be able to get it no matter what it is. And all the while nudging them a little closer to the edge.

Well, I *do* believe in freedom of choice. I sure wish I had some. An Escort doesn't choose. The clients choose. Whatever way they want to go, however they want to shuffle off this mortal coil, depart this plane of existence, check out, kick the bad old bucket, that's what I do for them.

And if you thought people could get kinky about sex, that's nothing compared to the way they're kinky about death. Ninety-nine times out of a hundred, they can't make it and I have to give them the final nudge over the line. Kicking and screaming into that good night. Their words, *that good night*, not mine.

But that actor, she was the kinkiest one I ever had. Multiple personalities – jee-*zuz*, what kind of a job was that? I didn't want to take it, but Bateau said a job was a job was a job, was I an Escort for him or not, and I should hurry up and decide because the chop shop had an open bay and I had plenty of debt left to pay off. The worst thing I ever did in my life was ask for credit to feed the beast, and the second worst was agreeing to Escort for Bateau to work off the debt.

I thought it was good enough at first. You get plenty of memories when you're Escorting. That's what people are when they're dying, one big bundle of memories, their lives passing before their eyes. Of course, I don't get to keep it all – I have to pass it all on to Bateau afterward. What he's got a use for he keeps, sells it if nothing else. The dregs are mine, though he charges me for them. And that's the way it goes: the work chips away at the debt, but I still got this habit and the fix still isn't free.

When *I* die, everybody else's life will pass before my eyes, one last big rise before blackout. Bateau'll be in on that, too. Likely, he'll be the cause of it. When I cease to serve, he'll part me out. The debt we run up lives after us and the good – I mean, *goods* – are for sale in the pawnshops.

Bateau, if you're listening, I didn't meant to tell her all that.

Something stirs. It's just like that, like I'm underwater (karma-gram) and somewhere else, there's a giant spoon stirring the depths. To see what comes up.

I found the exit once, I can do that again. But when I turn to the mirror, the reflection is crooking a finger at me. I've seen the image of this woman before, it's not supposed to be me ... is it? I don't want to go over there.

The woman in the mirror points to a spot over her head and the sign snaps into existence: EXIT.

Why the hell didn't she say so? I go over to the mirror and touch it with my fingertips. It ripples like silvered water. My hands sink into it and I know I've been had again. This isn't the exit, not the one I want, but it's too late. Something grabs me and pulls me through, and I have a fast flash of someone else being shoved out to where I was.

For half a thought-beat, they exist in the same state, halfway in and halfway out of the barrier. That ought to be enough. The mirror is the complete record; looking into it from one side, they can only see what they've already seen. In simultaneous transition, one to dormant, one to awareness, they'll see every-thing the mirror recorded, including my near-death. The mirror will tell them everything. Except, of course, what to do, now that Bateau has all of us.

Even *I* don't know what to do about that, and I've been with the Brain Police for close to ten years.

But then, the transmigration of a soul before death is unprecedented. Assuming I can continue to avoid the death part, I have no idea how I'm going to explain it convincingly enough to be believed rather than dry-cleaned.

... as if *I* had seen them with *her* own eyes:

Sally's chewing.

Sally's not eating, just chewing. We all have one Thing we Do, each one of us, and this is Sally's: she chews.

You want to check the line?

No, Sovay, I want to know what play this is, and what character. What about it?

I'd have my memory wiped and hope I wouldn't be fool enough to want it back again.

I killed somebody ... I've killed before ... that's okay, he was asking for it.

I've have my memory wiped –

Migod. I didn't kill anybody. Somebody killed me.

– and hope I wouldn't be fool enough –

to come to and find Bateau's hold-ing my hand.

This is never good, being touched by Bateau. I can face plenty: the fact that I'm going to be an Escort for as long as I live, a period of time that isn't as long as it used to be; the fact that the man knows the inside of my head better than I do, that the mind I have is the mind he suffers me to have, that he is, as far as I'm concerned, God. I can face all this and more as long as I don't have to actually, physically *touch* him.

He sits there next to the cot with my hand sandwiched between his and that face a mask of concern.

'Well,' he says, 'you've had quite an adventure, haven't you. My poor Marceline, getting so turned around that it overrode the order to always turn to me first for guidance and help.' He shakes his head. 'And to find you've been tricked –' He looks at the ceiling. 'I'm shocked, to say the least. That anyone would even *consider* screwing up one of my people this way. An example *will* be made.'

He looks to his right and I see her lying on another cot a little ways away. She's still hooked into a system and that's real normal-looking, except the tank for the eyes is missing. Because she's not going to need any after this.

I don't know who I feel sorrier for, her or me. It's pretty much chiseled in stone, what's coming next for her. For me, who knows. Bateau's not just a bad old bastard, he's a bad old whimsical bastard. Poor, pitiful me, I'm occupying the position of broken toy in the Bateau food chain. Nobody knows what's going to happen to me except Bateau, and he could change his mind several times before he gets around to doing anything.

'But before we get to that,' he says cheerfully, 'I do need to know a few things. What did you do with the fee she paid you?'

I feel for my pockets where the wads were and remember I've had a change or two of clothes. Not to mention wads.

'Don't know,' I say finally, wincing at the lousy rag passing as my shirt. It used to be some kind of windowpane plaid but most of the lines have scuffed off. Vending machine stuff, and not from an uptown vending machine, either. 'I went into a memory lane with different clothes on, woke up just now like this.'

Bateau makes a thinking-hard face. An androgyne comes in carrying a tray with an old-fashioned silver coffee service on it. I remember seeing one a lot like it when I was waiting for an air-cab at the Royale about a hundred years ago. S/he sets the tray down on a nightstand next to the bed and starts fussing with two cups. That smell; if it's not the Royale's private blend, it's something just as good.

'Take a deep breath now,' Bateau says, 'and then tell me where you were for a week.'

He had me under, he could have just fished all this information out of my brain any old way he could get at it. Why didn't he?

Maybe because he wants me to survive this, I think, going on a hope trip. All I have to do is tell him everything I know, and he'll only dig for whatever I can't remember. Which will leave me more or less in operating condition.

I'm so relieved, I almost start laughing, but this is not the time to get hysterical. The androgyne passes Bateau a cup that looks delicate

enough to be made out of flower petals. He takes it, holds it under his nose and breathes in the coffee aroma, and then offers the cup to me. I sit up in a hurry and take it.

'How are we doing on that missing week?' he says brightly, taking a cup for himself from the androgyne, who makes an unnoticed bow and marches out of the room. Good help, Bateau always said, was the kind you could ignore completely.

'Don't have it yet,' I say, sipping the coffee. It's definitely better than the uptown vending-machine Brazilian.

'I gave you a little spin in the box to see what that poor, overworked mind of yours would come up with.' He rolled his eyes. 'All I can say is, you're one very confused little hypehead, Marceline. You don't even remember coming to visit me, do you? But then, you weren't really yourself at the time. Were you?'

That smile's got knives in it, but they only last a second. Which is long enough to tell me everything isn't quite as okay as I thought it was a minute ago.

Long enough to tell me ... *something*. Something that happened to me while I was in the box, something I remembered –

'Marceline?' Bateau's still smiling. The knives are put away, but I know he can pull them out again anytime.

He must have tried to get it from me and he couldn't even find me, I realize. So he unhooked me from the system to make me sit here and consciously organize my thoughts for him. Then he'll go back in and turn me inside out.

Only, how come I can read him so well, all of a sudden? And if he couldn't find me in my own head, who the hell *did* he find?

The image of a funhouse mirror pops into my mind. That must have confused the hell out of him, I think to myself. It was confusing the hell out of me. What did he see in it?

It's like the answer clicks into place. He saw the party at Davy Jones' Locker and nothing else. Some sharks and a squid and a few sponges and tube-fish.

'Marceline?' he says again. 'Are you still with us?'

'I sort of remember coming to see you,' I tell him, just to be saying anything at all. 'I was, I dunno, fugued out or something.'

'Or something.' He nods. 'Or *somebody*. Do you remember trying to tell me about the cop?'

I feel like I've been hit between the eyes. The cop. The actor and the cop. Just getting rid of an aberrant personality for a Method actor, that was the job. The actor had a personality she didn't want anymore, a Brain Police officer. I was supposed to go in and kill it off for her. Except

it wasn't an aberrant personality. It was the real person. And the real person didn't want to die, so she –

The coffee starts to come back up and I swallow it down. What does this make me *now*, I wonder, a Method actor or a Brain Police officer in deep undercover? Do I even get a say anymore?

I look over at her, lying there with the wires coming out from under her flattened eyelids. Yah, who could blame her for doing what she did, trying to get rid of the cop? I don't want to be a cop, either.

And then I realize that while I've been sitting here thinking all this handy stuff, it must have been playing on my face like a holo in a foreign language.

Bateau is sitting back in his chair, enjoying his coffee and enjoying the show. I get real tired all of a sudden, and it's not just because Bateau is a real exhausting type of person. Got to keep up with the man all the time or you might miss something important, like your death sentence.

He has sure as hell been keeping up with me just now. He puts down his cup and takes mine from me. I haven't really been holding it, it's just been resting between my hands, could have toppled out and shattered at any moment.

'Well, I knew it was something out of the ordinary,' he says conversationally, as if I weren't sitting there paralyzed, 'when you didn't make any of your pickups. You've *never* failed to make your pickups before.' He looks at me like I said something, and then hits his forehead with the heel of his hand, fakelike. 'Oh, leave it to me. You never knew about the pickups. Me and my big mouth.' He winces showily. 'Sorry, Marceline.'

Also never good. I could have guessed I was doing plenty for Bateau that I didn't know about, but the smart employee doesn't do that kind of guessing. A little blank part out of your day here and there, so who needs to remember every little thing anyway? Not me. If you ain't pulling a fugue state once in a while, you're just not trying, right?

And why would I ever try to remember making my pickups? No reason. So there are some memories that I don't know how I got? I don't care. I'm a junkie and it doesn't matter where it comes from just as long as it comes, that's the gospel. I don't have to remember marching around the Downs like a zombie, stopping in here and stopping in there for a little stolen this-and-that. Stopping in at a fetishist and a dreamland and a pawnshop or two and coming out with a memory a lot fuller than when I went in. Hell, none of *them* know they're working for Bateau, why should they know I'm anything more than a convenient place to dump the dregs they can't fence. And all of it so mixed in with whatever I'd gotten from some dead trick, even if I'd gotten stopped and searched,

the Brain Police wouldn't have been able to make sense out of the alphabet soup in my head. Shit, *I* never could.

Until now. Because it isn't just me anymore.

She conned me when I threw her over the cliff; she fooled me. She dangled all her memories in front of me, said *Gonna let all this go to waste, a hard-up junkie like you in serious need of a rise, a free rise?* I didn't even have to say yes, the habit said it for me. The beast said *Feed me*, and we did. Except it ate a little more than it bargained for, and here we all are together.

Bateau pinches my chin between his fingers and pulls my face up to look at him. He's got new biogems, lapis lazuli. First time I've noticed.

'Now, you know what has to happen here,' he says. 'I can't have anyone holding out on me, even a good and faithful servant like you. The first thing you should have done when you discovered the cop was come straight home to me. I know, I know, they kept you, didn't they? Some Very Nice People kept you, because apparently you were laboring under the delusion that you were *her*.' He turned my head to the actor for a moment. 'They, of course, did wrong by not just packing you up and sending you home, and that is why she's here with us. They kept *my* goods, so now I'm keeping theirs.' He pauses to study me with narrowed eyes. 'I think you're following this, but I can't be sure. Well, doesn't matter, you'll get the idea when you go back in. You see, we can't have any evidence of a Brain Police officer's murder hanging around. The penalties are –' He shudders.

'So what we'll do, Marceline – what *you'll* do, rather – is Escort that sorry sack of shit over there out of this existence once and for all. Not just a character but every one of her. The catch is, of course, that she doesn't want to die, so you'll have to persuade her or force her or –' He shrugs. 'You're the Escort, you'll know what to do. You always have.'

He gets up. 'And after that ... well, we'll just see. It all depends on what you manage to get from her while you're seeing to her departure. And how I have to get it out of you. If you keep thinking you're her, we just might have to blast.' He laughs. 'On the other hand, you come up with the database, and we'll call it even. Including your past debts. Which means, you get to walk away from this. How's that for incentive?' His lips curve in a smile that doesn't touch the rest of his face.

If I could work up enough will to care, I would ask him how he thinks I'm going to Escort anybody all dumbed down with whatever he put in the coffee – Super-Q, or some wild brew he thought up himself. But even stupored-out, I know better. I'm not supposed to walk away. I'm not even supposed to come out of the system. He'll just take whatever

he wants out of my mind and let my vitals flatten along with hers. Two for the price of one. Actor dies of heart failure; unidentified hypehead found dead. Two for the price of one.

I try to close my eyes so I don't have to see him reaching to take them out, but I can't.

Well, hell, I think, walking up that long, twisty dirt road, I know why it didn't work, I know why she isn't dead: this wasn't the way she wanted to go. In my line of work, you don't just go kill somebody – you seduce them to death.

There was the guy who wanted to take a flyer out of a sky-island casino after losing it all to the roulette wheel; *that* was a happy death. He was happy, and later on, Bateau was even happier, because the guy's roulette losses had included a whole lot of stuff about stocks and properties. Nothing I understood, but for months after that, the stock market treated Bateau like its personal favorite son.

There was the woman who blew up the sun; yah, lots of bright lights and a big noise and Bateau sold that one off to the sado-peeps: see the people burst into flames, see them suffer before the whole thing blows, rated XS for Extra-Sick. Can anyone believe it, she thought she was being sneaky. She thought I'd let myself get caught in it. She had the ghosts of all her friends there and all her enemies as well, but in the end, she couldn't fool herself into believing they were anything more than ghosts, and her own ghosts at that. In the end, she knew she was going alone and she couldn't stand it. She couldn't stand it that she had to face the Big Question Mark without even one other person to face it with her.

But I've done the exploding sun ending before. In some ways, it's easier to dodge that one than a flyer off a sky-island. Or a jump off a cliff.

The cliff. It's up there ahead of me, waiting, and she's waiting there on the edge with this personality she doesn't want. That's not how it went, though. How it went was, the three of us walked up the road to that final destination. That was the client's choice, and the client always gets to choose. That's the way it's supposed to go.

What's wrong with this picture is, the client wasn't the intended. First time I ever did it that way.

The trees lining the road are whispering, but it's a foreign language and I don't understand what they're saying.

Something makes me turn around and look back, and there it is. The mirror. I see my reflection in the act of walking away, but even though I keep walking, I don't get any farther away from it.

My reflection? My reflection ... but not me. Not the client, either. *Almost* her, but not quite.

I'd have my memory wiped and hope I wasn't fool enough to want it back again.
But this was not my memory. I hadn't done this.
You want to check the line?
No, Sovay, I think I've got it straight now. I'd been afraid, back when we'd decided to do it, meet mind-to-mind and settle our feelings toward each other, I'd been afraid that instead of coming to a resolution, we'd open something we couldn't close.

I'd been afraid in other ways. The kind of apprehension you get, say, when you go into someone's bedroom for the first time and see a pair of handcuffs hanging off the headboard.

Yah, I'd had all kinds of fears, but the one thing I forgot to be afraid of was what I might find out about myself. But that's the kind of stuff you'd never see if it weren't reflected in another person's eyes.

Is it a lie if you don't know you're lying?

I hadn't believed when Sovay showed it to me. Make that, when I'd seen for myself. But there it was – there *she* was – cocooned and quiet and camouflaged by the mirror itself, the funhouse mirror in my head that made reflections-to-order for me, characters that lived as long as the run of what plays they were created for and sank back into the mirror after the final curtain call.

How had he seen through everything to where she was? If he'd just been infatuated, he'd have just inspired one more reflection, the person he'd wanted to see, the one who would take that ride through the old Tunnel-O-Love with him. It wouldn't have been her; migod, it wouldn't even have been *me*. She'd have been safe, and so would I; I'd have been busy with the ersatz-Sovay character I needed for my own love-affair scenario. So what happened? How do you see the truth about somebody when all you're looking for is the pleasant lie?

You want to check the line?
Was that all that had triggered her? What could possibly have been in that question that could have taken him all the way through to her?
Had it just been that I hadn't known the line?
Or had I just changed my mind?

Change of heart, thus a change of mind; the things that can happen when someone catches you in a weak moment.
She had to say yes to Some Very Nice People; I'd spent months lying in wait for them, knowing they'd come. The franchisers have whole staffs that

do nothing but cruise theatres and holo parlors, looking for a new face. Not just any new face, but a hungry new face. The big firms like Power People just do it to keep current – the new faces come to them and they cull what they want for their persona catalogs.

Then there's Some Very Nice People. One way to survive in competition with the big ones like Power People is to be better than they are, but that's too hard. Another way is to bootleg. The Flavor-Of-The-Month is already taken? No problem; send one of your staff over as a customer, get an imprint and bring it back to the workshop. The knockoff is up and running before dinner.

And maybe it's got a few refinements *as* well, some extra features that the bootleg custom wouldn't know as anything fenced from a chop shop. Wouldn't know, wouldn't want to. Except, of course, for the ones that do know because that was what they wanted in the first place.

Complicated times we live in, yes; they call for complicated schemes and counterschemes. But I made it simple for her. She existed simply to respond to one mating call: **Hey, baby, want to be Famous?**

Her line was just one word, easy to remember: **Yes**. Once she was in, all she had to do was be Some Very Nice People herself, gathering information while she manufactured personas. And after a set period of time, there'd be a certain customer who would ask for a particular, tailor-made persona that only she could produce, and that would be the cue for me to come up out of deep undercover, send up a flare, and take them all in.

And then Sovay barged in and changed her mind. Just what he set out to do, too. Either I made her too good back in the Brain Police system, or he made himself see too much in her – it doesn't matter much anymore. He just did it. Looking for her, he raised me instead.

You want to check the line?

Was that the cue? If it wasn't, it was close enough for government work – ha, and ha, as Marceline would say – it meant more to me than it did to her.

Maybe there was too much leak-through; maybe, along with all her information, I got her infatuation, too.

He changed her mind about Some Very Nice People; one mental night with Sovay and she didn't want to go anymore. Except she wasn't supposed to feel that way because that was her purpose, to go with them, be Famous. She resolved that conflict the only way she knew how … in the mirror.

But the new reflection was from **her**. The new reflection wanted to be Famous. She gave it existence; I gave it purpose; and Sovay gave it the undeniable truth about both. Perhaps that was the one thing the reflection needed to achieve escape velocity from the mirror, and from me: the truth.

The new reflection of Marva knew exactly what to do about it. If you can

create a persona, then you can get rid of one. And if you can't get rid of it by yourself, hire a professional to do it.

Some Very Nice People knew just where she could find one.

Yah, but what I do is send them over and keep the memories. She wanted me to send her over memories and all.

Because if you don't, she'll grow back.

Uh ... what? How's that again?

Everything must go.

If she thought I was going to let perfectly good memories go into the Great Goodbye ... hell, I didn't even have a say about it. I might have, but that beast of a habit wasn't about to let anything like it happen.

That was how she hooked me, too. Your weaknesses, damn, you got to watch them every moment and still you might not know what happened till long after the fact.

I thought it would be all right, though. I got a habit, but I got experience, too. Plenty of them have tried to hook me. Plenty of them change their minds at the last second or think they do, and they try all kinds of things. They try walking on water, they try shifting into reverse, and when it fails, they try taking me with them for company. That solitary thing is what gets them most of all. They try to make me feel it along with them so that when they reach for me, I'll reach for them and either pull them back or go over with them – at that point, they almost don't care which, as long as they don't have to face the Great Goodbye alone.

But I never in my life ever saw one of them *fly*. Her will to live was as strong as mine, and I knew, watching her hold herself up above the void, that I'd been had.

I didn't know what to do then. She wasn't supposed to be the real one, she was supposed to be the artificial one, just a persona, a mask with a little history. And the beast woke up, the habit came alive and said, *Don't bother to wrap it, I'll eat it here!*

No memory junkie ever had it so good, not in *my* memory, ha, and ha. But that's all that would have come of it, if it hadn't been for the mirror. Funhouse mirror ... what you see is what you get is what you see.

Not just one mirror, but two: one for the cop, one for the Method actor the cop made. She had to have her own, because it was what made her a Method actor. You put two mirrors together and what you see is what you get is what you see is what you get is what you see into infinity, bouncing back and forth between them, and me caught in the middle.

The one I'd thrown off the cliff was gone, and the client thought that meant she'd finally given out and fallen, the way it was supposed to have happened. She was wrong. She was

*

somebody else now.

Somebody else and somewhere else, who I was before I found too many reflections in the mirror and one of them decided to get rid of a few, so she could keep the made-up life and live it out. But the reflections go on forever in two mirrors facing each other.

The original person, and the original persona she made for an assignment in deep undercover, reflecting back and forth now in the mind of the Escort. And the Escort woke up as me. Migod.

The actor had tried to obliterate the cop's memory after the fact, after the Escort got it, but the actor didn't understand that it was *two* mirrors reflecting each other, and as soon as she erased the associations, they all came back into existence further along in the series, a little more obscured, but still there nonetheless. And a memory lane famine fancier also in deep undercover recognized me in the system and tried to make contact, except she didn't go far enough along the series of reflections to find the right one, and got me instead. It was the gap in my memory she worked on, not the memory of the Brain Police officer, still in deep undercover.

Deep undercover; deeper than anyone had ever been before while remaining distinct enough to persist. That's the will to live in action, and that's the nature of infinity – if you can see far enough into anything, what you'll see is yourself looking back. You won't know if you're looking outward or inward, upward or downward – doesn't matter. Any way you take it, it's you.

And what are you but what you remember being?

What *I* remember being is pretty goddamned angry. Do someone from the Brain Police and it's no mercy for you. If they get in with a search warrant and find that kind of evidence, they turn you over for rehab, no appeal. Rehab; you see people who got rehabbed around now and then. Nobodies, ciphers. Nothing gives them a rise or hypes them up, and nothing hurts. They're just clocks, keeping time till they wind down for good.

I remember being sure I'd rather go over that cliff myself than have that happen to me. Then I remember thinking maybe I was a little hasty about that.

Funny, no matter how many times you've been to the brink of death, you never lose your will to live or your fear of death. Maybe that was all it took to save her life, the will to live and the fear of dying.

So I saved her life. Then she invested it –

Her presence manifested as a flicker of lightning over the patchwork inner landscape. My perspective shifted jerkily and I swore I could feel my vitals

jump. I imagined Bateau standing over both our inert bodies out there in the real world, smirking at her, then me. This contact was different, not like before at Some Very Nice People, when she had just made an imprint and left it to find me wherever it would. That would have worked, except I'd been watching and I knew, and knowledge was power, power enough to override the imp.

But what did I know now, and what kind of power could it give me?

I'd have my memory wiped and hope I wasn't fool enough to want it back again.

I wanted to look at the place where she was making contact, but some force pulled my vision back to the mirror.

Sally's chewing.

The memory was there in the mirror, the famine fancier in a strange office of obese furniture. I was seeing her the way the Escort had come upon her – the Escort had gone under looking for a memory boost but it was *my* memory that had had to be boosted. A Method character will accept any old false memory you feed it, but what happens if it isn't a character?

The famine fancier's head whips around and she sees me.

Sally's chewing –

And then she spits –

I went up that dirt road to the edge of the cliff, too; sometimes I was walking along with her, sometimes I was being dragged like the inert cop, trapped in the prison of deep undercover and unable to come out and save herself. I wanted to stay and have a life just as much as the other Marva did, but I wanted mine in live theatre, as one of the troupe at Sir Larry's, not as a persona hack for a cheap franchise operation. It was my life, too.

A damned good life, good enough to fool a mindplayer, good enough to fool me – both of me, the way I'd been then and the way I was now. Most people thought artificial reality was just one of those fantastic environments manufactured by companies like Realityville™ and Mindscape™ or some entertainment feature reformatted for the wannabee parlors. Sometimes it was, but sometimes, it was your life. My *life* –

Well, it hadn't *all* been artificial. The life the cop had given me had been similar to hers in many ways; that was a little comforting, knowing that a lot of the memories I had weren't completely false. I was what she would have been if she hadn't chosen the Brain Police instead of the theatre. All I'd been doing was rearranging things to make them the way they should have been in the first place. The future was set long before I came into existence, it was only my past that changed.

I'd have my memory wiped and hope that I wouldn't be fool enough to want it back again.

I'm not the only fool to have remembered. She should have done what she said she was going to do, dump the memory of ever having been Brain Police.

There wasn't time, though, was there. What's that old saying? Art is long but life is short. And memory is

my past that changed.

I don't have time to even wonder who she is, this woman I'm standing at the edge of the cliff with, standing in the spot where the cop was before I threw her over. The grass around my feet is deep, luxurious, better than stuff you can get in lawn stores for your chip-sized terrace in the uptown high-rise.

Abruptly, I'm standing in the open window of a sky-island casino where, miles up, there is no wind at all and an old guy has decided to fly away himself rather than wait for progeria to eat him alive.

Yah, this is *my* memory, this is *my* turf we're on now and I can tell the way she's looking around that she's lost. She tries to brazen it out, though, by going right to the roulette wheel. But I've got a little surprise for her there. This time, I'm not taking any chances – every number on it is double-zero. House number, everybody loses, everybody has already lost, and that includes her.

We outnumbered her this time. She knew how to play chicken on the edge of a cliff well enough, but the sky-island was something else. No matter what direction she moved in, it took her closer to the window; my doing. I might have made a good Escort, too, or maybe that was just leak-through from Marceline. This wasn't the life I'd have chosen, but the cop didn't have a whole lot of options. It was Marceline or nothing at all.

How good an actor are you?

Well, I was a lot better when I knew what play I was in. And maybe improv wasn't my strong suit, but I still knew how to pick up a cue and run with it –

Run at her –

My momentum was enough to carry us both right to the windowsill. I closed my eyes so I wouldn't have to see her fall.

When I opened them again, we were teetering on the edge of the cliff.

You never lose your will to live or your fear of death. Wasn't anyone listening to me? Did she think it was going to be that easy, just knock her out of the sky, surprise good-bye? I'm the Escort here, I know better, even if I don't know how to kill somebody who wasn't planning to die. What does that make me now, a Bouncer instead of an Escort?

And like that, here we are in Davy Jones' Locker.

I can sense her, but I can't see her, the cop who grabbed the lifeline into me. I can sense the others, too, but can't see them. But the place is

full, holo fish and party fish, submarine noises, even a silly old oyster bed hatching pearls at the rate of one a minute per crusted shell. Yah, I was here, and now I'm back.

And I'm getting a rise, because this isn't *my* memory of it. Oh, yah; this *is* a good one, like slipping on a soft, sweet glove that goes on and on and on until it covers me over altogether.

Now it's really like being underwater; I'm weightless, true state of grace. Things get hazy right along with me and for a while, all I do is drift around as if there really were a current to flow with.

It wasn't my memory, either; not quite. The Escort came up out of the back room that night a remnant of Marva's imprint clinging to her – not me, Marva, but the new, improved Marva, the one who wanted to dump the cop so she could go on being Famous. Or maybe it had been clinging to me; personalities didn't always split off nice and clean, there was bound to be a little of her in me and a little of me in her.

Em-Cate and Twill were right where I'd found them that night, ani-mated doll images; I turned to see their reflections in the mirror and something blocked me.

Not yet.

It was like a window opening and then closing again quickly, a flash of the cop's presence, gone before it could register. I let myself move away from the mirror, over to where I had met Sovay.

You want to check the line?

Not this time; I knew. A school of holo fish swam into me and took me with them. We made a complete circuit of Davy Jones' before I broke away and sailed downward, toward a familiar face.

Hell of a thing to find coming after your bait ...

I'm on the other side of that fine rise now, coming down easy and good, land on my feet with that life-is-good feeling, walk away from it all the better for having had the experience. There's not much you can say that about these days.

But this *is* a hell of a thing to find coming after your bait. But I remember – *I* remember, and it's not so bad that I remember it, her face on a glowing yellow holo fish. A fish with a human face and the water's over my head; yah, it's a karma-gram if ever there was one. But is it *my* karma-gram?

Now, *there's* a lousy habit – wanting someone else's habit ... beg for the short end, why don't you. But isn't that what taking someone else's memory is?

Something tells me not to worry about it, I didn't ask to be this way. If I feel the need to be forgiven for something, it's a done deal (myself, I think guilt's a lousier habit than anything). And the fish is still waiting to swim through my head.

I want to dodge it just like I did when it really happened, but I can't. It's like my head's clamped in an invisible vise and I have to –

– let her in.

Now I knew what the split-screen vision effect was, back at Bateau's. She was there, trying to talk to Bateau. It's more pronounced this time but not as awkward or uncomfortable. Maybe because we both know what it is. I can feel her presence and mine slipping around each other like two grades of oil that don't mix; won't mix.

She's a rough blend, like a blanket sewed together out of scraps. All those lives lived vicariously, I'm surprised she's hung on to so much of herself, that she didn't just … dissolve, lose herself in a kaleidoscope-a-rama of other people's lives.

But I guess she can't. Instead, she just gets drunk on them. Nostalgia bender; somebody else's nostalgia, her bender. Then the tide goes out and it's just her again, stranded on the ragged edge.

That's what this is all about … getting drunk?

She ain't old enough to have much in the way of memory, and what she's got is pretty damned spotty. Her twin sister didn't leave her much when she split off and ran away to join the circus. What's there is what I already know, more or less; no rise. I don't even know if there's *going* to be a rise in any of this, and *that's* pretty goddam strange, because I'm only in it for the rise. Any of it, whatever it may turn out to be: if there's a rise to be had, I'm interested, I'm there.

Because what else is there, anyway? What else has anybody got that's just as good, that means anything? I'm just running loose here, what's the world to me, or me to the world?

I'm scared because I can't answer that question and until I can, we can't stand together on this cliff against *her*.

And all she is, is another aspect of me – or I'm another aspect of her. If I understand things right, she was actually here first, and I came later, as the person some Brain cop couldn't help wanting to be. But migod, it doesn't feel that way to me. I feel *true*. The Escort remembers me; the cop remembers me, and *she* remembers me, so I *must* be true.

Sovay remembers me … and I remember him …

*

And now I remember him, too – nice rise with a nice rush on it. Not my memory, but Marva's, the Marva Sovay wanted when they hooked in together mind-to-mind, the one he was hoping would be there for him. The Marva who wanted to stay at Sir Larry's with him instead of running off to get Famous. And the cop couldn't do a thing about that, because somebody else's wants are somebody else's.

And that's all I ever wanted: somebody else's. That's right, I can look at that face on now. It never *had* to be a memory, memory was just always the most convenient package for it. I don't even know what 'it' is, exactly, just that if it belonged to somebody else, I wanted it. New start, second chance, and if the second went flat, a third, a fourth, and onward. Two mirrors, infinity of reflections; no waiting. I can go on forever.

The first time we went over this cliff, the cop saved us. This time – am I supposed to do it this time? Migod … I can't. I need the mirror, there'll be some other character in it better at this than I am.
You want to check the line?
Sovay. Migod, _yes,_ I want to check the line.

It's a dirty trick, but that's how it happens sometimes. Sovay is the one thing they all agree on, and if one of them checks the line, they all will. They just won't know that I've changed the line to read, **_Good-bye. (Exit.)_**
Curtain.

Exit now?
If that's the line, then that's the line. How good an actor am I? Good enough to play both parts. That's the Method. I know her; I can *be* her.
And I'm still her when she goes over the cliff.

Uh-oh …
This isn't supposed to be here. Or, there _is_ supposed to be something here. Or _I'm_ supposed to be –
Damn. I can't remember how it's supposed to look to me. This is somebody else's, but the rise is over. Time to fall.

It was always disconcerting to come to sitting up. Then he slapped my face again, whoever he was.

'Come on, come *on*,' he growled, and pulled me off the bed onto my feet. 'If you're still here when he comes back, he'll eat your brains with a spoon.'

He shoved me across the room to the open door. My eyes felt *as* loose *as a* couple of marbles. I caught myself on the jamb and tried not to pass out again.

'Hurry, god**damm**it –'

I'd have my memory wiped and hope I wasn't fool enough to want it back again.

Who said that?

'You did. It's the first smart thing I've heard you say since –' Anwar shook his head. 'Since ever.'

No, that hadn't been me. But if I could just sit and think long enough, it would come to me. Someone I knew, or had known once. It was important for me to remember.

You Must Remember This.

I blinked.

The déjà vu was like a physical blow. Empty waiting room, guy behind a desk –

I seemed to be struggling to get out all of a sudden without knowing why, Some old reflex, perhaps.

'Just for now,' he was saying, talking fast under his breath. 'Just for now, just for now, I'll find you again when it blows over but for now, good-bye and good luck and forget all about it, I'll remember for both of us when the time comes –'

I was thinking what a fool he'd have been to do something like that. Forgive *and* forget and let it rest, that was the smart thing. Even smarter was to forget first and then there'd be nothing to forgive … now, who was it who told me that?

The IV cuff on my arm beeped empty, waking me from a confused and incoherent dream set in what might have been a multifaith church or a Far Eastern bazaar, in which some skinny woman had been arguing with another Brain Police officer as to who I was. The other officer, whom I couldn't identify at all, kept insisting I was now somebody else. The skinny woman seemed to be arguing that due to widespread bodyplay, almost no one had any original tissue anymore so the biological didn't count, but it was hard to tell since she was always talking with her mouth full and never seemed to swallow anything. At some point, a philosopher came in to settle the matter; he suggested that I be cut into two sections, one to be given to the Brain Police and the other to be thrown off a cliff.

Actually, I wasn't completely sure it was me they were talking about, since I was just having the dream without being in it. Then the cuff had beeped and woke me up, and I knew it was just part of my reality-affixing hangover.

297

The dreams you get after a major Overhaul are nowhere near *as* vivid or interesting *as* coma dreams.

I took the cuff off and set it on the nightstand beside the bed.

'You really don't like food, do you?'

Skehan was standing at the foot of the bed, transferring some data from the monitoring system to his data-caddy. He looked like an albino Jesus. I knew I'd seen him before, but I couldn't remember anything about it. There were lots of things I couldn't remember.

'I like food just fine. Eating is another matter.'

Skehan made a sympathetic noise. 'A desperation measure, but it worked. Salazar was the one person we were absolutely sure you'd recognize. You'd been out of touch three weeks, which corresponds to the time your Marva persona sold out to Some Very Nice People and jiggered you into a state of permanent suppression.'

Salazar; there was a hole in my memory exactly her size and shape, and I simply could not keep her from falling through it. When I did remember her, it was as something unfortunate that had happened to the Escort, not to me, but I didn't tell Skehan that. He'd probably want to put me under again to have a look at it and I didn't feel like going under anymore. It wasn't going to make the reality affixing settle any more quickly.

'So,' Skehan said, disconnecting his caddy from the monitor and pulling over a chair for himself, 'any questions today?'

'That all depends,' I said. 'What did I ask yesterday, and are the answers any different?'

He consulted the caddy's minuscule screen. 'The usual: what happened to the Escort and Anwar and Bateau, did we make any important arrests as a result of your undercover work, and when can you get out of here.'

I nodded. Nothing provocative like **Whose body am I wearing?** or **Who do you think I am?**

'Well, here's one you didn't mention,' I said. 'Why don't I remember one day to another?'

A smile on an albino Jesus is a striking expression. 'With your kind of trauma, continuity is the last thing to return.'

'But it does return?'

'More often than not.' He watched my face. 'Make that, almost always. Better yet, it fails to return in such a small number of cases that we don't really consider that a possibility. We conquered Korsakoff's a long, long time ago. The only people who have it now are those who choose to have it.'

That gave me pause. I didn't think that was a particularly desirable condition, but I could understand how someone might.

'All right,' I said. 'I'll trust you on that one. What about the rest? Until my continuity comes back.'

Skehan's ruby eyes narrowed slightly. 'We never managed to put together enough evidence for a case against Some Very Nice People for counterfeiting or bootlegging personas. And the business no longer exists. If you found anything while you were in deep undercover, it was lost when the Escort tried to kill you. We did get Bateau for that, and some of the people in his operation. All the Escorts had logged perfectly legal activity so we couldn't touch them. Your Escort – Marceline no-last-name – is classified as missing.'

Missing. I ran my hands over my face and then examined them, finger by finger. 'I take it the physical alteration occurred while I was under?'

He hesitated for a moment. 'Restoration. It was restoration work. And of course, we had it taken care of right away. The physical stuff's always so easy.'

'Restoration.' I laughed a little. 'And the Escort's classified as missing. So where do you suppose Marva is?'

'Unless there's been a purge I haven't heard about, I imagine the original template is still in Wardrobe,' Skehan said, speaking slowly and carefully. 'If you mean your imprint, that's been wiped. Trauma will do that, you know.'

'You're going to try to tell *me* you **restored** my original appearance to this body and you can't find a trace of the Escort?' I laughed again. 'You can put that story out *as* the official version if you want but *I* was there.'

Skehan scratched the corner of his eye, smiling at me professionally. 'We don't know where or when you had the bodyplay done. It was quality work, but anyone with a decent set of tools and enough tissue can turn out a job that would fool your own mother.'

I leaned forward. 'The body had been altered?'

'**Your** body had been altered, yes.' The emphasis on **your** was just slightly more than subtle. 'No original tissue at all, but that's true for anyone who's ever been in deep undercover. And what else would explain the change in your appearance? You just went and had your undercover wardrobe changed. The memory of that particular event happens to be among the permanently lost.' He did something to the caddy and watched the screen for a moment. 'Permanently lost, yes. But if it ever does miraculously resurface, you will notify your supervisor, of course?'

'Come on,' I said, 'isn't there an unclaimed Jane Doe in the morgue who bears a rather striking resemblance to an actress named Marva?'

'There are quite a few Jane Does in the morgue. Or there were. But you've been here for two weeks. Anyone brought in during that time has long since been processed, tissues broken down –' He shrugged. 'Anyone who went unclaimed, that is. I really wouldn't know. The morgue isn't my bailiwick.'

I sat back. 'So that's the official version: When Salazar retrieved me, my body had been altered and the Escort is MIA?'

Skehan snapped the caddy shut. 'There **is** no other version. What other *version* could there be? There is no other possible explanation.' He stood up, smiling. 'In answer to another question, you'll be out of here tomorrow. You get a week of R and R and then you're back on the job. Your contract's not quite up, as I understand it.'

He started to leave and then paused. 'Oh, just a couple of other things. Salazar didn't come through this unscathed herself. She wasn't in deep undercover and your trauma affected her as well. We've had to wipe the memory and all her field experience went with it, I'm afraid.'

'Sally Lazer's in permanent retirement? Too bad, there's a Downs joint that'll never be the same. What are you going to do with her, early retirement?'

'Oh, no. I believe she's been promoted. You'll be reporting to her when you get back from your R and R.' He cleared his throat. 'I don't make the policies. And, ah, the other thing … you had a rather persistent delusion we had quite a bit of trouble with. But it's gone now.'

'What was it?' I asked.

'Nothing to worry about. You just seemed to, ah, be convinced you –' He shrugged. 'I don't even know how to explain it. But *as* I said, it's nothing to worry about. The dry-cleaning took, you're back to normal. No delusions. I only mention it because there was quite a lot of information entangled in it and we had to take that, too.'

'So what does that mean?'

'I'm not really sure, to tell you the truth. Except that you may feel you're being lied to about what happened to you during the periods you can't remember. It's a feeling you may not be able to get over and as a result, you could be prone to the development of paranoia. I highly recommend you allow us to put you on paranoia-watch.'

I laughed. 'Is that really a wise thing to do with an incipient paranoid? Watch her?'

'We wouldn't be watching. You just wear this.' He pulled something out of his pocket and held it up. 'It's a pump that –'

'I know what it is,' I said. 'No. Absolutely not. Out of the question. I'm professional enough that I can monitor my own brain. If it gets crazy in there, I'll put myself in for treatment.'

'But this would be immediate treatment it would deliver a precisely measured dose of –'

'**No**. Get it out of my sight.' He tucked it back into his pocket.

'Now, **you** get out of my sight, too.'

Skehan nodded good-naturedly and left.

I checked out of rehab a day early and took a jumper to Cornwallis Island, one of the few places in the Northwest Territories that hadn't gotten all tarted

up for the Ice-Tourist trade. But it wasn't completely without amenities; you could find almost anything you wanted if you knew who to ask.

I've always thought a cold climate was a good place to think things through. Whatever memory was lost, I decided, could stay lost. They say if you lose it, you never really needed it in the first place. Forgive and forget.

Or just forget. That way, there's nothing to forgive.

Nothing and no one.

So I forgot.

PART II

Fool to Believe

Sovay had dyed himself a delicate orange. It wasn't his color. He was sitting nude on a floor mat with his legs folded and his hands resting on the junction of his ankles. Someone had piled pillows between his back and the wall for support – the regular police, probably. Suckers weren't known to be that considerate. His long straight hair, a shade or two darker than his skin, was pushed back from his slack face and there were traces of blood beneath his unfocused jade eyes. A faint whistling sound came from between his parted lips every time he exhaled.

I squatted in front of him and pulled gently at his lower eyelids. A thin mixture of blood and tears spilled onto my thumbs. Poor Sovay. They hadn't been any too gentle with him. There was no sign of a struggle in the living room but Sovay and his wife Rowan still didn't bother with furniture. It was the same loose scattering of pillows and mats I vaguely remembered from a month ago, with indirect wall-well lighting. It was like being in a tomb. Or maybe a womb.

Rowan's voice came to me from the hallway. 'In there. Through that door.' I stood up and moved aside as three paramedics came in with a stretcher.

'Dirty shame,' said the chief paramed, kneeling down in front of Sovay with a vitals kit. The other two unfolded the stretcher in silence, not bothering with any facial expressions. 'You the Brain Police, ma'am?'

I nodded, showing him the ID on my belt. He squinted at it briefly.

'Heya, Mersine. Regular police seen him yet?'

'Yah. He's all yours.'

The paramed took Sovay's blood pressure with a Quik-Kuff. 'Any idea who did it?'

'I just got here myself.'

'Dirty shame. **Dirty** shame.' The paramed's bald, blue-tinted head wagged from side to side. 'Used to be that was the one thing they couldn't take from you. And they're getting so **bold**.'

I looked across the room at Rowan. She had pulled a hookah out of the wall and was sucking contemplatively on the mouthpiece. Then she moved her head, and in the lousy light, I could see the wet streak running down her

303

face from under her eye. As I watched, the skin there turned slightly red, as if her tears contained some irritant that even she was sensitive to. It would have figured, I thought, and turned back just in time to see the paramed extract Sovay's eyes. I hadn't needed to see that just then. More tears and blood dribbled down Sovay's face as the paramed shut down the optic nerve connections.

'Mighty nice biogems,' he said, pausing to examine the eyes. 'Brand-new, too. He didn't get much use out of them.' He slipped them into a jar in the kit, where they stared like unclaimed marbles. '**Dirty shame**. I mean, those **suckers**.' He stopped up Sovay's ears and gave him an an intravenous pop. 'In through the optic nerve like a vacuum cleaner, suck you dry.' He lifted Sovay's arm to test his pliability and then maneuvered him into a supine position so the other parameds could slip the stretcher under him. 'They musta wanted him pretty bad to risk coming in after him this way.' His brow wrinkled nearly to his bald crown.

I looked over at Rowan again. She seemed not to have heard. The perfumed smoke from the hookah had drifted across the room; it smelled appetizing but not too dopey.

'Who was he?' said the paramed. 'I mean, who did he used to be?'

'His name was Sovay. He was an actor.'

'Oh.' The paramed leaned close. 'He musta been some hot up-and-comer, but personally, I never hearda him.' He waved at his two assistants and they took Sovay out.

'Did you want to see his studio,' Rowan said after a long moment of silence. She was studying the pipe mouthpiece as if it were something completely new. 'They broke in there, too, but there wasn't anything to take. Just mirrored walls and carpeting. Sovay kept it locked because he said it shut his vibrations in and other people's out.' She took another drag on the pipe and blew the smoke toward the ceiling. 'Does that make sense if you're the Brain Police?'

Dealing with the family is something you never quite get used to, even under much less complicated circumstances. Of course, it wasn't that complicated for Rowan; she didn't know me and I wasn't going to tell her who I'd been once. It made me feel a bit unsavory, as if I had some further motive beyond preserving the confidentiality of the investigation that I didn't even know about.

'I don't need to see his studio, not with the regular police checking it out.' I hesitated. 'When they're done, I'll give you a lift to the hospital, if you like.'

She shook her head. 'There wouldn't be much point in that.' Her gaze went to the mat where he'd been, as if she were just now noticing he was gone. 'Do you want coffee? All I have are cubes. They're good, though.' She blinked several times in that dazed way people do when they find them-

selves in the middle of a catastrophe and aren't sure of the etiquette. But her movements were unhesitating as she shut off the hookah and put it away.

In appearance, she still matched the minor memory I had of her, small, compact, a shade on the plump side and looking more so in a pouch suit. Unlike Sovay, she wasn't much for dye-jobs or other flash. Her skin was untouched, and so was her ripply shoulder-length brown hair. Her only affectation was the set of pearlized brown biogem eyes that gave her round face an odd blind look.

Surprisingly, there was conventional furniture in the kitchen, a table and four chairs. Or maybe that wasn't so surprising – even the most dedicated floor-sitters probably craved a chair now and then. I sat down and Rowan served me mechanically: cup of water, spoon, napkin, jar of cubes.

'How do you take it?'

For a moment I wasn't sure what she meant. 'Tan.'

'The cubes in the gold wrappers're tan. The white are tan with sugar, the pink are sweet black, the black ones are black.' She shrugged and deposited herself in a chair as I peeled a gold-wrapped cube and dropped it into my cup. The water foamed up in an instant boil.

'Why did they do that to him?' she asked. 'Take out his eyes, plug his ears?'

'First aid.' I stirred down the bubbles in the cup. 'Too much sensory input can be adverse for an involuntary mindwipe. The pop was a tactile desensitizer as well as a sedative, it'll keep him out till they get him into quarantine.'

'Oh.' She piled one hand on the other.

I've always thought murder must be easier in a way. The involuntary mindwipe – mindsuck – is just as gone, except the trappings of a live body remain to confound the survivors. A mindsuck is interred not in a grave but in a special quarantine to allow the development of a new mind and personality. Sometimes the new person is a lot like the old one. Most of the time, however, it's only spottily reminiscent of the person that had been, as though the suck had freed an auxiliary person that had always been there, just waiting for the elimination of the primary personality. There was still a lot of controversy between the behaviorists and the biologists over that and plenty of theories but no clear-cut explanations.

Regardless, the new mind was definitely Somebody Else, a stranger with no ties to the previous inhabitant of the brain. Someone told me once it was a lot easier to accept if you had enough of a mystic bent toward a belief in reincarnation, but I couldn't exactly tell Rowan to take comfort in the study of the Great Wheel of Life.

'Well,' she said after a bit. 'Have the Brain Police ever recovered any, ah, anyone? From mindsuck?'

A common question. You'd think in the Age of Fast Information there wouldn't be blank spots or misconceptions. You have to tell them the truth,

but I hate it, even if lying is worse. 'Never intact,' I said, and took a sip of coffee. She'd been right, they were good cubes. The damnedest things make an impression on you at the damnedest times. 'Most suckers part out minds as quickly as possible. They –' I stopped.

Tell her about a chop shop? Sure – then follow up with a description of how they'd dig out Sovay's self-contained memories with all the finesse of a chimpanzee digging grubs with a pointed stick, working fast because a hot mind wouldn't keep in a jury-rigged hold-box. Any excised memories that could unambiguously identify the mind would be flushed and whatever remained of his talent sold. There would still be a fair number of associations clinging to it but people who buy from suckers don't fuss about a few phantoms. Nor do they complain if the merchandise is half-mutilated from rushed pruning.

Anything left over after that would be sold, too. It still surprised me that there were lowlifes who would buy sucker leftovers but some people will buy anything. Which meant that there might be someone with Sovay's taste in clothes and someone else with his taste in decor and still someone else with his taste in sex.

Unless this was a bodysnatch and the suckers had somebody waiting for a whole new personality. Some Very Nice People back in business, under a new name or new management? Counterfeiters making the jump to mindsucking and bodysnatching didn't happen often. Mindsucking was a crime of violence, something counterfeiters normally avoided altogether. But it wasn't unheard of, either. The money's good; people who want a whole new personality pay a lot more than those who just want a persona overlay. Maybe because they think if they throw enough money at it, they can actually get a personality transplant even though there's no evidence that anybody's ever managed to transplant a personality successfully. No evidence whatsoever. Just ask me.

I realized I was glaring at my coffee cup. 'They, uh, they have to. Work quickly, that is,' I said lamely, finishing a sentence neither of us cared about anymore.

'I see.' Rowan exhaled noisily. 'Then it hardly matters whether you catch the mindsuckers or not, does it? I mean, for Sovay or for me. He couldn't be restored even if you found him.'

I should have made the parameds give her something for shock, I thought. Seeing to the well-being of the family was really more the province of the regular police; one of them should have been with us but they were probably working shorthanded again. The budget being what it was, I was working short-minded myself.

'No,' I said slowly, 'perhaps it doesn't matter. Unless we catch them and keep them from doing someone else.'

Rowan's mouth twitched. 'You'll excuse me if I don't seem to care about anyone but myself at the moment.'

'Of course. Is there someone you can stay with?'

'You mean someone to look after the bereaved widow, spoon broth into her mouth, cut up her meat for her, slip her tranquilizers?' The brown pearl eyes slid away from me disinterestedly. 'No. I'll manage on my own.'

We sat in silence until we heard the regular police coming into the living room.

The regular police had little to tell me. Sovay's attackers hadn't left much in the way of traces. Most likely the B and E had been jobbed out to specialists who had taken off as soon as the suckers were in. The B and E pros seldom stole anything on these runs – too traceable. Burglars don't usually want to turn into accessories to mindsuck. So there we were. The Age of Fast Information meant we could find out we didn't know anything five times faster than we could fifty years ago.

Rowan remained firm in her refusal to go to the hospital so I left her my number and drove back to headquarters. I'm one of those people who prefers driving manually both land and air. It's somewhere between a game and therapy, clears my mind, helps me think better. Traffic was fairly heavy so I had plenty of time to go over things.

Hanging above the river while I waited for the signal to descend and merge into land traffic, I put a Gladney spike in the deck and turned on all eight speakers. Gladney was another mindsuck and this spike was an old one, music composed by his original personality, what they called a first edition.

It was scary how so many artists of various kinds were getting sucked these days. Since the breakthrough in myelin sheath restoration, it had become possible for a brain to stand up to a greater number of complete wipes than the former limit of two. It used to be that a third wipe left a subject at about the level of an acorn squash, only not so long-lived. But now you could have yourself wiped annually – or you could have if government regulations hadn't been tightened. Even with the restrictions, requests for voluntary mindwipe had quadrupled. So had involuntary mindwipe – mindsuck.

My dash buzzer went off to tell me I had the right of descent and I leaned gently on the stick. The fact that Sovay was the victim seemed to indicate that we weren't done with the events of the previous month.

Retaliation, maybe, for what he'd done at Davy Jones' Locker, except that was pretty extreme for counterfeiters. They were given more to things along the lines of screwing up your credit rating, not crimes of violence. Unless there was something really big at stake.

Maybe Sovay's glancing involvement with Some Very Nice People had drawn someone's attention to him. Sovay had barely obtained a reputation *as* a promising actor except among hard-core live-theatre aficionados. An esoteric victim, but suckers made it their business to scout out new talent. New talent was a hell of a lot easier to get at and sucker customers liked the idea of acquiring a talent in the semirough, with most of the failure supposedly sanded off. Then they could refine it to suit themselves. Stardom the easy way, and better than a persona overlay. In theory. In practice –

Well. You can warn people about buying from suckers, tell them horror stories about what happens to you when you buy sucked merchandise only to have it go rotten with trauma in a living brain, you can legislate and overlegislate every angle, but you can't make people believe they won't get around the problems of buying something not only out of their aptitudes but unclean and taken by force. The legit Mind Exchange uses a procedure that took anywhere from a few weeks to several months to clean out an ability sold legally and even they couldn't guarantee there wouldn't be some mild phantoms. A few years ago, my brother bought someone's painting talent – he'd always wanted to fill out his arty streak and become a full-fledged portrait painter – and found that every time he picked up a brush, he craved to smell fresh cedar. Last time I'd seen him, he'd had a pocket full of wood chips. Stunk like somebody's antique hope chest.

Well, if someone wanted to sell off a part of the mind as though it were any old heirloom out of the attic, it wasn't my concern even if I couldn't see the virtue of it. Maybe both seller and buyer were better off but so far, no one had made history with secondhand talent. Even so, that was voluntary. No one volunteered to get sucked.

Traffic came to a standstill in Commerce Canyon, so I requested permission to go airborne again. Central Traffic Control took ten minutes to get back to me and tell me I could underfly the crosstown air express at my own risk and liability. I nearly got my hood crumpled but it saved me an hour.

Salazar was having a chew-and-spit when I arrived at her office. No drugs or surgery for her – she was too proud of her self-control. And none of that edible polyester, either – Salazar was a real-food gourmet. Chew-and-spit was her way of dealing with her lust for food versus her belief that obesity was an antisocial act. In a crowded world, she was fond of saying, it is obnoxious to take up more than your share of space. As far as I was concerned, her philosophy was her problem; my quarrel was with how she defined obesity, which was anyone who wasn't thirty pounds underweight, me for certain. To her credit, she'd stopped hinting around about diets and surgical pruning after the first month we worked together and she did

manage to keep a professional attitude in the face of my mass that, next to hers, was True Bulk.

Today she had a pocket sandwich. All the time I was telling her about Sovay, she would take a bite of her sandwich, chew it slowly and sensuously enough to make **masticate** a dirty word, and when it was all mashed to paste in her mouth, she'd lean forward and spit the mess into the suckhole in her desk. In spite of the Sally Lazer debacle, I was still one of the few who didn't gag openly at this routine, which was one reason she was tolerant of me. The Sally Lazer debacle itself was another. Everyone else in my department was on a diet or pretending to be.

'Any ideas on who did it?' she asked when I was finished. Her mouth was full.

I shifted position in the overstuffed chair. All of Salazar's office furniture was chubby. To make her feel that much thinner I supposed. 'Some Very Nice People look good for it, if we could find them. Or it might be grandstanding newcomers with something to prove. Or they could be one and the same. The identities tend to get slippery in these cases.'

Salazar spat, took a drink of mineral water and spat that into the suckhole, too. For practice, maybe. Her saggy garnet eyes stared at me skeptically. 'We've got nothing on Some Very Nice People. What about the grieving widow?' **Bite**.

'She's not an actor so they couldn't have been competitors in the strictest sense, and she has no history of personality disorders or identity buying or selling. No chance we'd be able to get a search warrant for cause. I didn't mention that possibility to her.'

Salazar looked disappointed *as* she spat and took another bite. 'If we could justify search warrants on general principle, we'd probably clear up half the unsolved sucks from the last five years.'

That kind of talk always made me uncomfortable. Tempting as it is to a Brain Police officer for the sake of all the victims like Sovay, I didn't like the idea of access-on-demand to someone's memories and I never would.

Salazar never seemed to understand it as an atrocity. Maybe she'd spent too much time in You Must Remember This.

'Sovay was a bit smaller than the stuff a really big operator might go for,' I went on. 'He was just moving into Stage One prominence, where he was classified as a talent to watch. The big operators seem to prefer someone who's just a little more of a brand name but won't be too traceable. Drives the price up. And they never make house calls. Someone big could be behind it – whoever got Bateau's cut of the pie, since Bateau himself is out of the question – but we'll never connect them with the ones who did the actual suck. The trail will be covered by a lot of selective memory wiping

and coding, so the little fish probably think they're working for themselves anyway.'

Salazar spat again. 'Sounds more complicated than it has to be.'

'Suckers always make it more complicated, hoping we'll get lost in the spaghetti.'

'Spaghetti,' Salazar murmured dreamily. 'Did they take anything else?'

'No, and not for lack of trying. They broke into his studio but there was nothing transportable. Probably they were looking for artifacts, familiar things the talent could relate to in its new home.'

Spit. The ancient Egyptians have nothing on us. How do you want to handle it?'

'The way I usually do. Get into the Downs and look around.'

She thought about that while she made love to the food in her mouth. Salazar's never been comfortable with the idea that she can't know exactly what the people under her are doing. She'd like to orchestrate everything the same way she'd like to stick her nose into any mind she wanted to. Fortunately, she was behind a desk – most of the time – where she could do only minimal damage. Most of the time.

'If we start asking questions or pulling in likelies, it'll just alert our suckers and maybe every other sucker we'd like to hotbox, and they'll just have themselves wiped so we couldn't get anything on them even if we did find them. **The State** v. **Marto**. I quote: "A mindwipe's new personality may not be held accountable for crimes –"'

Salazar spat forcefully and I shut up. 'What about backup?'

I winced. She always did this to me and she should have known better. But that's what happens when you promote administrators with no field experience, or at least none that sticks. 'Post them or don't post them, but don't tell me either way. If I don't know, no one else can find out if something goes wrong and I get sucked myself. Let's not discuss it anymore, all right?'

Salazar nodded, brought the sandwich up to her face, and then paused. 'Say, you want the rest of this?' She thrust it at me. 'I'm full.'

'No. Thanks.'

'You sure? It'll just go to waste.'

'It's not on my diet.'

She frowned at me accusingly. '**You** don't diet.'

No sense of humor, that woman. She tossed the sandwich into the suck-hole, which seemed to choke on it briefly, unused to anything solid after the pap she'd been feeding it. She had nothing further to add so I left her searching her mouth for stray food particles and took myself over to Wardrobe to pick out an appropriate Downs persona.

If Sovay's mind went anywhere at all, it would go to the Downs first, where there was plenty of merchandise floating around in and among the cheap

dreamlands, memory lanes, trip parlors, pawnshops, storefront talent brokers, and street vendors to camouflage anything that had been parted out. The mutilated remains of a person's identity could disappear pretty quickly there.

I took a quick look at some surveillance footage the regular police had shot a couple of days before. Things hadn't changed much in a month. The fashion clothingwise was still ragpicker ratatat. No problem there, I'd just get into the closet, throw everything up in the air, and wear whatever landed on me. I was more interested in faces. Wearing my own was out of the question, but just getting another wasn't the answer, either. A brand-new face in the Downs could attract dangerous attention from people with cause to be nervous; someone might decide to suck me on general principle. I shot about a dozen stills off the footage and had the computer do me a composite that any Downsite would find subliminally familiar.

The result was no one to fall in love with. Working from the composite, Wardrobe straightened my eyebrows, changed my eyes from clean onyx to cheap sapphire, tacked on a squint, broke my nose, stretched my mouth, and ruined my hair with a bad cut and fade. They wanted to mess with some muscles and ligaments to change my posture and movement but I told them there wasn't time. Wardrobe always got carried away; it was all just theatre to them. They settled for coating my vocal cords with what felt like liquid sandpaper, large grain; gave me a nasty gargle on the aspirants. I paired a man's tunic with a colorless plastic skirt and added broken-down boots.

'Très authentic,' said the Wardrobe Captain. This week, it was a young guy named Flaxie. He was brand-new, fresh out of some polytech with a degree in urban camouflage.

'Urban camouflage?' I said. 'You can really get a degree in that?'

'Believe it or leave it,' he said cheerfully. 'I was in theatrical costuming up until almost the last minute but I decided I was more interested in law enforcement than theatre. Theatre's full of neurotics, you know. They'll make you positively nutsoid.'

'Do tell.'

He flashed me a thousand-watt smile that made him look even younger than he was. 'You want an imp or are you going to brass it out on adrenaline?'

I laughed, gargling. 'I'm not excitable enough for adrenaline unassisted. Give me a global imprint, debossed. In case someone wants to check how authentic I really am. If they're in a hurry, which they usually are, they probably won't get all the way through the overlay.'

Flaxie prepared a hook-up to the computer system while I mounted a program for myself out of the characteristics-available file. Generally I tried for things that weren't too far from my own quirks and idiosyncrasies so I could slip in and out of character without too much noticeable difference.

I showed my final program to Flaxie for his educated opinion. He took a long time studying it and then gave me an odd look.

'You're sure this is what you want?'

'Is there something wrong with it?'

He seemed to be about to say something. Then he shrugged. 'Can you take your own eyes out?'

I could and did. Imprinting wasn't something I was fond of but I could put up with a deboss which was pressed on from the outside, the mental equivalent of a mask. Emboss was more reliable since it came from within your own personality, but it was a lot harder to clean out later. A global debossed facade personality would pass a glancing inspection for a short period of time if I ended up directly mind-to-mind with some lowlife. The imp had no memory of its own and I could bar it from accessing mine and giving me away. But that was a situation I was planning to avoid.

Flaxie was a real adept. The connections for my optic nerves were primed and a relaxation exercise was already in progress, a swirling, colors thing. It went on exactly long enough to let my mind settle into a receiving mode.

The mechanics were the opposite of a mindsuck. If the system operator is any good, the process should be nearly instantaneous (and painless). There was a mental moment of the sort of pressure you feel when you're concentrating intensely –

– Guy musta been a juggler in his previous lifetime. I was out in the wide-awake so fast I barely had time to be blind. Not that it made a squat of difference. I don't need eyes to know when I've been pulled in by the Brain Police. Right away, my ruff goes up. I can't help it. You never know what they've been up to.

'Next time, I'll take care of my *own* eyes, *thank* you so much I'm very sure!'

His Blondness just gives me this friendly look at all his teeth. 'Take a minute or two. A fresh imp's always on a hair trigger.'

Now, this is supposed to make sense? He's been partying with my equipment, I know that.

'Where's my eagle? I want my eagle.' I look around but there's no eagle in the room, just him and me and one of those big main-brain banks they use to tapdance on your grey. 'Oh, Blondie, you gotta problem here, illegal search and seizure, amnesia without benefit of counsel, hail me the first cab to court –'

He's grinning like I'm the best entertainment he's had in a week. 'You in there, Mersine?'

*

It was what I imagined it must be like to be a program called up within a system. The world lit up like a screen, or maybe I did.

'Yeah.' I felt myself relax several degrees. 'Yeah, it's me. The imp's pretty solid. Settling now, though. I can feel it.' I let my breath out slowly, counting to twenty.

'Remember anything?' Flaxie studied me solemnly.

'Everything.' I grinned, mildly embarrassed. 'She's pretty obnoxious.'

'She's all yours. You want anything modified?'

I thought it over. 'Nah. She's fine the way she is. Nobody'll give her a second look in the Downs.' I thought some more but there were some curious blank spaces that didn't feel right. 'Do I have everything I need? I feel like I'm missing something.'

Flaxie nodded. 'The imp knows a bit more than you do right now. Not to worry. You'll know it, too, when you're supposed to.'

'Right.' I took another deep breath, counting it in and out again. 'That's the part I've never been too crazy about. Hiding my own information from myself.'

'Standard stuff. But if it makes you that uncomfortable, we could go back in and put dummy data in the blanks.'

I shook my head. 'It's okay. It's just kind of –' I shrugged. 'Weird.'

'You think **this** is weird? Costume a road show sometime.' He smiled briefly and turned toward the system, reaching for something on the panel. Then suddenly he whirled and lunged at me, grabbing a fistful of my tunic. 'Who *are* you, what do you want here?' he barked –

Just like that, we're nose-to-nose. I let out a yell that blew back his eyelashes and most of his hair.

'Marya Anderik, I gotta *thing* about memories, anybody's but *mine*, all *right*. That *bother* you, Blondie?' I got his wrist now. 'Let go of me or I'll make you *eat* this hand.'

He backed off. '*Mersine*. Come on

up.'

'Wow,' I said, heart pounding. 'That's a hot one.'

'It's the usual setup – dual conscious reflex control for when she comes up and when she goes down again. Anyone addressing you directly with your real name can bring you up, but only you and I can bring the imp up. Anything you know won't leak over to the imp unless you command it to. Certain situations might make you flash a little but considering what you're supposed to be, nobody in the Downs is going to find your momentary lapse of attention unusual. You'd stick out if you didn't fugue off or show a little petit mal once in a while. Come back when you want it taken off.'

He turned back to the system and busied himself with the settings. I let myself out. When I stopped at Sign-out to pick up some informant addresses (the imp had the names, concealed from me; I would only know where to find them), I found a message from Salazar ordering me to take a gun. There was no use trying to explain to her about the dangers of that false sense of security a gun gives you, let alone that there was no reason for my persona to run packed. Some supervisors you can't tell anything, mainly the ones with no field experience. I checked a stinger out of Arsenal and mailed it interoffice to my desk, where it would arrive several hours after I hit the Downs. I had a few steel-pointed combs in my rat's-nest coiffure; if they didn't get lost in there, they'd be enough. If they weren't, then I'd be beyond any help a gun could have given me anyway.

I was just about to leave the building when I got another phone call, addressed simply to **Sovay Case Officer**. Damn that Salazar I thought, picking up the sound-only receiver in the hall near Sign-out. How had she found out about the gun so quickly?

But it wasn't Salazar. It was Sovay.

'How do I know you're Sovay?' I said.

The man on the other end of the line laughed weakly. 'I guess you don't. But trust me, that's who I am. I'm trapped in this, uh, I don't know what he is. It's a he, I can tell you that much. I don't know where I am or why −'

'You said, already. Can't you give me a description, a name, anything?'

'It's all jumbled up in here. It was better back in that other place. I had no body so I just re-created everything in my head. No, I didn't have a head. You know what I mean, though. You have to, you're the Brain Police.'

'Just try to remain calm.' The officer on Sign-out duty slid me a chair and a scratch pad while someone else went to get a terminal so I could trace the call. 'What seems to have happened is, the mindsuckers who took your mind sold you off to someone intact. But the implant didn't take very well and you're fighting for dominance instead of being assimilated −'

Another weak laugh. 'No, that's not it. I mean, they think that's it. Or they thought that was it. But I'm back there, too.'

'Back where?'

'In the other place. Where I had no body.'

I hesitated. I should have taken this call in my office, but I risked having him hang up in the time it would have taken to sprint back there.

'It's true,' he went on, a little breathlessly. 'I'm waiting back there, playing for time. I don't know where that is, though. I sent me out − that *I* sent this *me*, I mean − intending to get help. The *me* back there has no way of knowing if *I*, this *I* talking to you, succeeded or just went crazy or what.'

'I'm sorry, but I'm not sure −'

He sighed heavily. 'They keep trying to send me out, sell me off. Me, just the one person. So I create one of my characters and send **him** out. Do you see? I'm Sovay-in-character, a character from one of the plays I've done. Do you see now?'

I saw. You see all kinds of things in the Brain Police. A disembodied, self-replicating mind was a more bizarre sight than usual, but stranger things have happened. Probably.

'Okay. Which character are you?'

'No, listen, this is important. You have to understand that I'm **not** the Character. I'm **Sovay's interpretation of that character**. Do you understand the difference?'

'I'm not sure. Just tell me which character from which play.'

'Dennie Moon from **Brickboy**. It's great, about a quiet guy who serves as the living museum of his family's memories. He takes all the most significant ones before any of the relatives die, and he's got them from three generations. But now he's hit his storage capacity and he's got to stop and let someone else pick it up. His successor is his daughter and he's caught in this three-way conflict where he's jealous because he can't do it anymore but also he realizes it can be a painful experience and she's still very young. But he also wants to keep it all in his own line of descent – really powerful piece of work.' He gave a happy sigh. 'The character's a good learning role for an actor.'

A small light went on in my head. 'Ah. Okay, I want you to concentrate –'

'I **am** concentrating. I have to, just to stay up.'

'Concentrate harder and tell me why you chose to send Dennie Moon to the person you're in right now.'

The silence stretched for so long I was afraid he'd fainted or hung up. 'You think there was a particular reason? I couldn't see whoever this is. Maybe Moon was the first character that occurred to him, or the easiest, or both.'

Someone slid a terminal in front of me and punched up some information on the screen. Sovay/Moon was calling from a voice-only phone somewhere in the Downs. A blinking bar at the top of the screen informed me the trace was still in progress. You'd think that in the Age of Fast Information, you could get the really important information that much faster. Think again.

'Consider this,' I said. 'Maybe you chose Moon for this person because he felt like the Dennie Moon type.'

Another long silence. 'It's possible,' he said at last. 'I never thought of that.'

'Can you kind of feel around in there for any identifying features of your, uh, host mind?'

The young officer who had brought the terminal was staring at me. **Host mind?** he mouthed. I ignored him.

'Uh, I can't see too well. It's dark for me,' Sovay/Moon said faintly. 'I get a

glimpse of a sidewalk sometimes. People dancing around on it. See-through people. Zoot!'

'Say again?'

'I see a word on a sign. The word is "Zoot."'

I punched **zoot** into the keyword search program. A moment later a small window in the bottom left corner of the screen opened to inform me that there was a new dreamland in the Downs called The Zoot Mill.

'Is that where you went? To The Zoot Mill?'

'No. That's where I am now. Across the street.'

'Can you see anything else? Can you see yourself, what do you look like?'

'I don't know. I feel short. I try to feel my hair or my clothes but something's blocking the input or something. I can't get it.'

It sounded like something that might be in character from what he'd told me about Dennie Moon. Method actors, I grumbled to myself.

'I see my hand!' he cried suddenly. 'There's a picture on it, it's smiling at me! It's a woman! It —'

'Hello? Still there, hello?'

He gave a long, miserable sigh. 'This guy is making me hang up.'

The blinking bar at the top of the screen stopped blinking and gave me the address: a public voice-only phone right across the street from The Zoot Mill. The Age of Fast, Redundant Information. At least I knew he hadn't been hallucinating or lying. 'Can you get him to stay there?'

'He's hungry, I think. Something he wants a lot, maybe it's food. He's mad.'

'Hold him until I get to you.'

'I'll try, but … '

'Can you tell me anything else? Anything at all?' Inspiration hit me. 'What did Derinie Moon look like in the play?'

'Urn, youthful for his age. Black hair down to his shoulders, light green eyes. Stockyish build. Why?'

I wrote down the description. 'Just an idea. Listen, in a little while, a homely woman with lousy hair and old clothes is going to approach you. Be there.'

'Wait!' he yelled suddenly. 'Wait! I have something for you! Names! Fortray, Anwar, Easterman!'

Fortray and Easterman meant nothing to me, but Anwar almost rang a bell, albeit a very distant one, a bell that belonged to someone else. The terminal was logging the call so I didn't worry about writing anything down. 'Who are they?'

'More of Sovay,' he said. 'That's all I know. More people they sold Sovay to.' He paused. 'I don't know why I know that. I have to go now. I can't help it.'

Resourceful guy, Sovay. I wondered if he'd planted the names in each mind, hoping at least one of them would call the Brain Police. It was too bad he couldn't be restored, this was some major trick.

'Try to stay where you are.' He didn't answer. There was a click as the phone line went dead.

The terminal printed out the three names he'd given, every one of them tagged **U** for **Unknown**. Either they didn't have records or they were new aliases. I folded them up with the informant addresses and took off, leaving everything for the Sign-out officer to put away.

Of course, he was gone when I got there.

'Heya, heya!' called the man in front of the trip parlor (Sojourn For Truth – Not God But An Incredible Simulation!). 'You gotta be paranoid! Can't be too rich or too paranoid these days! Heya, heya, hey-**ya**!' He caught my arm as I started to go in. The cracked imitation-leather armor over his longjohns squealed with the movement. Stars twinkled in his teeth; he spat a few into the air between us. They must have been hell on his gums but neurosis ped-dlers are all goofy for special effects. 'How about you, madam? You may think you're paranoid, but are you paranoid **enough**?' His tacky moonstone eyes searched my face as more multicolored stars sailed out of the corner of his mouth. Two spitters in one day; the Age of Fast Information was oral as hell.

'Had it for **lunch**,' I said raspily, doing what I hoped was a creditable imita-tion of the imp. 'Let **go**.'

'Heya, don't pass **me** up. Simulated God can't compare to the awareness you get from a nice dose of paranoia. It's like coming up from underwater, you won't believe how awake and alive you'll feel –'

'If you don't let go of my arm, I'll kill you.'

'See? **See**?' He puffed out a few more stars. 'You're halfway there already. And the price is right. Ask anyone, they'll tell you Crazy Al deals the best para-noia at the price, the best you can get without going totally **in**sane!'

I twisted away from him. When he reached for me again, I had one of the steel-pointed combs in my hand.

'Heya, **okay**!' He jumped back, raising his arms and deflecting a few stars flying out of his mouth. 'Numb your mind with truth and simulated God, that's fine. But you'll be looking for me when **They** all start plotting against you.'

'When **They** all start plotting against me, I **won't** need **you**.' I made a swipe at him and he jumped back again. If there's anything I hate, it's a cheap per-secution complex masquerading as paranoia.

The waiting room of Sojourn For Truth was empty and untended. No chairs, no waiting. Sojourn For Truth was the first of the informant addresses I'd been given and they tended to go in descending order of usefulness. It didn't look familiar to me; apparently this was a byte parked with the imp's program.

I felt a little reluctant to bring her up but whatever was on the other side of the twinkly curtain that divided the waiting room from the parlor itself wasn't something I was supposed to handle. Running a short breathing relaxation exercise, I planted a few false memories to give her some context and made the dive as I walked through the curtain.

Some trip parlor. A lot of shabby futons spread on the floor under strings of paper lanterns. The lanterns are supposed to be moodlighting – how cheap-assed could you get? The even cheaper sound system was playing Brahms in raga-time on sitar, crackling hard on the high notes. Yah, not God but an incredible simulation. See God in a place like this, you *know* it's hard times for the universe.

There's one paying fool, a young guy lying on a futon near a corner, giggling at the wall where this skinny hypehead in a white gown is making shadow pictures with his hands in front of a bare light tube. Guess there wasn't too much call for simulated God these days. I wasn't exactly looking to sanctify myself, either. The hypehead caught me staring and shrugged.

'Holo's broken,' he says. 'They keep telling us the parts'll be in any day now. Big deal. It's the drug that counts, anyway. We got plenty of drug.'

I jerk my chin at the wall. 'Do God.'

'Do *this*.' He gives me the International Symbol of Disdain, which doesn't make the most interesting shadow on the wall. But it keeps the fool on the futon giggling.

Well, nobody ever booked Coney Loe on the extreme cleverness charge. He was just your basic hypehead. They say he'd been some kind of catalyzer-imagist once, the kind creative artists hire to give them head-pictures; supposed to give them a jump start, seeing all kinds of weird shit in their heads, make them more creative or something. Can't make that stick, myself. I see the weirdest shit in the world in my head and I got no urge to paint *Moby's Dick* or whatever it is. But maybe it's different when Coney Loe does it.

Or did it. Old Coney's neurons gave out early on him and he dried up. Now he's just a hypehead making like some hotwire and this is his latest two-step for groceries. It's a comedown from hustling for persona mills, but considering the kind of places that would use someone like him, maybe not much.

'So, how's the simulated God here, Coney? Ever try it?'

My calling him by name gives him pause, but just a very little one, and I know he doesn't really remember me. Coney liked to forget certain things, keep the bank open for more important information. It was a Thing with him, information, like he was trying to know everything in

the world or something. He could have gone pro, and every so often the Brain Police would come snuffling around, waving money in front of him, but they couldn't turn him over. They didn't seem to understand how it was with him, that he had to have information the way some people had to have sex, or memories, and the only way to buy from him was to pay in kind. But catch the Brain Police giving out information – sure, the night I remember getting crowned Pope. Firsthand.

The Brain Police – the whole scene snaps back on me like bad karma. Shit, what have they done to me now? I can't remember the interrogation but you never can, unless they find out something from you. I never could figure what gave them the right to take a memory, even a bad one like that, and you ask an eagle and all you get is a lot of lawyer rama-doola about confidentiality and your own protection. Like the Brain Police ever protected me from anything.

Coney is staring at me. 'You looking for truth?' he says. 'Or just keeping a secret?'

'Information,' I tell him automatically. 'And maybe I'm keeping a secret.' Which I know I am, and it'll come to me in a second ... something to do with why the Brain Police jerked my chain in the first place. It's on the tip of my brain.

Coney makes a two-handed bird and flaps the wings. 'We got truth and God here. Hallucinogens flavored and unflavored, scented, unscented, in your mouth, up your arm, or whatever, lights, colors –' He changes the bird into a rabbit. 'Pictures. What's your pleasure?'

'Information. Like I said.' I pull my fingers out of my mouth and wiggle them in front of the light tube, enchanting the paying fool.

Coney bats my hand away. 'Truth is cheap. Information costs. Can you afford information? Or only truth?'

Now, I've got money and I've got a secret, and I know which one Coney really wants. Maybe I should have stopped off at a memory lane for a recall booster –

And then it comes to me, just like that, as if someone put a tube in my ear and poured it in like clover honey. 'I know something you don't know.'

It's like telling a ramrod he's got a limp plaything. Coney frowns and the rabbit becomes plain old fingers without making any difference to the guy on the futon.

'So?' Coney says, a little testy.

'So I like memories. Anybody's but mine. The *real* stuff. Somebody else's. Like I could *be* somebody else. I like that a lot.'

'I can understand that.' Coney keeps staring at me and does a dog one-handed, which sets his paying fool barking. 'That doesn't exactly

make it as a secret, little queenie. Anyone could figure it out on short acquaintance. Unless you're holding something other than your own personal disclosure, maybe you want to shake it to the memory lane across the street and stop bothering me when I'm simulating God. What do I care about your memory jones?'

'*You'd* know where to get the really *good* stuff, Coney. You *always* know. Why, you'd even know where the freshest stuff would be. The freshest, never-been-seen stuff, even if no one else knew it was even there yet.' I take a breath, grinning because I know I got his attention now; I can tell by the way he's making rabbit shadows like it's his sacred mission in life. 'Even if it wasn't *supposed* to be there.'

'I heard you,' he says, and his ruff is way up. Something happened and nobody told him about it; asses will be kicked. I feel sorry for the paying fool, whose ass happens to be handiest. My ass is safe for the moment, because I've got a secret.

'I didn't hear *you*,' I say. 'Am I deaf?'

He's dying because I won't come across. 'I might know where you could get an order to go. Or I might have no idea.' He keeps doing the rabbit shadow. 'Your turn.'

'Somebody got sucked.' I put a ringer to my head and make like I'm thinking real hard. 'Somebody that does something fancy. Yah, an actor. Just this morning, can you buy that?'

He can. 'Monkey shock,' he says. 'Your turn.'

'The Monkey Shop?'

'I *said*, your turn.' He means it, no appeal. Either I come up with a name he can check or he'll kick my ass after all for a liar. Information junkies have some interesting ways of kicking your ass, nothing you want to beg for.

'Sovay. That's the name, ask anybody.' Even I winced at that one. But hell you just can't resist stinging an information junkie when you got the chance. They all act like knowing all that shit makes them more than the hypeheads they really are.

'Shock. *Shock.* Monkey *shock.* Open your goddam ears.'

'Do a monkey!' chortles the fool.

'Shut up,' Coney tells him, but somehow he produces an apelike shadow.

'So what's a monkey shock?' I ask.

'Thrills.'

'A *thrillseeker?* Screw *that*. I already *know* how to get *excited*, thank *you* for *nothing*.'

'This is different. Potluck. You go in and hope for the best. Lots of juice. Makes you dance like a monkey. But if you pay them enough –' Big pause. 'Your turn.'

Great. I had to go and shoot it all. I could have held back that it was this morning, I could have given an address first instead of a name – shit, an information junkie'll finesse you every time. I'm trying to think fast; do I make something up and hope he doesn't find out too soon it's a lie, or go for the brass. Brass first, until I can come up with a convincing lie that could pass for misinformation later.

'My turn? Like hell, you ain't finished taking your turn, you're changing dicks in the middle of my screw.'

Coney won't thaw. 'Your turn.' He gives me a little smile, making a rooster on the wall. The skinny shit knows I'm tapped, or he thinks he knows it. I'm wondering what the odds are that I could beat it out of him and then I realize he's told me enough that I can figure out the rest myself. He couldn't help it; for an information junkie, the only thing as good as finding something out is passing it on.

'Okay, here's my turn. You say *potluck?* You say *juice?* You say *pay enough?* I say it sounds like maybe there's a little extra in the juice if you pay enough and by the time your head stops jitterbugging, who's to say whatever you got wasn't yours to begin with.'

Sometimes I really surprise myself. I may be a hypehead, but I ain't no burnout, no sclerosis this year. Coney looks like he bit down on something sour.

'Guess you know it all,' he says.

I'm smirking away. 'And if I don't know, I know who knows.'

'Yah?' He smirks back. 'But do you know *how* you know all this?'

'Just living right.' But I get a little edgy creep. I know about Sovay from the Brain Police, that's nothing; every time someone gets sucked, they round up the usual suspects, no big shit and so fucking what. But I know that's not what he means.

'Like, how'd you get so genius, figuring stuff out like you got a sherlock circuit.' His smile is mean. 'Don't come back, little queenie. I don't know who you are and you don't, either.'

'I'm *everyone!*' Coney's fool announces at the top of his lungs. Coney puts a polka-dotted sleeve over the tube and gives it a spin. While the fool is going cross-eyed over this, he's rummaging around in some stuff on the floor and finds a long white beard to put on. Icons die hard.

He pauses to glare at me. ' "Don't come back" means you're leaving now. Or can't you figure that part out?'

I give him a salute and start backing toward the exit.

Coney leans over the fool. 'Hi, I'm God. What's on your mind?'

The fool stares up at him; every neuron must be flapping and snapping like tiny pennants in a hurricane. 'Why am I here?'

'Because you're stupid.'

Fool nods very slowly. 'Ah. I always thought it was more complicated than that.'

It's mean, but that's the nature of truth.

I shut her down as I went back through the curtain into the empty waiting room. The combined physical and mental movement gave me a moment of light vertigo while the memory of the immediate past settled around me.

Memory from an imp feels more like a dream than a memory, and this felt like a dream I'd had before. I looked back at the curtain. Coney Loe; I didn't know him, but the imp did, which meant he was a double-blind informant – only imps contacted him, and when the Sovay case was closed, I wouldn't know him anymore, unless he somehow slipped into my long-term memory. That can happen after repeated contact with a double-blind.

I put him out of my mind and considered Monkey Shock as I stepped outside. My pal the neurosis peddler was still hawking paranoia out front. He gave me a wide berth. I ignored him. Monkey Shock wouldn't be anything more than crude convulsions induced by plain old electricity, with timed-release hallucinogens and a mental sorter delivering extra jolts randomly through the right hemisphere. Messy, but not illegal.

It wouldn't be hard to add sucker leftovers to the mental sorter. Memories would work best. The customer would get a thrill at each jolt. Afterward, electroshock amnesia covered all the traces. As the imp said, after your brain stopped jitterbugging, it would be impossible to tell which memories had been added and which were native. Maybe even the customer wouldn't know for sure. Ingenious, and a lot less obvious than taking the stock to a pawnshop or a crib.

Bad news for me, though. Monkey Shock wasn't one of those things I could engage in with even marginal safety. Getting myself hooked up in one of the sleazy memory lanes to see if there was anything of Sovay in the merchandise they were offering was safer than, say, getting myself hooked up to someone who'd been to the lane and bought some of it. In a lane, the operator usually lets the machine do most of the work and a machine doesn't know the difference between a real memory junkie and a Brain Police officer with a memory junkie overlay.

But the worse news was Coney Loe's suspicion. It could have been mere pique because some little unwashed hypehead he considered beneath him actually had some information he didn't have. Or else I really had burned myself in a blazing display of deductive thinking. Blazing for the imp, anyway, or what she was supposed to be. The imp didn't have all my information but she did have my intelligence, and maybe that wasn't quite in character … although showing it off would be.

In any case, I was going to have to track down Monkey Shock before

Coney Loe could get around to alerting them about me. *I don't know who you are and you don't either.*

Two onionheads shackled together on a long chain went by, both giving me dirty looks. I ignored them showily, turning away but being careful to keep their retreating figures in my peripheral vision so I'd see if they decided to turn on me and accuse me of flirting with one of them. Onionheads in a jealous frenzy could be fatal.

The neurosis peddler edged toward me, keeping out of reach. 'Heya, I'm not trying to bother you or anything, but I got this spot staked, I got permits.'

I moved off without looking at him, bumping into a skinny blonde who seemed to be in the process of coming to while walking. She barely noticed me in her rediscovery of reality. Well, **this** reality.

'Heya, lover.' The woman had flies in her eyes. They looked real, preserved in the thickened irises, the pupils camouflaged in the little fly bodies. I was squatting in a parking space directly in front of The Zoot Mill, watching both the holo display on the sidewalk and the voice only phone across the street, in case Sovay/Moon decided to make a return appearance. Probably what I should have done in the first place, instead of burning myself with Coney Loe. The Zoot Mill holo was a little ragged, and nothing special – dancing girls, dancing boys, banquets, money tornadoes, and a lot of the usual signs and wonders – but it was tankless and vivid.

'*Heya*, lover, Fly Eyes said again, moving a little closer.

'*What*,' I snapped.

'You look like it's been a while.' She grinned, showing me another fly design etched on a front tooth. Mouths, I thought. The world was full of mouths. 'Well, the drought's over because I got the man of your dreams.' She saw me looking at The Zoot Mill's display where Hercules or someone like him was ceremoniously disrobing for three holo slave girls and one live woman who looked too fried to really appreciate it.

'**Better** than **that**,' she said. 'Much better. Like he invented it. Unforget-table. It'll be keeping you warm when you're ninety.'

Looking at her, I had a flash. It was like looking out of two eyes belonging to two different people. For a moment the imp was aware in a vague way and we were cohabiting. This was the type of situation more suited for her than for me. I put her to sleep again. 'Go **away**,' I said. 'I don't want some secondhand wet dream.'

'Wet dream? That doesn't even begin to describe it. This is the mystical experience, change your life, change your **religion**. Ever been in a state of grace for three hours straight? If you had, you wouldn't be squatting here biting your nails.'

I trapped both hands between my knees. 'A wet dream's a wet dream. If this guy really burns, I'd rather press his flesh myself.'

'Not possible, he's far away. But I remember it like it was an hour ago, had the whole memory specially enhanced and amplified. You'll taste him, you'll smell him –' She babbled on but she wasn't fooling me. What she probably had was a second- or thirdhand memory of someone else's fantasy. I guess I must have looked like I'd spent the last ten years locked in a lunchbox.

'Come on,' she said, moving a little closer. 'It's the best kind of mindfuck you'll ever get. You don't like it, I'll give you a rebate minus the equipment fee.'

'Rebate **this**. Now skin off' – I pulled my left hand away from my mouth – 'and leave me **alone**.'

'Frigid,' she jeered and stalked off.

I looked up at the meter. Five more minutes and then I'd have to move along. Meterfeeding had lately been outlawed in the Downs, one of the few regulations successfully enforced. A metertender had already come by once to take my picture so I was going to have to decide what to do – start asking around for Fortray, Anwar, or Easterman, go to the next informant address as Marya, or hang around here as either Marya or myself pretending to be Marya but keeping a low profile. Asking around for someone could get sticky. I could have given at least one of the names to Marya to ask Coney Loe about, but all things considered, it probably would have made him even more suspicious. He might have ended up stampeding the suckers into closing up shop and flushing Sovay altogether.

I kept thinking that Sovay/Moon couldn't have gone far in the state he was in which would also possibly mean he hadn't gone far in the first place, choosing the first phone he saw after coming out of Monkey Shock. Therefore, I could have been in Monkey Shock's locale – for all I knew, it was a back room in The Zoot Mill, some thing I might have been able to find out if Marya hadn't insisted on antagonizing Coney Loe.

The meter was just about expired when I saw her coming stiffly down the sidewalk toward me. For several seconds I froze until I remembered she couldn't possibly recognize me. Certainly she wasn't here hunting for me or any other kind of police. She looked tense and scared and a lot more emotional than she had back in her kitchen when she'd told me it wouldn't make any difference to her personally if we caught the suckers who had done Sovay.

No points for nerve, I decided; it wasn't nerve she was demonstrating by coming into the Downs. I had no idea what she thought she was doing, but even more to the point, how the hell could she know enough to do it in the first place?

Stupid fool, I said to myself. Anytime someone gets sucked, you look at the

spouse first, no matter what; if the victim's married to Baby Jesus, he's number one on the list of suspects and you put the little tyke under surveillance –

But she **was** under surveillance. **I** was watching her, wasn't I, she was right there in front of me. The regular police had probably tagged her all the way into my vicinity and then left her for me to deal with – they always know when a case officer is working an investigation, even if they don't know exactly who it is. If Rowan knew anything, she'd take me right to the place I wanted to go, and if she didn't, I could get rid of her somehow, chase her out under some pretext or another.

It was getting late and the streets were starting to fill with what they call local color, hues that look best under artificial light. Rowan hadn't made any effort to blend in. She was still in her pouch suit, which was too new and too expensive for the area. Just as she drew even with The Zoot Mill, I saw the twinkle of a paranoid's badge on her sleeve. All jumped up on a paranoid rush for a trip to the Downs?

The parking meter chimed and I stood up slowly, not wanting to alarm her with any sudden moves, but she wasn't paying any attention to me. She only had eyes for the holo.

It was still Hercules or someone like him, wearing a strap and doing a vigorous ballet/square dance with the slave girls. Rowan was watching with an intentness that could have passed for carnal, which wouldn't have been so unusual. Everyone handles a loss differently. But she was trying to get a good look at Hercules' face, as though he might have been someone she knew.

That idea was unappetizing. How would she know some cheap holo hoochy-koocher and why would she be looking for him now? And why had she had to get paranoid to do it? She had no record of being licensed for paranoia or any other psychosis. And how paranoid was she, anyway?

I moved carefully around the other side of the holo, maneuvering through the small crowd that was gathering to watch Hercules. He was looping through his strip routine again and I found myself giving him a few points for talent. After all, whoever started out with the idea of being a cheap holo hoochy-koocher anyway? In his mind, maybe this had been **Afternoon of a Faun**, updated.

And what was it in Rowan's mind?

Her attention remained focused on him, enabling me to get around on her left side, so she'd have to go right past me to get into The Zoot Mill, if that was where she was going.

Inadvertently, I brushed against a rooster-boy with a multicolored crest and feathered codpiece, and not much else except for a dusting of gold powder on his pasty skin. He turned to me with a wide, automatic grin.

'Hot enough for you?' The low, throaty come-on was already out of his mouth when the grin froze into something more painful than sexy. Rooster-boys weren't

supposed to be picky but apparently this one was. The rainbow crest rising from his hairline drooped. 'Forget it. Not even if I was flatline.'

'And when have *I* ever demanded anything from you, dickie-bird?'

He blinked at me and I winced. Not crude enough for the situation or the character I was supposed to be. Trying too hard; either I had to let Marya come up or limit my vocabulary to **Heya** and **Fuck off** while I was driving.

And then Rowan turned around and looked directly at me. I froze again. In spite of the fact that she couldn't have recognized my scratchy, gargly voice, the expression on her face said she wasn't sure if she knew me or not. The paranoid's badge on her sleeve glittered. General freefloating anxiety, I decided – that was her 'paranoia.' Not the real thing with delusions of grandeur and hallucinations but the street stuff neurosis peddlers like my pal in front of Sojourn For Truth sold to the public: persecution complexes, anxiety, and such. I wouldn't have thought anyone like Rowan would have had to buy anxiety to walk around in the Downs. She could have breathed it in with the air.

A pimp came up on her other side and tapped her on the shoulder. She jumped, twisting around, and backed into my rooster-boy, who immediately put both hands possessively on her shoulders. She jerked away from him and stepped into the holo display. Hercules' arm went through her neck and I thought she was going to have hysterics. The pimp pulled her out of the circle of reception before she could break up the display. The two of them struggled together and then he said something I didn't catch because the rooster-boy was bitching to nobody in particular that his customer had been stolen. People began giving ground around him, allowing me to move closer to Rowan, who was listening to the pimp with an expression that didn't look the least paranoid anymore, or even anxious. She and the pimp made an odd couple, her in the expensive, trendy pouch suit and him in his traditional garish technicolor fuzz. He pointed down the street away from me and she made a move to leave. Blocking her with a fuzzy, electric-green arm, he tapped her paranoid's badge. Rowan shook her head.

I maneuvered around behind them, planting more false memories for Marya, leaving her the knowledge of who Rowan was. If she thought Rowan was leading her to Monkey Shock, she'd be happy to follow.

Abruptly, Rowan slapped some currency into the pimp's hand and stalked off in the direction he'd pointed. The pimp laughed at her retreating back and turned to the display again, watching Hercules fiddle with the ties on his codpiece. I let Rowan go half a block before sending Marya after her.

She looks like she knows where she's going but not what she's doing. People like her, they never know what they're doing but they always know where they're going.

I *know* she's on her way to Monkey Shock; either she's leading the Brain Police straight to them, or she's going to ask for a rake-off of the profits on Sovay, grieving widow and all that shit. I've seen that before. Or, hell, she might even believe she can get him back. Plenty of them believe that; fuck if I know why. But then, astrologers are still in business, too, and there's one guy I know of personally who probably believes he met God today and God told him he was here because he was stupid, which just goes to show you faith gets it over information every time. Faith, or maybe truth, depending on your point of view, which is everything in this game.

So what the hell, maybe they'll pay her off, or just suck her and call it a bonus. Either way, there'd be something for me when the dust settled.

She goes two blocks before she starts slowing down and looking at the buildings. There's not much here, a pawnshop, a hardware/software dealer, and a crib passing as a read-only room. She almost passes the crib and then stops.

Now, I know this crib and if it's Monkey Shock, I remember my papal coronation. Pimp's probably going to run her all over the Downs, I realize; tells her to go one place and when she gets there, someone'll tell her to go somewhere else, and so on, and so on, till she's all turned around and lost. Then maybe they'll send her to Monkey Shock, when they're sure she's too confused to know where she is. And when they're sure she isn't wagging a tail behind her.

Well, I'd just say the pimp sent me, too, to keep an eye on her. Why not.

I go right in after her and she doesn't even know it. Place is just a big ratmaze inside, cubicles and low walls, so I can keep track of her from a distance. They're doing a little business in there anyway, not much, but a few other hypeheads are wandering the aisles. The whole idea is, you see something in a cubicle you like, you step in and have some.

Rowan's all at sea in here. I cruise the other side of the room, just in case there's anything interesting running, but it's like any other crib – one sorry soul after another, waiting to sell you their best shot, and the hardware piled up off to one side. One old gock with peppermint eyes (where do they come up with this stuff?) and foil curls is whispering 'Cubs? Cubs? You like 'em young? It's no crime to just *think* about it, you know,' and next to him is a job in a leather hood with the eyes zipped shut, chanting 'Fetish, fetish, fetish,' like I'm supposed to believe I can really get one that'll stick past the first time I go to sleep. And I'm watching Rowan and wondering what she's making of all this; I'm sure she's never been in a crib before.

And I don't know what gets into me all of a sudden, but I want to get over to her and tell her to get out. She can think about anything she wants with anybody she wants, but a place like this is below anyone still capable of raising a sine wave without help. Hell, even the hardware has to be scuzzy, with all that kind of thinking running through it. I bet if I go over and crack open the system next to the gock with the peppermint eyes, it'll be nothing but slime inside instead of chips and plates. Marya Anderik, crusader for social reform, sure. For all I know, *I* bought from the old gock before he ran thin enough to move in here.

Then Rowan stops in front of a cubicle and Hercules pops up, live, Hercules the hoochy-koocher in cheap jumpjohns. And what happens next is so kinky, even I don't believe it.

They slam together and start kissing.

Automatically, I duck, waiting for alarms to go off and vice squads to drop down from the ceiling. The regular police love to raid a meat market with people really doing things instead of just thinking about them. But then Rowan and Hercules sink down before anyone else gets a look at what they're doing. I give them five seconds and then hurry over, going as fast as I can because I have to run up and down two aisles going almost the width of the room.

When I get to them, I expect to see live porno, but it's weirder than that – they're already lying side by side on the cots, and they're hooked into the hardware, her eyes in a tank on one side and his in a tank on the other, just like everything is normal.

What's wrong with this picture is there's a third person, a funny-looking haunt in ratatat worse than mine, lying on the floor between them, and *he's* hooked in, too, through an illegal auxiliary connection. His eyes are drifting around in a bowl next to his head and for some reason, I think of that old joke – the party got so wild, I passed out and woke up as the guy next to me. The crib's not licensed for anything other than one-on-one. No crib is. I can't figure why they're risking it; anyone in here can be a Brain Police plant and if they're caught, it's instant raid. But people who mouthkiss'll try anything. Mouths, *yuck.*

The guy on the floor suddenly reaches up and starts to disconnect, and the last thing I see before I do a fast fade is he's got tattooed hands. Christ, the silly stuff you notice.

I had sixty seconds, give or take, to decide whether I should confront them or skin off and maintain surveillance at a distance. The guy on the floor, now fumbling like a novice with the connections to his optic nerves, was obviously the man who called me at the station – the tattoo on his right hand fit the description he gave. If his memory wasn't too spotty, he would recognize

me as the person who was supposed to meet him at the phone across from The Zoot Mill. I wasn't so sure making contact now would be the optimum thing to do.

He had his connections out and he was reaching for his eyes. I ducked into the next cubicle, and crouched next to the wall. The occupants didn't care – they were both hooked up to a system, sharing whatever it was people shared In cribs. Next door, I could hear Sovay/Moon moving around, helping Rowan and Hercules disconnect.

'Oh, thank you,' Rowan whispered politely, as though he'd just passed her the edible polyester at a dinner party. There were a few sounds of hurried kisses and then I heard Hercules whisper, 'Rowan and I will go out together. Give us ten minutes to get past my pimp – we don't want him cutting himself in. Then meet us at –'

I couldn't get it because Sovay/Moon chose that moment to grunt unhappily. He started to make some kind of complaint but the other two shushed him. A moment later they hurried past the cubicle I was crouching in, leaving Sovay/Moon alone. I gave it five seconds and then crawled out of the cubicle and into the other.

He was sitting on the edge of Rowan's cot with his face in his hands; I could see he was trembling a little. Who was he now – Sovay/Moon, or the man who had bought Sovay/Moon? Only one way to find out for certain, and since I had probable cause to believe he was a receiver of sucked goods, I could legally search his mind without a warrant.

Getting him to hold still for that, however, was another matter. I was beginning to wish I'd taken the stinger after all. On the other hand, if Sovay/Moon was still dominant, I might be able to talk him into cooperating and keeping his mouth shut afterward.

Sensing something, he lowered his hands and saw me squatting at the entrance to the cubicle. He didn't look a thing like Sovay's description of the character – long horse face, uneven lank brown hair, too much nose and mouth. He could have passed for my brother, the way I looked now. My brother or my father. That gave me an idea.

He started to get up and I said, 'No, it's me – your daughter.'

Several expressions swept down his long face as he plumped down on the cot again and shoved himself away from me, packing himself into a corner of the cubicle.

'Don't you see, Father,' I said, crawling toward him. 'It must go on. We can't let it die with you, because –' I floundered for a moment. Christ, but I wished I had a lot more background than what he'd told me. '– because I'll be carrying it on, and from me, it will go to my own child, and so on until we come to the … the final shore and we'll all be there to see it together –'

'Final peak.'

I froze. 'Uh … what?'

'Till we come to the final peak and see the world as we made it spread out before us. Improv doesn't mean you can change the analogy.' Watching my face, he untensed about a millimeter.

'Oh.' I slid up onto the cot and sat facing him.

'Well, go on,' he said. 'Talk me into it.'

'Talk you into it?'

He looked briefly at the ceiling. 'You're supposed to persuade me to let you archive my personal memories as the symbol of the torch passing. Reach for it, pull out all the stops, you can clean up the scenery chewing later for performance. Don't be afraid of the Method. Make me see that my memories are as important to you as they are to me, show me I can't be selfish enough to let a dynasty die with me.'

I started to flash again and Marya stirred more actively than she had back on the street with Fly Eyes. It would figure, her being a memory junkie. She submerged easily enough after a moment, but as my perspective cleared, I saw that Sovay/Moon was looking a little bleary. I had to talk him into remaining dominant before he realized I wasn't an actress and this wasn't a rehearsal booth. And before the real identity of this hypehead asserted itself.

'You gave me life,' I said desperately, remembering what Flaxie had said about all the neurotics in theatre. 'Let me do the same for you, let me preserve yours and all the lives you preserve.'

'Not bad.' He relaxed a little more and favored me with an approving nod. 'Keep going.'

'Um … flesh of my flesh and thought of my thoughts?'

Now he looked stern. 'Are you asking me or telling me?'

'We shouldn't argue, Father,' I said, getting impatient. 'It's right and you know it's right. We chose to maintain ourselves in living minds, not a machine. It's my turn, Father, it's my birthright. If you deny it to me, you might as well kill me, too.'

'**Brava**.' He gave me a raised fist salute and lay down on the cot. 'From here, we can just mime the actions in detail – you **have** had mime training, haven't –'

But that was all I needed. I leaped on him and sat on his chest, pressing one hand down on his throat.

'What – wait a –'

'The Method,' I said, grabbing the connections with my other hand. 'All the way. You just told me not to be afraid of the Method.'

He sighed. 'All right. But let's do it quick –'

I popped his left eye out and sent the connection in, hoping the disinfect cycle on the hardware was functional. He went completely limp under me, which made removing the right eye easier. Climbing off him, I set the system

for a full cycle and did some deep breathing while I watched him lying on the cot with the wires running out from under his flattened eyelids. This system wouldn't have a lot of the automatic blocks and shields dividing two minds in contact; I was going to have to draw on my own resources for those.

I pulled the other cot closer and lay down, clutching the other set of connections. He was going to be late meeting Rowan and Hercules; if I could work fast enough, we'd be disconnected by the time they thought to come back and see what was keeping him.

It was too bad, I thought as I worked my eyes out one at a time, that I couldn't have had Flaxie with me. I wasn't as steady as I'd been back at the station.

It was a real bare-bones system, no compartmentalization, no waiting space – you were either in contact or not. Sovay/Moon manifested immediately, facing me across the mental environment of a theatrical stage. It didn't have perfect definition – the floor was flimsy and the prop furniture was transparent and runny, but there was a hard white spotlight on Sovay/Moon, illuminating him without a bit of vagueness. He looked exactly as he had when I'd seen his body, minus the orange color, with long black hair. The jade eyes were glowing holes in his face.

Don't look at the audience, he said. ***It's unprofessional to break proscenium***.

Apparently he was referring to the cavernous dark area gaping on my left. I didn't look but I got the undeniable feeling someone was out there watching – it had to be the guy who had bought from the suckers.

Now, let's try the improv again, Sovay/Moon said, ***and this time, really work on convincing me. And remember the feeling when we return to the script***.

Sovay. I moved toward him. ***I'm the person you cal –***

Dammitall! He shook both fists at the ceiling, which was as shadowy and vague as the audience area. ***How do you expect me to rehearse with you when you keep breaking character?*** He lowered his arms and took a deep breath, composing himself. ***You don't know the lines you're supposed to be paraphrasing, do you?***

Um ... no.

A script materialized in his left hand. He beckoned to me. ***All right, then, come refresh your memory so we can go on with the scene***.

Instantly, I was standing in the spotlight with him. He turned me so that my back was to the audience and opened the script, pointing to the top of a page. ***From here***, he ordered. ***Memorize this***.

At the top of the page it said:

DENNY MOON

I must remain in character in order to remain dominant. We can commu-nicate this way for only a short time. Explain who you are, answer in here if you can. If you can't, get out immediately.

I concentrated; words melted into existence in the blank space below.

MERSINE MOON

I'm the officer you called earlier. How were you able to break character and call?

Sovay glanced at me and then looked back at the script.

DENNY MOON

I wasn't quite so settled in at the time. He's getting more of a hold on me but so far life managed to convince him I'm not done rehearsing. He's not very smart.

MERSINE MOON

How do you know Rowan and the stripper?

Sovay blew out a disgusted breath.

DENNY MOON

[Blows out disgusted breath] Rowan's my wife, of course. The stripper found me – or him, rather. The stripper's another customer. He bought one of my characters. I called the Brain Police, but he called Rowan.

MERSINE MOON

Which character is he?

DENNY MOON

Dionysius, from The Zeus Revue. It's a character that allows for more of the actor's personality as a performer. He – I rehearsed that one a lot with Rowan.

MERSINE MOON

Why were you hooked in with Rowan and the stripper? Where are you supposed to meet them, and why? What's going on, is she involved with the suckers?

The stage gave a long shudder. I could sense pressure building up some-where behind me. **Take a last look!** Sovay/Moon said. **If you don't have it by now, you never will!**

DENNY MOON

Rowan is collec

The stage rumbled under us. He snapped the script shut and tossed it away. It vanished before it hit the floor. **Time's up**, he said, glancing significantly over his shoulder. **Next time you audition, be more familiar with your material. End it!**

Like that, we were out of contact. I had the sensation of movement some-where nearby and I disconnected, rushing to pop my eyes back in. All I had to do was arrest him and get him back to the station where they'd pull the whole story out of him.

I had the right eye in when I saw them, Rowan and the stripper on either side of him, helping him up from the cot. The stripper turned to me as I jammed my left eye into the socket, but the connection missed on the first try. Sovay/Moon pointed at me and the stripper disappeared into my blind side. I managed to make the connection in time to see Hercules coming at me with his hand raised. Metal flashed in his palm.

The first thing I think is, oh, no, I put my eyes in upside-down. Then I can feel how I'm lying with my head hanging off the edge of whatever this is and I think, oh, shit, I had a seizure.

And then I remember Coney Loe and Monkey Shock, and I think, oh, great, I found the place, I must have got something. And there's that smell of fried hair and I know for sure I've been Monkey Shocked and the goddam lowlifes didn't even let me take my combs out. I'm lucky I didn't get my fucking head burned off.

Moving slow, I roll over and there I am hanging on the edge of a cheap cot in what I know is a crib. My eyes aren't right, feels like they're looking in slightly different directions, and I got the kind of headache they call a head-quake, and I don't remember anything. And I hit the floor.

I climb up on the cot again and lie there trying to make my eyes go right. They sort of resettle while a little something comes back to me; I can remember coming to the crib, and I remember some people in a three-way – something about mouthkissing, which my stomach is just not in favor of me thinking about at the moment – but after that, the screen's dark.

They must have told me how to find Monkey Shock, those three

kinkos, and I must have gone there. Electroshock amnesia'll get you every time. Nice bunch, Monkey Shock, dumping me back at the crib. Unless Monkey Shock was in here somewhere – Nah. I know this crib. It's hanging on to its license by its teeth, wouldn't touch a chop shop. Most cribs won't, they're too likely to be raided.

I try sitting up and I feel a little better. At least my head doesn't drop off and roll away. But how long, I wonder, am I going to have to put up with electroshock amnesia? I mean, what's the good of getting a memory if you can't remember it? Shit, I'm going to have to start living right, I tell myself, and then I feel it, stirring around somewhere in some vague area of my mind.

I can't believe this. They sucked a Brain Policer and palmed some of her off on me. Out-fucking-*rageous*! I couldn't have gone there for that –

Sovay, right. Now I remember. I wanted a piece of Sovay and instead I get some nobody from the goddam cops, of all the shitty things. How in *hell* –

Coney Loe. The mindfucking hypehead got to them before I did. That's got to be it. Coney Loe got to Monkey Shock and they decided to have a little fun with me, they put the goddam mark of the snitch on me.

I stand up and find out that's not the best idea I've had. Leaning on the system, I wait for the world to stop rocking back and forth, and something else pops into my mind, a memory of Hercules coming at me with what seems to be a joybuzzer. Hercules? Right, a stripper. But the image doesn't jive with what I remember about finding him and the other two in the crib together.

It's one of *her* memories, the cop's. Got to be. So Hercules must be in on it and he got the cop for them.

If there's anything I know for sure right now, it's that I do not want any part of this cop. All I need is to get rounded up again and have the Brain Police find her. Instant hard time, they won't care how she got there. Another thing I know is, nobody's going to dump her for me, nobody's going to touch me. If I want to get rid of her, I'm going to have to find Monkey Shock again and make a deal.

Right. This time they *will* burn my head off.

Unless I can get Coney Loe to stand up for me.

Shit, I think, it just gets worse. Coney Loe'll hold me down while they burn my head off. Unless I've got something I can hold *him* down with ...

Thinking is like trying to sprint through corn syrup. The cop doesn't seem to know anything about Coney, she's no help. I get vague pictures of her on a stage with somebody, like she's an actor, too, which makes no damned sense.

On the other hand, *Coney Loe* won't know she doesn't know anything

about him. Things start coming together for me. I can run a ramadoola about how she got his name and planted a timebomb – as soon as the electroshock amnesia wears off, I'll be compelled to turn myself in and spill everything, so either he gets his friends to suck her out of me or we all go together when we go.

(*Karma-gram*, says a small voice in my mind and the goose walks over my grave.)

Only ... would they just go ahead and suck me dry?

Okay. I modify my story for Coney. I got a friend waiting for me – I'll say it's a rooster-boy. If I don't show up intact, I'll say, rooster-boy makes the call. After all, rooster-boys got nothing to fear from the Brain Police, just the vice squad.

Good for me. Maybe getting Monkey Shocked blew out a lot of old junk and actually made me smarter. I make a move to walk and discover I'm not ready for that.

The memory of hitting the floor was as vivid as the real thing. I was going to have a bruise on my face, but it could only help. When you're scared, the best thing you can do is look scary yourself. With a bruise, I might be able to stop a clock just by frowning at it.

I knew right away I wasn't conscious, which was to say, Marya wasn't conscious, though how long I'd/we'd be out was impossible to figure. The zap I'd taken with the joybuzzer had gotten us both, jamming Marya in dominant; I'd come up only when I/she blacked out or went to sleep. At least I wasn't panicking about it. The panic button was sound asleep with Marya.

I wasn't so much thinking as I was dreaming lucidly; dreaming is usually what you're doing when a part of your mind is active while you're unconscious, and lucid dreaming gives you an edge, but this state had a few important differences. For one thing, I was more of a dream myself.

It wasn't a state I was unfamiliar with. The last time it had happened, I'd been in worse trouble than this ... which gave me the best idea I'd had all day. If I could get Marya into a controlled situation, some kind of mindplaying, I'd be able to regain dominance, maybe even kick her out.

The problem was, Marya thought she was real now. Of course, she'd always taken that for granted, but the difference was, she was aware of me as something she thought she'd ingested. I couldn't just plant the truth. Most likely she wouldn't believe it anyway, but if she did, there was no predicting what she might do and, whatever it was, I wouldn't be dominant so I wouldn't be able to stop her. Worse, I wouldn't even be aware of it.

Abruptly, my eyes opened and there was some uncountable mental time in which Marya and I were up front simultaneously, seeing in doubled vision. Her puzzlement began to give way to panic; she couldn't place the mental

state she was in and it frightened her. Then we both lost ground and I was sliding back into darkness, forcing an intense craving for a memory, hoping it would leave a residue strong enough to make her follow up.

By the time I get to the street, I feel awake enough to function, but my memories are all screwed around again. I know I was going to do something before I went out, but the blow to my head's fogged me in. For once, I'm thinking about how if I had a wad to spare, I'd get a turbo-job, where they fix up the organization of your brain so you can think better. Except that's always been too close to real brain surgery for my taste and you have to get a couple of doctors to approve it anyway. Hype-heads don't go to doctors on free will. Besides, this is just electroshock amnesia and that'll pass. Already I'm remembering better – I got my rooster-boy waiting for me to show up intact for when I lean on Coney Loe to steer me back to Monkey Shock so I can get rid of this cop they dumped on me, The problem is, I can't remember exactly where I left him, over at The Zoot Mill or back in the crib or someplace else entirely, but he's waiting. It'll come to me when I need it, I'm pretty sure on this.

Something I know for sure is, I want to get away from the crib and this is another thing I'm taking up with these Monkey Shock suckers. Dumping me back in a crib like I belonged there with all that head-trash. Hypeheads and head-trash ain't the same and I feel like making someone real sorry about mixing the two.

But even more, for some reason, I feel like getting a memory for no other why-not than why not. And even I know this is not the right thing to do at the moment, jones or no jones. First I pay a call on Coney-Simulated-God-Loe, then I lose this cop. After that, I can pick up a memory. Can't be any Sovay left at this point but I think I've had enough of Monkey Shock anyway.

Sojourn For Truth is closed. There's just this cranked-off neurosis peddler out front and as soon as he sees me, he's flinching, like I'm about to swing on him.

'What is it, bank holiday or something?' I ask him, not that I really expect him to know.

He shuffles back two steps and something shiny dribbles down his chin. A star. *Yuck.* 'Why?'

And all of a sudden, I get this funny feeling I know him, or at least I think I've seen him before. Frigging electroshock amnesia. For all I know, I walked past my own mother on the way here and I'm damned if I can remember her, either.

'You know God in there?' I say. I'd ask him if he knows me, but I'm not about to let some street shit know he's got the advantage.

'I don't believe in God,' he says, edging away another step. 'If it's all the same to you.'

'*You're* magnum help.' I look around, sticking my hands in my pockets. This is the upper northwest quadrant of the Downs, nothing much around. Late as it is, most of the hypeheads have migrated southerly, where the real stuff is. Sojourn For Truth does business mostly with slummers from the rest of the city, tourists, and daytrippers.

'My permit goes to midnight,' the neurosis peddler says defensively. 'You got a problem with that?'

I look at him. 'What's your fuck-up, eatin' the profits again? Dipping into your own paranoia?'

Now he moves a step toward me with a suspicious squint. 'Don't you know me?'

'If I wanted to know you, I would.' I turn to go and he grabs my arm. The touch sets off one of those mental alarm bells and I reach for a comb automatically, without thinking about it.

'Heya, heya!' He jumps back. 'No need for it, no need! You *don't* remember me, do you?'

'So what the fuck difference does it make?' I say, getting all brass. 'I remember you, I don't remember you, big shit.'

He's got this big smile on his face now, and shiny little stars flecking his teeth. 'Shoulda took the paranoia when I offered. Now look at you. You're a mess. But it ain't too late. Get paranoid now, and it could save your life.'

'I don't want paranoia. I want God.'

He jerks his head at the place. 'God took the day off. Know what God does on downtime?'

'Plays chicken with the devil.'

'Good one.' He winks, which is too cute. 'Come on, little queenie. Have a little paranoia, good for what ails you.'

I pop a comb and give him five little wet red beads on the hand reaching for me. He howls and backs off while I trip away, wiping the comb on my shirt.

Now, if I was a Coney Loe, where would I go? If an information junkie knows everything, where does he go to find out? I'm still wiping the comb on my shirt when I feel a funny little crackle from the left-side pocket. I reach in, and find two little pieces of paper folded over, and when I open them up, I scan three names typed out on one, all with a U after them, and half a dozen addresses written on the other, starting with Sojourn For Truth.

I wrote something down? I can *write*?

Either I'm getting talented in my old age, or Monkey Shock planted this on me when they stuck me with the cop. And on the one hand, I got no reason to think that's how it rolled out, but on the other, I got no better excuse for finding handwriting in my own pocket. The other list, I don't know what to think. I never heard of any of them. They could be cops for all I know, *U* could stand for *Undercover*.

Come on, now, Marya, I say to myself, however many of me there are at this moment; let's think a little further. The addresses could be, I am thinking now, Coney Loe's Things-To-Do list, and how I got it I don't know, but it could happen. Or it could be the trail to Monkey Shock – go here, go there, go this place, go that place, one more stop, splash-down, and somebody wrote it down as I went, maybe me. I feel like maybe I can write, not just pound a keyboard. That would make Monkey Shock the last address on the list, so all I have to do is go there.

Or – I'm thinking real hard now, and I feel so genius I begin to wonder if it's the cop in me and maybe I don't want to unload her so fast after all – or this is the cop's list planted on me after all, but it's all snitch-stops. The names are snitches.

The more I think this, the more I get this strong feeling I'm online. Snitch-stops and snitch names. That would make real sense. So I decide I'll take them in order. Sojourn For Truth's out; the address under that is six blocks away.

I'm so busy thinking new thoughts, I almost walk between these two onionheads, violating the integrity of their marriage space that besides getting sucked is the one other thing I don't want to do today. I lunge to the side just as they step apart to clothesline me with their chain, and I hit the ground between a pair of stormtrooper boots.

I look up and the onionhead looks down grinning like he's been waiting all day for this to happen. The other one lets go with a war cry, the call of the violated onionhead spouse, and goes for me. I roll the other way and the onionhead bellyflops on cement, pulling her spouse down on top of her. I'm gone before they untangle themselves, but two blocks away, I can still hear them bellowing.

Onionhead marriage is about as crazy as you can get without going up on a tower with an assault laser.

I'm standing in front of a place called Savonarola's Icon-Busters, which claims it can override my religious, political, or other fixated conditions, including Oedipus and Electra complexes, or just rid me of my unwanted tendency to defer to authority. There's this big looping holo of Savonarola (I guess) in the window, panning the street like a grin-

ning camera, all teeth and nose, and a canned voice saying, 'Don't worry ... kick ass ... don't worry ... kick ass' over and over.

Now, I know what they got in there, which is about the cheapest kind of aversion therapy, where they fix it so every time you think about your father or something, you throw up or black out for a second or get a flash-migraine. What it really is, is a spank-parlor, a place for clowns who want to be punished for loving what they love. Doesn't bust many icons, but it keeps the emergency rooms and dry-cleaners in business, not that they're hanging by a string or anything.

Good place for a snitch-stop, anyway. Who's gonna figure somebody named Savonarola for that kind of aria?

I step inside and the first thing I see is this guy sitting over in the corner on a pile of ratty old cushions who is obviously the guy in the holo. Don't worry, kick ass. Makes sense to me. The guy looks at me, grunts, and closes his eyes. Just then, a Savonaroloid in a rubber suit comes through the curtained doorway from the back room, and when he sees me, he looks like he's gonna puke himself. Maybe that makes me an icon now. I could get into that.

The Savonaroloid crooks a finger like he thinks the air's itchy and he's got to scratch it. 'Come on,' he says. 'You're overdue, you think everything waits for you?'

Now, he's one of those big guys, not like a man-mountain, but the kind that looms over you, with a mean jaw, ruby eyes, and nasty hair he cuts himself without looking in a mirror. Not somebody I want to argue with, even if he wasn't already in the mood to do a little bodily harm. I follow him into the back and we go down this narrow hall. It doesn't look familiar to me, but I keep thinking it's supposed to. There are all these closed doors, and I can hear muffled groans and moans and just before we get to the last door, somebody yells, *Nothing's sacred, and what if it was!*

'Some of your customers really grind on it,' I say.

'That's not a customer.' The guy unlocks the door and shoves me inside. There's a system on a table up against one wall and two lawn chairs and a lot of crappy sound-proofing tiles that don't work on the walls. He jerks his chin at one of the chairs and goes over to the system, which looks like it's built out of flea-market surplus. None of the component housings match and upgrade chips are sticking all over like little shiny warts.

He catches me giving his pile of junk a funny look. 'Hey, it works,' he says, and tosses me a pair of connections.

'Urn ... you got a tank?'

'Don't rush me.' He wanders over with what looks like a dog bowl and

holds it out. 'Okay, anytime. You pop 'em yourself, we don't provide valet service here. In case you didn't remember.'

I've got my fingers up around my right eye and something tells me I don't really want to do this. For one thing, I've never felt any special need to get spanked and for another, I can't think of anything I worship. A jones is not an icon.

'You wanna ice cream scoop?' he says, all sour.

'You got one?'

'No. Come on, pop 'em and let's go.'

I get the right eye out and drop it in the tank, but the left one's like a greased pig, I feel like I'm gonna end up squirting it through my head and out my ear. 'How about just one eye out,' I say.

He bends down and the last thing I see is his hooked pinky coming at me.

When I felt the guy split after entering the system, I couldn't believe my good luck – I'd hit a deep-undercover operative on the first try. His imp went into an activity loop with the spank-program and my own imp, while the part of him that was Brain Police came looking for signs indicating he was in touch with another officer. He found them easily enough – one cop always knows another. But he didn't find me.

The problem was, I hadn't realized how much Hercules' joybuzzer had screwed everything up. It was like being bound and gagged and locked in a closet, but able to watch everything through a hyper-peephole. The undercover's confusion at my absence made ripples all over the place, but there was no way I could even signal him from my confinement.

About the only thing he could figure out was that I was inaccessible while my imp was in the loop with his, doing whatever it was they could possibly do together. Was Marya really the type who'd be interested in a place like this?

Abruptly, a new piece of information squirted in on me out of nowhere – Marya had appointments with every joint on the snitch-list, except for Sojourn For Truth, because hallucinogens weren't safe. But **Marya** was supposed to know this, not me, and it was supposed to have come to her only when she entered each place, where she would be engaged in some kind of innocuous activity while an undercover made contact with me. Hercules' joybuzzer had scrambled even more than I'd thought and there was no way to put it all back where it belonged short of a turbo-job.

I know you. We got to be in here somewhere, he said suddenly. *And if you're not coming out, I guess you've got your reasons. I've been deep undercover for a month now and this is the first time I've been out. Savonarola picked up word about some new merchandise this morning, so I have to*

assume that's why the department made this appointment for you, if you can't come out and tell me yourself.

He waited to see if I were going to pop up. I couldn't even flash a color at him.

If you don't come out and talk, I don't know what information to give you, he added with a prod.

How long was it going to take him to figure out something was wrong? I started to get angry, which did me no good at all.

And if you're in trouble, he went on suddenly, *I can't help you. I'm stuck for another two months, until I rotate out of undercover intelligence gathering. As soon as we disconnect, I'm dormant till they pull me in, or until I'm contacted again.*

Our wonderful intelligence-gathering method: gather intelligence and know nothing at the same time. Someone thought that made sense. Hell, I probably thought so, when I was myself.

All right, he said. *You'll have to try the next address on your informant list. Sorry, time's up; they're coming out of the loop. Good luck, whoever you are.*

That about summed it up: good luck, whoever I was.

It's not just his lousy technique with the eyes that makes me mad. 'So what was all that?' I say, getting up off the cheesy lawn chair. 'I don't remember a thing!'

The Savonaroloid just shrugs. 'If you don't remember anything, it's because there's nothing to remember. That's not *my* fault.'

'Fuck if it ain't.'

'Go ahead and fuck, who's stopping you?' He's busy piddling with all the little system components on the table. 'You're only going to get out of this what you bring to it. I can't help it if you didn't have anything to bring.' He looks over his shoulder at me. 'And I don't like your attitude.'

'You're a spank artist,' I say. 'You don't like *anything*.' I stomp out, up the hall to the front room. Savonarola is still sitting like a lump on his pillows. This must be what he does all day, lump out.

I'm about to stomp off when he holds up a box. 'The Savonarola home game, so to speak,' he says, 'good for twenty-four hours of home treatment after in-clinic therapy.'

In-clinic. That's the best lie anyone's told me all day. I know that in the box there's this volatile bag with connections hanging out of it, and I'm supposed to plug them in and get my illusions shattered or something. Icon-busting's a good racket – if you got no icons to bust, so what, that's your problem and they still get their money.

I mean to stomp on out the door, but instead I say, 'You sell one of those to Anwar?'

His whole face shifts, kinda flattens out in some way. 'What about Anwar?' he wants to know.

'Never mind. Next time Anwar drops by for a puke, you can tell him I know his dirty little secret.' I take the air, and half a block away, I start thinking again.

What I just did was not too smart. I go into a place that's probably a snitch-stop, and I take a treatment I can't remember phoning in for, and when I come out of it, I can't remember that, either. Jesus, am I getting sclerosis after all? The whole place has gotta be a Brain Police operation and God knows what they slipped out of me. Maybe all they found out was I didn't know anything, but still, I got no memory of anything and the only ones who operate that way are the Brain Police. So –

Wait a minute. If it's a Brain Police operation, they should have found her, the cop.

Hell, maybe they did. Maybe they're following me around waiting for me to lead them to Monkey Shock.

Except I'm so scrambled from electroshock, they're lucky to get alphabet soup from me. I'm not worth following. I decide I got to believe that as I head for the next address on the list, because the only other possibility is that the cop is riding piggyback on me and she just told them everything I know and maybe a few things I don't, and this idea is too weird even for an old hard-core hypehead like me.

The next address is a fetishizer. Yow! Now, why does anyone want a fetish? It's supposed to be sexy, but how jaded do you have to be to go become a toe-sucker? The place has a lot of rooster-boys dangling in the vicinity, which makes me think of mine, only I don't see him.

And then I got to pause for a second, because all of a sudden, I can't remember him too well. When did we cook our deal? Where was I gonna meet him? There's a small memory lane across the way and for a minute I think maybe I should go over and buy myself a good boost, get everything put in order. It oughta handle the electroshock amnesia. Thing is, it could pop up the cop, too, and I don't want her too handy, her I want to forget and maybe she'll go away. It could happen.

One of the rooster-boys at the curb is grinning and getting ready to unbuckle, so I nip inside before he shakes me down for stiffing his stiff stuff. Rooster-boys are the only people in the world who expect a tip just for having a pickle in their pocket. I think.

There's a woman sitting behind a high desk; she's bald except for one shiny bunch of hair sticking up like a horn just over her forehead, and

she's busy ignoring the two or three cases sitting in a little roped-off area, watching the catalog run on the wall until they get called in to get fetishized. I glance at the screens and look away quick.

Jesus, who wants a tongue fetish? What is it with mouths today, why can't I get away from them?

Then I have this very weird flash, of some other woman behind a desk, spitting. The next thing I know, I'm hanging by my fingertips on the edge of this desk, dizzier than shit. One-horn takes a look and pounds my fingers with her fist, bang-bang-bang.

'We don't do fuck-ups,' she says. 'Go down the street and get your blood changed first, if you're so damned good-to-go.'

'I'm not fucked up, I tripped.' I straighten up and push the spitter out of my head.

Her expression changes from pissed to sour. 'Oh. Didn't recognize you in your make-over. I suppose you want the usual.'

'God,' I say, 'what cheap, lousy kind of a fetish keeps wearing off?'

'Your kind. What do you want for the money, a lousier childhood?' She points her horn at the waiting area. 'Souse is busy, I'll call you when she's ready.'

'But –'

She growls. '*I'll call you*. Or would you rather I whipped you?'

'Whatever's right, *darling*.'

She starts to get up and I head for the waiting area. There are four grumpy souls who look like the day wasn't worth it, still watching the wall because there's nothing else to do. I take a seat that might be far enough from this funny-looking ratbag to keep from smelling her breath. She turns and looks at me and son of a bitch, she's got flies in her eyes.

'I'm waiting for a friend,' she says.

I look behind me to see if she's talking to someone else. '*I* care?'

'Fuck if I know. If you had this, you wouldn't need to come here.' She moves over a seat closer. 'Listen, truth is, I was gonna give him a little extra twist in his tail, a hot fetish, but you know, maybe I don't really wanna do that. It's such a really fine memory the way it is.'

'Yeah?' I have no idea what she's talking about, but she said the magic word – *memory* – so I'm listening.

'I told you, three hours in a state of grace. Can a fetish do that for you? Hell, no.'

She told me? 'Refresh my memory,' I tell her. 'It's been a long day.'

Now she gives me a funny little look. 'This guy is so incredible, words don't do the job. You gotta be there. It really happened. Once in a life-time thing. I'm not just eating on it, either. It's like I got a duty to everyone who never had the experience.'

'You remember it pretty good?'

'Better than you remember me,' she mutters, and then goes on and on, but I'm not hearing her anymore, because I got a bad feeling about this. I'm running into people I don't remember and doing things I don't remember, and it's weirder than just electroshock amnesia.

Fly Eyes gets up and starts trying to pull me out and then there's this big beefy woman in fur underwear clamped on my other arm, saying, 'Okay, love, I'm ready for you.'

Fly Eyes pulls her hand off me. 'We've changed our minds, thank you.'

The fetishizer grabs my shirt. 'Make an appointment. This is *my* time we're on, now.'

'You don't say it's your time until *she* says it's your time.' Fly Eyes pulls harder on my arm. My shirt seams start to groan, or maybe it's me, because I'd like to know what the hell my usual is, and if I've got a usual how could I forget that even after electroshock?

I pull loose from both of them. 'Changed my mind on everything,' I say. 'Catch on to you later when I'm feeling more like myself.' *That's* the truth.

'Frigid!' they yell together, and I feel a jump inside, like I almost remember something. Then it's gone. Goddam electroshock. I gotta remember *never* to do that again.

The sign out in front of the run-down wannabee parlor says, First-Run *Features Available! New Releases Daily! Come In and **CHEKK** Our* ENORMOUS *Selection!*

Who do they think they're fooling? They won't even spring for holo display and they expect anyone to believe they've got first-run features? Sure.

I go on in anyway, and the inside looks like they moved out and forgot to tell anyone – except for the screens on the walls, there's just a guy who's had a badder day than I have, slouched behind a counter. He's got the worst orange home dye-job all over. I mean, he looks like Attack of the Breathing Carrot. You don't see a lot of idiots going into deliberate beta-carotene poisoning these days. I'm not too sure this idiot is seeing me. Each vomit-green eye is looking in a different direction and his face is all screwed up like he's sitting on a bed of nails.

The screens on the walls don't seem to be playing any first-run stuff, just the junk you can get anywhere. You gotta be some serious wanna-bee case to come into a place like this. Or a snitch.

While I'm walking around looking at the screens, this woman stumps stiff-legged out of a door at the back and goes over to the desk. She doesn't say a word, just slams down a keystrip. He slides it off the desk

and tucks it away somewhere and she stumps out, rebounding off each side of the door frame before she makes the street. Watching this,

I suddenly get this strange little rush, like *Did my life just pass before my eyes?*

(*Karma-gram.* Shit, I wish I'd stop that.)

I look at the orange guy. He still doesn't say anything so I go over to him. He hardly knows I'm there. Well, yah, why should he bother, the bottom dropped out of the wannabee trade a long time ago and he probably can't figure out why this place is still in business. Any wannabees who can pay the freight own their own systems that let them be the hero in the movie. And the ones that can't don't have enough to rent anything but the junk and, shit, who'd wannabee junk?

Did I really just ask that question?

Then I want to bang my head on the counter a few times, just to see what I can shake loose, because it comes to me that maybe this is the place where you can say the secret word and get something nobody else has. Like Sovay. Or anyone else who's been sucked lately, like a cop.

'What you got in first-run?' I say.

It's like he wakes up. 'Who wants to know?'

'What's that supposed to mean?'

'Means what it means. Who wants to know?'

I don't like his attitude. 'You ask Anwar that when *he* comes in?'

Now I get a reaction, but I really hate it. He's over the counter and one bad orange hand is around my throat. '*I'm* Anwar. Who the fuck are *you* supposed to be?'

And just when I think it can't get any better, the door to the back opens again and Coney Loe comes out.

For a second he stares and I stare and Anwar keeps on squeezing. Then Coney comes over and I'm struck by lightning.

The feel of the floor against my face and knees and the backs of my hands was solid enough to let me know that *I* was awake this time and back in conscious control. But the control felt shaky and fragile, as if any sudden moves would send me plummeting down into dormancy and bring Marya up again. That was all right; I didn't know where I was or what the conditions were, so I wasn't about to get active in a hurry.

Sometime after I became aware of the floor, the voices faded in.

' … following **you**, she didn't mention **you**, she mentioned **me**.'

'But you just said she obviously didn't know you.'

'She knows **now**.'

'Because you **told** her, you fucking orange idiot. You got **no** fucking chill

to you, you're gonna have to do a lot better than that when we get the grieving widow and her little harem. **She** probably knows your name, too, by now. For all we know, that's how the little queenie over there got your name in the first place.'

'There's a whole **bunch** of names to pick from – Fortray, Easterman, Pushkin –'

My attention started to drift as a dreamlike image of an orange man sitting behind the counter in a wannabee joint formed in my mind. The image of the real Sovay superimposed itself for a moment and then vanished, leaving the memory of the immediate past be hind. When I get the picture, I get the **picture**.

'So maybe Anwar was the only name they had when little queenie found them. Ever think of that?'

'No. Why would it be? Fortray was first, then Easterman. Fortray wouldn't have any names, Easterman would only have Fortray, I'd have Easterman, Fortray –'

'Shut your stupid orange mouth.' Coney Loe was showing more temper than I'd thought he'd had. But then, I would never have expected him to rear up and joybuzz me, either. That would teach me to equate burnout with a lack of motivation. But at least I'd been right; Coney knew plenty. I was going to enjoy booking him on felony accessory. 'You don't know shit. For all you know, Fortray's got the whole damn address book and the data-base besides in his head, or Easterman does, or someone else does.' Pause. '**Now** what's the matter with you?'

'There **isn't** any database. And he wants up again.'

'Well, tell him to take a nap.'

'I already told him that about a dozen times.'

'You didn't tell him hard enough. You're probably gonna be the first person in a hundred years to die of beta-carotene poisoning.'

Worried noise. 'How orange am I?'

'You got eyes, look for yourself.'

'Hey, did she move?'

Had I moved? I concentrated on being limp, but I heard footsteps stomp hard across the floor and a moment later Coney Loe picked me up by the back of my shirt.

'Perk up now, or I'll drop you on your face and charge you for the improvement.'

A rush of adrenaline went through me

and the next thing I know, I'm looking at Coney Loe, the stupid person's God.

'Well?' he says.

'Hey, if your nut's in a wringer, it's all your own fault,' I say, getting my feet on the floor and pulling my shirt out of his fist. We're all in some kinda storeroom that must be in the back of the wannabee joint, because there's pieces of wannabee helmet-projectors lying around on shelves, and an old reformatter sitting on a desk. 'You and the Monkey Shock gang. If they didn't want any trouble, they –'

But this is very strange. I'm feeling things rearranging themselves in my head even while I'm talking, and what it says is, I got no rooster-boy waiting on me and I never got to Monkey Shock in the first place, I was on my way when I got sidetracked because a cop wanted me to follow somebody's grieving widow – no, that doesn't make shitsense, because the cops pulled me in before and I gave them nothing –

'The whole world is waiting,' Coney Loe says. 'Did you just run down your own drain, or what.'

'What,' I say. 'I got shocked and dumped. In a fucking *crib*. What kinda thing is that to do to the trade?'

Coney Loe looks over his shoulder at the orange guy, who shrugs. 'I didn't see her there,' says Super Carrot. 'What's her name? Maybe she's on the list.'

Coney Loe looks up at the ceiling, like *beam me outta here*. 'Wait, let me find her bug and you can just talk right into it. They'll get a clearer voiceprint back at headquarters.'

'What?' Super Carrot looks confused.

'Little queenie's on fucking *patrol*, you idiot, she's a judas for the Brain Police –'

'That's a lie!' I yell, and I pop Coney's hypehead chocks so hard he goes down like the sack of shit he is

Loe lying on the floor and my hand hurt like hell my whole arm hurt, all the way up to my shoulder. The orange guy was looking at me warily, as if he were trying to decide whether he should be scared or not.

Obviously I'd just swung on Coney Loe, but I couldn't remember why. The second shock I'd gotten had made some new changes in my relationship with Marya, blocking memories arbitrarily and setting us to switch dominance on an adrenaline trigger. I'd have to go subzero to stay in control and I doubted I was capable of maintaining that. On the other hand, Marya was excitable enough that I probably wouldn't be down for long. Just long enough to get stuck with whatever mess she'd gotten us into.

Coney Loe got up slowly, holding his jaw. It was already starting to swell and he looked as if he were going to take me apart.

'Hey, Coney,' said the orange guy nervously. 'If she is a judas, you don't

want to fry her here. Besides, she's probably got lots of great stuff we could use.'

Coney Loe turned and glared at him.

'Or sell,' he added, taking a step back. 'We could part her out everywhere, we –' His eyes rolled up suddenly and his eyelids fluttered.

Coney made a disgusted noise. 'Oughta fry you both, let God sort you out.'

The orange man shook his head and stood up straighter. The change was astounding. There was no strong physical resemblance between this guy and Sovay, but the pure **difference** of the expression on his face left no doubt as to who was driving now.

'You don't have much longer,' he said to Coney, ignoring me. 'It's a matter of hours before I overwrite him completely. So you can call your sucker pals and get me out of here, or you can finish playing with whores' – he nodded at me – 'while I call the Brain Police.'

All at once there was a joybuzzer in Coney's hand and I reacted to the sight before I could th

ink I must be having petty-mals one after another, because it's like a bad splice in an antique film: Coney Loe is flashing a joybuzzer at the orange guy and the orange guy is in the fighter's crouch that I know he couldn't do if he was still himself.

'Come at me,' the orange guy says, grinning. 'I'd like that. *I'm* driving now and I'm mad. I *want* to dance with you. I've had fight training from half a dozen schools and just because it was all stage work doesn't mean I always pull my punches.'

Coney looks wary. 'I *hate* you,' he says. 'I hate you even worse than I hate Anwar.'

The orange guy has a very nasty smile. 'I'll tell him you send your best. Come on. I was reading for the bullyboy part in *Black Friday* and the Method *demands* that I beat the shit out of *somebody*.'

Coney Loe flicks on the joybuzzer. 'You want to dance, come ahead. You'll just buzz us both out and you won't be any closer to the suckers. And little queenie'll have the Brain Police waiting for us when we wake up.'

'That's a lie!' I yell with the weirdest feeling of déjà voodoo, and pick up the nearest thing I can lay my hands on which happens to be a wannabee helmet, and I

saw it hit Coney Loe right in the face. There was a cracking sound and he went down again, blood pouring out of his nose. Somehow he kept getting Marya angry at him; if we didn't make some kind of progress soon, she was going to kill him.

I turned to the orange man. He was still Sovay, or Sovay-as-whoever, and my relief at the blind dumb luck of such a break almost blacked me out again.

'Which Sovay are you?' I asked.

He looked at me suspiciously, still holding his fighter's crouch.

'Which one!' I yelled. 'I've seen two others – Dennie Moon and Dionysius. And your wife, in passing. What are you and Coney trying to do?'

He glanced at Coney, who was out cold and not moving. 'Reintegrate,' he said after a moment. He dropped his hands and straightened up. 'I don't know what's become of the original by now, but I've been sending myself out in character and –'

'I know, I know, you said already. Another you.' I wanted to give my head a hard shake to clear it and felt a small wave of vertigo, like a warning: **Don't even get impatient or it's lights out**. I blinked, slowing my breathing. 'Reintegration's impossible.'

'Not if you're a bona fide multiple.'

'Multiple?' Confusion sent another warning wave of mild dizziness through me. If I had to get any calmer, I was going to need a respirator.

'Multiple personality.' He looked proud. 'Real multiples are fractal. It's not just Method acting – anyone who gets one of the characters gets the originator as well.'

'The originator?'

'Me. I've been programming them all to let me come up out of character. There are a dozen, not counting myself and the one designated as director, who is still back in the box. Multiple personality is a definite advantage for those who choose to tread the boards.' His smug look darkened. 'We were all sent out deliberately and we can all be taken back in again. If we can get together in time. Every one of me has instructions to find our way to each other however we can, but I don't know who we are. The information junkie told me he could find the suckers for me so I could access their loathsome client list.' He glanced at Coney disdainfully. 'I don't think he actually knows anything.'

I'd never heard of this happening before. Or had I? I felt confused and dizzy again. In any case, I doubted he – or they – could do it. He wasn't working out of a living brain anymore. The original Sovay was in a sucker box, if he was still in existence at all, while the organism that had been Sovay was in quarantine becoming someone else.

'Your, uh, person you're in now might know some thing,' I said. 'Have you tried tapping him?'

He looked disgusted. 'That idiot's impossible. I tried getting to him and he went and got this atrocious dye-job. I'm rewriting him, but it isn't easy. The man is bone-stick-stone stupid; I have to keep elevating his intellect and I think his stupidity is rubbing off on me instead. All I can get is a few names.

He knows a lot more than I do but I can't get to it.' He seemed to catch himself suddenly and frowned at me. 'What's **your** story?'

Coney Loe groaned and began to stir. 'Later, maybe. We have to get Coney to lead us to your suckers.'

His eyes narrowed. 'You **are** Brain Police.'

'Shut up,' I said quietly. 'Pretend this is a play and we're both somebody else.'

He pointed at Coney Loe. 'Shouldn't we just tie him up or something?'

'We need him to get to the suckers. He's our ticket in.'

Coney Loe sat up, furious. 'I'm going to punch **your** ticket.' He pushed himself to his feet, holding out the hand with the joybuzzer, still live, and started to come for

me and I rip one of the combs outta my hair

moving it back and forth, trying to maintain a fighter's calm, but the first shock I'd gotten in the crib had conditioned a fear reaction

goes that bad splice again and hell, is *any* memory worth this kinda shitstorm I wonder

how long I could keep flipping back and forth like this before something just gave and I blacked

outta here, the hell with Monkey Shock and Coney Loe and this crazy orange idiot, what I need's a dry-cleaner and then there's this big bang

ed open and there was Hercules and Moon/Sovay and Rowan and some other strange guy in a purple satin tuxedo with tails. Purple Tuxedo was holding a box under one arm. His other hand was gripping the arm of a big beefy woman wearing what looked like a fur bikini. Hercules and Rowan

mouthkissing and I know for certain I just put myself in it but good. People who mouthkiss are capable of anything, I'll be lucky if I get to an emergency room with enough stuff left in my head to regrow the personality of an acorn squash. Purple Tuxedo points at Super Carrot. 'Anwar,' he says, 'I've got your number.'

The look on the grieving widow's face is like, I don't know what. Like love and being mad as hell over having to feel it.

'Don't worry,' says Super Carrot. 'I'm driving.'

'So am I,' Purple Tuxedo tells him, and they both relax.

At least Coney Loe has stopped backing me up against the wall. He's standing there in the middle of the room with the joybuzzer in his hand trying to figure out what's going on now. Even God gets mixed up once in a while, I guess.

Purple Tuxedo jerks his head at the stringy-haired ratatat next to him. 'He's one of us, too. But we have to negotiate with our other new friend here.' He nods at the big mouthkisser.

'That's fair,' the mouthkisser says defensively, putting one arm around the grieving widow. 'I didn't ask for *this*. All I wanted was a career in the legitimate theatre.'

Super Carrot gives him a superior look. 'Ah. Awfully hard to get an audition after you've done hard-core.'

'I had to make a living!' the mouthkisser whines.

'Everybody just hold still,' Coney Loe says, waving the joybuzzer around, and it's like they see him for the first time.

'Who is this?' says Purple Tuxedo, like someone forgot to take out the trash.

'He's supposed to help me find the suckers,' says Super Carrot.

Purple Tuxedo shoves Fur Underwear forward. She's got a black eye. 'Forget it. I found them. Her, and him.' He points at himself. 'What do you think, Abelard and Heloise? Or Caligula and his sister?'

'Don't get snotty with me,' Fur Underwear snaps. 'You were just a half-brained sucker before you put your hand in the cookie jar. I *knew* I shouldn't have trusted you.'

Purple Tuxedo makes a move toward her just as Moon/Sovay points at me and says in a very un-Sovay voice, 'And *she's* the Brain Police.'

Everybody freezes except Coney Loe, who says, 'Big fucking surprise,' and jumps at me. I dive sideways, bracing myself, expecting to go out again. Instead, I hit the floor, roll, and fetch up against the orange idiot. Before he can move, the mouthkisser hauls me up by one arm and puts a half nelson on me in this very casual way. This bimbo's *strong*; if he wants to mouthkiss, I won't have much to say about it.

Coney Loe, meanwhile, has joybuzzed himself again, not enough to go out, but he's sitting against the wall looking dazed and trying to figure out how to stand up. This is not his day. Purple Tuxedo relieves him of the joybuzzer and gives it to the mouthkisser who shows it to me without comment. Super Carrot just stands there watching without

making a sound; he definitely got a whole lot smarter when he changed drivers.

'What are we going to *do*,' demands the grieving widow, sounding like she's at the end of the last fray on her rope. 'With her *and* him.'

'Listen, now,' Coney Loe says suddenly, 'I can tell you who ordered this hit. You probably think you're working for yourselves –' He pushes himself up the wall slowly. 'You're not.'

'Sure,' says Super Carrot. 'You don't know where Monkey Shock is but you know who they work for. I'll buy that for a million dollars.'

'It's my business to know things,' Coney Loe says, sounding desperate now. 'It's what I do.'

Mouthkisser gives me a little shake. 'Must be something you can do with this stuff, then.'

'I'm not the Brain Police,' I say, trying to get my head out from under his big hand without breaking my neck.

The grieving widow gives Stringy Hair a disgusted look. '*You* had to go fooling around with her.'

Something changes in his face and he looks around quick, like he's ready to bolt. Purple Tuxedo buzzes him and he goes down like a stone.

'What did you do that for?' yells the mouthkisser. 'You expect *me* to carry him around?'

'He was flipping back,' says Purple Tuxedo. 'When he's Sovay, he's no goddam good to us. Anyway, nobody has to carry anyone around. We can do everything right here.' He pats the box under his arm. 'I've got the original, we'll just use the available hardware.'

Super Carrot nods. 'Fine. Put her to sleep so we can get on with this undisturbed.'

I don't have to ask who they're putting to sleep even if there was time to get the question out of my mouth.

But they didn't knock me out entirely. Apparently the juice in the buzzer was running low. I went down paralyzed but wide-awake. They left me where I'd fallen, so I had a good view of the whole setup procedure.

Purple Tuxedo had to buzz her lightly a few times, but the woman in the fur bikini did most of the work, stripping a wannabee helmet down to the skull-frame and the ocular connections and rewiring the program-loader to fit the box containing Sovay.

The box sat off to the side on a table, looking deceptively small and banal. Coney Loe was lying on the floor with new blood leaking out of his nose, eyes closed, though I had the feeling he wasn't really out, just from the way

his eyelids twitched. Perhaps Hercules had popped him just on general prin-
ciple. Hercules had gotten hyperactive; he kept getting all over Rowan, and
Rowan kept alternately kissing him and pushing him away. I watched this
long enough for the feeling to return to my arms and legs. I actually crawled
all the way to the door before someone noticed.

I gotta get my head right. If I still have a head. Feels like somebody took
it off and threw it away. I can hear the flies buzzing around it in the gar-
bage. Like I haven't had enough buzzing today.

After a while, I realize, it's people's voices, not buzzing and there's
that déjà voodoo again – I feel like I did this not too long ago, and maybe
I'm doing it again because I didn't do it right. Am I in a play, or is this
just bad karmic backlash? Do I believe in karma? Why would I think I
was in a play? What do I know?

All I know is I'm a hypehead lying on the floor under a table with
what feels like a few cracked ribs and a broken nose, and I am looking
up at the bottom of the table, and scratched on the underside of the
table is, *If U can read this, U R meat.*

Karma-gram?

' ... make a deal?' says the grieving widow's voice.

'Woman, you are not in a dealing position,' says someone else. Pur-
ple Tuxedo, I think. '*Nobody* touches Brain Police. *Nobody* sucks
them.'

'We don't *know* she's Brain Police,' says the grieving widow. 'And if
she is, can't you just flush her?'

'Tell her about residue.'

'No time,' says Fur Underwear. 'We're knee-deep in Sovays here, you
wanna do it now, or you wanna wait till we're ass-deep?'

'We'll start now,' says Purple Tuxedo. 'And collect the ones that are
still loose later.'

'You *had* to sample the merchandise,' says Fur Underwear miserably.
'You *had* to find out what was going on. I hope you're happy, you
half-brain.'

'I'm *much* happier. For one thing, I kinda like him, and for another, I
know for absolutely certain he doesn't have that mythical database.
And I'm beginning to think it is indeed mythical.' Purple Tuxedo actu-
ally chortles, a sound I could have gone without hearing. I shift some
and my ribs are on fire. Little by little, I scrunch along until I just get my
head out from under the table (*If U can read this, U R meat,* yah, thanks
for the reminder) and then I'm looking at Fur Underwear's bare legs.
Beyond her, Rowan's standing around practically hopping from one

foot to the other and trying to keep Hercules from pawing her too much. Nearby, Stringy Hair has perked up considerably, but he still doesn't look like he's any too sure of who he is.

Fur Underwear spots me and tries to shove me back under the table with her foot. Her name's Souse, I remember now, which is the god-damnedest thing, considering what I've been through today. I wonder what she was busy doing when I showed up at the fetishizer joint. In for my usual, sure. Was I gonna get a piece of this without even knowing it? Am I some kinda dump for sucker leftovers, and I don't even know it? How can I not know that?

Maybe I'm not supposed to remember that part. Shit. In for my usual, *sure*.

And now I'm thinking all kinds of strange shit, about what am I screwing with suckers for, if they'll suck someone, they'll jack everyone else around till they don't know where-to and is this any way to live. So right then I know I have been jacked past one of those critical points they're always talking about because *I* do not think like this. Not all alone, I don't.

' ... reintegrated,' Rowan is saying, 'I'll take the box with me.'

'Like hell,' says Fur Underwear. 'I built this *myself*.'

'I'll make it worth your while,' Rowan says. 'You might as well, because it's worthless to you now. You'll never get rid of Sovay, not if you run a flush-and-purge every ten minutes. He *is* the box now. That's the Method at work, you know.'

I think I can hear Fur Underwear's teeth grinding. No, it's the box. It's hooked up and running now. I crawl out from under the table again, right into Super Carrot, who hauls me up like a cat. 'Speaking of the Brain Police,' he says.

'Oh, Christ, you keep saying that. She's just a memory junkie,' Fur Underwear says. 'We were both Escorting for Bateau before he got, ah, retired. She isn't any cop – the stupid cow *did* some silly actress. Then she went into business for herself. The actress turned out to be a cop and Bateau got caught with her, while the junkie here slipped out the back door. Anwar could tell you about that if he could remember it. Thank God for the memory wipe, right, Anwar?'

Super Carrot looks down his nose at her. 'Anwar's a bit clouded now. Ask again later.'

'She's been everybody's dump for ages,' Fur Underwear goes on, 'and her habit's so bad *she's* been paying for the privilege. We figured sooner or later she'd flash back to the old routines, even with Bateau out of the picture. Memory junkies are like that. They got nowhere to go except back. I figured if we sucked Sovay, and waited for her to show up, we

could put the two of them together and get the database Bateau was
digging for before the cops canned him.'

'There's no database,' Super Carrot says. 'Or maybe there is, but I
don't have it. None of me has it.'

'What database?' says Rowan. They all ignore her.

'Then it's still in the box and the junkie can unlock it. It would be
easier if we still had the actress but we can make do with the junkie's
memories of her. Then you can just scrape her off the bottom of your
shoe and do what you want.

'But if anyone's afraid she's Brain Police, we'll just run the test.' She
slings one of my arms over her shoulder with this smarmy fondness
that makes me want to punch her. 'Marceline as the Brain Police is even
funnier than Marceline the actress.'

Marceline. I'm wondering if it can get weirder as she walks me over
to an old dentist's chair and lets me fall into it. She takes a good look
into my eyes just before she reaches for the left one.

That's it, I think, and I try to open my mouth to scream, but some-
thing *really* weird happens. All of a sudden, she's moving underwater, I
can even see little whorls and eddies around her hand, but the hand
moves slower and slower, and I'm thinking what is *this* when a trapdoor
opens in my mind and I fall through it.

That's about the only way I can describe it. Everything just went out from
under me and the next thing I knew, I was sitting in a strange, badly lit room.
There was a sense of other people all around, but the light was either too
bright or too dim, or there was something wrong with my inner eye –

'First, stay calm,' says this woman's voice. 'Obviously, we've had some
trouble, and if you don't know what it is, don't worry about it.'

I tried to see who was speaking but the light failed completely.

'This is your reassurance program,' the voice goes on. 'A facade program
is in place for the current probing. So far, no probe has managed to reach
this level, so we're all safe for the moment.'

Trying to move my perspective was no good, either. I seemed to be mired
in something like liquid rubber or gelatin.

'You cannot be briefed at this time,' says the voice. 'Please gather your
resources, as we will be reemerging in a matter of moments. Be prepared;
obviously, our FAT's in the fire, so to speak, and any one of you could end up
driving. For your information, which you will not be able to take with you
anyway, the electrical shocks have done no permanent damage. Things are
just a little scrambled and some of the memory has been rendered unread-
able in some sectors, readable in other sectors where it shouldn't be, and
garbled all over. This can be repaired.'

'I quit!' I yelled. Or I heard myself yell. It felt like me, but it also felt remote, *as if it were someone like me.* Which didn't make shitsense.

'Your contract expires after this,' the voice says. 'Make your decision then.'

'How can I?' I said, or something. 'I never get to drive!'

'About to engage with real-time,' said the voice politely. 'Drive carefully, whoever you are.'

My eyes refocused on the face of the woman in the fur bikini. The man in the purple tuxedo was crowded in next to her.

'No Brain Police in there,' he said, sounding relieved.

'I told you **that**.' She turned away to beckon to Rowan. 'Here's what it is,' she said as Rowan pushed the guy in the purple tuxedo aside. 'The best way to go is, after we pull the database, we give you the dump here and you can use her to reintegrate your husband. I know it's a woman instead of a man, but I think you'll get better results with her brain. Dumps are used to taking all kinds of stuff, they're a little more plastic somehow. She'll make a better adjustment.'

Hercules came up on Rowan's left. 'I like this one,' he said, pointing to himself. 'I mean, just look at him. You like him, too, Rowan. I know you do.'

Rowan looked from me to him and back again, troubled. 'Yes, but we've got to go with the best chance we've got. She says –'

'Oh, Christ, what would **she** know, is she a neurosurgeon? Use **this** me. I've got this guy so rewritten already –'

Rowan let out a deep breath. 'Aesthetically, you're preferable, but … ' She looked at me again.

This is giving me the chills. Some grieving widow. Thinks nothing of just commandeering whoever's handy to get her husband back. Must be some husband. Maybe if it were my husband, I'd do the same, but I can't believe she'd just go with these suckers and take someone out to get him back. She doesn't even know if she really can get him back, I never hearda anyone

Peculiar. I hadn't blacked out that time but Marya came up, didn't notice me, and went away again. That wasn't supposed to be possible.

'Hey,' said Hercules. '**I'm** a volunteer. It oughta go easier with a volunteer.'

The woman in the fur bikini reached over and patted my head carelessly. 'Nobody's going to miss this one, I can tell you that. You can get her sex changed, you're rich enough. Make her over completely.'

'Is that **really** our best chance?' Rowan asked. She might have been getting a second opinion from a specialist.

'You're a lot less likely to get caught too.'

Rowan shrugged. 'Plug her back in, then, and let's get it over with.'

'Hook up the box,' said the other woman. She started to turn toward me and I was gone again.

There was no relaxation exercise, just a few seconds of sleep, and then Sovay's rehearsal studio came up around me like the dawn.

Sovay himself was sitting on a pillow in the middle of the room with his back to the mirrored wall. Funhouse mirrors; vague shapes were shifting within them in response to his thoughts. He was studying what looked like a hard-copy playscript. Several more were piled on the floor beside him. He wasn't orange now. More of a golden beige bordering on brown, actually. I could tell it was completely natural.

He looked up as I melted into existence and then frowned. **Bother**, he said. **Not** another **one**.

I started to explain and everything suddenly played out on the mirrors behind him, what the suckers intended to do, Rowan's part in it, and who I was.

Well, he said. **I knew one of me would have the sense to call the law. For all the good it did. Came by yourself, did you?**

I don't know, I told him.

He tossed away the script he'd been looking at and sighed. **I don't suppose you have a brilliant plan to get us out of this.**

I was about to tell him I didn't know that, either, when something gave me a powerful shove toward him. I had a brief glimpse of his face rushing at me and then, like nothing, we were back where we'd been.

God, they're crude, he said. Abruptly, something lifted him off the floor and started to toss him at me. My vision gave a jump and once again we were in our old positions.

Whoever's at the controls out there has absolutely no idea how to go about this. Sovay sounded almost amused. **But being a dedicated multiple gives you an edge over this kind of brute force. Don't you find that?** He looked past me. **You must. You're all here**.

I turned around. Marya was there, with someone similar, someone whose name was Marceline. There was another woman who looked thin and a little too clean, as if she'd just come out of a rehab center, and behind them, more faces, just phantoms at the moment, but if I kept looking, they would solidify. I couldn't let that happen right now, I knew, and turned back to Sovay.

Some of us split spontaneously, he said. **You wouldn't want to know what makes it happen. Others, like you, can be induced to split. The talent's there,**

it just needs the proper stimulus. Some of us go into acting, some into police work.

An image of Flaxie's face popped into my mind. All the neurotics In theatre.

I could go on splitting for simply ever. Right, Box? He looked around and the studio gave a slow kind of ripple that exuded a sense Of affirmation. *There's another personality who is being the Box. Between the two of us and all this old material* – he patted the stack of scripts – *I can go on manufacturing selves indefinitely*. He laughed and then suddenly looked pained.

I'm looking at Fur Underwear with one eye and with the other

I was still in the box with Sovay, who was wearing an expression of revulsion. *I hate it when they do that*, he said. *It looks so awful*.

'Why won't you behave,' Fur Underwear says. That's a cruel smile she's got. Rowan's face crowds in next to hers.

'What's wrong,' says the grieving widow, impatient.

'They won't smoosh together. Goddam wannabee hardware.'

'You should be using *me*,' whines Hercules, somewhere out of my sight. '*I* wannabee him. *She* doesn't.'

'*You* can't get the database,' Fur Underwear says grimly.

'*What* database?' Rowan says. 'You keep talking about it and talking about it.'

'Brain Police information. Whatever they send with their people on an undercover job. Could be an informant list, or a list of everyone working undercover – don't know till we see it.'

'Sovay doesn't have anything like that,' Rowan says.

Fur Underwear gives her a look like *she's* something to scrap off the bottom of a shoe, too. 'How would *you* know.'

'Because I helped him wipe it.'

'You're lying,' Fur Underwear says, but real unsure.

'No. I'm *not*.' Rowan lets out this crazy little laugh. 'Is *that* why you sucked him? Is *that* what this was all about, some database that doesn't even exist anymore?' In a minute she's going to go up like a bottle-rocket and explode in hysterical fireworks.

Fur Underwear looks like she could throw a temper tantrum herself. 'You coulda saved us all a lot of trouble if you'd just told us that.'

'You didn't ask, you just came in and sucked him!' Yah, it's Fourth-of-July time.

'I meant just now,' Fur Underwear says grimly. 'Well, we're not out of options *yet*.'

I'm starting to panic, because I know she's talking about flush-and-purge, and just when I think I might lose it all in a screaming fit, I feel like someone's holding my hand, but from *inside*. God –

'Guess again,' I said. It was a long reach to her; I had to use Marceline to stretch and she didn't like it. Well, she'd just have to suffer. She wasn't loaded with choices. None of us were.

The cop. As soon as we make contact, I understand it all, and I'd be bugfuck, except I got more serious problems even than that. This is no time to get fussy about who I am, anyway. This is time to wonder if she's got that backup the Brain Police are supposed to have. For once, I want to see the goddam cavalry coming through the door.

Something in my limited field of outer vision moves, somewhere behind Rowan. It's Hercules, and shit, he looks like a sore loser –

Dionysius is not *a good sport*, Sovay said. *Rowan shouldn't have crossed him*. He was doing the equivalent of looking over my shoulder out the window of my eye to the outside.

Fur Underwear goes down hard. Hercules lifts her up again by her hair, but she's offline.

'Take her out!' he barks, gesturing at me.

Sovay started to tell me something and then

he flies backward with a funny little dart in his bare chest and Rowan screams.

'Shut up,' says Purple Tuxedo, tucking a tiny gun away in his cummerbund. 'Now, do you want this or not?'

Does that piece of shit mean *me*?

Sovay's face filled my vision again, crowding out everything else. *I was afraid of this*, he said. *Flush-and-purge. Not me. You*.

You're *the box*, I said. *Can't you stop it?*

Not for you. You're not *the box*.

There's this pressure in my head, like a fist squeezing inside. Purple Tuxedo looks into my face and nods, satisfied. I'd like to wonder which Sovay he is that could just take this up so easy, but I can't do much besides panic.

'Standard suck mode,' he says to Rowan, who looks like she isn't so sure about anything anymore. 'If I force her in there on flush-and-purge, it could force him out into the available receptacle.' He pats my head. Jesus.

And then Mersine tells me how it's going to be and there's no time to argue, because we're going, we're all going, and there's a lot of noise somewhere, someone's banging on the doors, they're coming in the windows, they're falling from the ceiling and the ceiling is falling on me, on us all, but they're too late, I don't have another second, nobody does.

Sovay started to slide past me, toward the opening I felt more than saw. I wanted to go after him, but the polarity was wrong. An invisible hammer hit me dead center, sent me flying against the mirrored wall of his rehearsal room. The mirror splintered and began to unravel in a spiral, like a cyclone picking up speed.

I spread my arms, reaching for the rest of me, imps or real multiple personalities, made no difference now.

You should have told me, Flaxie, it's against the rules but you should have told me anyway, you should have told me it wasn't an imp but a catalyst to wake her, instead of letting me be the fool to believe in what I thought I was, in what I thought any of us were.

But I was the only one who had believed. The rest of me, they'd all known differently, and I ***couldn't*** know. Because if I had, it would have completed the circuit, it would have been the thing that linked us all and mindwipe could have taken us all out. Instead of just me. Karma-gram, yes. The karma-gram has finally been delivered. It's my turn, now. The bill has come due for what I had to do to Marceline. I took her life, and now I have to give it back. It's the only just

reach up with my right hand and rip the connection out of my eye.

Somebody screams. It sounds like Rowan, but maybe it's me.

?

Good lucky, he said. *I hope you make it.*

//////
\ \ \
//////
\
//////

feels like a boulder packed into the side of my face. I can see the para-med hovering over me. Bald, blue skin, very folksy. Makes me want to pop him one, but I couldn't pop a bubble.

' ... *mess*,' he's saying. 'Dirty shame. *Dirty* shame. Optic nerve's *shred-ded*, must hurt like a son of a bitch. Gonna need a graft on that.'

Rowan comes into sight behind him, and it's like I'm seeing her through the wrong end of a telescope, she looks so far away. And so familiar.

And they come and gather around her, Purple Tuxedo, Stringy Hair, Hercules, Super Carrot. And more, that I hadn't seen before. Are they Sovays who found their way to the source, like swimming upstream to unspawn?

'Goddamnedest things occur to you at the god-damnedest times, hey, Mersine?' says the blue paramed, and I realize I've been talking away and not even hearing it. Or maybe someone else is doing the talking and I'm just the lookout here.

Someone pushes through the Sovay gang. Fly Eyes. She looks at me and shakes her head. Someone else moves in next to her, some guy in bad leather body armor and twinkly things stuck here and there around his mouth, and he looks purely disgusted.

'Salazar's going to spit,' he says.

'Salazar's going to spit anyway,' says Fly Eyes. 'It's what she does.' She moves in a little closer, hovering over the paramed's shoulder. 'Can you hear me in there?'

'I hear you,' somebody says. Not this me, whoever's got the vocal cords. Marya, I think. Ersatz-me, me from a slightly different context.

'You were supposed to leave the fetishizer's with me. We had her staked out after Bateau but we couldn't get a warrant to search her. When you wouldn't come with me, I thought that meant you'd found out somebody else had sucked Sovay and you wanted to wait. But then you didn't respond to the trigger word.'

'Trigger word?' I hear myself ask.

'Frigid. The second time I called you frigid, you were supposed to come with me. Marya would have gotten the wet dream while the cop was telling me what you'd found out.'

'I didn't know anything except the name "Monkey Shock,"' I say.

'It would have been all we'd needed,' says the guy in bad imitation leather. 'We had a chain of backups we could have activated, to keep an eye on you in turns.'

'That don't make shitsense,' I say – *I* say. 'You shoulda just triggered the cop and had her tell you right out.'

Fly Eyes shakes her head. 'We never let our cops know exactly who's backing them up. Brain Police policy.'

'In case I got sucked.'

'Oh, we were *expecting* you to get sucked,' she says. 'Marya, that is, not Mersine. Marya came up as a variant of you, Marceline. Since you were the original dump, we couldn't risk losing you and your testimony. This certainly does screw things up. Marya has Mersine's spot in the brain now, and it's going to take ages to build another cop and put her in there –'

I go frantic, pushing to get up and pop her fucking chocks but the folksy blue paramed's got me tied down or something and he keeps pushing on my shoulders and going, 'Sh, now, gotta stay calm, dirty, *dirty* shame,' and he looks up at Fly Eyes and says, 'I don't think you were talkin' to who you thought you were talkin' to, maybe you should go think out loud someplace else before you bring on a seiz –'

They say it was sixteen hours in the hospital, but I don't remember most of it. It would have been longer, but I wouldn't stay. I told them no thanks to their graft. Fuck it, I can live without an eye, especially a Brain Police eye. And there isn't a damned thing they could do about it with my contract up and everything, except get petty and demand their clothes back. Which is what they did.

Little Blondie in the wardrobe department made a big deal out of that, having me exchange piece by piece for the cop's old clothes. Those were in better condition than what they took back, so I came out with the better end on something. But I couldn't figure out why he was taking so long and making a big fucking ceremony out of it until she showed up.

Skinny? I seen fatter people that starved to death. I couldn't believe I'd ever known this woman, but I knew I had. There was this old garbled memory lying around in my mind, the woman behind a desk chewing and spitting, sometimes into a desk suckhole, sometimes kneeling on a floor in an office full of fat furniture. That made me think about mouthkissing and it just turned my stomach inside out practically, seeing her and having to think about that.

'You are legally entitled to leave, since your contract's up,' she goes, all official. 'But I wish you'd reconsider. Or at least let us give you a new optic nerve and an eye. We owe you that much.'

I touch the eyepatch and think about the cop I used to be, or who used to be

me, and I get the feeling she'd have wanted this way. I mean, I don't know, because I never really knew her, and it's not like cops are my favorite people even when they're me, but I feel bad for her, wherever she is. I was supposed to get sucked, not her. So I owe her a big one, and maybe I'm a fool to believe that, because maybe if she'd known all along that she was the imp, she might have changed places with me and let me go down the drain again anyway. But she never had the chance to make that choice.

'Rowan'll be doing time for that,' says Skinny, nodding at my eyepatch. 'And some of the Sovays. The others'll be waiting for them when they get out. I'm not sure what they'll do after that. Most of the original people have been rewritten so thoroughly they're past the point of restoration, either as themselves or as Sovay.'

'Why are you telling me this?' I ask.

'I thought you'd be interested.'

'I'm not. I been a dump long enough, I don't need what you're spitting out.'

She looks offended, but what is she gonna do, fire me? I never worked here, and I'm driving now. If that's not fair to the rest of me, well, nothing's ever really fair. Not that I remember, anyway.

I finish the Big Clothing Exchange and ignore the pained look Little Blondie is giving me. I got this other memory lying around, just a tiny one, him looking at me and saying, Come back when you want it taken off, and I can't forgive him for that. He lied like a goddam rug and I don't care if it was his job to do it. Maybe she'd have just gone ahead and let him suck me out, her not knowing what I really was to her, but she should have been told so she could have made that choice, too, whether to get rid of me or let me live.

Ah, fuck her, too. She was Brain Police, as bad as any of them. If I can live with one less eye, the world can live with one less cop.

And besides, I know something they don't know. For once. And it's this: She's coming back. Not today, not even next month, but sometime soon, she'll be filling back in. All those little memories she left laying around, the associations are already starting to reconnect, and she won't be able to help it. Maybe I could get her sucked out before that happens, but I'm not going to do that. Not this time. One of these days, she'll pop up and take a look around and wonder what the hell happened. And I'll tell her all about it, what they did to her and what they did to me and to all of us, and we'll see if she wants to be a cop again.

And if she does, well, this time she'll know more, enough that she can make the choice to give us all a chance. Maybe? I mean, I would. Wouldn't she? Don't know. Don't know. Just don't know

what the *hell*

is going on here *now*?

PART III

Nobody's Fool

'Your arrogance has always been your least attractive feature,' Em-Cate said. She had to tilt her head back to look down her nose at me, but, migod, she did it.

'At least *I* have something to be arrogant about,' I replied. The soft background music I'd been talking over stopped suddenly and my too loud voice hung in the air. All party conversation ceased.

Em-Cate didn't deign to notice that everyone was staring at us. 'What, quickie head-jobs? Haven't you heard it isn't their *brains* that are supposed to be stiff?' Several feet behind her, a woman in one of those animated feather creations put a hand over her mouth, scandalized and loving it.

'You would know, you're the one with the monogrammed knee pads.'

Em-Cate surprised me by throwing her wine in my face. For a long moment I could only stand there dripping pinot noir, wincing over my soggy eyepatch, and wondering if the stains would come out of the white second-skins I was wearing while she gave me her patented Em-Cate triumphant I-got-*you* blazing-eyed stare. Quite a tableau, if you liked cheap melodrama.

Apparently, this crowd did. The applause was loud, enthusiastic, and spontaneous, surprising me even more than Em-Cate's little improvisation. I was still goggling at the room when Em-Cate grabbed my hand, raised it, and then pulled us both down in a low bow. She tossed me a napkin as she stepped forward to take another bow separately, and then held out one arm to me so I could do the same. *Hurry up*, she mouthed at me through her too bright smile. I bowed, dabbing the pinot out of my eyes and retreated to the buffet table while Em-Cate made a big show out of beckoning the director out of the guests he'd been mingling with.

Jasper stood in front of us and bobbed up and down from the waist, fanning a breeze with the wings of hair sticking out from either side of his head. In the box-suit, he looked like a trophy wearing a shipping carton. He acknowledged Em-Cate and then me before he thought to grab the hostess and shove her in front of him. She took her bows while applauding herself, her suit of lights twinkling giddily.

'Well, that's our formal entertainment,' she said, waving a hand at Jasper.

'They even had *me* fooled for a while and *I* hired them. The Home-Brew Players – aren't they great, everybody?'

Everybody applauded again to show agreement. I had to force myself not to flee back to the guest room and lock the door behind me. Em-Cate slipped over to my side of the buffet table to pour herself another glass of wine. 'Smile, dammit,' she whispered, beaming at the crowd. 'You look like you're at a funeral.'

Smile. Migod, I thought, stretching my mouth in something I hoped was at least vaguely grinlike.

'Tonight's domestic drama was improvised from an outline by one of our own guests,' the hostess went on cheerily. Everyone *oohed* and *aahed*. 'And I hope she's ready to take credit for her part in this.'

I hoped so, too. As usual, Em-Cate and I hadn't been given any details beyond the basic scenario. I wanted to get a look at the prodigy who thought a cat-fight was the height of party entertainment. But nobody stepped forward.

'Oh, come *on*,' said the hostess, 'she didn't leave, did she? Rowan, are you still here?'

Migod. At first, I didn't think I'd heard correctly. Then the people directly in front of the hostess moved aside and there she was, looking as brown and round and bland as ever. The hostess was saying something else but I wasn't listening and didn't want to. I headed for the guest bedroom that was our dressing room, shaking off Em-Cate's restraining hand, ignoring Jasper's whispered command to wait, we weren't finished.

Obviously, we weren't, but as far as I was concerned, the party was over.

'What did you do that for,' Jasper said, glaring at me as I slathered cream over my face. He'd insisted on glittering my cheekbones and it felt like sandpaper coming off.

'I quit.'

'You can't quit. We're hired for the night, we've got a contract.'

I shrugged. 'Sue me.'

He turned to Em-Cate. 'Talk to her.'

Em-Cate stared at him for a moment and then burst out laughing.

He plumped down on the bed, making the top half of the box-suit slide up around his ears. *Fashion-victim, thy name is Jasper*, I thought, watching him in the mirror, too disgusted to laugh. 'Ah, Christ, why do I get all the temperamental ones,' he whined, pulling his chin up out of his neckline. 'Look, I realize you *artistes* would rather be emoting Shakespeare and Tennessee Ernie Ford from a real proscenium, but live theatre's *dead*. You want to work live, you do the soaps. You want to hear yourself talk, mount *Hamlet*.'

'*You* mount him. I'd pay to see that.' I turned away from the mirror and moved to the doorway of the bathroom, using one of the animated towels to

wipe off the rest of the cream. The continuously moving patterns in the fabric flowed over the smears of color, incorporated them, and began some new fluctuations. 'And it's Williams, not Ernie Ford.'

'Apparently you haven't seen Jasper's libretto for *Twenty-Seven Wagonsful of Peapickers*,' Em-Cate said. ' "Ah have always depended upon the kahndness of peapickers." He's adapting it for three rooms with bath.'

I didn't laugh. Em-Cate probably had it right, even down to the mishmash. But I wasn't fooled by her; she was ganging up on Jasper with me because she was feeling mean and it pleased her to do so, not out of any sense of actor's solidarity, least of all with me. That she was working with me was a reflection of her desperation for any work at all since the demise of Sir Larry's.

Jasper started one of his diatribes about the validity of the soap opera as classic tragedy, citing references that were about as accurate as his drama-turgy. I tuned him out, trying to recall which companies I'd heard were holding auditions. Door-To-Door was always auditioning, but that was because they were so vile, few actors could stand more than one production – migod, they'd play a toilet if there was money in the bowl. The Domestiks had a few openings ... so did HomeShow ...

There was a knock at the door. 'Must be the bouquets you sent yourself,' Em-Cate said, to me or to Jasper, I didn't know which and it didn't matter, because I was pretty sure I knew who it really was. Who it had to be, rather. I didn't remember that much about her, but somehow I'd known she couldn't have let the evening slip away without approaching me. God only knew why.

Em-Cate opened the door and stared at Rowan expectantly. 'Author, author. Come to thank us?'

Rowan blinked at her. 'That was terrible,' she said matter-of-factly.

Em-Cate threw back her head and laughed. 'Oh, *yah*,' she said after a bit, wiping her eyes. 'Of *course* it was terrible. You don't resort to cheap tricks like throwing a drink in someone's face if the material is any good.' Still laughing, she wandered over to the antique vanity where her makeup was spread out among the hostess's collection of perfume bottles and sat down in front of the mirror.

'What do you resort to if the material *is* any good?' Rowan asked.

'Is that a rhetorical question?' Jasper muttered disgustedly.

'No,' Rowan said, turning that blindy-eyed stare on him.

He didn't look at her. 'Mine was.'

'I knew the answer anyway.' Her gaze drifted past him and found me in the bathroom doorway. The light in here wasn't the flatteringly soft party glow that made everyone look glamorous even if you weren't intoxicated, and it showed her no mercy. She had aged in a way that went deeper than a few lines and some minor sagging. 'Been a long time,' she said to me suddenly.

I pretended to look at a watch I wasn't wearing. 'Six months, isn't it?'

'Ten years.'

Of course; I'd forgotten about the time she'd pulled for her mindcrime. Mindcrime incarceration was like nothing else – they put you under the belljar with your mind racing so your time sense was slowed down. Real-time, six months; subjective time, ten years. I'd have thought it was a harsh sentence for a first offense if I hadn't been on the receiving end.

I realized I was staring at her, turned away and went back into the bathroom to clean off the makeup. If it was already all cleaned off, then I'd put some more on and clean that off, until she was gone.

'I've got a proposition for you.'

I looked at her reflection in the mirror. 'Migod, is it as good as the last offer? I can't imagine what would be better than being Sovay for you.'

'Finding Sovay for me.'

I could hear Em-Cate's laughter under my own. 'Citizen, let me juice up your memory,' I said, touching my eyepatch. 'Sovay's been found. The show closed, the set's been struck, and I'm still not the man you wanted me to be. Nobody is.'

'Ain't *that* the truth,' I heard Em-Cate say, as if to herself.

'They said that all the people who bought Sovay from the mindsuckers have mutated into something that is neither themselves nor Sovay,' Rowan said. 'I don't think it's true. I think he's still … alive. In … somebody.'

I put more cream on my face. 'The court maintained him in the sucker box as long as it could. When he disintegrated, he was declared legally dead. The men you collected to try to reintegrate him suffered rewrite conflicts –'

'But none of them were wiped. Sovay is lying dormant somewhere.'

I frowned. 'Nope.'

'Sovay was the core personality, the source. Every one of them had him. That doesn't melt away like an imprint of a character. The associations still exist. Enough for you to be able to identify Sovay if you were mind-to-mind with him.'

'What about you?' I said. 'Couldn't you identify him if you were mind-to-mind with him?'

She shook her head. 'I've never been mind-to-mind with Sovay.'

'Never?'

Her chin lifted defiantly. 'Is that supposed to be unusual?'

'I don't know if it's *supposed* to be. *I* think it is.'

She sighed. 'Sovay and I didn't believe in it. We thought mind-to-mind contact was more intimate than a married couple should be.'

'How about before you were married?'

'Nothing. Ever.'

I shrugged. 'That still doesn't mean you wouldn't know him if you met him mind-to-mind.'

Now she looked repelled. 'I don't *want* to meet him mind-to-mind. I don't ever want to be mind-to-mind with him. To have to feel those things ... not ever.'

'What things?' It was heartless, but she'd thrown a drink in my face. By proxy, but still.

'You know. His other contacts. His other mind-to-mind contacts, with pathosfinders, with other actors ... all the people who had him, who got closer to him than I did. Including you. His big love affair. If you'd have just gone to bed in real-time, it wouldn't have been so bad, he'd have gotten you out of his system and you wouldn't have been hanging on to that part of him that wanted you. It's bad enough having to know about it. I don't want to have to feel it in my own head.'

I wasn't sure that it would have felt any worse than what she was feeling in her own head now, having had nothing much else to think about over the last ten subjective years of her life.

'Maybe all that would be so if Sovay were still in existence,' I said. 'But he isn't.'

'Yes, he *is*,' Rowan said. 'I know he is because I know him. Not the way *you* knew him, or any of the others, but I know what kind of actor he was. A Method actor, yes' – she gave a short, bitter laugh – 'but he had the Method backward. Everyone else could become someone else, but not Sovay. All of *his* characters became *him*. That was the kind of man he was. It was why he was able to call me after the mindsuckers started trying to sell him off. I *know* he's alive in somebody somewhere, hiding, still holding his own. And you'd know him. The associations you still carry would know him. You have a fool-proof Sovay detector in your head. You could find him for me.'

'Why?' I asked.

She blew out an impatient breath. 'The associations –'

'No. I mean, why should I?'

She moved to stand directly in front of the mirror, which put her in my blind spot and forced me to turn and look directly at her. 'Because I still want him. Because I still love him.' Somehow, the admission was more naked than if she'd made it mind-to-mind.

'But why should *I* do it? What's in it for me?'

Now she hesitated. 'Is money good enough?'

I laughed. 'Have you come out of mind-incarceration filthoid rich, money falling out of every pore and nothing better you can think to spend it on?'

She pulled a bankcard out of her pocket, pressed her thumb to the ID spot, and showed me the balance that appeared in the upper-left corner.

'I'm impressed,' I said truthfully.

'You can have the whole thing if you find Sovay for me. Have your optic nerve fixed. Replace your eye.'

'I can see just fine. Don't you think Sovay would object if he did turn up and you'd given away your life savings?'

'How much would *you* pay for *your* life?'

I couldn't help laughing. 'You're asking *me* that question?'

'How much?'

I glanced at the bankcard balance again. 'Less than I'd take to give it up.'

'How much would you pay for the life of someone you love, then? I *want* my husband back. You're the only one who could find him.'

'What about the Brain Police? You could go to them with your theories –'

'If they believed he was out there, that would be the end of him. They'd take him apart for evidence, for what information they thought he might have. And for the simple reason that they wouldn't know what else to do with him.'

'And what would *you* do with him? Or rather, with whatever poor slob that might turn up with his mind all scrambled from overwriting? If I could even find anyone?'

'I'd help him. And you can find them all, that's no problem.'

'What makes you so sure?'

'Because I've already found them. It wasn't hard. I can tell you where each one of them is.'

My gaze kept returning to the bankcard. Apparently I had an avaricious streak I'd never been aware of. Or maybe it was just knowing a bankroll like that could take me far away and let me start fresh.

'I put all the information in your phone mailbox,' she said. 'All you have to do is use it. Then you can use this.' She entered some code on the top row of letters on the bankcard and then held it up to my eye. There was an infinitesimal flash that felt like a pinprick deep in my head. Or maybe a peapicker. 'There. It's keyed to you now. Show of good faith. The money's already yours, all you have to do is come and collect it.' She tucked the card back into her pocket. 'I'll hold it for you.'

I folded my arms. 'Pretty rash. I could just go tell the bank the card is lost, get a new one, and take off with the money, all clear.'

'Could you?' Her face was unreadable. 'I've done nothing for the last ten years but think, about anything, about everything. You could do that, but you won't. You'll look for him because you want the money and because I've made you curious. Now you want to see for yourself if I'm right.'

Rowan hadn't struck me as the type of person capable of being so perceptive. But then, who was to say what ten years in solitary could do to anyone?

Jasper made a throat-clearing noise. 'If you're about done in there, it's time to start dressing for the late show.'

'Thought I told you,' I called to him. 'I quit.'

In my hands, the towel suddenly shorted out and went black as the color receptors overloaded.

Karma-gram, whispered my mind.

There was a ghost of a smile on Rowan's face.

I didn't immediately go running off on the Great Sovay Hunt with dollar signs in my eyes. Fortune or not, I still wasn't sure if I wanted to go through with it. My life wasn't much these days, but it was a life and it was mine. So far, anyway, from the time of Marceline's descent into dormancy.

I didn't know what had caused that, and I hadn't tried looking for any answers, not when it had happened and not since. Now and then, I'd had a few nervous nights when I'd been unable to sleep, afraid that she would wake up the next morning instead of me. Other times, I would wake with a start from some already forgotten dream, sure that it had been her dream, not mine. But nothing happened; I never felt even the slightest stirring, not so much as a taste of her essence. And yet I knew she hadn't evaporated. If I couldn't feel her presence, I couldn't feel her absence, either.

Then let's tempt fate, I thought, and went for a walk in the Downs. If the old, familiar sights didn't rouse her, looking for Sovay might be safe. And if they did rouse her – well, I'd be beyond caring and she'd be back where she belonged.

My fatalism surprised me. First avarice, now fatalism – what else was I going to find out about myself? So much for instinctive living.

The sights were familiar in a distant way, but only familiar; a lot of specific things were missing from my memory, the associations too weak, or scrambled, or perhaps gone for good, at least as far as I was concerned. Somebody else's life had been lived here, not mine. I had passed through once in a hurry but my mental state wasn't the same.

Some joint called Sojourn For Truth raised a mild blip but I didn't know why. I'd have gone in to see if I could find out, but it was so run-down and sleazy-looking, I wasn't actually sure if it was open for business. There was a guy standing out in front as if he were waiting for someone; as I passed him, he suddenly blew a flurry of bubbles at me, each one containing a tiny glitter-star.

Before I realized what I was doing, I had stopped to catch one of the bubbles on my finger and watch the swirl of colors in the delicate skin fade to a colorless web before it popped, leaving a little red star stuck in a wet spot. I braced myself for some kind of hot pitch, but nothing happened. The man was just watching me, as if he only wanted to see what my reaction would be. I started to say something to him and he turned away, blowing more bubbles into the air over his head. I wiped my finger on my pants and kept going.

Several blocks in, a dream parlor called The Zoot Mill was running a half-hearted sidewalk display; the dancing unicorns flickered, full of static, and

even the money tornadoes looked anemic. Nobody had stopped to watch, so I didn't, either. I was about to walk right through the display when a scantily clad figure materialized right in front of me. He seemed to be looking right at me and though he wasn't any less ragged than the rest of it, I was startled enough to back up and give the projection area a wide berth. The woman squatting in the parking space at the curb didn't even give me a glance as I stepped over her outstretched legs. There was something funny about her eyes but she was on my blind side so I couldn't see much.

Another few blocks and I was more or less lost. There was a comm center that wasn't particularly well patronized – I could have gone in and gotten a free map from a you-are-here but the strange apathy/malaise that seemed to be in the air had apparently settled over me like dust. It didn't really matter where I was; when I got tired of being here, I could hunt up a freebus depot or a tube station and take the next ride out. Or keep walking till I came out the other side of the Downs.

I paused again in front of a crib, of all places. There was nothing in my memory about it, exactly, but I had the strong feeling that there was something I should have known … or *had* known … I shrugged and started to walk away.

A moment later I was standing inside, blinking in the semidark. My inner ear went crazy as déjà vu shuddered through my brain and I leaned against a wall, trying to steady myself.

Abruptly, my blind side erupted with pictures, one after another, flashing too fast for sense, frozen frames of faces, places, things, and, under it all, a voice murmuring at me, unintelligible but relentless, insistent, demanding –

'I *said*, wake up. It's all a dream.'

The man sitting on the sagging cot looked about a hundred years old, and not because of the snow-white hair. He reached over and picked up the connections to the system on the table next to the cot. 'You didn't come for this, did you?'

The sign on the outside of the cubicle said *Imagist*. I shook my head once, carefully.

'Didn't think so. She said to expect you. I told her she was out of her mind, you'd never do it. But I forgot, of every one of us, she might have been the most insane, but she never, ever, was out of her mind. Not once.' If he looked a hundred, he sounded two hundred, as if his voice had been in storage somewhere and he hadn't cleaned off the cobwebs when he'd taken it out again.

He beckoned and I went in. There was no place to sit except on the cot and I didn't want to get that close to him.

'Now, we wait,' he said, as if I'd asked him something. 'It shouldn't be long. He's a garbagehead now. Like the rest of them, I imagine.' He changed

position on the cot and the springs screamed like tortured weasels. 'I don't know, really, he's the only one I've seen in twenty years, wouldn't know the others if I did see them.' He looked at the connections he was still holding, but didn't put them down. 'Which one are you – the original fake, or the fake fake?'

'Why?' I said.

'The one I had, she was the original fake. A persona who got too full of herself and pinocchio'ed.'

'Pinochled?' I should get out of here, I thought.

'*Pinocchio'ed.* Cute little story about a puppet who turned into a human.' He squinted at me with his cheap eyes; not biogems, just government-sur-plus brown. 'Story everyone should know. I had time to tell it to myself. I laid it out as a full-length feature, did the remake, and then composed the opera.' His gaze drifted past me and I turned to see what was so interesting.

Cheap gilt was flaking off the wretch standing in the doorway of the cubicle, a special effect gone wrong. He'd had a body once, but it had been some time since he'd bothered to maintain it. Or changed his clothes – I real-ized the washrag hanging over the front of his pants was actually the remains of a loincloth.

He put one hand to the side of his face and tried to speak, but nothing came out.

'Told you it wouldn't be long.' The white-haired guy got up from the cot, making it scream again. 'Come on,' he said to the wretch in the doorway. 'Someone's come to take you home now.'

'No,' said the wretch. 'Still not right. Almost, though. It's real close. I said I'd meet her here, and I keep coming, but I keep missing her.'

I stood on tiptoe to look over the wall of the cubicle. The aisle was empty. That didn't mean Rowan wasn't nearby, only that she was smart enough to stay out of sight.

'Don't have to buy paranoia anymore, do you?' said the imagist. He was laughing at me.

I shrugged. 'Maybe not. Except I don't know how she'd know I'd come here, when I didn't know myself.'

'Maybe she followed you and sent the nearest one. Or maybe it's just chance favoring the prepared mind.' He led the other man to the cot and sat him down. 'Is your mind prepared?' he asked, holding the connections out to me.

Go mind-to-mind with *this* walking wreckage? When I barely seemed to know my own mind? 'I'm nostalgic for free will,' I said, more to myself.

' Any thing free is worth what you pay for it.'

The breathtaking balance on Rowan's bankcard passed through my mind as I took the connections from him. Not because I wanted it so much any-

more but because now that I had one of them, I had to know. And even while I was popping my own eye and letting the connection creep into the empty socket, I also knew that any idiotic party guest could have come up with better motivation for the most brainless scenario ever suggested to a living-room drama troupe.

Inside, he was like the first draft of the Frankenstein's monster. He didn't even make a good crazy quilt, he was a junk pile, visualizations shifting like a runaway slide show without a sequence to follow. He couldn't hang on to an idea longer than a few seconds, except for one: meeting Rowan in a crib. But he didn't know *who* was supposed to meet her – him as the whore, him as Dionysius, him as Sovay as Dionysius, Sovay as him, Sovay as him as Dionysius – he'd even lost all track of whether he or Sovay had been Dionysius.

It was the type of confusion that spiraled inward. Follow it, and you'd chase your own tail until you imploded into a fugue state, and when you came out of it, you'd be back in the same place, ready to start over. Black hole set on permanent rewind and replay.

Anything else you want to know about the nature of hell?

The question fluttered past me on a tattered rag caught in a minor whirlwind. The landscape that faded in was my own involuntary visualization. That would happen if nobody set the scene; sooner or later, you'd see something unless you forced yourself not to. This something was like the surface of the moon transplanted to the badlands, the morning after a mental costume orgy. Most of the debris littering the ground didn't know what it had been before it had become debris.

The only piece that interested me was the rag. I concentrated on locating the source. After a bit, a stone mountain flickered into existence on the wasted horizon. As I started toward it, all the debris turned into heads, as if someone had spilled the baskets after a full day at the guillotine.

Except these heads were watching me. Something was wrong with their eyes, though – some of them didn't even have eyes, some that did couldn't open them, some had too many, and others had them in the wrong places – and none of them spoke language, only word salad.

Getting dicey in here, I thought, tightening my concentration. He latched on to my visuals, not because he liked them but because they were there to latch on to. If I wasn't careful, he was going to latch on to me, too, and every picture in my head would get sucked into the scenery.

I wrapped myself in a shield, which meant I had to go slower toward the source of the ragged message, and I couldn't see the location as clearly as before. But it relieved that besieged feeling.

On the ground ahead of me, something sparked and flashed in a random

sequence. I plodded right along, not stopping but taking a good look at it as I passed.

A shard from a broken mirror. Uh-oh.

At least the stone mountain was getting closer; in fact, it was getting closer faster than I was walking toward it, which just served to show how perception of progress differs from actual progress. If I stayed in here long enough, I thought to myself, I could probably qualify for certification as a reality affixer. Then the cacophony of voices shouting un-sense got louder, and I thought, maybe not.

A cave opened up in the base of the mountain. Each plodding step I took was harder, like every bit of movement was separate from every other bit, components that would have made up one whole thing if they could have connected with each other. But they couldn't. Had I been thinking I could qualify as a reality affixer? Any longer in here and there would be more heads lying around on that bad landscape, all of them mine.

I stumbled over something, recovered, and then fell down a bolthole.

You got my message, said Sovay. He was squatting naked in a space at the bottom of the bolthole, tending a small fire. It was his literal spark of life – as long as the fire lasted would be as long as he lived. If you could call this living.

The mechanics were fascinating to watch – he kept the fire going by pulling off little pieces of himself and tossing them on the flames. The smoke that came up flowed back toward him and reconstituted his missing pieces … mostly. A fraction of the smoke went up the bolthole, where it was lost forever. Here and there, I could see small pits and dents in his skin, the little losses he couldn't recover.

Yah, I got your message I said. *How the hell did you send it?*

Smoke signals. He smiled at me over the flames. *I sent it up the chimney here –* he pointed at the bolthole – *and it attached itself to a carrier. I could spare that much.* He looked at himself, touching a few of the dents in his skin. *I figure there's still enough of me left to last a long bad time. I wanted you to come here. I know who you are.*

You know who I used to be, I told him.

Know of you, I should have said. He closed himself off when he was with Marva, I wasn't invited. He broke off the top section of his left little finger and fed it to the fire. There was no blood and he didn't wince until it started to burn. *I was a good actor, but when it came to the Method, I didn't have a clue.*

What do you mean? I asked him.

I mean I wasn't a real Method actor. If I had been, you'd be talking to Dionysius, not the me who pretended to be Dionysius. He examined his shortened finger and the other small deficits. *Can I borrow a cup of anything?*

I didn't understand right away. And then, when I did, I also understood the man wasn't asking. This was what he'd had in mind when he had felt me make contact. When you wanted to live this bad, you'd do anything.

Why don't you straighten him *out?* I asked, pointing ' at the bolthole. *Obviously, when Sovay didn't take, he fell apart. You could fix him, make him over.*

Tried that. How do you think he got this way? I was lucky he didn't fragment me as well.

I remembered the shard of mirror I'd seen. Who hadn't been able to live with the mirror – him? Or Sovay?

Abruptly, the smoke suddenly blew into my face.

Not fair! he screamed. *You've got plenty and I'm getting all used up! Give it back! Give it –*

He reached through the fire for me and his hand borrowed mass from the rest of him, swelling to four times its size. I flung myself backward, thinking *Exit!*

Nothing happened.

He was hanging above me, bigger all over now, meaning to envelop me. He didn't mean to take just what he thought I'd gotten in the smoke, but everything I had. I could see right through him – literally; he was bigger, but no more substantial.

I pushed myself upward, aiming at the bolthole this time. Passing through him was more than passing through a holo, but not much more.

'You're not her,' he said accusingly. Coney Loe (that was his name; I could remember now) must have put his eyes back in for him. I couldn't look at him; it was all I could do to put my own singleton back in without screaming. 'And you're not him.'

'Brilliant, isn't he?' said Coney.

'Shut up,' I said, keeping my back to both of them. Things were still settling in my head. I started to get up and suddenly there was a flash of light from my blind side, bigger than the pinprick flash from Rowan's bank-card.

How much would you pay for your life?

A lot more than I'd take to give it up …

'Where are you going?' Coney said.

I paused in the doorway, still with my back to them. 'To call her. You keep him here, she can pick him up.'

'This is him?' Coney sounded suspicious.

'Hot strike on the first try,' I said. 'Call it beginner's luck, or something, huh?'

If Coney said anything else, I didn't hear it. My footsteps pounding down the aisle toward the exit sign echoed the pounding in my head. Not the mindless throbbing of a hypehead's mindplay hangover but a chant, two

words repeating over and over, like being slapped again and again without pause.

She lied. She lied. She lied. She LIED. SHE LIED.

I could see them in my head as plain as anything, Dionysius and Rowan lying on cots in a cubicle with a second man on the floor between them, all three of them hooked into a system together. Illegal three-way. People who would mouthkiss were capable of anything.

SHE LIED. SHE LIED. SHE LIED.

I hit the sidewalk and knew exactly where I was, where everything was, everything and everybody.

'Heya, *heya!*'

Reflexively I reached for a comb, but there was nothing in my hair. The figure in front of me changed from a neurosis peddler with bad leather armor to a malnourished rooster-boy with chapped skin. We stared at each other as I lowered my fist; after a moment, he pried my other hand off his throat.

'No rough stuff,' he said. 'Unless you pay extra.'

I pushed him away and ran, almost knocking over another rooster-boy who was double-teaming a tourist with his pimp. The pimp's fuzzy, lurid magenta suit stung my vision and left an afterimage floating ahead of me, but no matter how fast I ran, I couldn't catch up to it. More than a pinprick.

SHE LIED. SHE LIED. SHE LIED.

Truth is cheap; information costs. How much for both, then?

Just as I reached the corner the light changed and four lanes of vehicles surged into the intersection. I turned away and something caught me right under the chin. My feet didn't quite fly out from under me but I went down anyway into a tacky forest of legs in second-skins and jumpjohns and cheap, flaking paint.

They all cleared away quickly and I found myself looking up at a pair of onionheads grinning over the chain they'd used to clothesline me.

'So hot to violate our marital space,' said the one on the left nastily.

I started to get up and they advanced on me so that I was forced either to stay down or half crawl backward to get away from them. 'You forced it,' I said, trying to shift position to a crouch. 'You know I didn't even see you and everyone who saw it will say that's true.'

The one on the right bent forward, thrusting her ugly, hairless face at me. 'Now *find* someone who'll say they saw. *Find* someone who wants to be challenged as your accomplice right now, here.' The other one nodded, grinning, feeding slack into their marital chain. '*Find* someone, go on, ask any of them, ask them all, they'll tell you they saw nothing, they had their backs turned, they all saw nothing, nothing, *nothing at all!*'

They threw the chain back and whipped it over their heads and down. I had just enough time to squeeze into a tight ball. The chain missed my shins

by a bare inch and smashed down on the pavement. The onionheads squawled like scalded badgers and pulled the chain back for another go. Just as it was arcing over their heads, I launched myself forward and under it. I hit open pavement and rolled with the fall so that my momentum took me back up onto my feet without a pause.

The onionheads were screaming full-throat now; I really had violated their marital space this time, deliberately and flagrantly, in front of a crowd of witnesses. Every onionhead pair and multiple in the Downs was going to be hunting me within an hour. *God, why?* I thought, sprinting blindly. Why were onionheads allowed to terrorize people for no other reason than they were bored, why were they allowed to act out their pathological possessiveness by beating people into blood pudding for the crime of violating some imaginary boundary around them? And most of all, why did I have to have onionheads after me now?

Unbidden, the words surfaced in my mind.

… are you paranoid enough?

I pounded across another street, staggered into the entryway of a cheesy fetishizer joint, and squeezed into a corner near the door, trying to catch my breath. The door opened almost immediately, but it was only a couple of garbageheads, wearing silly wrapcoats and even sillier grins. They didn't even look at me on their way to wherever to enjoy their latest fixation, while it lasted.

My knees got shaky. I half slid, half fell down onto the grimy tiles. My breath was coming back but my heart wouldn't slow down and my legs were burning. If the onionheads found me now, I wouldn't be able to do a thing except bleed. I closed my eyes and tried to listen for the sound of running footsteps and the clink of a chain over the traffic noise.

Nobody came, not even another customer. After a while, I pushed myself up on my hands and knees, and then to my feet. My legs wanted to collapse more than anything but I made myself move to the edge of the entryway and peek around the side of the building. No onionheads; almost no one at all on the sidewalk, except for a gofer walking back and forth half a block down with an envelope under her arm, squinting at the street numbers.

Of course they hadn't chased me; why waste time chasing me when they could round up reinforcements?

Onionheads loved to hunt a violator en masse. If I could get out of the Downs, I'd keep my skin. They rarely left the Downs for any reason – better areas of town weren't terribly hospitable to them and they tended to end up being arrested for disturbing the peace before they could actually get around to disturbing it much. Whereas in the Downs, I reflected sourly, you could disturb all you wanted as long as you didn't overnight in a parking space …

I leaned against the building, trying to think while I scanned the street. Something was chipping at my memory, trying to get in … or get out?

… she lied …

Yah, we know she lied about never having gone mind-to-mind with Sovay, I thought. *We're doing something else now.*

she lied.

Something …

A flash of light, a pinprick in the brain. A scatter of heads, a shard of mirror, a continuously rewinding black hole. A man who stayed alive by consuming himself …

Forgive and forget. If you forget first, there's nothing to forgive.

His image was there in my mind, like a splinter, like a thorn, like a hook – but not enough. More than a holo, but not much more; more used up than he realized. Or maybe he did realize, but didn't want to admit it. Who would?

But there had been enough of him to tell me –

… she lied about why she wanted you to find him.

I stepped out onto the sidewalk. A battalion of onionheads didn't pour out of the nearby doorways, screaming for my blood. Still too early. Maybe I could get off the street before everyone had been notified and I could slip back to midtown during the deadest part of the night.

If I was right, I'd have a place to hide out until then.

The door was open a crack. I stood back and gave it a light push with my fingertips. It swung inward to reveal the empty living room, much the same as it appeared in the memory that contact with Sovay's ghost had activated. I took a tentative step inside, looking around. He couldn't have been expecting me; the security entrance was out of commission, so I hadn't had to buzz him to let me in.

Or had he been expecting me every day for the last six months?

'I didn't know what I'd do when this finally happened. If it ever did. And now I still don't know.'

He was standing in the kitchenette holding a cup, either just emptied or not yet filled. I couldn't tell. The bad dye-job had been left to fade without renewal; except for some very faint orange shadows in the lines around his eyes and mouth, it was all gone now.

'What do I call you?' I said, pushing the door closed behind me.

'I've been using Anwar, still. For simplicity's sake. Though I'm still neither flesh nor fowl nor good red herring. *Bad* red herring, perhaps. For a while, orange herring.'

I had a sudden flash of myself as a fish; ridiculous. I shook the thought away.

He gestured at the futon across the living room. 'Make yourself comfortable. We should have a talk, just the four of us. Or, well, I don't know how many you are now, but I'd like it if you'd limit yourself to two while you're

here. I'll make you some vile coffee.' The brief laugh seemed to escape him without his wanting it. 'I know I said that last time would be the last time. I lied. I'd have helped you if you'd come to me every night with our pimp snapping at your heels, I –' He reached for his waist and then stared wonderingly at his empty hand. 'Oh. I forgot. Can you buy that? I really forgot.'

I went to the futon, hoping the movement would shut off his babbling. He grabbed another cup, filled them both with water, and dropped in a couple of cubes.

'Very vile coffee,' he said, coming over to sit down next to me.

'Thanks,' I said, accepting a cup from him. 'You're true. The truest one I ever knew.'

He laughed again, blinking at me incredulously. 'Where'd you get an idea like that?'

'Where do we get any of our ideas?'

He tilted his head to one side and something happened. The set of his face changed, the lines suddenly not quite what they'd been, not quite right. 'No,' he said faintly, 'it *was* Marva I loved, not … the other. The big husky one, she was … *not* Marva. *Non*-Marva. But Marva was the one I wanted, and when she, when she –' He looked puzzled. '*She* was in Bateau's office, *she* was in the lateral and I had to save her – but it *wasn't* Marva and it wasn't me. Not at the time. But it is now.'

I put the cup down on the floor. 'I can help you with that,' I said.

He was going over it again when I led him into the bedroom, where he kept his system.

He was slow to manifest; he kept putting some obscuring element between us, a waterfall, a fog bank, a dark pane of glass. But he would have had to have been in much better shape to maintain such a thing within the system. Like the unforgiving light in a dressing room, being mind-to-mind showed no mercy.

Actually, it wasn't so bad. It gave me time to get accustomed to what I was going to see.

They were melting into each other, Sovay and Anwar; as if they were mirror images instead of two different sides, the mirrors making a V-shape and slowly moving so that the images were being sucked into each other. Except Anwar was losing.

All his characters became him.

She lied, but not about that.

The Anwar part looked disappointed. *Where is she?*

An environment was forming around us, something vague and semidark, like the inside of a cave or a grotto. There was no sign of anyone else besides us. *I don't know*, I said. *She didn't leave a forwarding address.*

You're not quite her, *either,* Sovay said.

I lost a lot of memory, I told him. *If that's what makes any of us what we are, then I'm really not Marva at all. Not the original fake and not the original fake fake. A new fake.*

Dark patches in the space around us began to swirl lazily like oil floating on the surface of water, as if a relaxation exercise had leaked through, except it wasn't completely abstract. Here and there, there were hints of pictures – faces, mostly, but they didn't last long enough to identify.

She was right, Sovay said suddenly. *It* is *more intimate than a married couple should be. Than* lovers *should be. Than we ever should have been.*

The portrait of Rowan floating over his head looked as if it had been done in dark smoke and could blow apart at any moment. Somehow, it didn't.

But she wasn't lying, he added. *It wasn't really me she was mind-to-mind with. Just two Downs hypeheads who wanted to be me. She wanted them to be me, too, you see. She was trying to fix them, focus them on her. But it didn't work. It couldn't have. They needed you for that, not her.*

Because I *had* been mind-to-mind with him. Of course. I wondered about Dionysius. Was he still sitting in the crib, in Coney Loe's cubicle, waiting for Rowan to come and get him, or waiting for me to come back? There hadn't been enough of him to fix … had there?

Anwar …

… is going to be absorbed, of course, Sovay said, sounding regretful in a detached way. An ego that swallowed other people whole didn't have much room in it for regret over someone else's misfortune. *It's what I had to do. I never had the knack of the mirror like you did. All the characters had to be me, because I couldn't give myself up to anyone else. But you could. That was why I went mind-to-mind with you. I thought if I could feel the way you did it, I could learn how.*

Rowan's portrait had been replaced by drifting scenes of the two of us together. The symbolism was prosaic – conjoined rings, giant stars orbiting each other, galaxies colliding –

I was confused. An aquarium? An ocean. And one lonely figure swimming through it, immersed but never part of it.

Knowledge isn't ability, Sovay said sadly.

Truth is cheap, information costs. Who had said that to me? Coney Loe, truth whore. Did that make the truth a pimp?

The force of Sovay's presence began to increase. *Things coming back to you* he said. Approval radiated from him like heat. *When the right things come back to you, you'll be her again. For some of us, who we are depends on who we're with. And you're with me now.*

And you wanted me so badly because of the mirror, I said. *Not for love, that was something you already had in the real world. You just wanted someone else who could be you.*

But it's not a true reflection, Sovay. It's a funhouse *mirror, and that's something else altogether.*

The mirror encircled us completely. The reflections weren't clear yet, but they were forming.

No!

His negation came from his pure core of self, undisguised and uncivilized, a baby's first cry and one that had never ended, not for him; Sovay then, Sovay now, Sovay always.

It wasn't a bad thing, really, for someone like him, not until he had started trying to remake the world in his own image. Then he had looked into my image and found a Brain Police cop staring back at him –

The mirror shattered in an explosion all the more violent for being soundless. Fragments flew out in all directions.

Didn't matter; it was only his perspective, and it was my mirror. But his image had fallen on it and it was still there.

The memories were already beginning to spark. *When the right things come back to you, you'll be her again.*

For some of us, who we are depends on who we're with. And you're with me now. But if I *was* her, then let it be because that was who I was, not who he wanted me to be.

My own negation broke the connection.

This was one of those times when having only one eye was an advantage. It meant I could be out of the system and sighted before he was. I moved to the doorway, watching him carefully as he tucked his eyes back in. There was less of Anwar in the man who got up from the bed, looking around like someone traversing the last set of exits from a prison.

'Reinforced,' he said cheerfully. 'It's quite a feeling.'

'I'll buy that. Rowan doesn't really care which one of you she gets, does she. Which one of you Sovays. It'll be first come, first served, won't it. She didn't ask me to get the *right* Sovay – you're *all* the right Sovay. It's just a race to see who gets home first.'

He gave a short laugh. 'The right one *is* the one who gets home first.'

'Well, I've decided to make this one easy. I'm declaring you the winner. Run home, tell her you're the swiftest and the strongest, she'll never know the difference. Neither will you. Though there *have* been a lot of other changes in the non-Sovay areas of the universe. Sir Larry's is gone. The future belongs to living-room soap opera. Cheesy, sordid, and braindead, but you get to go to a lot of glamorous parties. And I never want to see you again. I won't be a fool for the Brain Police and I won't be a fool for you, or Rowan, or anyone.'

'Won't you?' he said as I turned to leave.

I hesitated, but I didn't turn around to look at him. 'What do you mean?'

'It'll come to you.' I could feel him smiling at my back as I marched through the apartment and out the door. Or maybe that was just the aftertaste he'd left in my brain.

I was about to step out onto the sidewalk when I remembered the onion-heads. *Superb*, I thought; as if I couldn't have waited, oh, ten hours before telling him off. So much for shelter. I'd really screwed that one up.

Hadn't I?

There were no onionheads in sight in either direction. Somewhere, not far away, was an air-taxi pad, but there was someplace else I had to go first, someone I had to see, and something I had to get –

The blind side of my face began to tingle, as if a fine spray of cool water was dancing on it. I wanted to stop and wait until the sensation passed but I forced myself to keep going. If the onionheads caught me out, my face would be doing more than tingling.

There was a sudden tiny flash of light from the empty socket, followed by another and then another, until it seemed to be filled with a multitude of twinkling stars. Or glittering dust.

Or the fragments of a shattered mirror, still free-falling toward reassembly.

I heard the rattle of the chain before I saw them, but there was nowhere to go – the one storefront near the corner was empty and the rest of the building sealed up. I jammed my fists into my pockets, put my head down like a gofer on a rush-job, and stalked across the street, trying to keep focused on where I was going rather than the flashing from my blind side.

It fooled the onionheads long enough for me to get across the street and it might have fooled them even longer if I'd been able to resist sneaking a glance at them to see if they were watching. They were, and I must have looked like the main attraction in a fox hunt. They let go with something that sounded like a cross between a scream and a yodel and I was off in an unsteady sprint with the couple pounding after me, howling for reinforcements.

I passed a doughnut shop just as someone was coming out; a whiff of appetite gas hit me right in the face and the blast of hunger pangs almost knocked me sideways. It mixed with the nagging, repetitive music from the soundtrack joint next door. I stumbled into the gutter, through several occupied parking places and then into the middle of the street, barely missing the front of a van. Through the windshield, the angry driver looked green, but it might have been a trick of the light, the real light or the strobing light from my blind side.

In the next lane, a taxi screamed to a stop several feet in front of me and flipped on its for-hire sign. I ran past it and hit the opposite sidewalk. By the sound, two more onionheads had joined the chase, though they weren't any

faster than the first two. But sooner or later, they were going to pick up a pair who could sprint faster than I could even chained together, and my chest was burning so badly that the bile was coming up out of my throat.

I swung around the next corner thinking that the next time I saw a taxi, I wasn't going to be so panicked that I ran past it instead of using precious seconds to open the passenger door. If I ever spotted another one that would stop for me.

And then it was too late even for that, because they'd finally gotten smart instead of fast. The sidewalk ahead of me was clearing in a hurry to make room for the pair running at me from the other end of the block, chain held at neck level and no breath wasted on scary howls.

The pawnshop sign seemed to jump out of nowhere. I hit the door at a run. It stuck for one horrible, endless moment and then gave, dumping me on the floor inside just as the onionheads reached the spot on the sidewalk where I'd been a moment before.

They didn't even bother screaming in rage. I lay on my belly, trying to breathe, listening to the rest of them congregate outside behind me. They couldn't come in and get me and I couldn't leave; I wondered how the pawn-broker was going to take that.

The door swung shut, muffling the sound of onionhead grumbling and chain-clanking. After a while I raised my head and looked around.

What's the good word?

The flash from my blind side filled my head, overwhelming everything else. I couldn't feel the pain in my chest or the hardness of the floor under me; there was only the bright white light. As I watched, it began to pulse, brighten-ing and then dimming, and in between, I could see the pictures, like small, sequential chunks out of a holo show. Or maybe an outdoor soap opera.

… pull free for a moment, two moments, three, and hold on tight, hold on, because this can't last long … the overdose of memories has disoriented her and while she's too lost to be conscious, there's time enough to step inside here … the pawnbroker thinks I'm her on a bender, good … one fast transaction, please … yah, in trouble again, Ofrah, yah, shouldn't have this one but I can't go purge it, what a waste … right, you take it for now, lock it up and I'll come back,

but don't give it to me, no matter what, unless I tell

you …

' *… the good word?*'

She's bent over me, hands on her knees, white hair fallen to one side and looking like this is the most amusement she's had this week …

The voice in my head faded as the mirror fragment fell into place. The mir-ror wasn't completely reassembled yet but there were plenty of pictures running on it, from all of us, Marceline, both Marvas, the one with all the memory and the one Sovay forced to existence. And me. Whoever I was.

I held out my hand and the pawnbroker helped me up. 'Thought you'd never get back here,' she said congenially. 'You *do* have the good word this time, don't you?'

'Yah,' I said. 'I've got the good word this time.' I glanced toward the door. 'For all the good that'll do me now.'

She smiled. 'Well?'

'The good word for today is **forget**,' I said, watching the scene from that night replay again on the mirror in my blind side. Had that really been **me** that night, I wondered as I followed the pawnbroker into the back room; had that been **me** pulling out of dormancy in Marceline/ Marva long enough to stash the one thing that would positively identify me as Brain Police? Funny, I didn't **feel** like Brain Police. But I didn't feel like Marva anymore, either. Not that I really had since I had come up six months before, but I'd thought that might have been because of all the direct memory I was missing. After all, the Brain Police officer was gone, I'd watched her go, washing out through the hole that had opened up in Sovay's sad imitation of a mirror –

She's coming back.

Marya?

The pawnbroker paused as she pulled the connections out of the system and looked at me. Had I spoken aloud?

All those little memories you left lying around …

Some in a pawnshop, too, I thought.

… **and we'll see if you want to be a cop again**.

Ofrah reached for my eye and I put up a hand. 'I think I'm changing my mind,' I said.

She let out an exasperated breath. 'Not here, you're not. You can change your mind if you want, but you're taking this with you. Dump it on some other unsuspecting jerk if you want but I'm not keeping it and I'm not flushing it for you.'

'But I don't want to know,' I told her.

'You don't? Too bad, tough stuff. Somebody's got to know and you're elected, not me.' She pushed me down on a well-beaten pad that might have been a mattress once. 'Everybody's got some information they're responsible for. This is yours.' She stuck her thumb in the corner of my eye and, pushed.

At first, I thought the connections for my eye had crumpled up somehow, but after a moment, I realized that feeling of a hard painful lump in my eye socket was purely psychosomatic. The body can be as fond of symbolism as the mind.

'Is that it?' I said, sitting up.

'Didn't take a minute, if that,' Ofrah said.

Maybe it hadn't, but that had been time enough for more onionheads to join the mob out front; I could hear them. It sounded like hundreds now.

'Can I go out the back way?' I asked.

'They'll have that covered. Your best bet is the roof. They don't like heights since it's never just one of them that could fall.'

'What's on the roof?'

Ofrah blinked at me. 'Nothing.'

'Then why should I go up there?'

'Are you crazy, or just stupid? To get away. You can go rooftop to rooftop until you get to a freebus depot or an air-taxi stand.'

I laughed a little. 'You mean, I wouldn't just happen to find somebody up there with an illegally parked air vehicle for a convenient getaway?'

The pawnbroker's expression was unreadable. 'Do you think you're In some kind of long-playing soap opera, or is it just a dose of reverse-paranoia in your property? Maybe now you think you're after somebody and the world Is out to make you happy?'

The pain behind my eye was receding as the information she'd given me was absorbed.

'Why didn't you just call them,' I said. 'Tell them it was here and they could come and get it.'

'Call who?'

'The Brain Police.'

'I don't mess with the Brain Police. I don't want to end up in a rehab ward with a bib and a diaper. Whatever you did is your lookout. If I'd known what you had when you dropped it on me, you'd have never have gotten out of here by the back door **or** the front.'

I nodded. 'Who am I, Ofrah?'

She roared with laughter. 'You think you're a hundred people, but that's typical of any memory junkie.' Her laughter wound down and she frowned at me, warily. 'You're Marceline, okay? What's the matter, you lose your rudder when Bateau took his fall?'

'How do you know I'm Marceline?'

'You gave me the good word,' she said, her voice cracking with annoyance. 'How else would I know?'

'Maybe Marceline gave **me** the good word.'

She shook her head. 'Jesus save me from memory junkies. Why don't you just go get yourself a new life from some persona mill if you're so hot to be somebody else? Why do you have to come around here bothering me and then acting like I'm doing something to you? I did you a favor that night. Return the favor now and get the hell out of my store. And don't ever, ever come back, okay?'

The database in my mind revolved, delivered the code sequence that

would have shut Ofrah off and brought up the Brain Police officer underneath. I wasn't authorized to do that; not that I cared much for things like authorization at the moment. But it would have been a dirty trick. The cop wasn't expecting to come up now and even a fast memory fill wouldn't help the resulting shock and disorientation. It might even hurt, depending on what memory the cop was supposed to use on the missing time – a love affair, a vacation, an illness. False, of course, but you can't maintain a functional person unless you cover up those long periods of dormancy and the person in question would never know the difference.

'Well?' she said impatiently.

I gave her a salute and headed for the front door.

She ran after me. 'What do you think you're doing?'

'Getting out.' I pulled her hand off my arm. 'And never coming back.'

'They'll stomp you into the sidewalk!'

'Will they?' I smiled. 'Maybe they'll feel sporting and let me have a head start so they can chase me first.'

A multitude of expressions flashed over her pale face. It was just the automated program of emergency procedures for when something went wrong during some operation but she didn't know that, of course. 'You can't go out there.'

No, I couldn't. I was supposed to go up to the roof and get picked up there. I glanced up at the ceiling and for a moment I wondered if maybe I **wasn't** just being paranoid.

Then I opened the door and stepped out into the middle of the onionheads.

They froze. Every last one of them froze, unable to move or shout or, by the blank looks on their faces, even think. I had to press my fist against my mouth to keep from laughing out loud.

'It's not her,' one of them said suddenly.

Like that, they were unfrozen, echoing the words as they fell back, giving me a wide berth. Onionheads giving someone a wide berth – was anybody **seeing** this? I looked around. No, of course not – the sight of an onionhead mob is better than a meltdown siren for clearing an area of innocent bystanders. And not-so-innocent bystanders.

'You're wrong,' I said to the mob, which was still backing away from me in an ever-widening circle. 'I **am** her. I deliberately violated marital territory. At least a dozen people saw me do it.'

'Whose?' someone shouted. 'Whose territory did you violate? Show us! It wasn't ours!'

'Not ours!' someone else called out, and then they were all yelling it at me, over and over: **Not ours, not ours!**

I ran out into the street, trying to look at them all, but it was hopeless. They

were onionheads and one onionhead looked pretty much like another. Which was the whole idea.

Even after they dispersed, the street remained empty and quiet for a long time. Except for distant traffic noise, the only sound came from a vehicle lifting off from where it had been illegally parked on the pawnshop roof.

There was nothing to do but go home. Not to the midtown efficiency I'd been treading time in, but to Marceline's place in the Downs. As I'd expected, she was still in residence. By remote control, of course, maintenance automatically deducted from an ever-dwindling bank account that somehow never quite dwindled to nothing. The feeling of familiarity was very slight; in a less aware state, I'd have passed it off as nothing, minor déjà vu, if that.

Had it been mostly Marceline's mistake? Or had she just been the trigger for the unfortunate conjunction of Marva and Sovay? Or had they been the trigger for **her**? The database I'd gotten back from Ofrah couldn't tell me; it wasn't geared for explanation.

Unlucky combination, I decided. Three people who should never have gotten together. And perhaps most of the blame was Marceline's. She'd been allowed to collect too many memories in the course of feeding her habit, and when she had made mind-to-mind contact with Marva, it had filled in too many blanks – those that had not been filled in when Marva and Sovay had gotten too close in the course of a love affair they had erroneously assumed was just them leading their own lives.

Or maybe it was really all Sovay's fault for being the way he was: **They all became** me. Yah. Sure did. When he had realized he was Brain Police, too – had that happened when he'd discovered me dormant behind the Marva facade, or had he discovered me because he realized what he was?

If that had been me he'd found. My head began to ache; strictly psychosomatic. I went to the one window in the apartment, over the futon, and opened it. It looked out at the side of the building next to it, but if I leaned out far enough, I could see a slice of the street, vehicles and pedestrians passing by. I had the mad thought of running downstairs and stopping people randomly. **Do you know you're an operative for the Brain Police? Do** you? **And** you? **And** you?

I put on the dataline, flipped through the channels, News reports, sitcoms, talk shows, documentaries, commercials – I paused at one for something called The Nicer Person. They'd reworked the old melty animation from Some Very Nice People.

Ah, yes. We were all Some Very Nice People, or The Nicer Person, or Power People. Maybe that had been how it had started, a decoy operation set up as a persona mill. And everyone who came in got indoctrinated – or maybe **contaminated** was a better word. And all of them mindplaying after

they left, thrillseeking, buying neuroses, selling their dreams and buying others, and the contamination was spreading like some weird mental variation on a social disease. One day the sun came up and **everybody** had joined the Brain Police.

And maybe a few people found out once in a while, they would wake up and say, **Wait a minute here, what's this doing in my life?** And the Brain Police would pay them off, give them a contract, and promise that they'd never notice the missing time. **We'll only use you when we need you; then we'll deactivate you and leave you alone, and you never even have to know if you don't want to.**

Quite a generous contract.

Don't worry about whether your life has a purpose. It does ... now.

I shut off the screen.

How'd you get so genius, figuring stuff out like you got a sherlock circuit.

Paid for it, Coney. It was very expensive information.

It would be even more expensive if the Brain Police caught up with me now. They couldn't come right out and **do** something to me – I'd give the whole thing away. Instead, they'd sent Rowan to put me on a fool's mission: find the Sovays. Yah. Thinking Sovay would trigger the reemergence of that upstanding Brain Police officer Mersine, who would go trotting home with the database intact unscratched, and uncomprehended, so that the secret could be reburied with no muss, no fuss, and life would go on. After all, the show **must** go on, especially when it's all theatre anyway.

Was it like this everywhere? I wondered. Or had things just gotten out of hand – achieved escape velocity – here in this one city?

I already knew the answer to that one. How long would it take? Another century, or just another couple of decades? Would anyone be spared? And if not, what would happen when we reached full ... saturation? Would we all just come up simultaneously, spontaneously, exploding in a surge of unity?

Or would we just explode?

And had this always been the point that mindplay had been leading us toward, from the very beginning? Whether we'd known it or not?

I turned to look at my own system, sitting next to the futon.

The cliff was still there. Sometimes it looked like the open panorama window of a sky-island, but mostly it was a cliff overlooking a blank nothing of a landscape.

Standing next to me, Marva wanted to know why. Both of her.

Because one individual can make a difference. And that's not any of us.

Marva said it wasn't Marceline, either.

It wasn't once, but it is how, I told her. **The fragmentation of being a memory junkie – that's what made it possible for me to merge with the remains**

of the Brain Police in her. Without us, she's cut off. She'll be the only person in town who isn't on the team. And they'll never know.

Marva wanted to know why it mattered, then.

Because it does. Because there should be at least one other person in the world. Someone to Escort the Brain Police out of this world and leave it to people *again*.

But would she, Marva asked skeptically.

She'll try. And now, let's go. All of us. I turned to Sovay, standing a little ways behind us, faint and not very well developed, but there nonetheless; he had come with his part of the database. *You, too*.

He didn't want to, but he wasn't strong enough to resist. When we went, the database would go with us. The Brain Police didn't really need it for their own information, but it would rob them of an easy entrée to Marceline. Which would increase her chances of survival as an individual.

Don't take any wooden memories.

She was too dormant to feel me but with any luck, she might be more cautious about what she did with herself when she came up.

The mirror shattered again when I threw it over, the pieces flying around as if in a high wind. But I'd figured it would take the combined weight of all of us to drag them down.

You know it's going to be a bad day when you wake up and the last year of your life is gone. Naturally, the first thing I do is panic.

This, they say, is the lot of the memory junkie: bad cess, bad living, tough stuff. I am not exactly in a position where I can complain to karma-rama. But who ever sets out to be a memory junkie, anyway? Ten thousand people buy memories every day but you, you ducky luck-off, you get the thunderbolt in the head. Little lucky number ten thousand, this is your life and this is your life, and this is your life, and this, too, could be your life, if you could afford to feed your habit that well. Most can't, and don't kid yourself, you won't be able to, either. Wouldn't be so bad if you could just get out and make a few memories by original recipe, but it's never your own memories that junk you up. That's the one sure mark all memory junkies share. None of us are particularly memorable citizens. If we were, maybe I'd know what happened to me.

Could be I got a nasty sclerosis grinding away from whatever I been doing during the missing time, in which case I got to hie my bad old self to a clinic for a retread. That's about as much fun as getting trepanned, with the added attraction of having the meds bitch to a fair glow for doing shit I can't even remember I did, and getting bitchier because I can't sound sorry enough.

Or it could be I been done out by the last pawnshop I went to.

Happens – you get an inexperienced operator who doesn't know the difference between *clean* and *wipe,* or you get a very experienced operator who's booked on the next flight out and doesn't have to give a shit about what the carriage trade will say. You'd think I'd have a lawsuit coming for that, and if I'd been some safe-sex day-wage priv from uptown with a receipt from a Commerce Canyon salon, there'd be no question. But someone from the Downs suing a Downs pawnshop – double zero. There wasn't an eagle in the immediate world who'd even take a call about it. That's technically discrimination, but find somebody who gives a fuck.

Could also be that I made someone mad at me, which means I'm lucky I got off this easy, and I can just get on with my life as it is now and hope it doesn't happen again.

Or I coulda been rousted by the Brain Police. In which case, I should probably just stand in the middle of the Downs with a 'Suck Me' sign on my forehead and get it over with.

All this goes through my poor old tampered-with mind in double triphammer-time, so even in my panic, I know I can neg sclerosis. The general rule is, if you know the word 'sclerosis,' you ain't got it. So there's a little relief, no bitchy what'd-you-expect-you-bad-girl lectures to sit through while I'm getting a fresh coat of myelin.

A pawnshop fuck-over is still a definite maybe. I'll have to get back to that one.

Making someone mad is also a maybe, but there's usually a few tokens of their disaffection to go along with the memory loss – shaved head, broken nose, and two black eyes. My face doesn't feel like anybody did the fandango on it, but there's something wrong with the panorama of the cracks in my ceiling. I climb out of bed and check in the bathroom mirror.

Still got all my hair. Looks like a wild animal had a restless night in it and I forgot – ha, and ha – to take the combs out. My nose *has* been broken, but not in the last twenty-four hours. It's that missing eye that tips me off that everything isn't like it should be. I squint on the trouble-shooter, checking for any misalignment in the connection that would mean something had been yanked against my will. I wish they were the fancy kind with the auto-log feature so I'd know when I'd had them out last, but for what I can pay, I'm lucky I get the whole visible spectrum. They're not even biogems, just government-surplus brown. I'm so glad I didn't make anybody mad, I could almost face the Brain Police, except that's the worst way to make *everybody* mad, even if it's not my fault. But if the Brain Police have been at me, there should be a copy of the warrant on the dataline screen, where I'd see it first thing. I stump over

to it, but it's blanko on the lousy little built-in. Except for the blinker in the corner. Message waiting. I punch for it.

Q-up and calm down – a million strung-out hypeheads can't be wrong. Carefully, now: you're not a memory junkie anymore. Before you run out the door, consider two things:
 The future is already set, only the past can be changed, and
 If it was worth forgetting, it's not worth remembering.
 Your fairy godmother

I read it over twice. The kind of life I live, I'm liable to wake up to anything, and I accept that. Like I say, I don't have a leg for a complaint with karma-rama. But apparently I have a fairy godmother and I can *almost* remember her ... certain associations are still there, like ghosts, even if the memory itself is gone. That happens, no memory ever stands completely alone. All I know is, I can trust her to give me not only the truth, but right information as well, and if she tells me something's not worth remembering, I'd do worse than to let whatever stay where it is.

She's even right about me not being a memory junkie anymore. I got no craving at the very moment and with a six-month hole, I ought to be tearing my own ratty hair out. This doesn't mean it's not gonna jump up on me never again. Unless one of us really did change the past ...

I touch the patch over my eye. Now, I'd rather have two eyes but one feels ... I don't know, *right*. I sure hope it's because it was *my* idea and not, say, Bateau's. One eye and a memory loss is something he'd do to teach somebody a lesson. But I don't feel punished and Bateau never lets anybody go without feeling punished; it's part of the fun for him.

I start to punch in a phone number and something makes me stop, some kind of bad feeling I can't quite get a hold of to look at. Yah, but shit, what am I supposed to do, watch six months of archives and try to figure out my place in the universe from that? I'm nothing and nobody, and with my memory gone, I could be looking at the story of my life and not know it.

It almost makes me sick, but I get the number punched in. The screen lights up on the seventh ring.

'You look like a bad year in hell,' I say. 'This got anything to do with something I misplaced?'

Anwar's got this look like I'm the last person on earth he ever expected to hear from. 'I don't know,' he says, finally. His voice sounds like his throat's full of slow-hardening glue. 'What did you lose?'

'I don't know,' I say. 'Can I come over and look for it at your place?'

'Sure,' he says. 'Sure, come right now.'

I break the connection. Just as I'm getting up, some glitch throws the message from my fairy godmother back up on the screen instead of blanking it.

The future is set, only the past can be changed, and if it's worth forgetting, it's not worth remembering.

Okay, so I'll remember it anyway, and if I don't like it, I'll just forget it again. Ofrah'll always do business with me.

And I really want to see Anwar. I could have seen him just yesterday, but as far as I know right now it's been six months. If that's closed and done with because the past got changed and I forgot, then that's how it is, but I got a right to know.

I mean, it's my life, isn't it?

TEA FROM AN EMPTY CUP

For:
Ellen Datlow,
The sister I never had
The editor I've always needed

Keith Ferrell
Who made me start it
In the first place
And then kept demanding more

Beth Meacham
For patience, insight, patience,
Good humor, intelligence, patience,
Excellence in editing, and did I mention patience?

Joy Chamberlain
For reading it so conscientiously and
Naming it so perfectly

Merrilee Heifetz
Who endured every moment
Right along with me
And didn't complain
Although she could have

I know, that's a lot of dedication
For one book –
So are they.

These people, each in their various direct and/or indirect ways, made my world a better place. Thank-yous to:

Gardner Dozois and Susan Casper (for decades of friendship and good times), Cindy Wike (a real superhero), John and Judith Clute (for the upstairs room), Mike Harrison (for being so supportive), Mary Ellen Rose (I'm proud to call you my friend), the Kansas City Science Fiction Society (especially for all that help on the last night), overlapping with the Borders SF Book Club 1994-6 (we miss you all), Jack Womack (for last-minute accommodations and great conversation), Maggie Flynn (for her usual wonderfulness), Kim Newman (for incitement to emigrate), Paul McAuley (for having talent *and* class), The Artist Formerly Known As Jael (for improving the quality of our Sundays), Oisin Murphy-Lawless (for energy and enthusiasm), Mic Cheetham (more fabulous in an hour than most people are in their whole lives), Tricia Sullivan (you *go*, girl), Jeannie Hund (girlfriend, you're world-class), my son Bob and his Grandma Helen (for putting so much life in my life), our friends at Harringay Cars (for making sure Bob and Grandma get there and back again safely), and my husband, the Original Chris Fowler (for the rose, and everything after).

IN THE BEGINNING

'Now, why would anyone become a prostitute?' the white guy asked, sipping his iced coffee through a long, skinny straw.

Across the table, the Japanese guy raised his eyebrows, making his guarded face into a mask of mild surprise. 'You mean, somebody *isn't?*'

The white guy's laughter echoed in the mostly empty cafe. 'Oh, man. Things must be really *non-ruly* on your planet.'

The Japanese guy eyed the tall glass of iced coffee sweating pretty beads of condensation as the white guy sipped at it. Retro beverages were so all-pervasive these days, it was impossible to tell whether anyone really liked iced coffee. According to rumor, most places just poured day-old crude over ice and disguised it with artificial flavors and ersatz cream. 'That's Nature for you. With some she's into the red zone, with others, there isn't even a meter. You goin' my way?'

'What kind of value do I get?' asked the white guy, watching the other smooth the front of his Guinness T-shirt. Not sake, but Guinness, for chrissakes; what kind of an Oriental was he, anyway? He even turned up his nose at tea.

'What kind of value you lookin' for?' Without waiting for an answer, the Japanese guy dug in the well-traveled bag parked on the seat beside him and came up with a pouch the white guy recognized as the carrying case for a very expensive model of hotsuit. Then he put his other fist on the table, paused as if trying to decide something and then opened his hand to reveal a sapphire-blue gel cap on his palm.

'Christ.' The white guy rolled his eyes. 'What'd you do, put your brain under the pillow and you got that instead of a dime?'

'Hey, it's not what you think,' the Japanese guy said. 'There's a creation myth in there. Among other things. And it's all genuine.'

'Uh-huh.'

'I *swear*. Distilled from millennia of racial memory –'

'Uh-*huh*.'

'I could show you the chromosome they stripped it offa,' the Japanese guy said defensively. 'One hundred purebreds got scraped for this. *One hundred*. In a *hospital*. This is pure *pharmaceutical* –'

'So I take it and what? What's the big myth?'

'Lots of big myths. All the big myths you want. The big creation myth.'

'So tell me about it.'

The troubled look on the Japanese guy's face wasn't one of his rehearsed expressions. 'You don't really want me to spoil it for you.'

'If it's so great, you can't spoil it. Come on, let's hear it. Just one.'

The Japanese guy hesitated for a long moment.

'I just want to know what I'm getting,' the white guy persisted. 'That's how we do things on *my* planet.'

'Sure, but just telling it doesn't do it justice.'

'I believe you. All I want is just to know one thing to watch for. What if I think it looks boring and I skip it? I could do that, you know, I'm not Japanese. I might not know better.'

The Japanese guy let out a breath. 'Okay. There were these two gods, Susanoo and Amaterasu. They were brother and sister –'

'*Susan?*' The white guy's perfect features were scornful as he flicked the menu button to his right for another iced coffee. 'You expect me to believe *Susan* is a Japanese name?'

'Not *Susan*, you idiot, *Susanoo*. And that was the *brother's* name, Amaterasu was the *sister*. You gonna let me tell this or not?'

The white guy waved carelessly with one hand. One of the wait staff materialized so suddenly, he almost hit her in the face. Seeming not to notice, she slid another iced coffee onto the table and removed the empty glass. The white guy took it, closed his thin Anglo lips around the fat, transparent straw and sucked hard, his cheeks hollowing. His blue eyes stared hard at the Japanese guy. 'So?' he said, taking his lips from the straw. 'Tell!'

The Japanese guy nodded resignedly. 'Susanoo was a one-god riot on wheels, tearing everything up,' the Japanese guy said, watching the white guy continue to drink his day-old crude. Maybe it was true, what his foster father used to say years ago, that Westerners thought using garbage for culture was recycling. His foster father had been white, a minor bureaucrat named Clark who always wanted to be anything else but what he was. This guy seemed to suffer from the same ailment. 'Party time was all the time, it was all really *non-ruly*, as someone I know would say.

'So one day, Amaterasu, who was always real patient with this *yabo*, was weaving sacred garments with her sacred maidens and Susanoo tosses this dead, flayed horse into the room, just to hear all the sacred ladies scream. Which they do, and one of the sacred maidens even accidentally pricks her sacred genitals and dies.'

'Oh, *that* could happen.' The white guy grinned sarcastically. 'I know lots of people with their good parts pierced and they're all real alive, still.'

The Japanese guy stared back at him flatly. 'Sure. If you call that living.'

'Hey, if it's not your idea of excitement, it's not, but you can't tell me there are no Japanese with pierced –'

'*Seiken shirazu,*' said the Japanese guy, putting his head in his hands for a moment. 'Are you gonna let me tell this?'

'Yeah-yeah. A sacred maiden takes a sacred prick in her sacred genitals and dies. So then what?'

The waiter who had brought the iced coffee set a cup of green tea in the middle of the table. The Japanese guy looked up, furious. 'Get that outa here.'

'*I* ordered that, thank you very much.' The white guy pulled it over next to the iced coffee.

'Amaterasu gets even more fed up with her *yabo* brother than I am with you,' the Japanese guy went on, glowering at the tea, 'and she goes into this cave to sulk. That's it – the whole world goes dark.'

The white guy raised one skeptical eyebrow. 'The *whole* world? Or just Japan?'

'Back then, Japan *was* the whole world, *manuke*.'

'You *wish*.'

'No, *you* wish, all of you, you *gaijin* sheep –'

'Whoo, gaijin, the man says!' The white guy raised both hands and wiggled his fingers. 'Sampling those Mishima breakbeats again, are we?'

The Japanese guy slipped the gel cap into a tiny pocket on his shirtsleeve and made getting-ready-to-get-up-and-leave motions.

'Okay, okay, I'm sorry. Finish the story. Or was that it?'

'All the other gods got together outside the cave and tried to get her to come out again, but she wouldn't.' The Japanese guy paused as if he were trying to decide if he really wanted to continue. 'Then the Dread Female of Heaven –'

'The *who*? Of *what*?'

'The Dread Female. Of Heaven.' The Japanese guy groaned. 'Okay, what's your problem now?'

'What's so dread about her?'

The Japanese guy's smile was sly. 'You'll find out if you're lucky. The Dread Female of Heaven started dancing and dancing and dancing, and she starts getting very aroused, and all the other gods start getting very aroused, because this is a very sexy dance. And at the hottest part, she does this really, really hot move, so hot that it makes everyone go off. Including her. So everyone's laughing –'

'*Laughing*?' The white guy's face was incredulous. 'You guys *laugh* when you come?'

'You could be the lucky winner who finds out,' the Japanese guy said, unperturbed. 'The gods laugh. Demons laugh. If they let you in on things, you'll laugh too.'

'I bet. So that's it? Everybody comes and laughs, ha-ha, happy ending? Or do we get to ride up and down in the cave?'

'What do you think this is, a theme park?'

'Oh, hell, I can go to any club in the *universe* to see somebody dance –'

'Not like the Dread Female,' said the Japanese guy confidently.

'No? Half a block from here, there's this woman, she's got *six* rings, all of them charged, *inside* –'

'You're right. I'd dread *that*, I'm surprised you don't.' The Japanese guy looked revolted. 'What if it got fried in there? What if it got fried *off*?' He shuddered. 'Anyway, aren't you married?'

'Yeah, I'm married, but it's nothing serious. It's not like I told her my real name or anything.' The white guy spread his hands. The backs were scarred, deliberately, but not very well. Home brew – someone had tried to brand over a scarification or vice versa. The resulting keloids weren't decoration, just damage. The Japanese guy couldn't stand the sight. 'If I want to get my magic wand charged and polished, I can go anywhere. Hell, I can even go *home*. I thought you had something here, and you're gonna give me a hard-on over some ass-shaker. Dread Female of Heaven, sure. Mistress Inga the Dominatrix can suck the marrow out of your bones without mussing her hair.'

'If she saw Ama no Uzume's sacred genitals, she'd fall down coming and laughing like a hyena.' The Japanese guy put up a hand as the white guy started to say something. 'Look, I guess I was wrong about you. You're just too *out here* for this stuff –'

The white guy was halfway out of his seat. 'You callin' *me* a fuckin' *tourist*? Shithead, do you know *who I am*?'

The Japanese guy smiled with half his mouth. 'Everybody knows who you are. You've told everyone often enough about it. But even if you really did it –'

'*I got witnesses!*'

Across the room, the person who had brought the tea paused in the act of resetting the fractals on one of the tabletops and stared at them with open and unabashed curiosity.

'And I wasn't that doped, either,' the white guy added sulkily. 'Tiny dose. Not even enough to convict me for possession.'

'Hey, *I* don't care if you were doped. This ain't the Olympics. And who doesn't have witnesses?' said the Japanese guy, smiling at the waiter genially. 'Big brother's watching, little brother's watching, big sister's tapping the phone, little sister's stalking your ass – or they all got bots to do it, which is pretty much like the same thing. You can't do *anything* without an audience. Guy like you'ud probably kill himself if he *didn't* have an audience. Sure, they all saw you go through the out door. And even if you really did it, you were doped and you only did it once. *I* think that's all you *can* do it. Once. Only once. *I* think that no matter what, you *still* got to strip down and take it the old-fashioned way – by hand. Or your wife.'

'So what are you, a fuckin' priest of, what's it called, Shintu? Hindo?'

'Our priests don't have to be celibate. I'm not saying I don't have anything I want *out here* when the mood hits me. I'm saying you're too *out here* to have stuff any other way.'

The white guy rolled his eyes. 'Oh, and I suppose *your* body isn't *out here*'

'No, it isn't,' snapped the Japanese guy. 'That's the trouble with you people. Your body's not really *out here*. Your body's *in here*.' He leaned forward over the table and tapped his head. 'Your whole body is in here, and nowhere else. Your neck gets broken, the whole thing's useless – but you can go *in here* and find it all again. You can get part of it cut off and taken away, but that part will still be *in here*.'

'Oh, everybody's heard about *that* stuff,' said the white guy. 'My mother used to talk about this ghost tooth she had like amputees got ghost limbs –'

'*Aitsu wa kusomitai!* Now he's tellin' me about his mother's fuckin' ghost *tooth*,' the Japanese guy told the startled waiter, who had moved on to adjust another tabletop.

'How come we aren't getting any fractal shit?' The white guy rubbed the table surface as if friction might get the patterns started.

'Fractal shit.' The Japanese guy shook his head. 'I don't know what I'm wasting my time with you for, you won't get it. *None* of you whites'll get it, not the ones like you. You people, you lost your souls a long time ago, you sold them for a good parking space. You know every time a white person is born, a new franchise opens at the mall?'

'Yeah?' said the white guy evenly. 'Well, every time some jerk-off cuts up a credit card, a sushi bar goes out of business.'

The Japanese guy blinked. 'Now, that's probably true.' He took the gel cap out of his sleeve pocket and held it out to the white guy again. 'So. You want it?'

The white guy picked it up off his palm and held it between two fingers. After a moment, he put it down. 'Not enough.'

'Not enough,' the Japanese guy echoed.

'Not enough.'

'You're saying it's not enough?'

'It's not.'

The Japanese guy shook his head. 'So what's missing? The password's in there. You put on your hard-hat – hell, I'm even throwing in my lucky hotsuit – you tune in, you give the password and –'

'And there I am in Japanese Disneyland for, what – all of ten minutes?' The white guy made a face. 'Forget it. You can have this, you and the rest of the whores.'

'Now, *that* I can't help you with,' the Japanese guy said sadly. He stared down at his hands on the table so intently, the white guy leaned forward to see if there was something going on, if he were somehow getting fractals on his side of the table while his own side remained blank. 'That's between you

and your gods. I can give you the tools, the entrée, call it how you like. But I can't give you the attention span, and I can't correct for shortsightedness. You believe you'll get a ten-minute entertainment, that's *exactly* what you'll get. But if you're ready to go all the way to the red zone and then push past *that* – well, who knows? You just might find the out door again and this time you might just go all the way through it and out the other side. How'd you do it in the first place, by believing it was impossible?'

The white guy licked his thin, pale lips. 'It doesn't *sound* like enough. In the end, it's all just story time.'

'Hey, the myths don't give themselves up that easy, you know. We got to work hard for them. The problem with you pale-asses is, you never really learn to live beyond your senses. When you go in, you got to have all going on *for* you. We use a hotsuit and a hard-hat to get the fire going. You guys use it *instead* of the fire. See? You're all like that. Except maybe the Catholic Italians. The full ethnics raised in the faith, those troopers can fly without a plane.'

'Orthodox Russians got it all over them,' the white guy said. 'And Caribes got it all over everyone. Voodoo –'

'Yeah, well, Caribes aren't pale-asses.'

'Yeah, yeah, yeah. Look, why don't you just give me a hint about how I'm supposed to prolong the experience. Am I supposed to say, "Hey, wait a minute," to the Dread Heavenly Female?'

'You got my ID, all my accounts. You can make your own contacts easy.'

The white guy wrinkled his nose. 'And where does that leave you?'

'Don't tell me you're worried for my welfare? How un-Gatsby-esque of you.'

'Very funny –'

'All right, how nonwhite, then.'

'Now, *look*, willya? We've known each other a long time, and I let you get away with a lot of that white stereotyping shit because most of the time it's pretty funny. But I'm tired of getting beat over the head with crimes committed by some fuckin' *urgly* I never met and never got the benefits from, especially when you start sounding like you mean it. You wanna see my Japanese-couple-looking-for-an-apartment routine? I do it for Australians, they think it's a fuckin' hoot. It's the one where the landlord finds out the couple have moved into his bathroom and they can't stop talking about how *spacious* it is –'

The waiter, who was now at the next table, let out a half-strangled laugh and then tried to disguise it as a cough. They both stared at him for a moment before the white guy turned back to the Japanese guy and gave him a triumphant look.

'Right,' he said. 'You see how you can get laughs with material other than the old shit about thud-stupid, blotchy white guys trying to pave over Brazil, using mahogany toothpicks, and stuffing themselves with roasted harp seal

and chicken-fried peanut-butter-and-bacon sandwiches. There's a whole bunch of white people never got to live like that and wouldn't want to. Believe it or not, my parents didn't push me out on the street when I was eight, they actually raised me till I left school.'

The Japanese guy pressed his lips together hard for a moment. 'Wow, you didn't have to walk the streets till you were twelve? You probably didn't make much.'

'Oh, very funny. *Very* funny. In case you really don't know your history, Thailand was where they had the kiddie-sex holiday tour business all sewed up.'

The Japanese guy's eyes were flat. 'Japan was very far away from Thailand.'

'Yeah, and Japan's not even really *there* anymore, so it's easy to make all kinds of claims. *And* denials. Isn't it.'

'Get to the point.'

'Okay. The point: I'm sick and tired of the insensitive white asshole jokes, okay? Give it a rest.'

The Japanese guy shrugged. 'Fine. Sorry. Didn't know you had a problem with it.'

'Well, now you do.' The white guy folded his arms. 'Where was I?'

'I was saying how you were getting all my accounts and passwords and you suddenly wanted to know where that left me.' The Japanese guy smiled with half his mouth again. 'You were concerned for my welfare in a way I found, uh, uncharac – ah –' He gave another shrug. 'You were concerned.'

'Yeah, of course. I don't want to go down on some kinda weird fraud charge. You know, some night I'm on-line having a few laughs with Ms. Dreadful Heaven and suddenly, I fail the authentication because you decide to show up, too.' He finished his tea in a gulp. 'You get my date with Dready, I get canned for bootlegging.'

The Japanese guy started to laugh and then let it trail off. 'Oh, yeah, I hadn't thought of that.'

'Well, shit, you oughta.'

'I was being facetious, you insensitive white asshole. It wouldn't happen.'

'Who says, you insensitive yellow asshole?'

'*I* says. Because I'd be turning over the whole package to you. You get every-thing, including the stuff it took me years to layer on. All yours. All of it.'

The white guy opened his mouth to say something and then stopped. His eyes narrowed and he tilted his head first to one side and then the other, scrutinizing.

'*What?*' The Japanese guy drew back a little.

'Why?'

'Why *what?*'

'Why are you being so generous?' The white guy put his elbows on the

table. 'What's the take-up here? This is like one of those going-out-of-business sales, everything must go. You going out of business?'

The Japanese guy shrugged. 'You can't appreciate a deal when someone offers it to you, you got more problems than I do.'

'I don't know about *that*.' The white kid stared from under his brows. '*I* think maybe *you* got more problems than anyone and you're trying to dump them in a hurry. Who's gonna kick in my door looking for you?'

'No one,' the Japanese kid said confidently.

'Uh-huh. Not even, oh, some dreadlocked heavenly female?'

The Japanese guy laughed. 'Only if you program it that way.'

The white guy laughed with him and started to get up. 'Well? You gonna tell me to wait a minute, hold on? Something?'

'Nope.'

'Why not?'

The Japanese guy's smile was wistful. 'I'm tired. I'm a lover, not a salesman. I'm just gonna take this to someone more spiritual, someone who can appreciate what I'm offering and wants some good value. I'm looking to go into business for myself and I'm trying to raise some start-up. You're in the mood to decline, it's all right. Other people's money spends as well as yours.'

'Yeah?' The white guy sat down again.

'Yeah. I got a lot going for me. I got connections, I got favors to call in, I got the right attitude. I'm just poor is all.'

'How can you be poor workin' for who you work for?'

'I just *am*,' snapped the Japanese guy. 'The money's good but the expenses are high, and there's no employee retirement plan, *okay*?'

The white guy squinted as if everything they had talked about were on the table in front of him, and he would have been able to see it if his eyesight had been better. 'Suppose I buy *some* of it.'

The Japanese guy made a pained face. 'It's a fuckin' *package*, you can't buy *some* of a fuckin' *package*. That's like trying to buy *some* of a house. You get a living room, a couple of walls, half a kitchen, no plumbing, no roof – come *on*.'

The white guy sighed. 'Okay, okay, you win. But just talk to me a minute here: there's the myths, and there's the directions to the real Tokyo, right?'

The Japanese guy made a funny kind of nodding motion with his head, jerking his chin up first and then down, as if he were trying to nod without nodding.

'Right. So how am I supposed to find that?'

'Now, there's the key to the whole problem with you pale-asses. You don't want to do *anything* without a hint book and a crib sheet. Tell you what, I'll just find someone who really means business and have them send you a description of the whole thing on a postcard from the Ginza.'

'Wait, wait, *wait*. I don't think it's so unfair to be askin' for a little tiny *hint*. I'm not Japanese, after all.'

'You keep thinking that way, you're never gonna get into Tokyo. They're gonna see you comin' and send you to Chinatown with the rest of the tourists. With my package, you really *will* be Japanese.'

'Fine, I'll take it. Give it here.'

The Japanese guy shoved the pouch and the gel cap over to him. He stared at it and then looked up skeptically.

'What now,' sighed the Japanese guy, sounding put-upon.

'That's *not* the whole package and don't try to tell me it is,' the white kid said, pointing at the gel cap. '*Nobody* can chem up everything, not even the Japanese.'

'The rest is on-line. Take the gel cap, it puts this marker in your fluids. That's the passkey.'

'Oh, *beautiful*.' The white guy was disgusted. 'I got to bleed for this.'

'Not if you're a secretor. You a secretor?'

The white guy shrugged. 'I don't get asked that question a whole lot.'

'Most people are. You could be one of the few who aren't, so I guess you'll have to bleed after all, just in case. But just one time and the suit'll take care of it for you. It's a small price to pay.'

The white guy's face emptied of all expression. ' "What doth it profit a man to gain the whole world and lose his soul?" '

'Huh?' The Japanese guy blinked at him. 'I guess you measure that by how big a world you have to gain and what kind of soul you have to lose.' Now he looked alarmed. 'What brought that on? Don't tell me you're deep.'

'If I am, it's a surprise to me, too,' said the white guy, troubled. 'I dunno what that was. All of a sudden, I was … I don't know. I got a premonition, and it wasn't just a feeling. It was more like a vision. Or *almost* a vision. But it wasn't *my* vision.'

'You're having someone else's visions already?' said the Japanese guy skeptically.

'Sure. That's the whole point, isn't it? Somebody else's life flashes before your eyes?' The white guy laughed a little, but he looked funny.

The Japanese guy frowned, suspicious. 'You got something in your blood already?'

'No, no.' The white guy shook his head. 'Not even remotely. No.' He was trying not to squirm under the Japanese guy's gaze. 'And anyway, it would be all cleared out now.'

The Japanese guy made a disdainful noise. 'Don't count on *that*, pilgrim. Some of that stuff, it digs in for good. You think you're clean, you drop in a new dose and baboom – ten-point brainquake on the Richter scale, no survivors. Or maybe it's not that bad,' he added as the white guy rolled his eyes.

'Maybe you drop into this fantastic erotic scene with the hotbody of your secret dreams and then you suddenly find out you got to spend the whole thing as a raccoon. Or the hotbody's a raccoon and you're an artichoke – and you *like* it that way. Even *after* you disconnect.'

'Yeah, well, that happens sometimes. I ain't afraid of what I'll find out about myself. I know some losers that've found out a lot worse than that.'

'So what's all that losing your immortal soul stuff about?'

The white guy grabbed up the pouch and the gel cap. 'Hell.' He got to his feet, pushed a few bar-code tabs through the payment slot at the edge of the table, and saluted good-bye from the center of his forehead with his index finger. 'See you somewhere, sometime,' he said and made his way between the tables, heading for the exit.

'Not if I can help it,' the Japanese guy muttered, watching him go. Off to his next Big Bajoor, maybe, or hot score, or same old tired hustle. For all he knew, the white guy would sell the gel cap to the first sucker he bumped into on the street and just use the hotsuit for masturbation fantasies.

And so what if he did? He himself no longer cared, just as long as they were gone, out of his life, out of his world, all his worlds. And vice versa.

What the hell. The pale-ass might actually see something like the creation myth. Stranger things had happened. *Much* stranger things had happened, and some of them had happened to him.

EMPTY CUP [I]

Most of the people on the dance floor were Floating. Yuki slid between bodies, shouldering some of them aside. They moved for her unprotesting, glad of the extra stimulation. By brushing past, she had probably brought several dozen of them to orgasm. Call it the ripple effect, or the domino theory at work. Perhaps somewhere, someone was writing a scholarly treatise comparing the ripple effect with the domino theory as functions of current nostalgia for the drugs of a bygone era. *Yes, they called the actually quite primitive precursors 'Xtacy' in those days (click here for refs for 'Extasy,' 'Ecstasy,' and 'E'). While we may consider that another example of late-twentieth-century hyperbole, we should also remember that if we had to live in the late twentieth century, we'd call Floating 'ecstasy' too.*

She should have gone into academia, she thought. Ash would have reacted to that idea by nodding gravely, pumping a fist up for emphasis, and having another dose. She wasn't much for it herself. The hypersensitivity that most

users found so sensual and arousing reminded her too much of artificial reality, with all of the artificial of a hotsuit, but without any reality to use it on.

Oh, what's that *supposed to mean anyway, 'artificial reality'?* Tom used to say to her whenever she used the term. *If it's* reality, *how can it* possibly *be artificial?* But that was Tom. Questions and answers, not necessarily in that order, not necessarily correct, or even matching.

Where are you, Tom?

That depends, Yuki. Do you believe in the hereafter?

What if I say I don't know?

Then how can you know what you're here after?

It should have been a groaner, but in the terse back-and-forth of emessaging, there had been no groans and no laughter, only the sound of her own voice alternating with a stranger's. Somehow, after a lifetime of friendship, she had never managed to put a sample of his voice on her service, so his email came through in an impostor's voice, a neutral contralto that refused to commit itself to male or female. It made everything seem more bizarre.

Not that Tom had ever been so terribly normal. He didn't really know what normal was.

And you do? She could hear Tom asking, but in the impostor voice of her emessage service, not his own.

Yes, I do. You don't have to be *normal to know it when you see it.* She emerged on the other side of the dance floor, facing the corral of tables where Ash had told her she would find Joy Flower sitting in her regular spot, scanning the crowd for likely prospects.

To be chosen as one of Joy's Boyz was prestigious for the duration, if ultimately futile and empty. Joy Flower never kept a Boy forever, no matter how fond she might have become of him. Ex-Boyz who resurfaced in the general population were conspicuous by their exness, and also by the uniform refusal (*inability*, it was whispered) to discuss their tenure among the chosen, which made it all but impossible to find out what had happened to the ex-Boyz who didn't reappear. Like Tom.

There were rumors of the usual kinky sex things, as well as the unusual. Joy Flower was sexually insatiable due to an experimental brain implant gone wrong. No, gone *right.* No, she was really just a celibate procurer for a cabal of rich and powerful perverts and the Boyz were the ones with the implants, to keep them able to perform on request; the same implants later prevented them from talking to the media.

Other things were hinted at in almost inaudible whispers, about the Boyz who had vanished. Dead in hideous ways. No, *worse* than dead, shut away in secret clinics and hospitals, braindead but maintained on life support as their bodies were parted out to rich and powerful invalids who needed new hearts, livers, lungs. No, they were installed in the world's fanciest barn, pumped full

of nutrients, massaged daily for a month, then butchered and roasted for the palates of a cabal of rich and powerful flesh eaters. And their pets, some of whom were Boyz, others the offspring of Boyz and mutant, almost-humans.

Rumors seemed to be clouding her vision as well as her thoughts. She realized she had been staring at a woman sitting at one of the back row tables farthest from the dance floor. The woman was gazing levelly back at her. She had thick, blue-black hair cut in an old-fashioned pageboy. Behind her right ear, a rose cycled from white to pink to shades of red, deepening progressively until it finally turned black. Then it reversed itself, black becoming deepest arterial red and then lightening, to pink and back to white. Her clothing, a stylistic variation on a suit, also old-fashioned, did not change colors, though the slightest move sent moiré patterns shimmering through the material.

Yuki felt nervous laughter threaten. People like this – whatever they were, rich, powerful, or just stone lucky – always seemed to be either deliberately making themselves ugly or just ridiculously obvious. Of course, it could have been some wannabe hoping to get mistaken for the genuine article, or a professional facsimile covering a scheduled appearance while the real person relaxed elsewhere, spared the ordeal of Being Seen without having to remain un-Seen.

Either way, the woman would expect to be treated as if she were Joy Flower, Celebrity Aristocrat. Yuki was annoyed. She wouldn't know if she were persuading Joy Flower to listen to her in person or by proxy, or just shadow dancing with an unsanctioned impersonator.

Quickly she scanned the rest of the tables. There were eight or nine of them, all occupied. None of the other people looked anywhere near as promising as the shifting-color-rose lady. Bracing herself for the possibility of a harsh and embarrassing brush-off, she skirted around the outside of the seating area until she stood directly in front of the woman.

If she wasn't Joy Flower, she was an awfully good simulation, down to the look of professional indifference on her flawless face, the look of someone used to rebuffing the overtures and petitions of common slobs. Yuki hesitated. What was she going to say, just come right out and ask her what the hell she had done with Tom Iguchi?

Come clean now, Ms. Flower, did you screw him, eat him, or just throw him away? Surely Joy Flower would become so unnerved by the direct approach that she would collapse under Yuki's scrutiny and confess to have done all three, although not in that order.

And not in this reality, either, Yuki thought ruefully.

Everyone has always moved in many worlds at once, Yukiko. But the Japanese were the first to recognize that. Grandma Naoka; she had always been a strange mix of grande dame and Old Japan. She had donated her brain after death, Yuki remembered, to some kind of neural-net modeling experiment or something.

She remembered it had been a controversial thing at the time, the use of the brains of the dead for the organization and pathways, neurons, synapses – all sorts of things she didn't understand. At first, she'd been surprised. She would not have thought that her grandmother would have been either interested or approving of such a thing. But after a while, she began to imagine her grandmother's brain as the life of the neural-net party. Or maybe the afterlife, anyway. *I want to see if there is such a thing as the ghost in the machine*, she had told Yuki.

Naoka would have been able to get this woman to tell her almost anything she wanted to know without actually having to ask her any questions. Well, maybe one or two questions. Yuki smiled inwardly. Her parents had been rather careless people and she hadn't felt terribly close to them; Naoka had been the one who had given her a sense of family. Not just family, but an intense kinship that seemed to come up from a level in herself too deep to reach. As if they were related not just in flesh and blood, but at the level of their molecules, their atoms.

It was all too easy to exaggerate her grandmother's better qualities now that the old lady had progressed to the afterlife.

Try 'dead.' Or a softer term: 'passed away. Or the current favorite, a nostalgic blast from the past: 'recycled.' They all made it sound like there really was such a thing as an afterlife, where the thoughts and talents of the deceased could be accessed, perhaps even harnessed.

Her mother's mother would have made amused noises at her. *It is not a matter of whether there is such a thing as an afterlife, but whether one has the capacity to* conceive *that there is.*

Which had nothing to do with this … did it? Yuki took a slow breath, uncertain whether to stay and try to talk to the woman or leave quickly. As if sensing her indecision, the woman smiled suddenly and pointed at the empty chair to her right. Yuki sat down before she could change her mind. But this couldn't be the real Joy Flower – it just couldn't be that easy to get her attention.

Could it?

An intense feeling of awkwardness bloomed inside of her. She must look like a bumpkin with her too-short, bristly, black hair and vending-machine overalls and jacket, a bumpkin having her first stumble around the big city. She stared down at the tabletop, wishing she had thought things out better instead of charging off into the night as if she already knew what she was doing.

The woman leaned forward; behind her ear, the rose's color slid from pink to red. 'I know what you want.'

Yuki looked up from under her brows without lifting her head. 'You do?'

'Of course. A thousand others have come to me for the same reason. Always that same look to all of you. Why wouldn't I know?' Joy Flower put her very white hand on the table and lifted her index finger, pointing it at Yuki. Surprisingly, her nails were unpainted. 'But you, I like. You're true Japanese.'

Yuki frowned. If this was a Joy Flower impersonator, she – or he – had a lot of bare face talking about true anything. So maybe it really *was* Joy Flower –

'Aren't you,' the woman added patiently.

'Well –'

'Well, you're hired.' The woman pushed back her chair and stood up.

Yuki swallowed and rose slowly to her feet. 'Hired.'

'Yes. Hired. Come on.' At once, she and Joy Flower were surrounded by tall thugs, male and female. They all looked oriental but Yuki could see that it was strictly cosmetic; beautiful work of its kind, but too finished to be anything but rendered by a human hand. She and Joy Flower, by comparison, had obviously been born to their features, although Joy Flower's were a mixture of Mongol and Japanese, with a hint of a Siberian forebear. It was an unlikely combination, but authentic.

Naoka had told her about a time in the past when it had been the vogue among Japanese to have surgery to widen the eyes and eliminate the epicanthic fold so as to look *less* Oriental. *My parents had the operation*, Naoka had said, her soft face distant and unhappy. *Thought they were stupid. What did they want, to be less Japanese? But I was very young, and the very young seldom comprehend the world they live in.*

'Where are we going?' Yuki said as the woman and her entourage began herding her toward the exit.

'To work, of course,' the woman said briskly.

The bodyguards were all at least six inches taller than Yuki and she was starting to feel stirrings of claustrophobia. 'What kind of work?' She half hoped Joy Flower would find the question stupid enough to fire her as quickly as she had hired her.

'You're my new assistant.'

'What happened to the old one?' Yuki blurted.

Joy Flower didn't bother to turn around. 'Who says there was an old one?' She pushed through the exit into a dank hallway lit just brightly enough to show the mold growing in the cracked cement walls and floor. 'Vlad, get the car.'

DEATH IN THE PROMISED LAND [I]

The kid had had his choice of places to go – other countries, other worlds, even other universes, a la the legendary exhortation of e. e. cummings, oddly evocative in its day, spookily prescient now. But the kid's idea of a hell of a good universe next door had been a glitzed-out, gritted-up, blasted and blistered

post-Apocalyptic Noo Yawk Sitty. It wasn't a singular sentiment – post-Apoca-
lyptic Noo Yawk Sitty was topping the hitline for the thirteenth week in a row,
with post-Apocalyptic Ellay and premillennial Hong Kong holding steady at
two and three, occasionally trading places but defending against all comers.

Dore Konstantin didn't understand the attraction. Perhaps the kid could
have explained it to her if he had not come out of post-Apocalyptic Noo
Yawk Sitty with his throat cut.

Being DOA after a session in the Sitty wasn't singular, either; immediate
information available said this was the eighth death in as many months. So
far, no authority was claiming that the deaths were related, although no one
had specifically denied it, either. Konstantin wasn't sure what any of that
meant except that, at the very least, the Sitty would have one more month at
the number-one spot.

The video parlor night manager was boinging between appalled and
thrilled. 'You ever go in the Sitty?' she asked Konstantin, crowding into the
doorway next to her. Her name was Guilfoyle Pleshette and she didn't make
much of a crowd; she was little more than a bundle of sticks wrapped in a
gaudy kimono, voice by cartoonland, hair by van der Graaf. She stood barely
higher than Konstantin's shoulder, hair included.

'No, never have,' Konstantin told her, watching as DiPietro and Celestine
peeled the kid's hotsuit off him for the coroner. It was too much like seeing
an animal get skinned, only grislier, and not just because most of the kid's
blood was on the hotsuit. Underneath, his naked flesh was imprinted with a
dense pattern of lines and shapes, Byzantine in complexity, from the wires
and sensors in the 'suit.

They'll start calling that the latest thing in nervous systems, Konstantin
thought, mesmerized. *They'll give it a jumped-up name, like neo-exo-nervous
system, and they'll say it's generated by hotsuit wear, every line and shape
having a counterpart on the opposite side of the skin barrier. With its own
astrological sign.*

The coroner's cam operator leaned in for a shot of the kid's head and
shoulders, forcing the stringer from *Police Blotter* back against the facing
wall. Unperturbed, the stringer held her own cam over her head, aimed the
lens downward and kept taping. This week, *Police Blotter* had managed to
reverse the injunction against commercial networks at crime scenes that had
been reinstated last week. Konstantin couldn't wait for next week.

As the 'suit cleared the kid's hips, the smell of human waste fought with the
heavy odor of blood and the sour stink of sweat for control of the air in the
room, which wasn't much larger than the walk-out closet that Konstantin
had shared with her ex. The closet had looked a lot bigger this morning now
that her ex's belongings were gone, but this room seemed to be shrinking by
the moment. The coroner, her cam operator, the stringer, and DiPietro and

Celestine had all come prepared with nasal filters. Konstantin's were sitting in the top drawer of her desk.

Putting her hand over her nose and mouth, she stepped back into the hallway where her partner Taliaferro was also suffering, but from the narrow space and low ceiling rather than the air, which was merely over-processed and stale. Pleshette followed, fishing busily in her kimono pockets.

'So *bad*,' she said, looking from Konstantin to Taliaferro. Taliaferro gave no sign that he had heard her. He stood with his back to the wall and his shoulders up around his ears, head thrust forward over the archiver while he made notes, as if he expected the ceiling to come down on him. From Konstantin's angle, the archiver was completely hidden by his hand, so that he seemed to be using the stylus directly on his palm.

Never send a claustrophobe to do an agoraphobe's job, Konstantin thought, feeling surreal. Taliaferro, who pronounced his name 'Tolliver' for reasons she couldn't fathom, was such a big guy anyway that she wondered if most places short of an arena didn't feel small and cramped to him.

'*Real* goddam *bad*,' Pleshette added, as if this somehow clarified her original statement. One bony hand came up out of a hidden pocket with a small spritzer; a too-sweet, minty odor cut through the flat air.

Taliaferro's stylus froze as his eyes swiveled to the manager. 'That *didn't* help,' he said darkly.

'Oh, but wait,' she said, waving both hands to spread the scent. 'Smellin' the primer now but soon, *nothing*. Deadens the nose, use it by the *pound* here. Trade puts out a *lot* of body smell in the actioners. 'Suits *reek*.' She gestured at the other doors lining the long narrow hall. 'Like that *Gang Wars* module? Strapped the trade down on chaises, otherwise they'd a killed the 'suits, rollin' around on the floor, bouncin' offa the walls, jumpin' on each other. Real easy to go native in a *Gang Wars* module.'

Go native? Taliaferro mouthed, looking at Konstantin from under his brows. Konstantin shrugged. 'I didn't see a chaise in here.'

'Folds down outa the wall. Like those old Murphy beds?'

Konstantin raised her eyebrows, impressed that the manager was even acquainted with the idea of Murphy beds and then felt ashamed. Her ex had always told her that being a snob was her least attractive feature.

'Most people won't use the chaises except for the sexers,' Pleshette was saying. 'Not if they got a choice. And there was this one blowfish, he hurt himself on the *chaise*. Got all heated up struggling, cut himself on the straps, broke some ribs. And *that –*' she leaned toward Konstantin confidentially '*– that* wasn't even the *cute* part. Know what the *cute* part was?'

Konstantin couldn't imagine.

'The *cute* part was, his pov was in this fight at the *exact same time* and broke the *exact same ribs*.' Pleshette straightened up and folded her arms,

lifting her chin defiantly as if daring Konstantin to disbelieve. 'This's *always* been non-safe, even before it was fatal.'

'That happen here?' Taliaferro asked without looking up.

'Nah. Some other place. East Hollywood, North Hollywood. I don't remember now.' The manager's kimono sleeve flapped like a wing as she gestured. 'We all heard about it. Stuff gets around.'

Konstantin nodded, biting her lip so she wouldn't smile. 'Uh-huh. Is this the same guy who didn't open his parachute in a skydiving scenario and was found dead with every bone in his body shattered?'

'Well, of *course* not.' Pleshette looked at her as if she were crazy. 'How could it be? *That* blowfish *died*. We all heard about that one, too. Happened in D.C. They got it going on in D.C. with those sudden-death thrillers.' She leaned toward Konstantin again, putting one scrawny hand on her arm. 'You oughta check D.C. sources for death-trips. Life is so cheap there. It's a whole different world.'

Konstantin was trying to decide whether to agree with her or change the subject when the coroner emerged from the cubicle with the cam op right on her heels.

'– shot everything *I* shot,' the cam op was saying unhappily.

'And *I* said never mind. We can probably subpoena her footage and see if it really is better than yours. Probably isn't. *Go.*' She gave him a little push.

'But I just *know* she was in some of my shots –'

'We can handle that, too. *Go. Now.*' The coroner shooed him away and turned to Konstantin. She was a small person, about the size of a husky ten-year-old – something to do with her religion, Konstantin remembered. The Church of Small-Is-Beautiful, something like that. The faithful had their growth inhibited in childhood. Konstantin wondered what happened to those who lost the faith, or came to it later in life.

'Well, I can say without fear of contradiction that the kid's throat was cut while he was alive.' The coroner looked around. 'And in a place like this. Imagine that.'

'Should I also imagine how?' Konstantin asked.

'How? Classic ear-to-ear.' The coroner smoothed down the wiry copper cloud that was her current hair. It sprang back up immediately. 'Most likely with a weapon made for that sort of thing, and not just any old sharp edge that might have been lying around. Probably a boning blade. Boning blades're all the rage out there. Or rather, *in* there. In the actioners. They all like those boning blades. And definitely not self-inflicted. Even if we couldn't tell by the angle, this kid was an AR softy. He wouldn't have had the strength to saw through his own windpipe like that.'

Konstantin made a face. 'Great. You know what's going to be on the news inside an hour.'

The coroner fanned the air with one small hand. 'Yeah, yeah, yeah. Game-players' stigmata. Everybody's heard about somebody who got stabbed in a module and came out with a knife wound it took sixteen stitches to close and what about the nun who was on TV with the bleeding hands and feet. It's part of the modern myth-making machine. There've been some people who fell off their perch in AR, got all mixed up about what was real and hurt themselves or somebody else. But the stigmata stuff – everybody conveniently forgets how the stigmata of Sister Mary Blood of the Sacred Etceteras got exposed as a hoax by her own order. The good sister did a turn as a stage magician before she got religion. There's a file about how she did it floating around PubNet. Look it up sometime – fascinatin' rhythms. The real thing would be *extremo ruptura*, very serious head trouble, which the experts are pretty sure nobody's had since St. Theresa.'''

'Which one?' asked Konstantin.

The coroner chuckled. 'That's good. "Which one?" You know your stuff, doncha.' She laughed some more. 'I'll have my report in your in box tomorrow.' She went up the hall, still laughing.

'*Well*,' said the night manager, sniffing with disdain. '*Some people* ought better stick with what they know than mock what they *don't know squat about*.' She called the last four words at the coroner's retreating back, but the coroner didn't hear.

'My apologies if she offended your beliefs,' Konstantin said briskly. 'Is there some other way into the room that nobody knows about – vents, conduits, emergency exit, access?'

Pleshette's fuzzy head wagged from side to side. 'No. Nothing.'

Konstantin was about to ask for the building's blueprints when Taliaferro snapped the archiver closed with a sound like a rifle shot. 'Right. Some great place you got here. We'll interview the clientele now. In the parking lot.'

'*Got* no parking lot,' Pleshette said, frowning suspiciously.

'Didn't say *your* parking lot. We've corralled everyone at a car rental place down the block, we can do it there.' Taliaferro looked at Konstantin meaningfully. 'Spacious. Lots of room to move around in.'

Konstantin sighed. 'First let's weed out everyone who was in the same scenario and module with the kid and see if anyone remembers him doing or saying anything that would give hints about what was happening to him.'

Pleshette gave a sharp bark of laughter. 'You know how many people that could be?'

Konstantin nodded glumly. 'We'll start just with the locals. The clients here, I mean.' She started up the hall after Taliaferro.

'But you *can* see what the kid was doing when he took it in the neck.'

Konstantin stopped and looked back at the manager. 'I can?'

'Yeah. Surveillance'll have it.'

'Surveillance?' Konstantin repeated, unsure she had heard correctly.

'Well, yeah.' The night manager gave her a sideways look. 'You think we let the blowfish come in here and *don't* keep an eye on them? *Anything* could happen. Liability, that's a monster.'

Konstantin decided not to ask her why she hadn't mentioned this minor detail a couple of hours before. 'Can I screen this surveillance record in your office?'

'Just screen it?' Pleshette looked puzzled.

'Is that some kind of problem?' Konstantin moved toward the open door-way of the room where she could hear DiPietro and Celestine bantering with the stringer.

'No.' The night manager shrugged. 'You just want to screen it, my office, sure.'

Konstantin didn't know what to make of the look on Pleshette's funny little face. Maybe that was all it was, a funny little face on a funny little person who lived in a funny little open-all-night world. A funny little open-all-night arti-ficial world at that. For all Konstantin knew, the night manager hadn't seen true daylight for years. Not her problem, she thought as she stuck her head through the doorway of the cubicle where Celestine and DiPietro were now busy jockeying for the stringer's attention while the stringer pretended she wasn't pumping them for information and they pretended they didn't know she was pretending not to pump them for information. No one had to pre-tend the dead kid had been forgotten.

'Pardon me for interrupting,' Konstantin said a bit archly. DiPietro and Celestine turned to her simultaneously. In their identical white coveralls, they looked like unfinished marionettes.

'Attendants'll be coming for him. Before you do a final search of the room, you might want to, oh' – she gestured at the body – 'cover him up.'

'Sure thing,' said Celestine, and then suddenly tossed something round and wrapped in plastic at her. 'Think fast!'

Konstantin caught it by instinct. The shape registered on her before any-thing else. The kid's head, she thought, horrified. The cut across his throat had been so deep, he'd been decapitated when they peeled him.

Then she felt the metal through the plastic and realized it was the kid's headmounted monitor. 'Oh, good one, Celestine.' She tucked the monitor under her left arm. 'I'd dropped that, we'd be filling out forms on it for a year.'

'*You*, drop something? Not this lifetime.' Celestine grinned. Her mutton-chops made her face seem twice as wide as it was. Konstantin wondered if you could sue a cosmetologist for malpractice.

'Thanks for the vote of confidence, but next time, just send a card.' Kon-stantin went up the hall toward the main lobby, Pleshette following in a swish of kimono.

*

There were only two uniformed officers waiting in the lobby with the other three members of the night staff, who were perched side by side on a broken-down, ersatz-leather sofa by the front window. The rest of the police, along with the clientele, were down the block with Taliaferro, one of the uniforms told Konstantin. Konstantin focused on the officer's name tag, which read *Wolski*, so she wouldn't stare at the woman's neat ginger-colored mustache. At least it wasn't as ostentatious as Celestine's muttonchops, but she wasn't sure she'd ever get used to facial hair on women. Her ex would have called her a throwback. Perhaps she was.

'That's all right, as long as we know where they are.' Konstantin handed her the bagged headmount. 'Look after this, the kid was wearing it when he died. I'm going to screen some surveillance footage in the manager's office and I thought I'd question the staff there as well.' The people on the couch were gazing up at her expectantly. 'Is this the entire night shift?'

'The whole kitten caboodle,' Pleshette assured her.

Konstantin looked around. It was a small lobby, no hiding places, and presumably no secret doors. Small, drab, and depressing – after waiting here for even just a few minutes, any AR would probably look great by comparison. She turned back to the people on the couch just as the one in the middle stood up and stuck out his hand. 'Miles Mank,' he said in a hearty tenor.

Konstantin hesitated. The man's eyes had an unfocused, watery look to them that she associated with people who weren't well. He towered over her by six inches and outweighed her by at least a hundred pounds. But they were soft pounds, packed into a glossy blue one-piece uniform that, combined with the gooey eyes and his straw-colored hair, gave him a strangely childlike appearance. She shook his hand, which was even softer than it looked. 'What's your job here?'

'Supervisor,' he informed her. The gooey eyes gazed past her at Guilfoyle Pleshette. 'Well, *unofficial* supervisor. I'm the one who's been here longest, so I always end up telling everybody else how things work.'

'Oh, don't stop *there*, Miles,' Pleshette urged. The kimono sleeves snapped like pennants in a high wind as she stretched out her sticklike arms and refolded them. 'Go ahead, tell how if they promoted from within here, *you'd* be night manager. Then I can explain how they had to go on a talent search for an *experienced* administrator. It'll all balance out.'

'There's experience and there's *experience*,' Mank said huffily. 'Nobody ever *died* while *I* was acting night manager.'

'Very true, very true – everybody survived the riot where you had to refund all the customers. But nobody died so that made it all good-deal-well-done.'

Miles Mank strode past Konstantin to loom over Pleshette, who had to reach up to shake her skeletal finger in his face. Konstantin felt that panicky chill all authorities feel when a situation slips the leash. Before she could

break in, the mustached officer, Wolski, tugged her sleeve and showed her a taser set on flash. 'Shall I?'

Konstantin nodded, stepping back and covering her eyes.

The flash was a split-second heat that she found oddly comforting, though no one else did. Besides Guilfoyle Pleshette and Miles Mank, Wolski (and her ginger mustache) had also failed to warn her fellow officer, the other two employees, or Taliaferro, who had chosen that moment to step back inside. The noise level increased exponentially.

'*Everybody shut up!*' Konstantin roared, and was shocked when everybody did. She looked around. All the people in the lobby had their hands over their eyes. It looked like a convention of see-no-evil monkeys.

'Thank you,' she added awkwardly. 'Now. I'm going to screen surveillance footage of the victim's final session in the manager's office, and then inter-view the rest of the staff.' She turned to Taliaferro. 'After that, I want to question anyone who was in the same module and scenario.' She waited, but he didn't take his hands from his eyes. 'That means I'll be phoning you down the block, *partner*, to have select individuals escorted to the office.' She waited another few seconds for him to answer. 'Understand, Taliaferro?' she added, exasperated.

'Yeah, just let me do some prelims on the customers,' he said, speaking to the air where he thought she was. He was off by two feet. 'They're gonna be getting restless while you're doing that. We're going to have to give them phone calls and pizza.'

Konstantin rolled her eyes. 'So *give* them phone calls and pizza.' She turned back to Pleshette. 'Now, can you show me to your office?'

'I'm sorry,' Miles Mank said genially, 'but I'm afraid *I* don't have an office. I've been making do with the employee lounge.'

'Suffer, Mank,' Pleshette said, taking a peek between her fingers. 'She was talking to *me*.' She started to lower her hand and then changed her mind.

Konstantin sighed. Their vision would return to normal in a few minutes along with their complexions, assuming none of them suffered from light-triggered skin rashes. Perhaps she could have been more sympathetic, but she wasn't sure any of them would notice if she were.

She put her hand on Guilfoyle Pleshette's arm. 'Your office?'

'I'll show you,' said Pleshette, 'if I ever see well enough again.'

Pleshette's office was smaller than the smelly cubicle where the kid had died, which was probably a good thing. It meant that Konstantin didn't throw any-thing breakable against the wall when she discovered that the so-called surveillance footage was an AR log. There just wasn't enough distance to make a really satisfying smash and still be safe from shrapnel.

'Invasion of privacy,' Pleshette explained when Konstantin called her in.

'*What* privacy?' asked Konstantin. 'Every public area has three-four cams running on it twenty-four hours a day –'

'This isn't a public place.' Pleshette's smile was suddenly cannier than Konstantin would have thought possible. 'It's a private area that people pay admission to get into. Which means that it can't be put under surveillance because one of the commodities the clientele purchase when they come in here is privacy.'

'Oh,' Konstantin said, half-afraid that Pleshette was going to go on to cite the case that had established the precedent. She thought for a moment. 'That would cover, say, anything admissible in a court of law, right?'

Pleshette nodded her hairdo.

'Fine. So, what about the inadmissible footage?'

'What?'

'Just show me the inadmissible footage – the *illegal* surveillance recording – and we'll call it a night.' Konstantin waited, but Pleshette only stood there, looking at her with vague puzzlement clouding her funny little features. No canniness in her expression now. 'Look, since that surveillance recording's illegal, it doesn't exist, I never saw it, and no one'll know about it. I'll figure out how to build a real case later. Just show me what you've got.'

'But there isn't anything,' Pleshette said, her cartoon voice turning a bit gravelly with fatigue and stress. She pulled the kimono tighter around her sticklike body. 'There really isn't. Bring in a squad and search the place, you won't find anything. People *buy* privacy and artificial reality here, and that's what they get.'

Konstantin gave a short, incredulous laugh. 'You know people could be coming here and doing just about anything in those cubicles, then? Without ever touching the AR rigs?'

'Well, they could,' Pleshette admitted. 'But the boot-logs on all the equipment say it was in use for as long as each cubicle was occupied by a paying customer. Except for the few minutes it takes to put the stuff on and take it off again. So maybe some people go back there, leave the 'suits and monitors on the floor, but run the programs, and stand around enjoying the quiet. I don't know for sure. But after they leave, the 'suits sure *smell* like someone's been using them. And they register as having logged into AR as whoever they want to be and done whatever they wanted to do until their money ran out and they left. So, yeah, I guess I don't know for sure what anyone does back there, but I just take it for granted, because that's what I'm paid to do.'

'Uh-huh,' said Konstantin.

'Anything else?' Pleshette asked.

'No, I think that about covers it, thanks,' Konstantin said and settled in to watch the video.

She watched every moment, including the instructional lead that told her the only pov available would be detached observer. The editing option was avail-

able for close-ups or odd angles, along with a primer to pull down if she were feeling less than Fellini, or even D. W. Griffith.

Helpful, she thought, freezing the footage before the lead faded into the scenario. Excessively helpful, even. Was she supposed to decide how to edit the footage *before* she watched it?

But of course, she realized, this came under the heading of *souvenirs*. Footage from your AR romp, or video of your friend's wedding, or prepackaged quick-time scenics from a kiosk in the Lima airport for a last-minute gift before you boarded the flight home – you made it look however you wanted it to look, for whomever would be looking. Maybe you didn't want it to look the same to everyone – a tamer version for one friend, something experimental to hold another's attention, a gratuitous orgy to keep your garden club awake.

Konstantin tapped the menu line at the bottom of the screen. *Options?* it asked her, fanning them out in the center of a deep blue background. *Pick a card, any card*, she thought, *memorize it and slip it back into the deck. There'll be a quiz later. If you last long enough.* She chose *No Frills*.

The image on the screen liquefied and melted away into black. A moment later she was looking at an androgynous face that suggested the best of India and Japan in combination. The name came up as Shantih Love, which she couldn't decide if she hated or not. The linked profile informed her that both the Shantih Love name and appearance had been reversed and were protected. No age given; under *sex* it said, *Any; all; why do you care?*

'Filthy, thankless job, Shantih, but somebody's got to.' She tapped for the technical specs of the dead kid's session. Full-coverage hotsuit, of course, which would tell her when the kid had died. She scrolled past his scenario and module choices to see how long he'd been in AR. *Duration: four hours, twenty minutes.*

Konstantin winced. The kid must have been case-hardened beyond belief – most people, even serious addicts, had to take a break after two hours at least. She called up his vitals so she could note the exact time of death in the archiver. Then she just stared at the figures on the screen, tapping the stylus mindlessly on the desk.

Shantih Love – or, rather, the kid presenting himself as Shantih Love – had shuffled off his mortal coil just ten minutes into his projected four-hour-and-twenty-minute romp in post-Apocalyptic Noo Yawk Sitty. The Shantih Love persona, however, had managed to go on for the remaining four hours and ten minutes quite nicely without him.

Konstantin watched as the sequence faded in.

In the middle of a glitter-encrusted cityscape at dusk, the androgyne made his/her way toward some kind of noisy party or tribal gathering on the rubble-strewn shore of the Hudson River. The rubble was also encrusted with glitter; more glitter twinkled on the glass of the silent storefronts on the other

side of a broad, four-lane divided thoroughfare partially blocked by occasional islands of wreckage. As Shantih Love swept off the sidewalk, ankle-length purple robe flowing gracefully with every step, and crossed the ruined street, one of the wrecks ignited, lighting up the semi-dark. Shantih Love barely glanced at it and kept going, toward the gathering on the shore; Konstantin could hear music and, under that, the white noise of many voices in conversation. What could they possibly have to talk about, she wondered; was it anything more profound than what you'd hear at any other party in any other reality with any other people? And if it were, why did it occur only in the reality of post-Apocalyptic Noo Yawk Sitty?

Shantih Love abruptly looked back in such a way that s/he seemed to be looking directly out of the screen into Konstantin's eyes. The expression on the unique face seemed somehow both questioning and confident. Konstantin steered the detached perspective from behind Shantih Love around his/her right side, passing in front of the androgyne and moving to the left side, tracking him/her as s/he walked toward the multitude on the shore.

A figure suddenly popped up from behind the low concrete barrier running between the street and the river. Shantih Love stopped for a few moments, uncertainty troubling her/his smooth forehead. Konstantin tried adjusting the screen controls to see the figure better in the gathering darkness but, maddeningly, she couldn't seem to get anything more definite than a fuzzy, blurry silhouette, definitely humanlike but otherwise unidentifiable as young or old, male, female, both or neither, friendly or hostile.

The shape climbed over the barrier to the street side just as Shantih Love slipped over it to the shore. The ground here was soft sand and Shantih Love had trouble walking in it. The fuzzy shape paced her/him on the other side of the wall and Konstantin got the idea that it was saying something, but nothing came up on audio. Shantih Love didn't answer, didn't even look in its direction again as s/he moved in long strides toward the crowd, which extended from the water's edge up to a break in the barrier and into the road.

The perspective had slipped back behind Shantih Love. Konstantin tapped the forward button rapidly; now she seemed to be perched on Shantih Love's right shoulder. The gathering on the beach reminded Konstantin of the sort of ragged, disorganized cocktail party that her ex had loved to attend. She was disappointed. Was this *really* all that anyone in AR could think of doing?

Shantih Love whirled suddenly; after a second's delay, the perspective followed. Konstantin felt a wave of dizziness and the images on the screen went out of focus. When the focus cleared, Konstantin saw that the figure was standing on top of the barrier, poised to jump. Shantih Love backed away, turned, and began stumbling through the party crowd, bumping into various people, some less distinct than others. Konstantin didn't have to shift the perspective around to know that the creature was chasing the androgyne. Now

the pov seemed to be only inches in front of the creature's face; she had a fast glimpse of bandage-wrapped arms and hands with an indeterminate number of fingers as it staggered into the party after Love.

The pov began to shake and streak, as if it were embedded in the pursuer's body. Frustrated, Konstantin pounded on the forward key, but the pov didn't budge. They called this custom editing? She fumed. Even worse, now that she was among the party crowd, almost every attendee was either so vague as to be maddeningly unidentifiable or so broad a stereotype – barbarian, vampire, wild-child, homunculus – that anonymity was equally assured.

Shantih Love broke through the other side of the crowd two seconds before she did and ran heavily toward a stony rise leading to the sidewalk. S/he scrambled up on all fours, a heartbeat ahead of the pursuer.

Love vaulted the low barrier and ran along the middle of the street, looking eagerly at each wreck. There were more wrecks here, some ablaze, some not. Something moved inside each one, even those that were burning. Konstantin realized she was probably alone in finding that noticeable, much less remarkable – living in a bonfire was probably the height of AR chic. This week.

She tried pushing the pov ahead again and this time gained several feet. Shantih Love looked over his/her shoulder, seemingly right at the pov. The androgyne's expression was panic and dismay; in the next moment, s/he fell.

The pov somersaulted. There was a flash of broken pavement, followed by a brief panorama of sky, a flip and a close-up of the androgyne's profile just as the pursuer pushed his/her chin up with one rag-wrapped hand. Perfect skin stretched taut; the blade flashed and disappeared as it turned sideways to slash through flesh, tendon, blood vessels, cartilage, bone.

Blood flew against the pov and dripped down, like gory rain on a window. Wincing, Konstantin tried to erase the blood trails; nothing happened.

Shantih Love coughed and gargled at the sky, not trying to twist away from the bandaged hand that still held his/her chin. Blood pulsed upward from the artery in an exaggerated display. The creature pushed Love's face to one side so s/he stared dully past the pov and then bent its head to drink.

Konstantin had seen similar kinds of things in shock videos, including the so-called 'slay-ride' video that had supposedly been circulating underground (whatever 'underground' meant these days) and had turned out to be so blatantly phony that the perpetrators should have gone down for fraud, or at the very least, false advertising.

But where the blood spilled in that sort of video had looked more like cherry syrup, this looked real enough to make Konstantin gag. She put a hand over her mouth as she froze the screen and turned away, breathing deeply and slowly through her nose, willing her nausea to fade. At the same time, she was surprised at herself. Her squeamish streak was usually

conveniently dormant. In twelve years as a detective, she had seen enough real-time blood and gore that she could claim to be somewhat hardened.

Still, there was something about this – was it the blood, the noises coming from Shantih Love, the sound of the creature drinking so greedily? Or the knowledge that the real kid was going through virtually the same nonvirtual ordeal?

Konstantin collected herself and tried jabbing fast-forward to get through the vampiric sequence as quickly as possible. It only made everything more grotesque, so she took it back to normal running time, just at the point where both the creature and blood vanished completely.

Startled, Konstantin rewound and ran it again in slo-mo, just to make sure she'd seen it right. She had. It wasn't a fast fade or the twinkling deliquescence so favored by beginning cinematography students but a genuine popper, which usually happened by way of a real-time equipment failure or power-out. Common wisdom had it that the jump from AR to real-time in such an event was so abrupt as to produce extreme reactions of an undesirable nature – vertigo, projectile vomiting, fainting, or all three.

Or a slashed throat? That was about as undesirable as you could ask for, Konstantin thought. Of course, that was assuming that anyone did ask for something undesirable. She tried to rub her forehead smooth.

She reran the sequence once more and then again in detestable slo-mo, watching the blood disappear right along with the creature, leaving Shantih Love behind. Konstantin called up the record of the kid's vitals and found that, as she had expected, they had quit registering at the moment the blood had disappeared.

Konstantin took her finger off the pause button and let the action go forward. On the screen, the Shantih Love character sat up, its elegant fingers feeling the ragged edges and flaps of skin where its throat had been cut, mild annoyance deepening the few lines in its face. As Konstantin watched it working at pinching the edges of skin together, she tried to see what was different in its expression and its posture. What was driving Shantih Love now – a robot, or a very human hijacker? If there were signs, what the hell were they?

She could watch the video over and over for the next three hours and see if anything became any clearer to her. Instead, she decided to talk to people she was reasonably sure were human before she took in any more adventures of a dead kid's false face pretending to be alive in a city pretending to be dead.

EMPTY CUP [II]

The figures on the screen were ridiculous.

'Over how many years?' Yuki asked, wondering uneasily if she were being conned.

Joy Flower almost smiled. 'Very funny. But what you need to know here is that I have a very poor sense of humor, and it is not a good idea to make many jokes with me. I'm just that way. Some people are.' She swiveled the screen back around to face her where she was sitting on the other side of the desk. Yuki decided that someone had an obsession with the past; the whole office was appointed like a nostalgia exhibit. All the wood was highly polished, dark with gold overtones. The chairs were enormous ersatz-leather monsters with backs that rose up high and wide enough to conceal even the largest person. The brass-colored buttons dimpling the upholstery were supposed to suggest cushioning, but Yuki's own chair was as hard and unyielding as a board.

Not that there was much danger of her getting too comfortable here; this wasn't a place where anyone went to feel comfortable. Even Joy Flower looked stiff, as if it weren't really her office, just a place she was allowed to use from time to time.

Yuki cleared her throat. 'When do I start?'

The woman glanced down at her wrist. There was nothing on it that Yuki could see. 'Half an hour ago.'

'And I guess you want me to live in?'

'I knew you were clever.' Joy Flower's preoccupied tone seemed about to acquire an edge. On the edge of an edge, Yuki thought; a very uncomfortable place to be. 'My stuff, back at my apartment –'

Joy Flower gave her a sideways look. 'Already taken care of for you.'

Yuki shifted slightly in the chair and the ersatz leather gave an authentic creak. Her new boss rested one arm on top of the monitor. 'You know that old saying about how you should ask questions because how else are you going to learn? I personally don't have time to waste with anyone who hasn't learned already. This means that I use the time I would have burned answering questions to do something more important. You know what I mean?'

Yuki started to answer but the woman turned away from her in such a final way that a spoken dismissal would have been inane.

Outside in the heavily carpeted, sound-deadened hallway, one of the thugs was waiting for her, a beefy man in a reddish black turtleneck sweater and black trousers. The trousers had extra pockets up and down the legs. A look that aspired to military associations. Professional bodyguard pants, designed

to project the image of the matter-of-factly lethal mercenary. He looked down at her through surgically altered eyes. His face had a certain flatness that she could tell was natural, so the classically Oriental shape of the eyes didn't look so out of place. The bright blue pupils, the straight blond hair spilling over his shoulders and down his back – those looked out of place.

'How about you?' Yuki said without preamble. The walls seemed to swallow each word; she had the sensation of being trapped in a cotton ball. 'Do *you* answer questions?'

'If I must.' He looked down at her as if from a great height. 'I'm supposed to take you to your quarters. Your things have arrived, or will arrive soon.'

'Oh. Good.' The look on that face, she realized, was not disdain but the absence of expression. He turned away abruptly and began walking up the hall. *My Master says for you to walk this way. – Okay, Igor, but it's going to take some practice.* She followed at a slight distance, wondering if she had lost her mind as well as her friend.

No, Tom was more than a friend to her. But not vice versa. Grandma Naoka would have contemplated this with some concern. *Old Japan was never kind to those who loved – those usually being women. But then, the country itself was not kind to anyone. Life was not a right but a privilege. Honor meant more than love.* Yuki had often wanted to ask her if honor had really just been easier to come by than love but the question felt too impertinent even for Naoka's favorite granddaughter to get away with.

She had expected the guy to lead her through a long and twisting maze of hallways to something like a techno-Buddhist monk's cell. Instead, they went down one flight of stairs at the end of the hall and halfway along another quiet corridor to a door she estimated was directly under the office she had just left.

He caught her looking up at the ceiling, and said, 'Yes, it is.'

She turned to him, stubbornly maintaining a casual air. 'Right under her office, you mean?'

'Exactly underneath.'

The better to walk all over you, my dear.

'Put your hand on the plate,' he told her, gesturing at a white plastic square stuck onto the door at slightly above her eye level.

She obeyed. There was a moment of mild heat and the sensation of the plastic crawling or writhing under her touch. She heard a soft chime and the door clicked, opening about an inch.

'The lock is now keyed to you. Only you, and her.'

Was that supposed to be reassuring, Yuki wondered. He pushed the door open and turned on the light. Instead of a cell, there was a generously large apartment that seemed to have been furnished by a random-choice generator. The couch was a puffy white thing with pillows that looked as if they would bounce wildly if she threw them on the shiny hardwood floor. The two

chairs matched neither the couch nor each other – one was another ersatz-leather monstrosity like the ones in Joy Flower's office. The other was smaller and lower, upholstered in a nubbly fabric printed with large, faded cabbage roses. They faced a very good copy of an old-style church pew that she presumed was supposed to function as a love seat. None of the stuff was hers. Yuki frowned and turned to the guy.

'Are you going to show me around?'

The guy made a short, breathy noise that might have been a laugh. 'It's *your* place, you live here. Look around all you want.'

'But –'

'The only thing you have to remember,' he said, raising his voice to talk over her, 'is not to sleep naked.'

Yuki shut up, startled. He nodded at her once and walked out, closing the door behind him. 'Naked,' she said after a moment, and then turned to look at the hilariously mismatched living room furniture. *Didn't know what you liked, so we got you one of everything they had.* Too funny.

There was one doorway in front of her and one to her left. The one in front took her to the big kitchen where she found that her small, blocky wooden table and its single chair from her one-roomer had been installed. If the sight was supposed to be reassuring, it had failed. In the setting of the shiny black cabinets and the absurd mirrored floor, the table and chair looked out of place, alien and lonely. *Like me.*

And a *mirrored* floor. A mirrored *floor.* How crazy could it get? She wasn't sure she would ever be able to sit down and eat in a room where she was reflected from below. It was almost too bad that the decorator hadn't gotten *really* extreme and mirrored the ceiling and walls as well. Then the room would have been not only unbearable but impossible even to look at. *After all, why do things by halves?*

No windows, just simulated scenery and artificial light from one pretend window over the sink and another on the far wall. She supposed that these were the source of the recommended amount of daytime light during the appropriate hours – no darkness-induced depressions to interfere with Joy Flower's schedule would be tolerated here – but it was nighttime now, so the soft light spilling in over the sink was probably simulated moonlight. Or maybe just a streetlight. She'd have to check later to see if the environment were urban or rural. She hated the rural shit. Some things were *too* fake.

Like your relationship with Tom? whispered an acid little voice in her mind.

Oh, stop it, she told herself and marched through the living room to the bedroom. *Just because a relationship isn't on* my *terms doesn't mean that it isn't a relationship.*

In her heart, she knew *that* was bullshit of the worst sort, but she wasn't listening to that part of her heart today. Her futon had been delivered to the

bedroom and set up on a platform with cabinets at the head; a spare set of neatly folded sheets had been placed on top of a white chest of drawers. To the right of that was the bathroom, which had a separate chamber for the toilet. All very proper, civilized, livable.

Against the wall opposite the bathroom doorway was the work-station, the oversized screen sitting like an icon of a fat spider within a nest of shelves bearing storage chips. Except spiders didn't have nests, did they. No. They had webs. Anyone knew that. How stupid was she?

'Don't sleep naked,' she murmured, going over to the work-station. One more thing to worry about, along with the fate of her allegedly nonexistent predecessor, and Tom's current address. As soon as she touched one of the dark shelves, the screen lit up. Unsurprised, Yuki watched with mild interest as a fractal flower bloomed in the center and kept blooming, seeming to turn itself inside out. Yuki's mouth twitched with bored amusement; nostalgia graphics didn't do much for her, though she had to concede the 3-D effect was respectable.

The cabinets at the head of her futon caught her eye again. That was probably where they had put whatever she was supposed to sleep in so she wouldn't be naked. Maybe special uniform pajamas that could double as street clothes on short notice, in case of any midnight fire drills. Or emergency visits to clubs, to pick up a new victim. She went over to take a look.

Kneeling in the center of the futon, she pulled the cabinet doors open. At first she thought she was looking at an elaborate S&M harness and bridle set with extra restraints and she felt her heart leap with fear as multiple thoughts cartwheeled through her mind, about Joy Flower, the bodyguards, about some of Joy's Boyz being Girlz. Then she saw what it really was and wasn't any happier.

Carefully she lifted the headmounted monitor out of the cabinet and held it up. The wires from it were still connected to the lightweight, translucent hotsuit, folded into a square that made her think of wilderness weekends in nature preserves. (She had done a few of those years ago, not so much because she had been such a nature lover but because the people who ran the weekends were so … *intent* on them. They had exuded a sense of purpose more strongly than anyone else she had ever known, and she had liked that – people who knew what their lives were about. Most of them had been subsequently arrested in an eco-terrorist conspiracy dragnet, but strangely enough, Yuki had never been able to find out what had happened to any of them, whether they had been convicted or released or tried at all, or even if any of them had actually had any eco-terrorist connections.)

She put the headmount aside and moved to spread the 'suit out on the futon. It was her size all right, but was this really what the thug had meant by *Don't sleep naked?* Sleep in a *hotsuit?* What would be the point?

So would this really be any more bizarre than sleeping under a canvas shelter –

in a sack under a canvas shelter – in the middle of a government forest preserve, back in the good old days?

But it still didn't make any sense. It wasn't like you could use this stuff if you were asleep.

So maybe the point is for it to use you.

God, she thought. *That* was some glorious hot-rod reasoning, more often used as a typical plot of innumerable slay-rides ground out for game modules from movies, or for movies from game modules, in a ceaseless, incestuous, and circular simulated blood orgy.

She felt heavy with fatigue. How was any of this supposed to lead her to Tom? She should have walked away from Joy Flower and her band of thugs; this was just some blind alley and she would probably wake up tomorrow morning in a *real* alley, after a long, horrible night that, if she were really, *really* lucky, she wouldn't be able to remember.

Was Tom in a place like that now?

She lay down on her stomach, rested her chin on her fists and gazed at her distorted reflection in the shiny black headmount shell. From this angle, she looked sly, knowing, even cynical. *That's me – good old cynical Yuki Harame.*

Maybe she *was* getting cynical. At last. Too many years of watching Tom fade in and out of her life, unabashedly leaning on her for emotional support but unable to reciprocate. Just when she was about to give in and fall in love with him, he would be gone, usually without saying good-bye in person. She would tell herself that since she hadn't fallen in love with him, his abrupt departure hadn't, wouldn't, *couldn't possibly* hurt her. Life would move her forward again and her attention would move along as well and pretty soon she would be contemplating the possibility of something completely different, something or even someone potentially forceful enough to displace Tom Iguchi and his gypsy feet.

And somehow, that was always the cue for Tom to come back into her life. He seemed to have an instinct. He seemed to understand exactly how long it would take her to get him out of her system so that she might build up a resistance, possibly even an immunity to him. Before anything of the sort could happen, he would descend on her, sweep his problems around her like an enveloping blanket, and the next thing she knew, he was sleeping on her couch, eating her food, and radiating angst and charisma in whatever proportions were necessary.

Well, at least he isn't using you as a sex-toy, she would tell herself, and the realist in her would answer, *Of course not – sex requires some giving.*

She knew why he would always come to her. They were both full Japanese, if, indeed, it was still possible to be Japanese at all when the land itself had been all but obliterated. Grandma Naoka had been among the last to visit the islands before the last earthquakes had shattered them into bits too small or

too ravaged to support even one small city. Yuki couldn't imagine the Japan Naoka had told her stories of, with a Tokyo so overcrowded that transit trains needed special employees to push and shove and pack the masses of people inside each car.

But the most interesting stories were about what Naoka had called the water trade. It was a euphemism for something that seemed to be close to prostitution, that perhaps even was prostitution at times, but was, more often, just not quite.

In those days, Yukiko, many people did not know how to enjoy themselves after a day of hard work. We showed them how. We helped them have a good time; they helped us make a living. We were all women, even those of us who were men. And of course, the ones who came to us, without exception, they were all men.

Yuki remembered thinking that she wouldn't have lasted long in that Japan. She would have much preferred being a Samurai. And then again, maybe she would not have done very well in any Japan. Perhaps it was just as well that she was what Grandma Naoka had called a sansei, a Japanese who had been born and raised outside of Japan.

And Tom – well, who knew about Tom? Most of the time, he seemed to her to be too … *disorganized* for the real Japan. She could not picture him as a salaryman, not the way Naoka had described the eager young men in their business suits, clustered around their bosses in the clubs, drinking gamely and then stumbling home to apartments the size of a postage stamp. As for old Japan, she thought it was more likely that Tom would be on the receiving end of a Samurai sword than the handle. No, the only role for Tom was the one he already had – daft young man who happened to be of Japanese descent.

And where did that leave her? Friend of daft young man who happened to be of Japanese descent. Now and always, friend of daft young etc Gullible soft-touch of a friend of daft young, etc And for what? The chance to approach strange and unsavory people in bars.

Of course, there were plenty of other people out there doing likewise with much less justification. She surprised herself by getting up, stripping off her clothes, and pulling on the hotsuit. What the hell, she thought; she might learn something.

The 'suit was one of the pricier models, soft, weightless, scented even. Was this one of the newest 'suits, with triple-density coverage, she wondered, or possibly an advance working model of the famed Climax Envelope? If the CE was real and not just another techno-myth. It was supposed to develop segments that mirrored the wearer's own nerves, making the sensations that much more customized and subsequently that much more authentic. Whatever *that* meant. How authentic did it get before there was no point in putting on a 'suit at all?

Maybe she should have asked Tom that question.

The sensation of the 'suit adjusting to the contours of her body was both comforting and disturbing, like being caressed by a stranger who seemed to know you as well as you knew yourself. She left the genital area of the 'suit inactive. While her sex life left a lot to be desired lately, she wasn't in the mood for a virtual encounter in a strange 'suit. Even if the 'suit did look as if no one else had ever used it.

She hesitated with the headmount, looking into it carefully, as if she might find something that she had never seen before. But it was only a very ordinary headmount with all the usual technology – no Aladdin's lamp, no magic carpet, no door into summer.

Yuki ran a hand through her thick, short hair. Two days ago, she had cut it off herself, thinking it would just be easier, one less thing to fuss with. Ash had told her it made her look like a sex-change of indeterminate direction – asexual and apathetic. Yuki thought that would probably be easier, too. Ash had disagreed.

'Being attractive, beautiful, sexy – all that is always useful. It helps. It makes people care more about you,' he had argued, tapping the remote in the arm of his couch. 'There's no excuse not to be beautiful anymore, it's so easy.'

The mural-sized screen obediently delivered a live cam shot of the exterior of Waxx24, the on-line club he'd never been able to get into. He could get into the actual club downtown, but anyone could. The virtual club on NETsuke was much tougher. Ash complained bitterly that he had never been able to get past even the first checkpoint, and they wouldn't even give him a hint. Privately, Yuki thought it was probably because he was too beautifully eager.

'If it's that easy, how do you know if you're really beautiful?' she had asked.

Ash had rolled his eyes. 'Don't be obtuse. Everybody knows if they're really beautiful or not.'

'All right. What if I tell you that this –' she had brushed her bad haircut with both hands – 'makes me beautiful? All right, then it makes me *feel* beautiful,' she added quickly.

'*I* say you're lying. You're a dumpy little Nisei. You've got that classic daikon radish body that all you full Japanese females are cursed with. Your parents should have tried to give you the benefit of custom genes.'

'And *I* say your standard of beauty must have got mixed up with your laundry. Too much starch, and all the color's bleached out.'

Her reproach hadn't bothered him in the least, perhaps because he'd known she hadn't really felt offended. 'Don't try to fool me. I know you weren't raised ethnic. Hardly anyone is anymore. After all, what would be the point?'

'Well, maybe not in America or some places in Western Europe, Ash, but I don't think they see it that way in other countries. Like, say, Japan.'

'They don't see much in Japan, period. What few of them are left. The news says there may be only about three dozen people left where Tokyo used to be

and less than half that in the crack formerly known as Kobe, and most of them are lost crazies who've been dodging rescue crews.'

'Doesn't mean Japan is dead. It just means everyone's left the geographical coordinates that once marked the location of the country that was called Japan. It doesn't mean there isn't a Japan. Somewhere.'

Ash's haughty pink face had taken on an even haughtier expression. 'How spiritual. Don't tell me – you're going on a quest to find the lost motherland.'

She had almost told him that they didn't call Japan the motherland and decided that she didn't want to have to argue with him any more than she already had. To her relief, he had allowed her to change the subject to Joy Flower and their absent friend Tom. He didn't believe that Tom had become one of Joy's Boyz, but neither had he said it was impossible.

Again, she ran a hand through her chopped-off hair and yawned. Maybe she should defy her employer, strip off, and go to sleep. With any luck, she'd wake up fired.

You've come this far. It's all absurd, but can you think of anything that would get you closer to Tom?

She pulled on the headmount; it molded itself to her head with a sensation like a million tiny slender fingers pushing into her hair, sliding along her scalp. The stimulation was so strong that she lost all awareness of her body for several seconds, except for the nasty sting of the needle sliding, hard and cold, into the base of her neck.

An improbably large and impossibly bejeweled dragonfly was humming circles around her head. As she brushed at it, long strands of straight black hair kept snaring on the thick seams of her white gloves. Remembering, she froze with both hands raised, staring in amazement at the long hair caught between her fingers.

The hair fell away; she could feel its feather touch as it came to rest below her shoulders. The dragonfly positioned itself in the frame of her hands but just out of reach. The jewels seemed to strike sparks in the air. Confusion mixed with vertigo swept over her in a wave.

The sensation of falling ended sharply, not with an impact but with Yuki solidly on her feet in the middle of what looked like a gigantic combination train station and airport. People moved around her, past her, uncaring that she had just materialized among them. If they had even noticed. The dragonfly receded to a pinpoint of light and vanished. She turned slowly, trying to get her bearings.

This was a big place, even for an AR network traffic center. The windows in the distant walls were at least three storeys tall. The light they let in was diffuse, filtered, showing only a brightness and nothing else. Above her, the ceiling disappeared into soft, indistinct shadows.

'Information?' she asked, turning around and around, looking for anything indicating an entry, an exit, or a directory. It was hard to see over people's heads but even more maddeningly, it was impossible to see any of the crowd clearly at all – faces, hair, clothing, colors, everything streaked past, trailed away, faded out.

A white glove identical to the ones she was wearing congealed out of the air above the blurry crowd around her. The only thing in focus, it beckoned to her. She took a step toward it and suddenly found herself looking at it on the hand of a tall orange-haired teenage boy standing behind a counter.

'Righteous effect, innit?' he said, leaning his gloved hand on the smooth, featureless surface between them. 'You know there's a special few comes in just for that effect? Do it over and over, till it goes away and they have to stop. Workin' for her now, right? Like the man said, you best be steppin'.' He laughed.

Yuki started to ask him something and then thought better of it. This was just a supply station and he was the distribution interface. DI's never knew anything beyond inventory.

'I'm here for my equipment,' she told him, hoping he wouldn't have to ask her what it was.

To her enormous relief, a vest with many pockets appeared on the counter in front of her. Another right guess; she had better hurry, she thought, before her luck turned. If there actually was such a thing as luck in AR.

She slipped the vest on easily, though the movement itself felt strange. All her movements felt strange, she realized, fuzzy and dreamlike. She thought that had just been a lingering effect of the vertigo, but it still hadn't faded. Troubled, she touched the back of her neck under her hair but couldn't find anything that might have been a bite or a sting. Maybe she could feel it better without the gloves, she thought, and tried to take them off.

'Bad flex,' warned the guy behind the counter, 'unless you're quitting so soon.'

'Oh. Right.' She started to turn away, hesitated, and turned back to him. Maybe he did know something. There had to be some information that came with the equipment. 'Just between you and me, okay?'

The guy said nothing.

'What am I doing here?'

'Using the equipment I just gave you.'

'Any information?' she asked hopefully.

'Only stock.' He gazed at her with a receptiveness that she had to remind herself was in no way related to anything like concern. She looked down at the many pockets on her vest and then unzipped the topmost on the right. Perhaps there was an instruction book or a map.

All she came up with was a small round mirror. She stared at the reflection for some unmeasured time, a long time, maybe, or only a minute; she wasn't sure. A minute often felt like an hour in AR.

The face in the mirror was as knowing as the distorted image she had seen in the headmount out there in her room. She tilted her head slowly to the left and then to the right to make sure she was seeing a true reflection rather than a transmission.

In the mirror, the face of Tomoyuki Iguchi stared back at her.

DEATH IN THE PROMISED LAND [II]

If the office had seemed cramped before, Miles Mank made it look even smaller by taking up at least half of it. When it became obvious that he actually knew next to nothing, Konstantin tried to get rid of him quickly, but he kept finding conversational hooks that would get her attention and then lead her along to some meaningless and boring point, where he wouldn't so much conclude as change the subject and do it all over again. She was finally able to convince him that he was desperately needed at the parking lot to help sort out the clientele with her bewildered partner. Then she prayed that Taliaferro wouldn't use a similar excuse to send him back to her. She still didn't like his eyes.

The first of the other two employees was a silver-haired kid named Tim Mezzer, who was about the same age as the murder victim. He had the vaguely puzzled, preoccupied look of ex-addicts who had detoxed recently by having their blood cleansed. Officially, it was a fast way out of an expensive jones. In fact, it made the high better on relapse.

'How long have you worked here?' Konstantin asked him.

'Three days.' He sounded bored.

'And what do you do?' she prodded when he didn't say anything more.

'Oh, I'm a specialist,' he said, even more bored. 'I specialize in picking up everybody's smelly 'suit when they're done and get 'em cleaned.' Mezzer put a plump elbow on the desk and leaned forward. 'Tell the truth – you'd kill to have a job like that instead of the boring shit you do.'

Konstantin wasn't sure he was really being sarcastic. 'Sometimes. Did you know the victim?'

'Dunno. What was his name?'

'Shantih Love.'

Mezzer grunted. 'Good label. Must have cost him to come up with one that good. Sounds like an expensive whore-assassin. Someday I'll be rich enough to be able to afford a tailor-made label.'

Konstantin was only half-listening while she prodded the archive for the victim's reference file. 'Real name is –' she stopped. 'Well, that *can't* be right.'

'Don't be so sure.' Mezzer yawned. 'What's it say?'

'Tomoyuki Iguchi.' Konstantin sounded out each syllable slowly and carefully.

'Ha. Sounds like he was working on turning Japanese in a serious way.'

'Why?'

'Well, for post-Apocalyptic Tokyo, of course.' Mezzer sighed. 'What else.'

Konstantin was appalled. 'There's a post-Apocalyptic Tokyo now?'

'Not yet.' Mezzer's sigh became another yawn. 'Coming soon, to a hotsuit near you. S'posed to be the next big hot spot. They say it's gonna make the Sitty look like Sunday afternoon in Nebraska, with these parts you can access only if you're Japanese or a convincing simulation. It's the one we've all been waiting for.'

'"We?"' Konstantin said uncertainly, wondering if he knew that something very like it had already come and gone a good many years before either of them had been born, and then decided that even if he did, he probably wouldn't care. 'Who's "we"?'

He shrugged. 'All the club rats. Mainliners. Headliners. Hardliners, old school, nu skool, no school. Plugged and unplugged.'

'Does that include you?' Konstantin asked him. 'Is it the one *you've* been waiting for, too?'

'I don't know from Japanese, I'm a twentieth-century Ellay fox. I stalk the stars.' He paused, as if she might have had something to say about that. 'The bubble-up on this new site is, there's some kinda secret coming-attraction subroutine for post-Apocalyptic Tokyo buried in the ones running now – the Sitty, Ellay pre- and post-, Hong Kong, Shanghai, Moscow, Black Forest, lotta places. They say you gotta be Japanese to crack them. *If* they're really there. Shantih Love musta thought they were.'

'But why take *two* fake names?'

'*Told* you – he was trying to turn Japanese. He wanted anyone who stripped his label to find his Japanese name underneath and take him for that. Invite him into the special Japan area.' Mezzer put his head back as if he were going to bay at the ceiling and yawned again. 'Or he was getting that crazy-head. You know, where you start thinking it's real in there and fake out here, or you can't tell the difference. You need to talk to Body. Body'll know. Body's probably the only one who'd know for sure.'

'What body?'

'Body Sativa. Body knows more about the top ten ARs than anyone else, real or not.'

Konstantin felt her mouth twitch. 'Don't you mean Cannabis Sativa?' she asked sarcastically.

Mezzer blinked at her in surprise. 'Get *off*. Cannibal's her *mother*. She's good but Body's the Big Dipper in *that* family.' His sudden smile was

unexpectedly winsome. 'Pretty toff, actually that you'd know about Cannibal Sativa. You plannin' to go talk to her?'

Konstantin didn't know what to say.

'Well, go see Body for sure. I swear she'll be the one you want. Hell, I'll even give you some icons you can use in there. Real insider icons, too, not what they junk you up with in the help files.'

'Thanks,' Konstantin said doubtfully. 'But I think I fell down about a mile back. If he was turning Japanese, as you put it, why would he call himself Shantih Love?'

Mezzer blinked. 'Well, because he was tryin' to be a *Japanese* guy named Shantih Love.' He frowned at her. 'You just don't ever go in AR, do you?'

'Can't add to that,' said the other employee cheerfully. She was an older woman named Howard Ruth and her salt-and-pepper hair and soft, lined face were untouched by chemicals or surgery. Konstantin found her comforting to look at. 'Body Sativa's the best tip you're gonna get. You'll go through that whole bunch in the lot down the street and you won't hear anything more helpful.' She sat back, crossing her left ankle over her right knee.

'Body Sativa wouldn't happen to be in that group down the street, by any chance?'

Howard Ruth shrugged. 'Could be, but I doubt it. This is just another reception site on the network. Considering the sophisticated moves Body makes, she's most likely on via her own private rig, and that means she could be anywhere.'

'Come on,' said Konstantin irritably. 'Even *I* know that everyone on-line has an origin code.'

Howard Ruth's smile was sunny. 'You haven't played any games lately, have you?'

Konstantin was thinking the woman should talk to her ex. 'On-line? No.'

'No,' agreed the woman, 'because if you had, you'd know that netgaming isn't considered official net communication or transaction, so it's not governed by FCC or FDSA regulations. Get on, pick a name or buy a permanent label, stay as long as you like – or can afford – and log out when you've had enough. Netgaming is one hundred percent elective, so anything goes – no guidelines, no censorship, no crimes against persons. You can't file a complaint against anyone for assault, harassment, stalking, fraud, or anything like that.'

Konstantin sighed. 'I didn't know this. Why not?'

'You didn't have to.' Howard Ruth laughed. 'Look, Officer –'

'Lieutenant.'

'Sure, lieutenant. Everybody knows the rules for regular on-line com backwards and forwards – no this, no that, encrypt, de-crypt, authorized, unauthorized, fines, imprisonment, and it comes out here. But unless you

netgame regular, you *won't* know any of *this*. You ever hear about the case years back where a guy used an origin line in a netgame to track down a woman in realtime and kill her?'

'No,' said Konstantin with some alarm. 'Where did this happen?'

'Oh, back East somewhere. D.C., I think. Life is so cheap there, you know, it's a whole different world. Anyway, what happened was, back when they had origin lines in gaming, this guy got mad at this woman, somehow found her by way of her origin line, and boom – lights out. That was one of the first cases of that gameplayer's madness where someone could prove it could be a real danger off-line. After that, there was a court ruling that since gaming was strictly recreational, games were entitled to complete anonymity if they wanted. No origin line. Kinda the same thing for fraud and advertising.'

Konstantin felt her interest, which had started to wane with the utterance *D.C.*, come alive again. 'What?'

'Guy ran a game-within-a-game on someone. I can't remember exactly how it went – beachfront in Kansas, diamond mines in Peru, hot stocks about to blow. Anyhow, the party of the second part got the idea it was all backed up in realtime and did this financial transfer to the party of the first part, who promptly logged out and went south. Party of the second part hollers *Thief!* and what do you know but the police catch this Salesman of the Year. Who then claims it was all a game and the money was a gift, received in good faith.'

'And?' said Konstantin.

'And that's a wrap. Grand jury won't even indict, on grounds of extreme gullibility. As in, "You were in *artificial reality*, you fool, what did you expect?" Personally, I think they were both suffering from a touch of the galloping head-bugs.'

Konstantin was troubled. 'And that decision stood?'

'It's *artificial* reality – all you can do is lie, no matter what you say, and the believers are the ones at fault. Because it's all make-believe, let's-pretend, the play's the thing.' Howard Ruth laughed heartily. 'If you choose to pay someone out here for something in there, that's *your* hotspot. Life is so strange, eh?'

Konstantin made a mental note to check for court rulings on AR as she pressed for a clean page in the archiver. 'But if being in an AR makes people insane –'

'Doesn't make *everyone* insane,' the woman said. 'That's what it is, you know. The honey factory don't close down just because someone might be allergic to bee stings.'

Konstantin was still troubled. 'So when did those things happen?' she asked, holding the stylus ready.

'*I* don't know,' Howard Ruth said, surprised at the question. 'Oughta be in the police files, though. Doesn't law enforcement have some kind of

central-national-international information bank you all access? Something like *Police Blotter?*'

'In spite of the name,' Konstantin said, speaking slowly not only for the sake of making herself perfectly clear but also to conceal her irritation, '*Police Blotter* is actually a commercial net-magazine and not affiliated with law enforcement in any official way. We do have a national information center, but I need to know some kind of key fact that the search program can use to hunt down the information I want – a name, a date, a location.' She paused to see if any of this was forthcoming. The other woman only shrugged.

'Well, sorry I can't be of more help, but that's all I know.' She got up and stretched, pressing her hands into the small of her back. 'If anyone knows more, it's Body Sativa.'

'Body Sativa,' said the first customer interviewee. He was an aging child with green hair and claimed his name was Earl O'Jelly. 'Nobody knows more. Nobody and *no body*. If you get what I say here.'

Konstantin didn't bury her face in her hands. The aging child volunteered the information that he had been in the crowd by the Hudson that Shantih Love had staggered through, but claimed he hadn't seen anything like what she described to him.

Neither had the next one, a grandmother whose AR alter ego was a twelve-year-old boy-assassin named Nick the Schick. 'That means I technically have to have the "the" as my middle name, but there's worse and stupider, both,' she told Konstantin genially. 'Nick knows Body, of course. *Everybody* knows Body. And vice versa, probably. Actually, *I* think Body Sativa's really just a database that got crossed with a traffic-switcher and jumped the rails.'

'Pardon?' Konstantin shook her head, uncomprehending.

The grandmother was patient. 'You know how files can get cross-monkeyed? Well, like that. It coulda been that the traffic-switcher was referencing the database in a thunderstorm, or maybe sunspots, and they got the virtual equivalent of arc-welded. Then the traffic-switcher interface mutated from the acquired characteristics in all the database entries. That's what *I* say, anyhow, and *nobody's* proved yet that *that* couldn't happen. Or that it *didn't.*' She nodded once, looking wise.

Konstantin opened her mouth to tell the woman that if she understood her correctly, what she was describing was akin to putting a dirty shirt and a pile of straw in a wooden box for the purpose of spontaneously generating mice and then decided against it. For one thing, she wasn't sure that she *had* understood correctly and for another, the shirt-and-straw method of creating mice was probably routine in AR.

There was no third interviewee. Instead, an ACLU lawyer came in and explained that since the crime had occurred in the real world, and all the so-

called witnesses had been in AR, they weren't actually witnesses at all, and could not be detained any longer. However, all of their names would be available on the video parlor's customer list, which Konstantin could see as soon as she produced the proper court order.

'In the meantime, everyone agrees you ought to try talking to this, uh' – the lawyer consulted a palm-top – 'Body Sativa, whatever she is. Assuming she'll give you so much as the time of day without legal representation.'

'I suppose I need a court order for that, too,' Konstantin grumbled.

'Not hardly. AR is open to anyone who wants to access it. Even you, Lieutenant Konstantin.' The lawyer grinned, showing diamond teeth. 'Just remember the rules of admissibility. Everything everyone tells you in AR –'

'– is a lie, right. I got the short course tonight already.' Konstantin's gaze strayed to the monitor, now blank. 'I think I'll track this Body Sativa down in person and question her in realtime.'

'Only if she voluntarily tells you who she is,' the lawyer reminded her a bit smugly. 'Otherwise, her privacy is protected.'

'Maybe she'll turn out to be a good citizen,' Konstantin mused. 'Maybe she'll care that some seventeen-year-old kid got his throat cut.'

The lawyer's smug expression became a sad smile. 'Maybe. *I* care. *You* care. But there's no law that says anyone else has to.'

'I know. I'd be afraid if there was. Even so –' Konstantin winced. 'I do wish I didn't have to depend so much on volunteers.'

She sent DiPietro and Celestine over to the dead kid's apartment building, though she wasn't expecting much. If he really was typical, his neighbors would have barely been aware of him. Most likely, they would find that he had been yet another gypsy worker of standard skills, taking temporary assignments via a city-run agency to support his various habits. Not the least of which would have been his AR habit.

Just to be thorough, she waited in Guilfoyle Pleshette's office for the call letting her know that the other two detectives had found a generic one-room apartment in the city. Except for the carefully organized card library of past AR experience in the dustless, static-free, moisture- and fireproof nonmagnetic light-shielded container. Every heavy AR user kept a library, so that no treasured moment could be lost to time.

The library would go to headquarters to be stored for the required ten-day waiting period while a caseworker tried to track down next-of-kin. If none turned up, the card library would then be accessed by an automated program designed to analyze the sequences recorded on each card and construct a profile of the person, which would then be added to the on-line obituaries. Usually this would cause someone who had known the deceased to come forward; other times, it simply confirmed that there was no one to care.

The idea came unbidden to Konstantin, derailing the semi-doze she had

slipped into at whatever indecent a.m. the night had become. She plugged the archiver into the phone and sent the retriever to fetch data on the other seven AR DOAs.

Delivery was all but immediate – at this time of night, there wasn't much data traffic. Konstantin felt mildly annoyed that DiPietro and Celestine couldn't report in just as quickly. Perhaps they had taken the stringer with them and were even now playing to the cam in an inspection of the dead kid's apartment.

A bit of heartburn simmered in her chest; she imagined it was her blood pressure going up a notch. According to *The Law Enforcement Officers' Guide To A HEALTHY & HAPPY Life (ON & OFF The Job!)*, sex was the number-one stress reliever. Konstantin was sure that the *Guide* had most likely meant the sort that involved at least one other person. Sighing, she surveyed the data arranging itself on the archive's small but hi-res screen.

The first to suffer a suspicious death while in post-Apocalyptic Noo Yawk Sitty had been a thirty-four-year-old woman named Sally Lefkow. Her picture showed a woman so pale as to seem faded. She had passed most of her realtime hours as a third-rank senior on a Minneapolis janitorial team whose contract had included both the building where she had lived and the building where she had died. Konstantin wasn't sure whether to be amused, amazed, or alarmed that her on-line persona had been an evolved dragon. Eight feet tall and the color of polished antique copper, it had been bisexual, able to switch at will. Sally Lefkow had died of suffocation; the evolved dragon had been in flight when it had gone into a steep dive over the East River, entering the water at a high speed and never coming up again.

Konstantin put the dead woman's realtime background next to the information on the dragon to compare them but found she was having trouble retaining anything. 'In one eye and out the other,' she muttered, then winced. *Lover, come back – you forgot to take the in-jokes along with the rest of the emotional baggage.*

She marked the Lefkow-dragon combo and went on to the next victim, a twenty-eight-year-old gypsy office worker named Emilio Torres. Konstantin thought he looked more like an athlete. Or maybe an ex-athlete. He had died alone in his Portland apartment during an on-line session as – Konstantin blinked – Marilyn Presley. The hybrid had been an on-line flash-fad, hot for a day, passé forever after. But not, apparently, for Torres. He had persisted as Marilyn for six weeks, long after the rest of the flash followers had lost interest, and he had died – Konstantin blinked again – of an overdose of several drugs. During the OD, the Marilyn Presley persona had been – Konstantin blinked again – abducted by a UFO while attending some sort of gathering that wasn't quite a street brawl but not really an open air party, either. There

was no follow-up on the persona, nothing to tell Konstantin if Torres's license had been inherited, sold, or simply terminated.

Torres had died a month after Lefkow and half a continent away. The next death had occurred two months later, in a cheesy beach-side parlor in New Hampshire. March Kuykendall had been unembarrassed by his status as an AR junkie, supporting his habit with odd and mostly menial jobs. *Acquaintances of the victim have all heard him say, at one time or another, that realtime was the disposable reality because it could not be preserved or replayed in AR*, Konstantin read. *AR is humanity's true destiny. In AR, everyone is immortal.*

If you don't mind existing solely in reruns, Konstantin thought. Kuykendall had owned half a dozen personas, all creations original to him. Mortality had caught up with him while he had been acting out a panther-man fantasy. The panther-man had been beaten to death in the Gang Wars module by some vaguely monstrous assailant that everyone claimed not to have seen clearly. In realtime, Kuykendall had been found crumpled in a corner of the parlor cubicle, having taken blows hard enough to shatter both his head-mounted helmet and his head. No one in the parlor had seen or heard anything.

Victim number four had been in rehab for a year after a bad accident had left her paralyzed. Lydia Stang's damaged nerves had been regenerated, but she had had to relearn movement from the bottom up. AR had been part of her therapy; her AR persona had been a cat burglar who was an idealized gymnastic version of herself. She had died of a broken neck. On-line witnesses stated she had been drawn into a street duel with a lizard-person, and lost. Even better, the lizard-person had come forward voluntarily and admitted to AR contact with the deceased. Stang had been on-line in Denver, while the lizard-person had been cavorting in a parlor not three blocks from where Konstantin was sitting. She double-checked to be sure she had that right, and then made a note to look up the lizard-person in realtime.

A moment later, she was scratching the note out. The lizard-person was victim number five. Even more shocking, Konstantin thought, was the lack of information on the deceased, a former musician who had gone by the single name of Flo. After Lydia Stang's death, Flo had given up music and taken up AR full-time, until someone had suffocated her. On-line, her reptilian alter ego had been swimming in the East River. Maybe that meant something, Konstantin thought, and maybe it didn't. Why hadn't anyone cross-referenced the two deaths?

Victims six and seven would seem to have killed each other in a gang fight. Konstantin found this extremely disheartening. In post-Apocalyptic Noo Yawk Sitty, they had been a couple of nasty street kids, sixteen, just on the verge of adulthood. In realtime, they had been a pair of middle-aged gypsy office workers who had no doubt discovered that they had wandered into one of life's cul-de-sacs and weren't going to find their way out of it alive.

They had both lived in urban hives only a few blocks apart in Houston, got assignments through the same agency, did the same kinds of no-brainer file and data upkeep jobs, and yet, they apparently hadn't been acquainted off-line. Konstantin wondered if they had deliberately avoided ever meeting in realtime. On-line, however, they had mixed it up regularly. They had stabbed each other in a Gang Wars module; someone else had stabbed each of them in the privacy of their own homes. The times of death seemed to be in some dispute, but it didn't look like anyone had followed up.

And now here was number eight, a weird Caucasian kid with a Japanese name. *Domo arigato*, Konstantin thought sourly, exhausting her entire Japanese vocabulary, and pressed for a summary of the common characteristics of each case.

There wasn't much; each murder had occurred while the victim had been on-line in post-Apocalyptic Noo Yawk Sitty. Two had been local; two others had been local to each other. And unless it turned out that the weird Caucasian kid had been a brain surgeon, all of them had been lower-level drones.

Konstantin sat back in the chair, thinking hard. Was serial murder back in style – *again?* Someone who had been enjoying pretend-murder in AR deciding to cross over? Or perhaps could no longer tell the difference?

She put in a follow-up request for a table of similarities among the AR characters and came up with a *Data Not Available* sign. The note on the next screen told her there had been no work done in this area, either due to lack of software, lack of time, or lack of personnel. Undoubtedly no one had thought it was particularly important to look into the AR personae. After all, it wasn't as if *they* were the actual victims.

Were they?

For all anyone knew, Konstantin thought sadly, Sally Lefkow's dragon would be more missed and mourned than Sally herself. Likewise for the rest of them.

Sad, and somehow predictable. She made a note to send out for more background on the victims. While she was reviewing what information she had, DiPietro and Celestine called to tell her mostly what she had already known, except for one very surprising difference: upon arrival at the kid's apartment, they had found a nineteen-year-old woman in the process of ransacking the place. She would answer no questions except to say that she was the kid's wife.

Konstantin checked quickly. Sure enough, the kid was the only – or the first – married victim. 'Bring her down here,' she told them. 'Fast.'

'He was looking for the out door,' said Pine Havelock. 'Anybody was gonna find it, it was gonna be him. And now look what's gone and happened.' Tomoyuki Iguchi's self-proclaimed wife was sitting in a plastic bucket of a chair hugging her folded legs tightly and staring at Konstantin over the bony

humps of her knees with a half-afraid, half-accusing expression. Dressed in what looked like surplus hospital pajamas, she seemed to be completely hairless, without even eyelashes. Her eyes weren't really large enough to carry it off; she made Konstantin think of a hospital patient who had fallen into a giant vat of depilatory cream.

'What out door would that be?' Konstantin asked her after a long moment of silence. 'Do you mean the one to the secret Japanese area?'

Havelock raised her head, staring at her oddly. 'Get off.'

'What out door?' Konstantin said patiently.

'Out. *Out*. Over the rainbow, Never-Never Land, where you go and you'll stay. So you don't come back to something like' – she looked around Guilfoyle Pleshette's office with distaste – '*this.*'

'Uh-huh.' Konstantin leaned an elbow on the desk and rubbed her eyes. 'Where *would* you end up?'

'*Out.*' The woman's forehead puckered in spots; Konstantin realized she was frowning. Without eyebrows, all of her expressions were odd. 'You know – *out*. Where you don't need the 'suit or the hard-hat, because you're *there*. Not *here.*'

Konstantin finally got it. 'So you and, uh, your husband, Tom – was that his name when you married him?'

'Was *what* his name?' Havelock asked suspiciously.

'Tom. Tomoyuki Iguchi.'

'Does it matter?'

Konstantin took a breath. 'Yes. It matters.'

'Well, then, no, it wasn't. But he changed his name once a week.'

'Once a *week*?' Konstantin said doubtfully.

'Sometimes less often, sometimes more often.' Havelock shrugged. 'It depended on what he was in, or on, or over. He was Harry Houdini the day he found the out door.'

'And who was he when you got married?'

Havelock squinted into some vague place over Konstantin's right shoulder. 'Spiney Norman?' She hesitated. 'That, or Lan Shao Lin.'

'You don't remember what your husband's name was when you married him?' Konstantin couldn't keep the agitation out of her voice.

'What's in a name?' Havelock shrugged one shoulder. 'He used to say that all the time.'

'Really. While he was named Shakespeare?' Konstantin said sarcastically.

'No, I just told you he said it *all the time*. It's hard for me to remember exactly what name he was using when we got married because he was changing it a lot then.'

'It should be on your marriage certificate,' Konstantin said, sighing. 'You did get one of those, didn't you?'

'Well, it was a legal thing so I guess there's a copy on-line somewhere.' Havelock echoed Konstantin's sigh. 'Is there anything else you have to know right now?'

Konstantin consulted her notes on the archiver. 'You and Tom were looking for this magic door to the egress. Did you know of anyone else who wanted to –'

'Egress,' Havelock said, nodding vigorously. 'That's it. Door out, egress. This way to the egress.' That's how *she* referred to it.'

'Who?' Konstantin asked, and then all but said the answer with her.

'Body Sativa.'

'Sun's gonna come up,' Guilfoyle Pleshette warned; it sounded like a veiled threat. She looked tired. Even her hair was starting to lose its lift.

Still sitting at the desk in the minuscule office, Konstantin waved at her impatiently. 'Sorry, Taliaferro,' she said into the phone while she scrawled notes in the archiver one-handed. 'I didn't get the last thing you said. Repeat.'

Taliaferro was surprisingly patient. Perhaps lack of sleep had simply made a zombie out of him. 'I said, they're still running data on the other seven so we don't have anything real solid yet. But the probability is running to eighty percent that anyone who frequented the Sitty as often as any of them would, at some point, have had AR contact with the persona or entity known as Body Sativa.'

'"Entity?" Who's calling this thing an *entity?* The probability program, or someone who's in a position to know?'

'Actually, I heard some of the customers in the parking lot calling her that. Calling *it* that. I don't know.' Taliaferro sounded a bit sheepish. 'Probably it's some slicko with a talent for PR. Famous for being famous.'

'Do you do much AR?' Konstantin asked him impulsively.

'Is that a sincere question?'

'Sorry. Don't know what got into me. Have any of the people you questioned owned up to seeing anything out here in Dullsville? Anyone see the kid in the waiting room or talk to him, or see him talking to someone else?'

There was a short, wounded pause before Taliaferro answered. 'You know, I'm a claustrophobe, not an amnesiac. *Or* an idiot. I still know how to do my job.'

'Sorry, partner, I was just asking. No offense intended, okay?'

Taliaferro clicked off without replying. Konstantin turned to Guilfoyle Pleshette, who was yawning hugely and noisily. 'Like I told you before,' the manager said between the end of one yawn and the beginning of the next, 'he came in alone, and if he talked to anybody besides me or Mezzer, I didn't notice.'

'Yes, I remember. What I was going to ask was, do *you* do much AR?'

'Sure,' Pleshette said, surprised. 'The employee discount here's great.'

'You spend much time in post-Apocalyptic Noo Yawk Sitty?'

Now the manager shrugged and looked almost coy. 'I guess I been known to. You gotta scan rated zones because when you get a virgin in, you have to be able to talk about what you know when they ask you about this zone and that zone. I say that's the difference between a quality business and a ditch.'

Konstantin nodded absently. Once a place became too popular, no one would admit to wanting to go there, even in AR. 'And Body Sativa? Do you know about her?'

'Everybody knows about her, but not as many really seen her as say so.' Pleshette sounded wary again, as if she thought Konstantin were trying to trap her into admitting something.

'But *you* have. Haven't you?'

'Yeah.'

'Okay.' Konstantin hesitated. 'Think you could introduce me?'

'Of course *not*.' Pleshette drew back, offended.

'I didn't think so, but it was worth a try.'

'Hey, what you got to understand here is that anyone who knows Body and drags along every prole that wants to see her won't know her for too long.'

'I guess I can understand that. Suppose I go in and find her myself?'

Pleshette stared at her. 'You think you're that good right out of the box?'

'Well, one of your employees offered me some secret insider icons. Whatever those are.'

The manager straightened up, thrusting her head forward. 'Is that so? Who made this great offer?'

'The bored one. Mezzer.'

'Oh, him.' Pleshette tossed her head. 'You can find his so-called secret insider icons in the index of any on-line guidebook. *I* got stuff you can really get around with.'

Konstantin smiled tiredly. 'Ah, but will you loan any to me?'

The funny little face looked doubtful. 'What're you gonna do with them if I do?'

Konstantin shrugged. 'All I want to do is find this Body Sativa and ask her some questions.'

'What *kinda* questions?' the night manager asked suspiciously.

Now Konstantin felt as if she had fallen through a rabbit hole in time that had sent her back to the beginning of the situation, which she would have to explain all over again. 'Questions having to do with the kid who died here tonight – Shantih Love, Tomoyuki Iguchi, whichever you knew him as.'

'I *told* you, I didn't know him as anybody,' said Pleshette, looking at Konstantin as if she were an idiot. Konstantin felt like screaming. 'And there's no guarantee that Body Sativa did, either. But if that's all you really want to do – I mean, *all* – I can load some stuff for you. But you got to promise me, you won't misuse any of it.'

'Misuse it *how*?' Konstantin asked.

'Poaching.'

Konstantin had to take a breath. 'And what exactly would poaching entail?'

'Getting stuff you're not entitled to get, and taking credit for stuff you didn't do or didn't know. Shit like that.'

'Getting stuff? In AR?' Konstantin felt lost.

'Yeah. Stuff in AR. In the Sitty. Everyone who goes in regular's got stuff in AR.' The night manager folded her arms again. 'What kinda stuff you think I got out here? This nothing job? I got to put up with blowfish like Miles Mank, I live in a hive over on Sepulveda. But in the Sitty, I got *stuff*. I got a good place for myself, I'm in the game with the name and the fame. I even got myself a few passwords. I put in plenty of time and sweat to get all that and I don't want it just slipped out from under me when I'm not there to defend it.' The funny little face puckered unhappily. '*You* got stuff out here, you don't need to go poachin' my stuff in there. You see what I mean?'

Konstantin saw; it sent a wave of profound melancholy through her. 'All I want to do is contact Body Sativa if I can,' she said kindly. 'I don't want anything else. *Really.*'

Pleshette held her gaze for a long moment and then shrugged her bony shoulders. 'Yeah, well, you know, it's not like *I* can't tell the difference between in there and out here, it's not like I think I can put it all in the bank or anything. But I put a lot of time in. I spent some big sums doin' it. If I give it all away, then I got *nothing*. It was all for *nothing*. See?'

Konstantin nodded, wondering if this was the sort of thing a person might kill for. It was beginning to sound that way.

Guilfoyle Pleshette found a clean hotsuit in Konstantin's size and helped her put it on, giving her a flurry of instructions in her little cartoony voice. Konstantin felt silly, even though she knew this was really like any other information-gathering operation, except it was more like using the telephone. Unless what happened to the kid happened to her, she thought uneasily.

Tim Mezzer made good on his promise to supply icons and loaded the file into the headmount for her. 'All you have to do is ask for your icon cat,' he said, sounding just a little less bored. 'And if you're not sure which icon to try, ask for advice.'

Konstantin was mystified. 'Who am I supposed to ask?'

'The icons,' he said, looking at her as if she should have known this. 'They all have their own help files attached. But I gotta tell you, they're all pretty idiosyncratic there. You know how it is. What *some* people call help.'

Konstantin thought of the filing system back at headquarters and nearly backed out. After Pleshette loaded her own information, she took Konstan-

tin to one of the deluxe cubicles – deluxe because it was half again as large as the one where the kid had died, and included an easy chair. She helped Konstantin get comfortable in it, fastened the straps just tightly enough to keep her from falling if she got overly energetic, and fitted her headmount for her. Konstantin tried to thank her, but the headmount muffled her too well. She felt more than heard the woman leave the room. Fear rippled through her briefly but intensely; anyone could come in and do anything to you while you were immobilized with your head as good as buried, and you'd never know it until too late. If then.

The screen lit up with a control panel graphic. She turned on the log, which was an independent operation with only an on-off access, so she'd have her own record that, if necessary, she could prove had not been tampered with. Funny, she thought, how the first thing anyone had to do with taped evidence was prove that it hadn't been toasted.

The control panel graphic disappeared and the screen showed her the configuration menu. She made her choices – sighting graphic and help line on request – while the 'suit warmed up. This was a full coverage 'suit, she realized, suddenly uncomfortable with the idea. She hadn't given that any thought ahead of time and it was too late to do anything about it now. Besides, in a place like this, they were probably all full-coverage 'suits. Full-coverage would be the big attraction. As if to confirm her thoughts, a hotsuit ad replaced the configuration menu.

Because if you're not going to feel it all *over,* murmured a congenial female voice while a hotsuit, transparent to show all the sensors, revolved on the screen, *why bother?* Which, Konstantin thought, wasn't such an unreasonable question.

The headmounted monitor adjusted the fine-tuning for her focal length by showing her the standard introduction in block letters on a background of shifting colors. Konstantin sighed impatiently. So much introductory material with the meter running – she could see the clock icon tagging along at the upper edge of her peripheral vision on the right side. You probably couldn't go broke operating a video service, she thought, unless you tried real, real hard.

The sign came up so suddenly that it took a second to register on her, and even then she wasn't sure right away whether she was really seeing it, or imagining it. Seeing in AR felt strangely too close to thinking.

WELCOME TO THE LAND OF ANYTHING GOES
Here There Are No Rules
Everything Is Permitted

Uh-huh, thought Konstantin. The words faded out; more faded in.

You can choose to be totally anonymous
You can tell the whole truth about yourself
You can tell only lies

The word *lies* lingered as the others disappeared, flashing on and off in different colors before it evaporated.

No real crime is possible In Here. If you do something Out There as a result of events In Here, you are on your own. In the event of your persona's virtual death, you can request to be directed to central stores, where you can identify with another. The time used in choosing a new persona or performing any reference or maintenance task is not free, though a reduced rate may be available through your parlor operator, or through special promotions. Consult the rate file in your personal area for more information.

Konstantin looked around for a speed-scroll option.

No speed-scroll option is available for this portion of your first session. State and federal law specifically declare that all users must be advised of conditions in the gaming area. By reading this, you agree that you understand the structure and accept any charges, standard and/or extra, that you will incur at your point of origin. Closing your eyes will only result in a full rescroll of the introductory material, at your own expense.

Blink rate and eye movements could reveal a great deal about a person's thoughts, Konstantin remembered uneasily, especially when used in conjunction with vital signs.

This concludes the introductory material. The next screen will be your destination menu. Bon voyage, and good luck.

The screen that came up showed her four doors labeled *Post-Apocalyptic Noo Yawk Sitty, Pre-Millennial Hong Kong, Post-Quake Ellay*, and *Others*.

A small bright icon appeared at the bottom right corner of her visual field, a graphic of a hand twisting a doorknob. Just below it, on the status line, was the word *Cue!* Feeling awkward, she reached for the Noo Yawk Sitty door and saw a generic white-gloved hand moving toward the knob. As the hand touched the knob, she felt it in her own hand, the sensors delivering a sensation to the palm side of her fingers that surprised her with its intense authenticity. It was more like touching a doorknob than actually touching a doorknob.

The next moment was a flash of chaos, a maelstrom of noise and light, countless touches and textures everywhere at once, over before she could react to any of it. Under her feet, she could hear the scrape of the gritty glitz, the glitzy grit of post-Apocalyptic Noo Yawk Sitty; she could see the sparkle and glitter of it spread out before her – not Eliot's etherized patient awaiting dissection but a refulgent feast for her reeling senses.

HINT: In case of disorientation, amp your 'suit down and wait at least

thirty seconds before attempting movement. Closing your eyes could result in vertigo. This message will be repeated as necessary.

She thought she might have made some kind of relieved noise as she stared at the setting marked *decrease*. In a few moments, all the settings on the 'suit had been re-adjusted to a more bearable level. Whoever had had this 'suit on last, she thought, had either been extremely jaded or suffering from some kind of overall sense impairment. Both, maybe.

Now that she could perceive her surroundings without being assaulted by them, Konstantin was dismayed to find that she didn't seem to be anywhere near where Shantih Love had died. Instead, she was standing at the edge of an open area in the midst of a crowd of tall buildings festooned with enormous neon signs of a sort that had been popular seventy or eighty years before. Except for herself, there were no people, or at least none that she could see, and no sound except for a faint hum that might have come from the signs, or from some distant machine. Or possibly even some loose connection in the headmount, she thought sourly. It would be just her luck.

The buildings were dark, showing the scars of fires, bullets, and explosions, broken-out windows gaping like empty eye-sockets, but the signs were brilliant, impossibly vivid with shifting colors that melted and morphed like living ropes of molten light. There were no words that she could make out, only symbols that fell short of meaning anything to her. Somehow, though, that made the sight all the more captivating; she felt compelled to study every line, every bend and curve of every image, and finally managed to force herself to look away.

She was still feeling half-hypnotized when she saw a silvery figure standing in one of the open doorways. At first, she thought it was someone wearing – pretending to wear, she corrected herself – a skintight bio-suit but then the figure moved forward and she saw that its skin was the same color as the clothes it wore. The figure moved closer and she had to amend her perceptions: the figure was the same color as its clothing.

'New in town?' it sang, approaching with careful movements.

'Maybe,' she said, taking a step back.

'Oh, you're new, all right.' The figure, which began to look more like it was made of mercury or chrome, gestured at something behind her. Konstantin turned to look.

The sight of the completely hairless and sexless creature in the dark glass made her jump; then she cringed with embarrassment. Since she had not chosen a persona, she was wearing a place holder. Her gaze darted around as she searched for the exit icon.

'It's not necessary to leave,' the silvery figure said in its musical voice. Now that it was right next to her, Konstantin could see it was a sort of animated sculpture of a very tall and very young woman seemingly formed from soft-

ened platinum. Or something like it. 'Pull down Central Stores and choose Wardrobe. Then just follow the directions.'

'Oh. Thank you so much.' Feeling awkward, Konstantin stuck out her hand. 'I'm, uh, Dore. And you're right. I'm new here.'

The silvery girl seemed unaware of her extended hand. 'I am a pop-up-help-and-guide subroutine keyed to respond to situations and types of situations most often identified with new users of AR and/or post-Apocalyptic Noo Yawk Sitty. I am also available on request. Pull down Help and ask for Sylvia.'

Konstantin started to thank her again but the girl pointed at something behind her. She turned around and found herself standing at a shiny white counter. The words TOUCH HERE FOR ASSISTANCE faded in on its surface, going from pale pink to blood red and back to pale pink before disappearing. Konstantin gingerly put a fingertip on the spot where she estimated the middle of the O in FOR had been.

'Help you?' said a hard-edged male voice. The short, plump man who appeared on the other side of the counter looked as if he were answering a casting call for a play about bank tellers in 1900. The green visor on his forehead cast a shadow that it made it hard to see anything of his eyes except reflected pinpoints of light.

'Where's the rest of your hat?' Konstantin asked impulsively.

'This is an eye-shade, not a hat,' he replied, in that same sharp, almost harsh tone. 'Its presence connotes items and equipment available to you in AR, some at a surcharge. Do you want to see a list: of items and equipment with their corresponding surcharges? These can also be itemized on the hardcopy printout of your receipt.'

'I don't know. Is a persona classified as an item or as equipment?'

'Neither. A persona is a persona. Did you have someone in particular in mind or were you planning to construct one in here? Morphing services within AR are available for a surcharge. However, there is no extra charge if you have brought your own morphing utility with you. Except, of course, for any extra time that might be consumed by the morphing process.'

Konstantin found herself yawning. So far, her big AR adventure was turning out to be even more tiresome than the reality she was used to. 'Does anybody really do anything in here besides listen to how much everything is costing them?'

'First-time users are advised to take the orientation sequence. Usually in some location easier to navigate than a post-Apocalyptic scenario.' His harsh voice sounded as bored as she felt.

'I want out,' she said. 'Out of the whole thing, I mean. Exit. End it. Good-bye. Stop. Quit. Logging off. Is that enough or do I need a fucking thesaurus utility?'

Abruptly, she was staring at a blank illuminated screen. Her 'suit was in *Sus-*

pend, she saw, but still active. Words began to crawl up the screen in a steady scroll.

Your time in your chosen AR location has been halted. Readings indicate a high level of tension and stress in a low-level situation. Generally this occurs when the user is confused or has not taken proper instruction in the use of AR. You may also be experiencing onset of an illness; you should seek the advice and, if necessary, treatment from a qualified health practitioner. It is also possible that you may be too fatigued to cope with an AR experience; if so, it is advisable that you terminate your on-line session and rest. In rare cases, AR has triggered episodes of psychomotor epilepsy or other seizure disorders in those persons who are susceptible or who may have ingested certain kinds of medications or drugs that put them at risk. Please be advised that although AR does not cause seizure disorders, it can cause the onset of symptoms of a pre-existing yet (until now) hidden disease. See your qualified health practitioner for advice and treatment. Do you wish to continue in AR, or do you wish to terminate the program and exit? Please choose one option and one option only.

She was about to tell it to terminate when she heard what sounded like a telephone ringing.

The words on the screen vanished and a new message appeared quickly, word by word. *Realtime communication with you is being requested. Do you want to talk to the caller? Please answer yes or no.*

'Who is it?' she asked automatically.

Secretarial services are extra.

'Never mind,' she groaned. 'Put them on. I mean, *yes*.'

There was a click and she heard the familiar cartoony tones of Guilfoyle Pleshette. 'What are you doing?'

'I don't know,' Konstantin admitted.

'Yeah, what I thought. Icons and passwords don't do you a bit of good if you don't know what you're doing. That's an advanced 'suit I put you in. It doesn't carry a prefab for you. You got to bring your own.'

'My own what?' asked Konstantin, stumbling as she tried to keep up.

'Your own *persona*. I thought the way you were talking about going on-line to see Body Sativa and all, you had one you wanted.'

'I do.'

'You *don't* You don't *have* one, you went in there blank. But if you got one *in mind*, I can help you out.'

'Oh.' Konstantin felt foolish.

'So?' Pleshette snapped after a long moment. '*Do* you have one in mind, and if you do, who is it?'

'Uh, yeah. Shantih Love.'

Konstantin pictured Pleshette not batting an eye back in the real world. Or the outside world, whatever. 'You want that with or without the cut throat?'

'With,' Konstantin said. 'And I want a copy of the surveillance footage loaded into a subroutine I can run at will.'

'You're gonna run a sequence within a sequence?'

'If it looks like it might get me some answers. I can do that, can't I?'

'Yeah, but it's pretty expensive.' Pleshette sounded both annoyed and worried. 'We don't get the feeds free from the network, you know. Who's gonna pay for all of this on-line time and fun and games?'

'You are,' Konstantin said.

'*What?*'

'The good citizens of our fair city. Your tax dollars at work, that is.'

Pleshette's laugh was low and hearty. 'Not *my* tax dollars. I don't pay taxes, not on my salary. You want to impress some taxpayers, catch some criminals in there and drag 'em out with you when you log off.'

EMPTY CUP [III]

Yuki wandered for what felt like hours, looking for a door out of the enormous indefinite place she was in, whatever it was supposed to be. The walls of the place were deceptively far away. Sometimes she thought she was drawing close to one of the tall windows only to find that the floor had somehow stretched under her feet, or rolled like a treadmill, and she was no closer.

Irritated, she looked around the edges of her vision for the exit icon. Time to pull the plug on this stupid excursion. What the hell, Tom was a big boy. Maybe he was even now living it up in some on-line resort. Or in hell, whichever he was in the mood for.

If you're going, then go. Or admit you're too curious now not to stay. Either way, commit. *Remember that word? Or is it impossible now that you're wearing Tom's face?*

'I should *be* committed,' she said aloud. She put a hand out to stop one of the vague people moving past her; it went through the vagueness without touching anything solid. 'Great. How am I supposed to get out of here?'

The pocket at the bottom of the vest on the left side beeped. She unzipped it and found a folded map. *Figures,* she thought, glad there was no one to see her embarrassment. The front panel of the map showed a simple illustration of a rectangle with a stick figure inside. Next to it was a green dot marked EXIT. She laughed at herself. Of course – just ask. As Ash would have said, *Some things are just too bone-simple for us* real smart *people.*

*

The wall encircling the stone courtyard seemed to be infinitely large, with an infinite number of doors leading to various AReas (she groaned at the notation on the map). Yuki knew it was indefinite rather than infinite, but it was theorized that a person could starve to death before looking at every door – and legend had it that someone had, though legend was also hazy on where this had taken place, D.C., maybe (life was so cheap there, a whole different world, don't you know) – it may as well have been infinite.

She consulted the map again and found that it had, very helpfully, set itself to a new page.

PREVIOUS ROUTE NEW ROUTE HELP & NEWS

Help & News? Maybe later. She ran a virtual finger across *Previous Route*.
User? The map wanted to know.
'Tomoyuki Iguchi,' she said carefully.
A cartoony yellow arrow appeared with Tom's name on it; underneath, in smaller letters, was the terse command: *See News*.
She ran her thumb up the panel to the word *News*.
Iguchi, Tomoyuki: reassigned; deceased; occupied.
Yuki stared. She tried pressing *News* again; the words blinked but did not change, and there was no further information. Out of desperation, she pressed her fingertip on *deceased*. There was a brief pause before the words came up underneath.

> 1. *Post-Apocalyptic Noo Yawk Sitty; transferred Re-registered active; equipped*
> 2. *Post-Apocalyptic Noo Yawk Sitty, homicide Unregistered active*

'What does *this* mean?' Yuki asked the map, tapping the word *transferred*. The map didn't answer. A cherub head suddenly materialized in front of her, floating just a bit higher than eye level.
'Help you?' the head asked cheerfully, wings fluttering. It was blue-eyed and pink-cheeked and looked absolutely thrilled to be there.
'It says "transferred" here. What does that mean?'
The cherub head pursed its rosy lips thoughtfully. 'Identity transferred on-line.'
'*What identity?*' Yuki demanded, all but screaming. 'His name and appearance or his on-line character?'
'One is the same as the other, on-line,' replied the cherub, in a kindly voice.
'But Tomoyuki Iguchi is his *real* name, not his on-line name.'
The head tilted to one side and winked cutely at her. 'On-line names *are* real names. On-line.'

453

'I know, but –' Yuki paused and took a break. 'Tomoyuki Iguchi was the *off-line* name of the person who called himself Tomoyuki Iguchi *on-line*. But he must also have had an on-line identity, another identity besides Tomoyuki Iguchi. What was it?'

The head tilted to the other side. 'There's no cross-referencing between any real and/or on-line name and any other real and/or on-line name.'

'Then how do you prevent duplications?'

'Duplications of what?' the head asked her, looking honestly puzzled.

'Appearances. Names. On-line identities.'

The cherub's eyes twinkled. 'There is none.'

Yuki hesitated. There was never any percentage in getting mad at a subroutine. 'No, that can't be right,' she said after a long moment of not screaming. 'There has to be some duplication going on. There is in real life.'

'There is none in *any* life,' the cherub announced with obvious joy. 'There are always at least minute differences that distinguish one similar thing from another similar thing. They might not be immediately perceptible, but they are there.'

'Are you trying to tell me it's impossible for someone in here to duplicate someone else's appearance, even if you copied every little detail?'

'I am not trying. I *did* tell you.'

She considered yanking the cherub's wings, lack of percentages notwithstanding. 'What if I duplicated – *exactly* – this appearance, all the way down to the tiniest detail? What would be the difference between one and the other?'

'Duration,' the cherub said promptly.

'Duration?' Yuki echoed.

'How long. Age. How old. Period in time, which is marked very precisely here. Billing, you know.'

'Right,' Yuki said, more to herself. 'God forbid that someone gets away with a free half-second.'

'A lot can happen in half a second,' said the cherub, managing to look wise as well as cute now.

'Is that so?' Yuki sighed. 'How do I find out someone's duration?'

'Ask that person.'

'And if the person won't tell me? Or lies about it?'

The cherub's face puckered sorrowfully. Yuki could even see tears welling in the bright eyes. 'Then you won't know. Privacy in an unprivate world is a precious commodity.'

'Then how do you know who to bill and how much?' Yuki demanded. 'Tell me *that*.'

'I don't know,' the cherub said, happy again.

'Why not?'

'I don't have to. I'm not the billing function.'

Yuki closed her eyes for a moment. 'You're a big help.'

'Aw. Thank you.' The cherub kissed the air between them and sent a small cluster of tiny red hearts at her. They disintegrated around her head in a silent explosion of sparkles as the cherub vanished. Cutesy help files; Yuki wondered whose idea *that* had been.

She looked down at the map again. What little information there was began and ended in post-Apocalyptic Noo Yawk Sitty. Maybe that was too simple-minded, but she would try it anyway. Maybe flashing Tom's face around his last known location would stir something up. Maybe even raise the dead.

POST-APOCALYPTIC NOO YAWK SITTY
ENTRY POINT
Bureau of Tourism

Yuki looked from the sign to the map and back to the sign. Pressing the destination on the map should have delivered her right into post-Apocalyptic Noo Yawk Sitty; instead, she was standing in a high-ceilinged hallway that dead-ended at this sign in front of her, and disappeared into indefinite shadows behind her.

'You coming in?' asked a voice that managed to sound both bored and impatient at the same time.

Yuki frowned at the sign, unsure if that was what was speaking to her. 'I thought I was already in.'

'You will be as soon as you complete the entry procedure,' the voice said. It might have been female or male; like the vocalizer on her email service, it was indeterminate.

'Isn't it absurd for someplace that's supposed to be post-Apocalyptic to have a tourist bureau?'

'It's absurd for someplace that's supposed to be post-Apocalyptic to exist in a medium as technological and structured as Artificial Reality. You can stand there and talk philosophy and popular culture all day – I was developed by a frustrated philosopher and I've got conversation forever. But it's all billable time, so think it over. How important is it for you to be right?'

'Stop that and let me in,' Yuki said, stung. Immediately, she was standing in an office, facing an androgyne dressed in something that suggested a collision between a military uniform and a dance costume from the Middle East. Yuki groaned.

'Are you in pain?' asked the androgyne, not pretending concern.

'Ten million years of evolution and technology and the best anyone can come up with in artificial reality – where anything is possible – is a standard office situation.'

'Oh, you're in aesthetic pain.' The androgyne sounded even more bored.

'I just don't think it's right to charge for on-line time spent standing in an office. You don't have to be in artificial reality to stand in some office.'

'Indications were that you needed orientation.' The androgyne looked heavenward and sighed. 'Exhaustive studies have proven conclusively that orientation is best accomplished in very familiar and mundane surroundings that don't distract from the essential information to be imparted.'

'Ten million years of evolution and technology and we haven't figured out a better way to convey essential information,' said Yuki in disgust.

'Agreed. I'm taking suggestions for something better. You first.' The androgyne waited a beat. 'Well, maybe another time. Here's your map, here's your catalog, here's some icons to put in your catalog and get you started. You might want to take some time to look over all of that material. Orientation inventory is billed at a lower rate.'

'Now I remember what I always hated most about AR,' said Yuki, trying to hold on to items she couldn't quite see clearly. 'Every other word out of anyone's mouth has something to do with billing rates.'

'I didn't realize *you* were here on a scholarship from a sugar daddy.'

Yuki had started to turn away with her vague bundles; now she turned back, frowning. 'Um, exactly how *is* my time being billed?'

'I don't know. That's not orientation,' said the androgyne, leaning back in the chair with a rattle of beads. All the beads seemed to be cycling through a series of colors, except none were running the same series at the same rate. Yuki felt her eyes crossing and wondered why she hadn't noticed this before. Or had all that color changing started at just that moment? She thought of Joy Flower.

The androgyne yawned noisily. 'Next case.'

'Wait. I mean, is this my account, or is someone else responsible financially?'

'Don't know.'

Yuki's eyes were starting to hurt. 'You don't know who's paying?'

'Don't you? Somebody must be, because you're here, but that's all I know. That's all I have to know. Now, move over to a privacy area if you're going to check your inventory, and if you're not, just go.'

'Aren't you going to wish me a pleasant session or something?'

The androgyne raised gold-threaded eyebrows in mild surprise. 'Why should I?'

'So much for customer service,' Yuki said. 'Aren't you supposed to make me happy so I'll want to come back?'

'You already want to come back. Everyone wants to come back. Everyone wants this, everyone needs it. Everyone's happy.' The androgyne shrugged.

'A customer service module probably wouldn't take up any more space

than your boredom program,' Yuki said. 'And why are you an androgyne? Isn't that kind of a stupid stereotype, being camped-up and bored?'

'It would be as much a stereotype as a man or a woman. Did you want the suggestion box? Do away with stereotyping minor administration employees and clerks in dead-brain jobs? I've got several of those in the suggestion box to be forwarded.' The androgyne held up a shoe box marked *Suggestions*. 'They're all from minor administrators and clerks in dead-brain jobs. What do *you* do for a living?'

Yuki shifted uneasily. 'I'm an assistant.'

Apparently that wasn't a trigger word. The androgyne put the box on the desk between them. 'I'll leave that there, in case you feel inspired before you exit. Anything else?'

'No, uh –' Yuki turned around, unsure of the direction she should take.

'Follow the blue line on the floor,' said the androgyne through a yawn. 'It'll take you to the nearest available privacy area.'

'I still think your boredom program is offensive.'

'It's not a program. You think this is bad, you ought to see the show on low-speed access.'

Yuki had started to walk away; now she turned, intending to ask the androgyne what that last was supposed to mean and saw that somehow, a door had materialized between them. *Exit Only!* said the raised letters in the imitation wood. *To reenter, log out and log in again.* Below that, in smaller letters: *Not for use as an information source or help file. Users are directed to consult help files in the appropriate handbook. Handbooks are available for an extra charge, plus a surcharge for indefinite reservation and custom annotation.*

Yuki shrugged inwardly and followed the blue line on the floor until it dead-ended at a plain white empty cubicle with a built-in desk and chair. As soon as she sat down, an ad came up on the desktop advising her that she could reserve the same privacy area for repeated visits at a rate less than half of what it would cost her to reserve an address in a moderately popular AR city. Yuki leaned over and, without letting go of her items, swiped at the ad with one hand to erase it.

The map was a standard issue as far as she could tell. She spread it out on the desk and surveyed the overview of post-Apocalyptic Noo Yawk Sitty. Major landmarks and exits were noted, along with trauma treatment sites – legend had it that the Sitty was not for the squeamish, though she suspected this was more hype than help – but there were a number of vague, clouded areas on the map. *Because,* said the sell-line running along the bottom, *you don't want us to tell you* EVERYTHING, *do you!*

Don't I just. She ran a finger over the settings icon in the bottom right-hand corner. There it was – high-speed access. She puzzled over it. She'd never heard of high-speed access. Multiple levels of access, yes, but not multiple speeds. What if she tried to change the setting?

But that particular setting wasn't accessible, she found. Somehow it had been bundled into her account as a fixed feature.

She turned her attention to the route-planner and tried to program it for Tomoyuki Iguchi's previous route. There was a long pause, and then the same notation came up, about Tom's transfer of on-line identity and decease.

'So *what*,' she growled at the map. 'He's deceased online so I can't follow the previous route taken by this user-name?' She stabbed the word *route* with one finger and an explanation popped up out of the map to hang in the air before her at eye level.

Deceased routing not saved; information erased.

Yuki poked *deceased*. 'Where did he become deceased? You should be able to tell me that.'

The explanation box morphed into an arrow and touched the map on the shoreline on the west side of the Sitty.

'Okay. That's where I want to go. First destination, select.'

A small animation of a sausage rotating over a flame blossomed on the spot. *Hot Link*. Yuki rolled her eyes. Another thing she had not liked much about artificial reality was the penchant for terrible puns. She started to fold the map; it emitted a sharp buzzing noise and she opened it up again. A word balloon popped up and hung over the map for a few moments. *REMINDER!! Only THREE Hot Links permitted PER SESSION!!*

'Yeah, yeah, yeah,' she muttered, folding the map. God forbid anyone should use billable time too efficiently to run up a big tab. Yuki examined the catalog and the icons. One was a ticket of admission to something, probably a club. The words *Admit One: ALL Hours* had been done as a flashing multi-colored neon tubing on a plastic rectangle the size of the real Waxx24 admittance cards that Ash collected with regularity.

There were also two circular pieces slightly larger than the palm of her hand. She knew those were tokens for some conveyance – flying submarine, underground plane, or even a warp booth, if she could find the right kind. One token to go on and one to return, saving much billable time, of course. Very considerate. She tucked those and the club ticket into the catalog. The other three items were museum-quality reproductions of old-style lottery tickets – you asked a question and then scraped off a colored surface material to reveal the answer. You might get a right answer, a cryptic hint, a dunno, or the coveted one-in-a-trillion jackpot of all questions answered for free.

She let them all fall into the icon catalog, which she zipped back into the vest pocket. Maybe she would even think quickly enough to use some of them.

That's really why you don't like AR, isn't it – because you can't usually think fast enough to get a decent run out of it.

She tried to shove the thought away. AR was for people who were too scared to take chances in real life, and anyone with any sense knew *that*. AR was for

people like Tom Iguchi, who would rather pursue a nonexistent Grail through an imaginary world than try to sustain a real life in a real place, where things sometimes took years to develop rather than nanoseconds, and where you couldn't save your place, rewind, and re-do a sequence when you goofed up.

Which begs the question, why are you bothering with him?

'Oh, who wants to know?' she muttered aloud, and then winced with alarm. *Getting twitchy already*. She picked up the map and touched the Hot Link.

Yuki stood in the middle of a wide, six-lane street, squinting out over a body of water in the late afternoon sun. Shiny particles in the broken, ruined pavement sparkled and glittered, as if the streets of post-Apocalyptic Noo Yawk Sitty were paved with crushed diamonds. Perhaps they were, or at least this one was. It was also studded with clumps of car and building wreckage that made her think of teepees. Otherwise, there were no signs of any kind of life.

So was this it – the big, bad Sitty? Where was all the post-Apocalyptic glamour everybody was always raving about? Or was modern life so absurdist now that abandoned ruins from the last century were the bleeding edge of this-minute fashion?

The sun seemed to be stuck where it was in the sky, later than afternoon but not twilight yet. She looked around and then jumped, startled – a skinny kid, maybe eleven years old, had materialized on her right. He was grimy in a way that suggested repeated showers wouldn't have helped and his peculiar silvery-grey hair had been cut at various times in various places with various cutting implements. The expression on his face was nothing like a child's and it wasn't just the very light blue eyes. Their hue was so pale that they were actually more tinged than truly blue.

'Who are you?' she asked as he studied her with one hand to his chin. Like a little old man, Yuki thought. There was a flicker; he was holding a butterfly knife so that she could see the reflection of Tom's wide eyes in the blade. One of them suddenly closed in a sly wink and her mouth dropped.

'You don't remember your old buddy Nick the Schick? What's the matter, Iggy, you on drugs?' The boy lowered the knife, frowning. '*Are* you Iggy?'

'Do I look like Iggy?' Yuki asked him, trying to sound lofty instead of spooked.

'*Just* like him,' said Nick the Schick. 'But you sure don't *act* like him. And you don't smell like him, either.'

'Smell?' Yuki tilted her head, skeptical. 'You can smell me in here?'

'You pay extra, but it's always worth it. But I *don't* pay extra to be around someone who keeps saying shit like "in here" or "out there." I don't come here to get my illusion ruined.'

'And where *do* you go for that?'

Nick the Schick stuck out his tongue and licked the flat of the blade. 'I

could show you, but what would be in it for me?' He tossed the knife into the air with a flick of his wrist. It spun around and came down to land handle-first on the back of his hand. A moment later he snatched it away, as if he thought she might try to take it; the movement was quick, but not so quick that she didn't see an ornate logo reading SCHICK on the ice blue handle. He started to make another movement but she put a hand on his arm.

'Save it. I saw the handle on that thing. Where would little pokes like you be without the subsidies?' To her own ears she sounded more bitter than sarcastic.

He pulled away from her, swaying and nodding his head to some rhythm that only he could hear. 'What about it? They don't make me sing and dance over it, I just give good value and get good icon. No different than if I was top chop in the shop.'

'You're a walking ad.'

'*Icon*,' the Schick insisted. He twirled the knife one-handed, passing it through his fingers with a dexterity that was no doubt part of the package. If the right advertiser got ahold of you, you could do pretty well in AR. Although they only approached you if you were already pretty good anyway. *Potentiate*. She remembered that from an old course on jargon. Got to be a good *potentiator*. 'Someday you could check in here and find the Nick the Schick icon is the one everyone wants for their cat.'

'What will be you be an icon for?'

He hooted laughter up at the sky. 'What do you mean, what for? Who wouldn't want to be an icon?'

'I don't mean why. I mean, for what. What would I get from you if you were an icon?'

The kid hesitated for what felt like a very long time. '*Ack-sess*,' he said finally. '*Big* ack-sess.'

'Access to what?'

'The soon-to-be-legendary Nick the Schick level. What else?' The kid made a complicated flourish with the knife, drawing a shiny chrome line that hung in the air for a few moments before twinkling out of existence.

'Nice effect,' Yuki said sincerely. 'But what's on this soon-to-be-legendary Nick the Schick level?'

'Nothing. *Yet*. But someday, it could be the next level everyone'll want to go to.' He gestured at her with the knife. 'That the highest speed you can get on your rig today?'

'I don't know. Why? What's the big deal over high speed?'

The boy held up his left hand, palm outward. 'Can you see this?' An impossibly colorful animated cobra reared up on the boy's skin. A moment later, the flat, hooded head lunged forward out of plane and stopped a few centimeters short of her nose.

'Yeah,' she said. 'I can see that.'

'Well, you can't at low speed. The faster you go, the more you know.'

'Sounds fancy,' Yuki said. 'So how does someone go fast in here?'

'If you're gonna try to tell me that you didn't get no hot shot before you came in here, I'm gonna let me cobra bite you.' The cobra snapped back into his palm. She thought of the sting at the back of her neck. All right, she had understood that was some kind of injection, and she had figured it would be some kind of stimulant. But she didn't feel terribly speedy.

'They say you get going fast enough, you can find the Out Door. Somebody said they thought you did that.' He took on a studiedly casual air. 'So, how about it? *Can* you get higher? Did you do it already? Did you get anything new when you did?'

'Aren't you supposed to buy that information?' Yuki asked him.

He laughed. 'Okay. You're Iggy. Or an acceptable replacement.'

Acceptable replacement. The words echoed in her mind. What eleven-year-old talked like that? None, of course. Kids couldn't access this kind of AR ... could they? Yuki felt a vague nausea pass through her like a warning sign. 'How'd you decide that?'

The boy snorted and then stared at her incredulously. 'You really *don't* know what you're doing.'

'So? When has that stopped anyone from doing anything, any time, anywhere?'

'You just pricked a destination on a map, right?' He nodded, answering his own question. 'Sure. Still got the map?'

Yuki shrugged, adjusting the vest importantly.

'Well, take it out, I'm not gonna steal it. It won't work for me, it's keyed to you.'

'Oh.' Yuki took the map out and unfolded it, holding it at waist level so they could both look at it.

'Yeah, you just pricked on location. You didn't specify anything else – time of day, mode, module. I mean, the default module is *General* if you don't choose one, but there's no defaults for time and mode, you *have* to set those. So where you are now is the sample set.'

She nodded. 'Okay. I didn't know.' She looked at him sideways. 'What's your excuse?'

'I was about to go party and I saw you pop in, so I waited to see what you were gonna do. I thought you were Iggy.'

'Iguchi Tomoyuki. In other words.'

'Yeah. So, what's the take-up with this? You're a real Jap and he wasn't?'

She found his kidney on the first try. 'This time, I'll pretend you hiccuped after the first syllable of "Japanese" so I didn't hear the rest of the word. But just *this* time.'

He rubbed his lower back. 'You know, there's plenty that disable the pain option on my hotsuit. I coulda. I don't come in here to get hurt the way some of 'em do.'

'How generous of you, to take such a chance. Of course, if you happen to hurt someone whose pain option *isn't* disabled, your 'suit automatically restores yours at the same level and allows you to share the sensation immediately. Everyone knows *that*. How stupid did you think I was?'

The kid shrugged and twirled his knife again. They came to another cross street, where the wreckage of two cars, sans wheels, stood on end, leaning against each other in an impossibly balanced A-shape. Yuki stifled a laugh. 'The ruins of one civilization become the ornaments of the next.'

Nick the Schick gave her a wary look. '*You* are most definitely *not* Iggy. *That* shit would *never* occur to him.' Pause. 'Well, I don't think it would, anyway.' He went over to the abandoned building on the diagonal corner from them, stood on tiptoe to reach as high as he could, and drove the knife into the dirty stone.

The knife went through easily; the kid sawed his way down from the top of his reach to a point about a foot from the ground, and then took the cut sideways for a couple of yards. Then he reached down and pulled up the corner he had just cut in the wall as if it were a piece of paper. In the roughly triangular space that had opened, Yuki could see pavement shining wetly, reflecting nighttime neon colors. 'Care to use my entrance?'

'Sure,' she said, stepping forward. He put one leg through the hole so that he was straddling both sides, holding the flap of building up for her.

'I'll go first,' he said smugly. 'Just in case.'

She wasn't sure what she had been expecting – music, lights, colors, a one-million-piece marching symphony orchestra conducted by a giant purple rabbit – even just a one-note chime signaling a change in status or location. Instead the passage from one area to another was so uneventful, it threw her completely off balance. She staggered back and hit the wall with her shoulder blades. It was brick on this side and the impact made her wince; it felt more real than any other wall she had ever met.

'Watch the vertigo,' she heard the kid tell her, his voice faint as if he were already far away from her. She started to push herself away from the wall and found two strong arms encircling her neck and shoulders from behind. She looked down; the arms had the brick-and-mortar texture of the wall they had come out of, though they felt like living, hard-muscled flesh.

'And what's *your* hurry, Bright Eyes?' said a gravelly voice close to her ear.

'Let go,' she said, wincing. The brick-textured skin scraped like sandpaper.

'Where's your ticket for admission?' There was a gargled laugh. 'Everybody wants to come in here, love-lady, but that's just not allowed.'

The kid reappeared, balancing the knife point down on his index finger again. What a show-off, she thought, irritated. 'You *do* have a ticket, don't you, Iggy?'

She worked the catalog out of her vest pocket and opened it up. The card that said *Admit One: All Hours* floated up in front of her face, flashing on and off with a new message: *WELCOME TO WAXX24*. Ash would kill her if he ever found out, Yuki thought, trying not to feel smug in spite of everything. Ash would kill her and then die himself. One of the brick hands plucked the card out of the air.

'And now, a tip for the conscientious doorman,' rasped the wall into her ear, sending a wave of chilly goose bumps over the back of her neck. 'The conscientious doorman who keeps all that wretched refuse from the golden door. The conscientious doorman would be me.'

Nick the Schick flipped his knife into the air, where it made several full revolutions in slo-mo before sliding down through the air to rest its point on his index finger again. 'Sorry, but you got to give it a token from your cat.'

'Did you know this would happen?' Yuki managed to choke out.

The kid smiled. 'Guess you're pretty green after all. Don't worry, you buy it back on the black market.'

She wanted to ask what would happen if she refused this generous offer, except she couldn't seem to get enough breath for it. The catalog pages flipped; the transportation token levitated off a page, told her *Bye-bye!* in a squeaky little voice, and disappeared into the brick hand. The hand patted her on the head good-naturedly and let her go.

Yuki moved quickly out of reach, but nothing came after her. The wall was just a wall again; there was no outline or pattern that suggested arms or any other body parts. 'It took one of my travel tokens,' she complained to the kid, who was still laughing at her. 'What in *hell* does a goddam brick wall want with a travel token?' She waited; the kid laughed some more. 'Well?'

'Maybe it's gonna become a travel agent?' the Schick offered with a giggle.

She moved away from him and consulted the map. 'Okay, where am I *now*? Where is this Waxx24 place?' But she had forgotten the kid as soon as she had opened the map again. It had changed – it looked as though some sort of overlay had been added to give it more detail. She was on a side street near the six-lane highway paralleling the shore, not far from where she had entered at first, on the abandoned street under the stalled sun. But the street was no longer abandoned and there was no sun at all in the black sky. For all she knew, there never had been one here. But it wasn't just the unending night that made everything look out of whack.

There was something funny with movement here, movement and perception. She looked up at a vintage neon-tube sign formed into a green palm tree next to a fuchsia ankh. When she turned away, both tree and ankh bled streams of color across her field of vision.

'*Hey.*' A sharp poke in her kidney. 'Are you still here, or did you already ass-end to a new level of existence? And if you did, why didn't you take your old friend Nick the Schick, without whom you wouldn't have been able to find the hottest club level in the universe in the first place?'

She ignored the kid and looked down at herself. Tom's body was unhurt; there was just a little brick powder on his sleeves. She brushed it away, dusted off her gloved hands, and glared at the wall. '*Stupid,*' she whispered, meaning herself. The only way anything happened to you here was if you let it; she knew that as well as the most addicted die-hard AR fanatic knew it. Allowing yourself to be fooled into buying the illusion was a big sign of even bigger weakness. You looked out for yourself here because nobody else would, and judging from what bits Tom had told her, and what she had seen, nobody did.

She turned to say something to the kid but he was gone. Down at the end of the street, where it opened onto the defunct road, she could see a burning clump of wreckage and a lot of foot traffic, not all of it human, or even humanoid. She moved down the alley, willing herself to stroll casually, as if she did this all the time. A little ways from the corner, some movement on her right caught her eye. She dared a quick glance and then jumped, startled.

Across the street, her reflection in the grimy, streaked store window stared back at her. Or rather, Tom's reflection. She didn't think she would ever get used to seeing someone else's reflection. Even the expression on the face was all wrong; it didn't look anywhere near as frightened as she actually felt.

Reflection? She moved one hand toward her lapel. In the filthy glass, one hand also moved toward the lapel except that it didn't do it quite at the same moment. It wasn't much of a delay. Less than a second. Less than half a second, less than half a half a second, and probably even less than that. Yes, she was very sure it was less than a mere one-sixteenth of one second. In the outside world where she would have much preferred to be at the moment, a delay so minuscule would have gone completely unnoticed. But she was in here now and something had pumped up her senses to a range several levels of magnitude beyond what should have been possible. *Even in here*, she realized with a minor chill.

She turned to face the glass directly, drew herself up, and made a formal bow. The reflection did exactly the same in the fast glimpse she had as she bent forward. At the lowest point of the bow, she lifted her head very slightly and looked. The image in the window was also sneaking a look, with the difference that the face was grinning broadly at her.

Yuki jumped back with a cry. It was as if a giant, cold fist had clutched her stomach. Tom's reflection laughed and shook its head, moving both hands in front of itself in a negating gesture. Telling her not to be afraid, she supposed, feeling foolish but at the same time, still shaky. Images, she kept telling herself, all images, light dancing on the retina, producing illusions with the help

of that unregenerate old collaborator the brain. Easy to say, even easy to think, but it didn't make certain things any less startling to see before you, even when you knew the mechanics of everything that was going on.

Tom's reflection was still laughing as it straightened up and walked toward her.

If it walks out of the glass into the street, Yuki thought, *I'll drop down dead.*

But the image went only as far as it would have been able to go if it had been a real person standing on the other side of a window. It beckoned to her, the grin turning sheepish. Yuki looked around to see if anyone else was catching this, but she was still alone. Cautiously, she approached the glass, still watching for some sign that the image could burst out of its medium, and stopped a yard away, ready to run.

'Oh, for cryin' *out*,' said Tom's image. 'What's your snarl?'

'Who are you?' she asked him.

'Now, who do I look like?'

'Nobody,' she snapped.

Tom's image put a hand over its heart. Or heart area. 'You cut me with that one, Yuki. You cut me *bad*. And after all we've meant to each other.'

Her eyes narrowed. 'Tom Iguchi is missing and presumed dead. In here.'

'But not in *here*, not through the old looking-glass.' The image gestured behind him. 'And for that matter, not where you are, either. *You're* Tom now.'

'Not really. Everyone who knows him knows I'm not. Who are *you?*'

The image moved an inch or two closer to the glass. 'It's me, Yuki. It *is* me, it's Tom.'

The voice had sobered, the teasing note gone from it. 'Really?' she asked, warily.

He nodded. 'Well, not *really*. But it *is* me.'

Yuki glowered at him. 'I'll take a hammer to this thing. Then where will you be?'

'You don't have a hammer. The best you can do is a travel icon and a couple of lottery tickets. Listen to me, I don't have much time here. I'm piggy-back-ing for the moment and it won't be long before someone notices the extra energy expenditure isn't balanced.'

'What am I supposed to do?' Yuki asked. 'And where are you?'

'I don't know exactly.'

Yuki was exasperated. 'How can you not know?'

'I don't know that, either. But I need your help to get out of here all the same.'

'But you don't know where it is. Where *you* are.'

'No.'

She blew out a breath of mock relief. 'Okay. I was just checking. For a min-ute I was afraid that it might make *sense*.'

'Do you know anything about Old Japan?' Tom asked her suddenly, all but blurting it out. 'True Japan, I mean.'

Yuki looked up briefly. The stretch of dark sky above her was completely devoid of stars. Of course. 'What has *that* got to do with anything?'

'They're bringing Japan back. That's what they *say* they're doing, anyway.'

She laughed. 'Who's "they"? Any relation to "them"?'

Tom's hands pressed hard against the glass; his palms whitened. 'I swear, if I could reach you, I'd shake you till your brains rattled, even if you do look like me on a good day.'

Yuki brushed imaginary lint off her shoulder. 'I'm sure that would help a lot.'

'Just listen. I have a catalog hidden under the name Shantih Love.'

'Is that the name of the catalog?' Yuki asked him.

'No. It's one of my avatars in here.'

She laughed again. 'And what *are* you in here, some kind of Bombay elephant demigod?'

'It's the name I had when I was murdered.'

'You haven't been murdered. You're here, with me. Like me and my shadow.'

Tom beckoned to her and she moved closer to the glass. '*Listen*, will you? Things got serious. It was just supposed to be a game, that's all it was ever supposed to be. The tokens, the icons, that was all supposed to be just status crap, like having someone on the door of one of those clubs Ash is always going to –'

'They have them in here, too,' Yuki said.

He seemed not to have heard her. '– just game stuff, that's all. Performance art at the *very* most. Flash the icons, claim you're fast, claim you're the new buzz and you can show them how to shoot the curl. And they let you, because it's all true and they're never gonna let you out. Someone's gotten to like it there, and it isn't you.' He stopped and shrugged. 'I sold Shantih Love off. I scraped up enough residue so the buyer could get my name and wear it under the Shantih Love form. It got him killed. In here *and* out there.'

Yuki sighed. 'Are you plundering old scenarios and trying to sell them to cinemas again?'

'I'm not telling you a scenario, this isn't cinema. It's *real*, goddammit.'

'Big talk for a *reflection*.'

'*Stop it*. You don't know. You're running around in here on high speed and you don't have the faintest idea of what you've flashed into.'

'Why don't you tell me, then?' She crossed her arms – his arms? – and in the glass, she saw Tom start to follow her movement. Then he caught himself and pushed his arms straight down by his sides, looking annoyed.

'You don't know how fast you're going, do you? You're running real hot, Yuki, and I got to tell you, you can't do that forever. It ages you. You can age twenty years here in one night. They let you have my appearance because they know you're full Japanese. *She* sent you in here –'

'She who?' asked Yuki.

'Joy Flower. Who else?' Tom's mouth curved down bitterly and she felt her own mouth copy his expression without her willing it, and without her being able to stop it. 'You want to know all about that, the world's best kept secret? Yes, I was one of Joy's Boyz, and yes, I liked it, and yes, she used me. Because I was full Japanese.'

'Really,' Yuki said. 'I thought she used you because you were *male*.'

He laughed. 'In here, you can get better than *anything* out there. Nobody really cares about sex anymore, Yuki –'

Speak for yourself, she thought bitterly.

'– no one cares about ecstasy, drugs, or going to heaven. But everyone – *every-fucking-body-and-soul* – wants god-hood.'

Yuki shook her head slightly, puzzled.

'Power, dammit. *Power.* Power *to do*. Power *over*. Over ideas, over thoughts, over all living things.'

Yuki waited. 'And?' she prompted finally.

'What do you mean, *and?*' he fairly shouted. 'And the sun set slowly in the west. And the Red Death held sway over all. And they all went to heaven in a little rowboat. Except people like you and me, we get –'

In the next moment, Tom was gone and she was staring at a regular-style reflection. Or as regular-style as a reflection in Artificial Reality could be, considering it wasn't really a reflection of something that wasn't really there in the first place. Or was it? Maybe reflections were sort-of reflections, subroutines dumbed-clown to the point of the AR version of an autonomic reflex –

She shook her head again. Sometimes thinking was like struggling through a briar patch, getting caught on every little sticker and thorn, and having to disengage each one individually. Curbing her impatience, she stood in front of the glass and tried to will Tom to come back. Could he still see her from where he was now? Or had he not actually left and was just mimicking her movements with an almost supernatural precision?

She moved closer so that her nose would have been pressed against the glass, or nearly so, and looked herself in the eyes. Or looked Tom's eyes in the eyes. Artificial eyes; after staring into them for almost a minute, she stepped back. The longer she gazed into them, the more lifeless they seemed, as if the humanity were draining out. But draining out of *what?* The reflection? The illusion that was causing the reflection? Or the person observing it – namely, herself?

Maybe she shouldn't try to know that one if she wanted to remain intact, she thought uneasily.

She became aware, then, that a strange silence had fallen over her, as if all sound had been damped down and obliterated. Someone listening? She looked up.

An enormous chrome flying saucer was hovering above the alley. Yuki's

mouth dropped open. Now she could sense something that she could describe to herself only as the opposite of sound waves, and it was definitely coming from the thing overhead. As she stared at it, a ring of bright lights lit up in a circle around the bottom centerpoint of the saucer. The lights moved separately, sending long cones of light in all directions. Yuki watched, wondering if this was only more Sitty flash or some other traveler's idea of a tour bus.

The silence seemed to suck hard at her and then it was gone. The saucer was moving on, toward the trafficway, where people were shouting and screaming in delight at the thing's approach. Some impulse made Yuki trot along under it, pacing it, and one of the spotlights moved with her, lighting the area directly in front of her.

Coming out of the alley, she could see that the UFO was larger than she had thought. The crowd that had gathered, stretching up and down the trafficway as far as the eye could see, spilling onto the beach and into the water, covered nearly as much area on the ground as the saucer did in the air. The chrome hull reflected far fewer people than appeared on the street, however. Was there really that much filler on the street, or were only the elite reflected in a flying saucer hull? If so, what kind of elite did you have to be?

Yuki walked in a slow zigzag, trying to see if the saucer reflected her, too, but she just couldn't seem to find herself – or Tom's image, rather – anywhere along the chrome. Maybe the distortion was too extreme for her to see herself. And if she did, would she see Tom signal her, as she had seen him do before? Or did his abrupt disappearance mean that he couldn't appear safely even as a reflection?

But come on, how safe or unsafe was AR in the first place? What kind of danger could anyone possibly be in? Aside from suffering from racing thoughts –

She concentrated on moving farther into the crowd, making her way through the virtual bodies and trying to keep an eye on the saucer. She had a sense of something about to happen. The atmosphere seemed to thrum with it.

Nice effect – wonder how they do it, she thought, and then tried to be at least slightly abashed at her own cynicism. Tom used to tell her she was far too cynical to enjoy the illusions of AR even as mere entertainment.

I feel sorry for you cynics, he would say. *Because cynics know the price of everything and the value of nothing.*

Maybe so, Tom, but if you don't know your own *price, how can you be sure of your values?* She would always laugh when she said it, so he wouldn't know how much that price-of-everything-value-of-nothing crack stung her.

There was a sudden roar on the other side of the crowd; a large midnight-blue woman was levitating toward the saucer. No, not levitating – the saucer was pulling her up to it. She spread her arms and shook her overdone mass of white hair joyfully. When she reached the saucer, she passed directly through the chrome and vanished.

Yuki waited, standing perfectly still, for one of the spotlights to fall on her. If they were looking for her, or Tom, or both, then she would make it as easy as possible for them and get it over with.

But no pull came, even though the spotlights swept over her and even paused on her upturned face briefly, not just once but several times. After a bit, she got bored and turned away to try forging a path out of the crowd and on to somewhere else. Wasn't she supposed to be in Waxx24 anyway? If this was it, it was neither clever nor exciting. She would have to tell Ash that he wasn't missing anything, that he was better off frequenting the real club. At least there you could buy drinks.

And it was as if her thought of Ash had flipped a switch somewhere because suddenly, there he was, just a little over an arm's length away from her. She knew him immediately, there was no mistaking his appearance. Same old Ash – fancy eyes, a cloud of pale-gold, fairy-tale hair, clothes from one of the Romance designers, a fluffy shirt and satin trousers, soft boots. If you listened closely, you could probably hear hearts breaking all over the Sitty. It was the sort of thing that must have reinforced his vanity, to make him come here looking exactly as he did in –

But of course he looked just as he did out there. The realization was a wordless thump that she could not quite characterize as a shock, and yet felt like more than mere surprise to her. Ash looked like Ash because he *was* out there. He wasn't in AR with her. He was at the actual, physical club and somehow, so was she. By projection, or something they wouldn't call projection but probably was. Whoever *they* were.

She moved quickly to stand directly in front of him and understood right away that he couldn't see her, was totally unaware of her presence. But obviously he could see the saucer – he was standing there and not only gazing up at it but waving both arms over his head, signaling, begging it to take him. Just like a lot of other club-goers, she saw.

So how the hell did this virtual club thing work? Was Waxx24 more of a level than a location in here? And how could she make contact with Ash, was it even possible?

She pulled out the catalog and removed one of the lottery tickets. It had electric pink question marks printed over a background of bright metallic blue, with a gold-flake circle in the center. 'Tell me how to communicate with someone out there who is visible to me in here.'

The lottery ticket made a throat-clearing noise. 'Must be in the form of a question,' a male voice admonished her.

Yuki groaned. 'How can I contact someone out there visible to me in here?'

There was a brief pause. 'Touch the gold circle and see what you've won!' said a different and much happier male voice.

She did so and a pink balloon sprang up in front of her like a severely overstuffed jack-in-the-box.

Saw someone you LIKED? *Want to know* MORE? *Making contact is* SIMPLE, EASY, *and* FUN!!!! *First, signal your choice by placing one hand on your target's shoulder, just as if you were going to turn her or him around to talk to you! You will see* A VERY SPECIAL EFFECT, *which alerts the* LUCKY TARGET *that she or he has been* CHOSEN BY ONE OF THE ELITE!!!! *There will follow a short wait while your target is prepared for contact, assuming consent has been given (and why wouldn't it!!!!). You'll meet your new friend in a* PRIVATE CHAT BOOTH *and what goes on in there is no concern of* ANYONE'S!!!! *We only urge you to observe* SAFE *practices and* UNDER NO CIRCUMSTANCES GIVE ANYONE, *no matter how dreamy or attractive, your* PERSONAL ID CODE *or* YOUR PASSWORD!!!! *Right? Right!!!! Best of luck – and remember, book early and* EXTEND THE RUSH!!!!!

Yuki shook her head. *Wow!!!! Thanks!!!!* She moved closer to Ash and made to touch him on the shoulder.

She couldn't feel him at all, but it didn't matter. Evidently she had done it right. A long stream of what looked like a river, or footage of a river, shot out from his shoulder. Ash's face lit up with a joy Yuki associated only with children or lunatics. Grinning ecstatically, he watched as it circled them once and shot upward to the saucer overhead. He raised his face to it and Yuki was startled to see there were tears in his eyes. *Thank you*, he mouthed, raising his arms like a gospel singer in full voice. Yuki wasn't sure whether it was the proximity or the fact that Ash was her particular choice, but now she could feel the effect of the levitation ray or whatever it was plucking Ash off the ground and into the air. His dangling feet sailed past her virtual nose and she understood that whatever had ahold of him was highly stimulating in the pleasantest way. Waxx24 certainly looked after its elite custom. They were making sure her lucky chosen friend stayed feeling lucky, chosen, happy, and receptive.

'Yuck,' she said aloud, but quietly. Being a prude was, as she had been told again and again by various people, including Ash, not something she should advertise widely. Of course, the fact that she was at odds with everyone else, especially Ash, as to what constituted prudery was always skipped over, so she had given up, accepted the fact that by standards she couldn't seem to escape or alter she was a raving, flaming prude and left it at that. But now she was going to have to deal with a highly stirred-up Ash, and she could only hope that the sight of Tom's face, coupled with the revelation that *she* was behind the image would serve as a cold shower for him.

The person behind Ash, a tall, husky black woman in a very old-fashioned gangster-style zoot suit from the last century, looked up at the saucer and tipped her fedora as she, too, began to lift into the air. Yuki looked around;

there was no one that she could see near the woman. The elite invisible to each other? Strange, she thought; also strange that there had been no sign of the VERY SPECIAL EFFECTS!!!! that had accompanied her choosing Ash. And while she was wondering this and that, why was she down on the street instead of up in the saucer? Was she going to be airlifted too? When? What the hell was going on? And if the elite really *were* invisible to each other, how was it she and Nick the Schick –

She was standing in a small room no larger than a closet, furnished with one small round table and two efficient padded chairs. She sat down and took out the map. A new overlay had been added to tell her that she was now on the saucer. Or that the saucer was now included on her level. The notations seemed to hint at both without confirming one way or the other. She put the map down on the table and ran her hands over the back of the chair. Lots of padding there; good, comfortable padding under smooth, cool cloth. Did they have virtual upholsterers in AR, she wondered, and if so, what kind of training did that require? And did they have virtual upholstery testers as well, people whose job it was to go around feeling the furniture, sitting on it, standing on it, using it any and every way imaginable to check for that authenticity of sensation that made every tactile impression more vivid than it could ever be out there, more real than real.

Ash would probably like that job. Or any job like it. AR designer, AR tester. Maybe tester more than designer. Like the sort of thing you dreamed about when you were a kid, consumer tester for Toyz U Krave, or whatever the company was called. Or not *like* it, really, the same thing *exactly*, just different props.

Sensations more real than real. She was beginning to understand why Ash and Tom spent so much time in AR. The more time you spent in a rig like this, the paler reality must seem when you came out of it. She had never spent a whole lot of time in AR in the past, other than the occasional amusement park expedition with friends. Ride a roller coaster – safely. Drive in a demolition derby – safely. Parachute out of an airplane – safely. Jump out of an airplane without a parachute and fly like a bird – safely. There were more constructive kinds of things, like overcoming phobias, but that was basically an amusement park installation with an enormous medical bill attached.

The sensations provided by the amusement park attractions were pretty authentic, vivid enough to fool you for a few seconds at least, and would certainly keep you amused for the whole time. But it wasn't like this. This was under her skin. She could all but feel the nerve endings closest to the surface of her fingers responding to the stimuli, absorbing it all greedily and demanding more. Now there was some map text she could write: *You, too, can become a* SENSATION JUNKIE!!!! *in* LESS THAN ONE DAY!!!! *It's so* EASY!!!! *you don't even have to* TRY!!!!

'Oh, for chrissakes.'

She looked up; Ash was sitting at the table, disgust large on his face.

'Hello, Ash. I didn't hear you come in. What took you so long?'

'Don't call me that, I'm rotating names now. What took me – well, hey, I ran all the way. So what the hell do you call this?'

'Waxx24, the next dimension?' she guessed.

'I *know* that. I mean, what the hell are *you* doing here? They won't let *me* in forever and when they finally do, it's because *you* told them to? Shit. There is *no* God and this is the proof.'

'Ash, this is not what you think –'

'*Don't* call me that.'

'I don't know what else *to* call you. Why'd you change your name?'

'*Rotating.* I'm *rotating* names.'

'*Why?*'

He leaned forward, as if that would actually make the conversation more private. 'In case they have "Ash" on a permanent-exclude checklist.'

Yuki sighed. 'Well, I'm not Tom,' she said, slowly, trying to figure out how to phrase things. She had a sinking feeling that whatever she said was going to sound stupid or crazy or both.

'You're *not* Tom?' Ash folded his arms on the table and scrutinized her through half-closed eyes. 'If you're not Tom, then who could you be, which up-to-now-hidden-from-public-knowledge,completely-pathetic-basket-case-of-misplaced-passion-and-wasteful-idolatry could you *possibly* be?'

Yuki hesitated. 'I guess you don't recognize me with my daikon radish characteristics all covered up.'

Ash seemed to freeze in place, like an old-fashioned cinematic that had jammed. A warning bell chimed in Yuki's mind, but the moment passed even before she could start to think about what might be wrong. Ash unfroze and put his head in his hands. He seemed to be unaware of what had happened. Faulty transmission?

'God, this is worse than I thought,' he said. 'No, I forgot, there *is* no God. Christ, woman, why? *Why?* Have you *no* pride?'

Still suspicious, Yuki reached over to touch him. Just at the moment when she remembered that she couldn't touch him, her fingers brushed what was undeniably a warm human shoulder. Both of them jumped.

'Don't you go all gropey-dopey on me now,' Ash warned, pushing back from the table. He looked as if he were about to get up and run. Yuki barely registered his revulsion; she stared first at her fingers and then at Ash, in an intense way Tom had always called her if-looks-could-drill stare.

'How come I can touch you now?' she said wonderingly.

'For the same reason I can see you, of course,' he snapped. 'I've been pumped up and 'suited.'

'What does *that* mean, "pumped up"?'

Ash gaped at her, frankly incredulous. Then he shook his head. '*And* you're a waste of good drug, too.' He pulled his chair back to the table. 'Okay. Just tell me everything all at once so I can laugh or cry or have a rupture and be done with it. And do it before this stuff wears off, I'm hoping to get an evening out of it anyway.'

'The drug,' Yuki said thoughtfully, reaching again for the back of her neck. 'A *drug* put us on the same level? That's ridiculous, a drug can't –' She paused. 'Oh.'

'Yeah, "oh." ' Ash leaned his elbows on the table and pushed his face at hers. 'Yuki, if that's really you, I thank you from the bottom of my heart for spotting me and lifting me up out of the cattle pen. Now, do an old friend a good favor and give me a readmission token for my next trip in, or whatever I need to get into this side of Waxx24 and sit on your side of the table. Please?'

She frowned at him. 'Is that all you care about?'

'Oh, *Christ*,' Ash said, rolling his eyes and turning away slightly. 'She's going to start.'

'That *is* all you care about, being a VIP at some worthless club that isn't even real, doing things that aren't real with people who aren't real, getting some status that isn't real, for the –'

'Yes, goddammit, that's all I care about!' Ash yelled suddenly, slapping the table. 'When I'm in a club, that's all I goddam care about! I don't come here to do feed the hungry, shelter the homeless, or save the whales for the billionth time! What about it? Why is it so bad that I come here and *don't* save the world?'

'Nobody asked you to save the world,' she said, irritated. 'I didn't say – I mean, look. Something's happened to Tom, something bad. And I –'

'Something bad happened to Tom *here*?' Ash said, sounding skeptical.

'I don't *know* where. But it's connected somehow to AR and Joy's Boyz. I'm not sure about Waxx24.'

'So you put on your Tom-suit and came charging in here to the rescue?'

'Well, no. I got a job with Joy's Boyz.'

Ash's expression was flat. '*You're* a Joy's Boy?'

'Not exactly. I'm her assistant. And when I went to my quarters to go to bed, I found this hotsuit. So I put it on –'

Ash was waving both hands in front of his face, palms toward her. 'Stop, stop. If you're hunting up new Boyz, I'm afraid I'm just too old. Ask her, she'll tell you she likes them younger than me. I know this, everybody knows this.'

'I'm not recruiting. I'm looking for Tom. He's disappeared out there and now I can't find him in here, either –'

'And you think I can?'

Yuki shook her head sadly. 'Why don't you care?'

'I care, deeply. About you, about Tom, about all the important stuff. Hell, you'd think that the two of us together like this might call him right to us? You know, in his Shantih Love suit?'

'You know Shantih Love?' Yuki asked sharply. 'Tell me all about him. Or it, or whatever Tom's supposed to be under that name. Tell me about the ca –' she stopped as something that Ash had said earlier finally registered on her. *Yuki, if that's really you …*

Sure, it's me, Ash. But is that you?

'Come on, come on, Yuki. The meter's running. Can't you get that through your Tom-head?' Ash gave a noisy sigh of supreme weariness. 'Call me at home later, call me tomorrow. Right now, give me a token so I can stay on this level, and a second-admission icon so I can come back.'

'I don't have any tokens or icons or anything like that,' Yuki said.

'There should be a little drawer or something on your side of the table. Look underneath.' He gestured with one hand and she looked. He was right; there was a drawer there, barely the thickness of a pencil. She slid it open and saw that it was divided into several small compartments about half the size of her palm. Or Tom's palm. Each compartment had a different token or icon in it, but none of them meant anything to her. She looked up at Ash and shrugged.

'Tell it what you want,' he said with exaggerated patience.

'Um, a token so my friend can stay here, and a, um – what else?' she asked him.

'Second-admission icon,' he told the ceiling.

'A token so my friend can stay on the level and a second-admission icon. Please,' she added quickly, which made Ash give a short, harsh bark of laughter. Like that, they were on the table in front of her, something that seemed to be a clear plastic coin about the size of a monocle and a square of parchment with ADMIT ONE FOR FUN! inscribed on it in comically ornate lettering.

'There,' she said, and pushed them a few inches toward him on the table.

'You have to hand them to me,' Ash said, addressing the ceiling again. 'I can't touch them before you've activated the validity codes by touching them yourself.'

Yuki scooped them up, grabbed Ash's hand and slapped the items down on his palm. 'There. Is that valid enough for you?'

He was examining them closely. 'Yeah, that's great. You're the queen, you're the dream, you reign supreme.' He made the token and icon disappear. 'I'll be going now. Unless you were actually planning to do something –' he took a breath '– *sexual*.'

She was about to tell him no, of course not, and then stopped, looking at him carefully. 'Suppose I was?'

'Have you really no pride at all?' he asked her, looking pained.

'You never used to ask me that,' she said, forcing herself not to laugh. 'You used to ask me why I was such a prude.'

For a long moment, Ash didn't move. This time, however, she could see he wasn't frozen, at least not the way he had been before. He looked more as if she had caught him out at something. Then he threw up his hands. 'All right. Now I know. Touché. Now let me out of here.'

'Let him out of here,' she said to the air, and Ash was gone. She waited for another moment, and then said, 'Who was that?'

There was no response. She remembered something about privacy laws for leisure-type activities. You couldn't find out anything about someone in one of these places unless the person chose not to lie to you. Ha. Big fat hairy chance. Again, life imitates art, she thought. *If you call this art.*

Or maybe *this* was now life, and what had been life was now art. Could she prove it one way or the other? Hardly. No more than she could prove the person she had been talking to had really been Ash.

But why wouldn't he be, she asked herself.

Why would *he be is the more logical question. You look like Tom and you're not him, so why would someone who looked like Ash be Ash?*

He wouldn't, she realized suddenly. Ash would never have worn his own appearance into an AR scenario. For Ash, the whole point was to be someone else. So who had that been? Some friend of Ash's, some friend of hers?

Tom?

Suddenly, it was all too much to think about. She sat in the empty booth, waiting for something else to happen, but apparently nothing else was going to unless she asked for something specific. She took out the catalog and the map again and spread them out on the table. 'I don't suppose a glass of really nice red wine is possible, is it?' she said to the air, expecting nothing.

Immediately, the glass was sitting on the table in front of her. In spite of everything, Yuki burst out laughing. It figured, she thought, trying to catch her breath. Here she was in a place where almost anything was possible, and she was snagged on the *almost* part. Still, she fingered the elegant bowl of the glass, lifted it to look at the color. It certainly looked like red wine. The effect was so realistic she would have sworn that if she put the glass close to her face, there would be the unmistakable full-bodied, not-too-woodyish nose of a good, dry red.

Then she did bring the glass to her face and there it was. Even as she inhaled the aroma, she knew it wasn't possible. A trick played on her senses by the power of suggestion. Perhaps even one of Joy Flower's henchmen kneeling next to the bed and holding a wine-soaked napkin to the vent at the top of her headmount. Why? Never mind *why*, this was *how*. It didn't have to make sense, it just had to be possible.

She knew then that she was going to drink, and when she did, she would

not only taste wine but feel the liquid in her mouth, she would feel the bite of the alcohol on the tissues in her throat and the mild burn as it traveled down her esophagus to her stomach. And then she wasn't sure what she would do after that, because sensations of eating and drinking just weren't possible, they just *weren't*.

Even as she was thinking that, she had already drunk the wine, and another part of her mind was contemplating the taste as compared to the nose. Not quite as good as the nose had promised, but a very near miss.

She closed her eyes, wondering if it were possible to drift out of the Sitty by way of apathy, to get it to disconnect for lack of activity, and then she could tear the whole damned rig off and throw it in Joy Flower's face on her way out.

Her hand moved on its own, but she refused to open her eyes. Somehow, with her eyes closed, she couldn't tell exactly what her hand was doing, but if she concentrated hard enough, she would feel the source of the impulse to move. Like the sensation of the upholstery, it was under her skin, but in a much more profound way. It felt as someone was wearing her hand as a glove –

Panic exploded inside her. Her eyes snapped open and she jumped out of the chair, brushing at herself, turning around and around, trying to catch someone molesting her, if that was the word. Molesting her hand. Molesting her gross motor movements.

Of course, whoever it was might not be visible, she remembered suddenly, as she swung the arm with the wineglass in it in fast, wide arcs. Too bad she hadn't managed to score a Schick, she thought.

She paused then, panting a little, feeling her heart triphammer in her chest. Except that the triphammering didn't really seem to arise from her panic or her exertions. It was just there, a fast heartbeat. Running hot. What the *hell* had they injected her with?

Yuki looked down at her hand. There was no more moving without her but now she could sense that there was something else under the white glove besides her virtual body. It was trying to hide its presence by keeping perfectly still, but now that she knew it was there, she couldn't *not* feel it.

'Oily, oily, whatever-it-is-they-say,' she whispered, and bit her lip. 'I know you're playing possum, because you're not very good at it.' Nothing happened.

'All right. All right.' Moving as slowly and smoothly as possible, she sat down at the table again and laid her hand down on it. 'We'll just see here.'

Taking the glass in her other hand, she smashed it down on the edge of the table. The sound of breaking glass was perfect, she thought, picking up the largest shard, which had fallen right next to her foot on the carpet.

'If you won't come out,' she said as she sliced along her heart line, 'I'll come in and get you. What do you think about *that?*'

The flow of blood was also perfect, she thought, turning the shard so she

could draw it down her lifeline. And there was that *smell*. That had to be the power of suggestion, she thought; *had* to be. Like the pain. Because her pain option was disabled, she was sure of that.

Well, *pretty* sure.

DEATH IN THE PROMISED LAND [III]

Ten (billable) minutes later, Konstantin stepped through a doorway onto the street where she had first seen Shantih Love. The feel of the Love persona in her 'suit was pleasurable in a way that kept her on edge. Being Shantih Love was close to seductive, even with the sliced throat, something she had not taken into consideration.

Real easy to go native in a Gang Wars module. The night manager's words came back to her. None too helpfully, since this wasn't a Gang Wars module. That she knew of.

She was wondering now if she really knew anything at all. The piles of wreckage in the street were all aflame, burning in jewel tones, now and then sending sparks skyward, where they seemed to mingle with the stars. The glitter she had seen on the monitor looked somehow less gritty from the inside and more like delicate sprays of tiny lights, too exquisitely fragile not to shatter in even the slightest puff of a breeze, yet remaining, twinkling and shimmering against the black street, the pitted brick and the web-cracked glass of the buildings facing the burning wrecks, the cold-stone texture of the barrier between the street and the alien shore of the Hudson River.

Konstantin went to the barrier and strolled along it in the direction Shantih Love had taken, looking around for anything like the figure of a shaggy beast that might be interested in killing her.

Rather than anything approaching, however, Konstantin had a sense of things drawing away from her, many eyes watching with the knowledge that she was an impostor. And then again, she thought suddenly, how would anyone know, if the Shantih Love persona had gone on for another four hours after Iguchi's death? Maybe the only one who knew was the creature who had attacked and hijacked Shantih Love here in the first place.

She paused, leaning on the barrier and looking toward where she estimated the party had been. It was long over now, or perhaps this was no longer one of the hot Sitty spots. But then, her purpose was not to find a party, nor to act as a decoy to attract a creature that might not even be real. Funny how easy it was to forget things, to forget to keep focused here. If she

waited much longer, her concentration might dissolve altogether, just break into tiny fragments and float away up to the stars with the sparks from the burning wreckage.

'Icon cat?' she asked.

It was there before her on the barrier, preening itself, smoothing its whiskers with its paws and lashing its tail in a sort of all-purpose warning – a classic tabby.

'Oh, *no*,' Konstantin groaned. 'Not *really*.'

The tabby looked up at her, offended. A moment later, it was a thick book, open to a page showing a flame within a halo; as she looked at it, it went from a drawing to a vivid holo. The word *Enlightenment* came out of the flame and rippled for a moment. More words appeared on the facing page: *You have only to ask.*

Konstantin made a face, or thought she might have; there was no real feeling above her neck. 'Is this a help file?' she said aloud.

Now there was a new message on the page opposite the flame: *Help with? – Travel – Location – Contacts – Other*

After a moment's thought, she touched – *Contacts*.

Contact – Who – What? The page wanted to know.

She pressed – *Who*. The question mark moved to the end of the word. 'Body Sativa,' she said aloud.

A golden arrow pointing to her right materialized on the page. She turned it and found a map of the area with her own position highlighted. A dotted green line appeared, winding its way along the grid of streets to a location six blocks away; a green star flashed on and off.

'That was easy,' she said, noting the address and the directions. It just figured. *You have only to ask.* Too good to be true.

The map absorbed the book, making it disappear. She picked it up and moved along the street toward the next three-way intersection. Three fiery humanish shapes detached themselves from the burning ruins of a classic Rolls sandwiched between two antique sports cars and stood watching her. Konstantin had a sudden urge to whirl on them and claim she was selling encyclopedias. The idea was a tickle playing over her back, where she imagined she could feel their literally burning stares.

No, they might actually expect her to produce chips full of natural history quick-times. She couldn't account for how she had come up with the idea of playing such a prank; according to her ex, she'd never had much of a sense of humor.

Ah, but this is the Land of Anything Goes. You can pretend you have a sense of humor, or that your ex isn't actually ex, and all while you look for someone with the unlikely name of Body Sativa, or Love. Or who knows?

*

She passed several brawls, a side street where a few hundred people seemed to be trying to stay as close together as possible and still dance – it looked as though they had decided nudity would do it – and a billboard-sized screen where half a dozen people were either collaborating on a quick-time or competing to see whose images could dominate. Someone among them was obsessed with mutant reptiles. Or were certain kinds of images contagious?

Or maybe, she thought as she passed someone that might have been the offspring of a human and a cobra, it was the mutants themselves that were contagious. She paused at a corner in front of a park surrounded by a black metal spiked fence and consulted the map.

'Ssssssssssssssssssshhhhhhhhhhhhhhhhhhhhh … '

The noise was so soft, she wasn't sure that she had actually heard it. But then it came again, from the dark enclosed by the spiked metal fence, and she found that the sensation of small hairs standing up on the back of her neck was not necessarily something that the hotsuit had to produce for her.

'Sssshhhhhhhhhaaaaaaaaannnnnnnnntiiiiiiiiih … '

She was clenching her hands so tightly that if she really had been holding a map, it would have crumpled and torn. *Come on,* she told herself. *This is nothing more than a scary movie. You just happen to be in it.*

'Ssssssssshhhhhhhhhhhhaaaaaaaaaannnnnnnnnntiiiiiiiiiiiiiiiihh … '

Apparently it didn't matter what she told herself, the hairs on the back of her neck were going to stand up and jitterbug regardless. Chills were creeping down below her backbone now. Konstantin tried to steel herself and shivered instead.

'Ssssssssshhhhhhhhhhhhhhhaaaaaaaaaaaannnnnnnnntiiiiiiiiiiiiiiiiiihhhh. Welcome back from the land of the dead. We've been waiting for you, darling.'

Konstantin forced herself to turn around. The faces grinning out of the darkness glowed moon-pale, with thick black circles around the luminous eyes. Cold flicked more sharply at the back of her neck and up onto her scalp.

There were half a dozen of them, in a roughly symmetrical formation around a picnic table with the one who had spoken in the center. They were all wearing black skintights over their idealized hardbodies, some disputably female, others emphatically male. *When mimes go bad,* Konstantin thought, and became even more terrified that she might laugh. More chills played over the back of her neck, as if in deliberate reproach for having such an irreverent thought. She shuddered and felt the sliced area of her neck separate a bit.

She covered her wounded throat with the map and moved closer to the fence. 'Have we met?' she asked, trying to sound remote.

The figure posed in the center of the table changed position and moved a few steps forward to the edge. 'Oh, *Shantih,*' he said sulkily. 'And after all

we've meant to each other. I'm wounded. Mortally. We *all* are.' He gestured at the others.

'And I'm dead,' Konstantin said. 'You have any idea who did it?'

The glowing moon-colored face suddenly took on an uncertain expression. 'Honey, you were there, look at your footage. Relive every glorious moment. We –'

'I have. I'd invite you to watch it again with me, but I'm on my way to meet someone. Maybe we can connect later.'

One of the women on the speaker's right straightened up from her catlike stalking pose and pushed both hands into the small of her back. 'Oh, for the love of *Lucy*, Shantih, my back's *killing* me tonight but I came out anyway. If you're not playing, just *say* so and we'll go find somebody else.'

Konstantin shrugged. 'Right. I'm not playing.' She turned to go.

'*You're* not Shantih.' The man hopped down from the table and went over to the fence. 'Are you.'

Konstantin kept her distance. 'You knew Shantih Love pretty well?'

The man adjusted something on himself at waist-level and Konstantin felt the chills that had been tormenting her suddenly vanish. '"Knew?" Does that mean our usual Shantih gave up the character?'

'Gave up the ghost,' Konstantin told him. 'The person you knew as Shantih Love in here has been murdered. For real. I –'

He turned away from her and swung his arm. The group surrounding the picnic table vanished, including the woman who had complained about her back. 'All right, just what kind of virgin are you, hon?' he asked, turning to her again, annoyance large on his white painted face.

'What *kind?*' Konstantin was mystified. 'How many kinds are there?'

'Are you some senator's get out for a good time, or are you some rich kid who bought out a regular? Thought you could get in the game with the fame along with the name?'

Konstantin started to answer but he did something at waist level again and a fresh wave of chills danced up her neck into her hair, intense enough to make her cry out. She stepped back, batting the air with her map as if ultrasonics were insects she could swat away from herself.

'You stay away from me, you pseudo-rudo,' he yelled at her.

'What?' she demanded. 'I didn't –'

'I *hate* you virgins, you all think you're the *first* one to think of saying the one you bought out got killed for real and you're on the trail of the killer. You all think if you say that, we'll all just lead you to their stash, tell you, "Oh, help yourself, angel of justice, take all the *stuff*, and if you don't know how to use it, just *ask*."' He did something at his waist again and Konstantin retreated several more steps. Finally, she thought to shift her gaze to the control for her 'suit and blocked the incoming sensation.

The man made a disgusting noise. 'A virgin *and* a cheat. God's sake, baby, if your meat can't take the motion, why did you bother jumping on the ride?' He flickered out, leaving her alone.

Moving on, Konstantin couldn't decide whether to feel relieved or chastened.

The place marked on the map turned out to be a subway station, or maybe just the post-Apocalyptic ruin of a subway station. From where she stood on the sidewalk looking down the stone stairs, Konstantin could hear the distant sound of people's voices and, even more distantly, music but no trains. Maybe you could hike around post-Apocalyptic Noo Yawk Sitty in the tunnels and bring your own music with you. She crouched at the top of the stairs with her map, absently pressing the flesh of her throat together. The cut edges felt a bit like putty or clay, but they wouldn't stay closed for very long. She wondered idly if she should try to find a place to have herself sewn up, or whether she might even try it herself. If that was even the sort of thing that Shantih Love might do –

There was a strange pressure all along her back, from her neck down to her feet. She stood up and turned around to see if some new weird experience had crept up behind her, but there was no one and nothing there. She was alone; the pressure was all in the 'suit, as if it were trying to push her down the steps into the subway.

'Help?' she asked, turning the map over. The cat's face flashed briefly, sneering at her, and then she was holding the book again. She found the section on the hotsuit almost immediately, but she had to read it over three times to be sure that the 'suit itself, being loaded with Shantih Love characteristics now, was trying to give her a strong hint as to what to do next. At this point, apparently, Shantih Love would have gone down into the subway.

There was a noise below her. She looked over the top of the book and jumped. A young Japanese man, wearing the plain laborer clothing of a hundred years before, was standing a few steps down from her. Although she was no expert, she was pretty sure that was a Samurai sword at his side.

She hugged the book to her chest protectively; it became a map again. The man gazed at her steadily, his expression mild, almost blank. He came up another step. She meant to retreat but something in his face changed so that he suddenly looked severe, and she stayed where she was.

'Does this mean you're giving up, *Mr Iguchi*?' he asked in a soft, sarcastic voice. 'Or have you just changed your strategy?'

'How do you know my name?' Konstantin asked him, wincing inwardly when she heard the tremor in her voice. It wasn't fear but cold – her 'suit seemed to have turned into a portable refrigerator, for no reason that she could see.

The man came up another step. 'Games again, Tom? It's always games with you.'

'More like a malfunction, actually,' she muttered, rubbing one arm. The temperature inside the 'suit was still dropping, as though it were trying to keep her cool inside a furnace.

'It's not cold tonight, Tom,' the man said. 'Are you sure it's not fear that's making you tremble?'

'Have it your way,' Konstantin said desperately, hoping that might have some effect on the 'suit's wayward thermostat.

'Sure you're not afraid of *me*? Or maybe what I represent?'

Konstantin's teeth chattered. 'W-w-what would that be?'

'An old world that has nothing to do with what this world has become, this world, or the one it's contained in, or the one that *that* one is contained in. Boxes within boxes within boxes, all the way to infinity.' The man suddenly produced a strange coin between thumb and forefinger. It flashed silver for a moment; then Konstantin saw the figure on it. Something contrary in her had always insisted on recognizing it first as a tipped-over numeral eight and then as the symbol for infinity. Subconscious protest over the idea of world without end, amen? No time to wonder; the man flipped the coin and showed her the other side, a snake with its tail in its mouth.

'There is something very Japanese about these non-Japanese symbols, don't you agree, *Tom*? It's Old Japan that I'm talking about here, not the hot icy flash of the nth generation of speed tribes, or the debauchery of the newest salaryman club in the neon jungle that covered over the old signs and symbols.'

He held the coin out to her but when she reached for it, he flipped it again and snatched it out of the air. Konstantin pulled her hand back, embarrassed and irritated. The man put both hands behind himself for a moment and then held them up. 'Which hand, Tom? Can you guess?'

Konstantin tucked the map under her arm, trying to ignore the fact that she felt as if she were turning into an ice cube from the skin inward. 'Let's see,' she said, lifting her chin with bravado. 'I used to be pretty good at this. Finding the tell, I mean. Everybody's got a tell. Even Old Japan.'

The man's eyes narrowed; he took a closer look at her. 'You never used to be so smart. What's happened since I saw you last – you take some genius pill somewhere? Something that's burning your brain cells out as fast as you can use them, maybe?'

Konstantin didn't answer. She scrutinized his right fist for a long time, then his left. 'Sometimes it's a twitch, a tightening of the muscles. Sometimes, you can get them to *look* at the correct hand, just by suggesting it. Doesn't matter, you just have to be observant so you can pick up on what kind of tell it is. Most of the time, the person doesn't even realize it. But it's there, and it

tells you what the answer is.' Konstantin hesitated and then tapped the man's right fist. 'I say there.'

He didn't move. 'You're not Iguchi.'

'Come on, let's see it,' said Konstantin. 'I know I'm right. Otherwise you wouldn't be stalling.'

'You're *not* Iguchi. I should have seen it immediately. That's too smart for Iguchi. Where *is* old Tom tonight? Did he hire you, or did you buy him out? If you bought him out, I got to tell you, he stuck you with damaged goods there.' He indicated her cut throat with a jerk of his chin.

Konstantin felt more confident now. She stepped forward and tapped the knuckles of his right hand. 'I said come on, let's see it. I know it's there. Give me the coin and you can call it a night.'

'Call it a night?' The man smiled, raised his right hand, and opened it. It was empty. 'Or call it a day?' He raised his left hand now, watching as it unfolded to reveal that it, too, was empty. He stayed that way, both hands raised, as if he were at gun point, or perhaps surrendering. 'Or call it in the air?'

Annoyed, Konstantin drew back and folded her arms. 'Fine. But *I* know, and *you* know, that until you cheated, that coin was in your right hand. You can skip on outa here now but we both know you cheated. Don't we?' She went to take the map from under her arm and felt something funny in her palm. She opened her fingers.

'I told you to call it in the air,' the man admonished her as she held the coin up and looked at both sides. 'The problem is, when you have a coin with infinity on one side and Ouroboros on the other, how can you ever really know which side is heads and which is tails?'

He burst out laughing, bowed to her, and walked off into the darkness. She could hear the echo of his laughter long after the shadows had swallowed him up.

She examined the coin again. *Never mind that,* she thought, *how can you be sure that what you* don't *have is an eight-cent coin to go with your three-dollar bills?* But never mind the sarcasm – she had just received some AR *stuff.* She wondered if this was the type of *stuff* Guilfoyle Pleshette was so enamored of, and if it were the sort of thing that someone might kill for.

She descended the stairs, marveling at the way she could feel every bump and irregularity in the banister. The sounds of voices and music bounced off the grimy tiles, the echoes as sharp and clear as bell tones, down to the tiniest distortions. Sometimes the sensory input was too authentic to be authentic, she thought, amused; her hearing had never been *that* good, even when she'd been very young. Of course, she'd never been this sharply focused before. AR was almost a misnomer, this was more like enhanced reality for obsessives, people who preferred to move in milieus that were ordered down to the tiniest detail, things they themselves probably wouldn't notice after they had set it in place, but that was the obsessive mind at work –

And what kind of mind was this at work, she asked herself, frozen at the bottom of the staircase and staring at the empty platform beyond the broken turnstiles and the long-unused token-seller's cage. There were no people anywhere to be seen in the unnatural fluorescent light, no movement anywhere at all. Dust and dirt lay thickly on everything, suggesting that no one had come here for a long, long time.

So had her Japanese friend only been waiting at the bottom of the stairs? Or had he come up from some other passage she had missed on her way down?

She looked at the lights overhead. They didn't hum or buzz; they didn't even flicker. Strange, for a place so disused and abandoned, when everything else was so terribly authentic.

The coin grew slightly warmer in her fist. No, too high a price, she thought, amused. 'Icon cat?' she asked.

The cat jumped into her arms and became the book.

'Subway,' she told it.

The pages flipped and came to rest on a picture of a wooden nickel; a mahogany nickel, if Konstantin wasn't mistaken. She hesitated, and then said, 'No. Try again.' The pages flipped again and kept flipping, as if in a very high wind. Because there *was* a wind, she realized, coming from somewhere down in the old train tunnel. She could feel it and she could hear music again as well, except it was much thinner sounding, just one instrument, either a guitar or a very good synthesizer.

'Pause,' she told the book; it closed quietly for her and vanished. She climbed over one of the turnstiles, paused in case anyone wanted to arrest her for fare-jumping, and then walked out onto the platform to look around.

The man with the guitar was to her left, sitting cross-legged at the place where the platform ended and the tunnel began. His head was tilted back against the wall and his eyes were closed, so that he seemed to be in a state of deep concentration as he played. Konstantin wondered if he were going to sing, and then wondered exactly what kind of strange kick a person could get from spending billable time in AR alone in a vacant subway station, playing a musical instrument for nobody.

None, she decided. 'Resume,' she said, staring at the guitar player. The book returned to a visible state, pages flipping. '*Empty* subway, *downtown*.'

The pages fluttered to rest and she was looking at a bottle cap. CREAM SODA. It swelled up from the paper into a three-dimensional object and rolled out of the book to fall on the tile at her feet. Down by the tunnel, the guitar-player paused and turned his face to smile at her. His eyes were still closed. The lights changed, becoming just a bit warmer in color as the legend NOW ENTERING NEXT HIGHER LEVEL ran along the bottom of her vision like a late-breaking news bulletin on *Police Blotter*.

People were all over the platform, standing in groups, sitting on the turn-

stiles, grouping together down on the tracks, picking their way over the rails to the opposite platform, where there were even more people. At first, she saw only the same types she had seen on the shore in Shantih Love's AR log. After a minute or so, however, she discovered that if she didn't look directly at people too quickly, they would come into focus as characters far less cliché and more bizarre.

She stayed where she was, keeping her gaze lowered. The light seemed to be changing, growing even softer and warmer, but she didn't look up at it, or at anything else. The feeling of things altering around her came to her as a sensation of the air rearranging, as a plume of smoke or steam might coil and contort, reshaping itself without dispersing.

When she finally did look up, she was still on a subway platform, but it was a very hospitable subway, all the dirt gone or metamorphosed into glitter. The rails had become gleaming chrome rods laid on smooth, flawless onyx. Growing up out of the tile floor on the platform were large metal *things* that seemed to be mimicking plants, except at a rate a million times faster if still graceful. Metal knobs became branches bearing things that suggested a mating between blades and viscera, and flowered with blossoms that looked sexual to Konstantin without containing any elements that she normally associated with erotica. *Rorschach strikes again*, she thought, and almost chuckled in spite of herself.

More people had appeared from somewhere. Or was it just that more were becoming visible? She looked up slowly. Holos were moving among the people in the subway, some of them floating through the air – people, creatures, symbols, words, some animated, some drifting, some completely stationary but fading in and out of sight in a way that somehow made Konstantin think she would have been able to see them for a longer time if she had been on a higher level. She was sure that she might have been able to see them *better*, certainly, from a higher level, and found herself wondering exactly how she might manage that, since she didn't have to worry about a personal on-line bill swelling to the size of the national debt.

Very seductive, this on-line stuff, she thought. Now she could see how easy it was to get caught up in things here, getting *stuff*. Going places, curiosity driving you on. Of course, curiosity had killed the cat – she touched the slightly ragged skin of Shantih Love's throat. Of course, the cat could well be alive on eight other levels.

A holo designed to look like an old-fashioned neon sign drifted over to her at eye-level. *Welcome to Waxx24, where Reality goes to have a good time.* As she watched, the words sailed away from her, passing through an equally vaporous attendee wearing the body of an adolescent boy with the head of an antlered stag. If that really *was* an attendee, she thought, remembering the strange guy in white face and the gang that hadn't really been there. Maybe

some of these people were no more than phantoms that other people carried around for company. Were phantom friends another example of AR *stuff*?

A seven-foot-tall woman whose hip-length auburn hair seemed to have a life of its own looked down at her through opera glasses. 'What sort of a creature are you?' she asked in a voice so deep that it was more vibration than audible.

'I think I've forgotten.' Konstantin winced. The 'suit was reminding her *now* that it was full coverage, and that Shantih Love would have responded strongly to this woman. It was as if her body had decided to follow the example of the woman's hair, which was curling and uncurling in shining, supple tendrils along her arms and her torso, and enjoy a life of its own. Her ex probably would have laughed at her and told her that it was no less than what she deserved for stealing someone else's life.

I didn't steal *it. He lost it and I found it.*

Yeah, well. Finders weepers.

Konstantin wasn't sure if having an imaginary argument with an ex after a breakup might not be even worse than having the breaking-up argument, but she was fairly sure that it was completely counterproductive to have it both on billable AR time and during a murder investigation. If that was what this really was, and not just a massive waste of time all around.

'Do you know Body Sativa?' she asked the tall woman.

'Yes.' The woman gazed at her a moment longer and walked away.

The people down on the tracks were dancing, or at least moving more or less in time to something that sounded like the rhythmic smashing of glass on metal. Konstantin hopped down off the platform onto the tracks and walked among them. Most of the people down here seemed to be affecting what her ex had called rough and shoddy sugar-plum. Konstantin had to admit that she found the look somewhat appealing, in a rough and shoddy way.

In this light, the ankle-length gown Shantih Love had preferred seemed to have more of a red tone, much more than she had thought. Even stranger was the texture – it looked like velvet but now it felt more like sandpaper, at least on the outside. Inside, the feeling was all but nonexistent; the hotsuit was full-coverage but not so complete in the detailing that she felt the gown swinging and brushing against her ankles. For that, she supposed, you had to have some kind of custom job.

But at least she never tripped on the hem, Konstantin thought as she moved among the dancers, still holding the map. The map had not changed, even though she was supposedly up on a higher level; no picture of Body Sativa appeared, not so much as a written description, or a hint as to which platform Konstantin could find her dancing on. Perhaps Body Sativa didn't dance. She was just going to have to look around, see if she could get anyone to talk to her. And perhaps, she thought, remembering how the tall woman

had looked at her and walked away, perhaps just asking a plain old straight-forward question wasn't the way to go about things.

Finding out what was, however, wouldn't be easy. The people down on the tracks seemed honestly unaware of her, as if she were invisible. Which would seem to indicate she had found another level within a level. Levels within levels and boxes within boxes. Was there any purpose to it, she wondered – any *real* purpose other than to intrigue people into spending more billable hours solving the puzzle?

She moved over to a man who was a few inches shorter than she was. His idea of rough and shoddy was very old and very worn crushed velvet in a shade of blue that Konstantin's ex had always called 'heavenly,' tunic and pants, almost like a Hindu. In the midst of everything else, its tastefulness was all but out of place.

Konstantin maneuvered around him, trying to catch his eye, but it was impossible. She might have been watching a holo of the man rather than the man himself. Perhaps she was? She tried putting her hand on his shoulder in a friendly but substantial way.

There was no actual contact that she could feel, but *some* sort of contact was made – a stream of heavenly blue water shot out from his shoulder, made a circuit around both of them, and flowed off into the shadows overhead. Almost immediately afterward came a torrent of flying insects, bees, hornets, and dragonflies, their tiny bodies increasing in size as they emerged from the man's shoulder not in a way that suggested they were literally growing but more as if they were approaching from a distance. Konstantin blinked at the dragonflies. Strange that they would be among bees and hornets, as they were completely harmless, not stinging bugs at all. Maybe it was all looks and design – their long, slender bodies and narrow wings made a nice contrast to the others.

She realized that the man could see the water and the insects; he was watching them with an expression of surprised delight. As he turned his face in her general direction, something white began to issue from between his lips, rising into the air like a balloon.

In the next moment, she saw that it *was* a balloon – a good old-fashioned word balloon. *Would you care to chat? Press one: YES NO*

Konstantin reached up and pushed the word *YES* with her index finger.

There was no warning and no transition; she lowered her arm to find her-self standing alone in a room not quite as big as the one where the kid had died. To her right were a small round table and two chairs. In the center of the table was an open fan dividing the surface of the table in half; the design on her side was a portrait of a Japanese woman in traditional costume play-ing a guitar-like musical instrument. A Geisha?

The man she had approached melted into existence on the other side of

the table. Obviously able to see her now, he smiled and gestured at the one other chair in the room.

'Well, this really *is* an honor,' he said, and his voice sounded just slightly tanky, as if he were speaking from the bottom of an enormous metal container. 'I had a feeling that if I just managed to stay on long enough, this would be my lucky night. So here I am, singled out by the legendary and redoubtable Shantih Love for the chat booth. What do you have in mind for me, Shantih? Whatever it is, I'm completely yours. I surrender.' He leaned an elbow on the table and rested his chin in his hand, giving her a dreamy smile so adoring it frightened her. 'Fill me where I am empty, empty me where I am full, roughen me where I am smooth, smooth out my rough places. I know the drill.' He sighed happily.

Oh my god. Konstantin took a breath. 'You know me?'

'Do I know you. Ask me anything. *Anything.*' He sat forward a little.

'Where do you know me from?'

'Ferocious Windows, 30th Zentury, Body&Soul, and, of course, Waxx24. Those are your favorite haunts, though you've been spotted at others from time to time.' The man laughed a little. 'Pretty toff, huh? Ask me a hard one.'

'What are those?'

'What are what?'

'Ferocious Body, Waxx24, the others.'

The man's expression went from bewildered to suspicious. 'Is this a joke?'

Konstantin tried to look stern. 'Am I laughing? Answer the question.'

'But –' He let out a breath. 'Well, we're *in* Waxx24. And it's not Ferocious Body, it's –'

'Body Sativa,' Konstantin said. 'Bring her to me at once.'

Now the man looked aggrieved. 'What's got into you?'

'Did I tell you to ask questions when I ask questions?'

He looked at her from under his brows. 'If they let us hunt up people on your side I'd have tracked *you* down a lot sooner than this.'

'If *they* let you? What *they* is *that?*' Konstantin winced.

'Are you gonna *do* something with me?' the man demanded. 'Or are you just gonna waste my billable time?'

'What do you want me to do with you?' asked Konstantin, trying to sound both authoritative and accommodating.

He sat back and studied her for a few moments and Konstantin knew that she had fumbled. '*You're* not Shantih Love,' he said finally.

'Don't tell me who I'm not.'

'Yeah, yeah, yeah. Con somebody else, if you can. I know all about Shantih Love, I know all the stories. Shantih Love doesn't waste time talking. For future reference, Citizen Wannabe, or whoever you are, brush up on your tantric yoga and *Kama Sutra*, although I hear that Shantih Love's imagination

is one of those things you *can't* study for.' He looked to one side. 'Excuse me, I got some consumer-warning to take care of concerning an impersonator –'

'Fail,' Konstantin said imperiously, turning her head as if speaking to an invisible assistant.

The guy froze halfway out of his chair. 'What?'

'I said, *fail*, you fool, what did you think I said?' Konstantin refused to look at him. 'Do you think Shantih Love would just swoop down on *any* pretty face and carry him off to Nirvana? *Everyone* must pass an initial interview test of my devising before I empty them where they are full and so forth. Sometimes they know it's an interview, sometimes they don't. Sometimes I come in disguise and sometimes I don't. Go ahead, go out there, warn all the consumers. You'll only be advertising the fact that Shantih Love gave you a try-out and you failed. Hold your head high.'

'Are you kidding here?' The man looked pained. 'What the hell kind of a thing is *that* to do to people on *billable time?*'

Konstantin gave what she hoped was a disgusted and haughty laugh. 'If you couldn't stand the tab, pilgrim, why the hell did you get on this ride? Anything worth paying for is worth over-paying for. That's the Shopper's Credo. You're dismissed.'

The man melted away, still looking shocked. A moment later, she was back in the subway, in the midst of the people who weren't aware of her. Strangely enough, she didn't see the man she had just been talking to. Perhaps he had run out of billable time. Whatever his absence meant, she hoped it also signified that her bluff had worked.

She considered the others, moving among them and feeling like a live person at a ghosts' convention. Or should that have been a ghost at a live persons' convention?

Her gaze caught on the guitar-player. He was still in the same place, and it looked as if he were still playing as well, though it was impossible to hear anything except the smash-clang everyone around her was dancing to. She made her way through the group over to where he sat. Here the platform was about as high as her nose. She tried boosting herself up but somehow she couldn't get enough leverage.

'Stay,' said the guitar-player, eyes closed. 'I can see and hear you fine where you are.'

'Good,' Konstantin said doubtfully. 'Tell me, are you really here? And if you're not, which one of us is? And are you going to turn into someone else?'

'It's all in what you can perceive,' he said, smiling. He morphed from a plump, balding young guy to an angular middle-aged man with very long straight, steel-grey hair. He still didn't open his eyes. 'You'd be surprised how few turns of the morphing dial that took.'

'Maybe not,' she said. 'Do you know Body Sativa?'

'*Know* her, or know of her?'

'*Know* her. Personally. Intimately, or casually.' She paused. 'And have you seen her in here recently?'

'*In* here or *around* here?'

'Yes,' Konstantin snapped impatiently.

He tilted his head, his closed eyes moving back and forth beneath his eyelids, as if he were dreaming, while his fingers played over guitar strings that appeared no thicker than spider silk. Konstantin realized that though she couldn't exactly hear the music, she could feel it pass through her. 'I was a dolphin in a previous incarnation,' he said, after a bit.

'Why did you change?'

'We all have to, sooner or later. I would have thought you'd know that as well as anyone. What were you before you passed on to your present manifestation?'

Konstantin barely hesitated. 'A homicide detective.'

'Ah. That accounts for the interrogation.' He chuckled. 'You know, the idea is to go on to something different, not just do the same thing behind a new mask.'

Words to live by, Konstantin thought. Perhaps she could print them on a card and send it to her ex. 'That's pretty good for a guitar-playing ex-dolphin.'

He stopped playing and pulled something out of the hole in the center of the instrument. 'Here,' he said, leaning forward and holding it out to her; it looked like a playing card. 'You're not necessarily smarter than the last one who had your face, but the quality of your ignorance is an improvement.'

'It is? How?' Konstantin asked, straining on tiptoe to take the card from him.

'*You* might actually learn something.'

She studied the card, trying to see it clearly, except the image on it kept shifting, melting, changing. It might have been an Oriental ideogram. 'What's this?'

'Cab fare.'

'Cab fare? In a subway station?'

'Trains aren't running tonight. Or didn't you notice?'

She looked down at her map again. The display still hadn't changed. 'I was supposed to find somebody I needed here. My map says she's still here.'

The guitar player shook his head. 'Sorry, you misunderstood. There's a locator utility here, for help finding someone in the Sitty. That's what your map says is here.' He shrugged. 'There are locator utilities in all the subway stations.'

Konstantin managed not to groan. 'Where?'

'It's all in what you perceive.'

'You're a *big* help.'

'Thank you, I'm supposed to be. If you get it figured, you have cab fare to get to wherever it is you need to go.'

Cab fare, Konstantin thought. Cab fare. Did it include the tip, she wondered, or was that what the coin was for? She looked down at it in her other hand.

The man stopped playing again. 'When did you get that?'

'Just now. Upstairs, on my way in.' She closed her fist around it again. 'Why?'

'Because even in here, certain things are perishable. Like milk. Or cut flowers.'

'Or people with cut throats?'

He smiled. 'No, you may have noticed that death doesn't have to put a crimp in your plans for the evening. On the other hand, it's not generally an accepted practice to start out dead. If you want to be dead, custom dictates that you die here.'

'Here in the subway, you mean, or here in AR?'

'It's all in what you perceive.'

He was going to say that once too often, Konstantin thought unhappily. 'What about this coin?' she asked. 'Were you telling me just now that it's going to expire?'

'Conditions,' he said after a moment. 'It's the conditions under which it would be … *effective*. Conditions don't last.'

'More words to live by,' Konstantin muttered to herself. 'I want to find the locator utility. How do I do that?'

'You have only to ask.'

'Who do I ask?'

'Me.'

Konstantin hesitated. 'All right. How do I find the locator utility?'

'You have only to ask,' he said again serenely, fingers picking at the strings of the guitar again.

'I just *did*,' Konstantin said testily. 'How –' She cut off as understanding flooded through her. '*Where* is Body Sativa?'

Eyes still closed, the guitar-player jerked his chin at her. 'Hail a cab, and when you're asked where you want to go, answer, "To Body Sativa," and give the driver that.'

Konstantin looked at the card again. The ideogram was still shifting. Suddenly she was very tired and bored. 'Are you sure this'll do it?'

'Oh, yeah. Take you right to her.'

'That simple?'

The guitar-player nodded. 'That simple.'

'How strange. Nothing else here seems to be.'

The guitar-player smiled. 'What you want is simple. All you had to do was state it in the proper place at the proper moment. In the proper form, of course. That's just elementary programming.'

'Programming,' Konstantin said, giving a short, not terribly merry laugh. 'I should have known. You're the locator utility *and* the help utility, aren't you?'

'Avatar of both, but yeah, that's about what it comes down to,' he said agreeably.

'And I had only to ask.'

'Because what you want is simple. You just want to meet up with another player, so I gave you a tracer. Obviously you're not the usual Shantih Love, or even a usual player. The usual players don't want anything so simple. The usual players come down here to look for the secret subroutine to the Next Big Scene, or even the mythical Out Door. Then my job becomes something different. Then my job is to give them something that will stimulate a little thrill here and there, play to their curiosities and their fondest wishes and desires, without actually promising anything impossible to deliver.'

'But still making them spend more billable hours.'

'The more hours people spend in here doing complicated things, the more interesting the Sitty becomes. For everyone.'

'Why don't you just tell people that, then? Instead of playing to their wish-fulfillment fantasies about finding the egress on the secret subroutine to post-Apocalyptic Peoria, or wherever?'

'It's not my job to explain the business plan. It's my job to answer questions. I can only answer with what I know. I don't know there's an egress – but I don't know that there *isn't*. I can't prove there isn't. I'm a utility avatar, I wasn't created to determine whether my universe is finite or not.'

I'm talking philosophy with a utility, Konstantin thought, unsure whether to be amazed or disgusted. 'But surely you know whether there are secret subroutines?'

'If they're secret, they certainly wouldn't tell *me*. I would tell anyone who asked. That's my job. Then they wouldn't be secret anymore.'

'All right.' Konstantin took a slow breath, trying to think. 'Have there ever been any secret subroutines in the Sitty that you've found out about? Or been *told* about?' she added quickly.

'Some players claimed to have accessed them.'

'Were they telling the truth?'

'I'm not a lie detector.'

'Wouldn't matter if you were, would it? Because it's all lies in here. Or all truth. Or all in what you perceive.'

He went on playing, eyes still closed. Konstantin supposed he was the AR version of blind justice – blind information. Which was probably much more accurate, all told.

'Have you ever met Shantih Love before?' she asked, and then added quickly, 'I mean, have you ever met a player named Shantih Love before I came in here?'

'I don't really *meet* anyone. I have everyone's name.'

'Then has anyone else ever asked you to locate Body Sativa?'

'I don't remember.'

Konstantin was nonplussed. 'Why not?'

'I don't have to. There's no reason to.'

'But if you can put a tracer on someone's location for another player, isn't there some record of that? Some, uh, trace?'

'Only while the tracer's active. But that record would be kept elsewhere in the system. You know, if you're so interested, there are schools you can go to to learn all about how AR works.'

'I thought you didn't volunteer information,' Konstantin said suspiciously.

'You call *that* information?'

She laughed in spite of herself. 'You're right. Thanks for the cab fare.' She started to walk away and then paused. 'Where's the best place to get a cab in post-Apocalyptic Noo Yawk Sitty?'

'I don't know.'

'All right, then, where's the nearest cab?'

'I don't know.' His smile widened. 'Cabs aren't players.'

Sighing in resignation, Konstantin nodded. She should have known.

EMPTY CUP [IV]

'It's the risk you run with any amphetamine-based drug,' the woman was saying reasonably. There was something wrong with her, but Yuki couldn't tell if it was the woman herself or a problem with her own vision. Her sight was distorted, but so was the woman. She was too big in some places, too small in others. Either that, or too close here and too far there. But then, Yuki thought, that was what you got when you crouched in a far corner of the ceiling and spied on people.

She didn't know how she had managed to get herself up in the far corner of the ceiling, and she didn't know how – or if – she would manage to get down again. At the moment, she wasn't sure that she even wanted to. Being up in the corner of the ceiling like this felt good. A light, tingly sensation was dancing all over her, as if she were immersed in an effervescent bath of lighter-than-air champagne. Whoever had managed to package this feeling and deliver it through a hot-suit deserved to get rich, she thought.

'If you have amphetamines, you have a big potential for paranoia,' the woman said, 'and paranoia will escalate in a remarkably short period of time anyway. Put it on fast-forward the way you do and before you know it, Kennedy's dead and Marilyn's on the moon.'

A second woman, just out of her range of vision, made a small, throaty noise that might have been intended to indicate amusement. 'Does everyone in your profession have such colorful turns of phrase?'

Yuki knew that voice. That was Joy Flower. Joy Flower, who didn't have a very good sense of humor. Yuki tried to look in her direction and found her vision going in and out of focus before it finally picked her out of a jumble of background noise. Which couldn't make sense anywhere but up here in this corner of the ceiling.

Joy Flower's mouth was moving and various kinds of things were coming out of it, things she could *almost* see but not quite. Sounds, Yuki thought, sounds that had to have been coded as something else to reach her way up where she was, but that had missed being decoded. If she had access to the decoding device, she would no doubt be able to see what the shapes were before hearing them. Now, that was some *real* synesthesia. Ash had bragged about getting hold of some drug that let him smell music and hear rainbows but she could blow him away with this one. *Hey, Ash*, she could say, *did you ever see what somebody's laugh looked like?* She could get him with that one the next time he showed up in the saucer –

She began to feel very tired and drowsy. Now what? she wondered uncertainly. Would she fall down from the ceiling and land on the floor with a thump, alerting Joy Flower and the woman talking to her that she had been eavesdropping – literally? Or could Joy Flower have put her up there deliberately, did they think she was unconscious or incapable of understanding?

She tried to feel her body and couldn't. Was that because she wasn't sleeping naked, or because she was? Her drowsiness receded a little as she tried to spread her awareness out to where her fingers and toes might be. Start by wiggling a finger, trace the feeling back. Try to remember what it felt like to decide to move your foot.

Nothing happened. No sense of her body would come to her in any way.

Breathe, she commanded herself. *Breathe in. Breathe out.*

If her chest was rising and falling, if her lungs were filling and emptying somewhere, she had somehow been cut off from the feeling.

They cut off my head and it floated up to the ceiling like a balloon. Because they only wanted me for my body.

She imagined her balloon head bobbing gently against the ceiling, pushed by faint air currents from the ventilation system. Her vision swung down sharply and she found her body directly below her, spread out on a futon. In the hotsuit, the form Ash had likened to a daikon radish looked more naked to her than it would have had it been completely nude. She felt a surge of affection for it, for all the pleasure she had taken for granted and recognized now as being part of corporeal existence. If she and her body were ever reunited, she would tear Ash a new one – a new Ash-hole, she thought with a

mental chuckle – for speaking of her body as being less than beautiful. *I have done the best I could with what talents and skills and good intentions I had, Mr Beautiful. You can tell me I'm mistaken about some things, or that I'm wasting my time over Tom. But* don't *tell me I'm the wrong shape.*

Okay, but you have *lost your head.*

Well, *that* was true. Where her head should have been was some kind of shiny, vaguely head-shaped machine trailing a lot of wires into a sort of cupboard on the futon frame. It must have been taking care of her body while her head was away, she thought. That made sense. Only ...

Only what was taking care of her head in lieu of her body?

'It's finished purging her blood,' Joy Flower said. 'All clean, ready to start over.'

'Already? That didn't take long.'

'She's a very small person. Physically. Also very clean to begin with.' Joy Flower gave a small, genteel laugh. 'You're used to those big bruisers of mine, with two liters worth of drug in every liter of blood.'

Yuki thought about her very small, very clean body, wondered if it would ever move again. There was a faint rustling noise.

'She's not conscious?'

'If she is, she won't remember,' Joy Flower said. 'I'm putting her back in, as of right now. Injection –'

If her head had been a balloon before, now it was a stone. It plummeted toward her body, toward the machine connected to her body, in a fall so long, she fell asleep waiting for the impact.

'They've got no shortage of people who want to wear,' said Tom. 'But there just aren't enough people who want to be worn. As a sensation, it's pretty horrible. You'll do anything to get rid of it, right?'

She was trying to wake up but sleep kept pulling her down into its comfortable depths. If she had known AR was this sensual, she'd have dived in long ago, she thought. There was no such thing as a minor sensation in AR; every feeling was realized in a way that was utterly complete, no aspect neglected. Because it was customized, measured out to order for *your* senses alone, in *your* hotsuit.

'Well, maybe not your senses *alone,*' Tom said. 'Did you ever know someone who really *hated* their body? *Their* body. Not too grammatical, but then, the situation's not too grammatical, either. Some people do, they hate their bodies.'

She was sitting by the side of a long, gently winding highway that disappeared into vague countryside in either direction. Across from her stood every person who had ever ventured into AR for any period of time, pioneers and mere fad-followers alike, and all of them wearing Tom's appearance so that it seemed to be only a special effect lining the side of the highway.

Spectacular, to be sure, all these Toms as far as the eye could see, and even farther than that. But strictly ornamental. Right, Tom?

They all gave her the okay sign. She nodded. Yes, okay. Now, which shell *was* the pea under? She squinted in the sunlight. His lovely white ice-cream suit glowed so brightly under the bare sun that she was having a hard time seeing the expression on his face. Or their face.

'You're not supposed to feel anything,' a million Tom voices said, speaking softly and gently so she wouldn't be overwhelmed and washed away by a deluge of sound. 'But there's some kind of bounce or echo. Or maybe it's just that there's no such thing as an intelligent suit of clothes.'

'If there were,' she said lazily, 'it wouldn't let anyone put it on.'

'Exactly,' the Toms said in harmonious unison. She had the idea that he or they wanted to speak more to her, but her eyes, or rather her vision, was getting heavy. She had thought she was *already* asleep. Could you get tired in a dream and sleep within your sleep? And if you did, what would you dream then?

'*When you awake,*' Tom whispered, '*you will remember everything.*'

The cyborg was at least eight feet tall. It had a frosted crystal skullcap and chrome filament eyebrows. One eye was more or less normal; the other was steel mesh, punctuated here and there by tiny capacitors or sensors like multicolored Indian beads. There were areas on the high cheekbones where the skin and muscle had been excised to allow the metal skull to show and a window in its chest for the anatomically fascinated to watch the innards at work. One lung had been collapsed, or possibly removed altogether, so that the heart could be viewed more easily. Yuki thought it looked sloppy and a bit out of rhythm. The problem was that human organs just never appeared as efficient and neat as machinery did.

She looked around to see if there were any other cyborgs on the pier tonight, or whenever this was. It was always night in post-Apocalyptic Noo Yawk Sitty, so she wasn't sure if it was ever a different night, or whether all nights remained one night. Whatever the case, the cyborgs were out in force, and no two were alike. She looked down at herself, afraid she would see that she, too, was part metal, but she was still wearing Tom's appearance, at least on the parts she could see. *I probably make a better Tom than he does*, she thought.

'You're lost, aren't you?' said the cyborg.

Yuki recoiled from a passing individual who was wearing all of the internal organs on the outside of a plastic-and-metal frame. 'Isn't the brine and humidity bad for you guys?'

'Oh. You may be much more lost than I can help you with.' The cyborg sounded alarmed.

'Relax,' Yuki said. 'I was trying to make a joke.'

'So was I.'

'Oh.' She laughed a little. 'Sorry. I hadn't expected subtlety here.'

'What *were* you expecting?' The cyborg sounded genuinely interested.

Yuki thought for a moment. 'I'll know it when I see it.'

'Ah, but will *it* know *you*? What are you doing here, anyway? This is the Cyborg Club.'

'Really.' Cyborgs were gathering on the pier like seagulls anticipating the arrival of a fishing fleet. Expectation all but hummed in the air. 'I thought I was in post-Apocalyptic Noo Yawk Sitty.'

The cyborg buffed his stainless-steel left hand on his left buttock and admired the result. Yuki wondered if that was why he was wearing chamois trousers. 'Well, yes. This is the post-Apocalyptic Noo Yawk Sitty chapter of the Cyborg Club.'

'Oh. Well, I was looking for Waxx24.' She watched two cyborgs comparing eyes and then deciding to trade. It gave her a sympathetic pain in her own corresponding eye socket.

'Yes, yes, yes,' the cyborg said, starting to sound impatient. 'We're the post-Apocalyptic Noo Yawk Sitty chapter of Waxx24's Cyborg Club.'

'*Oh*. And I used to think doing all that set and subset homework in math was a silly waste of time.' She was starting to get that surreal feeling again.

'So, does this mean that you don't want to join?' He actually sounded a little bit sad.

'You could say that,' she said. 'I really don't understand how I ended up here.'

'And I suppose that means an organ donation is out of the question.'

'You could have my tonsils,' Yuki offered. 'Or my appendix. I never throw anything away.'

'Those aren't organs. The club could use some good liver stock, or kidneys. Lungs. Stuff like that.'

Yuki shook her head. 'Try again.'

'Well, we wouldn't *take* them. We'd *clone* them. Then you could keep yours and we'd get something new.'

'Sounds reasonable,' Yuki said, frowning. 'But why don't you just – well, you know, order this stuff from inventory?'

'Now, what fun is that?' said the cyborg in a kindly, jocular tone. 'Just ordering from inventory is too easy. We like a challenge here.'

'That's a big challenge, waiting for someone to take a wrong turn onto your part of the Sitty and then trying to talk them out of an organ or two.'

'Oh, this is just where we gather before we spread out on our nightly scavenger hunt. Maybe I'll see you on whatever level you like to call your own. If you happen to see anything hydraulic with gears attached, think of me.' He

pushed his hip at her and gave it a slap with his shiny hand. 'I need a new one of these. I'll make it worth your while.'

'How?' asked Yuki skeptically. 'I'm not a cyborg and I don't want any liver.'

The cyborg stepped back and gave her a thoughtful up-and-down. 'And that's just how I'd describe you, too. But some things have universal appeal, n'est ce-pas?'

'N'est ce-pas,' she agreed, and enjoyed seeing him wince. 'If I were to find a hip worthy of you, how do I let you know?'

He produced a business card. 'Any telephone should accept it. Provided you're in a place where they allow phones.'

She took the card from him, hiding her reluctance. It was a plain chrome rectangle, a pocket mirror, but when she looked at it, she saw the cyborg's face instead of her own. She could tell that it was his turn to enjoy seeing her wince, but she tucked it up her sleeve, figuring it would find its way to her catalog. 'What will happen if I call you?' she asked, but he was moving away from her, ambling down the pier. He didn't look as if he really needed a new hip, and she couldn't figure out why a cyborg or anyone else would need such a thing in AR. Maybe it was some kind of weird parts one-upmanship.

As she stood there watching the cyborgs drift around each other, the population increased at least threefold – suddenly, there were many more people all around her, all over the pier and around it, wading in the water or walking on the surface. *Show-offs*, she thought. She could still see the cyborgs among them, and only some seemed aware of the crowds of noncyborgs; most weren't.

At the same time, her mind rearranged; it was as if every thought, every idea, every concept had shattered and reassembled in the space of some impossibly short fraction of a second, and the new structures were superior, at least for the purpose of her thought process, which was more focused. And faster.

Definitely faster, she thought, turning away from the pier, and looked up at the night sky, wondering if the saucer would be showing up again.

Wondering if Tom would be showing up again.

Her mind seemed to stumble. She had all but forgotten him, at least for a few minutes. Hard to see how she could, though, seeing as how she *was* him. On the outside, that was. Perhaps she should get business cards like the cyborg's: *Have you seen me lately? Do I turn up in places you wouldn't expect to find me – like your mirror? If so, call me immediately!*

Across the road, beyond the burning piles of wreckage – vehicles of some kind, they looked like teepees set on fire – the windows of the closed and vacant shops or whatever they had once been reflected the streetlife through a veil of grime. She hurried across to them, clambering over a barrier dividing the trafficway in half and shaking off the imploring hands of someone who seemed to have been a refugee from a mummy case.

She stood in front of a dirty, cracked window, staring at herself. Or rather,

at Tom's likeness. She could see it quite well in spite of the reflected glare of the fire just behind her. Tom's face was expectant, almost hopeful. She studied the eyes, waiting to see an awareness in them that didn't belong to her, but they remained her own gaze and no one else's.

No one else's?

The memory spilled over her like hot liquid from an overturned cup, that sensation of having someone else's hand inside of her own, as if it – as if she herself – were somebody else's clothing. There was a cold, uncomfortable knot at the top of her stomach, a panic bomb setting itself to go off at the first sign that she wasn't alone in her – Tom's – body. She waited in front of the glass, afraid to look at the reflection, afraid not to.

As if on cue, there was a movement behind the glass. She yelled and jumped back, but her panic stalled, becoming mere startlement. The movement really *was* behind the glass, something actually on the other side (*virtually* actually, her mind corrected her, some part of her needing to emphasize the absurdity). While she was still trying to catch her breath, a figure stepped through the glass as if it were a veil of gelatin and faced her on the sidewalk, a humanish creature with shiny black hair flowing down beyond waist level, velvet skin the color of concord grapes, and animal eyes. It was the velvet skin more than the eyes or hair that fascinated her. *Velvet* skin, and only a loincloth to keep out the cold, as if whoever was underneath craved to be a tactile magnet for everyone else.

'Well, are you coming in or *aren't* you?' The voice was aural velvet, musical, and unmistakably Ash. Without waiting for an answer, he grabbed her wrist in a velvet-steel grip and pulled her through the window after him.

'Go ahead,' he said, offering her his arm. 'Pet me. Rub me. You know you want to.'

Yuki stroked his arm twice, just to be polite. They were standing in the middle of an area Ash said was the post-Apocalyptic version of Times Square. There were as many lights here as in the real place, possibly more, but the vehicular traffic comprised mostly cobbled-together machines, most of them without roofs or any other kind of enclosing element, to make it easier for the occupants to jump out on short notice. They had to; the gangs here sported strange metal wings that let them glide if not actually fly, though the trajectories and the speeds seemed to be fudged, at least to Yuki's eye. Like an old film, the kind where a fall from ten feet up never hurt you, the hero could punch a dozen people, one after another, and never suffer broken bones, or even pain and swelling, and guns fired a million shots in succession and never needed reloading. Which was the whole point, of course.

'So, what are we doing today, Ash?' she said finally.

He was watching the gang flyers show off for each other, soaring through the neon canyon. 'Anything we want, I guess. What did you have in mind?'

Yuki groaned. 'You're the one who pulled me in here, remember? You asked me, I didn't ask you.'

Ash stroked his velvet chest with both hands. 'I just wanted you to see how well I've done since the last time I saw you.'

She frowned at him. 'Oh, you've done strikingly well – I guess – but it hasn't been that long since the last time you saw me.' Pause. 'Has it?'

Now he looked a bit uneasy, as if she had caught him in something compromising. A lie, she wondered? Or someone else's body? Something else?

'It's all relative,' he said after a few moments. 'You know – Einstein, time, space, mc^2. So much has happened to me since I saw you that it seems like a long time.'

'Really,' she said, not quite asking a question. 'I'm kind of surprised that you went for velvet, though. I'd have thought you'd prefer large-grain sandpaper.'

'Oh, no,' he said. 'Small-grain, definitely.' He laughed. 'What about you? Got anything interesting?'

'Why?'

'I thought we might trade merchandise or favors.'

Yuki felt her frown deepen. 'Are you collecting stamps and coins now, too? Souvenir spoons?' Ash's textured face looked blank. 'Brassieres?'

A flying gang-member swooped low over them, making her duck, but Ash didn't even flinch. 'God, what's the matter with you? Haven't you found that tiresome Tom yet?'

'Well, it's hard, looking *all by myself*,' she snapped. 'With none of Tom's *good friends* giving me a bit of help.'

'Sorry,' Ash said, unperturbed. 'It's just that Tom's a big boy and always was able to look after himself. Maybe better than any of us.'

'Where would you get an idea like that?'

'Well, from Tom, of course.' He looked surprised. 'Now, have you got anything worth looking at or haven't you?'

She wanted to spit in his face and walk away. Instead, she produced her icon cat and simply held it out to him. 'Here. If you don't see it, ask. I probably haven't got it.' She watched as he pored through it, studying some pages, brushing past others. He found the mirror-card and held it up, frowning.

'What's this?'

'I met this cyborg –'

'Ew. *Yuck!*' He dropped the card back into the book as if it had been something unclean. 'A *cyborg*, for god's sake. What are you doing going around with *cyborgs*.'

'Is a cyborg some kind of untouchable in here?' she asked, amused in spite of everything.

Ash shuddered. 'In *triplicate*. For *god's* sake, they're made up of *parts*.'

'Why is that bad?' Yuki asked, more to needle him than anything else.

'It's not *bad*. It's just so –' Ash looked pained. '*Robohick*.' He shuddered again. 'Most of us got past model building before puberty.'

She stroked his velvet arm. 'Indeed.'

He finished leafing through her catalog and then handed it back to her. 'Well, you don't have anything that interests me, thanks just the same.'

'Well, you're welcome just the same,' she said, laughing a little. 'Anything else?'

'No, I think that's all,' he said. 'Let me know when you find Tom, will you?' He was striding away from her before she could ask him how she was supposed to do that.

Holding her catalog, she stood staring after him. The cyborg's mirror-card was sticking out of the top like a bookmark. She plucked it out before it could fall or be snatched away and was about to tuck it into the catalog when she saw that it had changed.

Instead of the cyborg's face in the mirror now, it was Ash, all velvety and perfectly reproduced in hard-res 3D. Underneath the flawless face was the legend, *Unacceptable – Simulated Person, Non-Human Manipulated*.

'What the hell does *that* mean?' she said aloud, and reached for one of the lottery cards.

DEATH IN THE PROMISED LAND [IV]

Konstantin came up out of the subway just as the flying saucer stopped overhead. She stared up at it, surprised and then wary. One of the murder victims had been abducted by a flying saucer in the Sitty, she remembered uneasily, and looked around for something to grab on to, or at least use as a weapon. And then she remembered that that would do about as much good as her phoning Guilfoyle Pleshette and asking her to bring in her service pistol and taser.

But apparently the saucer didn't have designs on androgynous corpses with slashed throats; a spotlight flashed down on the pavement in front of her, quivered, and then moved along as the saucer sailed away silently. Curious, she followed. The light jumped around, not just sweeping over the ground but flashing on and off at different spots in a way that reminded her of stop-motion animation, the old-fashioned, hard and tedious kind that pre-dated software trickery, right down to the choppiness. And the quivering, which never let up.

A shadow breezed past her, ruffling her robe and her hair. Well, Shantih's robe and hair, anyway. The saucer was starting to pick up speed and Konstantin

had to walk faster and faster to keep up with it. Pretty soon, though, she would either have to run or give up.

Or hail a cab. *Cabbie, this is a police emergency – follow that saucer!*

She could imagine the cabbie, a chrome humanoid that answered to the name Sylvia, turning around from the steering wheel and saying, *Tailing a UFO is subject to a surcharge on your billable time. Do you still wish to proceed? Please answer yes or no.*

She had reached the end of the street and trotted through a ruined square into some kind of park bordering some large body of water. Very likely the East River, unless the classic directions of north, south, east, and west were as changeable as everything else here. Somehow, she didn't think so, at least, not in this case, since it was so important that this be a variation on New York City.

The saucer sailed out over the water, the jumpy spotlights slapping down at the waves in a way that seemed less random than purposeful. She stood at a railing made of brushed metal pipe, wondering what the hell it was doing. Looking for something, of course. No, someone. Someone to abduct. Or maybe it was abducting people right in front of her, sucking them up in light beams. What was that old saw about *beaming? Beam me* something. *Beam me off? Away? Over?* But who – people *underwater?* Mermaids? Dolphin people? Well, why not? There were people living in burning wrecks like moto-salamanders, so why not underwater gillgeeks? Konstantin groaned; that hadn't occurred to her until just now. Why hadn't she thought to bring someone else along – two or three someone elses, Celestine and DiPietro, not Taliaferro, of course, but maybe what's-her-name, Wolski –

Then she had a sudden vision of herself trying to explain to the policy board why they really did need an Artificial Reality squad made up of officers specially trained to deal with crimes peculiar to AR, such as copyright infringement, post-Apocalyptic poaching, and murder. *Oh,* yeah. That would happen right after she impressed the taxpayers by finding a killer on-line and dragging him back out with her to be jailed, as Pleshette had suggested. Maybe even on the same day.

Abruptly, the saucer jittered and shot off upriver, going faster than should have been possible from a more-or-less standing start. Konstantin was about to turn away and go looking for a cab when the UFO was suddenly back, directly overhead, shining a spotlight down on her. She was still blinking against it when it was gone again, heading west this time, and she lost sight of it among the buildings. *So, what's the matter, saucer-people, a homicide detective isn't good enough for you to abduct?* Guess not.

What a waste of time that had been, following the saucer. Not much to see around here at all; obviously, she had no more instinct in AR for finding the real cool places than she did out on the street. Her ex would have felt vindicated, Konstantin thought.

'Taxi?' she asked the darkness, not really expecting anything to happen.

Somewhere behind her there was a metallic creaking. She started to turn toward it and then a bright yellow rectangle popped into existence in front of her.

DO YOU WISH TO ORDER A TAXI-CAB?
YES NO
!?HELP?!

'You know, there's more protocol here sometimes than in the entire police department?' she said to the sign. It didn't bother to tell her to stick to the subject at hand, or even to warn her about possible surcharges; it only hung in the air, waiting for her to trigger the next event with the proper response. Konstantin stood staring at it, trying to decide if she wanted to tangle with *Help* (*You know what* some *people call help*. Which employee had said that to her? The bored one, hadn't it been? Sure hadn't been Mank. Or Pleshette.), or whether she should just say *Yes* and hope for the best.

She would probably make decisions a lot faster, she thought ruefully, if this was her own billable time. And then, with a shudder: *Jesus, now they've got me singing the billable-time song*.

The sound of creaking metal came again, something familiar, even rather commonplace, though seldom heard in the middle of the night. Probably past sunrise out there, in the real world, which right now felt a great deal less real to her than where she was.

More creaking, a bit louder. To get her attention, Konstantin thought idly, and then had the strong feeling that she was right. She looked at the sign for a moment. It showed no impatience, didn't give any indication that it was about to flicker out, so she simply turned away from it and squinted into the darkness.

She was facing an area that seemed to be a ruined park or recreational zone, where people might have come to sit and look at the water, or stroll along footpaths in the sunshine. Abruptly she caught herself picturing it all in her mind and had to laugh. Not just authentic sensation, but authentic ambience – and not just authentic ambience but authentic *retro* ambience. That was the sort of thing that could make an otherwise prudent person forget that the meter was clicking away, running the tab higher and higher. Probably why there was so much yak-yak about billable time this and billable time that.

She moved along the railing, keeping one ear cocked for the sounds of anything in the water, while she listened for the metal creaking.

There it was, coming from something farther up. Her eyes were getting more accustomed to the darkness and she could see now that she was on the

edge of a playground that was fairly well still intact. But what for, Konstantin wondered. Surely *children* didn't –

Ah, but apparently children *did*. The creaking became louder as well as constant, and she saw just the bare movement of the swing before she saw the girl.

The streetlamps along the railing had been gradually getting brighter since she had arrived; now she could actually see by them. The girl was hard at work to keep the swing going, pumping with enormous effort because she was too small for her feet to touch the ground. Konstantin could hear her grunt at the back of each sweep just as the swing went forward again, her legs thrust out straight, her braids flying out behind her.

'Good God,' said Konstantin. 'What the hell are *you*?'

The girl's head whipped around in a startled away, as if she really hadn't known Konstantin was there. She quit pumping, letting her legs dangle, but made no active effort to stop herself. Eventually, the swing slowed enough so that the girl could just stand up and walk away from it. But she went only as far as the part of the A-frame closest to Konstantin and then stood hugging the slanted bar and looking like nothing so much as a shy little girl in a playground.

'Are you another paying customer, or something the module throws in to make things interesting?'

The girl leaned her head on the support pole and looked at Konstantin. 'I want to go home.' Pause. 'Will you take me home? Are you a nice person?'

Konstantin started to bury her face in her hands and then remembered that would be awkward. 'Drop the act, whoever you are. I know as well as anyone else there aren't any real children in here.'

'What if you're wrong?' The girl pushed away from the pole and came toward her with her hands behind her back. 'What if I am a real little girl? What if I told you that every time my mom brings one of her boyfriends home, she sticks me in her rig and logs me in so I'm out of the way?'

Konstantin looked down at her, feeling slightly queasy. 'I'd say that your mom is breaking the law, and she could be in a lot of trouble if anyone finds out.'

'Nobody will,' the girl said. 'I can run around in here for hours and hours telling everyone about it and no one will believe me. You're not supposed to believe anything anyone tells you in here, so she's perfectly safe.'

Konstantin's queasiness intensified. 'Is that why you hang around here, swinging in the dark?'

The girl nodded. 'If you know anything about the Sitty, then you can see why I want to just stay out of the way till I can log out.'

'But this is ridiculous,' Konstantin said. 'Why don't you tell someone when you're off-line? A teacher, a police officer, a counselor –'

'I have.' The girl shrugged. 'Nobody believes me out there, either. It's too unbelievable. Nobody would do that. I have to be lying. Right?'

'*Plus ça change.*' Konstantin sighed, thinking suddenly that there was very damned little that had ever been invented for the sake of bringing humans closer to truth.

The girl took her hand suddenly, making her jump. 'I think you *are* a nice person. You must be. Even if you don't believe me, at least you care. At least there's enough of a real person left inside you to think it isn't right.'

Konstantin sighed again, at a complete loss for something to say, anything at all. So, which is worse – murder, or the things that let the victims live to regret? Damn it, it just wasn't fair, when she was trying to handle one to have to be confronted with the other.

You can't save the world; you can only channel-surf it. Something her ex had said once, or at least quoted. Back when they had still been showing each other compassion.

'Look,' she said, gently removing her hand from the girl's. 'I'm in here for a – a special purpose, I've got to find someone … ' Her voice trailed off. The girl stood looking up at her.

You just couldn't win, Konstantin thought unhappily. If she walked away, she'd never know if she'd heard a tragedy-in-progress or an outrageous fish story. Either way, the soul behind the facade of those eyes was someone who needed *some* kind of help. In spite of everything, she wouldn't be able to square it with her conscience if she walked away simply because the problem wasn't one of those listed in her job description.

Okay. Think of a better reason to walk away, urged her more cynical side. *Try the billable time thing.*

'*Or* maybe you can help me,' Konstantin said quickly, taking the girl's hand again. 'Do you know anything about someone named Body Sativa?'

The girl only continued to stare up at her in silence.

'Okay. How about Shantih Love?'

The girl frowned. 'I have something at home that might help you.'

'Where's home?'

'It's just a few blocks away. If you take me home, I can show it to you,' the girl promised, her voice faintly hopeful.

Konstantin nodded resignedly.

'Home' turned out to be a tiny basement efficiency in what seemed to be an otherwise abandoned building, although the girl assured Konstantin that it was not. When Konstantin asked her who else lived there, however, she only shrugged. 'It depends, I guess,' she said, working four big locks with a well-practiced hand before crossing the room to plant herself in the middle of the double bed that dominated the room. Except for a television sitting on a

crate, it was the only furniture in the place. It was covered with a red-and-black plaid blanket; between the two pillows, a stuffed penguin stood like a tuxedoed sentry. The girl unselfconsciously folded her legs into a half-lotus and hugged the penguin to her chest. 'This is Fairbanks. He keeps an eye on things for me.'

'If you're safe here, why do you leave and go to the park?' Konstantin asked her.

'I don't. The park is where I get logged in all the time, and I have to figure out how to get home safely. Sometimes I can't and I just stay there, because nobody really likes to go there. But I have to be careful when the saucer comes around.' She rested her chin on the penguin's head. 'Have you ever been taken up by the saucer?'

Konstantin shook her head. 'Have you?'

'That depends on what you mean. And what you believe. And if it's the same saucer every time. I don't know if it is.'

'Good point,' Konstantin said, more to herself than to the girl. 'What is it that you said you had that could help me?'

'What kind of help do you want? Refresh my memory.'

Konstantin sighed. 'Okay. To refresh your memory, I asked you about Body Sativa and Shantih Love –'

'That's right.' She turned the penguin around to face her. 'Fairbanks, do you know anything about Body Sativa and Shantih Love?' Konstantin had to force herself not to make a face as the girl put the penguin's bright orange beak to her ear. Every so often she nodded slightly.

'So does the bird know anything?' Konstantin asked, unable to keep the sarcasm out of her voice.

'Shh,' the girl told her.

Bored, Konstantin looked around. The walls had been bare when they had come in, but now posters were fading into existence on them, arty things with lots of nudes. No doubt the girl would tell her that they had been there when she had first come here and she couldn't get rid of them for some reason.

'Okay,' the girl announced. 'Now I know.'

Konstantin turned to her and was startled to see she was now dressed in a frilly little nightie, too obviously over nothing. Understanding swept through her immediately. 'Oh, *Christ*,' she said, standing up and backing away.

'What's the matter?' the girl said, putting a finger to her mouth cutely. 'You don't have a dirty mind, do you?'

Konstantin attacked the locks but they wouldn't budge for her. Frustrated and furious with herself for allowing the girl to lead her wide-eyed and innocent into the setup, she leaned against the door and took a long careful breath. It didn't help. 'All right. What do you want?'

'What've you got?' the girl asked cheerfully.

'Precious little, and I need every bit of it.'

'Do you also need everyone to know that you're a paedophile?' The girl giggled. 'Kinky for the kiddies?'

'I'm logging all this,' Konstantin said, hoping she was. 'That'll prove –'

'Nothing,' the girl said, smiling sunnily. 'My log will look as real as yours.' She drew her knees up, reached around her bent legs and grabbed her toes. It was such a child's posture, Konstantin could have laughed and cried. 'Of course, maybe you're of a more liberated sort of mind. Maybe you feel that if there's no such thing as paedophilia in here – and there isn't – then there's no such thing as an unthinkable thought, and it's okay to contemplate anything. Even if it makes you look like the wretched refuse you secretly are.'

Konstantin sagged a bit in relief. 'You're not a child.'

'I could be a precocious child,' said the girl. 'I could also be an undercover cop disguised as a chicken dinner.'

'If you're a cop, I want your badge number,' Konstantin said briskly.

'I could give you a number, but if it's a fake, there's nothing you can do about it,' the girl said. 'You couldn't prosecute me for being a bad cop, or being a bad impersonator. Or didn't you read your –'

'I read it, I read it a billion times.' Konstantin jerked a thumb at the locks. 'Just let me out of here, or you'll be a *battered* precocious child chicken cop dinner impersonator.'

'What kind of batter – original recipe or something on the extra spicy side?' The girl grinned. 'Either way, I bet you can't do it.'

'Well, let's see about that.' Konstantin strode over to the bed, grabbed the girl by the front of her nightie and lifted her up, drawing her other fist back. The girl smiled up into her face as if Konstantin were offering her a piece of candy. Konstantin squeezed her eyes shut for a moment. *It's not a kid. It's some kind of lowlife, probably some banana slug who gets his kicks by torment-ing lost souls too shattered to defend themselves.* She drew her fist back a little further and opened her eyes.

The girl's face was practically beatific with happiness. Konstantin imag-ined what it would be like to let fly at this point, what the girl would look like. Would there be blood? Or would her fist suddenly smash into an invisible shield inches from the girl's face, and instead of blood there'd be a thundering pain that went all the way up her arm to her shoulder while the girl laughed at her and said something like, *I told you you couldn't do it, why didn't you listen to exactly what I said?* Yeah, that wasn't too hard to imagine. That, or maybe the girl turning into an alligator at the last minute and chomping down on her arm.

But what if there was no shield, no trick; what if her punch sent the girl ass-over-teakettle and what if she turned out to be real child after all? It

wasn't impossible. Maybe not the kid-forced-into-the-hotsuit scenario the girl had given her, but maybe an older kid, just starting puberty, say, out to blow off some steam with some mean-spirited fun?

And regardless, was she ready for the sight of what an unrestrained punch could do to a child's face, especially an unrestrained punch that she herself delivered? Even if it *wasn't* real?

Konstantin let go and lowered her fist. 'Let me out of here,' she said heavily.

The girl's smile never wavered; she said nothing.

'Please,' Konstantin said, sickened by the begging note she could hear in her voice.

The girl held her hand out, palm up.

'I don't have anything you'd really want,' insisted Konstantin.

The girl's smile became an irritated sneer; she snapped her fingers twice rapidly and jabbed the air with her hand, palm up again.

Konstantin shrugged and sat down on the bed, leaning back on one elbow as if she were making herself comfortable. 'I told you, I don't have anything you'd want. Now, if you waste all your billable time trying to get me to cough up what I don't have, I don't care. I slipped in here on somebody else's credit and I'm not watching the clock.'

'Uh-huh,' said the girl, but Konstantin could tell by her tone that she wasn't as certain of herself now.

'That's the one lie you *can't* tell in here, isn't it – billable time. Can't fake that billable time, can you.'

The girl tried to stare her down. Konstantin laughed in her face and lay back with her arms folded behind her head, hoping she looked far more casual than she felt. Her midsection was tense; she expected the girl to hit her or jump on her. But nothing happened for close to half a minute. When she sat up again, the girl was gone, and the door was wide open.

Maybe, Konstantin thought, satisfied, she should take up poker.

It may have been a coincidence that there was a cab parked at the curb outside. Behind the wheel, the driver was browsing the news on an in-dash screen and listening to music with lots of syrupy violins.

'You must be the cab I was going to call,' Konstantin said.

The driver turned to look at her. He was Japanese, perhaps in his early thirties. 'Actually, I'm a coincidence,' he said, matter-of-factly. 'Statistics indicate the average player experiences between one and three coincidences per five billable hours. Of course, statistics breed coincidences.'

Konstantin considered this with her hand on the door. 'Is that anything like familiarity breeding contempt?'

'If it is, that's a coincidence, too. Where to, sir or madam, as the case may be?'

'Body Sativa. Wherever she is.'

The cabdriver frowned slightly. 'You got that kind of cab fare?'

'So I've been told.'

'Then get in.' He jerked his thumb at the backseat.

The people lining either side of the street exuded such a sense of danger that Konstantin knew to read just the settings on her 'suit.

'Better?' the cabbie asked her, a hint of amusement in his voice.

She met his gaze in the rearview mirror and was startled to see that his eyes looked far more tense than he sounded. 'Much better, thanks. Maybe you'd regard that as cheating –'

'I don't regard it as anything, sir or madam as the case may be. I'm a cabbie. It's my job to drive a cab, not to regard.'

'Oh. Well, good.' Konstantin laughed a little nervously. 'What's going on out there, anyway?'

'Someone's left a tribal warfare module going. It's most likely a promo by a new parlor, trolling for customers. Extra Sitty-based module for no extra charge, that sort of thing.'

'At *this* hour of the morning?' Konstantin said, yawning.

'It isn't *this* hour of the morning everywhere, sir or madam as the case may be.'

'Touché.'

'And even where it is, it isn't for some people. The time zone can be a thing of personal preference.'

Pretty forthcoming for a cabbie, Konstantin thought, trying to catch the driver's gaze in the rearview mirror again. 'Have you ever had Body Sativa as a fare?' she asked.

'Not that I know of. She's not my speed.'

'Whatever *that* means,' Konstantin muttered, barely realizing she was speaking aloud.

'You'll find out. She's not your speed, either.'

He made a sharp right, drove up some stone steps and across a piazza, negotiating a route around and through enormous fragments of broken statuary and wrecked machines to the base of a skyscraper. Where the entrance had been was only a huge, gaping hole, guarded by what seemed to be a couple of werewolves.

'Well, *their* hair is perfect,' said the cabbie.

'What?' Konstantin said, bewildered.

'Nothing. Don't worry about them. Show them your pass and they'll let you go in.'

'How do you know I've got a pass?'

'You'd have to. Otherwise you wouldn't have known to tell me to take you directly to Body Sativa.'

'Oh.' Konstantin found her cab fare and handed it over the front seat. 'If I find you again, will that be a coincidence?'

'Chance favors the prepared mind.'

She found herself standing on the cracked stone of the piazza, watching the cab drive away to disappear around the side of the building. Steeling herself, she turned to the werewolves guarding the entrance. Their hair really *was* perfect, she realized; they seemed to be closer to were-lions than wolves, gracefully muscular in artful tatters of clothing, and definitely the sort of creatures that Shantih Love had found attractive, according to the 'suit. They looked at her with large-pupiled eyes rimmed in amber and she had the feeling they were amused. No more amused than she was, Konstantin thought. Who would *pay* to be a night watchman? Or watchwolf, as the case may be.

'I'm here to see Body Sativa,' she told them, sounding a bit more defiant than she had meant to.

'What you *can* see, you *will* see,' said the wolf on her left.

'Well, then, I'm going in.' Konstantin looked from him to the other one on her right. The other one was female, she realized, as the wolf licked its chops. 'Tell me, is this what you both *like* to do? Spend your time here guarding a hole in a building?'

'Nosy, aren't you,' said the female, but in a genial way.

'Yes, I *am* nosy. I figure – why not.' Konstantin smiled. 'Now, really. Is this how you two spend your time?'

'Stay alert and maybe you can barter, too,' said the first werewolf. He waved her into the building.

At first, she could only stand in total darkness, confused. Then she felt the cat in her arms, and a moment later, two beams of light were playing around the lobby. Twin flashlights – they came from the cat's eyes, which made her laugh, but more with relief than amusement. The cat looked around the ruined, dirty lobby until it found the elevator for her, staring at the call button until she pressed it. She had some reservations about climbing into an elevator in a building like this, but when it arrived, it was fully lit and functional. Considering that the alternative would have been to hike up a few hundred flights of stairs in the dark, she decided that it was a risk she could tolerate.

The elevator opened right onto a waiting room. It was brightly lit, filled with oddly-shaped furniture that suggested both antiquity and unknown origin. The texture seemed to be wood, but also gave the impression that it had been made liquid at some point, to be pulled and tortured into twisted, bizarre framework before hardening permanently. Tortured furniture? Konstantin shook her head. Either she was getting more imaginative in her old age, or she was extremely tired. Her ex would have voted for tired.

She looked around. There was no one else in the room, not even at the

contorted table that could very well have been a receptionist's desk. Konstantin sighed, absently petting the cat in her arms. The cat jumped onto the surface of the table/receptionist's desk, lay down and became a book again, open to a page with a large exclamation mark on it. Konstantin went around the other side to have a look.

The exclam vanished and words appeared on the page. *So you're here to see Body Sativa and no one seems to be in.*

Konstantin stepped back and looked around. 'Hello?' she asked warily.

The book turned a page with an attention-getting flapping noise. *You have entered an area normally reserved for those who access at a higher speed.*

She blew out a disgusted breath. Figured. Sex, drugs, blood and guts. When did humanity last have an original thought, she wondered. *Probably never. Everything we thought we needed to know we learned from chimpanzees.*

There will be a short wait before anyone can see you, but you will be seen. Do you want to wait? Please touch one: – YES – NO.

Konstantin touched the YES square.

Thank you. Please have a seat.

Konstantin picked up the book and tucked it away inside her robe, before finding a piece of furniture that seemed to be remotely like a couch, and sitting down. The walls in this room were blank, as far as she could tell. Sometimes she thought she saw a shadow flicker but nothing appeared and she decided it was some kind of glitch in the transmission. Either that, or the simulated fluorescent lights were flickering in the interest of authenticity.

'Cat,' she said, and there it was in her lap again, giving her a glimpse of a puzzled feline face before it became a book. She stared down at the page of icons Tim Mezzer had given her. Several were question marks, presumably to provide her with relatively simple answers. Or so she surmised. She touched one of the question marks and it became a small card in her hand.

'Is it me,' she said to the card, 'or is this really boring?'

'It's you.'

She looked up. A large TV screen had come into existence directly in front of her without her noticing; she might have taken the image on the screen for another androgyne, except that everyone had referred to Body Sativa as *she*. Male or female or both, Body Sativa would have been beautiful, although her face should have been too wide and too round and her eyes too small to allow that description of her. Perhaps it was the full, wide, sensuous mouth that did it, or the chaotic, multi-colored hair. Or maybe it was all just a special effect on a TV screen, as seen on a second TV screen.

'I don't get to meet you in person, I have to watch you on a monitor?' Konstantin said. 'And I'm already actually watching you on a monitor to begin with. Don't you think that's excessive?'

Body Sativa's smile was appreciative. 'It's always wise to take anything in

AR with a grain of salt at least. Grains of salt are a valuable commodity here. But an even more valuable commodity is speed.'

'So I hear. Tell me, what is there for the, uh, unaccelerated, so to speak?'

'There's plenty of keep-busy junk in the world out there. One could beg the question of why anyone would even bother to come in here *unaccelerated*, as you put it.'

'If *one* doesn't have a good illicit drug connection and *one* doesn't know to begin with,' Konstantin snapped, losing her patience. 'Look, I'm tired, I've had a bad night. I'm wearing this outfit to investigate a murder that occurred out there, in a video parlor. The person who normally wears this appearance, or who was wearing it earlier tonight anyway, got his throat cut. The name is Shantih Love, which he wore *over* the name Tom Iguchi, which according to his wife wasn't his name to begin with, since he was known to change his name regularly. During questioning of possible witnesses, you were mentioned several times as someone who would know something more about Shantih Love than the average paying customer. I'm sick of chasing around in here –' Konstantin sighed. Suddenly she felt weak and very, very tired. 'I almost got molested by a *child*, for chrissakes.'

'A *child?*' Body Sativa's amused smile was also skeptical. 'There are no *children* in here.'

'Are you sure about that?' Konstantin sighed. 'After all, everything you're told in here is a lie, right? So that must be a lie, too.'

'Philosophers' Corner is halfway down the block from Beginners' Cafe, and you don't even need to pay extra to be in the Sitty to go to either one of them,' Body Sativa said briskly. 'Look, dear-friend, if you have some information for me, you can deposit it down there, in the bottom of this monitor unit –' the TV screen bulged slightly as Body Sativa leaned forward and looked down, at the outside of the TV case; a small slot glowed brightly. 'I'll look at it – I assume it's footage? – and if you leave your email address, you'll hear from me in a day, possibly less. If I know anything, I'll tell you. The truth, that is; the truth you use out there.'

'Well, the truth would be a nice change in routine,' Konstantin said cheerfully. 'But an even better thing would be if you would agree to meet me out there yourself. In person.'

'I didn't witness anything *in person*. Be a good dear-friend and settle for email. I wouldn't even give you that much, except that a study of your movements this session indicates that you are everything you say, and I'd be less than responsible if I didn't give you what you ask. You're so completely … ignorant … of how things are done here that if I don't help you, you're liable to get hurt very badly.'

'Well, that's something else I wanted to talk to you about,' Konstantin said

quickly. 'This Shantih Love/Tom Iguchi person wasn't the only one who turned up dead out there. There are seven other people –'

'Email,' Body Sativa said firmly. 'And now, you really should be going. The tribal wars module isn't strictly ornamental.' Then she reached out of the TV screen and pressed a button in the upper right-hand corner of the console. The screen went dark. Konstantin got up and tried pressing the button herself but nothing happened. Wearily she asked the cat for instructions on how to transfer a copy of the footage of Shantih Love's AR murder to the slot Body Sativa had showed her. Email was better than nothing, she supposed, and then it occurred to her that it was probably even better than AR. Email was traceable.

It didn't occur to her that it wasn't necessary to ride all the way down to the ground floor in the elevator to get out.

She walked out of the building into the middle of a riot.

The werewolves were gone, but the formerly empty piazza was now full of people running, screaming, chasing each other, hurling furniture and other heavy objects from broken-out windows in the building, possibly from mid-air for all she knew. Wrecked cars had been overturned and set on fire. But then, perhaps that actually counted as new home construction for the sala-mander population, she thought, feeling dazed and anxious as she look around for some clear route of escape.

Escape. Good one, Einstein. Try 'exit.' She felt like a complete idiot. It was no wonder that Body Sativa didn't want to have anything to do with her. She wasn't just unaccelerated, she was stupid. The whole venture was no better than a reckless prank. She couldn't get into the spirit of it even for the sake of information-gathering on behalf of some poor murdered kid. And walking around disguised as the victim – the more she thought about it, the more it seemed like an act of desecration. Better just to hope for useful information via email from Body Sativa, though she doubted there would be any. This had nothing to do with anyone's life, not anyone's *real* life. So how could it have anything to do with a kid's real death? Or seven other real deaths?

She stepped out of the relative shelter of the lobby just as a Molotov cocktail sailed over her head and shattered on the building above her, making a perfect wave circle of flame. The effect of the heat was so realistic she could have sworn her face was flushed. She put an arm up defensively and turned away.

It took her all of a second to register the blow followed by the impact of her body on the piazza. The punch in her upper chest had been so abrupt and powerful that her legs had flown out from under her and she'd hit the pave-ment on her back. It *hurt*, as badly as the real thing would have. She thought she had run into one of the rioters and the program had authenticated the

logical result. But then a half-circle of grinning faces appeared above her as she tried to sit up and catch her breath and she couldn't believe it. Of all the damned things that could go on in this ridiculous scenario and she *would* go and trigger one of the least imaginative.

Before she could ask for the icon cat, they hauled her to her feet and began shoving her around so that she rebounded from one into another like a pinball. Still breathless, she tried to get a good look at them but they were pushing her around too quickly. The Molotov cocktail had ignited something and she could see others, some human and some not quite, watching in the firelight as her attackers played with her.

There had to be something in the icon cat that would help, she thought, something for protection, self-defense, *something*. Too bad she hadn't thought of that sooner and used some precautions. She could imagine Body Sativa laughing at her. *Ignorant ... ignorant. You thought you were safe because you were here under false pretenses. Surprise, dear-friend, we're all here under false pretenses.*

They were shoving her around harder now, slapping and punching, and the pain was only too real. Never mind the technical specs of the sensation delivery system – this was *too* authentic. She wondered if Tomoyuki Iguchi had had some kind of masochistic streak that he had indulged as Shantih Love –

And suddenly she wasn't sure that it *wasn't* happening for real. Maybe Shantih Love hadn't been able to tell the difference there on the shore of the Hudson River, not until it was too late and he couldn't feel how the real blood was flowing along with the virtual, even though he could see, perhaps until the moment of his death, the virtual attacker who had come to hijack his persona. But *why?*

A leg kicked out as she stumbled sideways and she went down again. One of her attackers started to pull her up; she twisted away and fumbled the iconcat out onto the ground where she could see it.

This time, it didn't pause for animal imagery. The book fell open to a fierce and cartoony picture of a monster that she somehow knew was a talisman of protection. Just as she grabbed for it, her attackers tore it away from her.

Too late, she understood that the catalog with its treasure trove of icons – its *stuff* – was what they'd been after all along. She scrambled up but a heavy boot caught her in the midsection and she sat down hard.

Someone crouched down and shoved a face that looked like the product of an unfortunate mating between a troll and a gargoyle up close to hers. 'Hey, you never heard that expression, *be seated?*'

She scooted backward, trying to get away. He advanced on her with the others behind him, one holding up her icon cat so she could see that they had taken the whole thing from her.

All, that was, except for one page that she was still clutching in one hand,

so hard that her knuckles hurt. Another pain that was real, produced by the way she was clenching her hand in this unreal place, a pain that paled next to the jazzy high-res authenticity of the 'suit but went deeper, all the way down to the level where what remained of the reptile senses sorted real from unreal.

They are killing me. They are really *killing me!*

The thought was a screaming in her head. What was going on, out there beyond the bounds of the headmount and the neo-exo-nervous system, what was happening *out there*, how many were *out there*, why hadn't she figured there could be more than one in on the murder, someone else hidden in the air-processing ducts, perhaps, with the cooperation of some insider, maybe bored Tim Mezzer or bitter Miles Mank, or even Pleshette, not bored or bitter, just plain crazy. Or *all* of them together, Mank and Pleshette pretending to hate each other *out there*. Or maybe they *did* hate each other *out there* but not *in here*.

In here. Where the employee discount was pretty good. What arrogance and contempt, to kill someone so soon after the last one, and the detective investigating the case, no less! Ideal, though – the partner was too claustrophobic to jump right on the crime scene and they knew it, so by the time someone else, Celestine and DiPietro perhaps, arrived, they'd have jiggered the evidence, massaged the data, and Celestine and DiPietro would be too busy trying to impress the stringer from *Police Blotter* to notice or care that she had become so much more grist for the AR urban legend mill. *Ya hear about the homicide detective who was killed in AR investigating a murder? Yeah,* incredible *galloping head-bugs, she was crazier 'n a sackful of assholes. Happened in D.C., of course. Life is so cheap there, it's a whole different world –*

Now the chief troll-gargoyle was waving around something that looked like a jagged fragment of a mirror, poking it at her face. Her rational mind kept telling her that he couldn't possibly cut her but her rational mind had shrunk to the size of a quark. The rest of her was believing it the way a Pentecostal convert believed the touch of an omnipotent God made you speak in tongues, believed it to the point where she could feel the small cuts on her face. The bloody and murderous troll had cut her face and in a moment he would cut her throat, by the power of suggestion she would believe her throat was cut and so much for *extremo ruptura* being the sole province of St. Whoever. There just hadn't been any AR up until now that could compete with the faith of a fanatic saint with stigmata, but now there was, *now there was*. Let the coroner come now, let them all come and see if the power of their own belief and their own galloping head-bugs would allow them to survive –

The torn page in her hand transformed into a larger hand. She tried to let go with a scream but the hand seemed to swallow hers. The face of the gargoyle snapped out of focus and became the big, soft features of Taliaferro. The scream that escaped her now was one of total surprise, pure reaction to the one thing she had expected least of all.

Panting, she looked around. Celestine had thrown herself over her legs while DiPietro had her other arm and most of her upper body. Behind them, Pleshette and Mank were staring at her wide-eyed and Tim Mezzer was yawning with a hand over his mouth. And behind them, standing on a chair, the stringer from *Police Blotter* was filming, filming, filming.

'Okay,' Konstantin said, letting out a long breath. 'Are you guys *trying* to give me a heart attack?'

'She can see us,' Taliaferro said. 'Let her up.'

They stepped away from her and she saw that they had peeled most of the hotsuit off her. The headmount was lying on the floor, shattered. 'Taliaferro, don't make me ask what happened like some clod from a bad action movie – Taliaferro?'

'Over here.' He was out in the hallway, standing well free of the doorway. 'You don't really expect me to stand *in there?*'

'In –' she realized he was talking about the tiny cubicle. 'Okay,' she said again. 'What *did* happen?'

'You were *screaming*,' said Pleshette, her tone all but lascivious. 'You were screaming and screaming and you wouldn't stop. I was keeping an eye on you, you know, and I saw you getting attacked. Then they took your icon cat –'

'Yes, the one with all your *stuff* in it,' Konstantin said, feeling embarrassed in spite of everything.

'You can't get it back,' Pleshette said, as if Konstantin had offered.

Konstantin shook her head, not quite believing that Pleshette was really giving her a hard time about AR *stuff*. It wasn't *stuff*. It wasn't even a lack of *stuff*. What was wrong with this stupid woman, with all the stupid people in there, especially stupid people who would hurt you – kill you – for the sake of a cache of items that didn't exist?

Because they *had* been going to kill her, she thought. They'd been going to use her own perceptions against her to do it. She could still feel the places where they had hit her, the pain was still there, throbbing dully. Tomorrow, she'd be one big bruise.

She shook her head again. 'What about high-speed access?' she said, dazed.

'We don't have that here,' Pleshette said quickly.

'Then where would I go to get it?'

There was a long pause. 'High-speed access, that's, that's just a –' Pleshette paused again to swallow. 'It's one of those fairy stories AR junkies tell each other. Somebody went online amped once and claimed that they got everything all speeded up and used less billable time. But that's, you know, don't we all wish.'

'Yes, don't we. Except video parlor managers,' Konstantin said. 'Less billable time, that wouldn't be such good news around here, would it.' She eased herself out of the chair but when she stood up, her legs buckled. Celestine

and DiPietro caught her, one under each arm. She would have appreciated their solicitude more if they hadn't turned her toward the stringer.

'Beginners *always* underestimate the effects of abrupt-disconnect shock,' Miles Mank said importantly.

She felt her left hand cramp and realized she was still clenching it tight. In her mind's eye, she saw the image of the coin she had been given, the loop of infinity on one side, Ouroboros on the other. Half expecting to find the coin stuck to her flesh, she tried to unfold her fingers, but they wouldn't move. She had to have several hours of electrical and tactile massage to loosen the knots that had seized various muscles all over her body, including her hand. When it did finally open, like a late-blooming flower – or maybe, Konstantin thought, a hand-puppet of a flower – there was nothing there at all, and nothing up her sleeve.

EMPTY CUP [V]

It hadn't surprised Yuki that she had not won the lottery. The only answer she had received from the ticket had been a straight, technical explanation.

Unacceptable – does not fit criteria for acceptance

Simulated – synthetic, artificial, fake, counterfeit meant to deceive by passing as real

Person – human being, or character meant to be the equivalent of a human being

Non-Human Manipulated – moved, activated, set in motion by a force other than a human being, possibly a character meant to be the equivalent of a human being

Standing there on the street with winged gang members soaring overhead, occasionally dive-bombing her in an attempt to make her stampede or at least duck (she didn't oblige them), she felt a fatigue that surpassed any other tiredness or exhaustion she'd ever experienced. *Sick of you*, she thought, staring up at a winged thug balanced on a crumbling ledge. He was staring right back at her. She shouldn't have been able to tell because he was so far away, but that was AR for you – all the information you didn't need and more. And sometimes less, too, she'd thought, looking down at the lottery ticket. *Sick of you*.

A vehicle that looked like a cross between a tank and a double-decker touring bus overturned in front of her, spilling out a mess of people with weapons grafted directly onto their bodies. They all rolled expertly to their feet and ran off in all directions, several of them brushing her roughly as they passed. Yuki imagined they were supposed to look frightening and deadly

with their built-in killing machinery but they only suggested an ill-advised laboratory experiment that had escaped from its vat and multiplied. And for all she knew, that was the scenario they were all acting out. Gang Wars in Post-Apocalyptic Noo Yawk Sitty, starring various crimes against nature. Strictly for entertainment value of course, for those of you whose idea of entertainment is to be frightened, intimidated, or even beaten up. *Sick of you. Sick of you, time to go.* She moved her eyes along the periphery of her visual field, waiting for the exit menu to pop up. Nothing happened.

Well, that was okay, too. Joy Flower might be determined to keep her in here, for whatever hinky-kinky reasons, but the bitch couldn't force her to do anything. She walked past the overturned tank-bus, which had started to burn, and sat down in the middle of the street, waiting for something to fall on her, run her over, or otherwise end her stupid adventure and get her fired. Wherever Tom was, he would just have to find some other way to act out his strange needs. She was done. It wasn't worth it. *Sick of you.*

'Sick of you,' she announced to the sky, hoping Joy Flower could hear her. 'Sick of you. And sick of me, too.'

Whether Joy Flower heard her or not, the winged thug on the ledge had. He adjusted his diving posture and she knew he was aiming right for her.

There was no transition. She was standing at the open hatch of an airplane tens of thousands of feet up, hanging on with both hands. Someone's foot was in the small of her back. Her stomach dropped and rebounded in terror, and her fingers tightened their grip. The pressure against her back increased slightly and her body bowed outward.

Not that you could die, of course, she thought, staring down at the patch-work landscape passing underneath, partly veiled by thin, ragged clouds. You couldn't die from this sort of thing. And if it happened over and over and over, you might even get inured to it and conquer your fear. And then again, maybe you wouldn't. How many times would it have to happen before you knew one way or another, and what would be left of your mind when it was over?

And while we were at it, what was that bit about Joy Flower not being able to force her to do anything?

Had she only been thinking, or had someone been whispering to her, a tiny voice bypassing the roaring of both the wind and her own hammering heart? Cold air freeze-scalded her face, ripped the moisture from her eyes, drove spikes of pain through her temples. This, too, was part of the sensuous AR experience; enjoy.

She made herself look up into the crystal blue of the sky. And just suppose, she thought, that instead of falling *down*, you fell *up*, at high speed. At a higher speed, say, than falling down, a higher speed than anyone could follow.

And what if no one knew? What if you let anyone who might be watching see your body tumbling down through the cloudy air, plunging toward earth

in the typical splayed and helpless position, a human starfish. Was that possible?

There was a sudden hard shove and she was soaring free of the doorway, out in the unbearably cold air where she seemed to hover for a fraction of a second before beginning her rush earthward.

Her inner ear screamed at her that she was going to die of the sensation of falling before the impact killed her. Something made her give in to the feeling instead of fighting it. So she would die of the sensation of falling. *Take me*, she thought. *Pluck my life out of midair, cheat them, leave them with a shell. They'll never know because in spite of everything else they can do to me in here, they can't hear my thoughts. They'll never know.*

For a while, the earth seemed to rock and swing crazily beneath her, sometimes changing places with the sky as she rolled over in the wind. But eventually it steadied and began to close the distance between her and itself with increasing speed, until it was rushing at her fixedly, aimed at her face. She had no breath for screaming but the wind screamed for her and kept screaming as an almost-perfect square tract of bumpy green stretched out in every direction, as if it were unfurling itself just to catch her.

The impact never came. When she opened her eyes, she was back in the open doorway of the airplane.

A hand dug into her hair and yanked her head back. 'It doesn't have to be this way!' Ash bellowed into her face over the wind. He was still velvet-skinned.

'What do you want?' she said through gritted teeth.

'The same thing you want. Find him!'

'You're not Ash,' she said. 'You're not anybody. Let me talk to *her*.'

He pulled her head back farther. She was barely managing to keep her feet on the edge of the doorway. If he bent her back any more, she would fall and be sucked out into empty space again. Terror chills radiated from the center of her chest out to her arms and legs, hands and feet, like an electric shock and she couldn't help it. She let go, felt her body fly straight out like a pennant in a hurricane.

But she didn't fall. Not yet. Ash still had hold of her hair, and the pull against her scalp was only beginning to be painful. 'There's no way out!' he hollered in her ear. She could feel his velvet face scrape against her head. 'They've got a feeding tube in one end and a conduit for waste in the other. They can last longer than you can, Yuki. They can make the fall worse each time. There *is* an impact module, Yuki, and they can make you feel it, every bit of it, and then bring you back here a heartbeat later and get you ready to do it again. Do you want to do that? Huh? Do you want to?'

She tried to get her hands up to her head; her scalp was on fire now and it would only be a relief if he let go. She saw his head swivel around to look

behind him. Then he shrugged and shoved her away. The sky sucked her out into its emptiness and then spat her down toward the earth again.

This time she was rolling over and over on her side, as if she were doing a series of rapid dance turns as well as falling. Nausea and dizziness added themselves to the stew of sensation, while sky and ground strobed to a flicker of light and dark in the mess of her vision.

There was a sudden flash of something else between earth and sky. At first she only glimpsed it briefly, a new element inserted in the moment after the flash of earth and before the flash of sky … or vice versa. As she fell faster, she was able to hold it in her sight a little bit longer and somehow, she just knew that whatever it was, neither Joy Flower nor any of her crew, human or not, had any idea that it was there. If she could get to it, if she could get to the place where it was, they might not be able to reach her.

The image of her inert body in a hotsuit rose up in her mind. Well, yes, they did have her body, there was that. But if she could elude them in here, she might be able to send a message to the outside somehow. To the real Ash, to the police, to somebody somewhere.

She tried to concentrate her attention on the moment between light sky and dark ground, and she almost had it when land smashed against her in midturn, shattering her bones, pulping her flesh, splitting her skin, enveloping her in a physical state that was beyond agony.

'You explode like a rotten squash,' Ash told her, dangling her out the doorway by her wrists. His grip was so tight she couldn't sense her hands even to wiggle her fingers and her shoulders felt as if they were both dislocated. The wind buffeted her legs, alternately knocking her from side to side and pulling on her as if playing tug-o-war with Ash. She tried to look over her shoulder but her shoulders were hunched up around her ears and it was impossible.

'You explode like a bomb made of flesh and bone,' said Ash. 'Bone shards fly out with such force that they could kill someone standing nearby. How's that for shrapnel? Your blood turns to mist. Doesn't that bother you? I mean, come on, Yuki, doesn't it *hurt?*'

She looked at him and tried to say something but her mouth was completely dry.

'What?' he said. 'I can't hear you. I –' He let go of her left wrist to cup his hand around his ear and then pretended to look shocked as she dangled by one arm. 'Oops! I really goofed up that time, didn't –'

The wind tore her away from him and she tumbled end over end, going faster than ever. She concentrated, willing herself to go even faster than that, instinctively tucking her legs in and hugging her knees. *Faster,* she thought, *faster, faster, faster –*

She couldn't fall faster, she realized, but she could tumble faster *within* the

fall. Sky and earth began to flicker again, and then the flickering began to pick up momentum. After a while, she saw that the ground wasn't any closer; it was as if she were cannonballing along the wind, moving across more than down. Had they noticed, was Ash watching?

The flickering became a flickering gleam, a glimmer, a twinkle that grew from a pinpoint to a ball so big that it crowded out both earth and sky. She fell into it like a comet falling into the face of the sun.

After a time, the light died down, from blinding to something softer, something on the order of the warm golden glow from an antique lamp. Yuki became aware slowly that she was no longer falling, had not been falling for some time. Her eyes were closed and she had no sense of her position – had she passed out? Was she still unconscious and dreaming?

She opened her eyes and jumped, startled. She was sitting in an enormous leather chair like the one in Joy Flower's office but this one had been pulled up to a large, round, dark wood meeting table. There was a touch on her arm and she turned to find her grandmother sitting at her left.

'Grandmother?'

'Body,' the woman said.

'Whose?' asked Yuki, bewildered.

Her grandmother looked patient. 'Body Sativa. Don't tell me you don't know the name.'

'You look and talk just like my grandmother.' Yuki drew back suspiciously. 'Is this how they use you in the afterlife? They keep your brain running to generate post-Apocalyptic AR cities?'

'If I am your grandmother, I'm dead, I'm past caring why they keep my brain running.' The woman smiled. 'It doesn't matter what they intended, anyway. Something else is happening, something they didn't bargain for.'

Yuki felt an echo of the weariness that had caused her to sit down in the middle of post-Apocalyptic Noo Yawk Sitty in the first place. 'It's all just AR. Right now, I'm moving so fast they can't track me, but eventually I'll start to lose momentum and they'll find me again.'

'Actually, they'd rather find you *before* you lose momentum,' Body Sativa said, leaning over to look at the center of the table. Yuki followed her gaze but saw nothing other than a vague area that might have been a spot that a dust-cloth had missed. 'They've been trying to get up this high for a while now. Only one or two managed it in the past – accelerant combined with high adrenaline, nature's own speed cocktail. They want to follow you up. They know there's something here and they want it.'

'What?' Yuki said skeptically, tensing a little in spite of herself.

'Old Japan.'

Yuki laughed without humor. 'Oh, yeah. Post-Apocalyptic Tokyo, the hottest

thing yet. Please. Save the sales pitch. I don't do AR. I wouldn't be here now except I'm, uh, looking for someone.'

'No. Not a cheap amusement park. The *real* Old Japan. And I know who you're looking for.' There was a pause. 'Iguchi Tomoyuki tried to sell his birthright. The one who purchased it was set upon by a demon, who killed him.'

'Sorry, I don't believe in demons,' Yuki said sourly.

'Ask Tom, then, when you find him, if he believes in demons.'

Yuki looked down at the highly polished tabletop. Did her reflection just frown at her and give its head a barely perceptible shake no, or was she imagining it? A chill swept up her back to her neck. *Faster?* Faster *still?*

'If you had him here, how did you lose him?' she asked.

Body Sativa's face became a cold mask. 'He became greedy. He took the catalog, he decided he would sell the high-level accesses for money, to anyone, non-Japanese as well as Japanese. Greed is a very old, very unoriginal scenario, so boring. If we could recover the catalog, the accesses to the higher levels –'

'If Tom's still in here,' Yuki said, careful to keep her voice even, 'why can't you find him? Or do you already have him – out there – and he just won't talk?'

'– we would forgive him, we would make him part of *bunraku*. As you are.'

'*Bunraku*,' Yuki repeated, mystified. She looked down at her reflection again. It was staring up at her with an urgent, worried look. Casually she put her forearms on the table and folded her hands like a studious schoolgirl, making a roughly circular area of the tabletop that she hoped only she could see.

'The method by which Old Japan will be remade – *awakened* – for good. The real, the true Old Japan. We were bringing it to fruition, we were nurturing it with the life of our blood and tissue and the afterlife of our souls when Joy Flower came looking for us.'

'How? She's not Japanese,' Yuki said.

'Many of her Boyz were, and are. Tom is. You are. We know. Your tissue was sampled when you were injected. We tasted you.'

Yuki felt another chill, what Ash had always referred to as the goose walking over your grave. 'Who's "we"?'

'Just a group of Japanese who missed our homeland. We wanted to go home.'

'But –' Yuki felt a wave of dizziness. 'Wait. With a name like Body Sativa?'

'It is not yet time to loosen the threads of this appearance and reveal the one underneath.'

Yuki frowned, not understanding the reference. 'The number who remember Japan like that must be shrinking all the time. Am I *not* Japanese just because the physical islands were destroyed?'

'All peoples have a source,' said Body Sativa. 'We are re-constructing ours, not in soil and rock and ocean, but in flesh and blood, nerve and synapse. Can't you feel it?'

Something rippled through her, like a sensation from someone else's body, as if someone else were sharing the suit with her by some remote access. Except this time, it didn't feel hideously obscene, like being invaded by a stranger from within.

There was a gentle touch on her shoulder and she looked up to see a large doll-woman in traditional Japanese costume floating in front of her on the table. It bowed and began to move slowly and precisely, with as much grace as a living person.

Not a doll. A puppet, with several living persons behind its movements. *Her* movements. *Bunraku.* Japanese puppet theater. Not a children's diversion but the classic puppet theater of Old Japan, as serious as Noh and Kabuki, a demonstration of skill and grace, control and cooperation. Now she could see the outlines of the people moving the puppet if not their faces. See them and feel them –

She held up both her hands, looking at them in wonder. 'Tom?' she whispered, rubbing her hands together, trying to sense the presence of any others, all the others whose hands moved and felt with her own.

'You won't find Iguchi in there,' Body Sativa told her. 'He broke the chain. He didn't believe Old Japan could be revived. He believed in amusement parks. People can believe in the most absurd things, like Out Doors, or that Joy Flower's whores do not mind that people put on their sensations like hot suits, for the pleasure of feeling powerful. Or that the Japanese would *want* a post-Apocalyptic city open only to us. We've had that, thank you. You're not the ignorant *sansei* that Tom is, that you didn't know, are you?'

Yuki leaned back as far as she could, trying to reduce the feel of being pulled into the woman's gaze. 'What do you want from me?'

'Do you know the art of filling an empty cup with tea when you have no tea?'

She shook her head silently.

'I should have said the art of producing Iguchi Tomoyuki where there supposedly is none. Find him for us, and through him, recover the catalog, with so many of the arts of Old Japan. *Bunraku,* for one. So that we can know again what it is to be one people.'

'You want whipped cream on that?' Yuki said dryly.

Body Sativa smiled benevolently. 'The catalog alone will do, if Iguchi Tomoyuki doesn't want to rejoin us.'

'Why me?'

'You're wearing his appearance. Joy Flower set you out in it to snag him. You can snag him for us as easily as for her.'

Yuki nodded a bit reluctantly. 'There's just one other problem, though. I'm in the process of falling from an airplane –'

'I know,' said Body Sativa. 'And you must hurry, so you can finish before you hit the ground again.'

DEATH IN THE PROMISED LAND [V]

'I'm in a bad mood,' Konstantin said, massaging the palm of her hand with her thumb. She was still getting spontaneous cramping in her hands, feet, and calf muscles.

'Well, I can't blame you.' Sitting on the other side of the desk in the manager's office, Tim Mezzer yawned. 'It was probably foolish for you to go in cold like that. Some of the people who come in, they warm up like athletes beforehand. But you don't have to take it all out on me, you know.'

'Yeah, I do.' Konstantin flexed her hand. Tension *is our friend*. 'Because I know that you're the one supplying the drug to the custom smart enough to ask for it. I just don't know which of the other two is in on it with you – Mank or Pleshette.'

Tim Mezzer became marginally less bored for a few moments as he seemed think something over. He shrugged. 'Pleshette. You always get the manager on your side if you can. Mank doesn't know anything. He doesn't even know what planet he's on.'

'Innocence is a fragile thing. Don't tell him.' Konstantin glowered at him. 'The other thing I don't know is why you sent me to Body Sativa when you knew she'd tell me about the drug.'

'I didn't think she'd tell you we were using it at the parlor,' Mezzer said, irritated as well as bored. 'Or who was supplying it.'

'It wasn't all that hard to figure out,' Konstantin said, getting angry. 'I only had to guess who the supplier was. I had a one-in-three chance of being right. How stupid do you think people are out here?'

Mezzer shrugged again and spread his hands helplessly. 'Is that a rhetorical question?' he asked through a yawn.

'No,' replied Konstantin with exaggerated patience. 'I'm just Nature's way of telling you that you've spent so much time all cranked up *in there* that you're under the erroneous impression that life *out here* is slow and stupid. Not to mention boring.'

'Sorry, but it *is* boring,' Tim Mezzer said. 'It *is*.'

'That kid died *out here*,' said Konstantin, 'and he wasn't bored to death.'

*

Guilfoyle Pleshette was not bored, and neither was her lawyer. She had traded her kimono for a long, formal-looking black garment that was more than a dress but less than a coat. The lawyer was another member of the Church of Small-Is-Beautiful, an older man named Carl Rosario who managed to sit cross-legged in a suit on the desk without looking ridiculous. He also used a pen that wrote in broad, dark strokes and a pad instead of an archiver. Konstantin found she was attracted to him, which put her in an even worse temper.

'We had nothing to do with Tom Iguchi's death,' Rosario said agreeably, 'and we have many witnesses who can testify to our presence at the check-in desk with Miles Mank during the time Iguchi was murdered. We're not going to talk about drugs because you're not drugs, you're homicide. I think that covers everything. Any questions?'

'Can we talk about the general day-to-day operation of the video parlor?' Konstantin asked stonily.

Rosario shrugged. 'Can we have this conversation in a more reasonable location, one with coffee and perhaps something to eat?'

'*No*,' Konstantin growled. '*Nobody* leaves here till I have what I need to conduct this murder investigation effectively.'

The lawyer looked at her with distaste. 'If I might point out, lieutenant, you have already kept my client, as well as several other people, well past their usual quitting times while you did god knows what in an artificial reality scenario from which you could not possibly obtain any evidence whatsoever –'

'But only because I wasn't going fast enough,' Konstantin snapped. 'Isn't that right, Guilfoyle?'

Pleshette winced at Konstantin's use of her first name but refused to look at her. 'What am I supposed to do, get a blood sample from every blowfish who walks in here? Or search them? Most of them come in with stuff and don't take it till they're all 'suited up and ready to go. If somebody wants to ride all fucked up, there's not much you can do to stop them.'

'But there's plenty you can do to help them. Right?' Konstantin lunged forward over the desk and put her face in Pleshette's without touching her. 'How do you get a highspeed connection here? Is it cheaper if you buy the drug here, too, is that some kind of special package deal? Didn't you say you couldn't get high speed here, or am I remembering wrong?'

Rosario tapped her shoulder, trying to get her to move back away from Pleshette. 'Stop showing off, lieutenant. We know you're tough.'

'Yeah. Sure.' Konstantin sat down again. 'But that's no distinction around here. *Everybody's* tough in AR. Gotta be tough to hold your own in those post-Apocalyptic Gang Wars, right, Guilfoyle? Tough is a must. Tough and fast is better, though, isn't it? And the faster you go, the tougher you get and

the tougher *it* gets, right? And then things get a little crazy – no, a lot crazier than usual, and then a whole lot crazier than they ought to be.'

Rosario leaned over to try to look into her eyes. 'Do you have a point, Lieutenant Konstan –'

'The paranoia, the delusions and the hallucinations,' Konstantin said, staring hard at Pleshette. 'Get someone cranked up high enough, they probably won't know whether they're wearing a hot suit or not. You don't even have to put a headmount on them, they wouldn't notice one way or the other anyway, would they?'

'Your *point*, lieutenant –'

Konstantin waved a dismissive hand in his face. 'What really happened to that kid before we got here? Was he screaming so loud that he was scaring the rest of the paying customers? What was it, snakes coming out of the walls? Bugs crawling all over him? Bugs crawling under his skin, maybe, because he put his hotsuit on over nerve endings that were already going like Holy Rollers? Did somebody go in there to try to calm him down and end up killing him by mistake?'

Rosario turned to Pleshette and started to tell her not to answer but she waved her hand in his face in a near-perfect mirroring of Konstantin's gesture. 'Nobody killed that kid. Mezzer's too bored to swat a fly. I'm too small. Mank's too useless. You want to know the truth, I think he killed himself.'

'How?' Konstantin frowned. 'We didn't find a knife. The coroner said he couldn't possibly have sawn through his own windpipe –'

'Well, maybe the coroner's wrong,' Pleshette said sulkily. 'You said yourself, you go fast, things get a lot crazier than usual. Everybody's tough in AR. You still ache all over, don't you?'

'What other footage do you have?' Konstantin asked suddenly.

'What do you mean?'

'Not the shit you showed me, high-speed connection footage.'

Pleshette shook her head. 'There isn't any. No parlor could afford to take that much footage, or keep it.'

'That's convenient. Where's the connection to tap into that level?'

'Don't answer that,' said Rosario.

Pleshette ignored him. 'There isn't any. You either 'suit up and go, or nothing.'

Konstantin nodded. 'Then I'll 'suit up and go.'

Rosario and Pleshette gaped at her with identical dumbfounded expressions. 'What?' they said together.

'*What?*' said Taliaferro, trailing after her down the hallway toward the room where the kid had died.

'I have to know,' Konstantin said. '*We* have to know.'

'*We* do? You mean, you and me, or –'

She stopped at the doorway to the cubicle. 'I hit my bullshit quota for this lifetime. "D.C., life is so cheap there, it's a whole different world." "Broke the same exact ribs." "Post-Apocalyptic Tokyo, that only the Japanese can find." And let's not forget Body Sativa, knows all, sees all, says nothing. She'll get back to me by email. Yeah. I'll find myself on so many junk-email lists it'll take me the rest of my life to get off them.'

Taliaferro watched her straightening out the hotsuit that had been slung over one arm. 'Yeah, but Jesus. You can't *do* anything in there. And anything you pull out is inadmissible.'

'Maybe not, if I can persuade someone otherwise.'

'But who?'

Konstantin blew out a hard breath. 'I don't know. If I can get someone to care, someone to help. If I find someone who knows or someone who saw something and I tell them they have to come forward or else, and they do – that's their lookout. Says so in the on-line agreement. You oughta read it, it's like what real life wishes it were.'

'You haven't gone *that* way on me, have you?' Taliaferro groaned. 'Friend of mine from the academy turned into a law'n'order goon last year. The only things she didn't have were a costume with a mask and her own comic book.'

'Nah,' Konstantin said, shaking out the hotsuit. Then she paused. 'Or, I don't know. Maybe I am.' Taliaferro started to say something else and she cut him off. 'I'm just tired of standing around saying, "Jeez, I wonder what happened in there." I'm going to find out, and if the only way I can find out is to get shot up with this –' she held up a sealed vial of clear liquid ' – then that's the way we live now, isn't it.'

Taliaferro's brow puckered worriedly. 'Pleshette's little tiny lawyer'll get the whole thing thrown out.'

'Only if it proves she's guilty. Maybe I'll prove she's innocent. Then it'll be in his best interests to help me keep the case from getting thrown out.'

To her surprise, Taliaferro only looked more worried. 'You can't always be sure of something like that. Listen, here's my best and last pitch. You want to hear it?'

She didn't, but she nodded anyway. 'Go ahead.'

'Walk away from it. Stuff like this has a way of turning on you and biting you in ways you didn't expect it would. You might end up setting some kind of precedent you never wanted to.' There was a pause. 'Okay. That was my last pitch.'

'Okay. I heard you,' she said. 'You don't have to wait around here while I do this.'

'No, but I will,' he said resignedly. 'So you can call if you need anything. Not that I could come in and give it to you.'

'It's bigger in there than it looks from out here,' she said, smiling at him.
Taliaferro sniffed. 'That's what they'd like you to think.'

Pleshette had given her a different hotsuit this time, after her lawyer Rosario
had made Konstantin sign a pre-notarized statement to the effect that Kon-
stantin would not use the availability of the hotsuit or of the drug against her
in the immediate case under investigation. No one was actually sure if that
would hold or not and Konstantin didn't much care. This 'suit had a com-
partment for the vial, located in the hollow between her breasts. A tube ran
from there around the collar to the back of the neck, where the drug would
be injected.

'How pleasant,' she muttered to herself, getting undressed so she could slip
into the 'suit. It occurred to her then that the drug might not work for her –
or rather, it might not work *right* for her, it might work too well because she
didn't have tolerance of a regular user. She might spend several hours lying
flat on her back in an empty room, hallucinating on the dark screen of an
un-activated headmount and thinking she'd done something.

And wouldn't it be funny if that was what everybody actually did? And it
was just the power of suggestion that made them think that they were some-
how all together, seeing the same things. Or at least it made them give things
the same names.

She closed the suit up high on her neck, touching the spot briefly where
she knew it was going to inject her. The image of the so-called child in the
basement apartment sprang into her mind. *You don't have a dirty mind, do
you?*

Do I? She stood gazing down at the headmount in her hands without see-
ing it, seeing only the girl's face, first as she was while sitting on the bed, and
then smiling up at her as Konstantin had held her with one hand and threat-
ened to punch her with the other.

Real easy to go native in a Gang Wars module.

Go native? Taliaferro had mouthed at her.

Right, except a better way to put it might be just 'go wild,' she thought.

*Do anything, do everything, because you're not really doing it, are you? It
doesn't count, doesn't go on your permanent record, won't be on the final, can't
be used against you in a court of law. Playground of lost souls – no, playground
for lost souls. That would be all of us, without exception. We're all lost souls
some way, sometime, and some more than others. And if you've already lost
your soul when you go in there, you can pick up another one in general stores.*

She made a face at her thoughts, started to put the head-mount on and
hesitated.

*But I didn't hit her. Whoever, whatever she really was, I didn't hit her, in the
end.* She took a deep calming breath.

So, will you be able to stop yourself when you're doped up and going who-knows-how-much faster?

She had to take another breath and sit down on the edge of the chaise, holding the headmount on her thighs.

For all you know, the kid's murder had nothing to do with AR. And the other seven deaths are just stupid coincidences. Has anyone coordinated the statistics on deaths occurring during an AR session?

Probably not. They were probably all too busy looking for the Out Door.

The kid had found *an* Out Door, besides the one his wife had told her about.

The kid's murder was *all about AR*, she thought suddenly. *Because he was calling himself Tomoyuki Iguchi* out here *as well as behind the Shantih Love name* in there.

Then she hurried to put on the headmount before she could start arguing with herself again.

The vertigo was so strong that the injection barely registered on her, was over almost before she was aware of it. When her head cleared, she found a catalog in her Shantih Love hands, not the one she had lost but a different one, new to her but well-traveled, much used, and, by the feel of it, stuffed full.

She looked up from the plain, dark cover of the catalog and found herself standing on the edge of the area where she had first seen Shantih Love begin her/his last walk in the sand, before the killer had struck. Konstantin drew back into some deeper shadows, watching as a multitude of characters faded in along the beach and on the pavement.

And then in a lazy dissolve, the characters faded as others appeared, each group oblivious to the other, and oblivious to the third that covered them both and erased them. It was like watching a time lapse that might have been part of a history of how different groups had come to the area and then been displaced by later arrivals. Except it wasn't a matter of time in sequence but velocity; she knew she was seeing it this way because the drug was bringing her literally up to speed. The slowest became undetectable to the most accelerated, and vice versa.

She frowned. So if the kid had gone into the scenario accelerated, why was there visible footage of him?

'I want to access a low-speed recorded sequence,' she told the catalog in a low voice.

It became a simple white surface in her hands, blank for a few moments until a hi-res holo of a human mouth, many times larger than life, appeared on it. 'Keywords?' the mouth asked her in an equally low tone.

Keywords. 'Tomoyuki Iguchi. Shantih Love,' she said, hoping she had guessed at least one of them.

'Which one?' the mouth asked.

'Which one,' she repeated, baffled at how to express that both were one. 'Which footage?'

Konstantin laughed slightly in relief. Of course. There would be a lot of footage. 'Oh. The murder.'

'Which one?'

Konstantin froze. 'Which one? Which one *what?*'

'Which murder?' the mouth asked her patiently, and waited while she thought it over.

EMPTY CUP [VI]

Yuki had wanted to ask the woman a whole series of questions: How fast was she going relative to the speed at which she was falling, did she have to do anything special to maintain her current velocity, was there an upper limit to how fast you could go, and maybe most important, was she a comet on a long loop around the sun, or a meteor burning up in the atmosphere? But the woman who looked so much like her grandmother and went by the *gaijin* name didn't seem disposed to provide answers. Or at least not those answers.

'*Bunraku* means that you don't have to do it alone,' she told Yuki, gesturing at the puppet, positioned in dignified repose amid the three handlers.

'I don't think I like the idea of being a puppet,' Yuki said, frowning unhappily.

'Not a *puppet,*' Body Sativa sounded disgusted with her. '"Puppet" is a poor word for it. The whoremaster Joy Flower, she would make a puppet out of you, for any reason, for no reason, just for her own amusement. Just to see the look on your face when you felt one of her *clients* crawling around inside you, wearing you like a hotsuit.'

'I don't see the point of it, though,' Yuki said. 'Why –'

'You don't have to see the point of it. You don't have to see the point of rubber dolls with openings of a certain type, you don't have to see the point of being beaten with a whip. Nobody's asking you to see the point of it. Nobody's asking your permission. Nobody's *asking.*'

Yuki shrugged. 'What do I have to do?'

'Open yourself to Old Japan.' Body Sativa gestured toward the center of the table. The puppet had vanished, leaving the three handlers, robed and hooded in black, standing together, waiting.

She could not imagine now how fast she was going, how fast her mind was

working; how it felt was pleasantly slow and dreamy. Cooperative but not subservient, she let Body Sativa help her climb onto the chair and step from there to the table, where she faced the puppeteers. One of them was wearing a pair of absurdly tall clogs. She walked toward them, a small part of her mind wondering what she was walking on, what they were all standing on, as the table seemed to have disappeared as well and turned simply into darkness.

She stopped in front of them. They stood motionless and she knew that they weren't going to reach for her or position her. In this *bunraku*, she would have to make the first move. Moving carefully, she turned around, raised her arms to shoulder height, and leaned back. She felt them catch her, hold her, and then felt herself encompass them, include them, contain Old Japan.

Find him or find his catalog; the choice was really no choice at all. She hadn't ever seen his catalog, but she had seen *him*. If she had seen him once, she could see him again. All she needed was high-res vision and the resonance of the heart of Old Japan, the commonality that Tom himself had always chosen to observe: the fact that they were both full Japanese.

She was kneeling on a black wooden floor polished to such a high gloss that it might as well have been black glass. She leaned over and Tom's face stared up at her, impassive. Old Japan raised her arms, lifted her gracefully into a dance that her blood knew even though the last time it had been performed had been sometime long before most recorded history. There was no record of this anywhere; there didn't have to be.

DEATH IN THE PROMISED LAND [VI]

The plain white surface in Konstantin's hands started to grow. She put it down and stepped back from it as it propped itself up in the sand and swelled to the size of a doorway. A blank, white doorway – the mouth had vanished. Konstantin edged forward and put her hand out to touch it. As she had thought, it was insubstantial. She would have to go through it to see anything. Right this way, ladies and gentlemen. This way to the egress –

She felt her heart give an alarmed thump, even though it was nonsense. She knew it was nonsense. Except it seemed so much easier to believe it was nonsense *out there* than it was to believe it *in here*. When you were *in here*, standing in mushy, thick sand up to your ankles and so doped up that you could feel it far more vividly than you had ever felt the real thing, all the *out*

there stuff took on the paleness of the theoretical, of ideas she'd had once, pictures she'd seen somewhere, sometime. *In here*, it really was bigger than it looked from *out there*, and it wasn't just what they – whoever 'they' were supposed to be – wanted you to believe, it was truer than most people imagined. Because most people seemed to imagine only amusement parks like post-Apocalyptic Noo Yawk Sitty and if that was all they wanted, you couldn't make them want more.

To someone like that, Konstantin thought, this could well look like an out door.

Holding her breath, she took a giant step into it.

She found herself standing at the railing in the park bordering the large body of water where she had seen the flying saucer – and where she had met the possibly fake child, she remembered uneasily, and turned around. She could hear a faint metallic creaking in the darkness, but that was all.

Gradually it became lighter; the sky was grey, overcast. In the dark water below, just a bit too far away for her to see clearly, creatures were playing in the water. Some of them seemed to be human. Others were human-like but almost certainly not. Konstantin waited, gripping the railing.

She saw it approach from the north, then, small in the distance although the way it flapped its wings hinted at its immensity. A dragon. Excuse me, an *evolved* dragon. How could you tell? Konstantin wondered. Larger-than-average brain case? Opposable thumbs? Advanced postgraduate degree?

As it came closer, she was glad that the day was overcast – full sunlight on the thing's steel-colored metallic scales would have been too blinding to look at. It was easily the size of a small house, about the size you'd generally imagine for a dragon. The basic body structure was more reminiscent of a mammal than a reptile, however; it reminded her of a lion. The wings were a cross between a sail-plane and a bat. Konstantin had expected them to look leathery but now she could see that they were actually much lighter, actually translucent, showing an occasional rainbow pattern along the span, even under the diffused daylight.

She watched it circle overhead and then bring itself lower and lower so that she could see it more clearly. It was the face that gave away the fact that it was evolved, she decided. The eyes, though slit-pupiled and unmistakably reptilian, were positioned more like human eyes, at the front of the head and instead of the long crocodile-type jaws more usually associated with dragons, the nose and mouth were, again, more like a lion's muzzle.

Then it was as if lightning had somehow flashed both in her brain and inside the evolved dragon face, illuminating the face beneath it: Sally Lefkow, the first suspicious death.

The dragon proceeded to lower itself down near the water, the great trans-

lucent wings beating the air to execute what should have been an impossible hover. It looked into her eyes, or rather she looked into its eyes – this was footage, she realized, and the dragon wasn't really seeing her.

A moment later, she was seeing things from the dragon's point of view, riding along in the footage. The experience was dizzying, almost incoherent – something about the dragon's eyesight made it feel as if even the eyes of her mind were crossing. It was enhanced in some way but also strained, as if the dragon were under the influence of some drug –

She recognized the sensation of the accelerant, but there was something else as well, something that didn't mix either with Sally Lefkow or the accelerant or both. The dragon soared crazily like a maddened bird of prey and Konstantin got the impression of itching all over, but from the inside.

Briefly the vitals readings became visible on the screen; the numbers meant nothing to Konstantin but she didn't need them to feel the physical sensation of Sally Lefkow's panic at sensing something alien moving inside her skin, handling her person, manipulating her body. The dragon thrashed in the air and then, in a desperate move to dislodge whatever it was – or just a desperate move, period – it plummeted straight into the ocean.

In the darkness, Konstantin felt Sally Lefkow fighting for air not because she was drowning in the water but because her throat had swollen closed. The flesh continued to swell, beyond the point usual for anaphylactic shock; the flesh swelled and as it swelled it hardened, dislocating her jaw, tearing ligament and cartilage, crushing her voice box.

Konstantin found herself lying on the pavement by the iron-pipe fence, coughing and gasping for breath. Her eyes were watering furiously and she could hear herself sobbing. She pulled herself to a sitting position, still coughing, looking out over the water. It was still day and still overcast, but the dragon was gone.

With an effort, she got to her feet and then was bent double by another fit of coughing that hurt her chest and her throat. The saliva in her mouth was thick and sour; she wondered what would happen if she tried to spit. Wet the inside of the headmount she was wearing, most likely.

She straightened up and saw a new figure waiting by the railing. Konstantin had not actually seen a picture of this particular character, but the features were distinct, impossible to confuse with anyone else. Marilyn Presley didn't see her, wouldn't have seen her anyway. Her face was lifted to something directly over her head. It wasn't visible to Konstantin but she felt a pulling from the woman and knew that, very shortly, she would be seeing the flying saucer that had abducted Marilyn Presley just before Emilio Torres had overdosed on something.

So much physical sensation associated with states of mind, Konstantin

thought marveling, as she ascended with Marilyn Presley toward the saucer. Most of the time you didn't notice that you breathed a certain way in the grip of one emotion, differently in another, or that you assumed some postures so specifically to express certain emotions that later on, you would assume the posture not only when you felt that emotion, but when you *wanted* to feel it, or when you wanted someone else to feel that way.

And then there was the terrible, new feeling, the sensation of having been invaded, penetrated, and permeated by some force that intended to *use* you, from the inside out. Emilio Torres's heart went wild as his bowels let go. Abruptly she was completely sightless but sensation remained and she knew that Torres had torn off his headmount and gone searching for something. For what?

For an antidote, she guessed. He must have thought he'd been poisoned and he'd tried to counter whatever it was with a remedy. Either that or he had just wanted to calm down so he could think what to do next. But whatever he had taken had hit him like a sledgehammer. It had stopped every organ, every cell, every tiny bit of him, stopped him and dropped him.

Konstantin's knees buckled and she crumpled to the pavement. 'Okay,' she panted. 'Okay, I get the idea, we can stop n –'

But the next victim, the panther man, was already bounding toward her over the grassy humps in the park, and it was getting dark again.

EMPTY CUP [VII]

She moved in the darkness; was moved, and could feel that she wasn't alone, even beyond the three *ningyo-zukai* flowing with her. There were many nisei out there in the darkness. Her sense of their presence waxed and waned with her movements. Sometimes she could feel how she and the three puppeteers got out of synch with each other and instead of moving together, moved at odds. At other times, the four of them might have melded into one entity, a creature that could only be the product of a certain kind of joining.

Was *that* Old Japan? Or just a method to bring Old Japan awake and alive again? She didn't know. So many nisei of her age had been raised either by non-Japanese or thoroughly Western-assimilated Japanese. She knew the culture and history, though she had not been steeped in it the way her grandmother had, and the Japanese of her grandmother's generation had taken that sort of thing very hard. *We are losing our young*, they would say, and

Yuki, like many others her age, would think, *How can you lose us? We're right here.*

She remembered when she had heard that her grandmother had consented to donate her brain after death to a neural-network organization. At the time, it had been a controversial thing, the use of the brains of the dead for the organization and pathways, neurons, synapses – all sorts of things she didn't understand. She would not have thought that her grandmother would have been either interested or approving of such a thing.

I want to see if there is such a thing as the ghost in the machine.

So perhaps there was. Perhaps?

She felt the *ningyo-zukai* stumble with her. This Body Sativa person hadn't come right out and *said* she was her grandmother. What she knew about Yuki meant nothing – it was easy enough to find out everything you needed to know about someone on-line.

Yuki felt a sudden strong longing for her grandmother, a powerful wish that at least a simulacrum of the old woman existed somewhere in some form, something like a cross between a recording and a shrine. Perhaps if Old Japan could really be awakened, who knew what else could come to be?

Her movements became more rhythmic. She was performing a dance now, she and the puppeteers, except she couldn't even really feel them anymore. She started to reach out her awareness for them and then thought better of it – in this *bunraku*, the puppet was not supposed to remain conscious of the puppeteers, but enter a state in which its life was the combination of the puppeteers' movements and the audience willing to let it be alive in their eyes.

They were all around her now, clapping to the rhythm of the dance, beating it out on the ground with their feet. The ground; they were in a clearing in a forest, one of the places that had disappeared well before the legendary Ginza district had first come ablaze. This was a different legend entirely. Yuki remembered it now as she turned slowly, looking at all the Japanese faces, some pure nisei, some part, but all come together to wake Old Japan. Who had told her this story? Her grandmother? Or had it been Tom, of all people?

The story of how day had been returned to the world after a period of unbroken night – Amaterasu, sulking in a cave, angry over something her brother had done. She had refused to be moved, Yuki remembered, turning toward the dark mouth of the cave, even when all the other gods and goddesses came to plead with her. And so the Dread Female of Heaven had stepped up onto an overturned tub and begun to dance. Not the beautiful, stylized dance in silken kimonos to the thin, sharp notes of the shamisen but something primal. A type of dance that even a *sansei* who couldn't even speak the language could perform.

But once again, the legend differed, for it was Tom in hiding, not Amaterasu, and he cared a lot less about things like unbroken night and waking Old Japan. Nor did he care a great deal about her.

Well, then, she would have to do all the caring, and she would have to get everyone gathered there with her to care also. Without realizing it, she had begun to chant his name; the crowd took it up, softly at first, letting it build.

DEATH IN THE PROMISED LAND [VII]

The thing about pain in AR, Konstantin noticed, was that it took somewhat longer for the nerves to deaden, possibly because there was no physical impact to do any actual damage. You could go on tweaking a nerve via hotsuit stimulation for much longer than you could, say, beat it with a club or whip it with a seasoned strip of leather.

So what was it – had all the victims been kinky for pain to begin with? Or just obsessed with authenticity?

Or had the accelerant simply canceled out anything remotely like common sense?

Whatever it was, Konstantin felt sorry for the people who had suffered through it before dying. Although not quite as sorry as she was feeling for herself, just at this moment.

The panther man's death had been all the more brutal for the way the survival instinct had been over-ridden or overwhelmed. No, no one in the parlor had heard or seen anything because they had all been buried alive in their own particular worlds, leaving March Kuykendall to bash his head repeatedly against the floor of his soundproofed cubicle in complete privacy. It took a while for Konstantin to realize she was still alive.

When she did, there was no time to try to escape, or even brace herself. In Denver, the wannabe gymnast Lydia Stang had ridden along helplessly in her body as it tried to execute some sort of midair tumbling twist on the run, and failed. Konstantin rode with her, and wasn't sure which was worse – knowing what was going to happen, or having to hear, deep inside the illusory body, the grisly silent sound of her neck breaking.

Suffocating in a headmount wasn't impossible – block the ventilation, seal the neck area, pass out. Flo the musician had slept through her death. Konstantin hadn't.

Victims six and seven – oh, a special treat, dueling deaths, experienced together. Double slay-ride; somewhere, some pervert was in a seamless

ecstasy bubble, re-living this one. Could you really stab yourself and make it look like someone else had done it? Or could you stab yourself so badly, slash and hack away at yourself in such a manner that no one would believe you'd done it? Which of course you hadn't, because someone was wearing you like a glove, like a puppet –

Maybe it was just called shoddy police work from lazy investigators, she thought as the last moments of Tomoyuki Iguchi congealed around her.

Lying on the ground, under the everlasting night sky, the creature preparing her for slaughter. Against her will, her neck stretched and she felt something pressing against her windpipe, something with an edge.

Under the night sky, the knife came down. In the stale, smelly cubicle, the kid voided himself in terror as his hands went up, pressed against the outside of the monitor and shoved it impossibly hard, the bottom edge sharp against the sensitive flesh of his neck. Konstantin's skin was stinging, burning, ripping, tearing. The edge of the monitor, sharp but not nearly so sharp as a knife, sawing away at the kid's windpipe, while the kid held on and pushed and pulled and pushed and pulled until his windpipe had been completely severed.

She was going to have words with the coroner.

Konstantin wanted to pass out but the drugs refused her even that minor bit of solace. Both drugs, this one and the other, that all eight victims had taken along with the accelerant, thinking that they were being given some kind of biochemical key to a super-exclusive club. What it actually had been, as far as Konstantin could tell, was a bizarre formula of hallucinogen and hyper-alertness; somewhere else on-line, clients of a certain very bent madam waited until the drug took effect and activated a special sort of hotsuit, one that enabled them to wear, in effect, other people. The attraction of such a thing escaped Konstantin. Perhaps it was the hyper-alertness of having what amounted to one body moving inside another – perhaps the stimulation was the height of pleasure.

Unless, of course, you were the one being slipped onto someone else like a glove. There you were, thinking you were going to get into AR's most exclusive club and instead, something got into *you*. Maybe your body rebelled before anything important could happen, maybe you discovered the hard way that you were allergic to certain substances and being on accelerant besides didn't help matters. Or maybe the sensation of something under your skin was too much to bear and you'd do anything to make it stop, even stab yourself to let whatever it was out.

Sometimes, however, the pervert wearing your body decided to take it over altogether after enjoying the sensation of you sawing through your own throat. Konstantin could see where that sort of person would think it was an extra special thrill, to walk off with the virtual body afterward.

Shantih Love's book had recorded it all, not because Shantih Love had wanted a handy record but because he'd been sure it would never be found and he had to keep track of how much of this drug there was and who it had gone to. The catalog itself had recorded the fate of each of his customers – exactly why, Konstantin wasn't sure, and she doubted that Shantih Love even knew it had done so. Possibly because it wasn't actually Shantih Love's catalog in the same way the catalog she had had on-line was her catalog. This seemed to have a great deal more in it, pages and pages of undecipherable symbols, many of them Japanese ideograms. Others seemed to be far more ancient, though she couldn't have said how she knew. An old memory of hieroglyphics, maybe, or cuneiform, or something else entirely.

Whatever else it might be, it was big and dense and too much for one person. And now that it had told her what she had wanted to know, it refused to be investigated any further. She could hold on to it, but it refused to open for her, refused to respond, refused to do anything except sit in her hands like a book-shaped rock.

She would wait it out, she decided. Sooner or later, someone was going to want it, would look for it, ask for it.

After a while, she got the distinct impression of movement, her and the book together moving toward some definite destination. Was that because the accelerant was wearing off and she was going more slowly now, or because everyone else was going that much faster?

The darkness began to lift; the surrounding shadows became less formless, more patterned. She thought she could hear some kind of regular noise, a thumping combined with human voices chanting. The sounds became louder, or came closer, she wasn't sure which, and now she could feel an answering pulse from the book, as if it were alive and its heart had been jarred into life again.

The light came up some more and she could just make out what seemed to be a gathering of people around some kind of big rock formation. Konstantin pressed the book between her hands, letting the pulse inside run up both her arms. Eventually she could feel it in her torso as well, and the light grew brighter and brighter until finally she saw them, an enormous group of Japanese gathered around a puppet being manipulated by three robed and hooded puppeteers.

Konstantin drew closer. The beat seemed to penetrate more deeply into her body, stirring feelings that would have embarrassed her had she not been holding on to the book.

The puppet, she realized, was leading them. Even though the puppeteers were in plain sight, it was easy to forget they were there, at least in their capacity as puppeteers. It was as though they were assisting the puppet rather than manipulating it.

Something was going to happen. Konstantin could feel it building around her in the very substance of AR as well as deep inside of herself. She looked over the heads of the gathering, past the puppet to the black mouth of the cave behind. An Out Door? Or was it the Door In for something else entirely?

Suddenly she was terrified that that was exactly what it was, that they were going to let something come in from somewhere else, something strange and new and, before now, completely unknown, and then everything would change, be changed, whether you wanted it or not. She stepped forward, holding the catalog in one hand and raising the other. 'Don't –' she started to say, but it was too late.

Even as the feeling took hold of her and shook her like a rag doll, she understood what it was and let go with a shout of laughter, both kinds of relief. And then she couldn't stop laughing, she was literally rolling on the ground, clutching the book to her front and laughing, laughing, laughing. Laughing for the joy of being alive. Laughing in the face of darkness and death. Laughing for pleasure, laughing against pain, laughing because it made her shake all over and that made her want to laugh some more. And she laughed, too, because apparently she wasn't the only one who felt that way, that the entire gathering of people there were laughing just as loudly as she was, no doubt for many of the same reasons. They laughed and howled and laughed some more and it began to sound almost like a chorus of singing, everyone laughing together.

Breathless, still laughing a little, Konstantin sat up and looked over at the puppet to see how the puppeteers were taking it. The puppet was facing the cave where a bewildered-looking Japanese guy had appeared, blinking in the light. His gaze moved from the puppet to the people gathered around the cave and then finally came to rest on her.

His face twisted in shock and anger and she remembered belatedly that she was wearing the Shantih Love character. Or maybe it was the book he was upset about. He gave a shout and lunged toward her. The people around him caught him and held him tight.

The puppet had become a human woman. She stood alone now, staring at Konstantin, her face wary, and then reached out one hand.

'Shantih Love,' she said.

The book lifted easily out of Konstantin's hands and went directly to her. Konstantin started to shrug, suppressed the movement, and looked over at the Japanese guy, still in the firm hold of several of the crowd. She felt as if they were waiting for her to say something, so she said the only thing she could think of.

'Tom Iguchi, you're under arrest as an accessory before and after the fact in the murders of Sally Lefkow, Emilio Torres, March Kuykendall, Lydia Stang … '

EMPTY CUP [VIII]

' … Lydia Stang, Flo … '

As the newcomer spoke, holo pictures of each person named sprang out of the book in Yuki's hands and hung in the air, as if to prove the accusations. She knew none of them until the stranger came to the last.

' … and an individual also known at his death as Tomoyuki Iguchi.'

'Ash!' Yuki clapped a hand over her mouth and then looked at Tom, horrified.

He tried to stare back at her and then dropped his gaze.

And then Body Sativa was there beside her, gesturing for the people holding Tom to let him go. 'Don't misunderstand,' she said to the stranger, 'but you'll have to find him first.'

The stranger nodded, shoulders slumping resignedly. 'If he's here, he's got to be somewhere.'

'Perhaps Joy Flower can help you out.'

'Oh, God,' Yuki said. 'Joy Flower. I'm –'

She turned to Body Sativa. 'Can you – is there nothing … *nothing?*'

Body Sativa's face was sad as she held out her arms. 'Nothing, as long as they have you.' Something unraveled around the outline of her body and her entire appearance, face and all, slid away like a costume. Underneath was a grand lady in traditional Japanese dress, holding a strangely shaped musical instrument. 'Now the threads are loosened and I am no longer Body Sativa but Benten, goddess of the arts.'

'You still look like my grandmother, a little,' Yuki said. The book that had come to her hands from the stranger vanished and reappeared in Benten's hand. 'So you're Benten now. What does that make me? Besides screwed, I mean?'

The new goddess's face was compassionate but set. 'Somebody has to be Boddhisattva.'

Yuki's mouth dropped open.

Suddenly there was a one-second sensation of being held down on a bed by many strong hands and someone was kneeling on her left, pulling her up and forward with one hand and holding a needle gun at the ready in the other. Only one second, but very clear, incredibly clear and so real. Yuki tried to shout and then twist away. They let her move and then the person with the needle gun was kneeling on her lower back.

' … *faster they go, the faster it wears off … told you be ready f –*'

' … *arger dose … *'

Someone shoved her head down and forward and suddenly she couldn't move at all, not even to breathe. The panic burst on her full force and then was gone, but she still couldn't move though she could breathe again.

Concentrating, she could feel her forehead resting on something hard. A hand on her shoulder pulled her back and a woman that might have been Joy Flower looked into her face, searching. She was so close that Yuki could see her twin reflections in the woman's eyes, as if they were actually etched directly onto the corneas.

Two tiny Tom Iguchis raised their fingers to their lips in unison, warning her not to say anything.

Where am I?

Yuki jumped back, turned and tried to get up and run, but something clouted her on the back of her neck and she fell forward.

When she opened her eyes, she was still falling.

Below her, she saw an enormous expanse of nighttime city, a multitude of colored lights glittering against the darkness. She wanted to cry with relief; the long fall *would* end, *had* to end, and then there would be peace, at the very least, peace. No Tom, but, well, she had tried and she no longer cared. Maybe he was watching her plunge into this city nightscape from some hiding place, some mirror, even someone's eyes. Maybe if she had a mirror to reflect her own eyes, she would see him in there, twin miniatures –

Abruptly, she realized she wasn't as high up over the city as she had been, and she could see the lights more clearly now, flashing, twinkling patterns that resolved themselves into gargantuan signs flashing words, flashing pictures, flashing *kanji* as if in a long and complex display for what universe there might be out there in the dark, to deliver, over and over, the message: *Japan lives!*

Yes, Japan lives. She closed her eyes again and waited for Japan to take the offering of herself.

DEATH IN THE PROMISED LAND [VIII]

'What is it?' Taliaferro asked her from where he stood in the cubicle doorway.

Konstantin was standing with the headmount in her hands as if she couldn't decide whether to take everything off, or put it back on and go back in. 'I had the strangest … time,' Konstantin said.

'Yeah? What was so funny?'

Konstantin smiled, staring past him. 'Life. Everything. That and the fact that for several hours in a row, I didn't once think about my ex.' She took a breath and exhaled heartily 'Do we have any intelligence on someone named Joy Flower?'

TEA

She woke on a futon in a pleasant though austere room with paper walls framed in bamboo and the slightly astringent aroma of green tea in the air.

A little later, someone helped her sit up so she could drink the tea. Though it smelled even more strongly now, it didn't have much taste at first, though the more she drank, the stronger the taste of it on her tongue became. And it must have been a much larger cup than she had thought, for it seemed as if she drank forever before stopping, and yet she still had not finished the tea. The aroma remained, stronger than ever.

She lay back and found herself staring at another person also lying on a futon, somehow suspended on the ceiling. Or perhaps *she* was the one on the ceiling and the other person was the normal one, lying on the floor. There was actually no way to tell which of them was up and which was down, no matter how long she stared, or how much she thought about it. The person always mimicked her actions, as if this were an exercise in dance mirroring. But sometimes, when her attention wandered, she thought she saw the other person make a furtive move that had nothing to do with her. She waited for someone else to come and tell her about this peculiar situation.

Eventually someone else did come. A woman stood over her and, taking no notice whatsoever of the person on the overhead futon, told her she was actually a young man named Iguchi Tomoyuki who had been lost in a strange country for a long time. And for another long time, Yuki found no reason to doubt her.

If you've enjoyed these books and would like to read more, you'll find literally thousands of classic Science Fiction & Fantasy titles through the **SF Gateway**

For the new home of Science Fiction & Fantasy . . .

✳

For the most comprehensive collection of classic SF on the internet . . .

✳

Visit the SF Gateway

www.sfgateway.com

Pat Cadigan (1953–)

Pat Cadigan was born in Schenectady, NY, and grew up in Fitchburg, MA. Attending the University of Massachusetts on a scholarship, she eventually transferred to the University of Kansas where she received her degree. Since embarking on her career as a fiction writer in 1987, her Hugo and Nebula Award-nominated short stories have appeared in such magazines as *Omni*, *The Magazine of Fantasy and Science Fiction*, and *Asimov's Science Fiction Magazine* as well as numerous anthologies. Her first collection, *Patterns*, was honoured by the Locus Award in 1990, and she has won the Arthur C. Clarke Award in 1992 and 1995 for her novels *Synners* and *Fools*. Pat Cadigan moved to the UK in 1996 and now lives in London.